A Beautiful Wedding

MW00772519

BY JAMIE McGUIRE

Beautiful Disaster

Walking Disaster

Red Hill

A Beautiful Wedding

Beautiful Oblivion

A Beautiful Wedding

A Beautiful Disaster Novella

JAMIE McGUIRE

ATRIA PAPERBACK

New York London Toronto Sydney New Delhi

ATRIA PAPERBACK
A Division of Simon & Schuster, Inc.
1230 Avenue of the Americas
New York, NY 10020

First Atria Paperback edition November 2014

ATRIA PAPERBACK and colophon are trademarks of Simon & Schuster, Inc.

For information about special discounts for bulk purchases, please contact Simon & Schuster Special Sales at 1-866-506-1949 or business@simonandschuster.com.

The Simon & Schuster Speakers Bureau can bring authors to your live event. For more information or to book an event contact the Simon & Schuster Speakers Bureau at 1-866-248-3049 or visit our website at www.simonspeakers.com.

Manufactured in the United States of America

20 19 18 17 16

Library of Congress Control Number: 2014378668

ISBN 978-1-4767-5954-8
ISBN 978-1-5011-0307-0 (pbk)
ISBN 978-1-4767-5955-5 (ebook)

For Deana and Selena

If I was drowning you would part the sea
And risk your own life to rescue me . . .

—FROM JON BON JOVI, "THANK YOU FOR LOVING ME"

CHAPTER ONE

Alibi

Abby

I could feel it coming: a growing, persistent unease that crept just beneath my skin. The more I tried to ignore it, the more unbearable it became: an itch that needed to be scratched, a scream bubbling to the surface. My father said that the urgent need to run when things were about to go wrong was a like a tic, a defense mechanism inherent in the Abernathys. I'd felt it moments before the fire, and I was feeling it now.

Sitting in Travis's bedroom, just hours after the fire, my heart raced and my muscles twitched. My gut pulled me toward the door. Told me to leave; to get away, anywhere but here. But for the first time in my life, I didn't want to go alone. I could barely focus on that voice I loved so much describing how afraid he was of losing me, and how he was close to escaping when he ran in the opposite direction, toward me. So many people died, some of them

1

strangers from State but some were people I'd seen in the cafeteria, in class, at other fights.

We somehow survived and were sitting alone in his apartment, trying to process it all. Feeling afraid, feeling guilty . . . about those who died, and that we had lived. My lungs felt like they were full of cobwebs and flames, and I couldn't get the rancid smell of charred skin out of my nose. It was overpowering, and even though I'd taken a shower, it was still there, mixed in with the mint and lavender scent of the soap I used to scrub it away. Equally unforgettable were the sounds. The sirens, the wailing, the worried and panicked chatter, and the screams of people arriving on the scene to discover that a friend was still inside. Everyone looked the same, covered in soot, with identical expressions of bewilderment and despair. It was a nightmare.

Despite my struggle to focus, I did hear him say this: "The only thing I'm afraid of is a life without you, Pigeon."

We had been too lucky. Even in a dark corner of Vegas, being attacked by Benny's goons, we somehow still had the advantage. Travis was invincible. But being a part of the Circle, and helping to organize a fight in unsafe conditions that resulted in the deaths of countless college kids . . . that was a fight not even Travis Maddox could win. Our relationship had withstood so many things, but Travis was in real danger of going to prison. Even if he didn't know it yet, it was the one obstacle that could keep us apart. The one obstacle that we had no control over.

"Then you have nothing to be afraid of," I said. "We're forever."

He sighed, and then pressed his lips against my hair. I didn't think it was possible to feel so much for one person. He had protected me. It was my turn to protect him.

"This is it," he said.

"What?"

"I knew the second I met you that there was something about you I needed. Turns out it wasn't something about you at all. It was just you."

My insides melted. I loved him. I loved him, and I had to do whatever I could to keep him safe. Whatever it took—no matter how crazy. All I had to do was talk him into it.

I leaned against him, pressing my cheek against his chest. "It's us, Trav. Nothing makes sense unless we're together. Have you noticed that?"

"Noticed? I've been telling you that all year! It's official. Bimbos, fights, leaving, Parker, Vegas . . . even fires. Our relationship can withstand anything."

"Vegas?" I asked.

In that moment, the most insane plan formed in my mind, but the idea made sense as I stared into his warm, brown eyes. Those eyes made everything make sense. His face and neck were still covered in soot mixed with sweat, a reminder of how close we had come to losing everything.

My mind was racing. We would only need necessities

and we could be out the door in five minutes. We could buy clothes there. The sooner we left the better. No one would believe two people would get on a plane right after such an enormous tragedy. It didn't make sense, which was exactly why we had to do it.

I had to take Travis far enough away, for a specific reason. Something believable, even if it was crazy. Luckily, crazy wasn't that far a leap for Travis and me, and it was possible the investigators would second-guess the dozens of witnesses who saw Travis fighting in the basement of Keaton Hall that night—if they had proof that we were in Vegas hours later getting married. It was absolutely insane, but I didn't know what else to do. I didn't have time to come up with a better plan. We should already be gone.

Travis was staring back at me expectantly, waiting to unconditionally accept whatever came out of my crazy mouth. Goddammit, I couldn't lose him now, not after everything we'd fought through to get to this moment. By anyone's standards, we were too young to get married, too unpredictable. How many times had we hurt one another along the way, screamed at each other one minute and fallen into bed together the next? But we'd just seen how fragile life was. Who knew when the end would come along and sweep one of us away? I looked at him, resolute. He was mine, and I was his. If I knew anything at all, it was that only those two things mattered.

He furrowed his brow. "Yeah?"

"Have you thought about going back?"

His eyebrows shot up. "I don't think that's a good idea for me."

Weeks ago, I'd broken his heart. Travis chasing America's car when he realized it was over was still fresh in my mind. He was going to fight for Benny in Vegas, and I wouldn't go back there. Not even for him. He had gone through hell while we were apart. He'd begged me back on his knees, and I was so set on never returning to my life in Nevada, I'd walked away. I'd be a complete asshole if I asked him to go back. I half expected him to tell me to get the hell out for even mentioning it, but this was the only plan I had, and I was desperate.

"What if we just went for a night?" A night was all I needed. We just needed to be *somewhere else.*

He looked around his bedroom, searching the darkness for what he thought I wanted to hear. I didn't want to be that girl, the one who wasn't forthcoming and caused a huge, stupid misunderstanding. But I couldn't tell Travis the truth about what I'd just proposed to him. He would never agree to go.

"A night?" He clearly had no clue how to respond. He probably thought it was a test, but the only thing I wanted was for him to say yes.

"Marry me," I blurted out.

His mouth parted, forming a silent gasp. I waited

lifetimes until his lips curved upward, and he sealed his mouth on mine. His kiss screamed a thousand different emotions. My brain felt swollen with warring thoughts of relief and panic. This was going to work. We would get married, Travis would have an alibi, and everything would be okay.

Oh, hell.

Damn. Shit. *Fuck*.

I was getting married.

Travis

Abby Abernathy was famous for one thing: having no Tell. She could commit a crime and smile like it was any other day, lie without a twitch in her eye. Only one person in the world had any chance of learning her Tell, and that one person had to figure it out if he wanted to have any chance with her.

Me.

Abby had lost her childhood, and I'd lost my mom, so for two people who struggled to get on the same page, we were the same story. That gave me an edge, and after making this my goal over the past months, I'd arrived at an answer:

Abby's Tell was not having one. It might not make sense to most people, but it made perfect sense to me. It was the absence of that Tell that gave her away. The peace in her eyes, the softness in her smile, the relaxation of her shoulders alerted me that something was wrong.

If I didn't know her better, I might have thought this was just our happy ending, but she was up to something. Sitting in the terminal, waiting to board a plane to Vegas, with Abby snuggled into the curve of my body, I knew it was easy to try to ignore. She kept lifting her hand, staring at the ring I'd bought her, and sighing. The middle-aged woman across from us was watching my new fiancée and smiled, probably fantasizing about a time when she had her whole life ahead of her. She didn't know what those sighs really meant, but I had an idea.

It was hard to be happy about what we were about to do with the cloud of so many deaths hanging above our heads. No, really, it was literally above our heads. A television on the wall displayed the local news. Footage of the fire and the latest updates scrolled across the screen. They interviewed Josh Farney. He was covered in soot and he looked horrible, but I was glad to see he'd made it. He was fairly hammered when I saw him before the fight. Most of the people who came to the Circle either came drunk or worked their way up to a buzz while they waited for me and my opponent to trade blows. When the flames began to crawl across the room, adrenaline pumped into everyone's veins—enough to sober up even the most intoxicated.

I wished it hadn't happened. We'd lost so many, and

this wasn't exactly something you'd want your wedding to follow. From experience, I knew that the memory of a tragedy could be misplaced. Attaching this date to something we would celebrate year after year would keep it front and center in our minds. Damn, they were still bringing out bodies, and I was acting like this was an annoyance. There were parents out there who had no idea they'd never see their kids again.

That selfish thought led to guilt, and that guilt led to a lie. It was a sheer miracle that we were getting married right now, anyway. But I didn't want Abby thinking I was anything but super fucking pumped about getting married. Knowing her, she'd misread it and then change her mind. So I focused on her, and what we were about to do. I wanted to be a normal, so-excited-I-might-puke groom-to-be, and she deserved nothing less. It wouldn't be the first time I'd pretended not to care about something I couldn't get out of my head. The living proof was snuggled up next to me.

On the television screen, the anchorwoman standing outside Keaton Hall held the microphone with both hands, a frown line between her eyebrows. ". . . what the families of the victims will be asking: who is to blame? Back to you, Kent."

Suddenly the nausea became real. So many had died, of course they were going to hold someone accountable. Was it Adam's fault? Would he go to prison? Would I?

I hugged Abby to me and kissed her hair. A woman behind a desk picked up a mic and began to speak, and my knee started to bounce uncontrollably. If we weren't going to board soon, I might pick up Abby and run to Vegas. I felt like I could have made it there before the plane. The airline agent instructed us about boarding the flight, her voice rising and falling with the scripted announcement she'd probably read a million times. She sounded like the teacher in those *Peanuts* cartoons: bored, monotone, and impossible to understand.

The only thing that made sense were the thoughts on repeat inside my head: I was about to become the husband of the second woman I'd ever loved.

It was almost time. Damn. Shit, yeah! Fuck, yes!

I was getting married!

CHAPTER TWO

The Way Back

Abby

I stared at the sparkling rock on my finger and sighed again. It wasn't the airy sigh a young, newly engaged girl might make while staring at her rather large diamond. It was full of thought. A heavy, thoughtful thought that made me think heavier, thoughtful thoughts. But not second thoughts. We couldn't stay away from each other. What we were about to do was inevitable, and Travis Maddox loved me in a way most people dreamed about. The sigh was filled with worry and hope for my stupid plan. I wanted Travis to be okay so much that it was nearly tangible.

"Stop that, Pidge," Travis said. "You're making me nervous."

"It's just . . . too big."

"It fits just fine," he said, sitting back. We were wedged between a businessman talking softly on his cell phone and an elderly couple. An airline employee was standing behind the gate desk, talking into what looked like a CB radio. I wondered why they didn't just use a regular microphone. She announced a few names, and then hooked the device somewhere on the back of her desk.

"Must be a full flight," Travis said. His left arm was settled on the back of my chair, his thumb gently rubbing my shoulder. He was trying to pretend to be relaxed, but his bobbing knee gave him away.

"The diamond is excessive. I feel like I'm going to get mugged at any moment," I said.

Travis laughed. "First of all, no one is going to fucking touch you. Second, that ring was made to be on your finger. I knew when I saw it—"

"Attention passengers of American flight 2477 to Las Vegas, we are looking for three volunteers to take a later flight. We're offering travel vouchers good for one year from your departure."

Travis looked at me.

"No."

"You in a hurry?" he asked, a smug smile on his face.

I leaned in and kissed him. "Actually, I am." I reached up with my finger and wiped away the smudge of soot under his nose that he'd missed in the shower.

"Thanks, baby," he said, squeezing me against his side. He looked around, his chin lifted, his eyes bright. He was

in the best mood I'd seen him in since the night he'd won
our bet. It made me smile. Sensible or not, it felt good
to be loved so much, and I decided right then and there
I would stop apologizing for it. There were worse things
than finding your soul mate too early in life, and what was
too early, anyway?

"I had a discussion about you with my mom, once,"
Travis said, looking out the wall of windows to our left. It
was still dark. Whatever he saw wasn't on the other side.

"About me? Isn't that kind of . . . impossible?"

"Not really. It was the day she died."

Adrenaline burst from where adrenaline bursts from
and sped through my body, pooling in my fingers and toes.
Travis had never spoken about his mother to me. I often
wanted to ask him about her, but then I thought about the
sickening feeling that came over me when someone asked
me about my mother, so I never did.

He continued, "She told me to find a girl worth fighting for. The one that doesn't come easy."

I felt a little embarrassed, wondering if that meant
I was a huge pain in the ass. Truthfully, I was, but that
wasn't the point.

"She said to never stop fighting, and I didn't. She was
right." He took a deep breath, seeming to let that thought
settle into his bones.

The idea that Travis believed I was the woman who his

mother was talking about, that she would approve of me, made me feel an acceptance I'd never felt before. Diane, who had passed away almost seventeen years before, now made me feel more loved than my own mother.

"I love your mom," I said, leaning against Travis's chest.

He looked down at me, and after a short pause, kissed my hair. I couldn't see his face, but I could hear in his voice how much he was affected. "She would have loved you, too. No doubt in my mind."

The woman spoke into her CB again. "Attention passengers of American flight 2477 to Las Vegas: We will begin boarding soon. We'll start with anyone needing boarding assistance, and those with young children, and then we'll begin boarding first class and business class."

"How about exceptionally tired?" Travis said, standing. "I need a fuckin' Red Bull. Maybe we should have kept our tickets for tomorrow like we'd planned?"

I raised an eyebrow. "You have a problem with me being in a hurry to be Mrs. Travis Maddox?"

He shook his head, helping me to my feet. "Hell no. I'm still in shock, if you wanna know the truth. I just don't want you to be rushing because you're afraid you'll change your mind."

"Maybe I'm afraid you'll change your mind."

Travis's eyebrows pulled in, and he wrapped his arms around me. "You can't really think that. You gotta know there's nothing I want more."

I rose up on the balls of my feet and pecked his lips. "I think we're getting ready to board a plane for Vegas so we can get married, that's what I think."

Travis squeezed me against him, and then kissed me excitedly from cheek to collarbone. I giggled as he tickled my neck, and laughed even louder when he lifted me off the ground. He kissed me one last time before taking my bag off the floor, lowered me to the ground, and then led me by the hand to the line.

We showed our boarding passes and walked down the Jetway hand in hand. The flight attendants took one look at us and offered a knowing smile. Travis passed our seats to let me by, placed our carry-on bags in the overhead bin, and collapsed next to me. "We should probably try to sleep on the way, but I'm not sure I can. I'm too fucking amped."

"You just said you needed a Red Bull."

His dimple caved as he smiled. "Stop listening to everything I say. I'm probably not going to make sense for the next six months while I try to process the fact that I've gotten everything I've ever wanted."

I leaned back to meet his eyes. "Trav, if you wonder why I'm in such a hurry to marry you . . . what you just said is one of the many reasons why."

"Yeah?"

"Yeah."

He scooted down in his seat, and then laid his head on

my shoulder, nuzzling my neck a few times before relaxing. I touched my lips to his forehead, and then looked out the window, waiting as the other passengers passed by and silently praying for the pilot to hurry the hell out of there. I'd never been so thankful for my unrivaled poker face. I wanted to stand up and scream for everyone to sit down and for the pilot to get us off the ground, but I forbid myself to even fidget, and willed my muscles to relax.

Travis's fingers found their way to mine, and intertwined with them. His breath heated up the spot it touched on my shoulder, sending warmth throughout my body. Sometimes I just wanted to drown in him. I thought about what might happen if my plan didn't work. Travis being arrested, tried in court, and the worst case scenario: being sent to prison. Knowing it was possible to be separated from him for a very long time, I felt that a promise to be with him forever didn't seem like enough. My eyes filled with tears, and one escaped, falling down my cheek. I wiped it away quickly. Damn fatigue always made me more emotional.

The other passengers were stowing their bags and buckling their seat belts, going through the motions with no idea that our lives were about to change forever.

I turned to look out the window. Anything to get my mind off the urgency to get off the ground. "Hurry," I whispered.

Travis

It was easy to relax when I rested my head in the crook of Abby's neck. Her hair still smelled a little bit like smoke, and her hands were still pink and swollen from trying to force the basement window open. I tried to push that image from my head: the soot smudges on her face, her frightened eyes red and irritated from the smoke, emphasized by the smeared black mascara surrounding them. If I hadn't stayed behind, she might not have made it. Life without Abby didn't sound like much of a life at all. I didn't want to even wonder what losing her would be like. Going from a nightmare situation to one I'd dreamed about was a jarring experience, but lying there against Abby as the plane hummed and the flight attendant deadpanned the announcements over the PA system made for a somewhat easier transition.

I reached for Abby's fingers, lacing mine with hers. Her cheek pressed against the top of my head so subtly that if I'd been paying attention to what string to pull to trigger the automatic inflation of my life vest, I might have missed her tiny display of affection.

In just a few months' time, the petite woman next to me had become my whole world. I fantasized about how beautiful she would be in her wedding dress, returning home to watch Abby make the apartment her own, buying our first car, and doing those everyday, boring things that married people did, like the dishes and grocery shopping—together. I imagined watching her walk across the stage at her graduation. After we both found jobs, we would likely start a family. That was just three or four years away. We both had broken homes, but I knew Abby would be a damn good mother. I thought about how I would react when she broke the news to me of being pregnant, and I already felt a little emotional about it.

It wouldn't all be sunshine and rainbows, but struggling through a rough patch was when we were at our best, and we'd had enough rough patches to know we could get through them.

With thoughts of a future in which Abby was swollen with our first child running through my mind, my body relaxed against the itchy airplane seat, and I fell asleep.

What was I doing here? The smell of smoke burned my nose, and the cries and screaming in the distance made my blood turn to ice, even though sweat was pouring down my face. I was back in the bowels of Keaton Hall.

"Pigeon?" I yelled. I coughed and squinted my eyes, as if that would help me see through the darkness. "Pigeon!"

I'd felt this feeling before. The panic; the pure adrenaline of being truly afraid of dying. Death was just moments away, but I didn't think about what it would feel like to suffocate or burn alive. I only thought about Abby. Where was she? Was she okay? How would I save her?

A single door came into view, highlighted by the approaching flames. I turned the knob and pushed into the ten-by-ten room. It was just four walls of concrete blocks. One window. A small group of girls and a couple of guys were against the far wall, trying to reach for their only escape.

Derek, one of my frat brothers, was holding up one of the girls, and she was desperately reaching for the window. "Can you get it, Lindsey?" He grunted, breathing hard.

"No! I can't reach it!" she cried, clawing above her. She was wearing a pink Sigma Kappa T-shirt, damp from sweat.

Derek nodded to his friend. I didn't know his name, but he was in my humanities class. "Lift Emily, Todd! She's taller!"

Todd bent over and laced his fingers together, but Emily had flattened herself against the wall, frozen with fear. "Emily, get over here."

Her face compressed. She looked like a little girl. "I want my mom," she whimpered.

"Get. The fuck. Over here!" Todd commanded.

After taking a tiny moment to find her courage, Emily pushed away from the wall and climbed onto Todd. He pushed her up, but she couldn't reach it, either.

Lainey watched her friend reach for the window, noticed the approaching flames, and then balled her hands into fists at her chest. She squeezed them so tight, they shook. "Keep trying, Emily!"

"Let's try another way!" I said, but they didn't hear me. Maybe they'd already tried several routes, and this was the only window they could find. I ran into the dark hallway and looked around. This was the dead end. We had nowhere else to run.

I went back in, trying to think of something to save us. Dusty sheets covered stored furniture that lined the walls, and the fire was using them as a pathway. A pathway straight to the room we were in.

I backed up a few steps, and then turned to face the kids behind me. Their eyes widened, and they retreated against the wall. Lainey was trying to climb up the cement blocks out of pure terror.

"Have you seen Abby Abernathy?" I said. They didn't hear me. "Hey!" I yelled again. None of those kids acknowledged me. I walked up to Derek and screamed at him. "Hey!" He looked right through me at the fire, a horrified look on his face. I looked at the others. They didn't see me, either.

Confused, I walked over to the wall, and jumped, trying to reach the window, and then I was kneeling on the ground outside, looking in. Derek, Todd, Lainey, Lindsey, and Emily were still inside. I tried to open the window, but it wouldn't budge. I kept trying, anyway, hoping at any moment it would pop open and I could pull them out.

"Hold on!" I yelled. "Help!" I yelled again, hoping someone would hear.

The girls hugged, and Emily began to wail. "This is just a bad dream. This is just a bad dream. Wake up! Wake up!" she said over and over.

"Get one of the sheets, Lainey!" Derek said. "Roll it up and shove it under the door!"

Lainey scrambled to pull a sheet off a desk. Lindsey helped her, and then watched Lainey shove it desperately under the door. They both backed away, watching the door.

"We're trapped," Todd said to Derek.

Derek's shoulders fell. Lainey walked over to him, and he touched her dirty cheeks with both hands. They stared into each other's eyes. Thick, black smoke snaked under the door and seeped into the room.

Emily jumped for the window. "Lift me up, Todd! I want out! I want out of here!"

Todd watched her jump with a defeated expression on his face.

"Mommy!" Emily screamed. "Mommy help me!" Her eyes were trained on the window, but still she looked past me.

Lindsey reached out for Emily, but she wouldn't be touched. "Sssh . . ." she said, trying to comfort her from where she stood. She covered her mouth with her hands and began to cough. She looked at Todd, tears streaming down her face. "We're going to die."

"I don't want to die!" Emily screamed, still jumping.

As the smoke filled the room I punched the window, over and over. The adrenaline must have been unbelievable, because I couldn't feel my hand hitting the glass, even though

I was using every bit of strength I had. "Help me! Help!" *I yelled, but no one came.*

Smoke bumped and swirled against the window, and the coughs and crying silenced.

My eyes popped open, and I looked around. I was on the plane with Abby, my hands clenching the armrests, and every muscle in my body clenched.

"Travis? You're sweating," Abby said. She touched my cheek.

"I'll be right back," I said, quickly unbuckling my seat belt. I rushed to the back of the plane and jerked open the lavatory door, and then locked it behind me. Flipping up the sink lever, I splashed water on my face, and then stared into the mirror, watching the drops of water slide off my face and onto the counter.

They were there because of me. I knew Keaton wasn't safe, and I knew too many people were in that basement, and I let it happen. I contributed to dozens of deaths, and now I was on a plane to Las Vegas. What the fuck was wrong with me?

I walked back to my seat and buckled in next to Abby.

She stared at me, noticing right away that something was wrong. "What?"

"It's my fault."

She shook her head, and kept her voice low. "No. Don't do that."

"I should have said no. I should have insisted on a safer place."

"You didn't know that was going to happen." She glanced around, making sure no one was listening. "It's awful. It's horrific. But we couldn't stop it. We can't change it."

"What if I get arrested, Abby? What if I go to jail?"

"Sssh," she said, reminding me of the way Lindsey tried to comfort Emily in my dream. "It won't happen," she whispered. Her eyes were focused; resolute.

"Maybe it should."

CHAPTER THREE

Lucky One

Abby

When the wheels of the airplane touched down on the runway of McCarran International Airport, Travis was finally relaxed and leaning on my shoulder. The bright lights of Las Vegas had been visible for the past ten minutes, signaling us like a beacon toward everything I hated—and everything I wanted.

Travis roused slowly, glancing out the window quickly before kissing the cusp of my shoulder. "We're here?"

"Viva. I thought maybe you'd go back to sleep. It's going to be a long day."

"There's no way I was going back to sleep after that dream," he said, stretching. "I'm not sure I want to sleep again."

My fingers squeezed his. I hated to see him so shaken. He wouldn't talk about his dream, but it didn't take much

25

to figure out where he was while he was sleeping. I wondered if anyone that had escaped from Keaton would be able to close their eyes without seeing the smoke and the panicked faces. The plane arrived at the gate, the SEAT BELT light dinged, and the cabin lights came on, signaling everyone to stand up and dig for their carry-on luggage. Everyone was in a hurry, even though no one was getting out of there before the people seated ahead of them.

I sat, feigning patience, watching Travis stand to pull out our luggage. His T-shirt rose when he reached up, revealing his abs shifting and then contracting when he pulled down the bags.

"You got a dress in here?"

I shook my head. "I thought I'd find one here."

He nodded once. "Yeah, I bet they have plenty to choose from. A better selection for a Vegas wedding than home."

"My line of thinking exactly."

Travis held out his hand and helped me take the two steps to the aisle. "You'll look great no matter what you put on."

I kissed his cheek and took my bag just as the line began to move. We followed the other passengers down the gateway and into the terminal.

"Déjà vu," Travis whispered.

I felt the same. The slot machines sung their siren's song and flashed brightly colored lights, falsely promising luck and big money. The last time Travis and I were here, it was easy to pick out the couples who were getting married, and I wondered if we were just as obvious.

Travis took my hand as we passed baggage claim, and then followed the sign marked TAXIS. The automatic doors parted and we walked into the desert night air. It was still stifling hot, and dry. I breathed in the heat, letting Las Vegas saturate every part of me.

Marrying Travis would be the hardest easiest thing I'd ever done. I needed to awaken the parts of me that were molded in the darkest corners of this city to make my plan work. If Travis thought that I was doing this for any reason other than just wanting to commit to him, he would never let me go through with it, and Travis was not exactly gullible, and worse, he knew me better than anyone else; he knew what I was capable of. If I pulled the wedding off, *and* kept Travis out of prison without him knowing why, it would be my best bluff yet.

Even though we'd bypassed the crowd waiting for baggage, there was a long line for taxis. I sighed. We should have been getting married by now. It was still dark, but it had been over five hours since the fire. We couldn't afford more lines.

"Pidge?" Travis squeezed my hand. "You okay?"

"Yeah," I said, shaking my head and smiling. "Why?"

"You seem . . . a little tense."

I took stock of my body; how I was standing, my facial

expression, anything that might tip him off. My shoulders were so tight they were hanging up around my ears, so I forced them to relax. "I'm just ready."

"To get it over with?" he asked, his eyebrows pulling in infinitesimally. Had I not known better, I would have never caught it.

"Trav," I said, wrapping my arms around his waist. "This was my idea, remember?"

"So was the last time we went to Vegas. You remember how that turned out?"

I laughed, and then I felt terrible. The vertical line his eyebrow formed when he pushed them together deepened. This was so important to him. How much he loved me was overwhelming most of the time, but tonight was different. "I'm in a hurry, yes. Aren't you?"

"Yes, but something's off."

"You're just nervous. Stop worrying."

His face smoothed, and he hugged me. "Okay. If you say you're okay, then I believe you."

Fifteen long minutes later, and we were at the front of the line. A taxi pulled to the curb and stopped. Travis opened the door for me, and I ducked into the backseat and slid over, waiting for him to get in.

The cabdriver looked over his shoulder. "Short trip?"

Travis situated our single carry-on bag in front of him on the floorboard. "We travel light."

"Bellagio, please," I said calmly, keeping the urgency out of my voice.

With lyrics I didn't understand, a cheery, circuslike melody hummed through the speakers as we drove from the airport to the strip. The lights were visible miles before we reached the hotel.

When we arrived at the Strip, I noticed a river of people trekking up and down the sides of the road. Even in the wee hours of the morning, the sidewalks were packed with bachelors, women pushing strollers with sleeping babies, people in costumes taking pictures for tips, and businessmen—apparently looking to unwind.

Travis put his arm around my shoulders. I leaned against him, trying not to look at my watch for the tenth time.

The taxi pulled into the circle drive of the Bellagio, and Travis leaned forward with bills to pay the driver. He then pulled out our roller carry-on, and waited for me. I scooted out, taking his hand and stepping out onto the concrete. As if it weren't in the early AM, people were standing in the taxi line to go to a different casino, and others were returning, weaving and laughing after a long night of drinking.

Travis squeezed my hand. "We're really here."

"Yep!" I said, pulling him inside. The ceiling was distractingly ornate. Everybody in the lobby was standing around with their noses in the air.

"What are you—?" I said, turning to Travis. He was letting me pull him while he took in the ceiling.

"Look, Pidge! It's . . . wow," he said, in awe of the huge, multicolored flowers kissing the ceiling.

"Yep!" I said, tugging him to the front desk.

"Checking in," I said. "And we need to schedule a wedding at a local chapel."

"Which one?" the man asked.

"Any one. A nice one. A twenty-four-hour one."

"We can arrange that. I'll just get you checked in here, and then the concierge can help you with a wedding chapel, shows, anything you'd like."

"Great," I said, turning to Travis with a triumphant grin. He was still staring at the ceiling.

"Travis!" I said, pulling on his arm.

He turned, snapping out of his hypnotic state. "Yeah?"

"Can you go over to the concierge and get the wedding scheduled?"

"Yeah? I mean yeah. I can do that. Which one?"

I laughed once. "Close. Open all night. Classy."

"Got it," he said. He pecked my cheek before pulling the carry-on to the concierge desk.

"We're under Maddox," I said, pulling out a piece of paper. "This is our confirmation number."

"Ah, yes. I have a honeymoon suite available if you'd like to upgrade?"

I shook my head. "We're good." Travis was across the

room, talking with a man behind the desk. They were looking at a brochure together, and he had a huge smile on his face while the man pointed out the different venues.

"Please let this work," I said under my breath.

"What was that, ma'am?"

"Oh. Nothing," I said as he returned to clicking away on his computer.

Travis

Abby leaned in with a smile when I kissed her cheek, and then continued with check-in while I popped over to the concierge to nail down a chapel. I glanced over at my soon-to-be wife, her long legs propped up by those wedge heel shoes that make a nice pair of legs look even nicer. Her flow-y, thin shirt was just see-through enough that I felt disappointed to see a tank top under it. Her favorite sunglasses were perched on the front of her favorite fedora, and just a few long locks of her caramel hair, a little wavy from drying naturally after her shower, were cascading out from under the hat. My God, that woman was fucking sexy. She didn't even have to try, and all I wanted was to be all up in her business. Now that we were engaged that didn't sound like such a bastard thing to think.

"Sir?" the concierge said.

"Oh, yeah. Hey," I said, taking a last glance at Abby

before giving the guy my full attention. "I need a chapel. Open all night. Classy."

He smiled. "Of course, sir. We have several for you right here at the Bellagio. They are absolutely beautiful and—"

"You don't happen to have Elvis at a chapel here, do you? I figure if we're going to get married in Vegas, we should either get married by Elvis, or at least invite him, ya know?"

"No, sir, I apologize, the Bellagio chapels do not offer an Elvis impersonator. However, I can find a few numbers for you to call and request that one appear at your wedding. There is also, of course, the world famous Graceland Chapel, if you prefer. They have packages that include an Elvis impersonator."

"Classy?"

"I'm sure you'll be very pleased."

"Okay, that one. As quickly as possible."

The concierge smiled. "In a hurry, are we?"

I started to grin, but I realized I was already smiling, and probably had been, like an idiot, since I arrived at his desk. "Do you see that girl over there?"

He glanced at her. Quickly. Respectfully. I liked him. "Yes, sir. You're a lucky man."

"I sure as shit am. Schedule the wedding for two . . . maybe three hours from now? She'll need time to pick up a few things and get ready."

"Very thoughtful of you, sir." He clicked a few buttons on his keyboard and then grabbed the mouse, moving it around and clicking it a few times. His smile faded as he concentrated, and then it lit up his face again when he finished. The printer buzzed, and then he handed me a piece of paper. "There you are, sir. Congratulations." He held up his fist, and I bumped it, feeling like he'd just handed me a winning lottery ticket.

CHAPTER FOUR

Three Hours

Travis

Abby held my hand, pulling me along as we walked through the casino to the elevators. I was dragging my feet, trying to take a look around before we went up-stairs. It had only been a few months since the last time we'd been in Vegas, but this time was less stressful. We were here for a much better reason. Regardless, Abby was still all-business, refusing to pause long enough for me to get too comfortable around the tables. She hated Las Vegas and with good reason, which made me question even more why she chose to come here, but as long as she was on a mission to be my wife, I wasn't going to argue.

"Trav," she said, huffing. "The elevators are right . . . there . . ." She tugged on me a few times toward her final destination.

"We're on vacation, Pidge. Cool your jets."

"No, we're getting married, and we have less than twenty-four hours to get it done."

I pressed the button, pulling us both into an open space to the side of the crowd. It shouldn't have been surprising that there were so many people just ending their night this close to sunrise, but even a buck wild frat boy like myself could be impressed here.

"I still can't believe it," I said. I brought her fingers to my mouth and kissed them.

Abby was still looking above the elevator doors, watching the numbers descend. "You've mentioned that." She looked over to me and one corner of her mouth turned up. "Believe it, baby. We're here."

My chest rose while my lungs filled with air, preparing to let out a long sigh. In recent memory, or maybe ever, my bones and muscles had never been so relaxed. My mind was at ease. It felt strange to feel all of those things, knowing what we'd just left behind back on campus, and at the same time feeling so responsible. It was disorienting, and unsettling, this feeling happy one minute, and like a criminal the next.

A slit formed between the elevator doors, and then they slowly slid away from each other, allowing the passengers to bleed out into the hallway. Abby and I stepped on together with our small roller duffle bag. One woman had a large purse, a large carry-on that was the size of two of ours, and a four-wheeled, vertical suitcase that could fit at least two small children.

"Moving here?" I asked. "That's cool." Abby jammed her elbow into my ribs.

She took a long look at me, and then Abby, and then spoke in a French accent. "No." She looked away, clearly unhappy I'd spoken to her.

Abby and I traded glances, and then she widened her eyes, silently saying *Wow, what a bitch.* I tried not to laugh. Damn, I loved that woman, and I loved that I knew what she was thinking without her saying a word.

The French woman nodded. "Press floor thirty-five, please." Almost the Penthouse. Of course.

When the doors opened on the twenty-fourth floor, Abby and I stepped out onto the ornate carpet, a bit lost, doing the search-walk that people always do when looking for their hotel room. Finally, at the end of the hall, Abby inserted her keycard and pulled it out quickly.

The door clicked. The light turned green. We were in.

Abby flipped on the light and pulled her purse over her head, tossing it on to the king-size bed. She smiled at me. "This is nice."

I let go of the bag handle, letting it topple over, and then took Abby into my arms. "That's it. We're here. When we sleep in that bed later, we're going to be husband and wife."

Abby looked into my eyes, deep and thoughtful, and then cupped one side of my face. A corner of her mouth turned up. "We sure will."

I couldn't begin to imagine what thoughts were swirling behind her beautiful gray eyes, because almost immediately that thoughtful look disappeared.

She rose up on the balls of her feet and pecked me on the mouth. "What time is the wedding?"

Abby

"*Three* hours?" I kept my muscles relaxed even though my entire body wanted to tense up. We were wasting too much time, and I had no way to explain to Travis why I needed to get it over with.

Get it over with? Is that how I really felt about it? Maybe it wasn't just that Travis needed a plausible alibi. Maybe I was afraid I would chicken out if there was too much time to think about what we were doing.

"Yeah," Travis said. "I figured you'd need time to get a dress and your hair done and all that girly shit. Was that . . . was I wrong?"

"No. No, it's fine. I guess I was just thinking we'd get here and just go. But, you're right."

"We're not going to the Red, Pidge. We're gettin' married. I know it's not in a church, but I figured we'd . . ."

"Yeah." I shook my head and closed my eyes for a second, and then looked at him. "Yes, you're right. I'm sorry. I'll go downstairs, find something white, and then I'll come back here and get ready. If I can't find something here, I'll go to Crystals. There are more shops there."

Travis walked toward me, stopping just a few inches away. He watched me for several moments, long enough to make me squirm.

"Tell me," he said softly. No matter how I tried to explain it away, he knew me well enough to know—poker face or not—that I was hiding something from him.

"I think what you're reading is exhaustion. I haven't slept in almost twenty-four hours."

He sighed, kissed my forehead, and then went to the mini fridge. He bent over, and then turned, holding up two small cans of Red Bull. "Problem solved."

"My fiancé is a genius."

He handed me a can, and then took me into his arms. "I like that."

"That I think you're a genius?"

"Being your fiancé."

"Yeah? Don't get used to it. I'll be calling you something different in three hours."

"I'll like the new name even better."

I smiled, watching Travis open the bathroom door.

"While you find a dress, I'm going to take another shower, shave, and then try to find something to wear."

"So you won't be here when I get back?"

"Do you want me to be? It's at the Graceland Chapel, right? I thought we'd just meet there."

"It'll be kind of cool to see each other at the chapel, just before, dressed and ready to walk down the aisle."

"You're going to walk around Vegas by yourself for three hours?"

"I grew up here, remember?"

Travis thought for a moment. "Isn't Jesse still working as a pit boss?"

I lifted an eyebrow. "I don't know. I haven't talked to him. But even if he was, the only casino I'll be anywhere near is the Bellagio's, and that's just long enough for me to walk through to our room."

Travis seemed satisfied with that, and then nodded. "Meet you there." He winked at me, and then shut the bathroom door.

I grabbed my purse off the bed and the room keycard, and, after glancing at the bathroom door, picked up Travis's cell phone off the nightstand.

Opening his contacts, I pressed on the name I needed, sent the contact information to my phone via text, and then deleted the text message the second it went through. When I set his phone down, the bathroom door opened, and Travis appeared in just a towel.

"Marriage license?" he asked.

"The chapel will take care of it for an extra fee."

Travis nodded, seeming relieved, and then shut the door again.

I yanked the room door open and made my way to the elevator, inputting and then calling the new number.

"Please pick up," I whispered. The elevator opened,

revealing a crowd of young women, probably just a little older than me. They were giggling and slurring their words, half of them discussing their night, the others deciding if they should go to bed or just stay up so they wouldn't miss their flight home.

"Pick up, damnit," I said after the first ring. Three rings later, voicemail chimed in.

You've reached Trent. You know what to do.

"Ugh," I huffed, letting my hand fall to my thigh. The door opened, and I walked with purpose to the Bellagio shops.

After searching through too fancy, too trashy, too much lace, too many beads, and too . . . much of everything, I finally found it: the dress I would wear when I became Mrs. Maddox. It was white, of course, and tea length. Fairly plain, really, except for the sheer bateau neckline and a white satin ribbon that tied around the waist. I stood in the mirror, letting my eyes study each line and detail. It was beautiful, and I felt beautiful in it. In just a couple of hours, I would be standing next to Travis Maddox, watching his eyes take in every curve of the fabric.

I walked along the wall, scanning the numerous veils. After trying on the fourth, I placed it back into its cubby, flustered. A veil was too proper. Too innocent. Another display caught my eye, and I walked toward it, letting my fingers run over the different beads, pearls, stones, and metals of various hairpins. They were less delicate, and more . . . *me*. There were so many on the table, but I kept coming back to one in particular. It had a small, silver comb, and the rest of it was just dozens of different-size rhinestones that somehow formed a butterfly. Without knowing why, I held it in my hand, sure it was perfect.

The shoes were in the back of the store. They didn't have a huge selection, but luckily I wasn't super picky and chose the first pair of silver strappy heels I saw. Two straps went over my toes, and two more around my ankle, with a group of pearls to camouflage the belt. Thankfully they had size six in stock, and I was on to the last thing on my list: jewelry.

I chose a simple but elegant pair of pearl earrings. At the top, where they fastened to my ear, was a small cubic zirconia, just flashy enough for a special occasion, and a matching necklace. Never in my life had I wanted to stand out. Apparently even my wedding wouldn't change that for me.

I thought about the first time I stood in front of Travis. He was sweaty, shirtless, and panting, and I was covered in Marek Young's blood. That was just six months ago, and now we're getting married. And I'm nineteen. I'm only nineteen.

What the fuck am I doing?

I stood at the register, watching the receipt being printed out for the dress, shoes, hairpin, and jewelry, trying not to hyperventilate.

The redhead behind the counter tore off the receipt and handed it to me with a smile. "It's a gorgeous dress. Nice choice."

"Thank you," I said. I wasn't sure if I smiled back or not. Suddenly dazed, I walked away, holding the bag against my chest.

After a quick stop into the jewelry store for a black titanium wedding ring for Travis, I glanced at my phone and then tossed it back into my purse. I was making good time.

When I walked into the casino, my purse began to vibrate. I placed the bag between my legs and reached for it. After two rings, my searching fingers grew desperate, clawing and shoving everything to the side to get to the phone in time.

"Hello?" I screeched. "Trent?"

"Abby? Is everything okay?"

"Yeah," I breathed as I sat on the floor against the side of the closest slot machine. "We're fine. How are you?"

"I've been sitting with Cami. She's pretty upset about the fire. She lost some of her regulars."

"Oh, God, Trent. I'm so sorry. I can't believe it. It doesn't seem real," I said, my throat feeling tight. "There were so many. Their parents probably don't even know, yet." I held my hand to my face.

"Yeah." He sighed, sounding tired. "It's like a war zone down there. What's that noise? Are you in an arcade?" He sounded disgusted, as if he already knew the answer, and he couldn't believe we were that insensitive. "What?" I said. "God, no. We . . . we hopped on a flight to Vegas."

"*What?*" he said, incensed. Or maybe just confused, I couldn't be sure. He was excitable.

I cringed at the disapproval in his voice, knowing it was just the beginning. I had an objective. I had to set my feelings aside as best I could until I achieved what I came for. "Just listen. It's important. I don't have a lot of time, and I need your help."

"Okay. With what?"

"Don't talk. Just listen. Promise?"

"Abby, stop playin'. Just fucking tell me."

"There were a lot of people at the fight last night. A lot of people died. Someone has got to go to prison for it."

"You thinkin' it's gonna be Travis?"

"Him and Adam, yeah. Maybe John Savage, and anyone else they think coordinated it. Thank God Shepley wasn't in town."

"What do we do?"

"I asked Travis to marry me."

"Uh . . . okay. How the hell is that going to help him?"

"We're in Vegas. Maybe if we can prove we were off getting married a few hours later, even if a few dozen drunken frat boys testify that he was at the fight, it will sound just crazy enough to create reasonable doubt."

"Abby." He sighed.

A sob caught in my throat. "Don't say it. If you don't think it'll work, just don't tell me, okay? It was all I could think of, and if he finds out why I'm doing this, he won't do it."

"Of course he won't. Abby, I know you're afraid, but this is crazy. You can't marry him to keep him out of trouble. This won't work, anyway. You didn't leave until after the fight. "

"I said not to say that."

"I'm sorry. He wouldn't want you to do this, either. He would want you to marry him because you want to. If he ever found out, it'd break his heart."

"Don't be sorry, Trent. It's going to work. At least it will give him a chance. It's a chance, right? Better odds than he had."

"I guess," he said, sounding defeated.

I sighed and then nodded, covering my mouth with my free hand. Tears blurred my vision, making a kaleidoscope out of the casino floor. A chance was better than nothing.

"Congratulations," he said.

"Congrats!" Cami said in the background. Her voice sounded tired and hoarse, even though I was sure she was sincere.

"Thank you. Keep me updated. Let me know if they come sniffing around the house, or if you hear anything about an investigation."

"Will do . . . and it's really fucking weird that our baby brother is the first to get married."

I laughed once. "Get over it."

"Fuck off. And, I love ya."

"Love you, too, Trent."

I held the phone in my lap with both hands, watching the people walking by stare at me. They were obviously wondering why I was sitting on the floor, but not enough to ask. I stood up, picked up my purse and bag, and inhaled a deep breath.

"Here comes the bride," I said, taking my first steps.

CHAPTER FIVE

Caught

Travis

I dried off, brushed my teeth, and slipped on a T-shirt and shorts, and then my Nikes. Ready. Damn, it was good to be a man. I couldn't imagine having to blow-dry my hair for half an hour, and then burn it with whatever handheld metal hot iron I could find, and then spend fifteen to twenty minutes getting my makeup just right before finally getting dressed. Key. Wallet. Phone. Out the door. Abby had said there were shops downstairs, but she hinted strongly that we shouldn't see each other until the wedding, so I headed for the Strip.

Even when in a hurry, if the Bellagio fountains are dancing to the music, it is un-American not to stop and stand in awe. I lit a cigarette and puffed on it, resting my arms on a large, concrete ledge that lined the viewing platform. Watching the water sway and spray to the music reminded me of the last time I was there, standing with

Shepley while Abby efficiently kicked the asses of four or five poker veterans.

Shepley. Damn, I was so glad he wasn't at that fight. If I'd have lost him, or if he'd lost America, I'm not sure Abby and I would have been here. A loss like that would change the whole dynamic of our friendships. Shepley couldn't be around Abby and me without America, and America couldn't be around us without Shepley. Abby couldn't not be around America. If they hadn't decided to stay with his parents over spring break, I could be suffering the loss of Shepley instead of preparing for our wedding. Thoughts of calling Uncle Jack and Aunt Deana with news of their only son's death made a cold shiver crawl down my spine.

I shook the thought away as I remembered the moment before I called my dad's phone, standing in front of Keaton, the smoke billowing out of the windows. Some of the firefighters were holding the hose to pour water inside, others were bringing out survivors. I remembered what it felt like: knowing that I was going to have to tell my dad that Trent was missing and probably dead. How my brother had run the wrong way in the confusion, and Abby and I were standing outside without him. Thoughts of what that would have done to my dad, to our entire family, made me feel sick to my stomach. Dad was the strongest man I knew, but he couldn't take losing anyone else.

My dad and Jack ran our town when they were in high school. They were the first generation of badass Maddox brothers. In college towns, the locals either started fights or were picked on. Jim and Jack Maddox never experienced the latter, and even met and married the only two girls at their college that could handle them: Deana and Diane Hempfling. Yes, sisters, making Shepley and me double cousins. It was probably just as well that Jack and Deana stopped at one, with Mom having five unruly boys. Statistically, our family was due for a girl, and I'm not sure the world could handle a female Maddox. All the fight and anger, plus estrogen? Everyone would die.

When Shepley was born, Uncle Jack settled down. Shepley was a Maddox, but he had his mother's temperament. Thomas, Tyler, Taylor, Trenton, and I all had short fuses like our dad, but Shepley was calm. We were the best of friends. He was a brother who lived in a different house. He pretty much was, but he looked more like Thomas than the rest of us. We all shared the same DNA.

The fountain died down and I walked away, seeing the sign for Crystals. If I could get in and out of there quick, maybe Abby would still be in the Bellagio shops and wouldn't see me.

I picked up the pace, dodging the extremely drunk and tired tourists. One short escalator ride and a bridge later, I was inside the stories-tall shopping center. It had glass rectangles displaying colorful water tornados, high-end shops, and the same odd range of people. Families to strippers. Only in Vegas.

I popped in and out of one suit shop without any luck, and then walked until I hit a Tom Ford store. In ten minutes, I'd found and tried on the perfect gray suit but had trouble finding a tie. "Fuck it," I said, taking the suit and a white button-up to the register. Who said a groom had to wear a tie?

Walking out of the shopping center, I saw a pair of black Converse in the window. I went in, asked for my size, tried them on, and smiled. "I'll take them," I said to the woman helping me. She smiled with a look in her eyes that would have turned me on just six months ago. A woman looking at me that way usually meant any attempts I made to get in her pants had just been made a thousand times easier. That look meant: take me home.

"Great choice," she said in a smooth, flirtatious voice. Her dark hair was long, thick, and shiny. Probably half of her five feet. She was a sophisticated, Asian beauty, wrapped in a tight dress and sky-high heels. Her eyes were sharp, calculating. She was exactly the kind of challenge my old self would have happily taken on. "Are you staying in Vegas long?"

"Just a few days."

"Is this your first time here?"

"Second."

"Oh. I was going to offer to show you around."

"I'm getting married in these shoes in a couple of hours."

My response snuffed out the desire in her eyes, and she smiled pleasantly, but she'd clearly lost interest. "Congratulations."

"Thanks," I said, taking my receipt and bag with the shoe box inside.

I left, feeling much better about myself than I would have had I been here on a guys' trip and leading her back to my hotel room. I didn't know about love back then. It was fanfuckingtastic to go home to Abby every night, and see the welcoming, loving look in her eyes. Nothing was better than coming up with new ways to make her fall in love with me all over again. I lived for that shit now, and it was way more satisfying.

Within an hour of leaving the Bellagio, I had picked up a suit and a gold band for Abby, and was right back where I started: in our hotel room. I sat on the end of the bed and grabbed the remote, clicking on the power to the TV before bending over to untie my sneakers. A familiar scene lit up the screen. It was Keaton, quartered off with yellow tape, and still smoking. The brick around the windows were charred, and the ground surrounding was saturated with water.

The reporter was interviewing a tearful girl, describing how her roommate had never returned to the dorm, and she was still waiting to hear if she was among the dead. I couldn't hold it in anymore. I covered my face with my hands and rested my elbows on my knees. My body shook as I mourned my friends and all the people I didn't know who'd lost their lives, as I apologized over and over for being the reason why they were there, and being too much of a fucking bastard for choosing Abby over turning myself in. When I couldn't cry anymore, I retreated to the shower, standing under the steaming water until I got back into the frame of mind Abby needed me to be in.

She didn't want to see me until just before the wedding, so I got my shit straight in my head, got dressed, slapped on some cologne, tied my new kicks, and headed out. Before letting the door close, I took one long, last look at the room. The next time I came through this door, I'd be Abby's husband. That was the only thing that made the guilt bearable. My heart began to pound. The rest of my life was just hours away.

The elevator opened, and I followed the loudly patterned carpet through the casino. The suit made me feel like a million bucks, and people were staring, wondering where the fine-looking asshole sporting Converse was off to. When I was about halfway through the casino, I noticed a woman sitting on the floor with shopping bags, crying into her cell phone. I stopped dead in my tracks. It was Abby.

Instinctively, I stepped to the side, partially hiding myself at the end of a row of slot machines. With the music, the beeping, and the chatter, I couldn't hear what she was saying, but my blood ran cold. Why was she crying? Who was she crying to? Didn't she want to marry me? Should I confront her? Should I just wait it out and hope to God she doesn't call it off?

Abby picked herself off the floor, struggling with her bags. Everything in me wanted to run to her and help, but I was afraid. I was fucking terrified that if I approached her in that moment, she might tell me the truth, and I was afraid to hear it. The selfish bastard in me took over, and I let her walk away.

Once she was out of sight, I sat on an empty slot machine stool and pulled the pack of cigarettes out of my inside pocket. Flicking the lighter, the end of my cigarette sizzled before it glowed red while I pulled in a long drag of smoke. What was I going to do if Abby changed her mind? Could we come back from something like that? Regardless of the answer, I was going to have to figure out a way. Even if she couldn't go through with the wedding, I couldn't lose her.

I sat there for a long time, smoking, slipping dollar bills into the slot machine while a waitress brought me free drinks. After four, I waved her away. Getting drunk before the wedding wouldn't solve a damn thing. Maybe that's why Abby was having second thoughts. Loving her wasn't enough. I needed to grow the fuck up, get a real job, quit drinking, fighting, and control my goddamn anger. I sat alone in the casino, silently vowing that I would make all of those changes, and they would start right then.

My phone chimed. Just an hour was left before the wedding. I texted Abby, worried how she might respond.

> *I miss u*

Abby

I smiled at the phone display, seeing the text was from Travis. I clicked a response, knowing that words couldn't convey what I was feeling.

> I miss u too

> *T-minus one hour. U ready yet?*

> Not yet. U?

> *Hells yes. I look ducking amazing. When u c me u will want 2 marry me 4 sure.*

> Ducking?

> *Fucking* goddamn auto correct. Pic?*

> No! It's bad luck!

> *Ur lucky 13. You have good luck.*

Ur marrying me. So clearly u don't. And don't call me that.

Love u baby.

Love u too. See u soon.

Nervous?

Of course. Aren't you?

Only about ur cold feet.

Feet r toasty warm.

I wish I could explain to u how happy I am right now.

U don't have to. I can relate.

☺

<3

I sat the phone on the bathroom counter and looked into the mirror, touching the end of the lip gloss wand to my bottom lip. After pinning one last piece of my hair back, I went over to the bed, where I'd laid the dress. It wasn't what my ten-year-old self would have chosen, but it was beautiful, and what we were about to do was beautiful. Even why I was doing it was beautiful. I could think of much less noble reasons to get married. And, besides that, we loved each other. Was getting married this young so awful? People used to do this all the time.

I shook my head, trying to shake off the dozens of conflicting emotions swirling around my mind. Why go back and forth? This was happening, and we were in love. Crazy? Yes. Wrong? No.

I stepped into the dress and then pulled up the zipper, standing in front of the mirror. "Much better," I said. In the store, as lovely as the dress was, without hair and makeup done, the dress didn't look right. With my red lips and painted lashes, the look was complete.

I pinned the diamond butterfly into the base of the messy curls that made up my side bun, and slipped my feet into the new strappy pumps. Purse. Phone. Trav's ring. The chapel would have everything else. The taxi was waiting.

Even though thousands of women were married in Las Vegas every year, it didn't keep everyone from staring at me as I walked across the casino floor in my wedding dress. Some smiled, some just watched, but it all made me uncomfortable. When my father lost his last professional match after four in a row, and he announced publicly that it was my fault, I'd received enough attention to last two lifetimes. Because of a few words spoken in frustration, he'd created "Lucky Thirteen" and given me an unbelievable burden to bear. Even when my mother finally decided to leave Mick and we moved to Wichita three years later, starting over seemed impossible. I enjoyed two whole weeks of being an unknown before the first local reporter figured out who I was and approached me on the front lawn of my high school. All it took was one hateful girl a single hour of Friday Night Googling to figure out why anyone in the press cared enough to try to get a "Where Is She Now?" headline. The second half of my high school experience was ruined. Even with a mouthy, scrappy best friend.

When America and I left for college, I wanted to be invisible. Until the day I'd met Travis, I was enjoying my newfound anonymity immensely.

I looked down from the hundredth pair of eyes watching me intently, and I wondered if being with Travis would always make me feel conspicuous.

CHAPTER SIX

Dead or Alive

Travis

The limo door slammed hard behind me. "Oh, shit. Sorry. I'm nervous."

The driver waved me away. "No problem. Twenty-two dollars, please. I'll come back with the limo."

The limo was new. White. Abby would like it. I handed him thirty. "So you'll be right back here in an hour and a half, right?"

"Yes, sir! Never late!"

He drove away, and I turned around. The chapel was lit up, glowing against the early morning sky. It was maybe a half hour before sunrise. I smiled. Abby was going to love it.

The front door opened, and a couple came out. They were middle-aged, but he was in a tux, and she was in a huge wedding dress. A short woman in a light pink suit dress was waving them good-bye, and then she noticed me.

"Travis?"

"Yes," I said, buttoning my jacket.

"I could just eat you up! I hope your bride appreciates what a looker you are!"

"She's prettier than me."

The woman cackled. "I'm Chantilly. Pretty much run things around here." She put her fists at her side, somewhere in the area of her hips. She was as wide as she was tall, and her eyes were nearly hidden under thick, fake lashes. "Come on in, sugar! Come in! Come in!" she said, rushing me inside.

The receptionist at the desk offered a smile and a small stack of paperwork. Yes, we want a DVD. Yes, we want flowers. Yes, we want Elvis. I checked all of the appropriate boxes, filled in our names and information, and then handed the paper back.

"Thank you, Mr. Maddox," the receptionist said.

My hands were sweating. I couldn't believe I was here.

Chantilly patted my arm, well, more like my wrist, because that's the highest she could reach. "This way, honey. You can freshen up and wait for your bride in here. What was her name?"

"Uh . . . Abby . . ." I said, walking through the door Chantilly had opened. I looked around, noting the couch and mirror surrounded by a thousand huge lightbulbs. The wallpaper was busy but nice, and everything seemed clean and classy, just like Abby wanted.

"I'll let you know when she arrives," Chantilly said with a wink. "You need anything? A water?"

"Yes, that would be great," I said, sitting down.

"Be right back," she lilted as she backed out of the room and closed the door behind her. I could hear her humming down the hall.

I leaned back against the couch, trying to process what had just happened, and wondering if Chantilly had just chugged a 5-hour ENERGY, or if she was just naturally that chipper. Even though I was just sitting, my heart was pounding against my chest. This is why people had witnesses: to help them keep calm before the wedding. For the first time since we'd landed, I wished Shepley and my brothers were there with me. They would have been giving me all kinds of shit, helping to keep my mind off the fact that my stomach was begging to throw up.

The door opened. "Here you are! Anything else? You look a little nervous. Have you eaten?"

"Nope. I haven't had time."

"Oh, we can't have you passing out at the altar! I'll bring you some cheese and crackers, and maybe a little fruit plate?"

"Uh, sure, thanks," I said, still a little bewildered by Chantilly's enthusiasm.

She backed out, shut the door, and I was alone again. My head fell back against the couch, my eyes picked out different shapes in the wall texture. I was grateful for anything that kept me from glancing down at my watch. Was she coming? I closed my eyes tight, refusing to go there.

She loved me. I trusted her. She would be here. Goddammit, I wished my brothers were here. I was going to go out of my everlovin' mind.

Abby

"Oh, don't you look pretty," the driver said as I slid into the backseat of the taxi.

"Thank you," I said, feeling relieved to be out of the casino. "Graceland Chapel, please."

"Did you want to start out the day married, or what?" the driver said, smiling back at me from the rearview mirror. She had short, gray hair, and her backside filled up all of the seat, and then some.

"It was just the quickest we could get it done."

"You're awfully young to be in such a hurry."

"I know," I said, watching Las Vegas pass by outside my window.

She clicked her tongue. "You look pretty nervous. If you're having second thoughts, just let me know. I don't mind turning around. It's okay, honey."

"I'm not nervous about getting married."

"No?"

"No, we love each other. I'm not nervous about that. I just want him to be okay."

"You think he's having second thoughts?"

"No," I said, laughing once. I met her eyes in the mirror. "Are you married?"

"Once or twice," she said, winking at me. "I got married in the same chapel that you are the first time around. But so did Bon Jovi."

"Oh, yeah?"

"You know Bon Jovi? *Tommy used to work on the docks!*" she sang, very much to my surprise.

"Yep! Heard of him," I said, amused and grateful for the distraction.

"I just love him. Here! I have the CD." She popped it in, and for the rest of the drive we listened to Jon's greatest hits. "Wanted Dead or Alive," "Always," "Bed of Roses"; "I'll Be There for You" was just finishing up as we pulled over to the curb in front of the chapel.

I pulled out a fifty. "Keep the rest. Bon Jovi helped."

She gave me back the change. "No tip, honey. You let me sing."

I shut the door and waved to her as she left. Was Travis already here? I walked up to the chapel and opened the door. An older woman with big hair and too much lip gloss greeted me. "Abby?"

"Yes," I said, fidgeting with my dress.

"You're stunning. My name is Chantilly, and I'll be one of your witnesses. Let me take your things. I'll put them away, and they'll be safe until you're finished."

"Thank you," I said, watching her take away my purse. Something swished when she walked, though I couldn't pinpoint what exactly. "Oh, wait! The . . ." I said, watching as she walked toward me holding out my purse. "Travis's ring is in there. I'm sorry."

Her eyes were barely slits when she smiled, making her fake lashes even more noticeable. "It's fine, honey. Just breathe."

"I don't remember how," I said, sliding his ring over my thumb.

"Here," she said, holding out her hand. "Give me your ring and his. I'll give them to each of you when it's time. Elvis will be by shortly to take you down the aisle."

I looked at her, blank faced. "Elvis."

"As in The King?"

"Yes, I know who Elvis is, but . . ." My words trailed away as I pulled off my ring with a small tug, and placed it in her palm next to Travis's ring.

Chantilly smiled. "You can use this room to freshen up. Travis is waiting, so Elvis will be knocking any minute. See you at the end of the aisle!"

She watched me as she shut the door. I turned, startled by my own reflection in the huge mirror behind me. It was bordered by large, round lights like one an actress might use before a Broadway show. I sat down at the vanity, staring at myself in the mirror. Is that what I was? An actress?

He was waiting. Travis is at the end of the aisle, waiting for me to join him so we can promise the rest of our lives to each other.

What if my plan doesn't work? What if he goes to prison and this was all for nothing? What if they didn't so much as sniff in Travis's direction, and this was all pointless? I no longer had the excuse that I had gotten married, before I was even legal to drink, because I was saving him. Did I need an excuse if I loved him? Why did anyone get married? For love? We had that in spades. I was so sure of everything in the beginning. I used to be sure about a lot of things. I didn't feel sure now. About anything.

I thought about the look on Travis's face if he found out the truth, and then I thought about what bailing would do to him. I never wanted him to hurt and I needed him as if he were a part of me. Of those two things I was sure.

Two knocks on the door nearly sent me into a panic attack. I turned, gripping the top of the chair back. It was white wire, swirls and curves formed a heart in the middle.

"Miss?" Elvis said in a deep, southern voice. "It's time."

"Oh," I said quietly. I don't know why. He couldn't hear me.

"Abby? Your hunka hunka burnin' love is ready for ya."

I rolled my eyes. "I just . . . need a minute."

The other side of the door was quiet. "Everything okay?"

"Yes," I said. "Just one minute, please."

After a few more minutes, there was another knock on the door. "Abby?" It was Chantilly. "Can I come in, honey?"

"No. I'm sorry, but no. I'll be okay. I just need a little more time, and I'll be ready."

After another five minutes, three knocks on the door caused beads of sweat to form along my hairline. These knocks were familiar. Stronger. More confident.

"Pidge?"

CHAPTER SEVEN

Cash

Travis

The door blew open. "She's here! I just showed her to a dressing room to freshen up. Are you ready?"

"Yeah!" I said, jumping to my feet. I wiped my sweaty palms on my slacks and followed Chantilly out to the hallway, and into the lobby. I stopped.

"This way, honey," Chantilly said, encouraging me toward the double doors that led into the chapel.

"Where is she?" I asked.

Chantilly pointed. "In there. As soon as she's ready, we'll get started. But, you have to be at the other end of the aisle, sugar."

Her smile was sweet and patient. I imagined she dealt with all kinds of situations, from drunks to jitters. After one last look at the door to Abby's room, I followed Chantilly down the aisle and she gave me the rundown on where to stand. While she was talking, a man with thick chops and an Elvis costume pushed open the door in grandiose fashion, curling his lips and humming "Blue Hawaii."

"Man, I really like Vegas! You like Vegas?" he said, his Elvis impression spot-on.

I grinned. "Today I do."

"Can't ask for better than that! Has Ms. Chantilly told you everything you need to know to be a mister this mornin'?"

"Yeah. I think."

He slapped my back. "No worries, fella, you're gonna do just fine. I'll go get your missus. Be back in a flash."

Chantilly giggled. "Oh, that Elvis." After a couple of minutes, Chantilly checked her watch, and then walked back down the aisle toward the double doors.

"This happens all the time," the officiant assured me.

After another five minutes, Chantilly popped her head through the doors. "Travis? I think she's a little . . . nervous. Do you want to try to talk to her?"

Fuck. "Yeah," I said. The aisle seemed short before, but now it felt like a mile. I pushed through the doors, and raised my fist. I paused, took a breath, and then knocked a few times. "Pidge?"

After what felt like two eternities, Abby finally spoke, her voice on the other side of the door. "I'm here." Even though she was only inches away, she sounded miles away, just like the morning after I brought those two girls home from the bar. Just the thought of that night made me feel a burning sickness in my gut. I didn't even feel like the same person I was then.

"You okay, baby?" I asked.

"Yes. I just . . . I was rushed. I need a moment to breathe."

She sounded anything but okay. I was determined to keep my head, to fight away the panic that used to cause me to do all kinds of stupid stuff. I needed to be the man Abby deserved. "You sure that's all?"

She didn't reply.

Chantilly cleared her throat and wrung her hands, clearly trying to think of something encouraging to say.

I needed to be on the other side of that door.

"Pidge . . ." I said, followed by a pause. What I would say next could change everything, but making everything all right for Abby trumped my own epically selfish needs. "I know you know I love you. What you may not know is that there is nothing I want more than to be your husband. But if you're not ready, I'll wait for you, Pigeon. I'm not going anywhere. I mean, yeah. I want this, but only if you do. I just . . . I need you to know that you can open this door and we can walk down the aisle, or we can get a taxi and go home. Either way, I love you."

After another long pause, I knew it was time. I pulled an old, worn envelope from my inside jacket pocket, and held it with both hands. The faded pen looped around, and I followed the lines with my index finger. My mother had written the words *To the future Mrs. Travis Maddox*. My dad had given it to me when he thought things between Abby and me were getting serious. I'd only pulled this letter out once since then, wondering what she'd written inside, but never betraying the seal. Those words weren't meant for me.

My hands were shaking. I had no clue what Mom had written, but I really needed her right now, and was hoping that this one time, she could somehow reach out from where she was and help me. I squatted down, sliding the envelope under the door.

Abby

Pidge. The word used to make my eyes roll. I didn't know why he started calling me that in the first place, and I didn't care. Now, Travis's weird little nickname for me spoken in his deep, gritty voice made my entire body relax. I stood and walked over to the door, holding my palm to the wood. "I'm here."

I could hear my breath; wheezing, slow, like I was sleeping. Every part of me was relaxed. His warm words fell slowly around me like a cozy blanket. It didn't matter what happened after we got home, as long as I was Travis's wife. It was then that I understood that whether I was doing this to help him or not, I was there to get married to the man who loved me more than any man loved any woman. And I loved him—enough for three lifetimes. In the Graceland Chapel, in this dress was almost exactly where I wanted to be. The only place better would be next to him at the end of the aisle.

Just then, a small, white square appeared at my feet.

"What's this?" I said, bending down to pick it up. The paper was old, yellow. It was addressed to the future Mrs. Travis Maddox.

"It's from my mom," Travis said.

My breath caught. I almost didn't want to open it, it had obviously been sealed and kept safe for so long.

"Open it," Travis said, seeming to read my thoughts.

My finger carefully slid in between the opening, hoping to preserve it as best I could, but failing miserably. I pulled out the tri-folded paper, and the entire world stopped.

We don't know each other, but I know that you must be very special. I can't be there today, to watch my baby boy promise his love to you, but there are a few things that I think I might say to you if I were.

First, thank you for loving my son. Of all my boys, Travis is the most tender hearted. He is also the strongest. He will love you with everything he has for as long as you let him. Tragedies in life sometimes change us, but some things never change.

A boy without a mother is a very curious creature. If Travis is anything like his father, and I know that he is, he's a deep ocean of fragility, protected by a thick wall of swear words and feigned indifference. A Maddox boy will take you all the way to the edge, but if you go with him, he'll follow you anywhere.

I wish more than anything that I could be there today. I wish I could see his face when he takes this step with you, and that I could stand there with my husband and experience this day with all of you. I think that's one of the things I'll miss the most. But today isn't about me. You reading this letter means that my son loves you. And when a Maddox boy falls in love, he loves forever.

Please give my baby boy a kiss for me. My wish for both of you is that the biggest fight you have is over who is the most forgiving.

Love,
Diane

"Pigeon?"

I held the letter to my chest with one hand, and opened the door with the other. Travis's face was tight with worry, but the second his eyes met mine, the worry fell away.

He seemed stunned by the sight of me. "You're . . . I don't think there's a word for how beautiful you are."

His sweet, chestnut eyes, shadowed by his thick eyelashes, soothed my nerves. His tattoos were hidden under his gray suit and crisp, white button-up. My God, he was perfection. He was sexy, he was brave, he was tender, and Travis Maddox was mine. All I had to do was walk down the aisle. "I'm ready."

"What did she say?" he asked.

My throat tightened so a sob wouldn't escape. I kissed him on the cheek. "That's from her."

"Yeah?" he said, a sweet smile sweeping his face.

"And she pretty much nailed everything wonderful about you, even though she didn't get to watch you grow up. She's so wonderful, Travis. I wish I could have known her."

"I wish she could have known you." He paused a moment in thought, and then held up his hands.

His sleeve inched back, revealing his PIGEON tattoo. "Let's sleep on it. You don't have to decide right now. We'll go back to the hotel, think about it, and—" He sighed, letting his arms and shoulders fall. "I know. This is crazy. I just wanted it so bad, Abby. This crazy is my sanity. We can . . ."

I couldn't stand watching him stumble and struggle any longer. "Baby, stop," I said, touching his mouth with three of my fingertips. "Just stop."

He watched me. Waiting.

"Just so we're straight, I'm not leaving here until you're my husband."

At first his brows pulled in, dubious, and then he offered a cautious smile. "You're sure?"

"Where's my bouquet?"

"Oh!" Chantilly said, distracted by the discussion. "Here, honey." She handed me a perfectly round ball of red roses.

Elvis offered his arm, and I took it. "See you at the altar, Travis," he said.

Travis took my hand, kissed my fingers, and then jogged back the way he'd come, followed by a giggly Chantilly.

That small touch wasn't enough. Suddenly I couldn't wait to get to him, and my feet quickly made their way to the chapel. The wedding march wasn't playing, instead "Thing for You," the song we danced to at my birthday party, came through the speakers.

I stopped and looked at Travis, finally getting a chance to take in his gray suit and black Converse sneakers. He smiled when he saw the recognition in my eyes. I took another step, and then another. The officiant gestured for me to slow down, but I couldn't. My entire body needed to be next to Travis more than it ever had been before. He must have felt the same way. Elvis hadn't made it halfway before Travis decided to stop waiting and walked toward us. I took his arm.

"Uh . . . I was gonna give 'er away."

Travis's mouth pulled to one side. "She was already mine."

I hugged his arm, and we walked the rest of the way together. The music quieted, and the officiant nodded to both of us.

"Travis . . . Abby."

Chantilly took my rose bouquet, and then stood to the side.

Our trembling hands were knotted together. We were both so nervous and happy that it was almost impossible to stand still.

Even knowing how much I truly wanted to marry Travis, my hands were trembling. I'm not sure what the officiant said exactly. I can't remember his face or what he wore, I can only recall his deep nasally voice, his northeastern accent, and Travis's hands holding mine.

"Look at me, Pidge," Travis said quietly.

I glanced up at my future husband, getting lost in the sincerity and adoration in his eyes. No one, not even America, had ever looked at me with that much love. The corners of Travis's mouth turned up, so I must have had the same expression.

As the officiant spoke, Travis's eyes poured over me, my face, my hair, my dress—he even looked down at my shoes. Then, he leaned over until his lips were just a few inches from my neck, and inhaled.

The officiant paused.

"I wanna remember everything," Travis said.

The officiant smiled, nodded, and continued.

A flash went off, startling us. Travis glanced behind him, acknowledged the photographer, and then looked at me. We mirrored each other's cheesy grins. I didn't care that we must have looked absolutely ridiculous. It was like we were getting ready to jump off the highest high dive into the deepest river that fed into the most magnificent, terrifying waterfall, right onto the best and most fantastic roller coaster in the universe. Times ten.

"True marriage begins well before the wedding day," the officiant began. "And the efforts of marriage continue well beyond the ceremony's end. A brief moment in time and the stroke of the pen are all that is needed to create the legal bond of marriage, but it takes a lifetime of love, commitment, forgiveness, and compromise to make marriage durable and everlasting. I think, Travis and Abby, you've just shown us what your love is capable of in a tense moment. Your yesterdays were the path that led you to this chapel, and your journey to a future of togetherness becomes a little clearer with each new day."

Travis leaned his cheek to my temple. I was grateful he wanted to touch me where and whenever he could. If I could have hugged him to me and not disrupted the ceremony, I would have. The officiant's words began to blur together. A few times, Travis spoke, and I did, too. I slipped Travis's black ring onto his finger, and he beamed.

"With this ring, I thee wed," I said, repeating after the officiant.

"Nice choice," Travis said, admiring his ring.

When it was Travis's turn, he seemed to have trouble, and then slid two rings onto my finger: my engagement ring, and a simple, gold band.

I wanted to take a moment to appreciate that he'd gotten me an official wedding band, maybe even say so, but I was having an out-of-body experience. The harder I tried to be present, the faster everything seemed to happen.

I thought maybe I should actually listen to the list of things I was promising, but the only voice that made sense was Travis's. "I damn sure do," he said with a smile. "And I promise to never enter another fight, drink in excess, gamble, or throw a punch in anger . . . and I'll never, ever make you cry sad tears again."

When it was my turn again, I paused. "I just want you to know, before I make my promises, that I'm super stubborn. You already know I'm hard to live with, and you've made it clear on dozens of occasions that I drive you crazy. And I'm sure I've driven anyone who's watched these last few months crazy with my indecision and uncertainty. But I want you to know that whatever love is, this has got to be it. We were best friends first, and we tried not to fall in love, and we did anyway. If you're not with me, it's not where I want to be. I'm in this. I'm with you. We might be impulsive, and absolutely insane to be standing here at our age, six months after we met.

This whole thing might play out to be a completely wonderful, beautiful disaster, but I want that if it's with you."

"Like Johnny and June," Travis said, his eyes a bit glossed over. "It's all uphill from here, and I'm going to love every minute of it."

"Do you—" the officiant began.

"I do," I said.

"Okay," he said with a chuckle, "but I have to say it."

"I've heard it once. I don't need to hear it again," I said, smiling, never taking my eyes from Travis. He squeezed my hands. We repeated more promises, and then the officiant paused.

"That's it?" Travis asked.

The officiant smiled. "That's it. You're married."

"Really?" he asked, his eyebrows raised. He looked like a kid on Christmas morning.

"You may now kiss your—"

Travis took me in both arms and wrapped me tightly, kissing me, excitedly and passionate at first, and then his lips slowed, moving against mine more tenderly.

Chantilly clapped with her petite, chubby hands. "That was a good one! The best one I've seen all week! I love it when they don't go as planned."

The officiant said, "I present to you, Ms. Chantilly and Mr. King, Mr. and Mrs. Travis Maddox."

Elvis clapped, too, and Travis lifted me in his arms. I took each side of his face into my hands and leaned over to kiss him.

"I'm just trying not to have a Tom Cruise moment," Travis said, beaming at everyone in the room. "I now understand the whole jumping on the couch and punching the floor thing. I don't know how to express how I feel! Where's Oprah?"

I let out an uncharacteristic cackle. He was grinning ear to ear, and I'm sure I looked just as annoyingly happy. Travis set me down, and then glanced around at everyone in the room.

He seemed a little shocked. "Woo!" he yelled, his fists shaking in front of him. He was having a *very* Tom Cruise moment. He laughed, and then he kissed me again. "We did it!"

I laughed with him. He took me into his arms, and I noticed that his eyes were a little glossy.

"She married me!" he said to Elvis. "I fucking love you, baby!" he yelled again, hugging and kissing me.

I wasn't sure what I expected, but this definitely wasn't it. Chantilly, the officiant, and even Elvis were laughing, half in amusement, half in awe. The photographer's flash was going off like we were surrounded by paparazzi.

"Just a few papers to sign, a few pictures, and then

you can start your happily-ever-after," Chantilly said. She turned and then faced us again with a wide, toothy grin, holding up a piece of paper and a pen.

"Oh!" Chantilly said. "Your bouquet. We're going to need that in the pictures."

She handed me the flowers, and Travis and I posed. We stood together. We showed off our rings. Side by side, face-to-face, jumping in the air, hugging, kissing—at one point Travis held me up in his arms. After a quick signing of the marriage certificate, Travis led me by the hand to the limo waiting for us outside.

"Did that really just happen?" I asked.

"It sure as hell did!"

"Did I see some misty eyes back there?"

"Pigeon, you are now Mrs. Travis Maddox. I've never been this happy in my life!"

A smile burst across my face, and I laughed and shook my head. I'd never seen a crazy person be so endearing. I lunged at him, pressing his lips against mine. Since his tongue had been in my mouth in the chapel, all I could think about was getting it back there.

Travis knotted his fingers in my hair as I climbed on top of him, and I dug my knees into the leather seat on each side of his hips. My fingers fumbled with his belt while he leaned over to press the button to lift the privacy window.

I cussed his shirt buttons for taking so long to undo,

and then began working impatiently on his zipper. Travis's mouth was everywhere; kissing the tender parts of skin just behind my ear, running his tongue down the line of my neck, and nibbling my collarbone. With one motion, he turned me onto my back, immediately sliding his hand up my thigh and hooking my panties with his finger. Within moments, they were hanging off one of my ankles, and Travis's hand was moving up the inside of my leg until he paused at the tender skin between my thighs.

"Baby," I whispered before he silenced me with his mouth. He was breathing hard through his nose, holding me against him like it was the first and the last time.

Travis pulled back onto his knees, his ripped abs and chest, and his tattoos on full display. My thighs instinctively tensed, but he took my right leg in both of his hands, gently moving them apart. I watched as his mouth hungrily worked from my toes, to my heel, my calf, my knee, and then to my inner thigh. I lifted my hips to his mouth, but he lingered on my upper legs for several moments, far more patient than I was.

Once his tongue touched the most sensitive parts of me, his fingers slid between my dress and the seat, gripping my ass, lightly tugging me toward him. Every nerve melted and tensed at the same time. Travis had been in that position before, but he had clearly been holding back; saving his best work for our wedding night. My knees bent, shook, and I grabbed at his ears.

He paused once, only to whisper my name against my wet skin, and I faltered, closing my eyes and feeling as if they were rolling to the back of my head in pure ecstasy. I moaned, making his kisses more eager, and then he tensed, lifting my body closer to his mouth.

Every passing second became more intense, a brick wall between wanting to let go and needing to stay in that moment. Finally, when I couldn't wait any longer, I reached up and buried Travis's face into me. I cried out, feeling him smiling, overcome by the intense jolts of electricity bolting throughout my body.

With all of Travis's distractions, I didn't realize we were at the Bellagio until I heard the driver's voice over the speaker. "I'm sorry, Mr. and Mrs. Maddox, but we've arrived at your hotel. Would you like me to take another drive down the Strip?"

CHAPTER EIGHT

Finally

Travis

"No, just give us a minute," I said.

Abby was half-lying, half sitting on the black leather seat of the limo, her cheeks flushed, breathing hard. I kissed her ankle, and then pulled her panties off the toe of her high heel, handing them to her.

God damn, she was a beautiful sight. I couldn't take my eyes off of her while I buttoned up my shirt. Abby flashed me a huge grin while she shimmied her panties back over her hips. The limo driver knocked on the door. Abby nodded and I gave him the green light to open it. I handed him a large bill, and then lifted my wife into my arms. We made it through the lobby and then the casino in just a few minutes. You might say I was a little motivated to get back to the room—luckily having Abby in my arms provided cover for my bulging dick.

She ignored the dozens of people staring at us while we

entered the elevator, and then planted her mouth on mine. The floor number was muffled when I tried to say it to the amused couple closest to the buttons, but I saw out of the corner of my eye that they'd pushed the right one.

As soon as we stepped into the hall, my heart began to pound. When we reached the door, I struggled with keeping Abby in my arms and getting the keycard out of my pocket.

"I'll get it, baby," she said, pulling it out and then kissing me while she unlocked the door.

"Thank you, Mrs. Maddox."

Abby smiled against my mouth. "My pleasure."

I carried her into the room and lowered her down to stand at the foot of the bed. Abby watched me for a moment while she kicked off her heels. "Let's get this out of the way, Mrs. Maddox. This is one article of clothing of yours that I don't want to ruin."

I turned her around and then slowly unzipped her dress, kissing each piece of skin as it was exposed. Every inch of Abby was already ingrained in my mind, but touching and tasting the skin of the woman that was now my wife made it new all over again. I felt an excitement I'd never felt before.

The dress fell to the floor, and I picked it up, tossing it over the back of a chair. Abby unsnapped the back of her bra, letting it fall to the floor, and I tucked my thumbs between her skin and the lacey fabric of her panties. I grinned. I'd already had them off once.

I leaned down to kiss the skin behind her ear. "I love you so much," I whispered, slowly pushing her panties down her thighs. They fell to her ankles, and she kicked them away with her bare feet. I wrapped my arms around her, taking a deep breath in through my nose, pulling her bare back against my chest. I needed to be inside her, my dick was practically reaching out for her, but it was important to take our time. We only got one shot at a wedding night, and I wanted it to be perfect.

Abby

Goose bumps formed all over my body. Four months earlier, Travis had taken something from me I'd never given to any other man. I was so hell-bent on giving it to him, I didn't have time to be nervous. Now, on our wedding night, knowing what to expect and knowing how much he loved me, I was more nervous than I had been that first night.

"Let's get this out of the way, Mrs. Maddox. This is one article of clothing of yours that I don't want to ruin," he said.

I breathed out a small laugh, remembering my buttoned-up, pink cardigan, and the pattern of blood spatters down the middle of it. Then I thought about seeing Travis in the cafeteria the first time.

"*I ruin a lot of sweaters,*" he'd said with his killer smile and dimples. The same smile I wanted to hate; the same lips that were making their way down my back right now.

Travis moved me forward, and I crawled onto the bed, looking behind me, waiting, hoping he would climb on. He was watching me, pulling off his shirt, kicking off his shoes, and dropping his slacks to the floor. He shook his head, turned me onto my back, and then settled on top of me.

"No?" I asked.

"I'd rather look into my wife's eyes than be creative . . . at least for tonight."

He brushed a loose hair from my face, and then kissed my nose. It was a little amusing watching Travis take his time, pondering how and what he wanted to do to me. Once we were naked and settled under the sheets, he took a deep breath.

"Mrs. Maddox?"

I smiled. "Yes?"

"Nothing. I just wanted to call you that."

"Good. I kind of like it."

Travis's eyes scanned my face. "Do you?"

"Is that a real question? Because it's kind of hard to show it more than taking vows to be with you forever."

Travis paused, confliction darkening his expression. "I saw you," he said, his voice barely a whisper. "In the casino."

My memory instantly went into rewind, already sure he had crossed paths with Jesse, and he'd possibly seen a woman with him who resembled me. Jealous eyes play tricks on people. Just when I was ready to argue that I hadn't seen my ex, Travis began again.

"On the floor. I saw you, Pidge."

My stomach sank. He'd seen me crying. How would I possibly explain that away? I couldn't. The only way was to create a diversion.

I pushed my head back into the pillow, looking straight into the eyes. "Why do you call me Pigeon? I mean *really*?"

My question seemed to take him off guard. I waited, hoping he would forget all about the previous topic. I didn't want to lie to his face, or admit what I'd done. Not tonight. Not ever.

His choice to allow me to change the subject was clear in his eyes. He knew what I was doing, and he was going to let me do it. "You know what a pigeon is?"

I shook my head in a tiny movement.

"It's a dove. They're really fucking smart. They're loyal, and they mate for life. That first time I saw you, in the Circle, I knew what you were. Under the buttoned-up cardigan and the blood, you weren't going to fall for my shit. You were going to make me earn it. You would require a reason to trust me. I saw it in your eyes, and I couldn't shake it until I saw you that day in the cafeteria. Even though I tried to ignore it, I knew it even then. Every fuckup, every bad choice, were bread crumbs, so that we found our way to each other. So that we found our way to this moment."

My breath faltered. "I am so in love with you."

His body was lying between my open legs, and I could feel him against my thighs, only a couple of inches from where I wanted him to be.

"You're my wife." When he said the words, a peace filled his eyes. It reminded me of the night he won the bet for me to stay at his apartment.

"Yes. You're stuck with me, now."

He kissed my chin. "Finally."

He took his time as he gently slid inside of me, closing his eyes for only a second before gazing into mine again. He rocked against me slowly, rhythmically, kissing my mouth intermittently. Even though Travis had always been careful and gentle with me, the first few moments were a little uncomfortable. He must have known that I was new to this, even though I'd never mentioned it. The whole campus knew about Travis's conquests, but my experiences with him were never the wild romps everyone talked about. Travis was always soft and tender with me; patient. Tonight was no exception. Maybe even more so.

Once I relaxed, and moved back against him, Travis reached down. He hooked his hand behind my knee and pulled up gently, stopping at his hip. He slid into me again, this time deeper. I sighed, and lifted my hip to him. There were much worse things in life than promising to feel Travis Maddox's naked body against and inside of mine for the rest of my life. Much, much worse.

He kissed me, and tasted me, and hummed against my mouth. Rocking against me, craving me, pulling at my skin as he lifted my other leg and pushed my knees against my chest so he could press himself into me even deeper. I moaned and shifted, unable to keep quiet while he positioned himself so he was entering me at different angles, working his hips until my nails were digging into the skin of his back. My fingertips were buried deep into his sweaty skin, but I could still feel his muscles bulging and sliding beneath them.

Travis's thighs were rubbing and bumping against my backside. He held himself up on one elbow, and then sat up, pulling my legs with him until my ankles were resting on his shoulders. He made love to me harder, then, and even though it was a little painful, that pain shot sparks of adrenaline all over my body. It took every bit of pleasure I was already feeling to a new level.

"Oh, God . . . Travis," I said, breathing his name. I needed to say something, anything to let go of the intensity building up inside me.

My words made his body tense, and the rhythm of his movements became faster, more rigid, until beads of sweat formed on our skin, making it easier to slide against each other.

He let my legs fall back to the bed as he positioned himself directly over me again. He shook his head. "You feel so good," he moaned. "I wanna make this last all night, but I . . ."

I touched my lips to his ear. "I want you to come," I said, ending the simple sentence with a soft, small kiss.

I relaxed my hips, letting my knees fall even farther apart and closer to the bed. Travis pressed deep inside me, over and over, his movements building as he groaned. I gripped my knee, pulling it toward my chest. The pain felt so good it was addictive, and I felt it build until my whole body tensed in short but strong bursts. I moaned loudly, not caring who might hear.

Travis groaned in reaction. Finally, his movements slowed, but they were stronger, until he finally called out. "Oh, fuck! Damn! *Agh*!" he yelled. His body twitched and trembled as he pressed his forehead hard against my cheek.

Both out of breath, we didn't speak. Travis kept his cheek against mine, twitching one more time before burying his face in the pillow under my head.

I kissed his neck, tasting the salt on his skin.

"You were right," I said.

Travis pulled back to look at me, curious.

"You were my last first kiss."

He smiled, pressed his lips against me hard, and then buried his face against my neck. He was breathing heavily but still managed to sweetly whisper, "I fucking love you, Pigeon."

CHAPTER NINE

Abby

A buzzing pulled me out of a deep sleep. The curtains kept out all but the slivers of sun bordering them. The blanket and sheets were hanging halfway off our king-size bed. My dress had fallen off the chair onto the floor, joining Travis's suit that was scattered all over the room, and I could only see one of my high heels.

My naked body was tangled with Travis's, after the third time we consummated our marriage we passed out from sheer exhaustion.

Again with the buzzing. It was my phone on the night-stand. I reached over Travis and flipped it over, seeing Trent's name.

Adam arrested.
John Savage on the list of dead.

That was all he said. I felt sick as I deleted the messages, worried that maybe Trent didn't offer more because the police were at Jim's now, maybe even telling their dad that Travis might be involved. I glanced at the time on my phone. It was ten o'clock.

John Savage was one less person to investigate. One more death for Travis to feel guilty about. I tried to remember if I'd seen John after the fire broke out. He was knocked out. Maybe he'd never gotten up. I thought of those frightened girls Trent and I saw in the hall of the basement. I thought about Hilary Short, who I knew from calc class, and was smiling as she stood next to her new boyfriend near the opposite wall of Keaton Hall five minutes before the fire. How long the list of the dead really was and who was on it was something I'd tried *not* to think about.

Maybe we should all be punished. The truth was, we were all responsible, because we were all irresponsible. There is a reason why fire marshals clear these kinds of events and safety precautions are taken. We ignored all of that. Turning on a radio or the television without seeing the images on the news was impossible, so Travis and I avoided them when possible. But all this media attention meant investigators would be all the more motivated to find someone to blame. I wondered if their hunt would stop with Adam, or if they were out for blood. If I were a parent of one of those dead students, I might be.

I didn't want to see Travis go to jail for everyone's irresponsible behavior, and right or wrong, that wouldn't bring anyone back. I had done everything I could think of to keep him out of trouble, and I would deny his presence in Keaton Hall that night to my dying breath.

People had done worse for those they loved.

"Travis," I said, nudging him. He was facedown with his head buried under a pillow.

Uggggghhhhh, he groaned. "You want me to make breakfast? You want eggs?"

"It's just after ten."

"Still qualifies as brunch." When I didn't respond, he offered again. "Okay, an egg sandwich?"

I paused, and then looked over at him with a smile. "Baby?"

"Yeah?"

"We're in Vegas."

Travis's head popped up and he flipped on the lamp. Once the last twenty-four hours finally set in, his hand emerged from under his pillow and he hooked his arm around me, pulling me beneath him. He nestled his hips between my thighs, and then bent his head down to kiss me; softly, tenderly, letting his lips linger on mine until they were warm and tingly

"I can still get you eggs. Want me to call room service?"

"We actually have a plane to catch."

His face fell. "How much time do we have?"

"Our flight is at four. Checkout is at eleven."

Travis frowned, and looked over at the window. "I should have booked an extra day. We should be lying in bed or by the pool."

I kissed his cheek. "We have classes tomorrow. We'll save up and go somewhere later. I don't want to spend our honeymoon in Vegas, anyway."

His face screwed into disgust. "I definitely don't wanna spend it in Illinois."

I conceded with a nod. Couldn't exactly argue that. Illinois wasn't the first place that came to mind when I thought *honeymoon*. "St. Thomas is beautiful. We don't even need passports."

"That's good. Since I'm not fighting anymore, we'll need to save where we can."

I smiled. "You're not?"

"I told you, Pidge. I don't need all that when I have you. You've changed everything. You're tomorrow. You're the apocalypse."

My nose wrinkled. "I don't think I like that word."

He smiled and rolled onto the bed, just a few inches from my left side. Lying on his stomach, he pulled his hands under him, settling them under his chest, and he lay his cheek against the mattress, watching me for a moment, his eyes staring into mine.

"You said something at the wedding . . . that we were like Johnny and June. I didn't quite get the reference."

He smirked. "You don't know about Johnny Cash and June Carter?"

"Sort of."

"She fought him tooth and nail, too. They fought, and he was stupid about a lot of stuff. They worked it out and spent the rest of their lives together."

"Oh yeah? I bet she didn't have Mick for a dad."

"He'll never hurt you again, Pigeon."

"You can't promise that. Just when I start settling in somewhere, he shows up."

"Well, we're going to have regular jobs, broke like every other college student, so he won't have a reason to sniff around us for money. We'll need every dime. Good thing I still have a little left in savings to carry us through."

"Any ideas where you'll apply for a job? I thought about tutoring. Math."

Travis smiled. "You'll be good at that. Maybe I'll tutor science."

"You're very good at that. I can be a reference."

"I don't think it'll count coming from my wife."

I blinked. "Oh my God. That just sounds crazy."

Travis laughed. "Doesn't it? I fucking love it. I'm going to take care of you, Pidge. I can't promise that Mick will never hurt you again, but I can promise that I'll do everything I can to keep that from happening. And if it does, I'll love you through it."

I offered a small smile, and then reached up to touch his cheek. "I love you."

"I love you," he said right back. "Was he a good dad . . . before all that?"

"I don't know," I said, looking up at the ceiling. "I guess I thought he was. But what does a kid know about being a good parent? I have good memories of him. He drank for as long as I can remember, and gambled, but when his luck was up, he was kind. Generous. A lot of his friends were family men . . . they also worked for the mob, but they had kids. They were nice and didn't mind Mick bringing me around. I spent a lot of time behind the scenes, seeing things most kids don't get to see because he took me everywhere then." I felt a smile creep up, and then a tear fell. "Yeah, I guess he was, in his own way. I loved him. To me, he was perfect."

Travis touched his fingertip to my temple, tenderly wiping the moisture away. "Don't cry, Pidge."

I shook my head, trying to play it off. "See? He can still hurt me, even when he's not here."

"I'm here," he said, taking my hand in his. He was still staring at me, his cheek against the sheets. "You turned my world upside down, and I got a brand-new beginning . . . like an apocalypse."

I frowned. "I still don't like it."

He pushed off the bed, wrapping the sheet around his waist. "It depends on how you look at it."

"No, not really," I said, watching him walk to the bathroom.

"I'll be out in five."

I stretched, letting all of my limbs spread in every direction on the bed, and then I sat up, combing my hair out with my fingers. The toilet flushed, and then the faucet turned on. He wasn't kidding. He would be ready in a few minutes and I was still naked in bed.

Fitting my dress and his suit in the carry-on proved to be a challenge, but I finally made it work. Travis emerged from the bathroom and brushed his fingers across mine as we passed.

Teeth brushed, hair combed, I changed and we were checking out by eleven.

Travis took pictures of the lobby ceiling with his phone, and then we took one last look around before leaving for the long taxi line. Even in the shade it was hot, and my legs were already sticking to my jeans.

My phone buzzed in my purse. I checked it quickly.

> *Cops just left. Dad's @ Tim's but I told them you guys were in Vegas getting married. I think they fucking bought it.*

> Srsly?

> *Yeah! I should get an Oscar for that shit. JS*

I breathed a long sigh of relief.

"Who's that?" Travis asked.

"America," I said, letting the phone slip back into my purse. "She's pissed."

He smiled. "I bet."

"Where to? The airport?" Travis asked, holding his hand out for mine.

I took it, turning it enough so that I could see my nickname on his wrist. "No, I'm thinking we need to make a pit stop first."

One of his eyebrows pulled up. "To where?"

"You'll see."

CHAPTER TEN

Inked

Abby

"What do you mean?" Travis said, blanching. "We're not here for me?"

The tattoo artist stared at us both, a little surprised at Travis's surprise.

The entire taxi ride over, Travis assumed I was buying him a new tattoo as a wedding present. When I told the driver our destination, it never occurred to Travis that I would be the one getting inked. He talked about tattooing ABBY somewhere on him, but since he already had PIGEON on his wrist, I thought it would be redundant.

"It's my turn," I said, turning to the tattoo artist. "What's your name?"

"Griffin," he said in a monotone.

"Of course," I said. "I want MRS. MADDOX here." I touched my finger to my jeans on the right side of my lower abdomen, just low enough not to be seen, even in a bikini. I

99

wanted Travis to be the only one privy to my ink, a nice surprise every time he undressed me.

Travis beamed. "Mrs. Maddox?"

"Yes, in this font," I said, pointing to a laminated poster on the wall featuring sample tattoos.

Travis smiled. "That fits you. It's elegant, but not fussy."

"Exactly. Can you do that?"

"I can. It'll be about an hour. We have a couple people ahead of you. It'll be two fifty."

"Two fifty? For a few scribbles?" Travis said, his mouth falling open. "What the fuck, chuck?"

"It's Griffin," he said, unaffected.

"I know, but—"

"It's okay, baby," I said. "Everything is more in Vegas."

"Let's just wait until we get home, Pidge."

"Pidge?" Griffin said.

Travis sent him a death glare. "Shut up," he warned, looking back at me. "This'll be two hundred bucks cheaper back home."

"If I wait, I won't do it."

Griffin shrugged. "Then maybe you should wait."

I glared at Travis and Griffin. "I'm not waiting. I'm doing this." I pulled out my wallet and shoved three bills at Griffin. "So you take my money"—I frowned at Travis—"and you hush. It's my money, my body, and this is what I want to do."

Travis seemed to weigh what he was about to say. "But . . . it's going to hurt."

I smiled. "Me? Or you?"

"Both."

Griffin took my money and then disappeared. Travis paced the floor like a nervous expectant father. He peeked down the hall, and then paced some more. It was as cute as it was annoying. At one point he begged me not to do it, and then became impressed and touched that I was so hell-bent on going through with it.

"Pull down your jeans," Griffin said, getting his equipment ready.

Travis shot a piercing look at the short, muscular man from under his brow, but Griffin was too busy to notice Travis's most frightening expression.

I sat on the chair, and Griffin pushed buttons. As the chair reclined, Travis sat on a stool on the other side of me. He was fidgeting.

"Trav," I said in a soft voice. "Sit down." I held out my hand and he took it, also taking a seat. He kissed my fingers, and offered a sweet but nervous smile.

Just when I thought he couldn't take the waiting anymore, my cell phone buzzed in my purse.

Oh, God. What if it was a text message from Trent? Travis was already digging for it, grateful for the distraction.

"Leave it, Trav."

He looked at the display and frowned. My breath caught. He held out the phone for me to take. "It's Mare."

I grabbed it from him and would've felt relief if it

weren't for the cold cotton swab running over my hip bone. "Hello?"

"Abby?" America said. "Where are you? Shepley and I just got home. The car is gone."

"Oh," I said, my voice an octave higher. I hadn't planned on telling her yet. I wasn't sure how to break the news, but I was sure she was going to hate me. At least for a little while.

"We're . . . in Vegas."

America laughed. "Shut up."

"I'm totally serious."

America grew quiet, and then her voice was so loud, I flinched. "WHY are you in Vegas? It's not like you had a good time when you were there last!"

"Travis and I decided to . . . we kind of got married, Mare."

"What! This isn't funny, Abby! You better be fucking joking!"

Griffin placed the transfer onto my skin and pressed. Travis looked like he wanted to kill him for touching me.

"You're silly," I said, but when the tattoo machine began to hum my entire body tensed.

"What's that noise?" America said, steaming.

"We're at the tattoo parlor."

"Is Travis getting branded with your real name this time?"

"Not exactly . . ."

Travis was sweating. "Baby . . ." he said, frowning.

"I can do this," I said, focusing on spots on the ceiling. I jumped when Griffin's fingertip's touched my skin, but I tried not to tense.

"Pigeon," Travis said, his voice tinged with desperation.

"All right," I said, shaking my head dismissively. "I'm ready." I held the phone away from my ear, wincing from both the pain, and the inevitable lecture.

"I'm going to kill you, Abby Abernathy!" America cried. "Kill you!"

"Technically, it's Abby Maddox, now," I said, smiling at Travis.

"It's not fair!" she whined. "I was supposed to be your maid of honor! I was supposed to go dress shopping with you and throw a bachelorette party and hold your bouquet!"

"I know," I said, watching Travis's smile fade as I winced again.

"You don't have to do this, you know," he said, his eyebrow pulling together.

I squeezed his fingers. "I know."

"You said that already!" America snapped.

"I wasn't talking to you."

"Oh, you're talking to me," she fumed. "You are soooo talking to me. You are never going to hear the end of this, do you hear me? I will never, ever forgive you!"

"Yes you will."

"You! You're a . . . ! You're just plain mean, Abby! You're a horrible best friend!"

I laughed, causing Griffin to pull back. He breathed through his nose.

"I'm sorry," I said.

"Who was that?" America snapped.

"That was Griffin," I answered matter-of-factly.

"Is she done?" he asked Travis, annoyed.

Travis nodded once. "Keep it up."

Griffin just smiled, and continued. My whole body tensed again.

"Who the hell is Griffin? Let me guess: you invited a total stranger to your wedding and not your best friend?"

I cringed, from both her shrill voice and the needle stabbing into my skin. "No. He didn't go to the wedding," I said, sucking in a breath of air.

Travis sighed and shifted nervously in his chair, squeezing my hand. He looked miserable. I couldn't help but smile.

"I'm supposed to be squeezing your hand, remember?"

"Sorry," he said, his voice thick with distress. "I don't think I can take this." He opened his hand a bit and looked to Griffin.

"Hurry up, would ya?"

Griffin shook his head. "Covered in tats and can't take

your girlfriend getting a simple script. I'll be finished in a minute, mate."

Travis's expression turned severe. "Wife. She's my wife."

America gasped, the sound as high-pitched as her tone. "You're getting a tattoo? What is going on with you, Abby? Did you breathe toxic fumes in that fire?"

"Travis has my name on his wrist," I said, looking down at the smeared, black mess on my stomach. Griffin pressed the tip of the needle against my skin, and I clenched my teeth together. "We're married," I said through my teeth. "I wanted something, too."

Travis shook his head. "You didn't have to."

I narrowed my eyes. "Don't start with me."

The corners of his mouth turned up, and he gazed at me with the sweetest adoration I'd ever seen.

America laughed, sounding a bit insane. "You've gone crazy." *She should talk.* "I'm committing you to the asylum when I get home."

"It's not that crazy. We love each other. We have been practically living together on and off all year." *Okay, not quite all year . . . not that it matters now. Not enough to mention it and give America more ammunition.*

"Because you're nineteen, you idiot! Because you ran off and didn't tell anyone, and because I'm not there!" she cried.

For one second, guilt and second thoughts crept in. For one second, I let the tiniest bit of panic that I'd just made a huge mistake simmer to the surface, but the moment I looked up at Travis and saw the incredible amount of love in his eyes, it all went away.

"I'm sorry, Mare, I have to go. I'll see you tomorrow, okay?"

"I don't know if I want to see you tomorrow! I don't think I want to see Travis ever again!"

"I'll see you tomorrow, Mare. I know you want to see my ring."

"And your tat," she said, a smile in her voice.

I handed the phone to Travis. Griffin ran his thousand tiny knives of pain and anguish across my angry skin again. Travis shoved my phone in his pocket, gripping my hand with both of his, leaning down to touch his forehead to mine.

Not knowing what to expect helped, but the pain was a slow burn. As Griffin filled in the thicker parts of the letters I winced, and every time he pulled away to wipe the excess ink away with a cloth, I relaxed.

After a few more complaints from Travis, Griffin made us jump with a loud proclamation. "DONE!"

"Thank God!" I said, letting my head fall back against the chair.

"Thank God!" Travis cried, and then sighed in relief. He patted my hand, smiling.

I looked down, admiring the beautiful black lines hiding under the smeared black mess.

Mrs. Maddox

"Wow," I said, rising up on my elbows.

Travis's frown instantly turned into a triumphant smile. "It's beautiful."

Griffin shook his head. "If I had a dollar for every inked-up new husband who brought his wife in here and took it worse than she did—well, I wouldn't have to tat anyone ever again."

Travis's smile disappeared. "Just give her the postcare instructions, smart-ass."

"I'll have a printout of instructions and some A and D ointment at the counter," Griffin said, amused by Travis.

My stare kept returning to the elegant script on my skin. We were married. I was a Maddox, just like all of those wonderful men I had grown to love. I had a family, albeit full of angry, crazy, lovable men, but they were mine. I belonged to them, as they belonged to me.

Travis held out his hand, peering down at his ring finger. "We did it, baby. I still can't believe you're my wife."

"Believe it." I beamed.

I reached out to Travis, pointed to his pocket, and then turned my hand over, opening my palm. He handed me my phone, and I pulled up the camera to snap a picture of my fresh ink. Travis helped me from the chair, careful to avoid my right side. I was sensitive to every movement that caused my jeans to rub against my raw skin.

After a short stop at the front counter, Travis let go of me long enough to push the door open for me, and then we walked outside to a waiting cab. My cell phone rang again. America.

"She's going to lay on the guilt trip thick, isn't she?" Travis said, watching me silence my phone. I wasn't in the mood to endure another tongue-lashing.

"She'll pout for twenty-four hours after she sees the pictures—then she'll get over it."

"Are you sure about that, Mrs. Maddox?"

I chuckled. "Are you ever going to stop calling me that? You've said it a hundred times since we left the chapel."

He shook his head as he held the cab door open for me. "I'll quit calling you that when it sinks in that this is real."

"Oh, it's real all right. I have wedding night memories to prove it." I slid to the middle and then watched as he slid in next to me.

He leaned against me, running his nose up the sensitive skin of my neck until he reached my ear. "We sure do."

CHAPTER ELEVEN

The Road Home

Travis

A bby watched Las Vegas pass by her window. Just the sight of her made me want to touch her, and now that she was my wife, that feeling was amplified. But I was trying very hard not to make her regret her decision. Playing it cool used to be my superpower. Now I was dangerously close to being Shepley.

Unable to stop myself, I slid my hand over and barely touched her pinky finger. "I saw pictures of my parents' wedding. I thought Mom was the most beautiful bride I'd ever see. Then I saw you at the chapel, and I changed my mind."

She looked down at our fingers touching, intertwined her fingers in mine, and then looked up at me. "When you say things like that, Travis, it makes me fall in love with you all over again." She nuzzled up against me, and then kissed my cheek. "I wish I could have known her."

"Me, too." I paused, wondering if I should say the thought that was in my head. "What about your mom?"

Abby shook her head, leaning into my arms. "She wasn't all that great before we moved to Wichita. After we got there, her depression got worse. She just checked out. If I hadn't met America, I would have been alone."

She was already in my arms, but I wanted to hug my wife's sixteen-year-old self, too. And her childhood self, for that matter. There was so much that had happened to her that I couldn't protect her from.

"I . . . I know it's not true, but Mick told me so many times that I ruined him. Both of them. I have this irrational fear that I'll do the same to you."

"Pigeon," I scolded, kissing her hair.

"It's weird though, right? That when I started playing, his luck went south. He said I took his luck. Like I had that power over him. It made for some seriously conflicting emotions for a teenage girl."

The hurt in her eyes caused a familiar fire to come over me, but I quickly doused the flames with a deep breath. I wasn't sure if seeing Abby hurt would ever make me feel anything less than a little crazy, but she didn't need a hotheaded boyfriend. She needed an understanding husband. "If he had any fucking sense, he would have made you his lucky charm instead of his enemy. It really is his loss, Pidge. You're the most amazing woman I know."

She picked at her nails. "He didn't want me to be his luck."

"You could be my luck. I'm feeling pretty fucking lucky right now."

She playfully elbowed me in the ribs. "Let's just keep it that way."

"I have not a single doubt that we will. You don't know it yet, but you just saved me."

Something sparked in Abby's eyes, and she pressed her cheek against my shoulder. "I hope so."

Abby

Travis hugged me to his side, letting go just long enough for us to move forward. We weren't the only overly affectionate couple waiting in line at the check-in counter. It was the end of spring break, and the airport was packed.

Once we got our boarding passes, we made our way slowly through security. When we finally reached the front of the line, Travis kept setting off the detector, so the TSA agent made him take off his ring.

Travis grudgingly complied, but once we passed through security and sat on a nearby bench to put on our shoes, Travis grumbled a few inaudible swear words, and then relaxed.

"It's okay, baby. It's back on your finger," I said, giggling at his overreaction.

Travis didn't speak, only kissed my forehead before we left security for our gate. The other spring breakers appeared just as exhausted and happy as we were. And I spotted other arriving couples holding hands who looked just as nervous and excited as Travis and I were when we arrived in Vegas.

I grazed Travis's fingertips with mine.

He sighed.

His response caught me off guard. It was heavy, and full of stress. The closer we got to the gate, the slower he walked. I worried about the reaction we'd face at home, too, but I was more worried about the investigation. Maybe he was thinking the same thing and didn't want to talk to me about it.

At Gate Eleven, Travis sat next to me, keeping his hand in mine. His knee was bouncing, and he kept touching and tugging at his lips with his free hand. His three-day scruff twitched every time he moved his mouth. He was either freaking out on the inside, or he'd drunk a pot of coffee without me knowing.

"Pigeon?" he said finally.

Oh thank God. He's going to talk to me about it.

"Yeah?"

He thought about what he might say, and then sighed again. "Nothing."

Whatever it was, I wanted to fix it. But if he wasn't

thinking about the investigation or facing the aftermath of the fire, I didn't want to bring it up. Not long after we took our seat, first class was being called to board. Travis and I stood with everyone else to get in line for economy.

Travis shifted from one foot to the other, rubbing the back of his neck and squeezing my hand. He so obviously wanted to tell me something. It was eating at him, and I didn't know what else to do but squeeze his hand back.

When our boarding group began to form a line, Travis hesitated. "I can't shake this feeling," he said.

"What do you mean? Like a bad feeling?" I said, suddenly very nervous. I didn't know if he meant the plane, or Vegas, or going home. Everything that could go wrong between our next step and our arrival back on campus flashed through my mind.

"I have this crazy feeling that once we get home, I'm going to wake up. Like none of this was real." Concern shone in his eyes, making them glassy.

Of all the things to worry about, and he was worried about losing me, just as I worried about losing him. It was then, in that moment, that I knew we'd done the right thing. That yes, we were young, and yes, we were crazy, but we were as much in love as anyone. We were older than Romeo and Juliet. Older than my grandparents. It might not have been that long ago since we were children, but there were people with ten or more years of experience who still didn't have it together. We didn't have it all together, but we had each other, and that was more than enough.

When we returned, it was likely that everyone would be waiting for the breakdown, waiting for the deterioration of a couple married too young. Just imagining the stares and stories and whispers made my skin crawl. It might take a lifetime to prove to everyone that this works. We'd made so many mistakes, and undoubtedly we would make thousands more, but the odds were in our favor. We'd proven them all wrong before.

After a tennis match of worries and reassurances, I finally wrapped my arms around my husband's neck, touching my lips ever so slightly to his. "I'd bet my firstborn. That's how sure I am." This was a wager I wouldn't lose.

"You can't be that sure," he said.

I raised an eyebrow, my mouth pulling to the side. "Wanna bet?"

Travis relaxed, taking his boarding pass from my fingers, and handing it to the attendant.

"Thank you," she said, scanning it and then handing it back. She did the same to mine, and just as we had little more than twenty-four hours before, we walked hand in hand down the Jetway.

"Are you hinting at something?" Travis asked. He stopped. "You're not . . . is that why you wanted to get married?"

I laughed, shook my head, and pulled him along. "God, no. I think we've taken a big enough step to last us a while."

He nodded once. "Fair enough, Mrs. Maddox." He squeezed my hand, and we boarded the plane for home.

CHAPTER TWELVE

Anniversary

Abby

Water beaded on my skin, mixing with the sunscreen and magnifying the texture of my tanned stomach. The sun beat down on us, and everyone else on the beach, making the heat dance in waves on top of the sand between the patches of brightly colored beach towels.

"Ma'am," the waiter said, leaning down with two drinks. Sweat dripped off his dark skin, but he was smiling. "Charging to the room?"

"Yes, thank you," I said, taking my frozen strawberry margarita and signing the check.

America took hers and stirred the ice with her tiny straw. "This. Is. Heaven."

We all deserved a little Heaven to recover from the last year. After attending dozens of funerals, and helping Travis deal with his guilt, we fielded more questions from investigators. The students who were at the fight kept Travis's name out of it when speaking with the authorities, but rumors spread, and it took a long time for Adam's arrest to be enough for the families.

It took a lot of convincing for Travis not to turn himself in. The only thing that seemed to hold him back was my begging for him not to leave me alone, and knowing Trent would be charged with misleading an investigation. The first six months of our marriage was far from easy, and we spent a lot of long nights arguing about what was the right thing to do. Maybe it was wrong for me to keep Travis from prison, but I didn't care. I didn't believe he was any more at fault than anyone who had chosen to be in that basement that night. I would never regret my decision, just like I would never regret looking straight into that detective's eyes and lying my ass off to save my husband.

"Yes," I said, watching the water climb up the sand and then recede. "We have Travis to thank. He was at the gym with as many clients as he could fit around his classes six days a week from five in the morning to ten o'clock at night. This was all him. It sure wasn't my tutoring money that got us here."

"Thank him? When he promised me a real wedding, I didn't know he meant a year later!"

"America," I scolded, turning to her. "Could you be more spoiled? We're on a beach, drinking frozen margaritas in St. Thomas."

"I guess it gave me some time to plan your bachelorette party and the renewal of your vows," she said, taking a sip.

I smiled, turning to her. "Thank you. I mean it. And this is the best bachelorette party in the history of bachelorette parties."

Harmony walked over and sat down in the lounge chair on the other side of me, her pixie short chestnut hair glistened in the sun. She shook the salt water out of it, making it feather out. "The water is so warm!" she said, pushing up her oversize sunglasses. "There is a guy over there teaching kids how to windsurf. He's stupid hot."

"Maybe you can talk him into being our stripper later?" America said, straight-faced.

Kara frowned. "America, no. Travis would be livid. Abby isn't *actually* a bachelorette, remember?"

America shrugged, letting her eyes close behind her sunglasses. Although Kara and I had grown very close since I moved out, she and America still weren't on the best of terms. Probably because both of them said exactly what they thought.

"We'll blame it on Harmony," America said. "Travis can't get mad at her. He's forever indebted to her for letting him into Morgan Hall that night you were fighting."

"Doesn't mean I want to be on the wrong end of a Maddox rage," Harmony said, shuddering.

I scoffed. "You know he hasn't lashed out in a long time. He's got a handle on his anger now."

Harmony and I had shared two classes that semester, and when I invited her to the apartment to study, Travis recognized her as the girl who'd let him into our dorm. Like Travis, her brother was also a member of Sigma Tau fraternity, so she was one of the few pretty girls on campus that Travis hadn't slept with.

"Travis and Shepley will be here tomorrow afternoon," America said. "We have to get our partying in tonight. You don't think Travis is sitting at home doing nothing, do you? We're going out and we're going to have a damn good time whether you like it or not."

"That's fine," I said. "Just no strippers. And not too late. This wedding will actually have an audience. I don't want to look hungover."

Harmony lifted the flag next to her chair, and almost immediately a waiter came over.

"How may I help you, miss?"

"A piña colada, please?"

"Of course," he said, backing away.

"This place is swank," America said.

"And you wonder why it took us a year to save up for this. "

"You're right. I shouldn't have said anything. Trav wanted you to have the best. I get it. And it was nice of Mom and Dad to pay my way. I sure as hell wouldn't have been able to come otherwise."

I giggled.

"You promised me I could be a bridesmaid and do everything you made me miss last year. I see them paying as a wedding present and an anniversary present to you, and a birthday present to me all rolled into one. If you ask me, they got off cheap."

"It's still too much."

"Abby, they love you like a daughter. Daddy is very excited about walking you down the aisle. Let them do this without ruining the spirit of it," America said.

I smiled. Mark and Pam treated me like family. After my father landed me in a dangerous situation last year, Mark decided that I needed a new father—and nominated himself. If I needed help with tuition or books or a new vacuum cleaner, Mark and Pam showed up at my door. Helping me also gave them an excuse to visit America and me, and it was obvious that they enjoyed that the most.

Not only did I now have the unruly Maddox clan as family, but I had Mark and Pam as well. I'd gone from belonging to no one, to being a part of two amazing families that were incredibly important to me. At first, it made me feel anxious. I'd never had so much to lose before. But over time, I realized that my new family wasn't going anywhere, and I learned how much good could come from misfortune.

"Sorry. I'll try to just accept this graciously."

"Thank you."

"Thank you!" Harmony said, taking her drink from the tray. She signed the bill and began sipping the fruity concoction. "I'm just so excited to be going to this one!"

"Me, too," America said, glaring in my direction. She had barely forgiven me for getting married without her. And, honestly, I hoped she'd never try to pull the same move on me. But marriage was still a long way off for her.

She and Shepley were going to get their own apartment, but both decided that even though they were always around each other, America would stay in Morgan, and Shepley would move into Helms, a men's dorm. Mark and Pam were happier about this arrangement. They loved Shepley but were worried that the stress of real-world bills and jobs would affect Shepley's and America's focus on school. America was struggling, even at the dorms.

"I just hope it goes smoothly. I hate the thought of standing in front of all those people staring at us."

America breathed out a laugh. "Elvis wasn't invited, but I'm sure it will still be beautiful."

"I still can't believe Elvis was at your wedding," Harmony said, giggling.

"Not the dead one," Kara deadpanned.

"He wasn't invited this time," I said, watching the children taking lessons celebrate windsurfing on their own.

"What was it like? Getting married in Vegas?" Harmony asked.

"It was . . ." I said, thinking about the moment we left, almost exactly a year earlier. "Stressful and frightening. I was worried. I cried. It was pretty much perfect."

Harmony's expression was one of combined disgust and surprise. "Sounds like it."

Travis

"Fuck you," I said, not amused.

"Oh, c'mon!" Shepley said, shaking with laughter. "You used to say I was the whipped one."

"Fuck you again."

Shepley turned off the ignition. He had parked the Charger on the far side of Cherry Papa's parking lot. Home of the fattest, dirtiest strippers in town. "It's not like you're going to take one of them home."

"I promised Pidge. No strippers."

"I promised you a bachelor party."

"Dude, let's just go home. I'm full, tired, and we've got a plane to catch in the morning."

Shepley frowned. "The girls have been lying on a beach in St. Thomas all day, and now they're probably partying it up in a club."

I shook my head. "We don't go to clubs without each other. She wouldn't do that."

"She would if America planned it."

I shook my head again. "No, she fucking wouldn't. I'm

not going into the strip club. Either pick something else, or take me home."

Shepley sighed, and squinted his eyes. "What about that?"

I followed his line of sight to the next block over. "A hotel? Shep, I love ya, man, but it's not a real bachelor party. I'm married. And even if I weren't, I still wouldn't have sex with you."

Shepley shook his head. "There's a bar in there. It's not a club. Is that permitted on your long list of marriage rules?"

I frowned. "I just respect my wife. And yes, douche bag, we can go in there."

"Awesome," he said, rubbing his hands together.

We walked across the street, and Shepley opened the door. It was pitch-black.

"Uh . . ." I began.

Suddenly the lights turned on. The twins, Taylor and Tyler, threw confetti in my face, music began to blare, and then I saw the worst thing I'd ever seen in my life: Trenton in a man thong, covered in about ten pounds of body glitter. He had on a cheap, yellow wig, and Cami was laughing her head off, cheering him on.

Shepley pushed me in the rest of the way. My dad was on one side of the room, standing next to Thomas. They were both shaking their heads. My uncle Jack was on the other side of Thomas, and then the rest of the room was filled with Sigma Tau brothers and football players.

"I said no strippers," I said, watching dumbfounded as Trenton danced around the room to Britney Spears.

Shepley burst into laughter. "I know, brother, but looks like the stripping happened before we got here."

It was a train wreck. My face screwed into disgust as I watched Trenton bump and grind his way across the room—even though I didn't want to. Everyone in the room was cheering him on. Cardboard cutouts of tits were hanging from the ceiling, and there was even a booby cake on a table next to my dad. I'd been to several bachelor parties before, and this one had to win some sort of a freak prize.

"Hey," Trenton said, breathless and sweaty. He pulled a few yellow strands of fake hair from his face.

"Did you lose a bet?" I asked.

"As a matter of fact, I did."

Taylor and Tyler were across the room, slapping their knees and laughing so hard they could barely breathe.

I slapped Trenton's ass. "You look hot, bro."

"Thanks," he said. The music started and he shook his hips at me. I pushed him away, and, undeterred, he danced across the room to entertain the crowd.

I looked at Shepley. "I can't wait to watch you explain this to Abby."

He smiled. "She's your wife. You do it."

For the next four hours, we drank, and talked, and watched Trenton make a complete ass out of himself. My dad, as expected, cut out early. He, along with my other brothers, had a plane to catch. We were all flying to St. Thomas in the morning for the renewal of my vows.

For the last year, Abby tutored, and I did some personal training at the local gym. We'd managed to save a little after school costs, rent, and the car payment to fly to St. Thomas and stay a few days in a nice hotel. We had plenty of things the money could have gone to, but America kept talking about it and wouldn't let us drop the idea. Then when America's parents presented us with the wedding gift/America's birthday present/anniversary gift, we tried to say no, but America was insistent.

"All right, boys. I'm going to be hurtin' in the morning if I don't call it a night."

Everyone groaned and taunted me with words like *whipped* and *pussy*, but the truth was they were all used to the new, tamer Travis Maddox. I hadn't put my fist to someone's face in almost a year.

I yawned, and Shepley punched me in the shoulder. "Let's go."

We drove in silence. I wasn't sure what Shepley was thinking about, but I couldn't fucking wait to see my wife. She'd left the day before, and that was the first time we'd been apart since we'd been married.

Shepley pulled up to the apartment and shut off the car. "Front door service, loser."

"Admit it. You miss it."

"The apartment? Yeah, a little. But I miss you fighting and us making shit tons of money more."

"Yeah. I do sometimes, too. See you in the morning."

"Pick you up right back here at six thirty."

"Later."

Shepley drove away while I slowly climbed the steps, searching for the apartment key. I hated coming home when Abby wasn't here. There was nothing worse after we met, and it was the same now. Maybe even more miserable because Shepley and America weren't even there to annoy me.

I pushed in the key and opened the door, locking it behind me and tossing my wallet onto the breakfast bar. I had already taken Toto to the pet hotel to be boarded while we were gone. It was too fucking quiet. I sighed. The apartment had changed a lot in the last year. The posters and bar signs had come down, and pictures of us and paintings went up. It was no longer a bachelor pad, but it was a good trade.

I went into my bedroom, stripped down to my Calvin Klein boxer briefs, and climbed into the bed, burying myself under the blue and green floral comforter—something else that would have never seen the inside of this apartment had Abby not had a hand in it. I pulled her pillow over and rested my head on it. It smelled like her.

The clock read 2:00 AM. I would be with her in twelve hours.

CHAPTER ~~THIRTEEN~~ FOURTEEN

Bachelorette

Abby

Those seated on the far edge of the restaurant began to scream, nearly pushing over tables and children to get away. Wineglasses broke and silverware clanged on the floor. A pineapple-shaped hurricane was knocked over, rolled off a table, and broke. America rolled her eyes at the twenty or so people gathered a few tables over. "Christ on the cross, people! It's just a little rain!"

The waitstaff and hostesses scrambled to release the rolled-up walls of the outdoor restaurant.

"And you were grumbling because we didn't have an ocean view," Harmony teased.

"Yeah, those snobby bitches aren't smirking now, are they?" America said, nodded and smiling to the six-pack of blondes now huddling and wet.

"Knock it off, Mare. You've had one too many glasses of wine," I said.

"I'm on vacation, and it's a bachelorette party. I'm supposed to be drunk."

I patted her hand. "That would be fine if you weren't a mean drunk."

"Fuck you, whore, I am *not* a mean drunk." I glared at her, and she winked at me and smiled. "Just kiddin'.'"

Harmony let her fork fall to her plate. "I'm stuffed. Now what?"

America pulled a small three-ring binder from her purse with a devious grin. It had small, foam letters glued to the front that read TRAVIS & ABBY and our wedding date. "Now we play a game."

"What kind of game?" I asked, wary.

She opened the binder. "Since Cami couldn't be here until tomorrow, she made you this," she said, turning the front over to read the words painted on the front. "The What Would Your Husband Say? Game. I've heard about it. Super fun, although typically it's about your *future* husband," she said, shifting excitedly in her seat. "So . . . Cami asked Travis these questions last week, and sent the book with me."

"What?" I shrieked. "What kind of questions?"

"You're getting ready to find out," she said, waving the waiter over. He brought a full tray of brightly colored Jell-O shots.

"Oh my," I said.

"If you get them wrong, you drink. If you get them right, we drink. Ready?"

"Sure," I said, glancing at Kara and Harmony.

America cleared her throat, holding the binder in front of her. "When did Travis know you were the one?"

I thought for a minute. "That first poker night at his dad's."

Errrr! America made a horrendous noise with her throat. "When he realized he wasn't good enough for you, which was the moment he saw you. Drink!"

"Aw!" Harmony said, holding her hand to her chest.

I picked up a small plastic cup and squeezed its contents into my mouth. Yum. I wasn't going to mind losing at all.

"Next question!" America said. "What is his favorite thing about you?"

"My cooking."

Errrrr! America made the noise again. "Drink!"

"You suck at this game," Kara said, clearly amused.

"Maybe I'm doing it on purpose? These are good!" I said, popping another shot into my mouth.

"Travis's answer? Your laugh."

"Wow," I said, surprised. "That's kind of endearing."

"What is his favorite part of your body?"

"My eyes."

"Ding, ding, ding! Correct!"

Harmony and Kara clapped, I bowed my head. "Thank you, thank you. Now drink, bitches."

They all laughed, and popped their shots.

America turned a page and read the next question. "When does Travis want to have kids?"

"Oh," I blew through my lips. "In seven . . . eight years?"

"A year after graduation."

Kara and Harmony made the same face, their mouths forming "oh."

"I'll drink," I said. "But he and I will have to talk about that one some more."

America shook her head. "This is a prewedding game, Abby. You should be much better at this."

"Shut up. Continue."

Kara pointed. "Technically she can't shut up and continue."

"Shut up," American and I said in unison.

"Next question!" America said. "What do you think Travis's favorite moment of your relationship was?"

"The night he won the bet and I moved in?"

"Correct again!" America said.

"This is so sweet. I can't take it," Harmony said.

"Drink! Next question," I said, smiling.

"What is one thing Travis said he'll never forget that you've said to him?"

"Wow. I have no idea."

Kara leaned in. "Just guess."

"The first time I said I loved him?"

America narrowed her eyes, thinking. "Technically,

you're wrong. He said it was the time you told Parker you loved Travis!" America burst into laughter, and so did the rest of us. "Drink!"

America turned another page. "What is the one item Travis can't live without?"

"His motorcycle."

"Correct!"

"Where was your first date?"

"Technically it was the Pizza Shack."

"Correct!" America said again.

"Ask her something more difficult, or we're going to get hammered," Kara said, throwing back another shot.

"Hmmm . . ." America said, thumbing through the pages. "Oh, here we go. What do you think Abby's favorite thing about you is?"

"What kind of question is that?" I asked. They watched me expectantly. "Um . . . my favorite thing about him is the way he always touches me when we sit together, but I bet he said his tats."

"Damn it!" America said. "Correct!" They drank, and I clapped to celebrate my small victory.

"One more," America said. "What does Travis think your favorite present from him is?"

I paused for a few seconds. "That's easy. The scrapbook he got me for Valentine's Day this year. Now, drink!"

Everyone laughed, and even though it was their turn, I shared the last shot with them.

Harmony wiped her mouth with a napkin, and helped me to collect the empty cups and place them on the tray. "What's the plan now, Mare?"

America fidgeted, clearly excited about what she was about to say. "We hit the clubs, that's what."

I shook my head. "No way. We talked about this."

America stuck out her lip.

"Don't," I said. "I'm here to renew my vows, not to get a divorce. Think of something else."

"Why doesn't he trust you?" America said, her voice very closely resembling a whine.

"If I really wanted to go, I would go. I just respect my husband, and I would rather get along than sit in a smoky club with lights that give me a headache. It would just make him wonder what went on, and I'd rather not go there. It's worked so far."

"I respect Shepley. I still go to clubs without him."

"No, you don't."

"Only because I haven't wanted to, yet. Tonight, I do."

"Well, I don't."

America's brows pulled together. "Fine. Plan B. Poker night?"

"Very funny."

Harmony's face lit up. "I saw a flyer for movie night tonight at Honeymoon Beach! They bring a screen right on the water."

America made a face. "Boring."

"No, I think it sounds fun. When does it start?"

Harmony checked her watch, and then her face fell, deflated. "In fifteen minutes."

"We can make it!" I said, grabbing my purse. "Check please!"

Travis

"Calm your tits, dude," Shepley said. He looked down at my fingers nervously beating against the metal armrest. We had landed safely and taxied in, but for whatever reason they weren't ready to let us off yet. Everyone was quietly waiting for that one, tiny *ding* that meant freedom. Something about the *ding* of the fasten seat belt light that made everyone jump up and scramble to get their carry-on luggage and stand in line. I actually had a reason to be in a hurry, though, so the wait was particularly irritating.

"What the fuck is taking so long?" I said, maybe a little too loud. A woman in front of us with a grade-school-age kid turned slowly to give me a look. "Sorry." She faced forward in a huff.

I looked down at my watch. "We're going to be late."

"No we're not," Shepley said in his typical smooth and calming voice. "We've still got plenty of time."

I stretched to the side, looking down the aisle, as if that would help. "The flight attendants haven't moved. Wait, one is on the phone."

"That's a good sign."

I sat upright and sighed. "We're gonna be late."

"No. We're not. You just miss her."

"I do," I said. I knew that I looked pitiful and I wasn't even going to attempt to hide it. This was the first time Abby and I had spent a night apart since before we were married, and it was miserable. Even after a year, I still looked forward to when she'd wake up in the morning. I even missed her when I slept.

Shepley shook his head in disapproval. "Remember when you used to give me so much shit for acting like this?"

"You didn't love them the way I love her."

Shepley smiled. "You really happy, man?"

"As much as I loved her back then, I love her even more, now. Like the way Dad used to talk about Mom."

Shepley smiled and then opened his mouth to respond, but the fasten seat belt light dinged, sending everyone into a flurry of standing up, reaching up, and getting situated in the aisle.

The mother in front of me smiled. "Congratulations," she said. "Sounds like you have it figured out more than most people."

The line began to move. "Not really. We just had a lot of hard lessons early on."

"Lucky you," she said, guiding her son down the aisle.

I laughed once, thinking about all the fuckups and let-downs, but she was right. If I had to do it all over again,

I'd rather endure the pain in the beginning than have had it easy and then have it all go to shit later on.

Shepley and I rushed to baggage claim, got our luggage, and then hurried outside to catch a cab. I was surprised to see a man in a black suit holding a dry erase board with MADDOX PARTY scribbled in red marker.

"Hey," I said.

"Mistah Maddox?" he said, smiling wide.

"That's us."

"I'm Mistah Gumbs. Right this way." He took my larger bag and led us outside to a black Cadillac Escalade. "You're staying at the Ritz-Carlton, yeah?"

"Yes," Shepley said.

We loaded the trunk with the rest of the bags, and then sat in the middle row of seats.

"Score," Shepley said, looking around.

The driver took off, buzzing up and down hills, and around curves, all on the wrong side of the road. It was confusing, because the wheel was on the same side as ours.

"Glad we didn't rent a car," I said.

"Yes, the majority of accidents here are caused by tourists."

"I bet," Shepley said.

"It's not hard. Just remember you are closest to the curb," he said, karate-chopping the air with his left hand.

He continued giving us a minitour, pointing out different things along the way. The palm trees made me feel enough out of our element, but the cars parked on the left side of the road were really messing with my head. Large hills seemed to touch the sky, peppered with little white specks—what I assumed were hillside houses.

"That's Havensight Mall, there," Mr. Gumbs said. "Where all the cruise ships dock, see?"

I saw the big ships, but I couldn't stop staring at the water. I'd never seen water such a pure blue before. I guess that's why they call it Caribbean blue. It was fucking unbelievable. "How close are we?"

"Gettin' there," Mr. Gumbs said with a happy grin.

Right on cue, the Cadillac slowed to a stop to wait for oncoming traffic, and then we pulled into a long drive. He slowed once more for a security booth, we were waved in, and then we continued on another long drive to the entrance of the hotel.

"Thanks!" Shepley said. He tipped the driver, and then pulled out his cell phone, quickly tapping on the screen. His phone made a kiss noise—must have been America. He read the message and then nodded. "Looks like you and I go to Mare's room, and they're getting ready in yours."

I made a face. "That's . . . odd."

"I guess they don't want you to see Abby, yet."

I shook my head and smiled. "She was that way last time."

A hotel employee showed us to a golf cart, and then he drove us to our building. We followed him to the correct room, and then we walked inside. It was very . . . tropical, fancy Ritz-Carlton tropical.

"This'll do!" Shepley said, all smiles.

I frowned. "The ceremony is in two hours. I have to wait two hours?"

Shepley held up a finger, tapped on his phone, and then looked up. "Nope. You can see her when she's ready. Per Abby. Apparently she misses you, too."

A wide grin spread across my face. I couldn't help it. Abby had that effect on me, eighteen months ago, a year ago, now, and for the rest of my life. I pulled out my cell phone.

Love you, baby.

OMG! You're here! Love u 2!

See u soon.

You bet ur ass.

I laughed out loud. I'd said before that Abby was my everything. For the last 365 days straight, she'd proved that to be true.

Someone pounded on the door, and I walked over to open it.

Trent's face lit up. "Asshat!"

I laughed once, shook my head, and motioned for my brothers to come in. "Get in here, you fuckin' heathens. I've got a wife waiting, and a tux with my name on it."

CHAPTER FIFTEEN

Happily Ever After

Travis

A year to the day after I stood at the end of an aisle in Vegas, I found myself waiting for Abby again, this time in a gazebo overlooking the rich blue waters surrounding St. Thomas. I pulled at my bow tie, pleased that I had been smart enough not to wear one last time, but I also didn't have to deal with America's "vision" last time.

White chairs with orange and purple ribbons tied around their backs sat empty on one side, the ocean sat on the other. White fabric lined the aisle Abby would walk down, and orange and purple flowers were pretty much everywhere I looked. They did a nice job. I still preferred our first wedding, but this looked more like what any girl would dream of.

And then, what any boy would dream of stepped out from behind a row of trees and bushes. Abby stood alone, empty-handed, a long, white veil streaming from her half-up, half-down hair, blowing in the warm Caribbean breeze. Her long, white dress was form fitting and a little shiny. Probably satin. I wasn't sure and I didn't care. All I could focus on was her.

I jumped the four steps that led up to the gazebo and jogged to my wife, meeting her at the back row of chairs.

"Oh my God! I've missed you like hell!" I said, wrapping her in my arms.

Abby's fingers pressed into my back. It was the best thing I'd felt in three days, since I'd hugged her good-bye.

Abby didn't speak, she just giggled nervously, but I could tell she was happy to see me, too. The last year had been so different from the first six months of our relationship. She had totally committed to me, and I had totally committed to being the man she deserved. It was better, and life was good. The first six months, I kept waiting for something bad to happen that would rip her away from me, but after that we settled into our new life.

"You are amazingly beautiful," I said after pulling back to get a better look.

Abby reached to touch my lapel. "You're not so bad yourself, Mr. Maddox."

After a few kisses, hugs, and stories about our bachelor/bachelorette parties (which seemed to be equally uneventful—except for the whole Trent stripper thing), the guests began to trickle in.

"Guess that means we should get in our places," Abby said. I couldn't hide my disappointment. I didn't want to be without her for another second. Abby touched my jaw and then rose up on her feet to kiss my cheek. "See you in a bit."

She walked off, disappearing behind the trees again.

I returned to the gazebo, and before long the chairs were all filled. We actually had an audience this time. Pam sat on the bride's side in the first row, with her sister and brother-in-law. A handful of my Sigma Tau brothers lined the back row, with my dad's old partner and his wife and kids, my boss Chuck and his girlfriend of the week, both sets of America's grandparents, and my Uncle Jack and Aunt Deana. My dad sat in the first row of the groom's side, keeping my brothers' dates company. Shepley stood as my best man, and my groomsmen, Thomas, Taylor, Tyler, and Trent, stood next to him.

We'd all seen another year pass, we'd all been through so much, in some cases lost so much, and yet come together as a family to celebrate something that had gone right for the Maddoxes. I smiled and nodded at the men standing with me. They were still the impenetrable fortress I remembered from my childhood.

My eyes focused on trees in the distance as I waited for my wife. Any second now she would step out and everyone could see what I saw a year before, and find themselves in awe, just like I was.

Abby

After a long embrace, Mark smiled down at me. "You are beautiful. I'm so proud of you, sweetheart."

"Thank you for giving me away," I said, a little embarrassed. Thinking about everything he and Pam had done for me made hot tears pool in my eyes. I blinked them away before they had a chance to spill down my cheeks.

Mark pecked my forehead. "We're blessed to have you in our lives, kiddo."

The music began, prompting Mark to offer his arm. I took it, and we walked down a small, uneven sidewalk that was lined with thick, flowering trees. America was worried it would rain, but the sky was nearly clear, and sun was pouring down.

Mark guided me to the end of the trees, and then we rounded the corner, standing just behind Kara, Harmony, Cami, and America. All of them but America were dressed in purple, strapless satin minidresses. My best friend wore orange. They were all absolutely beautiful.

Kara offered a small smile. "I guess the beautiful disaster turned into a beautiful wedding."

"Miracles do happen," I said, remembering the conversation she and I had what seemed like a lifetime ago.

Kara laughed once, nodded, and then gripped her small bouquet in both hands. She rounded the corner, disappearing behind the trees. Soon after Harmony, and then Cami, followed.

America turned, hooking her arm around my neck. "I love you!" she said with a squeeze.

Mark tightened his grip, and I did the same with my bouquet.

"Here we go, kiddo."

We rounded the corner, and the pastor motioned for everyone to stand. I saw the faces of my friends and new family, but it wasn't until I saw the wet cheeks of Jim Maddox that my breath caught. I struggled to keep it together.

Travis reached out for me. Mark held his hands over ours. I felt so safe in that moment, held by two of the best men I knew.

"Who gives this woman away?" the pastor asked.

"Her mother and I." The words stunned me. Mark had been practicing *Pam and I* all week. After hearing that, there was no holding back my tears as they welled up and spilled over.

Mark kissed my cheek, walked away, and I stood there with my husband. It was the first time I'd seen him in a tux. He was clean-shaven, and had recently gotten his hair cut. Travis Maddox was the kind of gorgeous every girl dreamed about, and he was my reality.

Travis tenderly wiped my cheeks, and then we stepped onto the platform of the gazebo, directly in front of the pastor.

"We are gathered here today to celebrate a renewal of vows . . ." the pastor began. His voice melted into the sounds of the ocean breaking against the rocks in the background.

Travis leaned in, squeezing my hand as he whispered, "Happy anniversary, Pidge."

I looked into his eyes, as full of love and hope as they were the year before. "One down, forever to go," I whispered back.

You fell in love with Abby and Travis.
Now, meet Cami and Trent.

Fiercely independent Camille "Cami" Camlin gladly left behind her childhood before it was over. Now living off campus and tending bar at the Red Door, Cami doesn't have time for much besides work and college classes—until a canceled trip to see her boyfriend leaves her with her first weekend off in a year.

Trenton Maddox was the king of Eastern State University—guys wanted to be him, and women wanted to tame him, but after a tragic accident turned his world upside down, Trent left campus to come to grips with the crushing guilt.

Eighteen months later, Trent is living at home with his widower father and working full-time at a local tattoo parlor to help with the bills. Just when he thinks his life is returning to normal, he notices Cami sitting alone at a table at the Red Door.

As the older sister of three rowdy brothers, Cami believes she'll have no problem keeping her new friendship with Trent Maddox strictly platonic. But everyone knows that when a Maddox boy falls in love, he loves forever . . .

Turn the page to read the first chapter of
Jamie McGuire's breathtaking new novel,
Beautiful Oblivion, **available now from**
Atria Paperback.

His words hung there, in the darkness between our voices. I sometimes found comfort in that space, but in three months, I'd only found unrest. That space became more like a convenient place to hide. Not for me, for him. My fingers ached, so I allowed them to relax, not realizing how hard I'd been gripping my cell phone.

My roommate, Raegan, was sitting next to my open suitcase on the bed, her legs crisscrossed. Whatever look was on my face prompted her to take my hand. *T.J.?* she mouthed.

I nodded.

"Will you please say something?" T.J. asked.

"What do you want me to say? I'm packed. I took vacation time. Hank has already given Jorie my shifts."

"I feel like a huge asshole. I wish I didn't have to go, but I warned you. When I have an ongoing project, I can be called out at any time. If you need help with rent or anything . . ."

"I don't want your money," I said, rubbing my eyes.

"I thought this would be a good weekend. I swear to God I did."

"I thought I'd be getting on a plane tomorrow morning, and instead you're calling me to say I can't come. Again."

"I know this seems like a dick move. I swear to you I

told them I had important plans. But when things come up, Cami . . . I have to do my job."

I wiped a tear from my cheek, but I refused to let him hear me cry. I kept the trembling from my voice. "Are you coming home for Thanksgiving, then?"

He sighed. "I want to. But I don't know if I can. It depends on if this is wrapped up. I do miss you. A lot. I don't like this, either."

"Will your schedule ever get better?" I asked. It took him longer than it should to answer.

"What if I said probably not?"

I lifted my eyebrows. I expected that answer but didn't expect him to be so . . . truthful.

"I'm sorry," he said. I imagined him cringing. "I just pulled into the airport. I have to go."

"Yeah, okay. Talk to you later." I forced my voice to stay level. I didn't want to sound upset. I didn't want him to think I was weak or emotional. He was strong, and self-reliant, and did what had to be done without complaint. I tried to be that for him. Whining about something out of his control wouldn't help anything.

He sighed again. "I know you don't believe me, but I do love you."

"I believe you," I said, and I meant it.

I pressed the red button on the screen and let my phone fall to the bed.

Raegan was already in damage control mode. "He was called into work?"

I nodded.

"Okay, well, maybe you guys will just have to be more spontaneous. Maybe you can just show up, and if he's called out while you're there, you wait on him. When he gets back, you pick up where you left off."

"Maybe."

She squeezed my hand. "Or maybe he's a tool who should stop choosing his job over you?"

I shook my head. "He's worked really hard for this position."

"You don't even know what position it is."

"I told you. He's utilizing his degree. He specializes in statistical analysis and data reconfiguration, whatever that means."

She shot me a dubious look. "Yeah, you also told me to keep it all a secret. Which makes me think he's not being completely honest with you."

I stood up and dumped out my suitcase, letting all the contents spill onto my comforter. Usually I only made my bed when I was packing, so I could now see the comforter's light-blue fabric with a few navy-blue octopus tentacles reaching across it. T.J. hated it, but it made me feel like I was being hugged while I slept. My room was made up of strange, random things, but then, so was I.

Raegan rummaged through the pile of clothes, and held up a black top with the shoulders and front strategically ripped. "We both have the night off. We should go out. Get drinks served to us for once."

I grabbed the shirt from her hands and inspected it

while I mulled over Raegan's suggestion. "You're right. We should. Are we taking your car, or the Smurf?"

Raegan shrugged. "I'm almost on empty and we don't get paid until tomorrow."

"Looks like it's the Smurf, then."

After a crash session in the bathroom, Raegan and I jumped up into my light-blue, modified CJ Jeep. It wasn't in the best of shape, but at one time someone had had enough vision and love to mold it into a Jeep/truck hybrid. The spoiled college dropout who owned the Smurf between that owner and me didn't love it as much. The seat cushions were exposed in some places where the black leather seats were torn, the carpet had cigarette holes and stains, and the hard top needed to be replaced, but that neglect meant that I could pay for it in full, and a payment-free vehicle was the best kind to own.

I buckled my seat belt, and stabbed the key into the ignition.

"Should I pray?" Raegan asked.

I turned the key, and the Smurf made a sickly whirring noise. The engine sputtered, and then purred, and we both clapped. My parents raised four children on a factory worker's salary. I never asked them to help me buy a car, instead I got a job at the local ice cream shop when I was fifteen, and saved $557.11. The Smurf wasn't the vehicle I dreamed about when I was little, but 550 bucks bought me an independence, and that was priceless.

Twenty minutes later, Raegan and I were on the opposite side of town, strutting across the gravel lot of the Red

Door, slowly and in unison, as if we were being filmed while walking to a badass soundtrack.

Kody was standing at the entrance, his huge arms probably the same size as my head. He eyed us as we approached. "IDs."

"Fuck off!" Raegan snarled. "We work here. You know how old we are."

He shrugged. "Still have to see IDs."

I frowned at Raegan, and she rolled her eyes, digging into her back pocket. "If you don't know how old I am at this point, we have issues."

"C'mon, Raegan. Quit busting my balls and let me see the damn thing."

"The last time I let you see something you didn't call me for three days."

He cringed. "You're never going to get over that, are you?"

She tossed her ID at Kody and he slapped it against his chest. He glanced at it, and then handed it back, looking at me expectantly. I handed him my driver's license.

"Thought you were leaving town?" he asked, glancing down before returning the thin plastic card to me.

"Long story," I said, stuffing my license into my back pocket. My jeans were so tight I was amazed I could fit anything besides my ass back there.

Kody opened the oversize red door, and Raegan smiled sweetly. "Thanks, baby."

"Love you. Be good."

"I'm always good," she said, winking.

"See you when I get off work?"

"Yep." She pulled me through the door.

"You are the weirdest couple," I said over the bass. It was buzzing in my chest, and I was fairly certain every beat made my bones shake.

"Yep," Raegan said again.

The dance floor was already packed with sweaty, drunk college kids. The fall semester was in full swing. Raegan walked over to the bar and stood at the end. Jorie winked at her.

"Want me to clear you out some seats?" she asked.

Raegan shook her head. "You're just offering because you want my tips from last night!"

Jorie laughed. Her long, platinum blond hair fell in loose waves past her shoulders, with a few black peekaboo strands. She wore a black minidress and combat boots, and was pushing buttons on the cash register to ring someone up while she talked to us. We had all learned to multitask and move like every tip was a hundred-dollar bill. If you could bartend fast enough, you stood a chance of working the east bar, and the tips made there could pay a month's worth of bills in a weekend.

That was where I'd been tending bar for a year, placed just three months after I was hired at the Red Door. Raegan worked right beside me, and together we kept that machine greased like a stripper in a plastic pool full of baby oil. Jorie and the other bartender, Blia, worked the south bar at the entrance. It was basically a kiosk, and they loved it when Raegan or I were out of town.

"So? What are you drinking?" Jorie asked.

Raegan looked at me, and then back at Jorie. "Whiskey sours."

I made a face. "Minus the sour, please."

Once Jorie passed us our drinks, Raegan and I found an empty table and sat, shocked at our luck. Weekends were always packed, and an open table at ten thirty wasn't common.

I held a brand-new pack of cigarettes in my hand and hit the end of it against my palm to pack them, then tore off the plastic, flipping the top. Even though the Red was so smoky that just sitting there made me feel like I was smoking an entire pack of cigarettes, it was nice to sit at a table and relax. When I was working, I usually had time for one drag and the rest burned away, unsmoked.

Raegan watched me light it. "I want one."

"No, you don't."

"Yes, I do!"

"You haven't smoked in two months, Raegan. You'll blame me tomorrow for ruining your streak."

She gestured at the room. "I'm smoking! Right now!"

I narrowed my eyes at her. Raegan was exotically beautiful, with long, chestnut-brown hair, bronze skin, and honey-brown eyes. Her nose was perfectly small, not too round or too pointy, and her skin made her look like she came fresh off of a Neutrogena commercial. We met in elementary school, and I was instantly drawn to her brutal honesty. Raegan could be incredibly intimidating, even for Kody, who, at six foot four, was over a foot taller than she was. Her personality was charming to those she loved, and repellent to those she didn't.

I was the opposite of exotic. My tousled brown bob and heavy bangs were easy to maintain, but not a lot of men found it sexy. Not a lot of men found me sexy in general. I was the girl next door, your brother's best friend. Growing up with three brothers and our cousin Colin, I could have been a tomboy if my subtle but still present curves hadn't ousted me from the boys-only clubhouse at fourteen.

"Don't be that girl," I said. "If you want one, go buy your own."

She crossed her arms, pouting. "That's why I quit. They're fucking expensive."

I stared at the burning paper and tobacco nestled between my fingers. "That is a fact my broke ass continues to make note of."

The song switched from something everyone wanted to dance to, to a song no one wanted to dance to, and dozens of people began making their way off the dance floor. Two girls walked up to our table and traded glances.

"That's our table," the blonde said.

Raegan barely acknowledged them.

"Excuse me, bitch, she's talking to you," the brunette said, setting her beer on the table.

"Raegan," I warned.

Raegan looked at me with a blank face, and then up at the girl with the same expression. "It *was* your table. Now it's ours."

"We were here first," the blonde hissed.

"And now you're not," Raegan said. She picked up the

unwelcome beer bottle and tossed it across the floor. It spilled out onto the dark, tightly stitched carpet. "Fetch."

The brunette watched her beer slide across the floor, and then took a step toward Raegan, but her friend grabbed both of her arms. Raegan offered an unimpressed laugh, and then turned her gaze toward the dance floor. The brunette finally followed her friend to the bar.

I took a drag from my cigarette. "I thought we were going to have a good time tonight."

"That was fun, right?"

I shook my head, stifling a smile. Raegan was a great friend, but I wouldn't cross her. Growing up with so many boys in the house, I'd had enough fighting to last a lifetime. They didn't baby me. If I didn't fight back, they'd just fight dirtier until I did. And I always did.

Raegan didn't have an excuse. She was just a scrappy bitch. "Oh, look. Megan's here," she said, pointing to the blue-eyed, crow-headed beauty on the dance floor. I shook my head. She was out there with Travis Maddox, basically getting screwed in front of everyone on the dance floor.

"Oh, those Maddox boys," Raegan said.

"Yeah," I said, downing my whiskey. "This was a bad idea. I'm not feeling clubby tonight."

"Oh, stop." Raegan gulped her whiskey sour and then stood. "The whine bags are still eyeing this table. I'm going to get us another round. You know the beginning of the night starts off slow."

She took my glass and hers and left me for the bar.

I turned, seeing the girls staring at me, clearly hoping I would step away from the table. I wasn't about to stand up. Raegan would get the table back if they tried to take it, and that would only cause trouble.

When I turned around, a boy was sitting in Raegan's chair. At first I thought Travis had somehow made his way over, but when I realized my mistake, I smiled. Trenton Maddox was leaning toward me, his tattooed arms crossed, his elbows resting on the table across from me. He rubbed the five o'clock shadow that peppered his square jaw with his fingers, his shoulder muscles bulging through his T-shirt. He had as much stubble on his face as he did on the top of his head, except for the absence of hair from one small scar near his left temple.

"You look familiar."

I raised an eyebrow. "Really? You walk all the way over here and sit down, and that's the best you've got?"

He made a show of running his eyes over every part of me. "You don't have any tattoos, that I can see. I'm guessing we haven't met at the shop."

"The shop?"

"The ink shop I work at."

"You're tattooing now?"

He smiled, a deep dimple appearing in the center of his left cheek. "I knew we've met before."

"We haven't." I turned to watch the women on the dance floor, laughing and smiling and watching Travis and Megan vertically dry fucking. But the second the song was over, he left and walked straight over to the blonde who claimed ownership over my table. Even though she'd seen Travis running his hands all over Megan's sweaty skin two seconds earlier, she was grinning like an idiot, hoping she was next.

Trenton laughed once. "That's my baby brother."

"I wouldn't admit it," I said, shaking my head.

"Did we go to school together?" he asked.

"I don't remember."

"Do you remember if you went to Eakins at any time between kindergarten through twelfth grade?"

"I did."

Trenton's left dimple sunk in when he grinned. "Then we know each other."

"Not necessarily."

Trenton laughed again. "You want a drink?"

"I have one coming."

"You wanna dance?"

"Nope."

A group of girls passed by, and Trenton's eyes focused on one. "Is that Shannon from home ec? Damn," he said, turning a one-eighty in his seat.

"Indeed it is. You should go reminisce."

Trenton shook his head. "We reminisced in high school."

"I remember. Pretty sure she still hates you."

Trenton shook his head, smiled, and then, before taking another swig, said, "They always do."

"It's a small town. You shouldn't have burned all of your bridges."

He lowered his chin, his famous charm turning up a notch. "There's a few I haven't lit a fire under. Yet."

I rolled my eyes, and he chuckled.

Raegan returned, curving her long fingers around four standard rocks glasses and two shot glasses. "My whiskey sours, your whiskey straights, and a buttery nipple each."

"What is with all the sweet stuff tonight, Ray?" I said, wrinkling my nose.

Trenton picked up one of the shot glasses and touched it to his lips, tilting his head back. He slammed it on the table and winked. "Don't worry, babe. I'll take care of it." He stood up and walked away.

I didn't realize my mouth was hanging open until my eyes met Raegan's and it snapped shut.

"Did he just drink your shot? Did that really just happen?"

"Who does that?" I said, turning to see where he went. He'd already disappeared into the crowd.

"A Maddox boy."

I shot the double whiskey and took another drag of my cigarette. Everyone knew Trenton Maddox was bad news, but that never seemed to stop women from trying to tame him. Watching him since grade school, I promised myself that I would never be a notch on his headboard—if the rumors were true and he had notches, but I didn't plan to find out.

"You're going to let him get away with that?" Raegan asked.

I blew out the smoke from the side of my mouth, annoyed. I wasn't in the frame of mind to have fun, or deal with obnoxious flirting, or complain that Trenton Maddox had just drunk the shot glass of sugar that I didn't want. But before I could answer my friend, I had to choke back the whiskey I'd just drunk.

"Oh, no."

"What?" Raegan said, flipping around in her chair. She immediately righted herself in the chair, cringing.

All three of my brothers and our cousin Colin were walking toward our table.

Colin, the oldest and the only one with a legit ID, spoke first. "What the hell, Camille? I thought you were out of town tonight."

"My plans changed," I snapped.

Chase spoke second, as I expected he would. He was the oldest of my brothers, and liked to pretend he was older than me, too. "Dad's not going to be happy that you missed family lunch if you were in town."

"He can't be unhappy if he doesn't know," I said, narrowing my eyes.

He recoiled. "Why are you being so pissy? Are you on the rag or something?"

"Really?" Raegan said, lowering her chin and raising her eyebrows. "We're in public. Grow up."

"So he canceled on you?" Clark asked. Unlike the others, Clark looked genuinely concerned.

Before I could answer, the youngest of the three spoke up. "Wait, that worthless piece of shit canceled on you?" Coby said. The boys were all only eleven months apart, making Coby just eighteen. My coworkers knew my brothers had all scored fake IDs and thought they were doing me a favor by looking the other way, but most of the time I wished they wouldn't. Coby in particular still acted like a twelve-year-old boy not quite sure what to do with his testosterone. He was bowing up behind the others, letting them hold him back from a fight that didn't exist.

"What are you doing, Coby?" I asked. "He's not even here!"

"You're damn right he's not," Coby said. He relaxed, cracking his neck. "Canceling on my big sister. I'll bust his fuckin' face." I thought about Coby and T.J. getting into a brawl, and it made my heart race. T.J. was intimidating when he was younger, and lethal as an adult. No one fucked with him, and Coby knew it.

A disgusted noise came from my throat, and I rolled my eyes. "Just . . . find another table."

All four boys pulled chairs around Raegan and me. Colin had light-brown hair, but my brothers were all redheads. Colin and Chase had blue eyes. Clark and Coby had green. Some redheaded men aren't all that great-looking, but my brothers were tall, chiseled, and outgoing. Clark was the only one with freckles, and they still somehow looked good on him. I was the outcast, the only child with mousy brown hair and big, round, light-blue eyes. More than once the boys tried to convince me that I'd been adopted. If I wasn't the female version of my father, I might have believed them.

I touched my forehead to the table and groaned. "I can't believe it, but this day just got worse."

"Aw, c'mon, Camille. You know you love us," Clark said, nudging me with his shoulder. When I didn't answer, he leaned in to whisper in my ear. "You sure you're all right?"

I kept my head down, but nodded. Clark patted my back a couple of times, and then the table grew quiet.

I lifted my head. Everyone was staring behind me, so I turned around. Trenton Maddox was standing there, holding two shot glasses and another glass of something that looked decidedly less sweet.

"This table turned into a party fast," Trenton said with a surprised but charming smile.

Chase narrowed his eyes at Trenton. "Is that him?" he asked, nodding.

"What?" Trenton asked.

Coby's knee began to bounce, and he leaned forward in his chair. "That's him. He fuckin' canceled on her, and then he showed up here."

"Wait. Coby, no," I said, holding up my hands.

Coby stood up. "You jackin' with our sister?"

"Sister?" Trenton said, his eyes bouncing between me and the volatile gingers sitting on each side of me.

"Oh, God," I said, closing my eyes. "Colin, tell Coby to stop. It's not him."

"Who's not me?" Trenton said. "We got a problem here?"

Travis appeared at his brother's side. He wore the same amused expression as Trenton, both flashing their matching left-sided dimples. They could have been their mother's second set of twins. Only subtle differences set them apart, including the fact that Travis was maybe an inch or two taller than Trenton.

Travis crossed his arms across his chest, making his already large biceps bulge. The only thing that kept me from exploding from my chair was that his shoulders relaxed. He wasn't ready to fight. Yet.

"Evening," Travis said.

The Maddoxes could sense trouble. At least it seemed that way, because whenever there was a fight, they had either started it, or finished it. Usually both.

"Coby, sit down," I commanded through my teeth.

"No, I'm not sittin' down. This dickhead insulted my sister, I'm not fuckin' sittin' down."

Raegan leaned over to Chase. "That's Trent and Travis Maddox."

"Maddox?" Clark asked.

"Yeah. You still got something to say?" Travis said.

Coby shook his head slowly and smiled. "I can talk all night long, motherfu—"

I stood. "Coby! Sit your ass down!" I said, pointing to his chair. He sat. "I said it wasn't him, and I meant it! Now everybody *calm* the *fuck* down! I've had a *bad* day, I'm here to drink, and relax, and have a good *goddamn* time! Now if that's a problem for you, back the fuck off my table!" I closed my eyes and screamed the last part, looking completely insane. People around us were staring.

Breathing hard, I glanced at Trenton, who handed me a drink.

One corner of his mouth turned up. "I think I'll stay."

About the Author

Jamie McGuire is the *New York Times* bestselling author of *Beautiful Oblivion*, *A Beautiful Wedding*, *Red Hill*, *Walking Disaster*, *Beautiful Disaster*, and *The Providence* trilogy. She and her husband, Jeff, live with their children just outside Enid, Oklahoma, with three dogs, six horses, and a cat named Rooster. Please visit JamieMcGuire.com.

 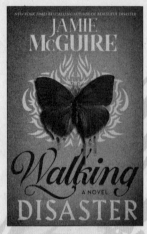
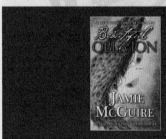

Walking
DISASTER

ALSO BY JAMIE McGUIRE

Beautiful Disaster

Walking DISASTER

A NOVEL

JAMIE McGUIRE

ATRIA PAPERBACK

New York   London   Toronto   Sydney   New Delhi

ATRIA PAPERBACK

A Division of Simon & Schuster, Inc.

1230 Avenue of the Americas

New York, NY 10020

First Atria Paperback edition April 2013

ATRIA PAPERBACK and colophon are trademarks of Simon & Schuster, Inc.

For information about special discounts for bulk purchases, please contact Simon & Schuster Special Sales at 1-866-506-1949 or business@simonandschuster.com.

The Simon & Schuster Speakers Bureau can bring authors to your live event. For more information or to book an event contact the Simon & Schuster Speakers Bureau at 1-866-248-3049 or visit our website at www.simonspeakers.com.

Designed by Rhea Braunstein

Manufactured in the United States of America

10   9   8   7   6

Library of Congress Cataloging-in-Publication Data

McGuire, Jamie.

    Walking disaster : a novel / Jamie McGuire. — 1st Atria Books trade paperback ed.

      p. cm.

1. Man-woman relationships—Fiction. 2. Love stories. I. Title.

   PS3613.C4994W35 2013

   813'.6—dc23   2012037231

ISBN 978-1-4767-1298-7

ISBN 978-1-4767-1299-4 (ebook)

To Jeff,
my very own
BEAUTIFUL disaster

PROLOGUE

Even with the sweat on her forehead and the skip in her breath, she didn't look sick. Her skin didn't have the peachy glow I was used to, and her eyes weren't as bright, but she was still beautiful. The most beautiful woman I would ever see.

Her hand flopped off the bed, and her finger twitched. My eyes trailed from her brittle, yellowing nails, up her thin arm, to her bony shoulder, finally settling on her eyes. She was looking down at me, her lids two slits, just enough to let me know she knew I was there. That's what I loved about her. When she looked at me, she really saw me. She didn't look past me to the other dozens of things she needed to do with her day, or tune out my stupid stories. She listened, and it made her really happy. Everyone else seemed to nod without listening, but not her. Never her.

"Travis," she said, her voice raspy. She cleared her throat, and the corners of her mouth turned up. "Come here, baby. It's okay. C'mere."

Dad put a few fingers on the base of my neck and pushed me forward while listening to the nurse. Dad called her Becky. She came to the house for the first time a few days ago. Her words were soft, and her eyes were kinda nice, but I didn't like Becky. I couldn't explain it, but her being there was scary. I knew she might have been there to help, but it wasn't a good thing, even though Dad was okay with her.

Dad's nudge shoved me forward several steps, close enough to where Mommy could touch me. She stretched her long, elegant fingers, and brushed my arm. "It's okay, Travis," she whispered. "Mommy wants to tell you something."

I stuck my finger in my mouth, and pushed it around on my gums, fidgeting. Nodding made her small smile bigger, so I made sure to make big movements with my head as I stepped toward her face.

She used what was left of her strength to scoot closer to me, and then she took a breath. "What I'm going to ask you will be very hard, son. I know you can do it, because you're a big boy now."

I nodded again, mirroring her smile, even if I didn't mean it. Smiling when she looked so tired and uncomfortable didn't feel right, but being brave made her happy. So I was brave.

"Travis, I need you to listen to what I'm going to say, and even more important, I need you to remember. This will be very hard. I've been trying to remember things from when I was three, and I . . ." She trailed off, the pain too big for a bit.

"Pain getting unmanageable, Diane?" Becky said, pushing a needle into Mom's IV.

After a few moments, Mommy relaxed. She took another breath, and tried again.

"Can you do that for Mommy? Can you remember what I'm about to say?" I nodded again, and she raised a hand to my cheek. Her skin wasn't very warm, and she could only keep her hand in place for a few seconds before it got shaky and fell to the bed. "First, it's okay to be sad. It's okay to feel things. Remember that. Second, be a kid for as long as you can. Play games, Travis. Be silly"—her eyes glossed over—"and you and your brothers take care of each other, and your father. Even when you grow up and move away, it's important to come home. Okay?"

My head bobbed up and down, desperate to please her.

"One of these days you're going to fall in love, son. Don't settle for just anyone. Choose the girl that doesn't come easy, the one you have to fight for, and then never stop fighting. Never"—she took a deep breath—"stop fighting for what you want. And never"—her eyebrows pulled in—"forget that Mommy loves you. Even if you can't see me." A tear fell down her cheek. "I will always, *always* love you."

She took a choppy breath, and then coughed.

"Okay," Becky said, sticking a funny-looking thing in her ears. She held the other end to Mommy's chest. "Time to rest."

"No time," Mommy whispered.

Becky looked at my dad. "We're getting close, Mr. Maddox. You should probably bring the rest of the boys in to say goodbye."

Dad's lips made a hard line, and he shook his head. "I'm not ready," he choked out.

"You'll never be ready to lose your wife, Jim. But you don't want to let her go without the boys saying their goodbyes."

Dad thought for a minute, wiped his nose with his sleeve, and then nodded. He stomped out of the room, like he was mad.

I watched Mommy, watched her try to breathe, and watched Becky checking the numbers on the box beside her. I touched Mommy's wrist. Becky's eyes seemed to know something I didn't, and that made my stomach feel sick.

"You know, Travis," Becky said, leaning down so she could look me in the eyes, "the medicine I'm giving your mommy will make her sleep, but even though she's sleeping, she can still hear you. You can still tell Mommy that you love her and that you'll miss her, and she'll hear everything you say."

I looked at Mommy but quickly shook my head. "I don't want to miss her."

Becky put her soft, warm hand on my shoulder, just like Mommy used to when I was upset. "Your mom wants to be here with you. She wants that very much. But Jesus wants her with him right now."

I frowned. "I need her more than Jesus does."

Becky smiled, and then kissed the top of my hair.

Dad knocked on the door, and then it opened. My brothers crowded around him in the hallway, and Becky led me by the hand to join them.

Trenton's eyes didn't leave Mommy's bed, and Taylor and Tyler looked everywhere *but* the bed. It made me feel better somehow that they all looked as scared as I felt.

Thomas stood next to me, a little bit in front, like the time he protected me when we were playing in the front yard, and the neighbor boys tried to pick a fight with Tyler. "She doesn't look good," Thomas said.

Dad cleared his throat. "Mom's been real sick for a long time, boys, and it's time for her . . . it's time she . . ." He trailed off.

Becky offered a small, sympathetic smile. "Your mom hasn't been eating or drinking. Her body is letting go. This is going to be very hard, but it's a good time to tell your mom that you love her, and you're going to miss her, and that it's okay for her to go. She needs to know that it's okay."

My brothers nodded their heads in unison. All of them but me. It wasn't okay. I didn't want her to leave. I didn't care if Jesus wanted her or not. She was my mommy. He could take an old mommy. One that didn't have little boys to take care of. I tried to remember everything she told me. I tried to glue it to the inside of my head: Play. Visit Dad. Fight for what I love. That last thing bothered me. I loved Mommy, but I didn't know how to fight for her.

Becky leaned into my dad's ear. He shook his head, and then nodded to my brothers. "Okay, boys. Let's go say goodbye, and then you need to get your brothers in bed, Thomas. They don't need to be here for the rest."

"Yes, sir," Thomas said. I knew he was faking a brave face. His eyes were as sad as mine.

Thomas talked to her for a while, and then Taylor and Tyler whispered things in each of her ears. Trenton cried and hugged her for a long time. Everyone told her it was okay for her to leave us. Everyone but me. Mommy didn't say anything back this time.

Thomas pulled on my hand, leading me out of her bedroom. I walked backward until we were in the hall. I tried to pretend she was just going to sleep, but my head went fuzzy. Thomas picked me up and carried me up the stairs. His feet climbed faster when Dad's wails carried through the walls.

"What did she say to you?" Thomas asked, turning on the tub faucet.

I didn't answer. I heard him ask, and I remembered like she told me to, but my tears wouldn't work, and my mouth didn't either.

Thomas pulled my dirt-soiled shirt over my head, and my shorts and Thomas the Train Underoos down to the floor.

"Time to get in the tub, bubby." He lifted me off the floor and sat me in the warm water, soaking the rag, and squeezing it over my head. I didn't blink. I didn't even try to get the water off of my face, even though I hated it.

"Yesterday, Mom told me to take care of you and the twins, and to take care of Dad." Thomas folded his hands on the rim of the tub and rested his chin on them, looking at me. "So that's what I'm gonna do, Trav, okay? I'm going to take care of you. So don't you worry. We're going to miss Mom together, but don't be scared. I'm going to make sure everything's okay. I promise."

I wanted to nod, or hug him, but nothing worked. Even though I should have been fighting for her, I was upstairs, in a tub full of water, still as a statue. I had already let her down. I promised her in the very back of my head that I would do all the things she had told me as soon as my body worked again. When the sad went away, I would always play, and I would always fight. Hard.

CHAPTER ONE
Pigeon

FUCKING VULTURES. THEY COULD WAIT YOU OUT FOR hours. Days. Nights, too. Staring right through you, picking which parts of you they will pull away first, which pieces will be the sweetest, the most tender, or just which part will be most convenient.

What they don't know, what they've never anticipated, is that the prey is faking. It's the vultures that are easy. Just when they think all they have to do is be patient, to sit back and wait for you to expire, that's when you hit them. That's when you bring in the secret weapon: an utter lack of respect for the status quo; a refusal to give in to the order of things.

That's when you shock them with how much you just don't give a fuck.

An opponent in the Circle, some random douche bag trying to expose your weakness with insults, a woman trying to tie you down; gets them every time.

I'd been very careful from a very young age to live my life this way. These bleeding heart assholes that went around giving their soul to every gold-digging banshee that smiled at them had it all wrong. But somehow I was the one swimming upstream. I was the man out. Their way was the hard way if you ask me. Leaving emotion at the door, and replacing it with numbness, or anger—which was much easier to control—was easy. Letting yourself feel made you vulnerable. As many times as I tried to explain this error to my brothers, my cousins, or my friends, I was met with skepticism. As many times as I had seen them crying or losing sleep over some dumb bitch in a pair of fuck-me heels that never gave a shit about them anyway, I couldn't understand it. The women that were worth that kind of heartbreak wouldn't let you fall for them so easy. They wouldn't bend over your couch, or allow you to charm them into their bedroom on the first night—or even the tenth.

My theories were ignored because that wasn't the way of things. Attraction, sex, infatuation, love, and then heartbreak. That was the logical order. And, it was always the order.

But not for me. No. Fucking. Way.

I decided a long time ago I would feed on the vultures until a dove came along. A pigeon. The kind of soul that didn't impede on anyone; just walked around worrying about its own business, trying to get through life without pulling everyone else down with its own needs and selfish habits. Brave. A communicator. Intelligent. Beautiful. Soft-spoken. A creature that mates for life. Unattainable until she has a reason to trust you.

As I stood at my open apartment door, flicking the last bit of ashes off my cigarette, the girl in the bloody, pink cardigan from the Circle flashed in my memory. Without thinking, I'd called her Pigeon. At the time it was just a stupid nickname to make her even more uncomfortable than she already was. Her crimson-spattered face, her eyes wide, outwardly she seemed innocent, but I could tell it was just the clothes. I pushed her memory away as I stared blankly into the living room.

Megan lay on my couch lazily, watching TV. She looked bored, and I wondered why she was still in my apartment. She usually got her crap and left right after I bagged her.

The door complained when I pushed it a little wider. I cleared my throat and picked up my backpack by the straps. "Megan. I'm out."

She sat up and stretched, and then gripped the chain of her excessively large purse. I couldn't imagine she had enough belongings to fill it. Megan slung the silver links over her shoulder, and then slipped on her wedge heels, sauntering out the door.

"Text me if you're bored," she said without glancing in my direction. She slipped on her oversize sunglasses, and then descended the stairs, completely unaffected by my dismissal. Her indifference was exactly why Megan was one of my few frequent flyers. She didn't cry about commitment, or throw a tantrum. She took our arrangement for what it was, and then went about her day.

My Harley glistened in the morning autumn sun. I waited for Megan to pull away from the parking lot of my apartment, and then jogged down the stairs, zipping up my jacket. Dr. Rueser's humanities class was in half an hour, but he didn't care if I was late. If it didn't piss him off, I didn't really see a point in killing myself to get there.

"Wait up!" a voice called from behind me.

Shepley stood at the front door of our apartment, shirtless and balancing on one foot while trying to pull a sock onto the other. "I meant to ask you last night. What did you say to

Marek? You leaned into his ear and said something. He looked like he swallowed his tongue."

"I thanked him for taking off out of town a few weekends before, because his mother was a wildcat."

Shepley stared at me, dubious. "Dude. You didn't."

"No. I heard from Cami that he got a Minor In Possession in Jones County."

He shook his head, and then nodded toward the couch. "Did you let Megan spend the night this time?"

"No, Shep. You know better than that."

"She just came over to get some morning nookie before class, huh? That's an interesting way to claim you for the day."

"You think that's it?"

"Anyone else gets her sloppy seconds." Shepley shrugged. "It's Megan. Who knows. Listen, I've gotta take America back to campus. Want a ride?"

"I'll meet you later," I said, slipping on my Oakleys. "I can take Mare if you want."

Shepley's face contorted. "Uh . . . no."

Amused at his reaction, I saddled up on the Harley and ripped the engine. Even though I had the bad habit of seducing his girlfriend's friends, there was one line I wouldn't cross. America was his, and once he showed interest in a girl, she was off my radar, never to be considered again. He knew that. He just liked to give me shit.

I met Adam behind Sig Tau. He ran the Circle. After the initial payout the first night, I'd let him pick up the tote returns the following day, and then give him a cut for his trouble. He kept the cover; I kept the winnings. Our relationship was strictly business, and we both preferred to keep it simple. As long as he kept paying me, I stayed out of his face, and as long as he didn't want to get his ass kicked, he stayed out of mine.

I made my way across campus to the cafeteria. Just before I reached the double metal doors, Lexi and Ashley stepped in front of me.

"Hey, Trav," Lexi said, standing with perfect posture. Perfectly tanned, silicone-endowed breasts peeked from her pink T-shirt. Those irresistible, bouncing mounds were what begged me to bag her in the first place, but once was enough. Her voice reminded me of the sound made by air being slowly let out of a balloon, and Nathan Squalor bagged her the night after I did.

"Hey, Lex."

I pinched the cherry off my cigarette and threw it into the bin before walking quickly past her through the doors. Not that I was eager to tackle the buffet of limp vegetables, dry meat, and overripe fruits. Jesus. Her voice made dogs howl, and children perk up to see what cartoon character had come to life.

Regardless of my dismissal, both girls followed.

"Shep." I nodded. He was sitting with America, laughing with the people around him. The pigeon from the fight sat across from him, poking at her food with a plastic fork. My voice seemed to pique her curiosity. I could feel her big eyes follow me to the end of the table where I tossed my tray.

I heard Lexi giggle, forcing me to restrain the irritation boiling inside me. When I sat, she used my knee for a chair.

Some of the guys from the football team sitting at our table watched in awe, as if being followed by two inarticulate tarts was an unattainable aspiration for them.

Lexi slid her hand under the table and then pressed her fingers into my thigh as she made her way up the inseam of my jeans. I spread my legs a little wider, waiting for her to reach her mark.

Just before I felt her hands on me, America's loud murmurs traveled down the table.

"I think I just threw up a little bit in my mouth."

Lexi turned, her entire body rigid. "I heard that, skank."

A dinner roll flew past Lexi's face and bounced off the floor. Shepley and I traded glances, and then I let my knee give way.

Lexi's ass bounced off the cafeteria tile. I admit, it turned me on a little hearing the sound of her skin slap against the ceramic.

She didn't complain much before walking away. Shepley seemed to appreciate my gesture, and that was good enough for me. My toleration for girls like Lexi only lasted so long. I had one rule: respect. For me, my family, and for my friends. Hell, even some of my enemies deserved respect. I didn't see a reason to associate longer than necessary with people who didn't understand that life lesson. It might sound hypocritical to the women that have passed through my apartment door, but if they carried themselves with respect, I would have given it to them.

I winked at America, who seemed satisfied, nodded to Shepley, and then took another bite of whatever was on my plate.

"Nice job last night, Mad Dog," Chris Jenks said, flicking a crouton across the table.

"Shut up, dumb ass," Brazil said in his typical low voice. "Adam will never let you back in if he hears you're talking."

"Oh. Yeah," he said, shrugging.

I took my tray to the trash, and then returned to my seat with a frown. "And don't call me that."

"What? Mad Dog?"

"Yeah."

"Why not? I thought that was your Circle name. Kind of like your stripper name."

My eyes targeted Jenks. "Why don't you shut up and give that hole in your face a chance to heal."

I'd never liked that little worm.

"Sure thing, Travis. All you had to do was say so." He chuckled nervously before gathering his trash and heading out.

Before long, most of the lunchroom was empty. I glanced down to see Shepley and America still hanging around, talking with her friend. She had long, wavy hair, and her skin was still bronzed from summer break. She didn't have the biggest tits I'd ever seen, but her eyes . . . they were a weird gray color. Familiar somehow.

There was no way I'd met her before, but something about her face reminded me of something I couldn't put my finger on.

I stood up and walked toward her. She had the hair of a porn star, and the face of an angel. Her eyes were almond shaped and uniquely beautiful. That was when I saw it: behind the beauty and fake innocence was something else, something cold and calculating. Even when she smiled, I could see sin so deeply ingrained in her that no cardigan could hide it. Those eyes floated above her tiny nose, and smooth features. To anyone else, she was pure and naive, but this girl was hiding something. I knew only because the same sin had dwelled in me my entire life. The difference was she held it deep within her, and I let mine out of its cage on a regular basis.

I watched Shepley until he felt me staring at him. When he looked my way, I nodded in the pigeon's direction.

Who's that? I mouthed.

Shepley only responded with a confused frown.

Her, I silently mouthed again.

Shepley's mouth turned up into the annoying asshole grin he always made when he was about to do something to piss me off.

"What?" Shepley asked, a lot louder than necessary.

I could tell the girl knew we were talking about her, because she kept her head down, pretending not to hear.

After spending sixty seconds in Abby Abernathy's presence, I discerned two things: she didn't talk much, and when she did she was kind of a bitch. But I don't know . . . I kind of dug that about her. She put on a front to keep assholes like me away, but that made me even more determined.

She rolled her eyes at me for the third or fourth time. I was annoying her and found it pretty amusing. Girls didn't usually treat me with unadulterated loathing, even when I was showing them the door.

When even my best smiles didn't work, I turned it up a notch. "Do you have a twitch?"

"A what?" she asked.

"A twitch. Your eyes keep wiggling around." If she could have murdered me with her glare, I would have bled out on the floor. I couldn't help but laugh. She was a smart-ass and rude as hell. I liked her more every second.

I leaned closer to her face. "Those are some amazing eyes, though. What color is that, anyway? Gray?"

She immediately ducked her head, letting her hair cover her face. Score. I made her uncomfortable, and that meant I was getting somewhere.

America immediately jumped in, warning me away. I couldn't blame her. She'd seen the endless line of girls come in and out of the apartment. I didn't want to piss America off, but she didn't look angry. More like amused.

"You're not her type," America said.

My mouth fell open, playing into her game. "I'm everyone's type!"

The pigeon peeked over at me and grinned. A warm feeling—probably just the insane urge to throw this girl on my couch—came over me. She was different, and it was refreshing.

"Ah! A smile," I said. Simply calling it a smile, like it wasn't the most beautiful thing I'd ever seen, seemed wrong, but I wasn't about to fuck up my game when I was just getting ahead. "I'm not a rotten bastard after all. It was nice to meet you, Pidge."

I stood, walked around the table, and leaned into America's ear. "Help me out here, would ya? I'll behave, I swear."

A French fry came hurdling toward my face.

"Get your lips outta my girl's ear, Trav!" Shepley said.

I backed away, holding my hands up to highlight the most innocent expression on my face that I could manage. "Networking! I'm networking!" I walked backward a few steps to the door, noticing a small group of girls. I opened the door, and they swarmed through like a herd of water buffalo before I could let myself out.

It had been a long time since I'd had a challenge. The weird thing was, I wasn't out to fuck her. It bothered me that she might think I was a piece of shit, but it bothered me more that I cared. Either way, for the first time in a long time, someone was unpredictable. Pigeon was the total opposite of the girls I'd met here, and I had to know why.

CHANEY'S CLASS WAS FULL. I TOOK THE STEPS TO MY seat two at a time, and then waded through the bare legs crowding my desk.

I nodded. "Ladies."

They hummed and sighed in harmony.

Vultures. Half of them I'd bagged my freshman year, the other half had been on my couch well before fall break. Except the girl on the end. Sophia flashed a crooked smile. It looked like her face had caught fire and someone had tried to put it out with a fork. She had been with a few of my frat brothers. Knowing their track records and her lack of concern for safety, it was best to consider her an unnecessary risk, even if I was habitually careful.

She leaned forward on her elbows to make better eye contact. I felt the urge to shudder with disgust, but I resisted. *No. Not even close to being worth it.*

The brunette in front of me turned around and batted her lashes. "Hey, Travis. I hear there's a date party coming up at Sig Tau."

"No," I said without pause.

Her bottom lip formed a pout. "But . . . when you told me about it, I thought you might want to go."

I laughed once. "I was bitching about it. Not the same."

The blonde next to me leaned forward. "Everyone knows Travis Maddox doesn't go to date parties. You're barking up the wrong tree, Chrissy."

"Oh yeah? Well, no one asked you," Chrissy said with a frown.

As the women argued back and forth, I noticed Abby rush in. She practically threw herself into a front-row desk just before the bell rang.

Before I took a second to ask myself why, I grabbed my paper and popped my pen in my mouth, and then jogged down the steps, sliding into the desk next to her.

The look on Abby's face surpassed amusing, and for a reason I couldn't explain, it caused adrenaline to rush through my body—the kind that I used to experience before a fight.

"Good. You can take notes for me."

She was utterly disgusted, and that only pleased me more. Most girls bored me outta my gourd, but this girl was intriguing. Entertaining, even. I didn't faze her, at least not in a positive way. My very presence seemed to make her want to puke, and I found that strangely endearing.

The urge came over me to find out if it was really hate she felt for me, or if she was just a hard-ass. I leaned in close. "I'm sorry . . . did I offend you in some way?"

Her eyes softened before she shook her head. She didn't hate me. She just *wanted* to hate me. I was way ahead of her. If she wanted to play, I could play.

"Then what is your problem?"

She seemed embarrassed to say what came next. "I'm not sleeping with you. You should give up, now."

Oh yeah. This was going to be fun. "I haven't asked you to sleep with me . . . have I?" I let my eyes drift to the ceiling, as if I had to think about it. "Why don't you come over with America tonight?"

Abby's lip turned up, as if she'd smelled something rotten.

"I won't even flirt with you, I swear."

"I'll think about it."

I tried not to smile too much and give myself away. She wasn't going to roll over like the vultures above. I glanced behind me, and they were all glaring at the back of Abby's head. They knew it as well as I did. Abby was different, and I was going to have to work for this one. For once.

Three doodles of potential tattoos, and two dozen 3-D boxes later, class dismissed. I slid through the halls before anyone could stop me. I made good time, but Abby had somehow ended up outside, a good twenty yards ahead of me.

I'll be damned. She was trying to avoid me. I quickened my pace until I was next to her. "Have you thought about it?"

"Travis!" A girl said, playing with her hair. Abby kept going, leaving me stuck listening to this girl's irritating babble.

"Sorry, uh . . ."

"Heather."

"Sorry, Heather . . . I'm . . . I've gotta go."

She wrapped her arms around me. I patted her backside, shrugged out of her grasp, and kept walking, wondering who she was.

Before I could figure out who Heather was, Abby's long, tan legs came into view. I popped a Marlboro into my mouth and jogged to her side. "Where was I? Oh yeah . . . you were thinking."

"What are you talking about?"

"Have you thought about coming over?"

"If I say yes, will you quit following me?"

I pretended to mull it over, and then nodded. "Yes."

"Then I'll come over."

Bullshit. She wasn't that easy. "When?"

"Tonight. I'll come over tonight."

I stopped midstep. She was up to something. I hadn't anticipated her going on the offensive. "Sweet," I said, playing off my surprise. "See you then, Pidge."

She walked away without looking back, not the least bit affected by the conversation. She disappeared behind other students making their own way to class.

Shepley's white ball cap came into view. He was in no hurry to get to our computer class. My eyebrows pressed together. I hated that class. Who doesn't know how to work a fucking computer anymore?

I joined Shepley and America as they merged into the flow of students on the main walkway. She giggled and watched him yap at me with stars in her eyes. America was no vulture. She was hot, yeah, but she could have a conversation without saying *like* after every word, and she was pretty funny at times. What I liked most about her is she wouldn't come to the apartment for several weeks after their first date, and even after they watched a movie all snuggled up at the apartment, she went back to her dorm room.

I had a feeling the probationary period before Shepley could bag her was about to end, though.

"Hey, Mare," I said, nodding.

"How's it going, Trav?" she asked. She acknowledged me with a friendly smile, but then her eyes were right back on Shepley.

He was one of the lucky ones. Girls like that didn't come along very often.

"This is me," America said, gesturing to her dorm around the corner. She wrapped her arms around Shepley's neck and kissed him. He gripped her shirt on each side and pulled her close before letting her go.

America waved one last time at both of us, and then joined her friend Finch at the front entrance.

"You're falling for her, aren't you?" I asked, punching Shepley in the arm.

He shoved me. "None of your business, dick."

"Does she have a sister?"

"She's an only child. Leave her friends alone, too, Trav. I mean it."

Shepley's last words were unnecessary. His eyes were a billboard for his emotions and thoughts most of the time, and he was clearly serious—maybe even a little desperate. He wasn't just falling for her. He was in love.

"You mean Abby."

He frowned. "I mean any of her friends. Even Finch. Just stay away."

"Cousin!" I said, hooking my elbow around his neck. "Are you in love? You're making me all misty-eyed!"

"Shut up," Shepley grumbled. "Just promise me you'll stay away from her friends."

I grinned. "I promise nothing."

CHAPTER TWO
Backfire

"WHAT ARE YOU DOING?" SHEPLEY ASKED. HE STOOD IN the middle of the room, a pair of sneakers in one hand, a dirty pair of underwear in the other.

"Uh, cleaning?" I asked, shoving shot glasses into the dishwasher.

"I see that. But . . . why?"

I smiled, my back turned to Shepley. He was going to kick my ass. "I'm expecting company."

"So?"

"The pigeon."

"Huh?"

"Abby, Shep. I invited Abby."

"Dude, no. No! Don't fuck this up for me, man. Please don't."

I turned, crossing my arms across my chest. "I tried, Shep. I did. But, I don't know." I shrugged. "There's something about her. I couldn't help myself."

Shepley's jaw worked under his skin, and then he stomped into his room, slamming the door behind him.

I finished loading the dishwasher, and then circled the couch to make sure I hadn't missed any visible empty condom wrappers. That was never fun to explain.

The fact that I had bagged a good portion of beautiful coeds at this school was no secret, but I didn't see a reason to remind them when they came to my apartment. It was all about presentation.

Pigeon, though. It would take far more than false advertising to bag her on my couch. At this point, the strategy was to take her one step at a time. If I focused on the end result, the process could easily be fucked up. She noticed things. She was farther from naive than I was; light-years away. This operation was nothing less than precarious.

I was in my bedroom sorting dirty laundry when I heard the front door open. Shepley usually listened for America's car to pull in so he could greet her at the door.

Pussy.

Murmuring, and then the closing of Shepley's door was my signal. I walked into the front room, and there she sat: glasses, her hair all piled on top of her head, and what might have been pajamas. I wouldn't have been surprised if they'd been molding in the bottom of her laundry hamper.

It was so hard not to bust into laughter. Never once had a female come to my apartment dressed like that. My front door had seen jean skirts, dresses, even a see-through tube dress over a string bikini. A handful of times, spackled-on makeup and glitter lotion. Never pajamas.

Her appearance immediately explained why she'd so easily agreed to come over. She was going to try to nauseate me into leaving her alone. If she didn't look absolutely sexy like that, it might have worked, but her skin was impeccable, and the lack of makeup and the frames of her glasses just made her eye color stand out even more.

"It's about time you showed up," I said, falling onto the couch.

At first she seemed proud of her idea, but as we talked and I remained impervious, it was clear that she knew her plan had failed. The less she smiled, the more I had to stop myself from grinning from ear to ear. She was so much fun. I just couldn't get over it.

Shepley and America joined us ten minutes later. Abby was flustered, and I was damn near light-headed. Our conversation had gone from her doubting that I could write a simple paper to her questioning my penchant for fighting. I kind of liked talking to her about normal stuff. It was preferable to the awkward task of asking her to leave once I bagged her. She didn't understand me, and I kind of wanted her to, even though I seemed to piss her off.

"What are you, the Karate Kid? Where did you learn to fight?"

Shepley and America seemed to be embarrassed for Abby. I don't know why; I sure as hell didn't mind. Just because I didn't talk about my childhood much didn't mean I was ashamed.

"I had a dad with a drinking problem and a bad temper, and four older brothers that carried the asshole gene."

"Oh," she said simply. Her cheeks turned red, and at that moment, I felt a twinge in my chest. I wasn't sure what it was, but it bugged me. "Don't be embarrassed, Pidge. Dad quit drinking. The brothers grew up."

"I'm not embarrassed." Her body language didn't match her words. I struggled to think of something to change the subject, and then her sexy, frumpy look came to mind. Her embarrassment was immediately replaced by irritation, something I was far more comfortable with.

America suggested watching TV. The last thing I wanted to do was to be in a room with Abby but unable to talk to her. I stood. "You hungry, Pidge?"

"I already ate."

America's eyebrows pulled in. "No, you haven't. Oh . . . er . . . that's right. I forgot. You grabbed a . . . pizza? Before we left."

Abby was embarrassed again, but her anger quickly covered it. Learning her emotional pattern didn't take long.

I opened the door, trying to keep my voice casual. I'd never been so eager to get a girl alone—especially to *not* have sex with her. "C'mon. You've gotta be hungry."

Her shoulders relaxed a bit. "Where are you going?"

"Wherever you want. We can hit a pizza place." I inwardly cringed. That might have been too eager.

She looked down at her sweatpants. "I'm not really dressed."

She had no idea how beautiful she was. That made her even more appealing. "You look fine. Let's go, I'm starvin'."

Once she was on the back of my Harley, I could finally think straight again. My thoughts were usually more relaxed on my bike. Abby's legs had my hips in a vise grip, but that was oddly relaxing, too. Almost a relief.

This weird sensation I felt around her was disorienting. I didn't like it, but then again it reminded me that she was around, so it was as comforting as it was unsettling. I decided to get my shit together. Abby might be a pigeon, but she was just a fucking girl. No need to get my boxers in a bunch.

Besides, there was something under the good girl facade. She hated me on sight because she'd been burned by someone like me before. No way was she a slut, though. Not even a reformed slut. I could spot them a mile away. My game face slowly melted away. I'd finally found a girl that was interesting enough to get to know, and a version of me had already hurt her.

Even though we'd just met, the thought of some jackhole hurting Pidge infuriated me. Abby associating me with someone that would hurt her was even worse. I gunned the throttle as I pulled into the Pizza Shack. That ride wasn't long enough to sort out the clusterfuck in my head.

I wasn't even thinking about my speed, so when Abby jumped off my bike and started yelling, I couldn't help but laugh.

"I went the speed limit."

"Yeah, if we were on the autobahn!" She ripped the wild bun down from the crown of her head, and then brushed her long hair with her fingers.

I couldn't stop staring while she rewrapped it and tied it back again. I imagined that this was what she looked like in the morning, and then had to think about the first ten minutes of *Saving Private Ryan* to keep my dick from getting hard. Blood. Screaming. Visible intestines. Grenades. Gunfire. More blood.

I held the door open. "I wouldn't let anything happen to you, Pigeon."

She angrily stomped past me and into the restaurant, ignoring my gesture. It was a damn shame; she was the first girl that I had ever wanted to open the door for. I'd been looking forward to that moment, and she didn't even notice.

After following her inside, I headed for the corner booth I usually commandeered. The soccer team was seated at several tables pushed together in the middle of the room. They were already howling that I had walked in with a date, and I gritted my teeth. I didn't want Abby to hear.

For the first time ever, I found myself embarrassed about my behavior. But it didn't last long. Seeing Abby sit across the table, cranky and annoyed, cheered me right up.

I ordered two beers. The look of disgust on Abby's face caught me off guard. The waitress was blatantly flirting with me, and Abby was unhappy. Apparently I could piss her off without even trying.

"Come here often?" she snapped, glancing at the waitress.

Hell, yeah. She was jealous. Wait. Maybe the way I was treated by women was a turnoff. That wouldn't surprise me, either. This chick made my head spin.

I leaned on the table with my elbows, refusing to let her see she was getting to me. "So what's your story, Pidge? Are you a man-hater in general, or do you just hate me?"

"I think it's just you."

I had to laugh. "I can't figure you out. You're the first girl that's ever been disgusted with me *before* sex. You don't get all flustered when you talk to me, and you don't try to get my attention."

"It's not a ploy. I just don't like you."

Ouch. "You wouldn't be here if you didn't like me."

My persistence paid off. Her scowl smoothed, and the skin around her eyes relaxed.

"I didn't say you're a bad person. I just don't like being a foregone conclusion for the sole reason of having a vagina."

Whatever it was that had come over me, I couldn't contain it. I choked back my laughter to no avail, and then burst out laughing. She didn't think I was a dick after all; she just didn't like my approach. Easily fixed. A wave of relief washed over me, and I laughed harder than I'd laughed in years. Maybe ever.

"Oh my *God*! You're killing me! That's it. We have to be friends. I won't take no for an answer."

"I don't mind being friends, but that doesn't mean you have to try to get in my panties every five seconds."

"You're not sleeping with me. I get it."

That was it. She smiled, and in that moment, a whole new world of possibilities opened up. My brain flashed like channels through Pigeon porn, and then the whole system crashed, and an infomercial about nobility and not wanting to screw up this weird friendship we'd just begun appeared in its place.

I smiled back. "You have my word. I won't even think about your panties . . . unless you want me to."

She rested her small elbows on the table and leaned onto them. Of course my eyes went right to her tits, and the way they now pressed against the edge of the table.

"And that won't happen, so we can be friends."

Challenge accepted.

"So what's *your* story?" Abby asked. "Have you always been *Travis 'Mad Dog' Maddox*, or is that just since you came here?" She used two fingers on each hand as quotation marks when she said that god-awful fucking nickname.

I cringed. "No. Adam started that after my first fight." I hated that name, but it stuck. Everyone else seemed to like it, so Adam kept using it.

After an awkward silence, Abby finally spoke. "That's it? You're not going to tell me anything about yourself?"

She didn't seem to mind the nickname, or else she just accepted the backstory. I never knew when she was going to get offended and freak out, or when she would be rational and stay cool. Holy hell, I couldn't get enough of it.

"What do you wanna know?"

Abby shrugged. "The normal stuff. Where you're from, what you want to be when you grow up . . . things like that."

I was having to work at keeping the tension out of my shoulders. Talking about myself—especially my past—was out of my comfort zone. I gave some vague answers and left it at that, but then I heard one of the soccer players make a crack. It wouldn't have bothered me nearly as much if I wasn't dreading the moment Abby realized what they were laughing about. Okay, that was a lie. That would have pissed me off whether she was there or not.

She kept wanting to know about my family and my major, and I was trying not to jump out of my seat and take them all out in a one-man stampede. As my anger came to a boil, focusing on our conversation became more difficult.

"What are they laughing about?" she finally asked, gesturing to the rowdy table.

I shook my head.

"Tell me," she insisted.

My lips pressed together into a thin line. If she walked out, I'd probably never get another chance, and those cheese dicks would have something more to laugh about.

She watched me expectantly.

Fuck it. "They're laughing about me having to take you to dinner, first. It's not usually . . . my thing."

"First?"

When the meaning sunk in, her face froze. She was mortified to be there with me.

I winced, waiting for her to storm out.

Her shoulders fell. "I was afraid they were laughing about

you being seen with me dressed like this, and they think I'm going to sleep with you," she grumbled.

Wait. What? "Why wouldn't I be seen with you?"

Abby's cheeks flushed pink, and she looked down to the table. "What were we talking about?"

I sighed. She was worried about me. She thought they were laughing about the way she looked. The Pigeon wasn't a hardass, after all. I decided to ask another question before she could reconsider.

"You. What's your major?"

"Oh, er, general ed, for now. I'm still undecided, but I'm leaning toward accounting."

"You're not a local, though. You must be a transplant."

"Wichita. Same as America."

"How did you end up here from Kansas?"

"We just had to get away."

"From what?"

"My parents."

She was running. I had a feeling the cardigan and pearls she wore the night we met were a front. But, to hide what? She got irritated pretty quick with the personal questions, but before I could change the subject, Kyle from the soccer team shot off his mouth.

I nodded. "So, why here?"

Abby snapped something back. I missed whatever it was. The chuckles and asshole comments from the soccer team drowned out her words.

"Dude, you're supposed to get a doggie bag, not bag the doggie."

I couldn't hold back anymore. They weren't just being disrespectful to me, they were disrespecting Abby. I stood up and took a few steps, and they started to shove each other out the door, tripping and stumbling over a dozen pairs of feet.

Abby's eyes penetrated the back of my head, bringing me back to my senses, and I planted myself back in the booth. She raised an eyebrow, and immediately my frustration and anger melted away.

"You were going to say why you chose this school," I said. Pretending that little sideshow didn't happen was probably the best way to continue.

"It's hard to explain," she said, shrugging. "I guess it just felt right."

If there was a phrase to explain the way I felt at that moment, that was it. I didn't know what the hell I was doing or why, but something about sitting across from her in that booth brought me a weird sense of calm. Even in the middle of a rage.

I smiled and opened my menu. "I know what you mean."

CHAPTER THREE
White Knight

SHEPLEY STOOD AT THE DOOR LIKE A LOVESICK IDIOT, waving to America as she pulled out of the parking lot. He shut the door, and then collapsed in the recliner with the most ridiculous smile on his face.

"You're dumb," I said.

"Me? You should have seen you. Abby couldn't get out of here quick enough."

I frowned. Abby didn't seem in a hurry to me, but now that Shepley had said something, I remembered that she *was* pretty quiet when we got back. "You think so?"

Shepley laughed, stretching back in the chair and pulling the footrest up. "She hates you. Give it up."

"She doesn't hate me. I nailed that date—dinner."

Shepley's eyebrows shot up. "Date? Trav. What are you doing? Because if this is just a game to you and you fuck this up for me, I'm going to kill you in your sleep."

I fell against the couch and grabbed the remote. "I don't know what I'm doing, but I'm not doing that."

Shepley looked confused. I wouldn't let him see that I was just as baffled as he was.

"I wasn't kidding," he said, keeping his eyes on the TV screen. "I'll smother you."

"I heard you," I snapped. The whole feeling-out-of-my-element thing was pissing me off, and then I had Pepé Le Pew over there threatening my death. Shepley with a crush was annoying. Shepley in love was almost intolerable.

"Remember Anya?"

"It's not like that," Shepley said, exasperated. "It's different with Mare. She's the one."

"You know that after a couple of months?" I asked, dubious.

"I knew it when I saw her."

I shook my head. I hated it when he was like this. Unicorns and butterflies flying out of his ass and hearts floating in the air. He always ended up getting his heart broken, and then I had to make sure he didn't drink himself to death for six months solid. America seemed to like it, though.

Whatever. No woman could make me blubber and get slobbering drunk over losing her. If they didn't stick around, they weren't worth it anyway.

Shepley stood and stretched, and then ambled toward his room.

"You're full of shit, Shep."

"How would you know?" he asked.

He was right. I'd never been in love, but I couldn't imagine it changing me that much.

I decided to turn in, too. I stripped down and lay back on the mattress in a huff. The second my head hit the pillow, I thought of Abby. Our conversation replayed verbatim in my mind. A few times she had showed a glint of interest. She didn't totally hate me, and that helped me relax. I wasn't exactly apologetic about my reputation, but she didn't expect me to pretend. Women didn't make me nervous. Abby made me feel distracted and focused at the same time. Agitated and relaxed. Pissed off and damn near giddy. I'd never felt so at odds with myself. Something about that feeling made me want to be around her more.

After two hours of staring at the ceiling, wondering if I would see her the next day, I decided to get up and find the bottle of Jack Daniel's in the kitchen.

The shot glasses were clean in the dishwasher, so I pulled out one and filled it to the brim. After hammering it back, I poured another. I tossed it back, set the glass in the sink, and turned around. Shepley stood in his doorway with a smirk on his face.

"And so it begins."

"The day you appeared on our family tree, I wanted to cut it down."

Shepley laughed once and shut his door.

I trudged to my bedroom, pissed that I couldn't argue.

MORNING CLASSES TOOK FOREVER, AND I WAS A LITTLE disgusted with myself that I had all but run to the cafeteria. I didn't even know if Abby would be there.

But, she was.

Brazil was sitting directly across from her, chatting it up with Shepley. A smirk touched my face, and then I sighed, both relieved and resigned to the fact that I was lame.

The lunch lady filled my tray with god-knows-what, and then I walked over to the table, standing directly across from Abby.

"You're sittin' in my chair, Brazil."

"Oh, is she one of your girls, Trav?"

Abby shook her head. "Absolutely not."

I waited, and then Brazil complied, taking his tray to an empty seat at the end of the long table.

"What's up, Pidge?" I asked, waiting for her to spit venom in my direction. To my extreme surprise, she showed no signs of anger.

"What is that?" She stared at my tray.

I looked down at the steaming concoction. She was making random conversation. Yet another good sign. "The cafeteria ladies scare me. I'm not about to critique their cooking skills."

Abby watched me poke around with my fork for something edible, and then seemed distracted by the murmurings of those around us. Granted, it was new for my fellow students to see me make a fuss over sitting across from someone. I still wasn't sure why I did.

"*Ugh* . . . that bio test is after lunch." America groaned.

"Did you study?" Abby asked.

America's nose wrinkled. "God, no. I spent the night reassuring my boyfriend that you weren't going to sleep with Travis."

Shepley immediately became sullen at the mention of the previous night's conversation.

The football players seated at the end of our table quieted down to hear our conversation, and Abby sunk down into her seat, shooting a glare at America.

She was embarrassed. For whatever reason, she was mortified by any attention whatsoever.

America ignored Abby and nudged Shepley with her shoulder, but Shepley's frown didn't fade.

"Jesus, Shep. You've got it that bad, huh?" I threw a packet of ketchup at him, trying to lighten the mood. The surrounding students turned their attention to Shepley and America then, hoping for something to talk about.

Shepley didn't answer, but Abby's gray eyes peeked up at me over a small smile. I was on a roll today. She couldn't hate me if she tried. I don't know why I was so worried. It wasn't like I wanted to date her or anything. She just seemed like the perfect platonic experiment. She was basically a good girl—albeit slightly angry—and didn't need me fucking up her five-year plan. If she had one.

America rubbed Shepley's back. "He's going to be okay. It's just going to take him a while to believe Abby is resistant to your charms."

"I haven't *tried* to charm her," I said. I was just getting ahead, and America was sinking my battleship. "She's my friend."

Abby looked to Shepley. "I told you. You have nothing to worry about."

Shepley met Abby's eyes, and then his expression smoothed. Crisis averted. Abby saved the day.

I waited for a minute, trying to think of something to say. I wanted to ask Abby to come over later, but it would be lame after America's comment. A brilliant idea popped into my head, and I didn't hesitate. "Did *you* study?"

Abby frowned. "No amount of studying is going to help me with biology. It's just not something I can wrap my head around."

I stood, nodding toward the door. "C'mon."

"What?"

"Let's go get your notes. I'm going to help you study."

"Travis . . ."

"Get your ass up, Pidge. You're gonna ace that test."

The next three seconds might have been the longest of my life. Abby finally stood. She passed America and tugged on her hair. "See you in class, Mare."

She smiled. "I'll save you a seat. I'll need all the help I can get."

I held the door open for her as we left the cafeteria, but she didn't seem to notice. Again, I was only horrifically disappointed.

Shoving my hands in my pockets, I kept pace with her during the short walk to Morgan Hall, and then I watched as she fidgeted with her door key.

Abby finally pushed the door open, and then tossed her biology book onto the bed. She sat down and crossed her legs, and I fell onto the mattress, noting how stiff and uncomfortable it was. No wonder all the girls at this school were cranky. They couldn't possibly get a good night's rest on these damn mattresses. Jesus.

Abby turned to the correct page of her textbook, and I went to work. We went over the key points of the chapter. It was kind of cool how she watched me while I talked. Almost like she was both hanging on to every word, and amazed that I knew how to read. A few times I could tell by her expression that she didn't understand, so I'd go back over it, and then her eyes would brighten. I started working hard for the lights-on look on her face after that.

Before I knew it, it was time for her to go to class. I sighed, and then smacked her playfully on the head with her study guide.

"You got this. You know this study guide backward and forward."

"Well . . . we'll see."

"I'm going to walk you to class. I'll quiz you on the way." I waited for a polite rejection, but she offered a small smile and nodded.

We walked into the hall, and she sighed. "You're not going to be mad if I flunk this test, are you?"

She was worried if I was going to be mad at her? I wasn't sure what I should think about that, but it felt pretty fucking awesome.

"You're not going to flunk, Pidge. We need to start earlier for the next one, though," I said, walking along with her to the science building. I asked her question after question. She answered most right away, some she hesitated about, but she got them all correct.

We reached the door of her classroom, and I could see the appreciation on her face. She was too proud to admit it, though.

"Kick ass," I said, not really knowing what else to say.

Parker Hayes passed by and nodded. "Hey, Trav."

I hated that douche. "Parker," I said, nodding back.

Parker was one of those guys that liked to follow me around and use his White Knight status to get laid. He liked to refer to me as a womanizer, but the truth was, Parker just played a more sophisticated game. He wasn't honest about his conquests. He pretended to care and then let them down easy.

One night our freshman year, I took Janet Littleton home from the Red Door to my apartment. Parker was trying to get lucky with her friend. We went our separate ways from the club, and after I bagged her and didn't pretend to want a relationship afterward, she called her friend all pissed off to come get her. The friend was still with Parker, so he ended up taking Janet home.

After that, Parker had a new story to tell his conquests. Whatever girl I bagged, he usually swept up my sloppy seconds by recounting the time he saved Janet.

I tolerated him, but only just barely.

Parker's eyes targeted Pigeon and immediately lit up. "Hey, Abby."

I didn't understand why Parker was so insistent on seeing if he could land the same girls I did, but he'd had class with her for several weeks and was just now showing interest. Knowing it was because he saw her talking to me nearly sent me into a fury.

"Hi," Abby said, taken off guard. She clearly didn't know why he was suddenly talking to her. It was written all over her face. "Who's that?" she asked me.

I shrugged casually, but I wanted to tear across the room and beat his preppy ass. "Parker Hayes," I said. His name left a bad taste in my mouth. "He's one of my Sig Tau brothers." That left a bad taste, too. I had brothers, both frat and blood. Parker felt like neither. More like an archenemy that you kept close enough to keep an eye on.

"*You're* in a *frat?*" she asked, her little nose wrinkling up.

"Sigma Tau, same as Shep. I thought you knew."

"Well . . . you don't seem the . . . fraternity type," she said, eyeing the tattoos on my forearms.

The fact that Abby's eyes were back on me immediately put me in a better mood. "My dad is an alumnus, and my brothers are all Sig Tau. It's a family thing."

"And they expected you to pledge?" she asked, skeptical.

"Not really. They're just good guys," I said, flicking her papers. I handed them to her. "Better get to class."

She flashed that flawless smile. "Thanks for helping me." She nudged me with her elbow, and I couldn't help but smile back.

She walked into the classroom and sat next to America. Parker was staring at her, watching the girls talking. I fantasized about picking up a desk and hurling it at his head as I walked down the hall. With no more classes for the day, there was no reason for me to stick around. A long ride on the Harley would help keep the thought of Parker sleazing his way into Abby's good graces from driving me crazy, so I made sure to take the long way home to give me more time to think. A few couch-worthy coeds crossed my path, but Abby's face kept popping into my mind—so many times that I began to annoy myself.

I had notoriously been a piece of shit to every girl with whom I'd had a private conversation over the age of sixteen—since I was fifteen. Our story might have been typical: Bad boy falls for good girl, but Abby was no princess. She was hiding something. Maybe that was our connection: whatever it was that she had left behind.

I pulled into the apartment parking lot and climbed off the bike. So much for thinking better on the Harley. Everything I'd just unraveled in my head made no fucking sense. I was just trying to justify my weird obsession with her.

Suddenly in a very bad mood, I slammed the door behind me and sat on the couch, and became even more pissed off when I couldn't find the remote right away.

Black plastic landed beside me as Shepley passed to sit in the recliner. I picked up the remote and pointed it at the TV, turning it on.

"Why do you take the remote to your bedroom? You just have to bring it back in here," I snapped.

"I don't know, man, it's just habit. What's your problem?"

"I don't know," I grumbled, flipping on the TV. I pressed the mute button. "Abby Abernathy."

Shepley's eyebrow pushed up. "What about her?"

"She gets under my skin. I think I just need to bag her and get it over with."

Shepley eyed me for a while, unsure. "It's not that I don't appreciate you not fucking up my life with your newfound restraint, but you've never needed my permission before . . . unless . . . don't tell me you finally give a shit about someone."

"Don't be a dick."

Shepley couldn't contain his grin. "You care about her. I guess it just took a girl refusing to sleeping with you for more than a twenty-four-hour period."

"Laura made me wait a week."

"Abby won't give you the time of day, though?"

"She just wants to be friends. I guess I'm lucky she doesn't treat me like a leper."

After an awkward silence, Shepley nodded. "You're scared."

"Of what?" I asked with a dubious smirk.

"Rejection. *Mad Dog* is one of us after all."

My eye twitched. "You know I fucking hate that, Shep."

Shepley smiled. "I know. Almost as much as you hate the way you feel right now."

"You're not making me feel any better."

"So you like her and you're scared. Now what?"

"Nothing. It just sucks that I finally found the girl worth having and she's too good for me."

Shepley tried to stifle a laugh. It was irritating that he was so amused about my predicament. He straightened his smile and then said, "Why don't you let her make that decision for herself?"

"Because I care about her just enough to want to make it for her."

Shepley stretched and then stood, his bare feet dragging across the carpet. "You want a beer?"

"Yeah. Let's drink to friendship."

"So you're going to keep hanging out with her? Why? That sounds like torture to me."

I thought about it for a minute. It did sound like torture, but not as bad as just watching her from afar. "I don't want her to end up with me . . . or any other dick."

"You mean or anyone else. Dude, that's nuts."

"Get my fuckin' beer and shut up."

Shepley shrugged. Unlike Chris Jenks, Shepley knew when to shut up.

CHAPTER FOUR

Distracted

The decision was crazy, but freeing. The next day I walked into the cafeteria, and without a second thought, sat in the empty seat across from Abby. Being around her was natural and easy, and other than having to put up with the prodding eyes of the general student population, and even some professors, she seemed to like having me around.

"We studying today or what?"

"We are," she said, unfazed.

The only negative about hanging out with her as friends was the more time I spent with her, the more I liked her. It was harder to forget the color and shape of her eyes, and the way her lotion smelled on her skin. I also noticed more about her, like how long her legs were, and the colors she wore most often. I even got a pretty good handle on which week I shouldn't give her any extra shit, which fortunately for Shepley, was the same week not to fuck with America. That way, we had three weeks to not be on guard instead of two, and we could give each other fair warning.

Even at her worst, Abby wasn't fussy like most girls. The only thing that seemed to affect her was the occasional questions about our relationship, but as long as I took care of it, she got over it pretty fast.

As more time passed, people speculated less. We ate lunch together on most days, and on the nights when we studied, I'd take her out to dinner. Shepley and America invited us to a movie once. It was never awkward, never a question of whether we were more than friends. I wasn't sure how I felt about that, especially since my decision not to pursue her in that way didn't stop me from fantasizing about making her moan on my couch—until one night I was watching her and America poke and tickle each other at the apartment and I imagined Abby in my bed.

She needed to get outta my head.

The only cure was to stop thinking about her long enough to land my next conquest.

A few days later, a familiar face caught my eye. I'd seen her before with Janet Littleton. Lucy was fairly hot, never missed a chance to show off her cleavage, and very vocal about hating my guts. Fortunately it took me thirty minutes and a tentative invite to the Red to get her home. I'd barely shut the front door before she was removing my clothes. So much for the deep well of hatred she had harbored toward me since last year. She left with a smile on her face and disappointment in her eyes.

I still had Abby on my mind.

Not even postorgasm fatigue was going to cure it, and I felt something new: guilt.

The next day, I rushed to history class and slid into the desk next to Abby. She already had out her laptop and book, barely acknowledging my presence when I sat down.

The classroom was darker than usual; the clouds outside robbed the room of the natural light that usually poured in

through the windows. I nudged her elbow, but she wasn't as receptive as usual, so I snatched her pencil out of her hand and
began doodling in the margins. Tattoos, mostly, but I scrawled
her name in cool letters. She peeked over at me with an appreciative smile.

I leaned over and whispered in her ear. "You wanna grab
lunch off campus today?"

I can't, she mouthed.

I scribbled in her book.

Y?

Because I have to make use of my meal plan.

BULLSHIT.

Seriously.

I wanted to argue but was running out of room on the page.
FINE. ANOTHER MYSTERY MEAL. CAN'T WAIT.

She giggled, and I enjoyed that on-top-of-the-world feeling I
experienced whenever I made her smile. A few more doodles and
a legit drawing of a dragon later, Chaney dismissed class.

I tossed Abby's pencil in her backpack as she packed away the
rest of her things, and then we walked to the cafeteria.

We didn't get as many stares as we had in the past. The student populace had grown accustomed to seeing us together on
a regular basis. When we went through the line, we made small
talk about the new history paper Chaney had assigned. Abby
ran her meal card and then made her way to the table. I immediately noticed one thing missing from her tray: the can of OJ she
picked up every day.

I scanned the line of husky, no-nonsense servers who stood
behind the buffet. Once the stern-looking woman behind the
register came into view, I knew I'd found my target.

"Hey, Miss . . . uh . . . Miss . . ."

The cafeteria lady sized me up once before deciding I was going to cause her trouble, as most women did right before I made their thighs tingle.

"Armstrong," she said in a gruff voice.

I tried to subdue my disgust as the thought of her thighs appeared in the dark corners of my mind.

I flashed my most charming smile. "That's lovely. I was wondering, because you seem like the boss here . . . No OJ today?"

"There's some in the back. I've been too busy to bring any more to the front."

I nodded. "You're always running your ass off. They should give you a raise. No one else works as hard as you do. We all notice."

She lifted her chin, minimizing the folds on her neck. "Thank you. It's about time someone did. Did you need orange juice?"

"Just a can . . . if you don't mind, of course."

She winked. "Not at all. I'll be right back."

I brought the can to the table and sat it on Abby's tray.

"You didn't have to do that. I was going to grab one." She peeled off her jacket and laid it across her lap, exposing her shoulders. They were still tan from the summer, and a little shiny, begging me to touch them.

A dozen dirty things flashed in my mind.

"Well, now you don't have to," I said. I offered one of my best smiles, but this time it was genuine. It was another one of those Happy Abby moments I sort of wished for these days.

Brazil snorted. "Did she turn you into a cabana boy, Travis? What's next, fanning her with a palm tree leaf, wearing a Speedo?"

I craned my neck down the table to see Brazil with a smart-ass grin. He didn't mean anything by it, but he ruined my moment, and it pissed me off. I probably did look a little bit like a pussy, bringing her a drink.

Abby leaned forward. "You couldn't *fill* a Speedo, Brazil. Shut the hell up."

"Easy, Abby! I was kidding!" Brazil said, holding up his hands.

"Just . . . don't talk about him like that," she said, frowning.

I stared for a moment, watching her anger subside a tiny bit as she turned her attention to me. That was definitely a first. "Now I've seen it all. I was just defended by a girl." I offered her a small smile and then stood, glaring at Brazil one last time before leaving to dump my tray. I wasn't that hungry, anyway.

The heavy metal doors easily gave way when I shoved through them. I pulled my cigarettes from my pocket and lit one up, trying to forget what had just happened.

I'd just made an ass of myself over a girl, and it was particularly satisfying to my frat brothers because I had been the one giving them a hard time for two years for even mentioning they might want to do more than just bag a girl. It was my turn now, and I couldn't do a damn thing about it—because I couldn't. Even worse? I didn't want to.

When the other smokers around me laughed, I did the same, even though I had no clue what they were talking about. Inside I was pissed off and humiliated, or pissed off that I was humiliated. Whichever. The girls pawed at me and took turns trying to make conversation. I nodded and smiled to be nice, but I really just wanted to get out of there and punch something. A public tantrum would show weakness, and I wasn't havin' that shit.

Abby passed, and I cut off one of the girls in midsentence to catch up with her. "Wait up, Pidge. I'll walk you."

"You don't have to walk me to every class, Travis. I know how to get there on my own."

I admit it: That stung a little. She didn't even look at me when she said it, completely dismissive.

Just then a girl with a short skirt and mile-high legs passed by. Her shiny dark hair swayed against her back as she walked. That's when it hit me: I had to give up. Bagging a random hot chick was what I did best, and Abby wanted nothing more than to be friends with me. I planned to do the right thing and keep things platonic, but if I didn't do something drastic, that plan would get lost in the mess of conflicting thoughts and emotions swirling inside of me.

It was time to finally draw a line. I didn't deserve Abby, anyway. What was the point?

I threw my cigarette to the ground. "I'll catch up with you later, Pidge."

I put on my game face, but it wouldn't take much. She had crossed my path on purpose, hoping her short skirt and hooker heels would get my attention. I got ahead of her and turned around, shoving my hands in my pockets.

"You in a hurry?"

She smiled. I already had her. "I'm going to class."

"Oh yeah? What class?"

She stopped, one side of her mouth pulling to the side. "Travis Maddox, right?"

"Right. My reputation precedes me?"

"It does."

"Guilty."

She shook her head. "I have to get to class."

I sighed, feigning disappointment. "That's a shame. I was just going to ask you for some help."

"With what?" Her tone was dubious, but she was still smiling. I could have just asked her to follow me home for a quick fuck and she probably would have gone for it, but a certain amount of charm went a long way for later.

"Getting to my apartment. I have a terrible sense of direction."

"Is that so?" she asked, nodding, frowning, and then smiling. She was trying hard not to be flattered.

Her top two buttons were loose, leaving the bottom curve of her breasts and a few inches of her bra visible. I felt that familiar swelling in my jeans, and I switched my weight to the other foot.

"Terrible." I smiled, watching her gaze drift to the dimple in my cheek. I don't know why, but the dimple always seemed to seal the deal.

She shrugged, trying to remain cool. "Lead the way. If I see you veering off course, I'll honk."

"I'm this way," I said, nodding in the direction of the parking lot.

She had her tongue down my throat before we got all the way up the apartment stairs and was pulling off my jacket before I could single out the right key. We were clumsy, but it was fun. I had plenty of practice opening the lock on the apartment door with my lips on someone else's. She shoved me into the living room the second the bolt unlatched, and I grabbed her hips and pushed her against the door to close it. She wrapped her legs around my waist, and I lifted her up, pressing my pelvis against hers.

She kissed me like she'd been starving and she knew there was food in my mouth. I don't know, I kinda dug it. She bit my bottom lip, and I took a step back, losing my footing and crashing into the end table beside the recliner. Various items knocked to the floor.

"Oops," she said, giggling.

I smiled and watched as she walked over to the couch and leaned forward over the back so her ass cheeks became visible along with the slightest trace of a thin strip of white lace.

I unbuckled my belt and took a step. She was going to make this easy. She arched her neck and whipped her long dark hair against her back. She was hot as hell, I'd give her that. My zipper could barely contain what was underneath.

She turned to look at me and I leaned over, planting my lips on hers.

"Maybe I should tell you my name?" she breathed.

"Why?" I panted. "I kinda like this."

She smiled, hooked her thumbs onto each side of her panties and then pulled them down until they fell down to her ankles. Her eyes connected with mine, refreshingly wicked.

Abby's disapproving eyes flashed in my mind.

"What are you waiting for?" she asked, excited and impatient.

"Absolutely nothing," I said, shaking my head. I tried to concentrate on her bare backside against my thighs. Having to concentrate to stay hard was definitely something new and different, and it was all Abby's fault.

She turned around and yanked my shirt over my head, and then finished unzipping my jeans. Damn. I was either working at a turtle's pace, or this woman was the female version of me. I kicked off my boots and then stepped out of the denim, kicking it all to the side.

One of her legs pulled up, and her knee hooked around my hip. "I've wanted this for a long time," she whispered against my ear. "Since I saw you at freshman orientation last year."

I ran my hand up her thigh, trying to think if I'd talked to her before. By the time my fingers reached the end of the line, they were drenched. She wasn't kidding. A year's worth of mental foreplay made my job a lot easier.

She moaned the second my fingertips touched her tender skin. She was so wet my fingers didn't get much traction, and my balls were starting to hurt. I had only bagged two women in as many weeks. This chick, and Janet's friend Lucy. Oh wait. Megan made three. The morning after I met Abby. Abby. Guilt swept over me, and it had a rather negative effect on my hard on.

"Don't move," I said, running in only boxers to my bedroom. I fished out a square package from my nightstand, and then jogged back to where the brunette stunner was standing, exactly the way I'd left her. She snatched the package out of my hand, and then got on her knees. After some creativity and rather surprising tricks with her tongue, I had the green light to put her on the couch.

So I did. Facedown with a reach around, and she loved every minute of it.

CHAPTER FIVE

Roommates

THE SEXAHOLIC WAS IN THE BATHROOM, GETTING dressed and primping. She didn't say much after we finished, and I was thinking I was going to have to get her number and put her on the very short list of girls—like Megan—that didn't require a relationship to have sex, and were also worth a repeat.

Shepley's phone chirped. It was a kiss noise, so it must have been America. She changed her text tone on his phone, and Shepley was more than happy to comply. They were good together, but they also made me wanna puke.

I was sitting on the couch clicking through channels, waiting for the girl to come out so I could send her home, when I noticed that Shepley was buzzing around the apartment.

My eyebrows pushed together. "What are you doing?"

"You might want to pick up your shit. Mare's coming over with Abby."

That got my attention. "Abby?"

"Yeah. The boiler went out again at Morgan."

"So?"

"So they're going to be staying here for a few days."

I sat up. "They? As in Abby's going to stay here? In our apartment?"

"Yes, buttmunch. Get your mind out of Jenna Jameson's ass and listen to what I'm saying. They will be here in ten minutes. With luggage."

"No fuckin' way."

Shepley stopped in his tracks and looked at me from under his brow. "Get your ass up and help me, and take your trash out," he said, pointing to the bathroom.

"Oh, fuck," I said, hopping to my feet.

Shepley nodded his head, his eyes wide. "Yeah."

It finally hit. If it pissed America off that I had a straggler still here when she arrived with Abby, it would put Shepley in a bad spot. If Abby didn't want to stay here because of it, it would become his problem—and mine.

My eyes focused on the bathroom door. The faucet had been running since she'd gone in there. I didn't know if she was taking a shit or a shower. No way was I going to get her out of the apartment before the girls came. It would look worse if I was caught trying to sweep her out, so I decided to change the sheets on my bed and pick up a little bit, instead.

"Where is Abby going to sleep?" I asked, looking at the couch. I wasn't going to let her sprawl out on fourteen months of body fluids.

"I don't know. The recliner?"

"She's not sleeping on the fucking recliner, assclown." I scratched my head. "I guess she'll sleep in my bed."

Shepley howled, his laughter spanning at least two blocks. He bent over and grabbed his knees, his face turning red.

"What?"

He stood up and pointed, shaking his finger and his head at me. He was too amused to talk, so he just walked away, trying to continue cleaning while his body shuddered.

Eleven minutes later, Shepley was jogging across the front room to the door. He made his way down the stairs, and then nothing. The faucet in the bathroom finally shut off, and it became very quiet.

After a few minutes more, I heard the door bang open, and Shepley complaining between grunts.

"Christ, baby! Your suitcase is twenty pounds more than Abby's!"

I walked into the hall, seeing my latest conquest emerge from the bathroom. She froze in the hallway, took one look at Abby and America, and then finished buttoning her blouse. She definitely wasn't freshening up in there. She still had makeup smeared all over her face.

For a minute, I was completely distracted from the awkwardness by the letters *W, T,* and *F.* I guess she wasn't as uncomplicated as previously thought, making America and Abby's unannounced visit even more welcome. Even if I was still in my boxers.

"Hi," she said to the girls. She looked down at their luggage, her surprise turning to total confusion.

America glared at Shepley.

He held up his hands. "She's with Travis!"

That was my cue. I turned the corner and yawned, patting my guest's ass. "My company's here. You'd better go."

She seemed to relax a bit and smiled. She wrapped her arms around me, and then kissed my neck. Her lips felt soft and warm not an hour ago. In front of Abby, they were like two sticky buns lined with barbed wire.

"I'll leave my number on the counter."

"Eh . . . don't worry about it," I said, purposefully nonchalant.

"What?" she asked, leaning back. The rejection in her eyes shone bright, searching mine for something other than what I truly meant. Glad this was coming out now. I might have called her again and made things very messy. Mistaking her for a possible frequent flyer was a bit startling. I was usually a better judge than that.

"*Every* time!" America said. She looked at the woman. "*How* are you surprised by this? He's Travis Fucking Maddox! He is *famous* for this very thing, and *every* time they're surprised!" she said, turning to Shepley. He put his arm around her, gesturing for her to calm down.

The woman's eyes narrowed, on fire with anger and embarrassment, and then she stormed out, grabbing her purse on the way.

The door slammed, and Shepley's shoulders tensed. Those moments bothered him. I, on the other hand, had a shrew to tame, so I strolled into the kitchen and opened the fridge as if nothing had happened. The hell in her eyes foretold a wrath like I had never experienced (not because I hadn't come across a woman who wanted to hand my ass to me on a silver platter, but because I'd never cared to stick around to hear it).

America shook her head and walked down the hall. Shepley followed her, angling his body to compensate for the weight of her suitcase as he trailed behind her.

Just when I thought Abby would strike, she collapsed into the recliner. *Huh. Well . . . she's pissed. Might as well get it over with.*

I crossed my arms, keeping a minimum safe distance from her by staying in the kitchen. "What's wrong, Pidge? Hard day?"

"No, I'm thoroughly disgusted."

It was a start.

"With me?" I asked with a smile.

"Yes, *you*. How can you just use someone like that and treat them that way?"

And so it began. "How did I treat her? She offered her number, I declined."

Her mouth fell open. I tried not to laugh. I don't know why it amused me so much to see her flustered and appalled at my behavior, but it did. "You'll have sex with her, but you won't take her number?"

"Why would I want her number if I'm not going to call her?"

"Why would you sleep with her if you're not going to call her?"

"I don't promise anyone anything, Pidge. She didn't stipulate a relationship before she spread-eagled on my couch."

She stared at the couch with revulsion. "She's someone's daughter, Travis. What if, down the line, someone treats *your* daughter like that?"

The thought had crossed my mind, and I was prepared. "My daughter better not drop her panties for some jackass she just met, let's put it that way."

That was the truth. Did women deserve to be treated like sluts? No. Did sluts deserve to be treated like sluts? Yes. I was a slut. The first time I bagged Megan and she left without so much as a cuddle, I didn't cry about it and eat a gallon of ice cream. I didn't complain to my frat brothers that I put out on the first date and Megan treated me according to the way I behaved. It is what it is, no sense in pretending to protect your dignity if you set out to destroy it. Girls are notorious for judging each other, anyway, only taking a break long enough to judge a guy for doing it. I'd hear them label a classmate a whore before the thought ever crossed my mind. However, if I took that whore home, bagged her, and released her strings-free, I was suddenly the bad guy. Nonsense.

Abby crossed her arms, noticeably unable to argue, and that made her even angrier. "So, besides admitting that you're a jack-ass, you're saying that because she slept with you, she deserved to be tossed out like a stray cat?"

"I'm saying that I was honest with her. She's an adult, it was consensual . . . she was a little too eager about it, if you want to know the truth. You act like I committed a crime."

"She didn't seem as clear about your intentions, Travis."

"Women usually justify their actions with whatever they make up in their heads. She didn't tell me up front that she expected a relationship any more than I told her I expected sex with no strings. How is it any different?"

"You're a pig."

I shrugged. "I've been called worse." Regardless of my indifference, to hear her say that felt about as good as her shoving a two-by-four under my thumb nail. Even if it was true.

She stared at the couch, and then recoiled. "I guess I'm sleeping on the recliner."

"Why?"

"I'm not sleeping on that thing! God knows what I'd be lying in!"

I lifted her duffel bag off the floor. "You're not sleeping on the couch or the recliner. You're sleeping in my bed."

"Which is more unsanitary than the couch, I'm sure."

"There's never been anyone in my bed but me."

She rolled her eyes. "Give me a break!"

"I'm absolutely serious. I bag 'em on the couch. I don't let them in my room."

"Then why am *I* allowed in your bed?"

I wanted to tell her. Jesus, did I ever want to mouth the words, but I could barely admit it to myself, much less her. Deep down I knew I was a piece of shit, and she deserved better. Part of me wanted to carry her to the bedroom and *show* her why she was different, but that was also the one thing that stopped me. She was my opposite: innocent on the surface, and damaged deep within. There was something about her I needed in my life, and even though I wasn't sure what it was, I couldn't give into my bad habits and fuck it up. She was the forgiving type, I could see, but she had lines drawn that I knew better than to cross.

A better option popped into my head, and I smirked. "Are you planning on having sex with me tonight?"

"No!"

"That's why. Now get your cranky ass up, take your hot shower, and then we can study some bio."

Abby's eyes stared me down, but she complied. She nearly shoved her shoulder into me as she passed, and then slammed the bathroom door. The pipes under the apartment immediately whined in response to her turning on the water.

She packed light: only the essentials. I found some shorts and a T-shirt and a pair of white cotton panties with purple stripes. I held them up in front of me, and then dug a little further. They were all cotton. She really didn't plan to get naked with me, or even to tease. A little disappointing, but at the same time it made me like her even more. I wondered if she had any thongs at all.

Was she a virgin?

I laughed. A virgin in college was unheard of these days.

A tube of toothpaste and her toothbrush, and a small tub of some sort of face cream was packed, too, so I took them with me down the hall, grabbing a clean towel from the hall linen closet on the way.

I knocked once, but she didn't answer, so I just walked in. She was behind the curtain, anyway, and she didn't have anything I hadn't seen before.

"Mare?"

"No, it's me," I said, setting her stuff on the counter beside the sink.

"What are you doing in here? Get out!" she squealed.

I laughed once. What a baby. "You forgot a towel, and I brought your clothes, and your toothbrush, and some weird face cream I found in your bag."

"You went through my stuff?" Her voice went up an octave.

The sudden laughter caught in my throat and I choked it back. I brought in Prudezilla's things to be a nice guy, and she was freaking out. Not like I was going to find anything interesting in her bag, anyway. She was about as naughty as a Sunday school teacher.

I squeezed some of her toothpaste onto my toothbrush and turned on the faucet.

Abby was strangely quiet until her forehead and eyes popped out from behind the curtain. I tried to ignore her, feeling her eyes burning a hole in the back of my head.

Her irritation was a mystery. To me, the whole scenario was oddly relaxing. That thought caused me to pause; domesticity was not something I thought I'd enjoy.

"Get out, Travis," she growled.

"I can't go to bed without brushing my teeth."

"If you come within two feet of this curtain, I will poke out your eyes while you sleep."

"I won't peek, Pidge." Actually, the thought of her leaning over me, even with a knife in her hand, was kind of hot. More the leaning over part than the knife.

I finished brushing my teeth and then made my way to the bedroom, smiling the whole way. Within minutes the pipes silenced, but it took forever for her to come out.

Impatient, I poked my head through the bathroom door. "C'mon, Pidge! I'm gettin' old, here!" Her appearance surprised me. I'd seen her without makeup on before, but her skin was pink and shiny, and her long, wet hair was slicked back away from her face. I couldn't help but stare.

Abby reared back her arm and chucked her comb at me. I ducked, and then shut the door, chuckling all the way down the hall.

I could hear her small feet padding down the hall to my room, and my heart began to pound in my chest.

"Night, Abby," America called from Shepley's room.

"Night, Mare."

I had to laugh. Nightmare was right. Shepley's girlfriend had introduced me to my very own form of crack. I couldn't get enough, and I didn't want to quit. Even though I couldn't call it anything but an addiction, I didn't dare sample even a crumb. I only kept her close, feeling better just knowing she was around. There was no hope for me.

Two small knocks brought me back to reality.

"Come in, Pidge. You don't have to knock."

Abby slipped in, her hair dark and damp, in a gray T-shirt

and plaid boxer shorts. Wide eyes wandered about the room as she decided different things about me based on the bareness of my walls. It was the first time a woman had been in there. That moment wasn't something I had thought about, but Abby changing the way the room felt was not something I expected.

Before, it was just where I slept. A place where I'd never spent much time at all. Abby's presence made the white, clutter-less walls obvious, to the point where I felt a lesser version of embarrassment. Abby being in my room made it feel like home, and the emptiness no longer seemed right.

"Nice pj's," I said finally, sitting on the bed. "Well, come on. I'm not going to bite you."

Her chin lowered and she raised her brows. "I'm not afraid of you." Her biology book landed beside me with a *thud*, and then she stopped. "Do you have a pen?"

I nodded to the night table. "Top drawer." The second I said the words, my blood turned cold. She was going to find my stash. I readied myself for the impending death match that would quickly follow.

She put one knee on the bed and reached over, pulling open the drawer and fishing around until her hand lurched back. In the next second, she grabbed the pen and then slammed the drawer shut.

"What?" I asked, pretending to scan over the words in the biology book.

"Did you rob the health clinic?"

How does a pigeon know where to get condoms? "No. Why?"

Her face twisted. "Your lifetime supply of condoms."

Here it comes. "Better safe than sorry, right?" She couldn't possibly argue with that.

Instead of the yelling and name calling I expected, she rolled her eyes. I turned the pages of the biology book, trying not to look too relieved.

"Okay, we can start here. Jesus . . . photosynthesis? Didn't you learn this in high school?"

"Kind of," she said, defensively. "It's Biology 101, Trav. I didn't pick the curriculum."

"And you're in calculus? How can you be so advanced in math and behind in science?"

"I'm not behind. The first half is always review."

I raised an eyebrow. "Not really."

She listened while I went over the basics of photosynthesis, and then the anatomy of plant cells. It didn't matter how long I talked, or what I said, she hung on to every word. It was easy to pretend that she was interested in me and not a passing grade.

"Lipids. Not lipides. Tell me what they are again."

She pulled off her glasses. "I'm beat. I can't memorize one more macromolecule."

Fuckin' A. Bedtime. "All right."

Abby suddenly looked nervous, which was curiously soothing to me.

I left her alone with her nerves to take a shower. Knowing she had just been standing naked in the same spot made for some arousing thoughts, so for the five minutes before I got out, the water had to be ice cold. It was uncomfortable, but at least it got rid of my hard-on.

When I returned to the bedroom, Abby was lying on her side, eyes closed, and stiff as a board. I dropped my towel, changed into my boxers, and then crawled into bed, flipping off the light. Abby didn't move, but she wasn't asleep.

Every muscle in her body was tense, but they tightened even more just before she turned to face me.

"You're sleeping in here, too?"

"Well, yeah. This is my bed."

"I know, but I . . ." she trailed off, weighing her options.

"Don't you trust me by now? I'll be on my best behavior, I swear." I held up my index, middle, and pinky finger, affectionately known by my frat brothers as the "shocker." She didn't get it.

As much as being good would suck, I wasn't going to run her off the first night by doing something stupid.

Abby was a delicate balance of tough and tender. Pushing her too far seemed to garner the same reaction as a cornered animal. It was fun to walk the tightrope she required, in a terrifying, driving-at-a-thousand-miles-per-hour, backward-on-a-motorcycle kind of way.

She turned away from me, karate chopping the blanket around every curve of her body. Another smile crept across my face, and I leaned into her ear.

"Good night, Pigeon."

CHAPTER SIX
Shots

The sun had just begun to cast shadows on the walls of my bedroom when I opened my eyes. Abby's hair was tangled and messy, and covering my face. I took a deep breath through my nose.

Dude. What are you doing . . . besides being creepy? I thought. I turned onto my back, but before I could stop myself, took in another breath. She still smelled like shampoo and lotion.

A few seconds later, the alarm bleated, and Abby began to rouse. Her hand ran across my chest, and then lurched back.

"Travis?" she said, groggily. "Your alarm." She waited for a minute, and then sighed, reaching across me, straining until she finally reached the clock, and then pounded against the plastic until the noise stopped.

She fell against her pillow and puffed. A chuckle escaped my lips, and she gasped.

"You were awake?"

"I promised I'd behave. I didn't say anything about letting you lay on me."

"I didn't lay on you. I couldn't reach the clock. That has to be the most annoying alarm I've ever heard. It sounds like a dying animal."

"You want breakfast?" I tucked my hands behind my head.

"I'm not hungry."

She seemed pissed about something, but I ignored it. She probably just wasn't a morning person. Although with that logic, she wasn't really an afternoon or night person, either. Come to think of it, she was kind of a cranky bitch . . . and I *liked* it.

"Well, I am. Why don't you ride with me down the street to the café?"

"I don't think I can handle your lack of driving skills this early in the morning." She wiggled her bony little feet into her slippers, and then shuffled to the door.

"Where are you going?"

She was instantly annoyed. "To get dressed and go to class. Do you need an itinerary while I'm here?"

She wanted to play hardball? Okay. I'd play. I walked over to her and cupped her shoulders in my hands. Damn, her skin felt good against mine. "Are you always so temperamental, or will that taper off once you believe I'm not just creating some elaborate scheme to get in your pants?"

"I'm *not* temperamental."

I leaned in, whispering in her ear. "I don't want to sleep with you, Pidge. I like you too much."

Her body grew tense, and then I left without another word. Jumping up and down to celebrate the thrill of victory would have been a bit obvious, so I restrained myself until I was sufficiently hidden behind the door, and then made a few celebratory air punches. Keeping her on her toes was never easy, but when it worked, I felt like I was one step closer to . . .

To what? I wasn't exactly sure. It just felt right.

It had been a while since I'd done any grocery shopping, so breakfast wasn't quite gourmet, but it was good enough. I scrambled eggs in a bowl, throwing in a concoction of onion, green and red pepper, and then poured it into a skillet.

Abby walked in and sat on a stool.

"You sure you don't want some?"

"I'm sure. Thanks, though."

She had just rolled out of bed and was still gorgeous. It was ridiculous. I was sure that couldn't be typical, but I wouldn't know, either. The only girls I'd seen in the morning were Shepley's, and I didn't look at any of them close enough to have an opinion.

Shepley grabbed some plates and held them in front of me. I scooped up eggs in the spatula and flopped them onto each plate. Abby watched with mild interest.

America puffed as Shepley sat the plate in front of her. "Don't look at me like that, Shep. I'm sorry, I just don't want to go."

Shepley had been moping for days about America's rejection of his invitation to the date party. I didn't blame her. Date parties were torture. The fact that she didn't want to go was kinda impressive. Most girls fell all over themselves to be invited to those things.

"Baby," Shepley whined, "the House has a date party twice a year. It's a month away. You'll have plenty of time to find a dress and do all that girl stuff."

America wasn't going for it. I tuned them out until I realized America had agreed to go only if Abby would. If Abby went, that meant she'd go with a date. America looked to me, and I raised an eyebrow.

Shepley didn't hesitate. "Trav doesn't go to the date parties. It's something you take your girlfriend to . . . and Travis doesn't . . . you know."

America shrugged. "We could set her up with someone."

I started to speak up, but Abby clearly wasn't happy. "I can hear you, you know," she grumbled.

America pouted. That was the face Shepley couldn't deny.

"Please, Abby? We'll find you a nice guy who's funny and witty, and you know I'll make sure he's hot. I promise you'll have a good time! And who knows? Maybe you'll hit it off."

I frowned. America would find her a guy? For the date party. One of my frat brothers. Oh, fuck, no. The thought of her hitting it off with *anyone* made the hairs on the back of my neck stand on end.

The pan made a clanging noise when I threw it into the sink. "I didn't say I wouldn't take her."

Abby rolled her eyes. "Don't do me any favors, Travis."

I took a step. "That's not what I meant, Pidge. Date parties are for the guys with girlfriends, and it's common knowledge that I don't do the girlfriend thing. But I won't have to worry about you expecting an engagement ring afterward."

America pouted again. "Pretty please, Abby?"

Abby looked like she was in pain. "Don't look at me like that! Travis doesn't want to go. I don't want to go . . . we won't be much fun."

The more I thought about it, the more I warmed to the idea. I crossed my arms and leaned back against the sink. "I didn't say I didn't want to go. I think it'd be fun if the four of us went."

Abby recoiled when all eyes turned to her. "Why don't we hang out here?"

I was okay with that.

America's shoulders slumped, and Shepley leaned forward.

"Because I have to go, Abby," Shepley said. "I'm a freshman. I have to make sure everything's running smoothly, everyone has a beer in their hand, things like that."

Abby was mortified. She clearly didn't want to go, but what scared me was that she couldn't say no to America, and Shepley was willing to say anything for his girlfriend to go. If Abby didn't go with me, she could end up spending the evening—or night—with one of my frat brothers. They weren't bad guys, but listening to the stories they've told, and imagining them talking about Abby was something I couldn't stand.

I walked across the tile and wrapped my arms around Abby's shoulders. "C'mon Pidge. Will you go with me?"

Abby looked to America, then to Shepley. It was only a few seconds until she looked into my eyes, but it felt like a goddamn eternity.

When her eyes finally met mine, her walls came crashing down.

"Yes." She sighed. The enthusiasm in her voice was nonexistent, but it didn't matter. She was going with me, and that knowledge allowed me to breathe again.

America screamed like girls do, clapped her hands, and then grabbed Abby to hug her.

Shepley offered an appreciative smile to me, and then to Pigeon. "Thanks, Abby," he said, placing his hand on her back.

I'd never seen someone less happy to go on a date with me, but then again, it wasn't me she was unhappy about.

The girls finished getting ready and left early for their eight o'clock class. Shepley stuck around to do the dishes, happy that he'd finally gotten his way.

"Dude, thank you. I didn't think America would go."

"What the fuck, Chuck? You guys are trying to set Pidge up with someone?"

"No. I mean, America might have. I don't know. What does it matter?"

"It matters."

"It does?"

"Just don't . . . don't do that, okay? I don't wanna see her making out in a dark corner with Parker Hayes."

Shepley nodded, scrubbing the egg from the skillet. "Or anyone else."

"So?"

"How long do you think that's going to fly?"

I frowned. "I don't know. As long as it can. Just don't step on my toes."

"Travis, do you want her or not? Doing what you can to keep her from dating someone else when you're not even with her is kind of an asshole thing to do."

"We're just friends."

Shepley shot a dubious smirk in my direction. "Friends talk about a weekend fuck. Somehow, I don't see that happening for you two."

"No, but that doesn't mean we can't be friends."

Shepley's eyebrows shot up in disbelief. "It kinda does, bro."

He wasn't wrong. I just didn't want to admit it. "There's just . . ." I paused, glancing to see Shepley's expression. Of all people, he would judge me the least, but it felt weak to admit what I'd been thinking about, and how often thoughts of Abby had crossed my mind. Shepley would understand, but it didn't make me feel any better about saying it out loud. "There's something about her I need. That's all. Is it weird that I think she's cool as hell and I don't want to share?"

"You can't share her if she's not yours."

"What do I know about dating, Shep? You. You and your twisted, obsessive, needy relationships. If she meets someone else and starts dating them, I'll lose her."

"So date her."

I shook my head. "Not ready yet."

"Why's that? Scared?" Shepley asked, throwing the dish towel in my face. It fell to the floor, and I bent down to pick it up. The fabric twisted and pulled tight in my hands as I wrung it back and forth.

"She's different, Shepley. She's good."

"What are you waiting for?"

I shrugged. "Just one more reason, I guess."

Shepley grimaced with disapproval, and then bent down to start the dishwasher. A mixture of mechanical and fluid sounds filled the room, and Shepley made his way to his room. "Her birthday's coming up, you know. Mare wants to put something together."

"Abby's birthday?"

"Yeah. In a little over a week."

"Well, we gotta do something. Do you know what she likes? Does America have something in mind? I guess I better buy her something. What the fuck do I get her?"

Shepley smiled as he closed his bedroom door. "You'll figure it out. Class starts in five. You riding in the Charger?"

"Nah. I'm going to see if I can get Abby on the back of my bike again. It's the closest I can get to the inside of her thighs."

Shepley laughed, and then shut the door behind him.

I headed to my bedroom, and slipped on a pair of jeans and a T-shirt. Wallet, phone, keys. I couldn't imagine being a girl. The bullshit routine they had to go through just to get out the door consumed half of their lives.

Class took for fucking ever, and then I rushed across campus to Morgan Hall. Abby was standing at the front entrance with some guy, and my blood instantly boiled. A few seconds later, I recognized Finch and sighed with relief. She was waiting for him to finish his cigarette, and laughing at whatever he was saying. Finch was waving his arms around, obviously in the middle of a grand story, the only pauses he took were to take drags of his cigarette.

When I approached, Finch winked at Abby. I took that as a good sign. "Hey, Travis," he sang.

"Finch." I nodded, quickly turning my attention to Abby. "I'm headed home, Pidge. You need a ride?"

"I was just going in," she said, grinning up at me.

My stomach sank, and I spoke before thinking. "You're not staying with me tonight?"

"No, I am. I just had to grab a few things that I forgot."

"Like what?"

"Well, my razor for one. What do you care?"

Damn, I liked her. "It's about time you shaved your legs. They've been tearing the hell outta mine."

Finch's eyes nearly popped out of their sockets.

Abby frowned. "That's how rumors get started!" She looked to Finch. "I'm sleeping in his bed . . . *just* sleeping."

"Right," Finch said with a smug smile.

Before I knew what happened, she was inside, tromping up the stairs to her room. I took two steps at a time to catch up with her.

"Oh, don't be mad. I was just kidding."

"Everyone already assumes we're having sex. You're making it worse."

Apparently her having sex with me was a bad thing. If I had questions of whether she was into me like that at all, she'd just given the answer: not just no, but hell no. "Who cares what they think?"

"I do, Travis! I do!" She pushed open the door to her dorm room, and then zoomed from one side of the room to the other, opening and shutting drawers, and shoving things into a bag. I was suddenly drowning in an intense feeling of loss, the kind where you either have to laugh or cry. A chuckle escaped from my throat.

Abby's gray eyes darkened and targeted me. "It's not funny. Do you want the whole school to think I'm one of your sluts?"

My sluts? They weren't mine. Hence them being sluts.

I took the bag from her hands. This wasn't going well. To her, being associated with me, not to mention being in a relationship with me, meant sinking her reputation. Why did she still want to be my friend if that was how she felt?

"No one thinks that. And if they do, they better hope I don't hear about it."

I held open the door, and she stomped through. Just as I let go and began to follow her, she stopped, forcing me to balance on the tips of my toes to keep from running into her. The door closed behind me, shoving me forward. "Whoa!" I said, bumping into her.

She turned. "Oh my God!" At first I thought our collision had hurt her. The shocked look on her face had me worried for a second, but then she continued, "People probably think we're to-gether and you're shamelessly continuing your . . . *lifestyle*. I must look pathetic!" She paused, lost in the horror of her realization, and then shook her head. "I don't think I should stay with you anymore. We should just stay away from each other in general for a while."

She took her bag from my hands, and I grabbed it back. "No one thinks we're together, Pidge. You don't have to quit talking to me to prove a point." I felt a little desperate, which was nothing less than unsettling.

She pulled on her bag. Determined, I yanked it back. After a few tugs, she growled in frustration.

"Have you ever had a girl—that's a friend—stay with you? Have you ever given girls rides to and from school? Have you eaten lunch with them every day? No one knows what to think about us, even when we tell them!"

I walked to the parking lot with her bag, my mind racing. "I'll fix this, okay? I don't want anyone thinking less of you because of me."

Abby was always a mystery, but the grieved look in her eyes took me by surprise. It was disturbing to the point where I wanted to make anything that didn't make her smile go away. She was fidgeting, and clearly upset. I hated it so much that it made me regret every questionable thing I'd ever done because it was just one more thing that got in the way.

That's when the realization hit: as a couple, we weren't going to work. No matter what I did, or how I finagled my way into her good graces, I would never be good enough for her. I didn't

want her to end up with someone like me. I would just have to settle for whatever scraps of time I could get with her.

Admitting that to myself was a jagged pill to swallow, but at the same time, a familiar voice whispered from the dark corners of my mind that I needed to fight for what I wanted. Fighting seemed much easier than the alternative.

"Let me make it up to you," I said. "Why don't we go to the Dutch tonight?" The Dutch was a hole-in-the-wall, but a lot less crowded than the Red. Not as many vultures hanging around.

"That's a biker bar." She frowned.

"Okay, then let's go to the club. I'll take you to dinner and then we can go to the Red Door. My treat."

"How will going out to dinner and then to a club fix the problem? When people see us out together, it will make it worse."

I finished tying her bag to the back of my bike and then straddled the seat. She didn't argue about the bag this time. That was always promising.

"Think about it. Me, drunk, in a room full of scantily clad women? It won't take long for people to figure out we're not a couple."

"So what am I supposed to do? Take a guy home from the bar to drive the point home?"

I frowned. The thought of her leaving with a guy made my jaw tense, as if I'd poured lemon juice in my mouth. "I didn't say that. No need to get carried away."

She rolled her eyes, and then climbed onto the seat, wrapping her arms around my middle. "Some random girl is going to follow us home from the bar? *That's* how you're going to make it up to me?"

"You're not jealous, are you, Pigeon?"

"Jealous of *what*? The STD-infested imbecile you're going to piss off in the morning?"

I chuckled, and then started the engine. If she only knew how impossible that was. When she was around, everyone else seemed to disappear. It took all of my focus and concentration to stay a step ahead of her.

We informed Shepley and America of our plans, and then the girls began their routine. I hopped in the shower first, realizing too late that I should have been last, because the girls took a lot longer than me and Shepley to get ready.

Me, Shepley, and America waited for an eternity for Abby to come out of the bathroom, but when she finally emerged, I nearly lost my balance. Her legs looked like they went on forever in her short, black dress. Her tits were playing peek-a-boo, just barely making their presence known when she turned a certain way, and her long curls hung off to the side instead of over her chest.

I didn't remember her being that tan, but her skin had a healthy glow against the dark fabric of her dress.

"Nice legs," I said.

She smiled. "Did I mention the razor is magic?"

Magic my ass. She was fucking gorgeous. "I don't think it's the razor."

I pulled her out the door by her hand, leading her to Shepley's Charger. She didn't pull it away, and I held it in mine until we got to the car. It felt wrong to let go. When we got to the sushi restaurant, I interlaced my fingers between hers as we walked in.

I ordered one round of sake, and then another. The waitress didn't card us until I ordered beer. I knew America had a fake ID, and I was impressed when Abby whipped hers out like a champ.

Once the waitress looked it over and walked away, I grabbed it. Her picture was in the corner, and everything looked legit as far as I knew. I'd never seen a Kansas ID before, but this one was flawless. The name read Jessica James, and for some reason, that turned me on. Hard.

Abby flicked the ID, and it popped out of my grasp, but she caught it midflight to the floor, and within seconds it was hidden away inside her wallet.

She smiled, and I smiled back, leaning on my elbows. "Jessica James?"

She mirrored my position, leaning on her elbows and matching my stare. She was so confident. It was incredibly sexy.

"Yeah. So?"

"Interesting choice."

"So is the California Roll. Pansy."

Shepley burst into laughter, but stopped abruptly when America chugged her beer. "Slow down, baby. The sake hits late."

America wiped her mouth and grinned. "I've had sake, Shep. Stop worrying."

The more we drank, the louder we became. The waitstaff didn't seem to mind, but that was probably because it was late and there were only a few others on the far side of the restaurant, and they were almost as drunk as we were. Except Shepley. He was too protective of his car to drink too much while driving, and he loved America more than his car. When she came along, he not only watched his intake, but he also followed every traffic law and used his blinkers.

Whipped.

The waitress brought the check, and I tossed some cash on the table, nudging Abby until she scooted out of the booth. She elbowed me back playfully, and I nonchalantly threw my arm around her while we walked across the parking lot.

America slid into the front seat next to her boyfriend, and began licking his ear. Abby looked at me and rolled her eyes, but regardless of being a captive audience to the peep show, she was having a good time.

After Shepley pulled into the Red, he drove through the rows of cars two or three times.

"Sometime tonight, Shep," America muttered.

"Hey. I have to find a wide space. I don't want some drunken idiot dinging the paint."

Maybe. Or he was just prolonging the tongue bath his inner ear was getting from America. Sick.

Shepley parked on the edge of the lot, and I helped Abby out. She pulled and tugged at her dress, and then shook her hips a little bit before taking my hand.

"I meant to ask you about your IDs," I said. "They're flawless. You didn't get them around here." I would know. I'd purchased many.

"Yeah, we've had them for a while. It was necessary . . ."

Why in the hell would it be necessary for her to have a fake ID?

". . . in Wichita."

The gravel crunched under our feet as we walked, and Abby's hand squeezed mine as she navigated the rocks under her heels.

America tripped. I let go of Abby's hand in reaction, but Shepley caught his girlfriend before she hit the ground.

"It's a good thing you have connections," America said, giggling.

"Dear God, woman," Shepley said, holding her arm before she fell over. "I think you're already done for the night."

I frowned, wondering what the hell it all meant. "What are you talking about, Mare? What connections?"

"Abby has some old friends that—"

"They're fake IDs, Trav," Abby said, interrupting before America could finish. "You have to know the right people if you want them done right, right?"

I looked to America, knowing something wasn't right, but she looked everywhere but at me. Pushing the issue didn't seem smart, especially since Abby had just called me Trav. I could get used to that, coming from her.

I held out my hand. "Right."

She took it, smiling with the expression of a hustler. She thought she'd just pulled one over on me. I'd definitely have to revisit that later.

"I need another drink!" she said, pulling me toward the big red door of the club.

"Shots!" America yelled.

Shepley sighed. "Oh, yeah. That's what you need. Another shot."

Every head in the room turned when Abby walked in, even a few guys with their girlfriends were shamelessly breaking their necks or leaning back in their chairs to get a longer look.

Oh, fuck. This is going to be a bad night, I thought, tightening my hand around Abby's.

We walked to the bar closest to the dance floor. Megan stood in the smoky shadows by the pool tables. Her usual hunting ground. Her big, blue eyes locked on me before I even recognized it was her standing there. She didn't watch me long. Abby's hand was still in mine, and Megan's expression changed the moment she saw. I nodded at her, and she smirked.

My usual seat at the bar was open, but it was the only one open along the bar. Cami saw me coming with Abby trailing behind, so she laughed once, and then brought my arrival to the attention of the people sitting on the surrounding stools, warning them of their impending eviction. They left without complaint.

Say what you want. Being a psychotic asshole had its perks.

CHAPTER SEVEN
Seeing Red

BEFORE WE REACHED THE BAR, AMERICA PULLED HER best friend to the dance floor. Abby's hot pink stilettos glowed in the black light, and I smiled when she laughed at America's wild dance moves. My eyes traveled down her black dress, stopping on her hips. She had moves, I'd give her that. A sexual thought popped into my mind, and I had to look away.

The Red Door was fairly crowded. Some new faces, but mostly regulars. Anyone new walking in was like fresh meat to those of us who didn't have the imagination for anything but showing up at the bar every weekend. Especially girls that looked like Abby and America.

I ordered a beer, chugged half of it, and then turned my attention back to the dance floor. Staring wasn't voluntary, especially knowing I probably had the same expression on my face as every schmuck watching them.

The song ended, and Abby pulled America back to the bar. They were panting, smiling, and just sweaty enough to be sexy.

"It's going to be like this all night, Mare. Just ignore them," Shepley said.

America's face was screwed in disgust, staring behind me. I could only imagine who was back there. Couldn't have been Megan. She wasn't one to wait in the wings.

"It looks like Vegas threw up on a flock of vultures," America sneered.

I glanced over my shoulder, and three of Lexi's sorority sisters were standing shoulder to shoulder. Another of them stood next to me with a bright smile. They all grinned when I made eye contact, but I quickly turned around, chugging the last half of my beer. For whatever reason, girls that acted that way around me made America pretty cranky. I couldn't disagree with her vulture reference, though.

I lit a cigarette, and then ordered two more beers. The blonde next to me, Brooke, smiled and bit her lip. I paused, unsure if she was going to cry or hug me. It wasn't until Cami popped the tops and slid the bottles over that I knew why Brooke had that ridiculous look on her face. She picked up the beer and started to take a sip, but I grabbed it from her before she could, and handed it to Abby.

"Uh . . . not yours."

Brooke stomped off to join her friends. Abby, however, seemed perfectly content, taking man-size gulps.

"Like I would buy a beer for some chick at a bar," I said. I thought it would add to Abby's amusement, but instead she held up her beer with a sour look on her face.

"You're different," I said with a half smile.

She clinked her bottle against mine, clearly irritated. "To being the only girl a guy with no standards doesn't want to sleep with." She took a swig, but I pulled the bottle from her mouth.

"Are you serious?" When she didn't respond, I leaned in closer for full effect. "First of all . . . I have standards. I've never been with an ugly woman. Ever. Second of all, I wanted to sleep with you. I thought about throwing you over my couch fifty different ways, but I haven't because I don't see you that way anymore. It's not that I'm not attracted to you, I just think you're better than that."

A smug smile crept across her face. "You think I'm too good for you."

Unbelievable. She really didn't get it. "I can't think of a single guy I know that's good enough for you."

The smugness melted away, replaced with a touched, appreciative smile. "Thanks, Trav," she said, setting her empty bottle on the bar. She could really put them back when she wanted to. Normally I would call that sloppy, but she carried herself with such confidence . . . I don't know . . . anything she did was hot.

I stood and grabbed her hand. "C'mon." I pulled her to the dance floor, and she followed behind me.

"I've had a lot to drink! I'm going to fall!"

Now on the dance floor, I grabbed her hips and pulled her body tight against mine, leaving no room between us. "Shut up and dance."

All the giggles and smiles left her face, and her body began to move against mine to the music. I couldn't keep my hands off of her. The closer we were, the closer I needed her to be. Her hair was in my face, and even though I'd drunk enough to call it a night, all of my senses were alert. The way her ass felt against me, the different directions and motions her hips made to the music, the way she leaned back against my chest and rested the back of her head on my shoulder. I wanted to pull her to some dark corner and taste the inside of her mouth.

Abby turned to face me with a mischievous smile. Her hands began at my shoulders, and then she let her fingers run down my chest and stomach. I nearly went insane, wanting her right then and there. She turned her back to me, and my heart beat even faster against my rib cage. She was closer that way. I gripped her hips and pulled her tighter into me.

I wrapped my arms around her waist and buried my face in her hair. It was saturated with sweat, and combined with her perfume. Any rational thought disappeared. The song was ending, but she showed no signs of stopping.

Abby leaned back, her head against my shoulder. Some of her hair fell away, exposing the glistening skin of her neck. All willpower vanished. I touched my lips to the delicate spot just behind her ear. I couldn't stop there, opening my mouth to let my tongue lick the salty moisture from her skin.

Abby's body tensed, and she pulled away.

"What, Pidge?" I asked. I had to chuckle. She looked like she wanted to hit me. I thought we were having a good time, and she was angrier than I'd ever seen her.

Instead of letting her temper fly, she pushed through the crowd, retreating to the bar. I followed, knowing I would find out soon enough what exactly I had done wrong.

Taking the empty stool beside her, I watched as Abby signaled to Cami that she wanted another beer. I ordered one for myself, and then watched her chug half of hers. The bottle clanged against the counter when she slammed it down.

"You think *that* is going to change anyone's mind about us?"

I laughed once. After all that bumping and grinding against my dick, she was suddenly worried about appearances? "I don't give a damn what they think about us."

She shot me a dirty look, and then turned to face forward.

"Pigeon," I said, touching her arm.

She jerked away. "Don't. I could *never* get drunk enough to let you get me on that couch."

Instant rage consumed me. I had never treated her like that. Never. She led me on, and then I gave her one or two little kisses on the neck, and she freaks out?

I started to speak, but Megan appeared next to me.

"Well. If it isn't Travis Maddox."

"Hey, Megan."

Abby eyed Megan, clearly taken off guard. Megan was an old pro at tipping the scales in her favor.

"Introduce me to your girlfriend," Megan said, smiling.

She knew damn good and well Abby wasn't my girlfriend. Ho 101: If the man in your sights is on a date or with a female friend, force him to admit to lack of commitment. Creates insecurity and instability.

I knew where this was going. Hell, if Abby really thought I was a criminal-grade douche bag, I might as well act like one. I slid my beer down the bar, and it fell off the edge, clinking into the full trash can at the end. "She's not my girlfriend."

Purposefully ignoring Abby's reaction, I grabbed Megan's hand and led her to the dance floor. She complied, happily swinging our arms until our feet hit the wood. Megan was always entertaining to dance with. She had no shame and let me do anything to her that I wanted, on and off the dance floor. As usual, most of the other dancers stopped to watch.

We usually made a spectacle, but I was feeling exceptionally lewd. Megan's dark hair slapped me in the face more than once, but I was numb. I picked her up and she wrapped her legs around my waist, and then bent back, stretching her arms over her head. She smiled as I pumped her in front of the entire bar, and when I set her on her feet, she turned and bent over, grabbing her ankles.

Sweat poured down my face. Megan's skin was so wet, my hands slipped away every time I tried to touch her. Her shirt was soaked, and so was mine. She leaned in for a kiss, her mouth slightly open, but I leaned back, looking toward the bar.

That was when I saw him. Ethan Coats. Abby was leaned in toward him, smiling with that drunken, flirty, take-me-home smile I could spot in a crowd of a thousand women.

Leaving Megan on the dance floor, I pushed through the mass that had gathered around us. Just before I reached Abby, Ethan reached over to touch her knee. Remembering what he'd gotten away with the year before, I balled my hand into a fist, standing between them, with my back to Ethan.

"You ready, Pidge?"

Abby put her hand on my stomach and pushed me to the side, smiling the instant Ethan came back into view. "I'm talking, Travis." She held her hand out, feeling how wet it was, and then wiped it on her skirt in dramatic fashion.

"Do you even know this guy?"

She smiled even wider. "This is Ethan."

Ethan extended his hand. "Nice to meet you. "

I couldn't take my eyes off of Abby while she stared at that sick and twisted fuck across from her. I left Ethan's hand hanging, waiting for Abby to remember I was standing there.

Dismissive, she waved her hand in my direction. "Ethan, this is Travis." Her voice was decidedly less enthusiastic about my introduction, which just pissed me off more.

I glared down at Ethan, and then at his hand. "Travis Maddox." My voice was as low and menacing as I could manage.

Ethan's eyes grew wide, and he awkwardly pulled back his hand. "Travis *Maddox?*"

I stretched my arm behind Abby to grip the bar. "Yeah, what of it?"

"I saw you fight Shawn Smith last year, man. I thought I was about to witness someone's death!"

My eyes narrowed, and my teeth clenched. "You wanna see it again?"

Ethan laughed once, his eyes darting back and forth between us. When he realized I wasn't kidding, he smiled awkwardly at Abby, and then walked away.

"Are you ready, now?" I snapped.

"You are a complete asshole, you know that?"

"I've been called worse." I held out my hand and she took it, letting me help her from the stool. She couldn't have been that pissed.

With a loud whistle, I signaled Shepley, who saw my expression and immediately knew that it was time to leave. I used my shoulder to cut through the crowd, shamelessly knocking over a few innocent bystanders to let off steam until Shepley headed us off and took over for me.

Once outside, I took Abby's hand, but she jerked it away.

I wheeled around and yelled in her face. "I should just kiss you and get it over with! You're being ridiculous! I kissed your neck, so what?"

Abby leaned back, and when that didn't create enough space, she pushed me away. No matter how pissed I was, she knew no fear. It was kinda hot.

"I'm not your fuck buddy, Travis."

I shook my head, stunned. If there was anything else I could do to keep her from thinking that, I didn't know what it was. She was special to me from the second I laid eyes on her, and I tried to let her know it every chance I got. How else could I get that across to her? How much different from everyone else could I treat her? "I never said you were! You're around me 24-7, you sleep in my bed, but half the time you act like you don't wanna be seen with me!"

"I *came* here with you!"

"I have never treated you with anything but respect, Pidge."

"No, you just treat me like your property. You had no right to run Ethan off like that!"

"Do you know who Ethan is?" When she shook her head, I leaned in. "I *do*. He was arrested last year for sexual battery, but the charges were dropped."

She crossed her arms. "Oh, so you have something in common?"

A red veil covered my eyes, and for less than a second, the rage inside me boiled over. I took a deep breath, willing it away. "Are you calling me a *rapist?*"

Abby paused in thought, and her hesitation made the anger melt away. She was the only one that had that effect on me. Every other time I'd been that angry, I had punched something or someone. I had never hit a woman, but I would have definitely taken a swing at the truck parked next to us.

"No, I'm just pissed at you!" she said, pressing her lips together.

"I've been drinking, all right? Your skin was three inches from my face, and you're beautiful, and you smell fucking awesome when you sweat. I kissed you! I'm sorry! Get over yourself!"

My answer made her pause, and the corners of her mouth turned up. "You think I'm beautiful?"

I frowned. What a stupid question. "You're gorgeous and you know it. What are you smiling about?"

The harder she tried not to smile, the more she did. "Nothing. Let's go."

I laughed once, and then shook my head. "Wha . . . ? You . . . ? You're a pain in my *ass*!"

She was grinning from ear to ear from my compliment, and the fact that I had gone from psycho to ridiculous in less than five minutes. She tried to stop smiling, and, in turn, that made me smile.

I hooked my arm around her neck, wishing to God I *had* just kissed her. "You're making me crazy. You know that, right?"

The ride home was quiet, and when we finally arrived at the apartment, Abby went straight to the bathroom, turning on the shower. My mind was too fuzzy to rifle through her shit, so I grabbed a pair of my boxers and a T-shirt. I knocked on the door, but she didn't answer, so I went ahead and walked in, laid it on the sink, and then left. I wasn't sure what to say to her anyway.

She walked in, swallowed by my clothes, and fell into bed, a residual smile still on her face.

I watched her for a moment, and she stared back, clearly wondering what I was thinking. The trouble was, even *I* didn't know. Her eyes slowly traveled down my face to my lips, and then I knew.

"Night, Pidge," I whispered, turning over, cussing at myself like never before. She was incredibly drunk, though, and I wasn't going to take advantage. Especially not after she'd forgiven me for the spectacle I'd made with Megan.

Abby fidgeted for several minutes before finally taking a breath. "Trav?" She leaned up on her elbow.

"Yeah?" I said, not moving. I was afraid if I looked into her eyes, all rational thought would go out the window.

"I know I'm drunk, and we just got into a ginormous fight over this, but . . ."

"I'm not having sex with you, so quit asking."

"What? No!"

I laughed and turned, looking at her sweet, horrified expression. "What, Pigeon?"

"This," she said, laying her head on my chest and stretching her arm across my stomach, hugging me close.

Not what I was expecting. At all. I held up my hand and froze in place, unsure what the hell to do. "You *are* drunk."

"I know," she said, shameless.

No matter how pissed she would be in the morning, I couldn't say no. I relaxed one hand against her back, and the other on her wet hair, and then kissed her forehead. "You are the most confusing woman I've ever met."

"It's the least you can do after scaring off the only guy that approached me tonight."

"You mean Ethan the rapist? Yeah, *I* owe *you* for that one."

"Never mind," she said, beginning to pull away.

My reaction was instantaneous. I held her arm against my stomach. "No, I'm serious. You need to be more careful. If I wasn't there . . . I don't even want to think about it. And now you expect me to apologize for running him off?"

"I don't want you to apologize. It's not even about that."

"Then what's it about?" I asked. I'd never begged for anything in my life, but I was silently begging for her to tell me she wanted me. That she cared about me. Something. We were so close. It would just take another inch or so for our lips to touch, and it was a mental feat not to give in to that inch.

She frowned. "I'm drunk, Travis. It's the only excuse I have."

"You just want me to hold you until you fall asleep?"

She didn't answer.

I turned, looking straight into her eyes. "I should say no to prove a point," I said, my eyebrows pulling together. "But I would hate myself later if I said no and you never asked me again."

She happily nestled her cheek against my chest. With my arms wrapped around her tight, it was hard to keep it together. "You don't need an excuse, Pigeon. All you have to do is ask."

CHAPTER EIGHT
Admission

Abby passed out before I did. Her breathing evened out, and her body relaxed against mine. She was warm, and her nose made the slightest, sweetest buzzing noise when she inhaled. Her body in my arms felt way too good. It was something I could get used to far too easily. As scared as that made me, I couldn't move.

Knowing Abby, she would wake up and remember she was a hard-ass, and yell at me for letting it happen or, worse, resolve to never let it happen again.

I wasn't stupid enough to hope, or strong enough to stop myself from feeling the way I did. Total eye-opener. Not so tough, after all. Not when it came to Abby.

My breathing slowed, and my body sank into the mattress, but I fought the fatigue that steadily overtook me. I didn't want to close my eyes and miss even a second of what it felt like to have Abby so close.

She stirred, and I froze. Her fingers pressed into my skin, and then she hugged herself up against me once before relaxing again. I kissed her hair, and leaned my cheek against her fore-head.

Closing my eyes for just a moment, I took a breath.

I opened my eyes again, and it was morning. Fuck. I knew I shouldn't have.

Abby was wiggling around, trying to unwedge herself out from under me. My legs were on top of hers, and my arm still held her.

"Stop it, Pidge. I'm sleepin'," I said, pulling her closer.

She pulled her limbs out from under me, one at a time, and then sat on the bed and sighed.

I slid my hand across the bed, reaching the tips of her small, delicate fingers. Her back was to me, and she didn't turn around.

"What's wrong, Pigeon?"

"I'm going to get a glass of water. You want anything?"

I shook my head, and closed my eyes. Either she was going to pretend it didn't happen, or she was pissed. Neither option a good one.

Abby walked out, and I lay there a while, trying to find the motivation to move. Hangovers sucked, and my head was pounding. I could hear Shepley's muffled, deep voice, so I decided to drag my ass out of bed.

My bare feet slapped against the wood floor as I trudged into the kitchen. Abby stood in my T-shirt and boxers, pouring chocolate syrup into a steaming bowl of oatmeal.

"That's sick, Pidge," I grumbled, trying to blink the blur from my eyes.

"Good morning to you, too."

"I hear your birthday is coming up. Last stand of your teenage years."

She made a face, caught off guard. "Yeah . . . I'm not a big birthday person. I think Mare is going to take me to dinner or something." She smiled. "You can come if you want."

I shrugged, trying to pretend her smile hadn't gotten to me. She wanted me there. "All right. It's a week from Sunday?"

"Yes. When's your birthday?"

"Not 'til April. April first," I said, pouring milk on top of my cereal.

"Shut up."

I took a bite, amused at her surprise. "No, I'm serious."

"Your birthday is on *April Fools'*?"

I laughed. The look on her face was priceless. "Yes! You're gonna be late. I better get dressed."

"I'm riding with Mare."

That small rejection was a lot harder to hear than it should have been. She had been riding to campus with me, and suddenly she was riding with America? It made me wonder if it was because of what had happened the night before. She was probably trying to distance herself from me again, and that was nothing less than disappointing. "Whatever," I said, turning my back to her before she could see the disappointment in my eyes.

The girls grabbed their backpacks in a hurry. America tore out of the parking lot like they had just robbed a bank.

Shepley walked out of his bedroom, pulling a T-shirt over his head. His eyebrows pushed together. "Did they just leave?"

"Yeah," I said absently, rinsing my cereal bowl and dumping Abby's leftover oatmeal in the sink. She'd barely touched it.

"Well, what the hell? Mare didn't even say goodbye."

"You knew she was going to class. Quit being a crybaby."

Shepley pointed to his chest. "I'm the crybaby? Do you remember last night?"

"Shut up."

"That's what I thought." He sat on the couch and slipped on his sneakers. "Did you ask Abby about her birthday?"

"She didn't say much, except that she's not into birthdays."

"So what are we doing?"

"Throwing her a party." Shepley nodded, waiting for me to explain. "I thought we'd surprise her. Invite some of our friends over and have America take her out for a while."

Shepley put on his white ball cap, pulling it down so low over his brows I couldn't see his eyes. "She can manage that. Anything else?"

"How do you feel about a puppy?"

Shepley laughed once. "It's not my birthday, bro."

I walked around the breakfast bar and leaned my hip against the stool. "I know, but she lives in the dorms. She can't have a puppy."

"Keep it here? Seriously? What are we going to do with a dog?"

"I found a cairn terrier online. It's perfect."

"A what?"

"Pidge is from Kansas. It's the same kind of dog Dorothy had in *The Wizard of Oz*."

Shepley's face was blank. "*The Wizard of Oz*."

"What? I liked the scarecrow when I was a little kid, shut the fuck up."

"It's going to crap everywhere, Travis. It'll bark and whine and . . . I don't know."

"So does America . . . minus the crapping."

Shepley wasn't amused.

"I'll take it out and clean up after it. I'll keep it in my room. You won't even know it's here."

"You can't keep it from barking."

"Think about it. You gotta admit it'll win her over."

Shepley smiled. "Is that what this is all about? You're trying to win over Abby?"

My brows pulled together. "Quit it."

His smile widened. "You can get the damn dog . . ."

I grinned. *Yes! Victory!*

". . . if you admit you have feelings for Abby."

I frowned. *Fuck! Defeat!* "C'mon, man!"

"Admit it," Shepley said, crossing his arms. What a tool. He was actually going to make me say it.

I looked to the floor and everywhere else except Shepley's smug ass smile. I fought it for a while, but the puppy was fucking brilliant. Abby would flip out (in a good way for once), and I could keep it at the apartment. She'd want to be there every day.

"I like her," I said through my teeth.

Shepley held his hand to his ear. "What? I couldn't quite hear you."

"You're an asshole! Did you hear that?"

Shepley crossed his arms. "Say it."

"I like her, okay?"

"Not good enough."

"I have feelings for her. I care about her. A lot. I can't stand it when she's not around. Happy?"

"For now," he said, grabbing his backpack off the floor. He slung one strap over his shoulder, and then picked up his cell phone and keys. "See you at lunch, pussy."

"Eat shit," I grumbled.

Shepley was always the idiot in love acting like a fool. He was never going to let me live this down.

It only took a couple of minutes to get dressed, but all that talking had me running late. I slipped on my leather jacket and put my ball cap on backward. My only class that day was Chem II, so bringing my bag wasn't necessary. Someone in class would let me borrow a pencil if we had a quiz.

Sunglasses. Keys. Phone. Wallet. I slipped on my boots and slammed the door behind me, trotting down the stairs. Riding the Harley wasn't nearly as appealing without Abby on the back. Dammit, she was ruining everything.

On campus, I walked a little faster than usual to make it to class on time. With just a second to spare, I slipped into the desk. Dr. Webber rolled her eyes, unimpressed with my timing, and probably a little irritated with my lack of materials. I winked, and the slightest smile touched her lips. She shook her head, and then returned her attention to the papers on her desk.

A pencil wasn't necessary, and once we were dismissed, I took off toward the cafeteria.

Shepley was waiting for the girls in the middle of the greens. I grabbed his ball cap, and before he could take it back, I tossed it like a Frisbee across the lawn.

"Nice, dick," he said, walking the few feet to pick it up.

"Mad Dog," someone called behind me. I knew from the scruffy, deep voice who it was.

Adam approached Shepley and me, his expression all business. "I'm trying to set up a fight. Be ready for a phone call."

"We always are," Shepley said. He was sort of my business

manager. He took care of getting the word out, and he made sure I was in the right place at the right time.

Adam nodded once, and then left for his next destination, whatever that was. I had never been in a class with the guy. I wasn't even sure if he really went to school here. As long as he paid me, I guess I didn't really care.

Shepley watched Adam walk away, and then cleared his throat. "So did you hear?"

"What?"

"They fixed the boilers at Morgan."

"So?"

"America and Abby will probably pack up tonight. We're going to be busy helping them move all their shit back to the dorms."

My face fell. The thought of packing Abby up and taking her back to Morgan felt like a punch in the face. Especially after the night before, she'd probably be happy to leave. She might not even speak to me again. My mind flashed through a million scenarios, but I couldn't think of anything to get her to stay.

"You okay, man?" Shepley asked.

The girls appeared, giggly and smiling. I tried a smile, but Abby was too busy being embarrassed by whatever America was laughing about.

"Hey, baby," America said, kissing Shepley on the mouth.

"What's so funny?" Shepley asked.

"Oh, a guy in class was staring at Abby all hour. It was adorable."

"As long as he was staring at Abby." Shepley winked.

"Who was it?" I asked before thinking.

Abby shifted her weight, readjusting her backpack. It was

overflowing with books, the zipper barely containing the contents. It must have been heavy. I slipped it off her shoulder.

"Mare's imagining things," she said, rolling her eyes.

"Abby! You big fat liar! It was Parker Hayes, and he was being *so* obvious. The guy was practically drooling."

My face twisted. "Parker *Hayes?*"

Shepley pulled on America's hand. "We're headed to lunch. Will you be enjoying the fine cafeteria cuisine this afternoon?"

America kissed him again in answer, and Abby followed behind, prompting me to do the same. We walked together in silence. She was going to find out about the boilers, they would move back to Morgan, and Parker would ask her out.

Parker Hayes was a cream puff, but I could see Abby being interested in him. His parents were stupid rich, he was going to med school, and on the surface he was a nice guy. She was going to end up with him. The rest of her life with him played out in my head, and it was all I could do to calm down. The mental image of tackling my temper and shoving it into a box helped.

Abby placed her tray between America and Finch. An empty chair a few seats down was a better choice for me than attempting to carry on a conversation like I hadn't just lost her. This was going to suck, and I didn't know what to do. So much time had been wasted playing games. Abby didn't have a chance to even get to know me. Hell, even if she had, she was probably better off with someone like Parker.

"Are you okay, Trav?" Abby asked.

"Me? Fine, why?" I asked, trying to get rid of the heavy feeling that settled in every muscle of my face.

"You've just been quiet."

Several members of the football team approached the table and sat down, laughing loudly. Just the sounds of their voices made me want to punch a wall.

Chris Jenks tossed a French fry onto my plate. "What's up, Trav? I heard you bagged Tina Martin. She's been raking your name through the mud today."

"Shut up, Jenks," I said, keeping my eyes on my food. If I looked up at his ridiculous fucking face, I might have knocked him out of his chair.

Abby leaned forward. "Knock it off, Chris."

I looked up at Abby, and for a reason I couldn't explain, became instantly angry. What the fuck was she defending me for? The second she found out about Morgan, she was going to leave me. She'd never talk to me again. Even though it was crazy, I felt betrayed. "I can take care of myself, Abby."

"I'm sorry, I . . ."

"I don't want you to be sorry. I don't want you to be anything," I snapped. Her expression was the final straw. Of course she didn't want to be around me. I was an infantile asshole that had the emotional control of a three-year-old. I shoved away from the table and pushed through the door, not stopping until I was sitting on my bike.

The rubber grips on the handlebars whined under my palms as I twisted my hands back and forth. The engine snarled, and I kicked back the kickstand before taking off like a bat out of hell into the street.

I rode around for an hour, feeling no better than before. The streets were leading to one place, though, and even though it took me that long to give in and just go, I finally pulled into my father's driveway.

Dad walked out of the front door and stood on the porch, giving a short wave.

I took both of the porch stairs at once and stopped just short of where he stood. He didn't hesitate to pull me against his soft, rounded side, before escorting me inside.

"I was just thinking it was about time for a visit," he said with a tired smile. His eyelids hung over his lashes a bit, and the skin beneath his eyes was puffy, matching the rest of his round face.

Dad checked out for a few years after Mom died. Thomas took on a lot more responsibilities than a kid his age should have, but we made do, and finally Dad snapped out of it. He never talked about it, but he never missed a chance to make it up to us.

Even though he was sad and angry for most of my formative years, I wouldn't consider him a bad father, he was just lost without his wife. I knew how he felt, now. I felt maybe a fraction for Pidge what Dad felt for Mom, and the thought of being without her made me feel sick.

He sat on the couch and gestured to the worn-out recliner. "Well? Have a seat, would ya?"

I sat, fidgeting while trying to figure out what I would say.

He watched me for a while before taking a breath. "Something wrong, son?"

"There's a girl, Dad."

He smiled a bit. "A girl."

"She kinda hates me, and I kinda . . ."

"Love her?"

"I don't know. I don't think so. I mean . . . how do you know?"

His smile grew wider. "When you're talking about her with your old dad because you don't know what else to do."

I sighed. "I just met her. Well, a month ago. I don't think it's love."

"Okay."

"Okay?"

"I'll take your word for it," he said without judgment.

"I just . . . I don't think I'm good for her."

Dad leaned forward, then touched a couple of fingers to his lips.

I continued. "I think she's been burned by someone before. By someone like me."

"Like you."

"Yeah." I nodded and sighed. The last thing I wanted was to admit to Dad what I'd been up to.

The front door slammed against the wall. "Look who decided to come home," Trenton said with a wide grin. He hugged two brown paper sacks to his chest.

"Hey, Trent," I said, standing. I followed him into the kitchen and helped him put Dad's groceries away.

We took turns elbowing and shoving each other. Trenton had always been the hardest on me as far as kicking my ass when we disagreed, but I was also closer to him than I was to my other brothers.

"Missed you at the Red the other night. Cami says hi."

"I was busy."

"With that girl Cami saw you with the other night?"

"Yeah," I said. I pulled out an empty ketchup bottle and some molding fruit from the fridge and tossed them in the garbage before we returned to the front room.

Trenton bounced a few times when he fell into the couch, slapping his knees. "What've you been up to, loser?"

"Nothin'," I said, glancing at Dad.

Trenton looked to our father, and then back at me. "Did I interrupt?"

"No," I said, shaking my head.

Dad waved him away. "No, son. How was work?"

"It sucked. I left the rent check on your dresser this morning. Did you see it?"

Dad nodded with a small smile.

Trenton nodded once. "You stayin' for dinner, Trav?"

"Nah," I said, standing. "I think I'm just going to head home."

"I wish you'd stay, son."

My mouth pulled to the side. "I can't. But, thanks, Dad. I appreciate it."

"You appreciate what?" Trenton asked. His head pivoted from side to side like he was watching a tennis match. "What'd I miss?"

I looked at my father. "She's a pigeon. Definitely a pigeon."

"Oh?" Dad said, his eyes brightening a bit.

"The same girl?"

"Yeah, but I was kind of a dick to her earlier. She kind of makes me feel crazy-er."

Trenton's smile started small, and then slowly stretched the entire width of his face. "Little brother!"

"Quit." I frowned.

Dad smacked Trent on the back of the head.

"What?" Trenton cried. "What'd I say?"

Dad followed me out the front door and patted me on the shoulder. "You'll figure it out. I have no doubt. She must be something, though. I don't think I've seen you like this."

"Thanks, Dad." I leaned in, wrapping my arms around his large frame as best I could, and then headed for the Harley.

The ride back to the apartment felt like it took forever. Just a hint of warm summer air remained, uncharacteristic for the time of year, but welcome. The night sky draped darkness all around me, making the dread even worse. I saw America's car parked in her usual spot and was immediately nervous. Each step felt like a foot closer to death row.

Before reaching the door, it flew open, and America stood with a blank look on her face.

"Is she here?"

America nodded. "She's asleep in your room," she said softly.

I slipped past her and sat on the couch. Shepley was on the love seat, and America plopped down beside me.

"She's okay," America said. Her voice was sweet and reassuring.

"I shouldn't have talked to her like that," I said. "One minute I'm pushing her as far as I can to piss her off, and the next I'm terrified she'll wise up and cut me out of her life."

"Give her some credit. She knows exactly what you're doing. You're not her first rodeo."

"Exactly. She deserves better. I know that, and at the same time I can't walk away. I don't know why," I said with a sigh, rubbing my temples. "It doesn't make sense. Nothing about this makes sense."

"Abby gets it, Trav. Don't beat yourself up," Shepley said.

America nudged my arm with her elbow. "You're already going to the date party. What's the harm in asking her out?"

"I don't want to *date* her; I just want to be around her. She's . . . different." It was a lie. America knew it, and I knew it. The truth was, if I really cared about her, I'd leave her the hell alone.

"Different *how?*" America asked, sounding irritated.

"She doesn't put up with my bullshit, it's refreshing. You said it yourself, Mare. I'm not her type. It's just not . . . like that with us." Even if it *was*, it shouldn't be.

"You're closer to her type than you know," America said.

I looked into America's eyes. She was completely serious. America was like a sister to Abby, and protective like a mother bear. They would never encourage anything for each other that could be hurtful. For the first time, I felt a glimmer of hope.

The wooden boards creaked in the hall, and we all froze. My bedroom door shut, and then Abby's footsteps sounded in the hall.

"Hey, Abby," America said with a grin. "How was your nap?"

"I was out for five hours. That's closer to a coma than a nap."

Her mascara was smeared under her eyes, and her hair was matted against her head. She was stunning. She smiled at me, and I stood, took her hand, and led her straight to the bedroom. Abby looked confused and apprehensive, making me even more desperate to make amends.

"I'm so sorry, Pidge. I was an asshole to you earlier."

Her shoulders fell. "I didn't know you were mad at me."

"I wasn't mad at you. I just have a bad habit of lashing out at those I care about. It's a piss-poor excuse, I know, but I *am* sorry," I said, enveloping her in my arms.

"What were you mad about?" she asked, nestling her cheek into my chest. Damn, that felt so good. If I wasn't a dick, I would have explained to her that I knew the boilers had been fixed, and the thought of her leaving here and spending more time with Parker scared the shit out of me, but I couldn't do it. I didn't want to ruin the moment.

"It's not important. The only thing I'm worried about is you."

She looked up at me and smiled. "I can handle your temper tantrums."

I scanned her face for several moments before a small smile spread across my lips. "I don't know why you put up with me, and I don't know what I'd do if you didn't."

Her eyes slowly fell from my eyes to my lips, and her breath caught. Every hair on my skin stood on end, and I wasn't sure if I was breathing or not. I leaned in less than a centimeter, waiting to see if she would protest, but then my fucking phone rang. We both jumped.

"Yeah," I said impatiently.

"Mad Dog. Brady will be at Jefferson in ninety."

"*Hoffman?* Jesus . . . all right. That'll be an easy grand. Jefferson?"

"Jefferson," Adam said. "You in?"

I looked at Abby and winked. "We'll be there." I hung up, stuck my phone in my pocket, and grabbed Abby's hand. "Come with me."

I led her to the living room. "That was Adam," I said to Shepley. "Brady Hoffman will be at Jefferson in ninety minutes."

CHAPTER NINE
Crushed

SHEPLEY'S EXPRESSION CHANGED. HE WAS ALL BUSINESS when Adam called with a fight time. His fingers tapped against his phone, clicking away, texting to the people on his list. When Shepley disappeared behind his door, America's eyes widened over her smile.

"Here we go! We'd better freshen up!"

Before I could say anything, America pulled Abby down the hall. The fuss was unnecessary. I'd kick the guy's ass, make the next few months' worth of rent and bills, and life would return to normal. Well, sort of normal. Abby would move back to Morgan Hall, and I would imprison myself to keep from killing Parker.

America was barking at Abby to change, and Shepley was now off the phone, Charger keys in hand. He bent backward to peek down the hall, and then rolled his eyes.

"Let's go!" he yelled.

America ran down the hall, but instead of joining us, she ducked into Shepley's room. He rolled his eyes again but was also smiling.

A few moments later, America burst out of Shepley's room in a short, green dress, and Abby rounded the hall corner in tight jeans and a yellow top, her tits bouncing every time she moved.

"Oh, hell, no. Are you trying to get me killed? You've gotta change, Pidge."

"What?" She looked down at her jeans. The jeans weren't the problem.

"She looks cute, Trav, leave her alone!" America snapped.

I led Abby down the hall. "Get a T-shirt on, and some sneakers. Something comfortable."

"What?" she asked, confusion distorting her face. "Why?"

I stopped at my door. "Because I'll be more worried about who's looking at your tits in that shirt instead of Hoffman," I said. Call it sexist, but it was true. I wouldn't be able to concentrate, and I wasn't going to lose a fight over Abby's rack.

"I thought you said you didn't give a damn about what anyone else thought?" she said, steaming.

She really didn't get it. "That's a different scenario, Pigeon." I looked down at her breasts, proudly pushed up in a white, lacy bra. Canceling the fight suddenly became a tempting idea, if only to spend the rest of the night trying to find a way to get them naked and against my chest.

I snapped out of it, making eye contact again. "You can't wear this to the fight, so please . . . just . . . please just change," I said, shoving her into the room and shutting myself out before I said fuck it and kissed her.

"Travis!" she yelled from the other side of the door. Sounds of scurrying could be heard on the other side of the door, and then what was probably shoes flying across the room. Finally, the door opened. She was in a T-shirt and a pair of Converse. Still hot, but at least I wouldn't be too worried about who was hitting on her to win my damn fight.

"Better?" she puffed.

"Yes! Let's go!"

Shepley and America were already in the Charger, ripping out of the parking lot. I slipped on my shades and waited until Abby was secure before taking off on the Harley into the dark street.

Once we reached campus, I drove down the sidewalk with my lights off, pulling up slowly behind Jefferson.

As I led Abby to the back entrance, her eyes widened, and she laughed once.

"You're joking."

"This is the VIP entrance. You should see how everyone else gets in." I hopped down through the open window into the basement, and then waited in the dark.

"Travis!" she half yelled, half whispered.

"Down here, Pidge. Just come in feetfirst, I'll catch you."

"You're out of your damn mind if you think I'm jumping into the dark!"

"I'll catch you! I promise! Now get your ass in here!"

"This is insane!" she hissed.

In the dim light, I saw her legs wiggle through the small rectangular opening. Even after all her careful maneuvering, she managed to fall instead of jump. A tiny squeal echoed down the concrete walls, and then she landed in my arms. Easiest catch ever.

"You fall like a girl," I said, setting her on her feet.

We walked through the dark maze of the basement until we arrived in the room adjacent to the main room where the fight

would be held. Adam was yelling over the noise with his bullhorn, and arms were sticking straight up from the sea of heads,
waving cash in the air.

"What are we doing?" she asked, her small hands wrapped
tight around my bicep.

"Waiting. Adam has to run through his spiel before I go in."

"Should I wait here, or should I go in? Where do I go when
the fight starts? Where's Shep and Mare?"

She looked extremely unsettled. I felt a little bad for leaving her here alone. "They went in the other way. Just follow me
out, I'm not sending you into that shark pit without me. Stay by
Adam; he'll keep you from getting crushed. I can't look out for
you and throw punches at the same time."

"Crushed?"

"There's going to be more people here tonight. Brady Hoffman is from State. They have their own Circle there. It will be
our crowd and their crowd, so the room's gonna get crazy."

"Are you nervous?"

I smiled at her. She was particularly beautiful when she was
worried about me. "No. You look a little nervous, though."

"Maybe," she said.

I wanted to lean down and kiss her. Something to ease that
frightened-lamb expression on her face. I wondered if she worried about me the first night we met, or if it was just because she
knew me now—because she cared about me.

"If it'll make you feel better, I won't let him touch me. I won't
even let him get one in for his fans."

"How are you going to manage *that*?"

I shrugged. "I usually let them get one in—to make it look
fair."

"You . . . ? You *let* people *hit* you?"

"How much fun would it be if I just massacred someone and they never got a punch in? It's not good for business, no one would bet against me."

"What a load of crap," she said, crossing my arms.

I raised an eyebrow. "You think I'm yankin' your chain?"

"I find it hard to believe that you only get hit when you *let* them hit you."

"Would you like to make a wager on that, Abby Abernathy?" I smiled. When I first said the words, it wasn't my intention to use them to my advantage, but when she flashed back an equally wicked smile, the most brilliant fucking idea I'd ever had slipped into my mind.

She smiled. "I'll take that bet. I think he'll get one in on you."

"And if he doesn't? What do I win?" I asked. She shrugged just as the roar of the crowd surrounded us. Adam went over the rules in his usual asshole way.

I stopped a ridiculous grin erupting across my face. "If you win, I'll go without sex for a month." She raised an eyebrow. "But if I win, you have to stay with me for a month."

"*What?* I'm staying with you, anyway! What kind of bet is that?" she shrieked over the noise. She didn't know. No one had told her.

"They fixed the boilers at Morgan today," I said with a smile and a wink.

One side of her mouth turned up. It didn't faze her. "Anything is worth watching you try abstinence for a change."

Her reply sent a rush of adrenaline through my veins that I'd only ever felt during a fight. I kissed her cheek, letting my lips linger against her skin for just a moment longer before walking out into the room. I felt like a king. No way was this fucker going to touch me.

Just as I had anticipated, there was standing room only, and the shoving and shouting amplified once we entered the room. I nodded to Adam in Abby's direction, to signal for him to watch out for her. He immediately understood. Adam was a greedy bastard, but he was once the undefeated monster in the Circle. I had nothing to worry about as long as he watched over her. He would do it so I wouldn't be distracted. Adam would do anything as long as it meant making a shit ton of money.

A path cleared as I walked to the Circle, and then the human gate closed behind me. Brady stood toe to toe with me, breathing hard and shaking like he'd just shot up with Red Bull and Mountain Dew.

Usually I didn't take this shit seriously and made a game of psyching my opponents out, but tonight's fight was important, so I put on my game face.

Adam sounded the horn. I balanced my core, took a few steps back, and waited for Brady to make his first mistake. I dodged his first swing, and then another. Adam popped something off from the back. He was unhappy, but I had anticipated that. Adam liked for fights to entertain. It was the best way to get more heads in the basements. More people meant more money.

I bent my elbow and sent my fist flying into Brady's nose, hard and fast. On a normal fight night, I would hold back, but I wanted to get this over with and spend the rest of the night celebrating with Abby.

I hit Hoffman over and over, and then dodged a few more from him, careful not to get so excited that I would let him hit me and fuck everything up. Brady got a second wind, and came back at me again, but it didn't take long for him to wear himself out throwing punches he couldn't land. I'd dodged punches from Trenton way faster than this bitch could throw.

My patience had run out, and I lured Hoffman to the cement pillar in the center of the room. I stood in front of it, hesitating just long enough for my opponent to think he had a window to nail my face with a devastating blow. I sidestepped as he put everything into his last throw, and slammed his fist straight into the pillar. Surprise registered in Hoffman's eyes just before he doubled over.

That was my cue. I immediately attacked. A loud thud signaled that Hoffman had finally hit the ground, and after a short silence, the room erupted. Adam threw a red flag on Hoffman's face, and then I was surrounded by people.

Most of the time I enjoyed the attention and hell yeahs of those that bet on me, but this time they were just in the way. I tried looking over the sea of people to find Abby, but when I finally got a glimpse of where she was supposed to be, my stomach sank. She was gone.

Smiles turned to shock when I shoved people out of my way. "Get! The fuck! Back!" I yelled, pushing harder as panic came over me.

I finally reached the lantern room, desperately searching for Abby in the darkness. "Pigeon!"

"I'm here!" Her body crashed into mine, and I flung my arms around her. One second I was relieved, the next I was irritated.

"You scared the shit out of me! I almost had to start another fight just to get to you! I finally get here and you're gone!"

"I'm glad you're back. I wasn't looking forward to trying to find my way in the dark."

Her sweet smile made me forget everything else, and I re-membered that she was mine. At least for another month. "I be-lieve you lost the bet."

Adam stomped in, looked at Abby, and then glowered at me. "We need to talk."

I winked at Abby. "Stay put. I'll be right back." I followed Adam into the next room. "I know what you're gonna say . . ."

"No you don't," Adam growled. "I don't know what you're doin' with her, but *don't* fuck with my money."

I laughed once. "You made bank tonight. I'll make it up to you."

"You're goddamn straight you will! Don't let it happen again!" Adam slammed cash into my hand, and then shouldered past me.

I shoved the wad of cash into my pocket, and smiled at Abby. "You're going to need more clothes."

"You're really going to make me stay with you for a month?"

"Would you have made me go without sex for a month?"

She laughed. "We better stop at Morgan."

Any attempt at covering my extreme satisfaction was an epic fail. "This should be interesting."

As Adam passed he handed Abby some cash before disap-pearing into the waning crowd.

"You put in?" I asked, surprised.

"I thought I should get the full experience," she said with a shrug.

I took her by the hand and led her to the window, and then jumped once, pulling myself up. I crawled on the grass, and then turned around, leaning down to pull up Abby.

The walk to Morgan seemed perfect. It was unseasonably warm, and the air had the same electric feel as a summer night.

I was trying not to smile the entire time like an idiot, but it was hard not to.

"Why on earth would you want me to stay with you, anyway?" she asked.

I shrugged. "I don't know. Everything's better when you're around."

Shepley and America waited in the Charger for us to show up with Abby's extra things. Once they took off, we walked to the parking lot and straddled the bike. She wrapped her arms around my chest, and I rested my hand on hers.

I took a breath. "I'm glad you were there tonight, Pidge. I've never had so much fun at a fight in my life." The time it took her to respond felt like an eternity.

She perched her chin on my shoulder. "That was because you were trying to win our bet."

I turned to face her, looking straight in her eyes. "Damn right I was."

Her eyebrows shot up. "Is that why you were in such a bad mood today? Because you knew they'd fixed the boilers, and I would be leaving tonight?"

I got lost in her eyes for moment, and then decided that it was a good time to shut up. I ripped the engine and drove home, slower than I had driven . . . ever. When a stoplight caught us, I found a strange amount of joy in putting my hands on hers, or resting my hand on her knee. She didn't seem to mind, and admittedly, I was pretty fucking close to heaven.

We pulled up to the apartment, and Abby dismounted the bike like an old pro, and then walked to the steps.

"I always hate it when they've been home for a while. I feel like we're going to interrupt them."

"Get used to it. This is your place for the next four weeks," I said, turning around. "Get on."

"What?"

"C'mon, I'll carry you up."

She giggled and hopped onto my back. I gripped her thighs as I ran up the stairs. America opened the door before we made it to the top and smiled.

"Look at you two. If I didn't know better . . ."

"Knock it off, Mare," Shepley said from the couch.

Great. Shepley was in one of his moods.

America smiled as if she'd said too much, and then opened the door wide so we could both fit through. I kept hold of Pidge, and then fell against the recliner. She squealed when I leaned back, playfully pushing my weight against her.

"You're awfully cheerful this evening, Trav. What gives?" America prompted.

"I just won a shitload of money, Mare. Twice as much as I thought I would. What's not to be happy about?"

America grinned. "No, it's something else," she said, watching my hand as I patted Abby's thigh.

"Mare," Shepley warned.

"Fine. I'll talk about something else. Didn't Parker invite you to the Sig Tau party this weekend, Abby?"

The lightness I was feeling immediately went away, and I turned to Abby.

"Er . . . yeah? Aren't we all going?"

"I'll be there," Shepley said, distracted by the television.

"And that means I'm going," America said, looking expectantly at me. She was baiting me, hoping I would volunteer to come along, but I was more concerned with Parker asking Abby out on a fucking date.

"Is he picking you up or something?" I asked.

"No, he just told me about the party."

America's mouth spread into a mischievous grin, almost bobbing in anticipation. "He said he'd see you there, though. He's really cute."

I shot America an irritated glance, and then looked to Abby. "Are you going?"

"I told him I would." She shrugged. "Are you going?"

"Yeah," I said without hesitation. It wasn't a date party, after all, just a weekend kegger. Those I didn't mind. And no fucking way was I going to let Parker have an entire night with her. She'd come back . . . ugh, I didn't even wanna think about it. He'd flash his Abercrombie smile, or take her to his parents' restaurant to parade his money, or find some other way to sleaze into her pants.

Shepley looked at me. "You said last week you weren't."

"I changed my mind, Shep. What's the problem?"

"Nothing," he grumbled, retreating to his bedroom.

America frowned. "You know what the problem is," she said. "Why don't you quit driving him crazy and just get it over with." She joined Shepley in his room, and their voices were reduced to murmuring behind the closed door.

"Well, I'm glad everyone else knows," Abby said.

Abby wasn't the only one confused by Shepley's behavior. Earlier he was teasing me about her, and now he was being a little bitch. What could have happened between then and now that had him freaked out? Maybe he would feel better once he figured out that I'd finally decided I was done with the other girls and just wanted Abby. Maybe the fact that I had actually admitted to caring about her made Shepley worry even more. I wasn't exactly boyfriend material. Yep. That made more sense.

I stood. "I'm going to take a quick shower."

"Is there something going on with them?" Abby asked.

"No, he's just paranoid."

"It's because of us," she guessed.

A weird floating feeling came over me. She said *us*.

"What?" she asked, eyeing me suspiciously.

"You're right. It's because of us. Don't fall asleep, okay? I wanna talk to you about something."

It took less than five minutes for me to wash up, but I stood under the stream of water for at least five more, planning what to say to Abby. Wasting more time wasn't an option. She was here for the next month, and that was the perfect time to prove to her that I wasn't who she thought I was. For her, at least, I was different, and we could spend the next four weeks dispelling any suspicions she might have.

I stepped out of the shower and dried off, excited and nervous as hell about what possibilities could spawn from the conversation we were about to have. Just before opening the door, I could hear a scuffle in the hall.

America said something, her voice desperate. I cracked open the door and listened.

"You promised, Abby. When I told you to spare judgment, I didn't mean for you two to get involved! I thought you were just friends!"

"We are," Abby said.

"No, you're not!" Shepley fumed.

America spoke, "Baby, I told you it will be fine."

"Why are you pushing this, Mare? I told you what's going to happen!"

"And I told you it won't! Don't you trust me?"

Shepley stomped into his room.

After a few seconds of silence, America spoke again. "I just can't get it into his head that whether you and Travis work out or not, it won't affect us. But he's been burned too many times. He doesn't believe me."

Dammit, Shepley. Not the ideal segue. I opened the door a bit more, just enough to see Abby's face.

"What are you talking about, Mare? Travis and I aren't together. We *are* just friends. You heard him earlier . . . he's not interested in me that way."

Fuck. This was getting worse by the minute.

"You heard that?" America asked, surprise evident in her voice.

"Well, yeah."

"And you believe it?"

Abby shrugged. "It doesn't matter. It'll never happen. He told me he doesn't see me like that, anyway. Besides, he's a total commitment-phobe, I'd be hard-pressed to find a girlfriend outside of you that he hasn't slept with, and I can't keep up with his mood swings. I can't believe Shep thinks otherwise."

Every bit of hope I'd had slipped away with her words. The disappointment was crushing. For a few seconds, the pain was unmanageable, until I let the anger take over. Anger was always easier to control.

"Because not only does he know Travis . . . he's talked to Travis, Abby."

"What do you mean?"

"Mare?" Shepley called from the bedroom.

America sighed. "You're my best friend. I think I know you better than you know yourself sometimes. I see you two together, and the only difference between me and Shep and you and Travis is that we're having sex. Other than that? No difference."

"There is a huge, *huge* difference. Is Shep bringing home different girls every night? Are you going to the party tomorrow to hang out with a guy with definite dating potential? You know I can't get involved with Travis, Mare. I don't even know why we're discussing it."

"I'm not seeing things, Abby. You have spent almost every moment with him for the last month. Admit it, you have feelings for him."

I couldn't listen to another word. "Let it go, Mare," I said.

Both girls jumped at the sound of my voice. Abby's eyes met mine. She didn't seem embarrassed or sorry at all, which only pissed me off more. I'd stuck my neck out, and she slit my throat.

Before I said something shitty, I retreated to my room. Sitting didn't help. Neither did standing, pacing, or push-ups. The walls closed in on me more every second. Rage boiled inside of me like an unstable chemical, ready to blow.

Getting out of the apartment was my only option, to clear my head, and try to relax with a few shots. The Red. I could go to the Red. Cami was working the bar. She could tell me what to do. She always knew how to talk me down. Trenton liked her for the same reason. She was the oldest sister of three boys, and didn't flinch when it came to our anger issues.

I slipped on a T-shirt and jeans, and then grabbed sunglasses, my bike keys, and riding jacket, and then shoved my feet inside my boots before heading back down the hall.

Abby's eyes widened when she saw me round the corner. Thank God I had on my shades. I didn't want her to see the hurt in my eyes.

"You're leaving?" she asked, sitting up. "Where are you going?"

I refused to acknowledge the pleading in her voice. "Out."

CHAPTER TEN
Broken

It DIDN'T TAKE CAMI LONG TO FIGURE OUT I WASN'T good company. She kept the beers coming as I sat in my usual stool at the bar of The Red. Colors from the lights above chased one another around the room, and the music was almost loud enough to drown out my thoughts.

My pack of Marlboro Reds was nearly gone, but that wasn't the reason for the heavy feeling in my chest. A few girls had come and gone, trying to strike up conversation, but I couldn't lift my line of sight from the half-burnt cigarette nestled between two of my fingers. The ash was so long it was just a matter of time until it fell away, so I just watched the remaining embers flicker against the paper, trying to keep my mind off of what sinking feelings the music couldn't muffle.

When the crowd at the bar thinned, and Cami wasn't moving a thousand miles per hour, she sat an empty shot glass in front of me, and then filled it to the brim with Jim Beam. I grabbed for it, but she covered my black leather wristband with her tattooed fingers that spelled BABY DOLL when she held her fists together.

"Okay, Trav. Let's hear it."

"Hear what?" I asked, making a feeble attempt to pull away. She shook her head. "The girl?"

The glass touched my lips, and I tilted my head back, letting the liquid burn down my throat. "What girl?"

Cami rolled her eyes. "What girl. Seriously? Who do you think you're talking to?"

"All right, all right. It's Pigeon."

"*Pigeon?* You're joking."

I laughed once. "Abby. She's a pigeon. A demonic pigeon that fucks with my head so bad I can't think straight. Nothing makes sense anymore, Cam. Every rule I've ever made's getting broken one by one. I'm a pussy. No . . . worse. I'm Shep."

Cami laughed. "Be nice."

"You're right. Shepley's a good guy."

"Be nice to yourself, too," she said, throwing a rag on the counter and pushing it around in circles. "Falling for someone isn't a sin, Trav, Jesus."

I looked around. "I'm confused. You talking to me or Jesus?"

"I'm serious. So you have feelings for her. So what?"

"She hates me."

"Nah."

"No, I heard her tonight. By accident. She thinks I'm a scumbag."

"She said that?"

"Pretty much."

"Well, you kinda are."

I frowned. "Thanks a lot."

She held out her hands, her elbows on the bar. "Based on your past behavior, do you disagree? My point is . . . maybe for her, you wouldn't be. Maybe for her, you could be a better man." She poured another shot, and I didn't give her the chance to stop me before throwing it back.

"You're right. I've been a scumbag. Could I change? I don't fucking know. Probably not enough to deserve her."

Cami shrugged, holstering the bottle back in its spot. "I think you should let her be the judge of that."

I lit a cigarette, taking a deep breath, and adding my lungfuls of smoke to the already murky room. "Toss me another beer."

"Trav, I think you've had enough already."

"Cami, just fucking do it."

I WOKE UP WITH THE EARLY AFTERNOON SUN SHINING through the blinds, but it might as well have been noon in the middle of a white sand desert. My lids instantly closed, rejecting the light.

A combination of morning breath, chemicals, and cat piss stuck to the inside of my dry mouth. I hated the inevitable cotton mouth that came after a hard night of drinking.

My mind instantly searched for memories from the night before but came up with nothing. Some type of partying was a given, but where or with who was a complete mystery.

I looked to my left, seeing the covers pulled back. Abby was already up. My bare feet felt weird against the floor as I trudged down the hall and found Abby asleep in the recliner. Confusion made me pause, and then panic settled in. My brain sloshed through the alcohol still weighing down my thoughts. Why didn't she sleep in the bed? What had I done to make her sleep in the chair? My heart began beating fast, and then I saw them: two empty condom wrappers.

Fuck. Fuck! The night before came crashing back to me in waves: drinking more, those girls not going away when I told them to, and finally my offer to show them both a good time—at the same time—and their enthusiastic endorsement of the idea.

My hands flew up to my face. I'd brought them here. Bagged them here. Abby had probably heard everything. Oh, God. I couldn't have fucked up any worse. This was beyond bad. As soon as she woke, she would pack her shit and leave.

I sat on the couch, my hands still cupped over my mouth and nose, and watched her sleep. I had to fix this. What could I do to fix this?

One stupid idea after another flipped through my mind. Time was running out. As quietly as I could, I rushed to the bedroom and changed clothes, and then snuck into Shepley's room.

America stirred, and Shepley's head popped up. "What are you doing, Trav?" he whispered.

"I gotta borrow your car. Just for a sec. I have to go pick up a few things."

"Okay . . . ," he said, confused.

His keys jingled when I took them from his dresser, and then I paused. "Do me a favor. If she wakes up before I get back, stall, okay?"

Shepley took a deep breath. "I'll try, Travis, but man . . . last night was . . ."

"It was bad, wasn't it?"

Shepley's mouth pulled to the side. "I don't think she'll stay, cousin, I'm sorry."

I nodded. "Just try."

One last glance at Abby's sleeping face before I left the apartment spurred me to move faster. The Charger could barely keep up with the speed I wanted to go. A red light caught me just before I reached the market and I screamed, hitting the steering wheel.

"God dammit! Turn!"

A few seconds later, the light blinked from red to green, and the tires spun a few times before gaining traction.

I ran into the store from the parking lot, fully aware that I looked like a crazy person as I yanked a grocery cart from the rest. One aisle after another, I grabbed at things that I thought she'd like, or remembered her eating or even talking about. A pink spongy thing hung in a line off of one of the shelves, and that ended up in my basket, too.

An apology wasn't going to make her stay, but maybe a gesture would. Maybe she would see how sorry I was. I stopped a few feet away from the register, feeling hopeless. Nothing was going to work.

"Sir? Are you ready?"

I shook my head, despondent. "I don't . . . I don't know."

The woman watched me for a moment, shoving her hands in the pockets of her white-and-mustard-yellow-striped apron. "Can I help you find something?"

I pushed the cart to her register without responding, watching her scan all of Abby's favorite foods. This was the stupidest idea in the history of ideas, and the only woman alive that I gave a shit about was going to laugh at me while she packed.

"That'll be eighty-four dollars and seventy-seven cents."

A short swipe of my debit card, and the sacks were in my

hands. I bolted into the parking lot, and within seconds the Charger was getting the cobwebs blown out of her pipes all the way back to the apartment.

I took two steps at a time and blew through the door. America's and Shepley's heads were visible over the top of the couch. The television was on, but muted. Thank God. She was still asleep. The sacks crashed against the countertop when I sat them down, and I tried not to let the cabinets crash around too much as I put things away.

"When Pidge wakes up, let me know, okay?" I asked softly. "I got spaghetti, and pancakes, and strawberries, and that oatmeal shit with the chocolate packets, and she likes Fruity Pebbles cereal, right, Mare?" I asked, turning.

Abby was awake, staring at me from the chair. Her mascara was smeared under her eyes. She looked as bad as I felt. "Hey, Pigeon."

She watched me for a few seconds with a blank stare. I took a few steps into the living room, more nervous than I was the night of my first fight.

"You hungry, Pidge? I'll make you some pancakes. Or there's uh . . . there's some oatmeal. And I got you some of that pink foamy shit that girls shave with, and a hairdryer, and a . . . a . . . just a sec, it's in here." I grabbed one of the bags and took it into the bedroom, dumping it out onto the bed.

As I looked for that pink loofah thing I thought she'd like, Abby's luggage, full, zipped, and waiting by the door, caught my eye. My stomach lurched, and the cotton mouth returned. I walked down the hall, trying to keep myself together.

"Your stuff's packed."

"I know," she said.

Physical pain burned through my chest. "You're leaving."

Abby looked to America, who stared at me like she wanted me dead. "You actually expected her to stay?"

"Baby," Shepley whispered.

"Don't fucking start with me, Shep. Don't you dare defend him to me," America seethed.

I swallowed hard. "I am so sorry, Pidge. I don't even know what to say."

"Come on, Abby," America said. She stood and pulled on her arm, but Abby stayed seated.

I took a step, but America pointed her finger. "So help me God, Travis! If you try to stop her, I will douse you with gasoline and light you on fire while you sleep!"

"America," Shepley begged. This was going to get bad from all sides real quick.

"I'm *fine*," Abby said, overwhelmed.

"What do you mean, you're *fine*?" Shepley asked.

Abby rolled her eyes and gestured to me. "Travis brought women home from the bar last night, so what?"

My eyes closed, trying to deflect the pain. As much as I didn't want her to leave, it had never occurred to me that she wouldn't give a fuck.

America frowned. "Huh-uh, Abby. Are you saying you're *okay* with what happened?"

Abby glanced around the room. "Travis can bring home whoever he wants. It's *his* apartment."

I swallowed back the lump that was swelling in my throat. "You didn't pack your things?"

She shook her head and looked at the clock. "No, and now

I'm going to have to unpack it all. I still have to eat, and shower, and get dressed," she said, walking into the bathroom.

America shot a death glare in my direction, but I ignored her and walked over to the bathroom door, tapping lightly. "Pidge?"

"Yeah?" she said, her voice weak.

"You're staying?" I closed my eyes, waiting for punishment.

"I can go if you want me to, but a bet's a bet."

My head fell against the door. "I don't want you to leave, but I wouldn't blame you if you did."

"Are you saying I'm released from the bet?"

The answer was easy, but I didn't want to make her stay if she didn't want to. At the same time, I was terrified to let her go. "If I say yes, will you leave?"

"Well, yeah. I don't live here, silly," she said. A small laugh floated through the wood of the door.

I couldn't tell if she was upset or just tired from spending the night in the recliner, but if it was the former, there was no way I could let her walk away. I'd never see her again.

"Then no, the bet's still in effect."

"Can I take a shower, now?" she asked, her voice small.

"Yeah . . ."

America stomped into the hall and stopped just short of my face. "You're a selfish bastard," she growled, slamming Shepley's door behind her.

I went into the bedroom, grabbed her robe and a pair of slippers, and then returned to the bathroom door. She was apparently staying, but kissing ass was never a bad idea.

"Pigeon? I brought some of your stuff."

"Just set it on the sink. I'll get it."

I opened the door and set her things on the corner of the sink, looking to the floor. "I was mad. I heard you spitting out everything that's wrong with me to America and it pissed me off. I just meant to go out and have a few drinks and try to figure some things out, but before I knew it, I was piss drunk and those girls . . ." I paused, trying to keep my voice from breaking. "I woke up this morning and you weren't in bed, and when I found you on the recliner and saw the wrappers on the floor, I felt sick."

"You could have just asked me instead of spending all that money at the grocery store just to bribe me to stay."

"I don't care about the money, Pidge. I was afraid you'd leave and never speak to me again."

"I didn't mean to hurt your feelings," she said, sincere.

"I know you didn't. And I know it doesn't matter what I say now, because I fucked things up . . . just like I always do."

"Trav?"

"Yeah?"

"Don't drive drunk on your bike anymore, okay?"

I wanted to say more, to apologize again, and to tell her that I was crazy about her—and it was literally driving me insane because I didn't know how to handle what I felt—but the words wouldn't come. My thoughts could only focus on the fact that after everything that had happened, and everything I just said, the only thing she had to say was to scold me about driving home drunk.

"Yeah, okay," I said, shutting the door.

I pretended to stare at the television for hours while Abby primped in the bathroom and bedroom for the frat party, and then decided to get dressed before she needed the bedroom.

A fairly wrinkle-free white shirt was hanging in the closet, so I grabbed it and a pair of jeans. I felt silly, standing in front of the mirror, struggling with the button at the wrist of the shirt. I finally gave up and rolled each sleeve to my elbow. That was more like me, anyway.

I walked down the hall and crashed into the couch again, hearing the bathroom door shut and Abby's bare feet slapping against the floor.

My watch barely moved, and of course nothing was on TV except daring weather rescues and an infomercial about the Slap Chop. I was nervous and bored. Not a good combination for me.

When my patience ran out, I knocked on the bedroom door.

"Come in," Abby called from the other side of the door.

She stood in the middle of the room, a pair of heels sitting side by side on the floor in front of her. Abby was always beautiful, but tonight not a single hair was out of place; she looked like she should be on the cover of one of those fashion magazines you see in the checkout line of the grocery store. Every part of her was lotioned, smooth, polished perfection. Just the sight of her nearly knocked me on my ass. All I could do was stand there, dumbfounded, until I finally managed to form a single word.

"Wow."

She smiled, and looked down at her dress.

Her sweet grin snapped me back to reality. "You look amazing," I said, unable to take my eyes off her.

She bent over to help one foot into her shoe, and then the other. The skintight, black fabric moved slightly upward, exposing just half an inch more of her thighs.

Abby stood and gave me a quick once-over. "You look nice, too."

I shoved my hands in my pocket, refusing to say, *I might be falling for you at this very moment*, or any of the other stupid things that were bombarding my mind.

I stuck out my elbow, and Abby took it, letting me escort her down the hall to the living room.

"Parker is going to piss himself when he sees you," America said. Overall America was a good girl, but I was finding out how nasty she could be if you were on her bad side. I tried not to trip her as we walked to Shepley's Charger, and I kept my mouth shut the entire trip to the Sig Tau house.

The moment Shepley opened the car door, we could hear the loud and obnoxious music from the house. Couples were kissing and mingling; freshmen pledges were running around, trying to keep the damage to the yard at a minimum, and sorority girls carefully walked by hand in hand, in tiny hops, trying to walk across the soft grass without sinking their stilettos.

Shepley and I led the way, with America and Abby just behind us. I kicked a red plastic cup out of the way, and then held the door open. Once again, Abby was totally oblivious to my gesture.

A stack of red cups sat on the kitchen counter beside the keg. I filled two and brought one to Abby. I leaned into her ear. "Don't take these from anyone but me or Shep. I don't want anyone slipping something in your drink."

She rolled her eyes. "No one is going to put anything in my drink, Travis."

She clearly wasn't familiar with some of my frat brothers. I'd heard stories about no one in particular. Which was a good thing, because if I'd ever caught anyone pulling that shit, I would beat the shit out of them without hesitation.

"Just don't drink anything that doesn't come from me, okay? You're not in Kansas anymore, Pigeon."

"I haven't heard that one before," she snapped, throwing back half the cup of beer before she pulled the plastic away from her face. She could drink, I'd give her that.

We stood in the hallway by the stairs, trying to pretend everything was fine. A few of my frat brothers stopped by to chat as they came down the stairs, and so did a few sorority sisters, but I quickly dismissed them, hoping Abby would notice. She didn't.

"Wanna dance?" I asked, tugging on her hand.

"No thanks," she said.

I couldn't blame her, after the night before. I was lucky she was speaking to me at all.

Her thin, elegant fingers touched my shoulder. "I'm just tired, Trav."

I put my hand on hers, ready to apologize again, to tell her that I hated myself for what I'd done, but her eyes drifted away from mine to someone behind me.

"Hey, Abby! You made it!"

The hairs on the back of my neck stood on end. Parker Hayes.

Abby's eyes lit up, and she pulled her hand out from under mine in one quick movement. "Yeah, we've been here for an hour or so."

"You look incredible!" he yelled.

I made a face at him, but he was so preoccupied with Abby, he didn't notice.

"Thanks!" She smiled.

It occurred to me that I wasn't the only one that could make her smile that way, and suddenly I was working to keep my temper in check.

Parker nodded toward the living room and smiled. "You wanna dance?"

"Nah, I'm kinda tired."

A tiny bit of relief dulled my anger a bit. It wasn't me; she really was just too tired to dance, but the anger didn't take long to return. She was tired because she was kept up half the night by the sounds of whoever I'd brought home, and the other half of the night she'd slept in the recliner. Now Parker was here, sweeping in as the knight in shining armor like he always did. Rat bastard.

Parker looked at me, unfazed by my expression. "I thought you weren't coming."

"I changed my mind," I said, trying very hard not to punch him and obliterate four years of orthodontic work.

"I see that," Parker said, looking to Abby. "You wanna get some air?"

She nodded, and I felt like someone had knocked the air out of me. She followed Parker up the stairs. I watched as he paused, reaching to take her hand as they climbed to the second floor. When they reached the top, Parker opened the doors to the balcony.

Abby disappeared, and I squeezed my eyes shut, trying to block out the screaming in my head. Everything in me said to go up there and take her back. I gripped the banister, holding myself back.

"You look pissed," America said, touching her red cup to mine.

My eyes popped open. "No. Why?"

She made a face. "Don't lie to me. Where's Abby?"

"Upstairs. With Parker."

"Oh."

"What is that supposed to mean?"

She shrugged. She'd only been there a little over an hour, and already had that familiar glaze in her eyes. "You're jealous."

I shifted my weight, uncomfortable with someone else besides Shepley being so direct with me. "Where's Shep?"

America rolled her eyes. "Doing his freshman duties."

"At least he doesn't have to stay after and clean up."

She lifted the cup to her mouth and took a sip. I wasn't sure how she could already have a nice buzz drinking like that.

"So are you?"

"Am I what?"

"Jealous?"

I frowned. America wasn't usually so obnoxious. "No."

"Number two."

"Huh?"

"That's lie number two."

I looked around. Shepley would surely rescue me soon.

"You really fucked up last night," she said, her eyes suddenly clear.

"I know."

She squinted, glaring at me so intensely that I wanted to shrink back. America Mason was a tiny blond thing, but she was intimidating as fuck when she wanted to be. "You should walk away, Trav." She looked up, to the top of the stairs. "He's what she thinks she wants."

My teeth clenched together. I already knew that, but it was worse hearing it from America. Before that, I thought maybe she'd be okay with me and Abby, and that somehow meant I wasn't a complete dick for pursuing her. "I know."

She raised an eyebrow. "I don't think you do."

I didn't reply, trying not to make eye contact with her. She grabbed my chin with her hand, squashing my cheeks against my teeth.

"Do you?"

I tried to speak, but her fingers were now squishing my lips together. I jerked back, and then batted her hand away. "Probably not. I'm not exactly notorious for doing the right thing."

America watched me for a few seconds, and then smiled. "Okay, then."

"Huh?"

She slapped my cheek, and then pointed at me. "You, Mad Dog, are exactly what I came here to protect her from. But you know what? We're all broken some way or another. Even with your epic fuckup, you just might be exactly what she needs. You get one more chance," she said, holding up her index finger an inch from my nose. "Just one. Don't mess it up . . . you know . . . more than usual."

America sauntered away, and then disappeared down the hall. She was so weird.

The party played out as they usually do: drama, a fight or two, girls getting in a tiff, a couple or two getting in an argument resulting in the female leaving in tears, and then the stragglers either passing out or vomiting in an undesignated area.

My eyes drifted to the top of the stairs more times than they should have. Even though the girls were practically begging me to take them home, I kept watch, trying not to imagine Abby and Parker making out, or even worse, him making her laugh.

"Hey, Travis," a high-pitched, singsong voice called from behind me. I didn't turn around, but it didn't take long for the girl to weave herself into my line of sight. She leaned against the wooden posts of the banister. "You looked bored. I think I should keep you company."

"Not bored. You can go," I said, checking the top of the stairs again. Abby stood on the landing, her back to the stairs.

She giggled. "You're so funny."

Abby breezed past me, down the hall to where America stood. I followed, leaving the drunk girl to talk to herself.

"You guys go ahead," Abby said with subdued excitement. "Parker offered me a ride home."

"What?" America said, her tired eyes lit like double bonfires.

"What?" I said, unable to contain my irritation.

America turned. "Is there a problem?"

I glared at her. She knew exactly what my problem was. I took Abby by the elbow and pulled her around the corner.

"You don't even know the guy."

Abby pulled her arm away. "This is none of your business, Travis."

"The hell if it's not. I'm not letting you ride home with a complete stranger. What if he tries something on you?"

"*Good!* He's cute!"

I couldn't believe it. She was really falling for his game. "*Parker Hayes*, Pidge? Really? *Parker Hayes*. What kind of name is that, anyway?"

She crossed her arms and lifted her chin. "Stop it, Trav. You're being a jerk."

I leaned in, livid. "I'll kill him if he touches you."

"I *like* him."

It was one thing to assume she was fooled, it was another to hear her admit it. She was too good for me—damn sure too good for Parker Hayes. Why was she getting all giddy over that idiot? My face tensed in reaction to the rage flowing through my veins. "Fine. If he ends up holding you down in the backseat of his car, don't come crying to me."

Her mouth popped open, she was offended and furious. "Don't worry, I *won't*," she said, shouldering past me.

I realized what I'd said, and then grabbed her arm and sighed, not quite turning around. "I didn't mean it, Pidge. If he hurts you—if he even makes you feel uncomfortable—you let me know."

Her shoulders fell. "I know you didn't. But you have *got* to curb this overprotective big-brother thing you've got going on."

I laughed once. She really didn't get it. "I'm not playing the big brother, Pigeon. Not even close."

Parker rounded the corner and pushed his hands inside his pockets. "All set?"

"Yeah, let's go," Abby said, taking Parker's arm.

I fantasized about running up behind him and shoving my elbow in the back of his head, but then Abby turned and saw me staring him down.

Stop it, she mouthed. She walked with Parker, and he held the door open for her. A wide smile spread across her face in appreciation.

Of course. When he did it, she noticed.

CHAPTER ELEVEN
Cold Bitch

RIDING HOME ALONE IN THE BACKSEAT OF SHEPLEY'S Charger was less than thrilling. America kicked off her heels and giggled as she poked Shepley's cheek with her big toe. He must have been crazy in love with her, because he just smiled, amused by her infectious laughter.

My phone rang. It was Adam. "I got a rookie lined up in an hour. Bottom of Hellerton."

"Yeah, uh . . . I can't."

"What?"

"You heard me. I said I can't."

"Are you sick?" Adam asked, the anger rising in his voice.

"No. I gotta make sure Pidge gets home okay."

"I went to a lot of trouble to set this up, Maddox."

"I know. I'm sorry. Gotta go."

When Shepley pulled into his parking spot in front of the apartment and Parker's Porsche was nowhere to be found, I sighed.

"You coming, cuz?" Shepley asked, turning around in his seat.

"Yeah," I said, looking down at my hands. "Yeah, I guess."

Shepley pulled his seat forward to let me out, and I stopped just short of America's tiny frame.

"You have nothing to worry about, Trav. Trust me."

I nodded once, and then followed them up the stairs. They went straight into Shepley's bedroom and shut the door. I fell into the recliner, listening to America's incessant giggling, and trying not to imagine Parker putting his hand on Abby's knee—or thigh.

Less than ten minutes later, a car engine purred outside, and I made my way to the door, holding the knob. I could hear two pairs of feet walking up the stairs. One set was heels. A wave of relief washed over me. Abby was home.

Only their murmuring filtered through the door. When it got quiet and the knob turned, I twisted it the rest of the way and opened it quickly.

Abby fell through the threshold, and I grabbed her arm. "Easy there, Grace."

She immediately turned to see the expression on Parker's face. It was strained, like he didn't know what to think, but he recovered quickly, pretending to look past me into the apartment.

"Any humiliated, stranded girls in there I need to give a ride?"

I glared at him. He had some damn nerve. "Don't start with me."

Parker smiled and winked at Abby. "I'm always giving him a hard time. I don't get to quite as often since he's realized it's easier if he can get them to drive their own cars."

"I guess that does simplify things," Abby said, turning to me with an amused smile.

"Not funny, Pidge."

"*Pidge?*" Parker asked.

Abby shifted nervously. "It's uh . . . short for Pigeon. It's just a nickname, I don't even know where he came up with it."

"You're going to have to fill me in when you find out. Sounds like a good story." Parker smiled. "Night, Abby."

"Don't you mean good morning?" she asked.

"That, too," he called back with a smile that made me want to puke.

Abby was busy swooning, so to snap her back to reality, I slammed the door without warning. She jerked back.

"*What?*" she snapped.

I stomped down the hall to the bedroom, with Abby on my tail. She stopped just inside the door, hopping on one foot, trying to take off her heel. "He's nice, Trav."

I watched her struggle to balance on one leg, and then finally decided to help before she fell over. "You're gonna hurt yourself," I said, hooking my arm around her waist with one hand, and pulling off her heels with the other. I pulled off my shirt and threw it into the corner.

To my surprise, Abby reached behind her back to unzip her dress, slipped it down, and then yanked a T-shirt over her head. She did some sort of magic bra trick to get it off and out of her shirt. All women seemed to know the same maneuver.

"I'm sure there's nothing I have that you haven't seen before," she said, rolling her eyes. She sat on the mattress, and then pushed her legs between the cover and the sheets. I watched her snuggle into her pillow, and then took off my jeans, kicking them to the corner, too.

She was curled in a ball, waiting for me to come to bed. It irritated me that she'd just rode home with Parker and then un- dressed in front of me like it was nothing, but at the same time, that was just the kind of fucked-up platonic situation we were in, and it was all my doing.

So many things were building up inside of me. I didn't know what to do with them all. When we'd made the bet, it didn't occur to me that she would be dating Parker. Throwing a tantrum would just drive her straight into his arms. Deep down, I knew I'd do anything to keep her around. If keeping a lid on my jealousy meant more time with Abby, that's what I would have to do.

I crawled into the bed beside her and lifted my hand, resting it on her hip.

"I missed a fight tonight. Adam called. I didn't go."

"*Why?*" she asked, turning over.

"I wanted to make sure you got home."

She wrinkled her nose. "You didn't have to babysit me."

I traced the length of her arm with my finger. She was so warm. "I know. I guess I still feel bad about the other night."

"I told you I didn't care."

"Is that why you slept on the recliner? Because you didn't care?"

"I couldn't fall asleep after your . . . *friends* left."

"You slept just fine in the recliner. Why couldn't you sleep with me?"

"You mean next to a guy who still smelled like the pair of barflies he had just sent home? I don't know! How selfish of me!"

I recoiled, trying to keep the visual out of my head. "I said I was sorry."

"And I said I didn't care. Good night," she said, turning over.

I reached across the pillow to put my hand on hers, caressing the insides of her fingers. I leaned over and kissed her hair. "As worried as I was that you'd never speak to me again . . . I think it's worse that you're indifferent."

"What do you want from me, Travis? You don't want me to be upset about what you did, but you want me to care. You tell America that you don't want to date me, but you get so pissed off when I say the same thing that you storm out and get ridiculously drunk. You don't make any sense."

Her words surprised me. "Is that why you said those things to America? Because I said I wouldn't date you?"

Her expression was a combination of shock and anger. "No, I meant what I said. I just didn't mean it as an insult."

"I just said that because I don't want to ruin anything. I wouldn't even know how to go about being who you deserve. I was just trying to get it worked out in my head."

Saying the words made me feel sick, but they had to be said.

"Whatever that means. I have to get some sleep. I have a date tonight."

"With Parker?"

"Yes. Can I please go to sleep?"

"Sure," I said, shoving myself off the bed. Abby didn't say a word as I left her behind. I sat in the recliner, switching on the television. So much for keeping my temper in check, but damn that woman got under my skin. Talking to her was like having a conversation with a black hole. It didn't matter what I said, even the few times that I was clear about my feelings. Her selective hearing was infuriating. I couldn't get through to her, and being direct just seemed to make her angry.

The sun came up half an hour later. Despite my residual anger, I was able to drift off.

A few moments later, my phone rang. I scrambled to find it, still half asleep, and then held it to my ear. "Yeah?"

"Asshat!" Trenton said, loud in my ear.

"What time is it?" I asked, looking at the TV. Saturday morning cartoons were on.

"Ten something. I need your help with Dad's truck. I think it's the ignition module. It's not even turning over."

"Trent," I said through a yawn. "I don't fucking know about cars. That's why I have a bike."

"Then ask Shepley. I have to go to work in an hour, and I don't want to leave Dad stranded."

I yawned again. "Fuck, Trent, I pulled an all-nighter. What's Tyler doing?"

"Get your ass over here!" he yelled before hanging up.

I tossed my cell to the couch and then stood, looking at the clock on the television. Trent wasn't far off when he guessed the time. It was 10:20.

Shepley's door was closed, so I listened for a minute before I knocked twice and popped my head in. "Hey. Shep. Shepley!"

"What?" Shepley said. His voice sounded like he'd swallowed gravel and chased it with acid.

"I need your help."

America whimpered but didn't stir.

"With what?" Shepley asked. He sat up, grabbing a T-shirt off the floor and slipping it over his head.

"Dad's truck didn't start. Trent thinks it's the ignition."

Shepley finished getting dressed and then leaned over America. "Going to Jim's for a few hours, baby."

"Hmmm?"

Shepley kissed her forehead. "I'm going to help Travis with Jim's truck. I'll be back."

"Okay," America said, falling back asleep before Shepley left the room. He slipped on the pair of sneakers that were in the living room and grabbed his keys.

"You coming or what?" he asked.

I trudged down the hall and into my bedroom, dragging ass like any man that had only four hours of sleep—and not great sleep at that. I slipped on a tank top, and then a hoodie sweat-shirt, and some jeans. Trying my best to walk softly, I gently turned the knob of my bedroom door, but paused before leaving. Abby's back was to me, her breathing even, and her bare legs sprawled in opposite directions. I had an almost uncontrollable urge to crawl in bed with her.

"Let's go!" Shepley called.

I shut the door and followed him out to the Charger. We took turns yawning all the way to Dad's, too tired for conversation.

The gravel driveway crunched under the tires of the Charger, and I waved at Trenton and Dad before stepping out into the yard.

Dad's truck was parked in front of the house. I shoved my hands in the front pockets of my hoodie, feeling the chill in the air. Fallen leaves crunched under my boots as I walked across the lawn.

"Well, hello there, Shepley," Dad said with a smile.

"Hey, Uncle Jim. I hear you have an ignition problem."

Dad rested a hand on his round middle. "We think so . . . we think so." He nodded, staring at the engine.

"What makes you think that?" Shepley asked, rolling up his sleeves.

Trenton pointed to the firewall. "Uh . . . it's melted. That was my first clue."

"Good catch," Shepley said. "Me and Trav will run up to the parts store and pick up a new one. I'll put it in and you'll be good to go."

"In theory," I said, handing Shepley a screwdriver.

He unscrewed the bolts of the ignition module and then pulled it off. We all stared at the melted casing.

Shepley pointed to the bare spot where the ignition module was. "We're going to have to replace those wires. See the burn marks?" he asked, touching the metal. "The wire insulation is melted, too."

"Thanks, Shep. I'm gonna go shower. I've gotta get ready for work," Trenton said.

Shepley used the screwdriver to assist in a sloppy salute to Trenton, and then he threw it into the toolbox.

"You boys look like you had a long night," Dad said.

Half of my mouth pulled up. "We did."

"How's your young lady? America?"

Shepley nodded, a wide grin creeping across his face. "She's good, Jim. She's still asleep."

Dad laughed once and nodded. "And your young lady?"

I shrugged. "She's got a date with Parker Hayes tonight. She's not exactly mine, Dad."

Dad winked. "Yet."

Shepley's expression fell. He was fighting a frown.

"What's this, Shep? You don't approve of Travis's pigeon?"

Dad's flippant use of Abby's nickname caught Shepley off guard, and his mouth twitched, threatening a smile. "No, I like Abby just fine. She's just the closest thing America has to a sister. Makes me nervous."

Dad nodded emphatically. "Understandable. I think this one's different, though, don't you?"

Shepley shrugged. "That's kind of the point. Don't really want Trav's first broken heart to be America's best friend. No offense, Travis."

I frowned. "You don't trust me at all, do you?"

"It's not that. Well, it's kind of that."

Dad touched Shepley's shoulder. "You're afraid, since this is Travis's first attempt at a relationship, he's going to screw it up, and that screws things up for you."

Shepley grabbed a dirty rag and wiped his hands. "I feel bad for admitting it, but yeah. Even though I'm rooting for you, bro, I really am."

Trenton let the screen door slam when he jogged out of the house. He punched me in the arm before I even saw him raise a fist.

"Later, losers!" Trenton stopped, and turned on his heels. "I didn't mean you, Dad."

Dad offered a half smile and shook his head. "Didn't think you did, son."

Trent smiled, and then hopped into his car—a dark red, dilapidated Dodge Intrepid. That car wasn't even cool when we were in high school, but he loved it. Mostly because it was paid off.

A small black puppy barked, turning my attention to the house.

Dad smiled, patting his thigh. "Well, c'mon, scaredy-cat."

The puppy took a couple of steps forward, and then backed into the house, barking.

"How's he doing?" I asked.

"He's pissed in the bathroom twice."

I made a face. "Sorry."

Shepley laughed. "At least he's got the right idea."

Dad nodded and waved with concession.

"Just until tomorrow," I said.

"It's fine, son. He's been entertaining us. Trent enjoys him."

"Good." I smiled.

"Where were we?" Dad asked.

I rubbed my arm where it throbbed from Trent's fist. "Shepley was just reminding me of what a failure he thinks I am when it comes to girls."

Shepley laughed once. "You're a lot of things, Trav. A failure is not one of them. I just think you have a long way to go, and between your and Abby's tempers, the odds are against you."

My body tensed, and I stood straight. "Abby doesn't have a bad temper."

Dad waved me away. "Calm down, squirt. He's not bad-mouthing Abby."

"She doesn't."

"Okay," Dad said with a small smile. He always knew how to handle us boys when things got tense, and he usually tried to mollify us before we were too far gone.

Shepley threw the dirty rag on top of the toolbox. "Let's go get that part."

"Let me know how much I owe you."

I shook my head. "I got it, Dad. We're even for the dog."

Dad smiled and started to pick up the mess Trenton left of the toolbox. "Okay, then. I'll see you in a bit."

Shepley and I left in the Charger, heading to the parts store. A cold front had come through. I clenched the ends of my sleeves in my fists to help keep my hands warm.

"It's a cold bitch today," Shepley said.

"Getting there."

"I think she's going to like the puppy."

"Hope so."

After a few more blocks of silence, Shepley nodded his head. "I didn't mean to insult Abby. You know that, right?"

"I know."

"I know how you feel about her, and I really do hope it works out. I'm just nervous."

"Yep."

Shepley pulled into the parking lot of O'Reilly's and parked, but he didn't turn off the ignition. "She's going on a date with Parker Hayes tonight, Travis. How do you think it's going to go when he picks her up? Have you thought about it?"

"I'm trying not to."

"Well, maybe you should. If you really want this to work, you need to stop reacting the way you want, and react the way that will work for you."

"Like how?"

"Do you think it's going to win you any points if you're pouting while she's getting ready, and then act like a dick to Parker? Or do you think she'll appreciate it if you tell her how amazing she looks and tell her goodbye, like a friend would?"

"I don't want to be just her friend."

"I know that, and you know that, and Abby probably knows it, too . . . and you can be damn sure Parker knows it."

"Do you have to keep saying that fuck stick's name?"

Shepley turned off the ignition. "C'mon, Trav. You and I both know as long as you keep showing Parker he's doing something to drive you nuts, he's going to keep playing the game. Don't give him the satisfaction, and play the game better than he does. He'll show his ass, and Abby will get rid of him on her own."

I thought about what he was saying, and then glanced over at him. "You . . . really think so?"

"Yes, now let's get that part to Jim and get home before America wakes up and blows up my phone because she doesn't remember what I told her when I left."

I laughed and followed Shepley into the store. "He is a fuck stick, though."

It didn't take Shepley long to find the part he was looking for, and not much longer for him to replace it. In just over an hour, Shepley had installed the ignition module, started the truck, and had a sufficiently long visit with Dad. By the time we were waving goodbye as the Charger backed out of the driveway, it was just a few minutes after noon.

As Shepley predicted, America was already awake by the time we made it back to the apartment. She tried to act irritated before Shepley explained our absence, but it was obvious she was just glad to have him home.

"I've been so bored. Abby is still asleep."

"Still?" I asked, kicking off my boots.

America nodded and made a face. "The girl likes her sleep. Unless she gets insanely drunk the night before, she sleeps forever. I've stopped trying to turn her into a morning person."

The door creaked as I slowly pushed it open. Abby was on her stomach, in almost the same position she was in when I left, just on the other side of the bed. Part of her hair was matted against her face, the other in soft, caramel waves across my pillow.

Abby's T-shirt was bunched around her waist, exposing her light blue panties. They were just cotton, not particularly sexy, and she looked comatose, but even so, seeing her crashed haphazardly on my white sheets with the afternoon sun pouring in through the windows, her beauty was indescribable.

"Pidge? You gonna get up today?"

She mumbled and then turned her head. I took a few more steps, deeper into the room.

"Pigeon."

"Hep . . . merf . . . furfon . . . shaw."

America was right. She wasn't waking up anytime soon. I closed the door softly behind me, and then joined Shepley and America in the living room. They were picking at a plate of nachos America had made, watching something girly on TV.

"She up?" America asked.

I shook my head, sitting in the recliner. "Nope. She was talking about something, though."

America smiled, her lips sealed to keep food from falling out. "She does that," she said, her mouth full. "I heard you leave your bedroom last night. What was that about?"

"I was being an ass."

America's brows shot up. "How so?"

"I was frustrated. I pretty much told her how I felt and it was like it went in one ear and out the other."

"How *do* you feel?" she asked.

"Tired at the moment."

A chip flew at my face but fell short, landing on my shirt. I picked it up and popped it in my mouth, crunching the beans, cheese, and sour cream. It wasn't half bad.

"I'm serious. What did you say?"

I shrugged. "I don't remember. Something about being who she deserved."

"Aw," America said, sighing. She leaned away from me, in Shepley's direction, with a wry smile. "That was pretty good. Even you have to admit."

Shepley's mouth pulled to one side; that was the only reaction she would get from him for that comment.

"You are such a grouch," America said with a frown.

Shepley stood. "No, baby. I'm just not feeling all that great." He grabbed a copy of *Car and Driver* from the end table, and headed for the toilet.

With a sympathetic expression America watched Shepley leave, and then turned to me, her face metamorphosing into disgust. "Guess I'll be using your bathroom for the next few hours."

"Unless you want to lose your sense of smell for the rest of your life."

"I might want to after that," she said, shivering.

America took her movie off pause, and we watched the rest of it. I didn't really know what was going on. A woman was talking something about old cows and how her roommate was a man-whore. By the end of the movie, Shepley had rejoined us, and the main character had figured out she had feelings for her roommate, she wasn't an old cow after all, and the man-whore, now reformed, was angry about some stupid misunderstanding. She just had to chase him down the street, kiss him, and it was all good. Not the worst movie I'd ever seen, but it was still a chick flick . . . and still lame.

In the middle of the day, the apartment was well lit, and the TV was on, albeit on mute. Everything seemed normal, but also empty. The stolen signs were still on the walls, hung next to our favorite beer posters with half-naked hot chicks sprawled in various positions. America had cleaned up the apartment, and Shepley was lying on the couch, flipping through channels. It was a normal Saturday. But something was off. Something was missing.

Abby.

Even with her in the next room, passed out, the apartment felt different without her voice, her playful jabs, or even the sound of her picking at her nails. I'd grown accustomed to it all in our short time together.

Just as the credits of the second movie began to roll, I heard the bedroom door open, and Abby's feet dragging along the floor. The bathroom door opened and closed. She was going to start getting ready for her date with Parker.

Instantly, my temper began to boil.

"Trav," Shepley warned.

Shepley's words from earlier in the day replayed in my head. Parker was playing the game, and I had to play it better. My adrenaline died down, and I relaxed against the couch cushion. It was time to put my game face on.

The whining sound of the bathroom pipes signaled Abby's intent to take a shower. America stood, and then nearly danced into my bathroom. I could hear their voices banter back and forth but couldn't quite make out what they were saying.

I walked softly into the hall, and held my ear close to the door.

"I'm not thrilled about you listening to my girl urinate," Shepley said in a loud whisper.

I held my middle finger up to my lips, and then turned my attention back to their voices.

"I explained it to him," Abby said.

The toilet flushed, and the faucet turned on, and then suddenly Abby cried out. Without thinking, I grabbed the doorknob and shoved it open.

"Pidge?"

America laughed. "I just flushed the toilet, Trav, calm down."

"Oh. You all right, Pigeon?"

"I'm great. Get out." I shut the door again and sighed. That was stupid. After a few tense seconds, I realized neither of the girls knew I was just on the other side of the door, so I touched my ear to the wood again.

"Is it too much to ask for locks on the doors?" Abby asked. "Mare?"

"It's really too bad you two couldn't get on the same page. You're the only girl that could have . . ." She sighed. "Never mind. It doesn't matter, now."

The water turned off. "You're as bad as he is," Abby said, her voice thick with frustration. "It's a sickness . . . no one here makes sense. You're pissed at him, remember?"

"I know," America replied.

That was my cue to get back to the living room, but my heart was beating a million miles an hour. For whatever reason, if America thought it was okay, I felt like I had the green light, that I wasn't a total dick for trying to be in Abby's life.

As soon as I sat on the couch, America came out of the bathroom.

"What?" she asked, sensing something was amiss.

"Nothing, baby. Come sit," Shepley said, patting the empty space next to him.

America happily complied, sprawling out next to him, her torso leaning against his chest.

The hairdryer turned on in the bathroom, and I looked at the clock. The only thing worse than having to be okay with Abby leaving on a date with Parker, was Parker having to wait on Abby in my apartment. Keeping my cool for a few minutes while she got her purse and left was one thing. Looking at his ugly mug while he sat on my couch, knowing he was planning how to get into her pants at the end of the night, was another.

A small bit of my anxiety was relieved when Abby walked out of the bathroom. She wore a red dress, and her lips matched perfectly. Her hair in curls, she reminded me of one of those 1950s pinup girls. But, better. Way . . . *way* better.

I smiled, and it wasn't even forced. "You . . . are beautiful."

"Thank you," she said, clearly taken off guard.

The doorbell rang, and instantly adrenaline surged through my veins. I took a deep breath, determined to keep my cool.

Abby opened the door, and it took Parker several seconds to speak.

"You are the most beautiful creature I've ever seen," he cooed.

Yep, I was definitely going to vomit before I ended up throwing a punch. What a loser.

America's grin spread from one ear to the other. Shepley seemed really happy, too. Refusing to turn around, I kept my eyes on the TV. If I saw the smug look on Parker's face, I would climb over the couch and knock him to the first floor without him hitting a step.

The door closed, and I came forward, my elbows on my knees, my head in my hands.

"You did good, Trav," Shepley said.

"I need a drink."

CHAPTER TWELVE
Virgin

LESS THAN A WEEK LATER, I HAD EMPTIED MY SECOND
bottle of whiskey. Between trying to cope with Abby spending
more and more time with Parker, and her asking me to release
her from the bet so she could leave, my lips were touching the
mouth of the bottle more than they were my cigarettes.

Parker had ruined the surprise of Abby's surprise birthday
party Thursday at lunch, so I had to scramble to move it to Friday night instead of Sunday. I was thankful for the distraction,
but it wasn't enough.

Thursday night, Abby and America were chattering in the
bathroom. Abby's demeanor toward America was a stark contrast to the way she regarded me: she'd barely spoken to me that
evening since I refused to let her out of the bet earlier that day.

Hoping to smooth things over, I popped into the bathroom.
"Wanna grab dinner?"

"Shep wants to check out that new Mexican place downtown
if you guys wanna go," America said, absently combing through
her hair.

"I thought me and Pidge could go alone tonight."

Abby perfected her lipstick. "I'm going out with Parker."

"Again?" I said, feeling my face compress into a frown.

"Again," she lilted.

The doorbell rang, and Abby burst out of the bathroom and rushed across the living room floor to open the front door.

I followed and stood behind her, making a point to give Parker my best death glare.

"Do you ever look less than gorgeous?" Parker asked.

"Based on the first time she came over here, I'm going to say yes," I deadpanned.

Abby held up a finger to Parker, and turned around. I expected her to snap back something shitty, but she was smiling. She threw her arms around my neck and squeezed.

At first I braced myself, thinking she was trying to hit me, but once I recognized she was hugging me, I relaxed, and then pulled her into me.

She pulled away and smiled. "Thanks for organizing my birthday party," she said, genuine appreciation in her voice. "Can I take a rain check on dinner?"

She had the warmth in her eyes I'd missed, but mostly I was surprised that after not speaking to me all afternoon and evening, she was in my arms.

"Tomorrow?"

She hugged me again. "Absolutely." She waved to me as she took Parker's hand and closed the door behind her.

I turned around and rubbed the back of my neck. "I . . . I need a . . ."

"A drink?" Shepley asked, an edge of worry in his voice. He looked to the kitchen. "We're out of everything but beer."

"Then I guess I'm making a trip to the liquor store."

"I'll go with you," America said, jumping up to grab her coat.

"Why don't you drive him in the Charger?" Shepley said, tossing her the keys.

America looked down at the collection of metal in her hand. "You sure?"

Shepley sighed. "I don't think Travis should drive. Anywhere . . . if you get my meaning."

America nodded enthusiastically. "Gotcha." She grabbed my hand. "C'mon, Trav. Let's get you liquored up." I began to follow her out the door, but she stopped abruptly, turning on her heels. "But! You have to promise me something. No fighting tonight. Drowning your sorrows, yes," she said, grabbing my chin and forcing me to nod my head. "Mean drunk, no." She pushed my chin back and forth.

I pulled back, waving her hand away.

"Promise?" She raised one eyebrow.

"Yes."

She smiled. "Then off we go."

My fingers against my lips, my elbow leaning against the door, I watched the world pass my window. The cold front brought with it wild wind, whipping through the trees and bushes, and causing the hanging streetlights to swing back and forth. The skirt of Abby's dress was pretty short. Parker's eyes had better stay in his head if it happened to fly up. The way Abby's bare knees look when she sat next to me in the backseat of the Charger came to mind, and I imagined Parker noticing her soft, shiny skin as I had, but with less appreciation and more salaciousness.

Just as the anger welled up within me, America pulled on the emergency brake. "We're here."

The soft glow of Ugly Fixer Liquor's sign lit the entrance.

America was my shadow down aisle three. It only took me a moment to find what I was looking for. The only bottle that would do for a night like tonight: Jim Beam.

"You sure you wanna go there?" America asked, her voice tinged with warning. "You do have a surprise birthday party to set up tomorrow."

"I'm sure," I said, taking the bottle to the counter.

The second my ass hit the passenger seat of the Charger, I twisted the cap and took a swig, leaning my head back against the headrest.

America watched me for a moment, and then shoved the gear into reverse. "This is going to be fun, I can tell."

By the time we reached the apartment, I'd drunk the whiskey in the neck of the bottle, and made headway at the top.

"You didn't," Shepley said, spotting the bottle.

"I did," I said, taking another swig. "You want some?" I asked, pointing the glass mouth in his direction.

Shepley made a face. "God no. I need to stay sober so I can react fast enough when you go all Travis-on-Jim-Beam on Parker later."

"No, he won't," America said. "He promised."

"I did," I said with a smile, already feeling better. "I promised."

The next hour Shepley and America did their best to keep my mind off things. Mr. Beam did his best to keep me numb. Halfway into hour two, Shepley's words seemed slower. America giggled at the stupid grin on my face.

"See? He's a happy drunk."

I blew air through my lips, and they made a puff sound. "I'm not drunk. Not yet."

Shepley pointed to the diminishing amber liquid. "If you drink the rest of that, you will be."

I held up the bottle, and then looked at the clock. "Three hours. Must be a good date." I lifted the bottle to Shepley, and then touched it to my lips, tilting it all the way back. The rest of the contents passed my numb lips and teeth, and burned all the way to my stomach.

"Jesus, Travis," Shepley said with a frown. "You should go pass out. You don't want to be up when she gets home."

The sound of an engine grew louder as it approached the apartment and then idled outside. I knew the sound well—it was Parker's Porsche.

A sloppy smile spread across my lips. "What for? This is where the magic happens."

America watched me warily. "Trav . . . you promised."

I nodded. "I did. I promised. I'm just going to help her out of the car." My legs were under me, but I couldn't feel them. The back of the couch proved to be a great stabilizer for my drunken attempt at walking.

My hand encompassed the knob, but America gently covered it with her hand. "I'm going to go with you. To make sure you don't break your promise."

"Good idea," I said. I opened the door, and instantly adrenaline burned through the last half of the whiskey. The Porsche rocked once, and the windows were fogged.

Unsure of how my legs moved so fast in my condition, I was suddenly at the bottom of the stairs. America took a fistful of my shirt. As small as she was, she was surprisingly sturdy.

"Travis," she said in a loud whisper. "Abby's not going to let it go too far. Try to calm down, first."

"I'm just going to check that she's okay," I said, taking the few steps to Parker's car. The side of my hand hit the passenger-side window so hard, I was surprised it didn't break. When they didn't open the door, I opened it for them.

Abby was fidgeting with her dress. Her hair a mess and gloss-less lips, a telltale sign of what they'd been doing.

Parker's face tensed. "What the hell, Travis?"

My hands balled into fists, but I could feel America's hand on my shoulder.

"C'mon, Abby. I need to talk to you," America said.

Abby blinked a few times. "About what?"

"Just come on!" America snapped.

Abby looked to Parker. "I'm sorry, I have to go."

Parker shook his head, angry. "No, it's fine. Go ahead."

I took Abby's hand as she stepped from the Porsche, and then kicked the door shut. Abby flipped around and stood between me and the car, shoving my shoulder. "What is *wrong* with you? Knock it off!"

The Porsche squealed out of the parking lot. I pulled my cigs out of my shirt pocket and lit one up. "You can go in, now, Mare."

"C'mon, Abby."

"Why don't you stay, *Abs*," I said. The word felt ridiculous to say. How Parker could utter it with a straight face was a feat in itself.

Abby nodded for America to go ahead, and she reluctantly complied.

I watched her for a moment, taking a drag or two from my cigarette.

Abby crossed her arms. "Why did you do that?"

"*Why?* Because he was mauling you in front of my apartment!"

"I may be staying with you, but what I do, and who I do it with, is *my* business."

I flicked my cigarette to the ground. "You're so much better than that, Pidge. Don't let him fuck you in a car like a cheap prom date."

"I wasn't going to have sex with him!"

I waved my hand toward the empty space where Parker's car sat. "What were you doing, then?"

"Haven't you ever made out with someone, Travis? Haven't you just messed around without letting it get that far?"

That was stupidest thing I'd ever heard. "What's the point in that?" Blue balls and disappointment. Sounded like a ball.

"The concept exists for a lot of people. Especially those that *date.*"

"The windows were all fogged up, the car was bouncing . . . how was I supposed to know?"

"Maybe you shouldn't spy on me!"

Spy on her? She knows we can hear every car that pulls up to the apartment, and she decided that right outside my door was a good place to suck face with a guy I can't stand? I rubbed my face in frustration, trying to keep my cool. "I can't stand this, Pigeon. I feel like I'm going crazy."

"You can't stand *what?*"

"If you sleep with him, I don't wanna know about it. I'll go to prison for a long time if I find out he . . . just don't tell me."

"Travis." She seethed. "I can't *believe* you just said that! That's a big step for me!"

"That's what all girls say!"

"I don't mean the sluts you deal with! I mean *me!*" She held her hand to her chest. "I haven't . . . *ugh*! Never mind." She took a few steps, but I grabbed her arm, turning her to face me.

"You haven't what?" Even in my current state, the answer came to me. "You're a *virgin*?"

"So what?" she said, blushing.

"That's why America was so sure it wouldn't get too far."

"I had the same boyfriend all four years of high school. He was an aspiring Baptist youth minister! It never came up!"

"A youth minister? What happened after all that hard-earned abstinence?"

"He wanted to get married and stay in . . . Kansas. I didn't."

I couldn't believe what Abby was saying. She was almost nineteen, and still a virgin? That was almost unheard of these days. I couldn't remember meeting one since the beginning of high school.

I held each side of her face. "A virgin. I would have never guessed, with the way you danced at the Red."

"Very funny," she said, stomping up the stairs.

I went after her but busted my ass on one of the steps. My elbow cracked against the corner of the concrete stair, but the pain never came. I rolled onto my back, laughing hysterically.

"What are you doing? Get up!" Abby said as she tugged on me until I was upright.

My eyes turned fuzzy, and then we were in Chaney's class. Abby was sitting on his desk wearing something that looked like a prom dress, and I was in my boxer shorts. The room was empty, and it was either dusk or dawn.

"Going somewhere?" I asked, not particularly concerned that I wasn't dressed.

Abby smiled, reaching out to touch my face. "Nope. Not going anywhere. I'm here to stay."

"You promise?" I asked, touching her knees. I spread her legs just enough to fit snugly between her thighs.

"At the end of it all, I'm yours."

I wasn't exactly sure what she meant, but Abby was all over me. Her lips traveled down my neck, and I closed my eyes, in a complete and total state of euphoria. Everything I had worked for was happening. Her fingers traveled down my torso, and I sucked in a bit just as she slipped them between my boxers and settled on my junk.

Whatever awesomeness I'd felt before, it had just been surpassed. I twisted my fingers in her hair, and pressed my lips against hers, wasting no time to caress the inside of her mouth with my tongue.

One of her heels fell to the floor, and I looked down.

"I have to go," Abby said, sad.

"What? I thought you said you weren't going anywhere."

Abby smiled. "Try harder."

"What?"

"Try harder," she echoed, touching my face.

"Wait," I said, not wanting it to end. "I love you, Pigeon."

My eyes blinked slowly. When my eyes focused, I recognized my ceiling fan. My body hurt everywhere, and my head was thumping with every beat of my heart.

From somewhere down the hall, America's excited, shrill voice filled my ears. In contrast, Shepley's low voice was then peppered between America's and Abby's voices.

I closed my eyes, falling into a deep depression. It was just a dream. None of that happiness was real. I rubbed my face, trying to produce enough motivation to drag my ass outta bed.

Whatever party I'd crashed the night before, I hoped it was worth feeling like pulverized meat in the bottom of a trash can.

My feet felt heavy as I dragged them across the floor to pick up a pair of jeans crumpled in the corner. I pulled them on, and then stumbled into the kitchen, recoiling at the sound of their voices.

"You guys are loud as fuck," I said, buttoning my jeans.

"Sorry," Abby said, barely looking at me. No doubt I'd probably done something stupid to embarrass her the night before.

"Who in the hell let me drink that much last night?"

America's face screwed into disgust. "You did. You went and bought a fifth after Abby left with Parker, and killed the whole thing by the time she got back."

Bits of memories came back to me in scrambled pieces. Abby left with Parker. I was depressed. Liquor store stop with America.

"Damn," I said, shaking my head. "Did you have fun?" I asked Abby.

Her cheeks flushed red.

Oh, shit. It must have been worse than I thought.

"Are you serious?" she asked.

"What?" I asked, but the second the word came out, I'd regretted it.

America giggled, clearly amazed at my memory loss. "You pulled her out of Parker's car, seeing red when you caught them making out like high schoolers. They fogged up the windows and everything!"

I pushed my memory as far as it would go into the evening. The making out didn't ring a bell, but the jealousy did.

Abby looked like she was about to blow her top, and I recoiled from her glare.

"How pissed are you?" I asked, waiting for a high-pitched explosion to infiltrate my already throbbing head.

Abby stomped to the bedroom, and I followed her, closing the door softly behind us.

Abby turned. Her expression was different from what I'd seen before. I wasn't sure how to read it. "Do you remember anything you said to me last night?" she asked.

"No. Why? Was I mean to you?"

"No you weren't mean to me! You . . . we . . ." She covered her eyes with her hands.

When her hand went up, a new, shimmering piece of jewelry fell from her wrist to her forearm, catching my eye. "Where'd this come from?" I asked, wrapping my fingers around her wrist.

"It's mine," she said, pulling away.

"I've never seen it before. It looks new."

"It is."

"Where'd you get it?"

"Parker gave it to me about fifteen minutes ago," she said.

Rage welled up within me. The I-need-to-punch-something-before-I'll-feel-better kind. "What the fuck was that douche bag doing *here*? Did he stay the night?"

She crossed her arms, unfazed. "He went shopping for my birthday present this morning and brought it by."

"It's not your birthday, yet." My anger was boiling over, but the fact that she wasn't at all intimidated helped me to keep it in check.

"He couldn't wait," she said, lifting her chin.

"No wonder I had to drag your ass out of his car, sounds like you were . . ." I trailed off, pressing my lips together to keep the rest from coming out. Not a good time to vomit words out of my mouth I couldn't take back.

"What? Sounds like I was *what*?"

I grit my teeth. "Nothing. I'm just pissed off, and I was going to say something shitty that I didn't mean."

"It's never stopped you before."

"I know. I'm working on it," I said, walking to the door. "I'll let you get dressed."

When I reached for the knob, a pain shot from my elbow up my arm. I touched it, and it was tender. Lifting it revealed what I'd suspected: a fresh bruise. My mind raced to figure out what could have caused it, and I recalled Abby telling me she was a virgin, me falling, and laughing, and then Abby helping me to get undressed . . . and then I . . . Oh, God.

"I fell on the stairs last night. And you helped me to bed . . . We," I said, taking a step toward her. The memory of me crashing against her while she stood in front of the closet half naked rushed into my mind.

I had almost fucked her, taken her virginity when I was drunk. The thought of what might have happened made me feel ashamed for the first time since . . . ever.

"No we didn't. Nothing happened," she said, emphatically shaking her head.

I cringed. "You fog up Parker's windows, I pull you out of the car, and then I try to . . ." I tried to shake the memory out of my head. It was sickening. Thankfully, even in my drunken stupor, I'd stopped, but what if I hadn't? Abby didn't deserve for her first time to be like that with anyone, least of all me. Wow. For a while there, I'd really thought I had changed. It only took a bottle of whiskey and the mention of the word *virgin* for me to return to my dick ways.

I turned for the door and grabbed the knob. "You're turning me into a fucking psycho, Pigeon," I growled over my shoulder. "I don't think straight when I'm around you."

"So it's *my* fault?"

I turned. My eyes fell from her face to her robe, to her legs, and then her feet, returning to her eyes. "I don't know. My memory is a little hazy . . . but I don't recall you saying no."

She took a step forward. At first she looked ready to pounce, but her face softened, and her shoulders fell. "What do you want me to say, Travis?"

I glanced at the bracelet, and then back at her. "You were hoping I wouldn't remember?"

"No! I was pissed that you forgot!"

She made No. Fucking. Sense. "*Why?*"

"Because if I would have . . . if we would have . . . and you didn't . . . I don't know why! I just was!"

She was about to admit it. She had to. Abby was pissed at me because she was going to give me her virginity, and I didn't remember what had happened. This was it. This was my moment. We were finally going to get our shit straight, but time was slipping away. Shepley was going to come tell Abby any minute to go run errands with America per our plans for the party.

I rushed toward her, stopping inches away. My hands touched each side of her face. "What are we doin', Pidge?"

Her eyes began at my belt, and then traveled slowly up to my eyes. "You tell me."

Her face went blank, as if admitting deep feelings for me would make her whole system shut down.

A knock on the door triggered my anger, but I stayed focused.

"Abby?" Shepley said. "Mare was going to run some errands; she wanted me to let you know in case you needed to go."

"Pidge?" I said, staring into her eyes.

"Yeah," she called to Shepley. "I have some stuff I need to take care of."

"All right, she's ready to go when you are," Shepley said, his footsteps disappearing down the hall.

"Pidge?" I said, desperate to stay on track.

She took a few steps backward, pulled a few things from the closet, and then slid past me. "Can we talk about this later? I have a lot to do today."

"Sure," I said, deflated.

CHAPTER THIRTEEN
Porcelain

ABBY DIDN'T STAY IN THE BATHROOM LONG. AS A matter of fact, she couldn't leave the apartment fast enough. I tried not to let it throw me. Abby usually spazzed out whenever something serious came up.

The front door shut, and America's car pulled out of the parking lot. Once again, the apartment seemed stuffy and too empty at the same time. I hated being there without her and wondered what I had done before we met.

I walked over to a small plastic bag from the pharmacy that I'd picked up a few days before. I'd uploaded some pics of me and Abby from my phone, and ordered some prints.

The white walls finally had some color. Just as the last picture was tacked in place, Shepley knocked on the door.

"Hey, man."

"Yeah?"

"We've got shit to do."

"I know."

We drove to Brazil's apartment, mostly in silence. When we arrived, Brazil opened the door, holding at least two dozen balloons. The long silver strings blew into his face, and he waved them away, spitting some away from his lips.

"I was wondering if you guys had canceled. Gruver is bringing the cake and liquor."

We walked past him into the front room. Their walls didn't look much different from mine, but their apartment had either come "fully furnished" or they got their couch from the Salvation Army.

Brazil continued, "I had some redshirts grab some food and Mikey's kick-ass speakers. One of the Sigma Cappa girls has some lights we can borrow—don't worry, I didn't invite them. I said it was for a party next weekend. We should be set."

"Good," Shepley said. "America would shit a wildcat if she showed up and we were here with a bunch of sorority girls."

Brazil smiled. "The only girls here will be a few of Abby's classmates and girlfriends of the team. I think Abby's going to love it."

I smiled, watching Brazil spread the balloons across the ceiling, letting the strings hang down. "I think so, too. Shep?"

"Yeah?"

"Don't call Parker until the last minute. That way, we invited him, but if he makes it at all, at least he won't be here the whole time."

"Got it."

Brazil took a breath. "Wanna help me move furniture, Trav?"

"Sure," I said, following him into the next room. The dining room and kitchen were one room, and the walls were already lined with chairs. The counter had a row of clean shot glasses and an unopened bottle of Patrón.

Shepley stopped, staring at the bottle. "This isn't for Abby, is it?"

Brazil smiled, his white teeth standing out against his dark olive skin. "Uh . . . yeah. It's tradition. If the football team is throwing her a party, she's getting the team treatment."

"You can't make her drink that many shots," Shepley said. "Travis. Tell him."

Brazil held up his hand. "I'm not making her do anything. For every shot she drinks, she gets a twenty. It's our present to her." His smile faded when he noticed Shepley's frown.

"Your present is alcohol poisoning?"

I nodded once. "We'll see if she wants to take a birthday shot for twenty bucks, Shep. No harm in that."

We moved the dining table to the side, and then helped the redshirts bring in the food and speakers. One of the guys' girlfriends started spraying air freshener around the apartment.

"Nikki! Knock that shit off!"

She put her hand on her hips. "If you guys didn't smell so bad, I wouldn't have to. Ten sweaty boys in one apartment starts stinking pretty quick! You don't want her walking in here when it smells like a locker room, do you?"

"She's right," I said. "Speaking of that, I need to get back and shower. See you in half an hour."

Shepley wiped his brow and nodded, pulling his cell phone from one jeans pocket, his keys from the other.

He tapped out a quick text to America. Within seconds, his phone beeped. He smiled. "I'll be damned. They're right on schedule."

"That's a good sign."

We rushed back to our apartment. Within fifteen minutes, I was showered, shaved, and dressed. Shepley didn't take much longer, but I kept checking my watch.

"Calm down," Shepley said, buttoning up his green plaid shirt. "They're still shopping."

A loud engine pulled up out front, a car door slammed shut, and then footsteps climbed the iron steps outside our door.

I opened it, and smiled. "Good timing."

Trenton smiled, holding a medium-size box with holes cut into the sides and a lid. "He's been fed, watered, took his daily man crap. He should be good to go for a while."

"You're awesome, Trent. Thanks." I looked past him to see my dad sitting behind the wheel of his pickup. He waved, and I waved back.

Trenton open the lid a bit and grinned. "Be good, little man. I'm sure we'll see each other again."

The puppy's tail banged against the box while I replaced the top, and then took him inside.

"Aw, man. Why my room?" Shepley asked, whining.

"In case Pidge happens to go into mine before I'm ready." I pulled out my cell and dialed Abby's number. The phone buzzed once, and then again.

"Hello?"

"It's dinnertime! Where the hell did you two run off to?"

"We indulged in a little pampering. You and Shep knew how to eat before we came along. I'm sure you can manage."

"Well, no shit. We worry about you, ya know."

"We're fine," she said, a smile in her voice.

America spoke somewhere close to Abby. "Tell him I'll have you back in no time. I have to stop by Brazil's to pick up some notes for Shep, and then we'll be home."

"Did you get that?" Abby asked.

"Yeah. See you then, Pidge."

I hung up and quickly followed Shepley out to the Charger. I wasn't sure why, but I was nervous.

"Did you call the douche bag?"

Shepley nodded, putting his car in gear. "While you were in the shower."

"Is he coming?"

"Later. He wasn't happy that it was late notice, but when I reminded him that it was necessary because of his big fucking mouth, he didn't have much to say after that."

I smiled. Parker had always rubbed me the wrong way. Not inviting him would make Abby unhappy, so I had to go against my better judgment and let Shepley give him a call.

"Don't get drunk and punch him," Shepley said.

"No promises. Park over there, where she won't see," I said, pointing to the side lot.

We jogged around the corner to Brazil's apartment, and I knocked. It was quiet.

"It's us! Open up."

The door opened, and Chris Jenks stood in the doorway with a stupid grin on his face. He weaved back and forth, already drunk. He was the only person I liked less than Parker. No one could prove it, but Jenks was rumored to have slipped something in a girl's drink once at a frat party. Most believed it, since that was the only way he could get laid. No one had come forward to say he had, so I just tried to keep an eye on him.

I shot a glare at Shepley, who raised his hands. He obviously wasn't aware Jenks was going to be there either.

I glanced at my watch, and we waited in the dark with dozens of silver strings in our faces. Everyone was so close together, smashed into the living room waiting for Abby, that just one person's movement made us all list one way or the other.

A few knocks at the door made us all freeze. I was expecting America to walk in, but nothing happened. People were whispering while others were shushing them.

Another knock spurred Brazil into action, and he took several quick steps to the door, swinging it wide open, revealing America and Abby in the doorway.

"HAPPY BIRTHDAY!" we all yelled in unison.

Abby's eyes grew wide, and then she smiled, quickly covering her mouth. America nudged her inside, and everyone gathered around.

As I made my way to Abby, the crowd split. She looked phenomenal, wearing a gray dress and yellow heels. The palms of my hands cupped each side of her smiling face, and I pressed my lips against her forehead.

"Happy birthday, Pigeon."

"It's not 'til tomorrow," she said, smiling at everyone around us.

"Well, since you were tipped off, we had to make some last-minute changes to surprise you. Surprised?"

"Very!"

Finch rushed up to wish her a happy birthday, and America elbowed her side. "Good thing I got you to run errands with me today or you would have shown up looking like ass!"

"You look great," I said, making a show of looking her over. *Great* wasn't the most poetic word I could have used, but I didn't wanna overdo it.

Brazil came over to give Abby a bear hug. "And I hope you know America's Brazil-is-creepy story was just a line to get you in here."

America laughed. "It worked, didn't it?"

Abby shook her head, still grinning and wide-eyed from the shock of it all. She leaned into America's ear and whispered something, and then America whispered back. I was going to have to ask her later what that was about.

Brazil cranked up the volume on the stereo, and everyone screamed. "Come here, Abby!" he said, walking to the kitchen. He picked up the bottle of tequila from the bar, and stood before the shot glasses lined up on the counter. "Happy birthday from the football team, baby girl," he smiled, pouring each shot glass full of Patrón. "This is the way we do birthdays: You turn nineteen, you have nineteen shots. You can drink 'em or give 'em away, but the more you drink, the more of these you get," he said, fanning out a handful of twenties.

"Oh my God!" Abby squealed. Her eyes lit up at the site of so much green.

"Drink 'em up, Pidge!" I said.

Abby looked to Brazil, suspicious. "I get a twenty for every shot I drink?"

"That's right, lightweight. Gauging by the size of you, I'm going to say we'll get away with losing sixty bucks by the end of the night."

"Think again, Brazil," Abby said. She lifted the first shot glass to her mouth and rolled the rim from the side of her bottom lip to the middle of her mouth. Her head tipped back to empty the glass, and then she rolled the rim across the rest of her lip, dropping it into her other hand. It was the sexiest thing I'd ever seen.

"Holy shit!" I said, suddenly turned on.

"This is really a waste, Brazil," Abby said, wiping the corners of her mouth. "You shoot Cuervo, not Patrón."

The smug smile on Brazil's face faded, and he shook his head and shrugged. "Get after it, then. I've got the wallets of twelve football players that say you can't finish ten."

She narrowed her eyes. "Double or nothing says I can drink fifteen."

I couldn't help but smile, and at the same time wondered how in God's name I was going to behave myself if she kept acting like a fucking Vegas hustler. It was hot as hell.

"Whoa!" Shepley cried. "You're not allowed to hospitalize yourself on your birthday, Abby!"

"She can do it," America said, staring at Brazil.

"Forty bucks a shot?" Brazil asked, looking unsure.

"Are you scared?" Abby asked.

"Hell no! I'll give you twenty a shot, and when you make it to fifteen, I'll double your total."

She popped back another shot. "That's how Kansans do birthdays."

The music was loud, and I made sure to dance with Abby to every song she'd agree to. The whole apartment was full of smiling college kids, a beer in one hand, and a shot glass in the other. Abby would veer off occasionally to hammer back another shot, and then return with me to our makeshift dance floor in the living room.

The birthday gods must have been pleased with my efforts, because just when Abby was getting a good buzz, a slow song came on. One of my favorites. I kept my lips close to her ear, singing to her, and leaning back to mouth the important parts I wanted her to understand were from me. She probably didn't catch that part, but that didn't stop me from trying.

I leaned her back, and her arms fell behind her, her fingers nearly touching the floor. She laughed out loud, and then we were upright, swaying back and forth again. She wrapped her arms around my neck and sighed against my skin. She smelled so good, it was ridiculous.

"You can't do that when I start getting into the double-digit shots." She giggled.

"Did I tell you how incredible you look tonight?"

She shook her head and hugged me, laying her head on my shoulder. I squeezed her to me, and buried my face in her neck. When we were like that, quiet, happy, ignoring the fact that we weren't supposed to be anything more than friends, it was the only place I wanted to be.

The door opened, and Abby's arms fell away. "Parker!" she squealed, running over to hug him.

He kissed her lips, and I went from feeling like a king to a man on the edge of murder.

Parker lifted her wrist and smiled, mouthing something to her about that stupid bracelet.

"Hey," America said loudly in my ear. Even though the volume of her voice was louder than normal, no one else could hear.

"Hey," I said back, still staring at Parker and Abby.

"Keep your cool. Shepley said Parker is just stopping by. He has something to do tomorrow morning, so he can't stay long."

"Oh, yeah?"

"Yeah, so keep it together. Take a breath. He'll be gone before you know it."

Abby pulled Parker to the counter, picked up another shot glass, and killed it, slamming it on the counter upside down like the five times before. Brazil handed her another twenty, and she danced into the living room.

Without hesitation, I grabbed her, and we danced with America and Shepley.

Shepley slapped her on the butt. "One!"

America added a second swat, and then the entire party joined in.

At number nineteen, I rubbed my hands together, making her think I was going to bust her a good one. "My turn!"

She rubbed her posterior. "Be easy! My ass hurts!"

Unable to contain my amusement, I reared my hand far above my shoulder. Abby closed her eyes, and after a moment, peeked back. I stopped just short of her ass, and gave her a gentle pat.

"Nineteen!" I yelled.

The guests cheered, and America started a drunken rendition of "Happy Birthday to You." When it got to the part for her name, the entire room sang "Pigeon." It made me kinda proud.

Another slow song came over the stereo, but this time Parker pulled her to the middle of the room for a dance. He looked like a robot with two left feet, stiff and clumsy.

I tried not to watch, but before the song was over, I caught them slip off to the hallway. My eyes met America's. She smiled, winked, and shook her head, silently telling me not to do anything stupid.

She was right. Abby wasn't alone with him for more than five minutes before they were walking to the front door.

The uncomfortable, embarrassed expression on Abby's face told me that Parker had tried to make those few minutes memorable.

He kissed her cheek, and then Abby shut the door behind him.

"Daddy's gone!" I yelled, pulling Abby to the center of the living room. "Time to get the party started!"

The room exploded into cheering.

"Hang on! I'm on a schedule!" Abby said, walking into the kitchen. She took another shot.

Seeing how many she had left, I grabbed one from the end and drank it. Abby took another shot, so I did the same.

"Seven more, Abby," Brazil said, handing her more cash.

The next hour we danced, laughed, and talked about nothing particularly important. Abby's lips were locked in a smile, and I couldn't help but stare at her all night.

Once in a while, I thought I'd catch her glance at me, and it made me wonder what would happen when we got back to the apartment.

Abby took her time drinking the next few shots, but by her tenth, she was in bad shape. She danced on the couch with America, bouncing and giggling, but then lost her balance.

I caught her before she fell.

"You've made your point," I said. "You've drunk more than any girl we've ever seen. I'm cutting you off."

"The hell you are," she said, slurring her words. "I have six hundred bucks waiting on me at the bottom of that shot glass, and you of all people aren't going to tell me I can't do something extreme for cash."

"If you're that hard up for money, Pidge . . ."

"I'm not borrowing money from you," she sneered.

"I was gonna suggest pawning that bracelet." I smiled.

She smacked me on the arm just as America started the countdown to midnight. When the hands of the clock superimposed on the twelve, we all celebrated.

I had never wanted to kiss a girl so much in my life.

America and Shepley beat me to it, kissing each of her cheeks. I lifted her off the ground, twirling her around.

"Happy birthday, Pigeon," I said, trying very hard not to press my lips against hers.

Everyone at the party knew what she was up to in the hall with Parker. It would be pretty shitty of me to make her look bad in front of them.

She watched me with her big gray eyes, and I melted inside of them.

"Shots!" she said, stumbling to the kitchen.

Her shout startled me, bringing all the noise and motion around us back into my reality again.

"You look torn up, Abby. I think it's time to call it a night," Brazil said when she arrived at the counter.

"I'm not a quitter," she said. "I wanna see my money."

I joined her as Brazil placed a twenty under the last two glasses. He yelled at his teammates, "She's gonna drink 'em! I need fifteen!"

They all groaned and rolled their eyes, pulling out their wallets to stack a pile of twenties behind the last shot glass.

"I would have never believed that I could lose fifty bucks on a fifteen-shot bet with a girl," Chris complained.

"Believe it, Jenks," she said, picking up a glass in each hand.

She knocked back each of the glasses, one at a time, but then paused.

"Pigeon?" I asked, taking a step in her direction.

She raised a finger, and Brazil smiled. "She's going to lose it," he said.

"No, she won't." America shook her head. "Deep breath, Abby."

She closed her eyes and inhaled, picking up the last shot remaining on the counter.

"Holy God, Abby! You're going to die of alcohol poisoning!" Shepley cried.

"She's got this," America assured him.

She tipped her head back, and let the tequila flow down her throat. The entire party erupted into whistles and yells behind us as Brazil handed her the stack of money.

"Thank you," she said with pride, tucking the money away in her bra.

I'd never seen anything like it in my life. "You are incredibly sexy right now," I said in her ear as we walked to the living room.

She wrapped her arms around me, probably letting the tequila settle.

"You sure you're okay?"

She meant to say "I'm fine," but the words came out garbled.

"You need to make her go throw up, Trav. Get some of that out of her system."

"God, Shep. Leave her alone. She's fine," America said, annoyed.

Shepley's brows pulled in. "I'm just trying to keep something really bad from happening."

"Abby? You okay?" America asked.

Abby managed a smile, looking half asleep.

America looked at Shepley. "Just let it run through her system, she'll sober up. It's not her first rodeo. Calm down."

"Unbelievable," Shepley said. "Travis?"

I touched my cheek to Abby's forehead. "Pidge? You want to play it safe and purge?"

"No," she said. "I wanna dance." She wrapped her arms around me tighter.

I looked at Shepley and shrugged. "As long as she's up and moving . . ."

Unhappy, Shepley barreled through the crowd on the make-shift dance floor until he was out of sight. America clicked her tongue and rolled her eyes, and then followed after him.

Abby pressed her body against mine. Even though the song was fast, we were slow dancing in the middle of the room, surrounded by people bouncing around and waving their arms. Blue, purple, and green lights danced with us, on the floor and along the walls. The blue lights reflected on Abby's face, and I had to really concentrate through the liquor not to kiss her.

When the party began to wind down a few hours later, Abby and I were still on the dance floor. She had sobered up a bit after I fed her some crackers and cheese, and tried to dance with America to some stupid pop song, but other than that, Abby was in my arms, her wrists locked behind my neck.

The bulk of the party had either left or passed out somewhere in the apartment, and Shepley and America's bickering had gradually gotten worse.

"If you're riding with me, I'm leaving," Shepley said, tearing toward the door.

"I'm not ready to leave," Abby mumbled, her eyes half closed.

"I think this night is spent. Let's go home." When I took a step toward the door, Abby didn't move. She was staring at the floor, looking a bit green.

"You're going to throw up, aren't you?"

She looked up at me, her eyes half closed. "It's about that time."

She weaved back and forth a few times before I scooped her up in my arms.

"You, Travis Maddox, are kinda sexy when you're not being a whore," she said, a ridiculous, drunken grin twisting her mouth in different directions.

"Uh . . . thanks," I said, readjusting her so I had a better grip.

Abby touched her palm to my cheek. "You know what, Mr. Maddox?"

"What, baby?"

Her expression turned serious. "In another life, I could love you."

I watched her for a moment, staring into her glassed-over eyes. She was drunk, but just for a moment it didn't seem wrong to pretend that she meant it.

"I might love you in this one."

She tilted her head, and pressed her lips against the corner of my mouth. She'd meant to kiss me, but missed. She pulled back, and then let her head fall against my shoulder.

I looked around, and everyone still conscious was frozen, staring in shock at what they'd just witnessed.

Without a word, I carried her out of the apartment to the Charger, where America stood, her arms crossed.

Shepley gestured to Abby. "Look at her! She's your friend, and you let her do something insanely dangerous! You encouraged it!"

America pointed at herself. "I know her, Shep! I've seen her do way more than that for money!"

I shot her a glance.

"Shots. I've seen her do more shots for money," she qualified. "You know what I mean."

"Listen to yourself!" Shepley yelled. "You followed Abby all the way from Kansas to keep her out of trouble. Look at her! She has a dangerous level of alcohol in her system, and she is unconscious! That isn't behavior you should be okay with!"

America's eyes narrowed. "Oh! Thanks for the public service announcement about what not to do in college, Mr. Eighteen-year-old-frat-boy-with-eleventy-billion-'serious'-girlfriends-under-his-belt!" She used her fingers to mark invisible quotations when she said *serious*.

Shepley's mouth popped open, unamused. "Get in the fucking car. You're a mean drunk."

America laughed. "You haven't seen me mean, mama's boy!"

"I told you we're close!"

"Yeah, so are me and my asshole! Doesn't mean I'm going to call it twice a day!"

"You're a bitch!"

All color left America's face. "Take. Me. Home."

"I'd love to, if you'd *get in the fucking car!*" Shepley screamed the last bit. His face turned red, and veins were popping out on his neck.

America opened the door and climbed into the back, leaving the door open. She helped me slide Abby in beside her, and then I fell into the passenger seat.

The ride home was short and completely silent. When Shepley pulled into his parking spot and threw the shifter in Park, I scrambled out of the car and pulled the seat forward.

Abby's head was on America's shoulder, her hair covering her face. I reached in and pulled Abby out, throwing her over my shoulder. America crawled out quickly after, and she walked straight to her car, pulling her keys from her purse.

"Mare," Shepley said, regret already obvious from the break of his voice.

America sat in the driver's seat, slammed the door in Shepley's face, and then backed away.

Abby was ass up, her arms dangling behind me.

"She's gotta come back for Abby, right?" Shepley asked, his face desperate.

Abby moaned, and then her body lurched. The awful groan/growl that always accompanied vomit preceded a splashing sound. The back of my legs felt wet.

"Tell me she didn't," I said, frozen.

Shepley bent back for a second, and then righted himself. "She did."

I jogged up the stairs two at a time, and rushed Shepley as he tried to find the apartment key. He opened it, and I raced into the bathroom.

Abby leaned over the toilet, emptying the contents of her stomach liters at a time. Her hair was already wet with puke from the incident outside, but I grabbed one of those round, black, stretchy things off the sink and pulled her long hair back into a ponytail. The damp pieces clung together in thick clumps, but I pulled it all back with my hands, anyway, and secured it with the black hair holder thingy. I'd seen enough girls twist it and pull their hair back through in class, it didn't take long for me to figure it out.

Abby's body lurched again. I wet a washrag from the hall closet, and then sat back down beside her, holding it against her forehead. She leaned against the tub and groaned.

I gently wiped her face with the wet rag, and then tried to sit still when she lay her head on my shoulder.

"You gonna make it?" I asked.

She frowned, and then gagged, keeping her lips together just long enough to position her head over the toilet. She heaved again, and more liquid splashed into it.

Abby was so small, and the amount she was expelling didn't seem normal. Worry crept into my mind.

I scrambled from the bathroom and returned with two towels, an extra sheet, three blankets, and four pillows in my arms. Abby moaned over the toilet bowl, her body trembling. I fashioned the linens against the tub in a pallet and waited, knowing we would more than likely end up spending the night in that little corner of the bathroom.

Shepley stood in the doorway. "Should I . . . call someone?"

"Not yet. I'm going to keep an eye on her."

"I'm fine," Abby said. "This is me not getting alcohol poisoning."

Shepley frowned. "No, this is *stupid*. That's what this is."

"Hey, you got the uh . . . her uh . . ."

"Present?" he said with one eyebrow up.

"Yeah."

"I got it," he said, clearly unhappy.

"Thanks, man."

Abby fell back against the tub once more, and I promptly wiped her face. Shepley wet a fresh rag and tossed it to me.

"Thanks."

"Yell if you need me," Shepley said. "I'm going to lie awake in bed, trying to think of a way to get Mare to forgive me."

I relaxed against the tub as best I could, and pulled Abby against me. She sighed, letting her body melt into mine. Even

with her covered in vomit, close to her was the only place I
wanted to be. Her words at the party replayed in my mind.

In another life, I could love you.

Abby was lying weak and sick in my arms, depending on me
to take care of her. In that moment I recognized that my feelings
for her were a lot stronger than I thought. Sometime between
the moment we met, and holding her on that bathroom floor, I
had fallen in love with her.

Abby sighed, and then rested her head in my lap. I made
sure she was completely covered with blankets before I let myself nod off.

"Trav?" she whispered.

"Yeah?"

She didn't answer. Her breathing evened out, and her head
fell heavily against my legs. The cold porcelain against my back
and the unforgiving tile under my ass were brutal, but I didn't
dare move. She was comfortable, and she would stay that way.
Twenty minutes into watching her breathe, the parts of me that
hurt started to numb, and my eyes closed.

CHAPTER FOURTEEN

Oz

ALREADY, THE DAY HADN'T STARTED OFF WELL. ABBY
was somewhere with America, trying to talk her out of dumping
Shepley, and Shepley was chewing off his fingernails in the living
room, waiting for Abby to work a miracle.

I'd taken the puppy out once, paranoid that America would
pull up at any moment and ruin the surprise. Even though I'd fed
him and given him a towel to snuggle up with, he was whining.

Sympathy wasn't my strong point, but no one could blame
him. Sitting in a tiny box wasn't anyone's idea of a good time.
Thankfully, seconds before they returned, the little mongrel had
quieted down and gone to sleep.

"They're back!" Shepley said, jumping off the couch.

"Okay," I said, quietly shutting Shepley's door behind me.
"Play it coo—"

Before my sentence was complete, Shepley had opened the
door and run down the stairs. The doorway was a great spot to
watch Abby smile at Shepley and America's eager reconciliation.
Abby shoved her hands into her back pockets and walked to the
apartment.

The fall clouds cast a gray shadow over everything, but Abby's smile was like summertime. With each step she took that brought her closer to where I stood, my heart pounded harder against my chest.

"And they lived happily ever after," I said, closing the door behind her.

We sat together on the couch, and I pulled her legs onto my lap.

"What do you wanna do today, Pidge?"

"Sleep. Or rest . . . or sleep."

"Can I give you your present, first?"

She pushed my shoulder. "Shut up. You got me a present?"

"It's not a diamond bracelet, but I thought you'd like it."

"I'll love it, sight unseen."

I lifted her legs off of my lap and went to retrieve her gift. I tried not to shake the box, hoping the puppy wouldn't wake up and make any noises to tip her off. "Ssshhhh, little man. No crying, okay? Be a good boy."

I sat the box at her feet, crouching behind it. "Hurry, I want you to be surprised."

"*Hurry?*" she asked, lifting the lid. Her mouth fell open. "A *puppy?*" she shrieked, reaching into the box. She lifted the puppy to her face, trying to keep hold of it as it wiggled and stretched its neck, desperate to cover her mouth with kisses.

"You like him?"

"Him? I love him! You got me a puppy!"

"It's a cairn terrier. I had to drive three hours to pick him up Thursday after class."

"So when you said you were going with Shepley to take his car to the shop . . ."

"We went to get your present." I nodded.

"He's wiggly!" She laughed.

"Every girl from Kansas needs a Toto," I said, trying to keep the fur ball from falling off her lap.

"He does look like Toto! That's what I'm going to call him," she said, wrinkling her nose at him.

She was happy, and that made me happy.

"You can keep him here. I'll take care of him for you when you're back at Morgan, and it's my security that you'll visit when your month is up."

"I would have come back anyway, Trav."

"I'd do anything for that smile that's on your face right now."

My words made her pause, but she quickly turned her attention back to the dog. "I think you need a nap, Toto. Yes, you do."

I nodded, pulled her onto my lap, and then lifted her with me as I stood. "Come on, then."

I carried her to the bedroom, pulled back the covers, and then lowered her to the mattress. The action itself would have been a turn-on, but I was too tired. I reached over her to pull the curtains closed, and then fell onto my pillow.

"Thanks for staying with me last night," she said, her voice a bit hoarse and sleepy. "You didn't have to sleep on the bathroom floor."

"Last night was one of the best nights of my life."

She turned to shoot me a dubious look. "Sleeping in between the toilet and the tub on a cold, hard tile floor with a vomiting idiot was one of your best nights? That's sad, Trav."

"No, sitting up with you when you were sick, and you falling asleep in my lap, was one of my best nights. It wasn't comfortable, I didn't sleep worth a shit, but I brought in your nineteenth birthday with you, and you're actually pretty sweet when you're drunk."

"I'm sure between the heaving and purging I was very charming."

I pulled her close, patting Toto, who was snuggled up to her neck. "You're the only woman I know that still looks incredible with your head in the toilet. That's saying something."

"Thanks, Trav. I won't make you babysit me again."

I leaned against my pillow. "Whatever. No one can hold your hair back like I can."

She giggled and closed her eyes. As tired as I was, it was difficult to stop watching her. Her face was makeup free except for the thin skin under her lower lashes that was still a little stained with mascara. She fidgeted a bit before her shoulders relaxed.

I blinked a few times, my eyes getting heavier each time they closed. It seemed I'd just fallen asleep when I heard the doorbell.

Abby didn't even stir.

Two male voices murmured in the living room, one of them Shepley's. America's voice was a high-pitched break between the two, but none of them sounded happy. Whoever it was wasn't just making a social call.

Footsteps sounded in the hall, and then the door blew open. Parker stood in the doorway. He looked at me, and then at Abby, his jaw tense.

I knew what he thought, and it crossed my mind to explain why Abby was in my bed, but I didn't. Instead I reached over and rested my hand on her hip.

"Shut the door when you're finished being in my business," I said, resting my head next to Abby's.

Parker walked away without a word. He didn't slam my door, instead putting his full force behind closing the front door.

Shepley peeked into my room. "Shit, bro. That's not good."

It was done; couldn't change it now. The consequences weren't a concern in the moment, but lying next to Abby, scanning over her perfectly content, beautiful face, the panic slowly crept in. When she found out what I'd done, she would hate me.

THE GIRLS LEFT FOR CLASS THE NEXT MORNING IN A rush. Pidge barely had time to speak to me before she left, so her feelings about the day before were definitely less than clear.

I brushed my teeth and got dressed, and then found Shepley in the kitchen.

He sat on a stool in front of the breakfast bar, slurping milk from his spoon. He wore a hoodie and the pink boxers America had bought him because she thought they were "sexy."

I pulled a glass from the dishwasher and filled it with OJ. "Looks like you two worked it out."

Shepley smiled, looking nearly drunk with contentment. "We did. Have I ever told you what America is like in bed right after we argue?"

I made a face. "No, and please don't."

"Fighting with her like that is scary as hell, but tempting if we make up like that every time." When I didn't answer, Shepley continued. "I'm going to marry that woman."

"Yeah. Well, when you're done being a pansy ass, we need to be on our way."

"Shut your face, Travis. Don't think I'm oblivious to what's going on with you."

I crossed my arms. "And what's going on with me?"

"You're in love with Abby."

"*Pft.* You were obviously making shit up in your head to keep your mind off America."

"You're denying it?" Shepley's eyes didn't flinch, and I tried to look everywhere but into them.

After a full minute, I shifted nervously but remained silent.

"Who's being a pansy ass, now?"

"Fuck you."

"Admit it."

"No."

"No, you're not denying that you're in love with Abby, or no you won't admit it? Because either way, asshole, you're in love with her."

". . . So?"

"I KNEW IT!" Shepley said, kicking the stool back, making it skid to where the wood floor met the rug in the living room.

"I . . . just . . . shut up, Shep," I said. My lips formed a hard line.

Shepley pointed at me while walking to his room. "You just admitted to it. Travis Maddox in love. Now I've heard everything."

"Just put your panties on, and let's go!"

Shepley chuckled to himself in his bedroom, and I stared at the floor. Saying it out loud—to someone else—made it real, and I wasn't sure what to do with it.

Less than five minutes later, I was fiddling with the radio in the Charger while Shepley was pulling out of the parking lot of our apartment complex.

Shepley seemed to be in an exceptionally good mood as we weaved through traffic and slowed down just enough to keep from tossing pedestrians over the hood. He finally found a suitable parking space, and we headed to English Comp II—the one class we shared.

The top row had been me and Shepley's new seating arrangement for several weeks in an attempt to break free of the flock of baggable females that usually crowded my desk.

Dr. Park breezed into the classroom, dumping off a tote bag, a briefcase, and a cup of coffee onto her desk. "Christ! It's cold!" she said, pulling her coat tighter around her tiny frame. "Is everyone here?" Hands shot up, and she nodded, not really paying attention. "Great. Good news. Pop quiz!"

Everyone groaned, and she smiled. "You'll still love me. Paper and pen, people, I don't have all day."

The room filled with the same sound as everyone reached for their supplies. I scribbled my name at the top of my paper and smiled at Shepley's panicked whispers.

"Why? Pop quiz in Comp Two? Fucking ridiculous," he hissed.

The quiz was fairly harmless, and her lecture ended with another paper being due by the end of the week. In the last minutes of class, a guy in the row directly ahead of me craned his neck back. I recognized him from class. His name was Levi, but I only knew that because I'd heard Dr. Park call on him several times. His greasy dark hair was always slicked back, away from his pockmarked face. Levi was never in the cafeteria, or in any fraternity. He wasn't on the football team, either, and never at any parties. Not any that I frequented, anyway.

I looked down at him, and then turned my attention back to Dr. Park, who was sharing a story about the latest visit from her favorite gay friend.

My eyes drifted down again. He was still staring.

"Need something?" I asked.

"I just heard about Brazil's party this weekend. Well played."

"Huh?"

The girl to his right, Elizabeth, turned too, her light brown hair bouncing. Elizabeth was the girlfriend of one of my frat brothers. Her eyes lit up. "Yeah. Sorry I missed that show."

Shepley leaned forward. "What? Me and Mare's fight?"

The guy chuckled. "No. Abby's party."

"The birthday party?" I asked, trying to think of what he could be referring to. Several things had happened that would have the rumor mills churning, but nothing some random guy from oblivion would hear about.

Elizabeth checked to see if Dr. Park was looking in our direction, and then turned back around. "Abby and Parker."

Another girl turned. "Oh, yeah. I heard Parker walked in on you two the next morning. Is it true?"

"You heard where?" I asked, adrenaline screaming through my veins.

Elizabeth shrugged. "Everywhere. People were talking about it in my class this morning."

"Mine, too," Levi said.

The other girl just nodded.

Elizabeth turned around a bit more, leaning in my direction. "Did she really go at it with Parker in Brazil's hallway, and then go home with you?"

Shepley frowned. "She's staying with us."

"No," the girl beside Elizabeth said. "Her and Parker were making out on Brazil's couch, and then she got up, danced with Travis, Parker left all pissed, and she left with Travis . . . and Shepley."

"That's not what I heard," Elizabeth said, visibly trying to contain her enthusiasm. "I heard it was a threesome sort of deal. So . . . which is it, Travis?"

Levi seemed to be enjoying the conversation. "I'd always heard it was the other way around."

"What's that?" I asked, already irritated with his tone.

"Parker getting *your* sloppy seconds."

I narrowed my eyes. Whoever this guy was, he knew way more about me than he should. I leaned down. "That's some more of your fucking business, asshole."

"Okay," Shepley said, putting his hand on my desk.

Levi immediately turned, and Elizabeth's eyebrows shot up before she followed behind him.

"Fucking dirtbag," I grumbled. I looked to Shepley. "Lunch is next. Someone's going to say something to her. They're saying we both bagged her. Fuck. *Fuck*, Shepley what do I do?"

Shepley immediately began shoving his things in his backpack, and I did the same.

"Dismissed," Dr. Park said. "Get the hell out and be productive citizens today."

My backpack thumped against my lower back as I sprinted across campus, making a beeline for the cafeteria. America and Abby came into sight, just a few steps from the entrance.

Shepley grabbed America's arm. "Mare," he puffed.

I grabbed my hips, trying to catch my breath.

"Is there a mob of angry women chasing you?" Abby teased.

I shook my head. My hands were trembling, so I gripped the straps of my backpack. "I was trying to catch you . . . before you . . . went in," I breathed.

"What's going on?" America asked Shepley.

"There's a rumor," Shepley began. "Everyone's saying that Travis took Abby home and . . . the details are different, but it's pretty bad."

"*What?* Are you serious?" Abby cried.

America rolled her eyes. "Who cares, Abby? People have been speculating about you and Trav for weeks. It's not the first time someone has accused you two of sleeping together."

I looked at Shepley, hoping he'd figured a way out of the predicament I'd gotten myself into.

"What?" Abby said. "There's something else, isn't there?"

Shepley winced. "They're saying you slept with Parker at Brazil's, and then you let Travis . . . take you home, if you know what I mean."

Her mouth fell open. "Great! So I'm the school slut now?"

I had done this, and of course it was Abby that was getting the shit end of the stick. "This is my fault. If it was anyone else, they wouldn't be saying that about you." I walked into the cafeteria, my hands in fists at my sides.

Abby sat, and I made sure to sit a few seats across and down from her. Rumors had been spread about me bagging girls before, and sometimes Parker's name was even mentioned, too, but I never cared until now. Abby didn't deserve to be thought of that way just because she was my friend.

"You don't have to sit down there, Trav. Come on, come sit," Abby said, patting the empty table space in front of her.

"I heard you had quite a birthday, Abby," Chris Jenks said, throwing a piece of lettuce onto my plate.

"Don't start with her, Jenks," I warned, glowering.

Chris smiled, pushing up his round, pink cheeks. "I heard Parker is furious. He said he came by your apartment yesterday, and you and Travis were still in bed."

"They were taking a nap, Chris," America sneered.

Abby's eyes darted to me. "Parker came by?"

I shifted uncomfortably in my chair. "I was gonna tell you."

"*When?*" she snapped.

America leaned into her ear, probably explaining what everyone else but Abby knew.

Abby put her elbows on the table, covering her face with her hands. "This just keeps getting better."

"So you guys really didn't do the deed?" Chris asked. "Damn, that sucks. Here I thought Abby was right for you after all, Trav."

"You better stop now, Chris," Shepley warned.

"If you didn't sleep with her, mind if I take a shot?" Chris said, chuckling to his teammates.

Without thinking, I jumped from my seat, and climbed over the table at Chris. His face metamorphosed in slow motion from smiling to wide eyes and an open mouth. I grabbed Chris by the throat with one hand, and a fistful of his T-shirt in the other. My knuckles barely felt the connection with his face. My rage was full blown and I was just short of letting everything fly. Chris covered his face, but I kept whaling on him.

"Travis!" Abby screamed, running around the table.

My fist froze midflight, and then I released Chris's shirt, letting him crumble into a ball on the floor. Abby's expression made me falter; she was afraid of what she'd just seen. She swallowed, and took a step back. Her fear only made me more angry, not at her, but because I was ashamed of myself.

I shouldered past her and shoved through everyone else in my way. Two for two. First, I'd managed to help start a rumor about the girl I was in love with, and then scared her half to death.

The solitude of my bedroom seemed like the only place fit for me. I was too ashamed to even seek the advice of my father. Shepley caught up with me. Without a word, he got into the Charger next to me and started the engine.

We didn't speak as Shepley drove to the apartment. The scene that would inevitably go down when Abby decided to come home was something my mind didn't want to process.

Shepley brought his car to a stop in its usual parking spot, and I got out, walking up the stairs like a zombie. There was no possible good ending. Either Abby was going to leave because she was afraid of what she saw, or even worse—I had to release her from the bet so she could leave, even if she didn't want to.

My heart had been back and forth between leaving Abby alone and deciding it was okay to pursue her more times than a freshly single sorority girl on the second floor of a frat house. Once inside, I threw my backpack against the wall, and made sure to slam the bedroom door behind me. It didn't make me feel better, in fact, stomping around like a toddler reminded me just how much of Abby's time I was wasting by pursuing her—if it could be called that.

The high-pitched hum of America's Honda idled briefly before she cut the engine. Abby would be with her. She would either come in screaming, or the complete opposite. I wasn't sure which would make me feel worse.

"Travis?" Shepley said, opening the door.

I shook my head, and then sat on the edge of the bed. It sank under my weight.

"You don't even know what she's going to say. She could just be checking on you."

"I said no."

Shepley closed the door. The trees outside were brown and beginning to shed what color remained. Soon they would be leafless. By the time the last leaves fell, Abby would be gone. Damn, I felt depressed.

A few minutes later, another knock on the door. "Travis? It's me. Open up."

I sighed. "Walk away, Pidge."

The door creaked when she cracked it open. I didn't turn around. I didn't have to. Toto was behind me, and his small tail was beating my back at the sight of her.

"What is going on with you, Trav?" she asked.

I didn't know how to tell her the truth, and part of me knew she wouldn't hear me, anyway, so I just stared out the window, counting the falling leaves. With each one that detached and floated to the ground, we were one more closer to Abby disappearing from my life. My own natural hourglass.

Abby stood beside me, crossing her arms. I waited for her to yell, or chastise me somehow for the meltdown in the cafeteria.

"You're not going to talk to me about this?"

She began to turn for the door, and I sighed. "You know the other day when Brazil mouthed off to me and you rushed to my defense? Well . . . that's what happened. I just got a little carried away."

"You were angry before Chris said anything," she said, sitting next to me on the bed. Toto immediately crawled into her lap, begging for attention. I knew the feeling. All the antics, my stupid stunts; everything was to somehow get her attention, and she seemed oblivious to it all. Even my crazy behavior.

"I meant what I said before. You need to walk away, Pidge. God knows I can't walk away from you."

She reached for my arm. "You don't want me to leave."

She had no idea how right—and how wrong—she was. My conflicted feelings about her were maddening. I was in love with her; couldn't imagine a life without her in it; but at the same time, I wanted her to have better. With that in mind, the thought of Abby with someone else was unbearable. Neither one of us could win, and yet I couldn't lose her. The constant back and forth made me exhausted.

I pulled Abby against me, and then kissed her forehead. "It doesn't matter how hard I try. You're going to hate me when it's all said and done."

She wrapped her arms around me, linking her fingers around the cusp of my shoulder. "We have to be friends. I won't take no for an answer."

She'd stolen my line from our first date at the Pizza Shack. That seemed like a hundred lifetimes ago. I wasn't sure when things had become so complicated.

"I watch you sleeping a lot," I said, wrapping her in both of my arms. "You always look so peaceful. I don't have that kind of quiet. I have all this anger and rage boiling inside of me—except when I watch you sleep.

"That's what I was doing when Parker walked in. I was awake, and he walked in, and just stood there with this shocked look on his face. I knew what he thought, but I didn't set him straight. I didn't explain because I *wanted* him to think something happened. Now the whole school thinks you were with us both in the same night. I'm sorry."

Abby shrugged. "If he believes the gossip, it's his own fault."

"It's hard to think anything else when he sees us in bed together."

"He knows I'm staying with you. I was fully clothed, for Christ's sake."

I sighed. "He was probably too pissed to notice. I know you like him, Pidge. I should have explained. I owe you that much."

"It doesn't matter."

"You're not mad?" I asked, surprised.

"Is that what you're so upset about? You thought I'd be mad at you when you told me the truth?"

"You should be. If someone single-handedly sunk my reputation, I'd be a little pissed."

"You don't care about reputations. What happened to the Travis that doesn't give a shit what anyone thinks?" she teased, nudging me with her elbow.

"That was before I saw the look on your face when you heard what everyone's saying. I don't want you to get hurt because of me."

"You would never do anything to hurt me."

"I'd rather cut off my arm." I sighed.

I relaxed my cheek against her hair. She always smelled so good, felt so good. Being near her was like a sedative. My entire body relaxed, and I was suddenly so tired, I didn't want to move. We sat together, our arms around each other, her head tucked in against my neck, for the longest time. Nothing beyond that moment was guaranteed, so I stayed there inside of it, with Pigeon.

When the sun began to set, I heard a faint knock at the door.

"Abby?" America's voice sounded small on the other side of the wood.

"Come in, Mare," I said, knowing she was probably worried about why we were so quiet.

America walked in with Shepley, and she smiled at the sight of us tangled in each other's arms. "We were going to grab a bite to eat. You two feel like making a Pei Wei run?"

"*Ugh* . . . Asian *again*, Mare? Really?" I asked.

"Yes, really," she said, seeming a little more relaxed. "You guys coming or not?"

"I'm starving," Abby said.

"Of course you are, you didn't get to eat lunch," I said, frowning. I stood, raising her up with me. "Come on. Let's get you some food."

I wasn't ready to let go of her yet, so I kept my arm around her for the ride to Pei Wei. She didn't seem to mind, and even leaned against me in the car while I conceded to share a number-four meal with her.

As soon as we found a booth, I unloaded my coat beside Abby and went to the bathroom. It was weird how everyone was pretending I hadn't just pummeled someone a few hours ago, like nothing had happened. My hands formed a cup under the water, and I splashed my face, looking into the mirror. The water dripped from my nose and chin. Once again, I was going to have to swallow the dysphoria and go along with everyone else's fake mood. As if we had to keep up pretenses to help Abby move through reality in her little bubble of ignorance where no one felt anything too strongly, and everything was cut-and-dried.

"Damn it! The food's not here yet?" I asked, sliding into the booth next to Abby. Her phone lay on the table, so I picked it up, turned on the camera, made a stupid face, and snapped a picture.

"What the hell are you doing?" Abby said with a giggle.

I searched for my name, and then attached the picture. "So you'll remember how much you adore me when I call."

"Or what a dork you are," America said.

America and Shepley talked most of the time about their classes and the latest gossip, taking care not to mention anyone involved in the scuffle earlier.

Abby watched them talk with her chin rested on her fist, smiling and effortlessly beautiful. Her fingers were tiny, and I caught myself noticing how naked her ring finger looked. She glanced over at me and leaned over to playfully shove me with her shoulder. She then righted herself, continuing to listen to America's chatter.

We laughed and joked until the restaurant closed, and then crowded into the Charger to head home. I felt exhausted, and even though the day seemed long as hell, I didn't want it to end.

Shepley carried America up the stairs on his back, but I stayed behind, tugging on Abby's arm. I watched our friends until they went into the apartment, and then fidgeted with Abby's hands in mine. "I owe you an apology for today, so I'm sorry."

"You've already apologized. It's fine."

"No, I apologized for Parker. I don't want you thinking I'm some psycho that goes around attacking people over the tiniest thing," I said, "but I owe you an apology because I didn't defend you for the right reason."

"And that would be . . . ," she prompted.

"I lunged at him because he said he wanted to be next in line, not because he was teasing you."

"Insinuating there is a line is plenty reason for you to defend me, Trav."

"That's my point. I was pissed because I took that as him wanting to sleep with you."

Abby thought for a moment, and then grabbed the sides of my shirt. She pressed her forehead against my T-shirt, into my chest. "You know what? I don't care," she said, looking up at me with a smile. "I don't care what people are saying, or that you lost your temper, or why you messed up Chris's face. The last thing I want is a bad reputation, but I'm tired of explaining our friendship to everyone. To hell with 'em."

The corners of my mouth turned up. "Our *friendship*? Sometimes I wonder if you listen to me at all."

"What do you mean?"

The bubble she surrounded herself with was impenetrable, and I wondered what would happen if I ever did make it through. "Let's go in. I'm tired."

She nodded, and we walked together up the stairs, and into the apartment. America and Shepley were already murmuring happily in their bedroom, and Abby disappeared into the bathroom. The pipes shrieked, and then the water in the shower beat against the tile.

Toto kept me company while I waited. She didn't waste time; her nightly routine was complete within the hour.

She lay on the bed, her wet hair resting on my arm. She breathed out a long, relaxing breath. "Just two weeks left. What are you going to do for drama when I move back to Morgan?"

"I don't know," I said. I didn't want to think about it.

"Hey." She touched my arm. "I was kidding."

I willed my body to relax against the mattress, reminding myself that for the moment, she was still next to me. It didn't work. Nothing worked. I needed her in my arms. Enough time had been wasted. "Do you trust me, Pidge?" I asked, a little nervous.

"Yeah, why?"

"C'mere," I said, pulling her against me. I waited for her to protest, but she only froze for a few moments before letting her body melt into mine. Her cheek relaxed against my chest.

Instantly, my eyes felt heavy. Tomorrow I would try to think of a way to postpone her departure, but in that moment, sleeping with her in my arms was the only thing I wanted to do.

CHAPTER FIFTEEN
Tomorrow

Two weeks. That was all I had left to either enjoy our remaining time together, or somehow show Abby that I could be who she needed.

I put on the charm; pulled out all the stops; spared no expense. We went bowling, on dinner dates, lunch dates, and to the movies. We also spent as much time at the apartment as possible: renting movies, ordering in, anything to be alone with her. We didn't have a single fight.

Adam called a couple of times. Even though I made a good show, he was unhappy with how short the fights lasted. Money was money, but I didn't want to waste any time away from Pidge.

She was happier than I'd ever seen her, and for the first time, I felt like a normal, whole human being instead of some broken, angry man.

At night we would lie down and snuggle like an old married couple. The closer it came to her last night, the more of a struggle it was to stay upbeat and pretend I wasn't desperate to keep our lives the way they were.

The night before her last night, Abby opted for dinner at the Pizza Shack. Crumbs on the red floor, the smell of grease and spices in the air, minus the obnoxious soccer team, it was perfect.

Perfect, but sad. It was the first place we'd had dinner together. Abby laughed a lot, but she never opened up. Never mentioned our time together. Still in that bubble. Still oblivious. That my efforts were being ignored was at times infuriating, but being patient and keeping her happy were the only ways I had any chance of succeeding.

She fell asleep fairly quickly that night. As she slept just a few inches away, I watched her, trying to burn her image into my memory. The way her lashes fell against her skin; the way her wet hair felt against my arm; the fruity, clean smell that wafted from her lotioned body; the barely audible noise her nose made when she exhaled. She was so peaceful, and had become so comfortable sleeping in my bed.

The walls surrounding us were covered with pictures of Abby's time in the apartment. It was dark, but each one was committed to my memory. Now that it finally felt like home, she was leaving.

The morning of Abby's last day, I felt like I would be swallowed whole by grief, knowing we would pack her up the next morning for Morgan Hall. Pidge would be around, maybe visit occasionally, probably with America, but she would be with Parker. I was on the brink of losing her.

The recliner creaked a bit as I rocked back and forth, waiting for her to wake. The apartment was quiet. Too quiet. The silence weighed down on me.

Shepley's door whined as it open and closed, and my cousin's bare feet slapped against the floor. His hair was sticking up in places, his eyes squinty. He made his way to the love seat and watched me a while from under the hood of his sweatshirt.

It might have been cold. I didn't notice.

"Trav? You're going to see her again."

"I know."

"By the look on your face, I don't think you do."

"It won't be the same, Shep. We're going to live different lives. Grow apart. She'll be with Parker."

"You don't know that. Parker will show his ass. She'll wise up."

"Then someone else like Parker."

Shepley sighed and pulled one leg onto the couch, holding it up by the ankle. "What can I do?"

"I haven't felt like this since Mom died. I don't know what to do," I choked out. "I'm going to lose her."

Shepley's brows pulled together. "So you're done fighting, huh?"

"I've tried everything. I can't get through to her. Maybe she doesn't feel the same way about me that I do about her."

"Or maybe she's just trying not to. Listen. America and I will make ourselves scarce. You still have tonight. Do something special. Buy a bottle of wine. Make her some pasta. You make damn good pasta."

One side of my mouth turned up. "Pasta isn't going to change her mind."

Shepley smiled. "You never know. Your cooking is why I decided to ignore the fact that you're fucking nuts and move in with you."

I nodded. "I'll give it a try. I'll try anything."

"Just make it memorable, Trav," Shepley said, shrugging. "She might come around."

Shepley and America volunteered to pick up a few things

from the grocery store so I could cook dinner for Abby. Shepley even agreed to stop by a department store to pick up some new silverware so we didn't have to use the mix and match shit we had in our drawers.

My last night with Abby was set.

AS I SET OUT THE NAPKINS THAT NIGHT, ABBY CAME AROUND the corner in a pair of holey jeans and a loose, flowing white shirt.

"I have been salivating. Whatever you're making smells so good."

I poured the Alfredo and pasta into her deep plate, and slid the blackened Cajun chicken on top, and then sprinkled over it some diced tomatoes and green onions.

"This is what I've been cooking," I said, setting the plate in front of Abby's chair. She sat down, and her eyes widened, and then she watched me fill my own plate.

I tossed a slice of garlic bread onto her plate, and she smiled. "You've thought of everything."

"Yes, I did," I said, popping the cork on the wine. The dark red liquid splashed a bit as it flowed into her glass, and she giggled.

"You didn't have to do all of this, you know."

My lips pressed together. "Yes. I did."

Abby took a bite, and then another, barely pausing to swallow. A small hum emanated from her lips. "This is really good, Trav. You've been holding out on me."

"If I told you before, you would have expected it every night." The contrived smile I'd somehow managed quickly faded.

"I'm going to miss you, too, Trav," she said, still chewing.

"You're still gonna come over, right?"

"You know I will. And you'll be at Morgan's, helping me study, just like you did before."

"But it won't be the same." I sighed. "You'll be dating Parker, we're going to get busy . . . go in different directions."

"It's not going to change that much."

I laughed once. "Who would have thought from the first time we met that we'd be sitting here? You couldn't have told me three months ago that I'd be this miserable over saying goodbye to a girl."

Abby's face fell. "I don't want you to be miserable."

"Then don't go."

Abby swallowed, and her eyebrows moved in infinitesimally. "I can't move in here, Travis. That's crazy."

"Says who? I just had the best two weeks of my life."

"Me, too."

"Then why do I feel like I'm never gonna see you again?"

She watched me for a moment, but didn't reply. Instead Abby stood up and walked around the breakfast bar, sitting on my lap. Everything in me wanted to look her in the eyes, but I was afraid if I did, I'd try to kiss her, and our night would be ruined.

She hugged me, her soft cheek pressing against mine. "You're going to realize what a pain in the ass I was, and then you'll forget all about missing me," she whispered in my ear.

I rubbed my hand in circles between her shoulder blades, trying to choke back the sadness. "Promise?"

Abby looked into my eyes, touching each side of my face with her hands. She caressed my jaw with her thumb. Thoughts of begging her to stay crossed my mind, but she wouldn't hear me. Not from the other side of her bubble.

Abby closed her eyes and leaned down. I knew she meant to kiss the corner of my mouth, but I turned so that our lips met. It was my last chance. I had to kiss her goodbye.

She froze for a moment, but then her body relaxed, and she let her lips linger on mine.

Abby finally pulled away, playing it off with a smile. "I have a big day tomorrow. I'm going to clean up the kitchen, and then I'm going to head to bed."

"I'll help you."

We did the dishes together in silence, with Toto asleep at our feet. I dried the last dish and set it in the rack, and then reached down for her hand to lead her down the hall. Each step was agony.

Abby pushed down her jeans, and then lifted her shirt over her head. Grabbing one of my T-shirts from the closet, she let the worn gray cotton slide over her head. I stripped down to my boxers like I'd done dozens of times with her in the room, but this time solemnness hung over the room.

We climbed into bed, and I switched off the lamp. I immediately wrapped my arms around her and sighed, and she nestled her face into my neck.

The trees outside my window cast a shadow across the walls. I tried to concentrate on their shapes and the way the light wind changed the shape of their silhouette against the different angles of the wall. Anything to keep my mind off the numbers on the clock, or how close we were to the morning.

Morning. My life was going to change for the worse in just a few hours. Jesus Christ. I couldn't bear it. I squeezed my eyes shut, trying to block that train of thought.

"Trav? Are you okay?"

It took me a while to form the words. "I've never been less okay in my life."

She pressed her forehead against my neck again, and I squeezed her tighter.

"This is silly," she said. "We're going to see each other every day."

"You know that's not true."

Her head tilted just a tiny bit upward. I wasn't sure if she was staring at me, or getting ready to say something. I waited in the darkness, in the silence, feeling like the world was going to crash around me at any second.

Without warning, Abby puckered her lips and touched them to my neck. Her mouth opened as she tasted my skin, and the warm wetness of her mouth lingered in that spot.

I looked down at her, completely taken off guard. A familiar spark burned behind the window of her eyes. Unsure of how it happened, I'd finally gotten through to her. Abby finally realized my feelings for her, and the light had suddenly come on.

I leaned down, pressing my lips against hers, soft and slow. The longer our mouths were melded together, the more over-whelmed I became by the reality of what was happening.

Abby pulled me closer to her. Each movement she made was further affirmation of her answer. She felt the same. She cared about me. She wanted me. I wanted to run around the block screaming in celebration, and at the same time, didn't want to move my mouth from hers.

Her mouth opened, and I moved my tongue inside, tasting and searching softly.

"I want you," she said.

Her words sunk in, and I understood what she meant. One part of me wanted to rip off every piece of fabric between us, the other set off full lights and sirens. We were finally on the same page. No need to rush it now.

I pulled back a bit, but Abby only became more determined. I retreated all the way upright on my knees, but Abby stayed with me.

I gripped her shoulders to hold her at bay. "Wait a sec," I whispered, breathing hard. "You don't have to do this, Pidge. This isn't what tonight is about."

Even though I wanted to do the right thing, Abby's unexpected intensity coupled with the fact that I hadn't been laid in a length of time that was sure to be my all-time record, my dick was proudly standing against my boxers.

Abby leaned in again, and this time I let her come close enough to touch her lips to mine. She looked up at me, serious and resolute. "Don't make me beg," she whispered against my mouth.

No matter how noble I'd intended to be, those words coming from her mouth destroyed me. I grabbed the back of her head and sealed my lips against hers.

Abby's fingers ran down the length of my back and settled on the elastic of my boxers, before seeming to contemplate her next move. Six weeks of pent-up sexual tension overwhelmed me, and we crashed into the mattress. My fingers tangled in her hair as I positioned myself between her open knees. Just as our mouths met again, she slid her hand down the front of my boxers. When her soft fingers touched my bare skin, a low groan erupted. It was the best fucking feeling I could imagine.

The old gray T-shirt Abby wore was the first thing to go.

Thankfully the full moon lit the room just enough that I could appreciate her bare breasts for just a few seconds before I impatiently moved on to the rest of her. My hand gripped her panties, and then slipped them down her legs. I tasted her mouth as I followed the inside line of her leg, and traveled the length of her thigh. My fingers slipped between Abby's soft, wet skin, and she let out a long, faltering breath. Before I went further, a conversation we'd had not too long before replayed in my mind. Abby was a virgin. If this was what she really wanted, I had to be gentle. The last thing I wanted to do was hurt her.

Her knees arched and twitched with each movement of my hand. I licked and sucked different spots on her neck while I waited for her to make a decision. Her hips moved from side to side, and rocked back and forth, reminding me of the way she danced against me at the Red. Her bottom lip pulled in, and she bit it, digging her fingers into my back at the same time.

I positioned myself above her. My boxers were still on, but I could feel her bare skin against me. She was so fucking warm, holding back was the hardest thing I'd ever made myself do. Not even an inch more and I could have pushed through my boxers and been inside her.

"Pigeon," I said, panting, "it doesn't have to be tonight. I'll wait until you're ready."

Abby reached for the top drawer of the nightstand, pulling it open. Plastic crackled in her hand, and then she ripped the square package open with her teeth. That was a green light if I'd ever seen one.

My hand left her back, and I pulled my boxers down, kicking them violently. Any patience I'd had was gone. The only thing I could think about was being inside of her. I slipped the latex on, and then lowered my hips between her thighs, touching the most sensitive parts of my skin to hers.

"Look at me, Pigeon," I breathed.

Her big, round, gray eyes peered up at me. It was so surreal. This was what I had dreamed about since the first time she rolled her eyes at me, and it was finally happening. I tilted my head, and then leaned down to kiss her tenderly. I moved forward and tensed, pushing myself inside as gently as I could. When I pulled back, I looked into Abby's eyes. Her knees held my hips like a vise grip, and she bit her bottom lip harder than before, but her fingers were pressing into my back, pulling me closer. When I rocked into her again, she clenched her eyes shut.

I kissed her, softly, patiently. "Look at me," I whispered.

She hummed, and groaned, and cried out. With each noise she made, it became more difficult to control my movements. Abby's body finally relaxed, allowing me to move against her in a more rhythmic motion. The faster I moved, the less in control I felt. I touched every part of her skin, and licked and kissed her neck, cheek, and lips.

She pulled me into her over and over, and each time I pressed deeper inside.

"I've wanted you for so long, Abby. You're all I want," I breathed against her mouth.

I grabbed her thigh with one hand and propped myself up with my elbow. Our stomachs slid easily against each other as beads of sweat began to form on our skin. I thought about turning her over, or pulling her on top of me, but decided I'd rather sacrifice creativity for being able to look into her eyes, and staying as close to her as I could.

Just when I thought I could make it last all night, Abby sighed.

"Travis."

The sound of her breathing my name unguarded me and put me over the edge. I had to go faster, press farther until every muscle in my body tensed. I groaned and jerked a few times before finally collapsing.

I breathed in through my nose against her neck. She smelled like sweat, and her lotion . . . and me. It was fucking fantastic.

"That was some first kiss," she said with a tired, contented expression.

I scanned her face and smiled. "Your last first kiss."

Abby blinked, and then I fell onto the mattress beside her, reaching across her bare middle. Suddenly the morning was something to look forward to. It would be our first day together, and instead of packing in poorly concealed misery, we could sleep in, spend a ridiculous amount of the morning in bed, and then just enjoy the day as a couple. That sounded pretty damn close to heaven to me.

Three months ago, no one could have convinced me that I would feel that way. Now, there was nothing else I wanted more.

A big, relaxing breath moved my chest up and down slowly as I fell asleep next to the second woman I'd ever loved.

CHAPTER SIXTEEN
Space and Time

A<small>T FIRST, I DIDN'T PANIC. AT FIRST, A SLEEPY HAZE</small> provided just enough confusion to foster a sense of calm. At first, when I reached for Abby across the sheets and didn't feel her there, I felt just a small bit of disappointment, followed by curiosity.

She was probably in the bathroom, or maybe eating cereal on the couch. She'd just given her virginity to me, someone with whom she'd spend a lot of time and effort pretending not to have more than platonic feelings. That was a lot to take in.

"Pidge?" I called. I lifted only my head, hoping she would crawl back in bed with me. But after several moments, I gave in, and sat up.

Having no idea what was in store, I slipped on the boxers I'd kicked off the night before, and slipped a T-shirt over my head.

My feet dragged down the hall to the bathroom door, and I knocked. The door opened a bit. I heard no movement but I called for her, anyway. "Pigeon?"

Opening the door wider revealed what was expected. Empty and dark. I then went into the living room, fully expecting to see her in the kitchen or on the couch, but she was nowhere.

"Pigeon?" I called, waiting for an answer.

Panic started to swell inside of me, but I refused to freak out until I knew what the hell was going on. I stomped into Shepley's room and opened the door without knocking.

America lay next to Shepley, tangled in his arms the way I imagined Abby would have been in mine at that point.

"Have you guys seen Abby? I can't find her."

Shepley raised himself up onto his elbow, rubbing his eye with his knuckle. "Huh?"

"Abby," I said, impatiently flipping on the light switch. Shepley and America both recoiled. "Have you seen her?"

Different scenarios ran through my mind, all causing different degrees of alarm. Maybe she had let out Toto, and someone had taken her, or hurt her, or maybe she'd fallen down the stairs. But Toto's claws were clicking against the floor down the hall, so that couldn't be it. Maybe she went to get something out of America's car.

I rushed to the front door and looked around. Then I jogged down the stairs, my eyes searching every inch between the front door of the apartment and America's car.

Nothing. She'd vanished.

Shepley appeared in the doorway, squinting and hugging himself from the cold.

"Yeah. She woke us up early. She wanted to go home."

I took the stairs back up two at a time, grabbing Shepley's bare shoulders, pushing him back all the way to the opposite side of the room, and grinding him into the wall. He gripped my T-shirt, a half-frowning, half-stunned expression on his face.

"What the—" he began.

"You took her home? To Morgan? In the middle of the fuck-ing night? Why?"

"Because she asked me to!"

I shoved him against the wall again, blinding rage beginning to take over my system.

America came out of the bedroom, her hair ratted and her mascara smeared below her eyes. She was in her robe, tightening the belt around her waist. "What the hell is going on?" she asked, pausing midstep at the sight of me.

Shepley jerked out his arm and held out his hand. "Mare, stay back."

"Was she angry? Was she upset? Why did she leave?" I asked through my teeth.

America took another step. "She just hates goodbyes, Travis! I wasn't surprised at all that she wanted to leave before you woke up!"

I held Shepley against the wall and looked to America. "Was she . . . was she crying?"

I imagined Abby disgusted that she'd allowed some asshole like me, someone she didn't give a shit about, taking her virginity, and then I thought maybe I'd somehow, accidentally hurt her.

America's face twisted from fear, to confusion, to anger. "Why," she said. Her tone was more an accusation than a ques-tion. "Why would she be crying or upset, Travis?"

"Mare," Shepley warned.

America took another step. "What did you do?"

I released Shepley, but he took a fistful of my shirt as I faced his girlfriend.

"Was she crying?" I demanded.

America shook her head. "She was fine! She just wanted to go home! What did you do?" she yelled.

"Did something happen?" Shepley asked.

Without thinking, I flipped around and swung, nearly missing Shepley's face.

America screamed, covering her mouth with her hands. "Travis, stop!" she said through her hands.

Shepley wrapped his arms around mine at the elbows, his face just a couple of inches from mine. "Call her!" he yelled. "Fucking calm down, and call Abby!"

Quick, light footsteps ran down the hall and back. America returned, her hand outstretched, holding my phone. "Call her."

I snatched it from her hand and dialed Abby's number. It rang until the voice mail picked up. I hung up and dialed again. And again. And again. She wasn't answering. She hated me.

I dropped the phone to the ground, my chest heaving. When tears burned my eyes, I picked up the first thing my hands touched, and launched it across the room. Whatever it was splintered into large pieces.

Turning, I saw the stools situated directly across from each other, reminding me of our dinner. I picked one up by the legs and smashed it against the refrigerator until it broke. The refrigerator door popped open, and I kicked it. The force caused it to spring open again, so I kicked it again, and again, until Shepley finally rushed over to keep it closed.

I stomped to my room. The messy sheets on the bed mocked me. My arms flung in every direction as I ripped them off the mattress—fitted sheet, top sheet, and blanket—and then returned to the kitchen to throw them in the trash, and then I did the same with the pillows. Still insane with anger, I stood in my room, willing myself to calm down, but there was nothing to calm down for. I'd lost everything.

Pacing, I stopped in front of the nightstand. The thought of Abby reaching into the drawer came to mind. The hinges squeaked when I opened it, revealing the fishbowl full of condoms. I had barely delved into them since I'd met Abby. Now that she'd made her choice, I couldn't imagine being with anyone else.

The glass was cold in my hand as I picked it up and launched it across the room. It made contact with the wall beside the door and shattered, spraying small foil packages in every direction.

My reflection in the mirror above my dresser looked back at me. My chin was down, and I stared into my eyes. My chest heaved, I was shaking, and by anyone's standards looked insane, but control was so far out of my reach at that point. I reared back and slammed my fist into the mirror. Shards stabbed into my knuckles, leaving behind a bloody circle.

"Travis, stop!" Shepley said from the hall. "Stop it, God dammit!"

I rushed him, pushed him back, and then slammed my door shut. I pressed my hands flat against the wood, and then took a step back, kicking it until my foot made a dent at the bottom. I yanked on the sides until it came off the hinges, and then I tossed it across the room.

Shepley's arms grabbed me again. "I said stop!" he screamed. "You're scaring America!" The vein in his forehead popped out, the one that appeared only when he was enraged.

I shoved him, and he shoved me back. I took another swing, but he ducked.

"I'll go see her!" America pleaded. "I'll find out if she's okay, and I'll have her call you!"

I let my hands fall to my sides. Despite the cold air filling the apartment from the open front door, sweat was dripping from my temples. My chest heaved as if I'd run a marathon.

America ran to Shepley's room. Within five minutes, she was dressed, knotting her hair into a bun. Shepley helped her slip on her coat and then kissed her goodbye, offering a nod of assurance. She grabbed her keys and let the door slam behind her.

"Sit. The fuck. Down," Shepley said, pointing to the recliner.

I closed my eyes, then did what he commanded. My hands shook as I brought them to my face.

"You're lucky. I was two seconds away from calling Jim. And every brother you've got."

I shook my head. "Don't call Dad," I said. "Don't call him." Salty tears burned my eyes.

"Talk."

"I bagged her. I mean, I didn't *bag* her, we . . ."

Shepley nodded. "Last night was tough for both of you. Who's idea was it?"

"Hers." I blinked. "I tried to pull away. Offered to wait, but she all but begged me."

Shepley looked as confused as I felt.

I threw up my hands and let them fall to my lap. "Maybe I hurt her, I don't know."

"How did she act after? Did she say anything?"

I thought for a moment. "She said it was some first kiss."

"Huh?"

"She let it slip a few weeks ago that a first kiss makes her nervous, and I made fun of her."

Shepley's brows pushed together. "That doesn't sound like she was upset."

"I said it was her last first kiss." I laughed once and used the bottom of my T-shirt to pinch the moisture from my nose. "I thought everything was good, Shep. That she had finally let me in. Why would she ask me to . . . and then just leave?"

Shepley shook his head slowly, as confused as I was. "I don't know, cousin. America will find out. We'll know something soon."

I stared at the floor, thinking about what could possibly happen next. "What am I gonna do?" I asked, looking up at him.

Shepley gripped my forearm. "You're going to clean up your mess to keep you busy until they call."

I walked into my room. The door was lying on my bare mattress, pieces of mirror and shattered glass on the floor. It looked like a bomb had gone off.

Shepley appeared in the doorway with a broom, a dustpan, and a screwdriver. "I'll get the glass. You get the door."

I nodded, pulling the large wooden plank from the bed. Just after making the last turn on the screwdriver, my cell phone rang. I scrambled off the floor to snap it up from the night table.

It was America.

"Mare?" I choked out.

"It's me." Abby's voice was small and nervous.

I wanted to beg her back, to beg for her forgiveness, but I wasn't sure what I'd done wrong. Then, I got angry.

"What the fuck happened to you last night? I wake up this morning, and you're gone and you . . . you just leave and don't say goodbye? *Why?*"

"I'm sorry. I—"

"You're *sorry?* I've been going crazy! You don't answer your phone, you sneak out and—wh-*why?* I thought we finally had everything figured out!"

"I just needed some time to think."

"About what?" I paused, afraid of how she might answer the question I was about to ask. "Did I . . . did I hurt you?"

"No! It's nothing like that! I'm really, really sorry. I'm sure America told you. I don't do goodbyes."

"I need to see you," I said, desperate.

Abby sighed. "I have a lot to do today, Trav. I have to unpack and I have piles of laundry."

"You regret it."

"It's not . . . that's not what it is. We're friends. That's not going to change."

"*Friends?* Then what the fuck was last night?"

I could hear her breath catch. "I know what you want. I just can't do that right now."

"So you just need some time? You could have told me that. You didn't have to run out on me."

"It just seemed like the easiest way."

"Easier for who?"

"I couldn't sleep. I kept thinking about what it would be like in the morning, loading Mare's car . . . and I couldn't do it, Trav."

"It's bad enough that you aren't going to be here anymore. You can't just drop out of my life."

"I'll see you tomorrow," she said, trying hard to sound casual. "I don't want anything to be weird, okay? I just need to sort some stuff out. That's all."

"Okay," I said. "I can do that."

The line went silent, and Shepley watched me, wary. "Travis . . . you just got the door hung. No more messes, okay?"

My entire face crumpled, and I nodded my head. I tried to be angry, that was much easier to control than the overwhelming, physical pain in my chest, but all I felt was wave after wave of sadness. I was too tired to fight it.

"What did she say?"

"She needs time."

"Okay. So, that's not the end. You can work with that, right?"

I took a deep breath. "Yeah. I can work with that."

The dustpan jingled with the shards of glass as Shepley walked with it down the hall. Left alone in the bedroom, surrounded by pictures of me and Abby, made me want to break something again, so I went into the living room to wait for America.

Thankfully, it didn't take her long to return. I imagined that she was probably worried about Shepley.

The door opened, and I stood. "Is she with you?"

"No. She's not."

"Did she say anything else?"

America swallowed, hesitating to answer. "She said she'll keep her promise, and that by this time tomorrow, you won't miss her."

My eyes drifted to the floor. "She's not coming back," I said falling to the couch.

America stepped forward. "What does that mean, Travis?"

I cupped the top of my head with both hands. "What happened last night wasn't her way of saying she wanted to be together. She was saying goodbye."

"You don't know that."

"I know her."

"Abby cares about you."

"She doesn't love me."

America took a breath, and any reservations she'd had about my temper vanished as a sympathetic expression softened her face. "You don't know that, either. Listen, just give her some space. Abby isn't like the girls you're used to, Trav. She gets freaked out easy. The last time someone mentioned getting serious she moved an entire state away. This isn't as bad as it seems."

I looked up at America, feeling the tiniest bit hopeful. "You don't think so?"

"Travis, she left because her feelings for you scare her. If you knew everything, it would be easier to explain, but I can't tell you."

"Why not?"

"Because I promised Abby, and she's my best friend."

"Doesn't she trust me?"

"She doesn't trust herself. You, however, need to trust *me*." America grabbed my hands and pulled me to stand. "Go take a long, hot shower, and then we're going out to eat. Shepley told me it's poker night at your dad's."

I shook my head. "I can't do poker night. They'll ask about Pigeon. Maybe we could go see Pidge?"

America blanched. "She won't be home."

"You guys going out?"

"She is."

"With who?" It only took me a few seconds to figure it out. "Parker."

America nodded.

"That's why she thinks I won't miss her," I said, my voice breaking. I couldn't believe she was going to do that to me. It was just cruel.

America didn't hesitate to intercept another rage. "We'll go to a movie, then, a comedy, of course, and then we'll see if the go-kart place is still open, and you can run me off the track again."

America was smart. She knew the go-kart track was one of the few places I hadn't been with Abby. "I didn't run you off the track. You just can't drive worth a shit."

"We'll see," America said, pushing me toward the bathroom. "Cry if you must. Scream. Get it all out of your system, and then we'll have fun. It won't last forever, but it will keep you busy for tonight."

I turned around in the bathroom doorway. "Thanks, Mare."

"Yeah, yeah . . . ," she said, returning to Shepley.

I turned on the water, letting the steam warm the room before stepping in. The reflection in the mirror startled me. Dark circles under my tired eyes, my once confident posture sagging; I looked like hell.

Once in the shower, I let the water run over my face, keeping my eyes closed. The delicate outlines of Abby's features were burned behind my eyelids. It wasn't the first time; I saw her every time my eyes closed. Now that she was gone, it was like being stuck in a nightmare.

I choked back something welling up in my chest. Every few minutes, the pain renewed itself. I missed her. God, I missed her, and everything we'd gone through played over and over inside my head.

My palms flat against the wall of the tile, I clenched my eyes shut. "Please come back," I said quietly. She couldn't hear me, but it didn't stop me from wishing she would come and save me from the terrible pain I felt without her there.

After wallowing in my despair under the water, I took a few

deep breaths, and got myself together. The fact that Abby left shouldn't have been such a surprise, even after what happened the night before. What America said made sense. Abby was just as new at this and as scared as I was. We both had a piss-poor way of dealing with our emotions, and I knew the second I realized I'd fallen for her that she was going to rip me apart.

The hot water washed away the anger and the fear, and a new optimism came over me. I wasn't some loser that had no clue how to get a girl. Somewhere in my feelings for Abby, I'd forgotten that fact. It was time to believe in myself again, and remember that Abby wasn't just a girl that could break my heart; she was also my best friend. I knew how to make her smile, and her favorite things. I still had a dog in this fight.

OUR MOODS WERE LIGHT WHEN WE RETURNED FROM THE go-kart track. America was still giggling about beating Shepley four times in a row, and Shepley was pretending to sulk.

Shepley fumbled with the key in the dark.

I held my cell phone in my hands, fighting the urge to call Abby for the thirteenth time.

"Why don't you just call her already?" America asked.

"She's still on the date, probably. I better not . . . interrupt," I said, trying to push the thought of what might be happening from my mind.

"You shouldn't?" America asked, genuinely surprised. "Didn't you say you wanted to ask her to go bowling tomorrow? It's rude to ask a girl on a date the day of, you know."

Shepley finally found the keyhole and opened the door, letting us inside.

I sat on the couch, staring at Abby's name on my call list.

"Fuck it," I said, touching her name.

The phone rang once, and then again. My heart pounded against my rib cage, more than it ever did before a fight.

Abby answered.

"How's the date goin', Pidge?"

"What do you need, Travis?" she whispered. At least she wasn't breathing hard.

"I wanna go bowling tomorrow. I need my partner."

"*Bowling?* You couldn't have called me later?" She meant her words to sound sharp, but the tone in her voice was the opposite. I could tell she was glad I'd called.

My confidence soared to a new level. She didn't want to be there with Parker.

"How am I supposed to know when you're gonna get done? Oh. That didn't come out right . . . ," I joked.

"I'll call you tomorrow and we can talk about it then, okay?"

"No, it's not okay. You said you wanna be friends, but we can't hang out?" She paused, and I imagined her rolling those gorgeous gray eyes. I was jealous that Parker could see them firsthand. "Don't roll your eyes at me. Are you coming or not?"

"How did you know I rolled my eyes? Are you stalking me?"

"You always roll your eyes. Yes? No? You're wasting precious date time."

"Yes!" she said in a loud whisper, a smile in her voice. "I'll go."

"I'll pick you up at seven."

The phone made a muffled thud when I tossed it to the end of the couch, and then my eyes traveled to America.

"You got a date?"

"I do," I said, leaning back against the cushion.

America tossed her legs off of Shepley, teasing him about their last race while he surfed through the channels. It didn't take her long to get bored. "I'm going back to the dorm."

Shepley frowned, never happy about her departure. "Text me."

"I will," America said, smiling. "See ya, Trav."

I was envious that she was leaving, that she had something to do. I'd already finished days earlier the only two papers I had due.

The clock above the television caught my eye. Minutes rolled by slowly, and the more I told myself to stop paying attention, the more my eyes drifted to the digital numbers in the box. After an eternity, only half an hour had passed. My hands fidgeted. I felt more bored and restless until even seconds were torture. Pushing thoughts of Abby and Parker from my head became a constant struggle. Finally I stood.

"Leaving?" Shepley asked with a trace of a smile.

"I can't just sit here. You know how Parker's been frothing at the mouth for her. It's driving me crazy."

"You think they . . . ? Nah. Abby wouldn't. America said she was . . . never mind. My mouth is going to get me in trouble."

"A virgin?"

"You know?"

I shrugged. "Abby told me. You think because we . . . that she'd . . . ?"

"No."

I rubbed the back of my neck. "You're right. I think you're right. I mean, I hope. She's capable of doing some crazy shit to push me away."

"Would it? Push you away, I mean?"

I looked up into Shepley's eyes. "I love her, Shep. I know what I'd do to Parker if he took advantage of her, though."

Shepley shook his head. "It's her choice, Trav. If that's what she decided, you're going to have to let it go."

I took my bike keys and clenched my fingers around them, feeling the sharp edges of the metal as it dug into my palm.

Before climbing on the Harley, I called Abby.

"You home, yet?"

"Yeah, he dropped me off about five minutes ago."

"I'll be there in five more."

I hung up before she could protest. The frigid air that rushed against my face as I drove helped to numb the anger that thoughts of Parker sparked, but a sick feeling still descended on my gut the closer I came to campus.

The bike engine seemed loud as the noise bounced off the brick of Morgan Hall. Compared to the dark windows and the abandoned parking lot, me and my Harley made the night seem abnormally quiet, and the wait exceptionally long. Finally Abby appeared in the doorway. Every muscle in my body tensed as I waited for her to smile or freak out.

She did neither. "Aren't you cold?" she asked, pulling her jacket tighter.

"You look nice," I said, noting she wasn't in a dress. She obviously wasn't trying to look all sexy for him, and that was a relief. "Did you have a good time?"

"Uh . . . yeah, thanks. What are you doing here?"

I gunned the engine. "I was going to take a ride to clear my head. I want you to come with me."

"It's cold, Trav."

"You want me to go get Shep's car?"

"We're going bowling tomorrow. Can't you wait until then?"

"I went from being with you every second of the day to seeing you for ten minutes if I'm lucky."

She smiled and shook her head. "It's only been two days, Trav."

"I miss you. Get your ass on the seat and let's go."

She contemplated my offer, and then zipped up her jacket and climbed on the seat behind me.

I pulled her arms around me without apology, tight enough that it was difficult to expand my chest enough to fully inhale, but for the first time all night, I felt like I could breathe.

CHAPTER SEVENTEEN
Lowball

THE HARLEY TOOK US NOWHERE IN PARTICULAR. Watching out for traffic and the sporadic police cruiser that crossed our path was enough to keep my thoughts occupied at first, but after a while we were the only ones on the road. Knowing the night would eventually end, I decided the moment I dropped her off at Morgan would be when I put in my last-ditch effort. Regardless of our platonic bowling dates, if she continued to see Parker, eventually those would stop, too. Everything would stop.

Pressuring Abby was never a good idea, but unless I laid all my cards on the table, I stood a very good chance of losing the only pigeon I'd ever met. What I would say and how I would say it played over and over in my mind. It would have to be direct, something Abby couldn't ignore, or pretend she didn't hear or understand.

The needle had been flirting with the empty end of the gas gauge for several miles, so I pulled into the first open gas station we came across.

"You want anything?" I asked.

Abby shook her head, climbing off the bike. She raked her fingers through the tangles of her long, shiny hair, and smiled sheepishly.

"Quit it. You're fucking beautiful."

"Just point me to the nearest 1980s rock video."

I laughed, and then yawned, placing the nozzle into the Harley's gas tank opening.

Abby pulled out her cell phone to check the time. "Oh my God, Trav. It's three in the morning."

"You wanna go back?" I asked, my stomach sinking.

"We better."

"We're still going bowling tonight?"

"I told you I would."

"And you're still going to Sig Tau with me in a couple weeks, right?"

"Are you insinuating that I don't follow through? I find that a little insulting."

I pulled the nozzle from the gas tank and hooked it on its base. "I just never know what you're going to do anymore."

I sat on the bike and then helped Abby to climb on behind me. She wrapped her arms around me, this time on her own, and I sighed, lost in thought before starting the engine. I gripped the handlebars, took a breath, and just when I got the balls to tell her, decided a gas station was not the appropriate backdrop to bare my soul.

"You're important to me, you know," Abby said, tensing her arms.

"I don't understand you, Pigeon. I thought I knew women, but you're so fucking confusing I don't know which way is up."

"I don't understand you, either. You're supposed to be this

school's ladies' man. I'm not getting the full freshmen experience they promised in the brochure."

I couldn't help but feel offended. Even if it was true. "Well, that's a first. I've never had a girl sleep with me to get me to leave her alone."

"That's not what it was, Travis."

I started the engine and pulled out into the street without saying another word. The drive to Morgan was excruciating. In my head, I talked myself in and out of confronting Abby so many times. Even though my fingers were numb from the cold, I drove slowly, dreading the moment when Abby knew everything, and then rejecting me for the final time.

When we pulled in front of the entrance to Morgan Hall, my nerves felt like they had been cut, lit on fire, and left in a raw, mangled mess. Abby stepped off the bike, and her sad expression made subdued panic blaze inside me. She might tell me to go to hell before I had a chance to say anything.

I walked Abby to the door, and she pulled out her keys, keeping her head down. Unable to wait another second, I took her chin gently in my hand, and lifted it, waiting patiently as her eyes rose to meet mine.

"Did he kiss you?" I asked, touching my thumb to her soft lips.

She pulled away. "You really know how to screw up a perfect night, don't you?"

"You thought it was perfect, huh? Does that mean you had a good time?"

"I always do when I'm with you."

My eyes fell, and I felt my features compress into a frown. "Did he kiss you?"

"Yes." She sighed, irritated.

My eyes closed tight, knowing my next question could result in disaster. "Is that all?"

"That is *none* of your business!" she said, yanking open the door.

I pushed it closed and stood in her way. "I need to know."

"No you don't! Move, Travis!" she jabbed her elbow into my side, trying to get by.

"Pigeon . . ."

"You think because I'm no longer a virgin, I'll screw anyone that'll have me? *Thanks!*" she said, shoving my shoulder.

"I didn't say that, damn it! Is it too much to ask for a little peace of mind?"

"*Why* would it give you peace of mind to know if I'm sleeping with Parker?"

"How can you not know? It's obvious to everyone else but you!"

"I guess I'm just an idiot, then. You're on a roll tonight, Trav," she said, reaching for the door handle.

I cupped her shoulders. She was doing it again, the oblivious routine I'd become so accustomed to. The time to show my cards was now. "The way I feel about you . . . it's crazy."

"You got the crazy part right," she snapped, pulling away from me.

"I practiced this in my head the whole time we were on the bike, so just hear me out."

"Travis—"

"I know we're fucked up, all right? I'm impulsive and hot tempered, and you get under my skin like no one else. You act like you hate me one minute, and then you need me the next. I never get anything right, and I don't deserve you . . . but I fucking *love* you, Abby. I love you more than I've loved anyone or anything, ever. When you're around, I don't need booze or money or the fighting or the one-night stands . . . all I need is you. You're all I think about. You're all I dream about. You're all I want."

She didn't speak for several seconds. Her eyebrows raised, and her eyes looked dazed as she processed everything I'd said. She blinked a few times.

I cupped each side of her face and looked into her eyes. "Did you sleep with him?"

Abby's eyes glossed over, and then she shook her head no. Without another thought, my lips slammed into hers, and I slipped my tongue inside her mouth. She didn't push me away; instead her tongue challenged mine, and she gripped my T-shirt in her fists, pulling me close. An involuntary hum emanated from my throat, and I wrapped my arms around her.

When I knew I had my answer, I pulled back, breathless. "Call Parker. Tell him you don't wanna see him anymore. Tell him you're with me."

She closed her eyes. "I *can't* be with you, Travis."

"Why the hell not?" I asked, letting go.

Abby shook her head. She had proven herself unpredictable a million times before, but the way she kissed me had meant more than friendship, and had too much behind it to just be sympathy. That left me with only one conclusion.

"Unbelievable. The one girl I want, and she doesn't want me."

She hesitated before she spoke. "When America and I moved out here, it was with the understanding that my life was going to turn out a certain way. Or, that it *wouldn't* turn out a certain way. The fighting, the gambling, the drinking . . . it's what I left behind. When I'm around you it's all right there for me in an irresistible, tattooed package. I didn't move hundreds of miles away to live it all over again."

"I know you deserve better than me. You think I don't know that? But if there was any woman made for me . . . it's you. I'll do whatever I have to do, Pidge. Do you hear me? I'll do anything."

She turned away from me, but I wouldn't give up. She was finally talking, and if she walked away this time, we might not get another chance.

I held the door shut with my hand. "I'll stop fighting the second I graduate. I won't drink a single drop again. I'll give you the happy ever after, Pigeon. If you just believe in me, I can do it."

"I don't *want* you to change."

"Then tell me what to do. Tell me and I'll do it," I pleaded.

"Can I borrow your phone?" she asked.

I frowned, unsure what she would do. "Sure." I pulled my phone from my pocket, handing it to her.

She fingered the buttons for a moment, and then dialed, closing her eyes as she waited.

"I'm sorry for calling you so early," she stammered, "but this couldn't wait. I . . . can't go to dinner with you on Wednesday."

She had called Parker. My hands trembled with apprehension, wondering if she was going to ask him to pick her up—to save her—or something else.

She continued, "I can't see you at all, actually. I'm . . . pretty sure I'm in love with Travis."

My whole world stopped. I tried to replay her words over. Had I heard them correctly? Did she really just say what I thought she had, or was it just wishful thinking?

Abby handed the phone back to me, and then reluctantly peered up into my eyes.

"He hung up," she said with a frown.

"You love me?"

"It's the tattoos," she said, flippant and shrugging, as if she hadn't just said the one thing I'd ever wanted to hear.

Pigeon loved me.

A wide smile stretched across my face. "Come home with me," I said, enveloping her in my arms.

Abby's eyebrows shot up. "You said all that to get me in bed? I must have made quite an impression."

"The only thing I'm thinking about right now is holding you in my arms all night."

"Let's go."

I didn't hesitate. Once Abby was securely on the back of my bike, I raced home, taking every shortcut, rushing every yellow light, and weaving in and out of the little traffic there was at that time of the morning.

When we reached the apartment, turning off the engine and lifting Abby into my arms seemed simultaneous.

She giggled against my lips as I fumbled with the bolt lock on the front door. When I set her down and closed the door behind us, I let out a long, relieved sigh.

"It hasn't seemed like home since you left," I said, kissing her again.

Toto scampered down the hall and wagged his shaggy tail, pawing at Abby's legs. He'd missed her almost as much as I had.

Shepley's bed squeaked, and then his feet stomped across the floor. His door flew open as he squinted from the light. "Fuck no,

Trav, you're not pulling this shit! You're in love with Ab . . ."—his eyes focused and he recognized his mistake—"by. Hey, Abby."

"Hey, Shep," Abby said with an amused smile, setting Toto on the floor.

Before Shepley could ask questions, I pulled Abby down the hall. We crashed into each other. I hadn't planned on anything but having her next to me in the bed, but she yanked my shirt up and over my head with intention. I helped her with her jacket, and then she stripped off her sweater and tank top. There was no questioning the look in her eyes, and I wasn't about to argue.

Soon we were both completely naked, and the small voice inside of me wanting to savor the moment and take things slow was easily overpowered by Abby's desperate kisses and the soft hums she made whenever I touched her pretty much anywhere.

I lowered her to the mattress, and her hand shot out toward the nightstand. Instantly, I remembered my unceremonious breaking of the fishbowl of condoms to pledge my intended celibacy.

"Shit," I said, panting. "I got rid of them."

"*What? All* of them?"

"I thought you didn't . . . if I wasn't with you, I wasn't going to need them."

"You're kidding me!" she said, letting her head fall against the headboard in frustration.

I leaned down, breathing hard, resting my forehead against her chest. "Consider yourself the opposite of a foregone conclusion."

The next moments were a blur. Abby did some weird counting, concluding that she couldn't get pregnant that particular week, and before I knew it, I was inside of her, feeling every part of her against every part of me. I had never been with a girl without that thin sheath of latex, but apparently a fraction of a millimeter made a lot of difference. Every movement created equally overpowering conflicting feelings: delaying the inevitable, or giving in because it felt so fucking good.

When Abby's hips rose against mine, and her uncontrolled groans and whimpers escalated to a loud, satisfied cry, I couldn't hold back anymore.

"Abby," I whispered, desperate. "I need a . . . I need to . . ."

"Don't stop," she begged. Her fingernails dug into my back.

I rocked into her again one last time. I must have been loud, because Abby's hand flew up to my mouth. I closed my eyes, letting everything go, feeling my eyebrows press together while my body convulsed and stiffened. Breathing hard, I looked into Abby's eyes. Wearing only a tired, satisfied smile, she peered up at me, waiting for something. I kissed her over and over, and then cupped each side of her face with my hands, kissing her again, this time more tenderly.

Abby's breathing slowed, and she sighed. I leaned my body to the side, relaxing next to her, and then pulled her against me. She rested her cheek against my chest, her hair cascading down my arm. I kissed her forehead once more, locking my fingers together at the small of her back.

"Don't leave this time, okay? I wanna wake up just like this in the morning."

Abby kissed my chest, but didn't look up. "I'm not going anywhere."

THAT MORNING, LYING WITH THE WOMAN I LOVED, A SI-lent promise was formed in my head. I was going to be a better man for her, someone she deserved. No more flying off the handle. No more temper tantrums, or violent outbursts.

Every time I pressed my lips against her skin, waiting for her to wake up, I repeated that promise in my mind.

Dealing with life outside the apartment while trying to stay true to that promise proved to be a struggle. For the first time, I not only gave a shit about someone, but I was also desperate to keep them. Feelings of overprotection and jealousy chipped away at the oath I'd made just a few hours before.

By lunchtime, Chris Jenks had pissed me off and I regressed. Abby was thankfully patient and forgiving, even when I threatened Parker not twenty minutes later.

Abby had proved more than once that she could accept me for who I was, but I didn't want to be the violent asshole everyone was used to. Mixing my rages with these new feelings of jealousy was more difficult to control than I could have imagined.

I resorted to avoiding situations that could throw me into a rage, and remaining oblivious to the knowledge that not only was Abby insanely hot, every dick on campus was curious how she had tamed the one man they thought would never settle down. It seemed they were all waiting for me to fuck up so they could try her out, which only made me more agitated and cantankerous.

To keep my mind occupied, I focused on making it clear to the coeds that I was off the market, which had pissed off half the school's female population.

Walking into the Red with Abby on Halloween, I noticed that the sharp, late fall air didn't hinder the number of women wearing an array of slutty costumes. I hugged my girlfriend to my side, grateful that she wasn't one to dress up as Prostitute Barbie, or a football-player-slash-transvestite-whore, which meant that the number of threats I would have to make for staring at her tits or worrying about her bending over would be kept to a minimum.

Shepley and I played pool while the girls looked on. We were winning again, after having already pocketed $360 from the last two games.

From the corner of my eye, I saw Finch approach America and Abby. They giggled for a while, and then Finch pulled them onto the dance floor. Abby's beauty stood out, even amid the bare skin, glitter, and glaring cleavage of the naughty Snow Whites and sleazy referees around her.

Before the song was over, America and Abby left Finch on the dance floor and headed toward the bar. I stretched up onto my toes to find the tops of their heads in the sea of people.

"You're up," Shepley said.

"The girls are gone."

"They probably went to pick up drinks. Get to stickin', lover boy."

With hesitation, I bent down, focused on the ball, but then missed.

"Travis! That was an easy shot! You're killin' me!" Shepley complained.

I still couldn't see the girls. Knowing about the two sexual assault incidents the year before, it made me nervous to let Abby and America walk around alone. Drugging an unsuspecting girl's drink was not unheard of, even in our small college town.

I set my pool stick on the table and made my way across the wooden dance floor.

Shepley's hand fell on my shoulder. "Where are you going?"

"To find the girls. You remember what happened last year to that Heather chick."

"Oh. Yeah."

When I finally found Abby and America, I saw two guys buying them drinks. Both short, one was thicker around the middle, with a week's worth of scruff on his sweaty face. Jealousy should have been the last thing I would feel when looking at him, but the fact that he was clearly hitting on my girlfriend made this less about his looks and more about my ego—even if he didn't know she was with me, he should have assumed by looking at her that she wouldn't be alone. My jealousy mixed with annoyance. I'd told Abby a dozen times not to do something so potentially dangerous as accept a drink from a stranger; anger quickly took over.

The one guy yelling to Abby over the music leaned in. "You wanna dance?"

Abby shook her head. "No, thanks. I'm here with my—"

"Boyfriend," I said, cutting her off. I glared down at the men. It was almost laughable trying to intimidate two men wearing togas, but I still unleashed my full-on *I Will Kill You* expression. I nodded across the room. "Run along, now."

The men cowered, and then looked to America and Abby before retreating behind the curtain of the crowd.

Shepley kissed America. "I can't take you anywhere!" She giggled, and Abby smiled at me.

I was too angry to smile back.

"What?" she asked, taken aback.

"Why did you let him buy your drink?"

America let go of Shepley. "We didn't, Travis. I told them not to."

I took the bottle from Abby's hand. "Then what's this?"

"Are you serious?" she asked.

"Yes, I'm fucking serious," I said, tossing the beer in the trash can by the bar. "I've told you a hundred times . . . you can't take drinks from random guys. What if he put something in it?"

America held up her glass. "The drinks were never out of our sight, Trav. You're overreacting."

"I'm not talking to you," I said, glaring at Abby.

Her eyes flashed, mirroring my anger. "Don't talk to her like that."

"Travis," Shepley warned, "let it go."

"I don't like you letting other guys buy you drinks," I said.

Abby raised an eyebrow. "Are you trying to pick a fight?"

"Would it bother you to walk up to the bar and see me sharing a drink with some chick?"

"Okay. You're oblivious to all women, now. I get it. I should be making the same effort."

"It would be nice," I said, my teeth clenched.

"You're going to have to tone down the jealous-boyfriend thing, Travis. I didn't do anything wrong."

"I walk up here, and some guy is buying you a drink!"

"Don't yell at her!" America said.

Shepley put his hand on Travis's shoulder. "We've all had a lot to drink. Let's just get out of here."

Abby's anger turned up a notch. "I have to tell Finch we're leaving," she grumbled, shouldering past me to the dance floor.

I took her by the wrist. "I'll go with you."

She twisted from my grip. "I am fully capable of walking a few feet by myself, Travis. What is *wrong* with you?"

Abby pushed her way out to Finch, who was flinging his

arms around and jumping around in the middle of the wooden floor. Sweat was pouring down his forehead and from his temples. At first he smiled, but when she yelled her goodbyes, he rolled his eyes.

Abby had mouthed my name. She had blamed it on me, which only made me more mad. Of course I would get angry if she did something that could get her hurt. She didn't seem to mind so much when I was bashing Chris Jenks's head in, but when I got pissed about her taking drinks from strangers, she had the audacity to get mad.

Just as my anger boiled to rage, some asshole in a pirate costume grabbed Abby and pressed himself against her. The room blurred, and before I knew it, my fist was in his face. The pirate fell to the floor, but when Abby went with him, I snapped back to reality.

Her palms flat on the dance floor, she looked stunned. I was frozen in shock, watching her, in slow motion, turn her hand over to see that it was covered in bright red blood gushing from the pirate's nose.

I scrambled to pick her up. "Oh shit! Are you all right, Pidge?"

When Abby got to her feet, she yanked her arm from my grip. "Are you *insane?*"

America grabbed Abby's wrist and pulled her through the crowd, only letting go when we were outside. I had to walk double-time to keep up.

In the parking lot, Shepley unlocked the Charger and Abby slid into her seat.

I tried pleading with her. She was beyond pissed. "I'm sorry, Pigeon, I didn't know he had a hold of you."

"Your fist was two inches from my face!" she said, catching the oil-stained towel Shepley had thrown at her. She wiped the blood from her hand, wringing the cloth around each finger, clearly revolted.

I winced. "I wouldn't have swung if I thought I could have hit you. You know that right?"

"Shut up, Travis. Just shut up," she said, staring at the back of Shepley's head.

"Pidge . . ."

Shepley hit his steering wheel with the heel of his hand. "Shut up, Travis! You said you're sorry, now shut the fuck up!"

I couldn't say anything back. Shepley was right: I had FUBARed the entire night, and suddenly Abby kicking me to the curb became a frightening possibility.

When we reached the apartment, America kissed her boyfriend good night. "I'll see you tomorrow, baby."

Shepley nodded in resignation and kissed her. "Love you."

I knew they were leaving because of me. Otherwise, the girls would be staying the night at the apartment like they did every weekend.

Abby walked past me to America's Honda without saying a word.

I jogged to her side, trying an awkward smile in an attempt to defuse the situation. "C'mon. Don't leave mad."

"Oh, I'm not leaving mad. I'm furious."

"She needs some time to cool off, Travis," America warned, unlocking her door.

When the passenger side lock popped, I panicked, holding my hand against the door. "Don't leave, Pigeon. I was out of line. I'm *sorry*."

Abby held up her hand, showing the remnants of dried blood on her palm. "Call me when you grow up."

I leaned against the door with my hip. "You can't leave."

Abby raised an eyebrow, and Shepley jogged around the car beside us. "Travis, you're drunk. You're about to make a huge mistake. Just let her go home, cool off . . . you can both talk tomorrow when you're sober."

"She can't leave," I said, desperately staring into Abby's eyes.

"It's not going to work, Travis," she said, tugging on the door. "Move!"

"What do you mean it's not gonna work?" I asked, grabbing her arm. The fear of Abby saying the words, ending it right there made me react without thinking.

"I mean the sad face. I'm not falling for it," she said, pulling away.

A short-lived relief came over me. She wasn't going to end it. At least, not yet.

"Abby," Shepley said. "This is the moment I was talking about. Maybe you should—"

"Stay out of it, Shep," America snapped, starting the car.

"I'm gonna fuck up. I'm gonna fuck up a lot, Pidge, but you have to forgive me."

"I'm going to have a huge bruise on my ass in the morning! You hit that guy because you were pissed at *me*! What should that tell me? Because red flags are going up *all* over the place right now!"

"I've never hit a girl in my life," I said, surprised she would ever think I could ever lay a hand on her—or any other woman for that matter.

"And I'm not about to be the first one!" she said, tugging on the door. "Move, damn it!"

I nodded, taking a step back. The last thing I wanted was for her to leave, but it was better than her getting so pissed off that she ended up telling me to fuck off.

America put the car in reverse, and I watched Abby through the window.

"You're going to call me tomorrow, right?" I asked, touching the windshield.

"Just go, Mare," she said, looking straight ahead.

When the brake lights were no longer visible, I retreated into the apartment.

"Travis," Shepley warned. "No messes, bro. I mean it."

I nodded, trudging to my room in defeat. It seemed that just when I was getting a handle on things, my fucking temper would rear its ugly head. I had to get it under control, or I was going to lose the best thing that ever happened to me.

To pass the time, I cooked some pork chops and mashed potatoes, but just rolled it all around on my plate, unable to eat. Laundry helped to knock out an hour, and then I decided to give Toto a bath. We played for a while, but then even he gave up and curled up on the bed. Staring at the ceiling, obsessing about how stupid I'd been, wasn't appealing, so I decided to pull all the dishes out of the cabinet and wash them by hand.

Longest night of my life.

The clouds began to turn colors, signaling the sun. I grabbed the bike keys and went for a drive, ending up in front of Morgan Hall.

Harmony Handler was just leaving for a jog. She watched me for a moment, keeping her hand on the door.

"Hey, Travis," she said with her typical small smile. It quickly faded. "Wow. Are you sick or something? Do you need me to take you somewhere?" I must have looked like hell. Harmony had always been a sweetheart. Her brother was a Sig Tau, so I didn't know her all that well. Little sisters were off-limits.

"Hey, Harmony," I said, trying a smile. "I wanted to surprise Abby with breakfast. Think you could let me in?"

"Uh," she trailed off, looking back through the glass door. "Nancy might freak. Are you sure you're okay?"

Nancy was Morgan Hall's dorm mom. I'd heard of her, but never seen her, and doubted she would even notice. The word around campus was that she drank more than the residents and was seldom seen outside of her room.

"Just a long night. C'mon." I smiled. "You know she won't care."

"Okay, but it wasn't me."

I held my hand to my heart. "I promise."

I made my way upstairs, knocking softly on Abby's door.

The knob turned quickly, but the door opened slowly, gradually revealing Abby and America across the room. Kara's hand slipped from the doorknob back under the covers of her bed.

"Can I come in?"

Abby sat up quickly. "Are you okay?"

I walked in and fell to my knees before her. "I'm so sorry, Abby. I'm sorry," I said, wrapping my arms around her middle and burying my head in her lap.

Abby cradled my head in her arms.

"I'm uh . . . ," America stuttered, "I'm gonna go."

Abby's roommate Kara stomped around the room, getting her shower supplies. "I'm always very clean when you're around, Abby," she said, slamming the door behind her.

I looked up at Abby. "I know I get crazy when it comes to you, but God knows I'm tryin', Pidge. I don't wanna screw this up."

"Then don't," she said simply.

"This is hard for me, ya know. I feel like any second you're going to figure out what a piece of shit I am and leave me. When you were dancing last night, I saw a dozen different guys watching you. You go to the bar, and I see you thank that guy for your drink. Then that douche bag on the dance floor grabs you."

"You don't see me throwing punches every time a girl talks to you. I can't stay locked up in the apartment all the time. You're going to have to get a handle on your temper."

"I will," I said, nodding. "I've never wanted a girlfriend before, Pigeon. I'm not used to feeling this way about someone . . . about *anyone*. If you'll be patient with me, I swear I'll get it figured out."

"Let's get something straight; you're not a piece of shit, you're amazing. It doesn't matter who buys me drinks or who asks me to dance or who flirts with me. I'm going home with you. You've asked me to trust you, and you don't seem to trust me."

I frowned. "That's not true."

"If you think I'm going to leave you for the next guy that comes along, then you don't have much faith in me."

I tightened my grip. "I'm not good enough for you, Pidge. That doesn't mean I don't trust you, I'm just bracing for the inevitable."

"Don't say that. When we're alone, you're perfect. We're perfect. But then you let everyone else ruin it. I don't expect a 180, but you have to pick your battles. You can't come out swinging every time someone looks at me."

I nodded, knowing she was right. "I'll do anything you want. Just . . . tell me you love me." I was fully aware of how ridiculous I sounded, but it just didn't matter anymore.

"You know I do."

"I need to hear you say it."

"I love you," she said. She touched her lips to mine, and then pulled a few inches away. "Now quit being such a baby."

Once she kissed me, my heart slowed, and every muscle in my body relaxed. How much I needed her terrified me. I couldn't imagine love was like this for everyone, or men would be walking around like lunatics the second they were old enough to notice girls.

Maybe it was just me. Maybe it was just me and her. Maybe together we were this volatile entity that would either implode or meld together. Either way, it seemed the moment I met her, my life had been turned upside down. And I didn't want it any other way.

CHAPTER EIGHTEEN

Lucky Thirteen

HALF EXCITED, HALF NERVOUS AS HELL, I WALKED INTO my father's home, my fingers intertwined with Abby's. Smoke from my father's cigar and my brothers' cigarettes drifted from the game room, mixing with the faint, musky smell of carpet older than I was.

Even though Abby was initially pissed that she didn't have much notice before meeting my family, she looked more at ease than I felt. Bringing home a girlfriend was not a habit of the Maddox men, and any prediction of their reaction was unreliable at best.

Trenton came into view first. "Holy Christ! It's the asshat!"

Any hope of my brothers even pretending not to be anything but feral was a waste of time. I loved them anyway, and knowing Abby, she would, too.

"Hey, hey . . . watch the language around the young lady," Dad said, nodding to Abby.

"Pidge, this is my dad, Jim Maddox. Dad, this is Pigeon."

"Pigeon?" Jim asked, an amused expression on his face.

"Abby," she said, shaking his hand.

I pointed to my brothers, all of them nodding when I said their name. "Trenton, Taylor, Tyler, and Thomas."

Abby seemed a bit overwhelmed. I couldn't blame her; I'd never really talked about my family, and five boys would be mind-boggling to anybody. In fact, five Maddoxes were downright frightening to most.

Growing up, the neighborhood kids learned early not to mess with one of us, and only once did someone make the mistake of taking on all of us. We were broken, but came together as a solid fortress if necessary. That was clear even to those we didn't mean to intimidate.

"Does Abby have a last name?" Dad asked.

"Abernathy," she said, nodding politely.

"It's nice to meet you, Abby," Thomas said with a smile. Abby wouldn't have noticed, but Thomas's expression was a front for what he was really doing: analyzing her every word and movement. Thomas was always on the lookout for someone that could potentially rock our already rickety boat. Waves weren't welcome, and Thomas had always made it his job to calm potential storms.

Dad can't take it, he used to say. None of us could argue with that logic. When one or a few of us found ourselves in trouble, we would go to Thomas, and he would take care of it before Dad could find out. Years of fostering a bunch of rowdy, violent boys made a man out of Thomas far earlier than anyone should be expected to be. We all respected him for it, including my father, but years of being our protector left him a little overbearing at times. But Abby stood, smiling and oblivious to the fact that she was now a target, under scrutiny by the family guardian.

"Really nice," Trenton said, his eyes roving over places that would have gotten anyone else killed.

Dad slapped the back of Trenton's head and he yelped.

"What'd I say?" he said, rubbing the back of his head.

"Have a seat, Abby. Watch us take Trav's money," Tyler said.

I pulled out a chair for Abby, and she sat. I glared at Trenton, and he responded with only a wink. Smart-ass.

"You knew Stu Unger?" Abby asked, pointing to a dusty photo.

I couldn't believe my ears.

Dad's eyes brightened. "You know who Stu Unger is?"

Abby nodded. "My dad's a fan, too."

Dad stood up, pointing to the dusty picture beside it. "And that's Doyle Brunson, there."

Abby smiled. "My dad saw him play, once. He's unbelievable."

"Trav's granddaddy was a professional. We take poker very seriously around here." Dad smiled.

Not only had Abby never mentioned the fact that she knew anything about poker, it was also the first time I'd ever heard her speak of her dad.

As we watched Trenton shuffle and deal, I tried to forget what had just happened. With her long legs, slight but perfectly proportioned curves, and big eyes, Abby was stunningly gorgeous, but knowing Stu Unger by name already made her a huge hit with my family. I sat up a little taller in my seat. No way would any of my brothers bring home anyone that could top *that*.

Trenton raised an eyebrow. "You wanna play, Abby?"

She shook her head. "I don't think I should."

"You don't know how?" Dad asked.

I leaned over to kiss her forehead. "Play . . . I'll teach you."

"You should just kiss your money goodbye, now, Abby." Thomas laughed.

Abby pressed her lips together and dug into her purse, pulling out two fifties. She held them out to Dad, waiting patiently while he traded them for chips. Trenton smiled, eager to take advantage of her confidence.

"I have faith in Travis's teaching skills," Abby said.

Taylor clapped. "Hells yeah! I'm going to get rich tonight!"

"Let's start small this time," Dad said, throwing in a five-dollar chip.

Trenton dealt, and I fanned out Abby's hand. "Have you ever played?"

"It's been a while." She nodded.

"Go Fish doesn't count, Pollyanna," Trenton said, looking at his cards.

"Shut your hole, Trent," I growled, throwing him a quick threatening look before returning to Abby's cards. "You're shooting for higher cards, consecutive numbers, and if you're really lucky, in the same suit."

We lost the first few rounds, but then Abby refused to let me help her. After that, she started to pick it up pretty quickly. Three hands later, she had kicked all of their asses without blinking.

"Bullshit!" Trenton whined. "Beginner's luck sucks!"

"You've got a fast learner, Trav," Dad said, moving his mouth around his cigar.

I took a sip of my beer, feeling like the king of the world. "You're makin' me proud, Pigeon!"

"Thanks."

"Those that cannot do, teach," Thomas said, smirking.

"Very funny, asshole," I murmured.

"Get the girl a beer," Dad said, an amused smile lifting his already puffy cheeks.

I gladly hopped up, pulled a bottle from the fridge, and used the already cracked edge of the countertop to pop off the cap. Abby smiled when I placed the beer in front of her and didn't hesitate to take one of her signature man-size swigs.

She wiped her lips with the back of her hand, and then waited on my dad to put in his chips.

Four hands later, Abby had tipped back the last of her third beer and watched Taylor closely. "The action's on you, Taylor. You gonna be a baby or you going to put in like a man?"

It was getting very difficult for me to keep from being excited in other places. Watching Abby own my brothers—and a poker veteran like my father—hand after hand was turning me on. I'd never seen a women so sexy in my life, and this one happened to be my girlfriend.

"Fuck it," Taylor said, throwing the last of his chips in.

"Whatdya got, Pigeon?" I asked with a grin. I felt like a kid at Christmas.

"Taylor?" Abby prompted, her face completely blank.

A wide grin spread across his face. "Flush!" He smiled, spreading his cards faceup on the table.

We all looked to Abby. Her eyes scanned the men around the table, and then she slammed her cards down. "Read 'em and weep, boys! Aces and eights!"

"A full house? What the fuck?" Trenton cried.

"Sorry. I've always wanted to say that," Abby said, giggling as she pulled in her chips.

Thomas's eyes narrowed. "This isn't just beginner's luck. She plays."

I watched Thomas for a moment. He wasn't taking his eyes from Abby.

I looked to her, then. "Have you played before, Pidge?"

She pressed her lips together and shrugged, letting a sweet smile turn up the corners of her mouth. My head fell back, and I burst into laughter. I started to tell her how proud I was, but the words were held hostage by the uncontrollable cackling shaking my entire body. I hit the table with my fist a few times, trying to get a hold of myself.

"Your girlfriend just fucking hustled us!" Taylor said, pointing in my direction.

"NO FUCKING WAY!" Trenton wailed, standing up.

"Good plan, Travis. Bring a card shark to poker night," Dad said, winking at Abby.

"I didn't know!" I said, shaking my head.

"Bullshit," Thomas said, his eyes still dissecting my girlfriend.

"I didn't!" I said.

"I hate to say it, bro. But I think I just fell in love with your girl," Tyler said.

Suddenly my laughter was gone, and I frowned. "Hey, now."

"That's it. I was going easy on you, Abby, but I'm winning my money back, now," Trenton warned.

I sat out the last few rounds, watching the boys try to win back their money. Hand after hand, Abby steamrolled them. She didn't even pretend to go easy on them.

Once my brothers were broke, Dad called it a night, and Abby returned a hundred dollars to each of them, except Dad, who wouldn't take it.

I took Abby's hand, and we walked to the door. Watching my girlfriend de-sack my brothers was entertaining, but I was still disappointed that she returned some of their money.

She squeezed my hand. "What's wrong?"

"You just gave away four hundred bucks, Pidge!"

"If this was poker night at Sig Tau, I would have kept it. I can't rob your brothers the first time I meet them."

"They would have kept your money!"

"And I wouldn't have lost a second of sleep over it, either," Taylor said.

From the corner of my eye, I caught Thomas staring at Abby from the recliner in the corner of the living room. He'd been even more quiet than usual.

"Why do you keep starin' at my girl, Tommy?"

"What did you say your last name was?" Thomas asked.

Abby shifted nervously but didn't answer.

I put my arm around her waist, and turned to my brother, not sure what he was getting at. He thought he knew something, and was getting ready to make his move.

"It's Abernathy. What of it?"

"I can see why you didn't put it together before tonight, Trav, but now you don't have an excuse," Thomas said, smug.

"What the fuck are you talking about?" I asked.

"Are you related to Mick Abernathy by any chance?" Thomas asked.

All heads turned to wait for Abby's response.

She raked her hair back with her fingers, clearly nervous. "How do you know Mick?"

My neck craned even more in her direction. "He's only one of the best poker players that ever lived. Do you know him?"

"He's my father," she said. It looked almost painful for her to answer.

The entire room exploded.

"NO FUCKING WAY!"

"I KNEW IT!"

"WE JUST PLAYED MICK ABERNATHY'S DAUGHTER!"

"MICK ABERNATHY? HOLY SHIT!"

The words rang in my ears, but it still took me several seconds to process. Three of my brothers were jumping up and down and screaming, but to me the entire room was frozen, and the world silent.

My girlfriend, who also happened to be my best friend, was the daughter of a poker legend—someone my brothers, father, and even my grandfather idolized.

Abby's voice brought me back to the present. "I told you guys I shouldn't play."

"If you would have mentioned you were Mick Abernathy's daughter, I think we would have taken you more seriously," Thomas said.

Abby peeked over at me from under her lashes, waiting for a reaction.

"You're Lucky Thirteen?" I asked, dumbfounded.

Trenton stood and pointed. "Lucky Thirteen is in our house! No way! I don't fucking believe it!"

"That was the nickname the papers gave me. And the story wasn't exactly accurate," Abby said, fidgeting.

Even amid the booming commotion from my brothers, the only thing I could think about was how fucking hot it was that the girl I'm in love with was practically a celebrity. Even better, she was famous for something outrageously badass.

"I need to get Abby home, guys," I said.

Dad peered at Abby over his glasses. "Why wasn't it accurate?"

"I didn't take my dad's luck. I mean, how ridiculous." She chuckled, twisting her hair nervously around her finger.

Thomas shook his head. "No, Mick gave that interview. He said at midnight on your thirteenth birthday his luck ran dry."

"And yours picked up," I added.

"You were raised by mobsters!" Trent said, smiling with excitement.

"Uh . . . no." She laughed once. "They didn't raise me. They were just . . . around a lot."

"That was a damn shame, Mick running your name through the mud like that in all the papers. You were just a kid," Dad said, shaking his head.

"If anything it was beginner's luck," Abby said.

I could tell by the look on her face she was bordering on feeling mortification from all of the attention.

"You were taught by Mick Abernathy," Dad said, shaking his head in awe. "You were playing pros, and winning, at thirteen years old for Christ's sakes." He looked at me and smiled. "Don't bet against her, son. She doesn't lose."

My mind instantly returned to the fight when Abby bet against me, knowing she would lose, and have to live with me for a month if she did. All that time I thought she didn't care about me, and just then I realized it couldn't have been true.

"Uh . . . we gotta go, Dad. Bye, guys."

I raced through the streets, weaving in and out of traffic.

The faster the needle inched up on the speedometer, the tighter Abby's thighs clamped, making me even more eager to reach the apartment.

Abby didn't say a word when I parked the Harley and led her upstairs, and still wasn't speaking when I helped her with her jacket.

She let her hair down, and I stood, watching her in awe. It was almost like she was a different person, and I couldn't wait to get my hands on her.

"I know you're mad," she said, her eyes to the floor. "I'm sorry I didn't tell you, but it's not something I talk about."

Her words stunned me. "Mad at you? I am so turned on I can't see straight. You just robbed my asshole brothers of their money without batting an eyelash, you have achieved legend status with my father, and I know for a fact that you purposely lost that bet we made before my fight."

"I wouldn't say that . . ."

"Did you think you were going to win?"

"Well . . . no, not exactly," she said, pulling off her heels.

I could barely contain the smile that inched across my face. "So you *wanted* to be here with me. I think I just fell in love with you all over again."

Abby kicked her heels into the closet. "How are you not mad right now?"

I sighed. Maybe I should've been mad. But I just . . . wasn't. "That's pretty big, Pidge. You should have told me. But I understand why you didn't. You came here to get away from all of that. It's like the sky opened up. Everything makes sense, now."

"Well, that's a relief."

"Lucky Thirteen," I said, grabbing the hem of her shirt and pulling it over her head.

"Don't call me that, Travis. It's not a good thing."

"You're fucking famous, Pigeon!" I unbuttoned her jeans and pulled them down around her ankles, helping her to step out of them.

"My father *hated* me after that. He still blames me for all his problems."

I yanked off my shirt and hugged her to me, impatient to feel her skin against mine. "I still can't believe the daughter of Mick Abernathy is standing in front of me, and I've been with you this whole time and had no idea."

She pushed me away. "I'm not *Mick Abernathy's daughter,* Travis! That's what I left behind. I'm Abby. *Just* Abby!" she said, walking over to the closet. She yanked a T-shirt off its hanger and pulled it over her head.

"I'm sorry. I'm a little starstruck."

"It's just me!" She held the palm of her hand to her chest, an edge of desperation in her voice.

"Yeah, but . . ."

"But *nothing.* The way you're looking at me right now? This is exactly why I didn't tell you." She closed her eyes. "I won't live like that anymore, Trav. Not even with you."

"Whoa! Calm down, Pigeon. Let's not get carried away." I took her in my arms, suddenly worried where the conversation was going. "I don't care what you were or what you're not anymore. I just want you."

"I guess we have that in common, then."

I pulled her gently to the bed, and then snuggled next to her, taking in the faint smell of cigar mixed with her shampoo. "It's just you and me against the world, Pidge."

She curled up beside me, seeming satisfied with my words. When she relaxed against my chest, she sighed.

"What's wrong?" I asked.

"I don't want anyone to know, Trav. I didn't want *you* to know."

"I love you, Abby. I won't mention it again, okay? Your secret's safe with me," I said, pressing my lips gently against her temple.

She nuzzled her cheek against my skin, and I pulled her tight. The night's events seemed like a dream. The first time I bring a girl home, and not only is she the daughter of a famous poker player, but she could also easily bankrupt us all in a single hand. For being the family fuckup, I felt like I had finally gained a little respect from my older brothers. And it was all because of Abby.

I lie in bed awake, unable to stop my mind long enough to doze off. Abby's breathing had evened out half an hour before.

My cell lit up and buzzed just once, signaling a text message. I opened it up, and immediately frowned. The sender's name scrolled across: Jason Brazil.

Dude. Parker's talkin smack.

Very carefully, I pulled my arm out from under Abby's head to use both hands to type a message back.

Says who?

Says me hes sittin right here.

Oh yeah? Whats he sayin?

Its about Pigeon. U sure u wanna know?

Dont b a dick.

He sd shes still calling him.

Negative.

Sd earlier hes waiting 4 u to screw up, and shes just waitin for a good time to kick u 2 the curb.

Did he now?

Sd just now that she told him the other day she was really unhappy but u were kinda crazy and she was worried about when to do it.

If she wasnt laying next to me id come over there n beat his fkn ass

Not worth it. We all know hes full of shit.

Still pisses me off

I heard that. Don't worry about the douche canoe. U got ur girl next 2 u.

Had Abby not been sleeping beside me, I would have jumped on my bike and went straight to the Sig Tau house and shoved my fist through Parker's five-thousand-dollar grill. Maybe taken a bat to his Porsche.

Half an hour passed before the rage shakes finally began to subside. Abby hadn't moved. That same subtle noise that she made with her nose when she slept helped to slow my heart rate, and before long I was able to take her back into my arms and relax.

Abby wasn't calling Parker. If she was unhappy, she would have told me. I took a deep breath and watched the shadow of the tree outside dance against the wall.

"HE DIDN'T," SHEPLEY SAID, STOPPING MIDSTEP.

The girls left us at the apartment alone so they could shop for a dress for the date party, so I talked Shepley into driving us to the local furniture store.

"He sure as shit did." I turned my phone for Shepley to see. "Brazil texted me last night and ratted his ass out."

Shepley sighed and shook his head. "He had to know that would get back to you. I mean . . . how could it not? Those guys are bigger gossips than the girls."

I stopped, seeing a couch that caught my eye. "I bet that's why he did it. Hoping it would get back to me."

Shepley nodded. "Let's face it. The old you would have gone into a jealous rage and scared her right into Parker's arms."

"Bastard," I said as a salesman approached.

"Good morning, gentleman. Can I help you find something in particular?"

Shepley threw himself onto the couch, and then bounced a few times before nodding his head. "I approve."

"Yeah. I'll take this one," I said.

"You'll take it?" he said, a little surprised.

"Yeah," I said, a little surprised myself at his reaction. "Do you deliver?"

"Yes, sir, we do. Would you like to know the price?"

"It says right here, doesn't it?"

"Yes."

"So, I'll take it. Where do I pay?"

"Right this way, sir."

The salesman tried unsuccessfully to talk me into some more items that matched the couch, but I had a few more things to buy that day.

Shepley gave them our address, and the salesman thanked me for being the easiest sale of the year.

"Where are we going now?" he asked, trying to keep pace with me to the Charger.

"Calvin's."

"You getting new ink?"

"Yep."

Shepley watched me, wary. "What are you doing, Trav?"

"What I always said I would do if I met the right girl."

Shepley stepped in front of the passenger door. "I'm not sure this is a good idea. Don't you think you should discuss it with Abby first . . . you know, so she doesn't freak out?"

I frowned. "She might say no."

"It's better she says no than you do it and she runs out of the apartment because you scared her off. Things have been going good between you two. Why don't you just let it ride for a while?"

I cupped my hands on Shepley's shoulders. "That doesn't sound like me at all," I said, and then moved him aside.

Shepley jogged around the front of the Charger, and then slid into the driver's seat. "I'm still taking the official position that this is a bad idea."

"Noted."

"Then where?"

"Steiner's."

"The jewelry store?"

"Yep."

"Why, Travis?" Shepley said, his voice more stern than before.

"You'll see."

He shook his head. "Are you *trying* to run her off?"

"It's going to happen, Shep. I just want to have it. For when the time is right."

"No time anytime soon is right. I am so in love with America that it drives me crazy sometimes, but we're not old enough for that shit, yet, Travis. And . . . what if she says no?"

My teeth clenched at the thought. "I won't ask her until I know she's ready."

Shepley's mouth pulled to the side. "Just when I think you can't get any more insane, you do something else to remind me that you are far beyond bat shit crazy."

"Wait until you see the rock I'm getting."

Shepley craned his neck slowly in my direction. "You've already been over there shopping, haven't you?"

I smiled.

CHAPTER NINETEEN

Daddy's Home

Friday, the day of the date party, three days after Abby smiled about the new couch and then minutes later turned to whiskey over my tats.

The girls were gone doing what girls do on the day of date parties, and I was sitting in front of the apartment, on the steps, waiting for Toto to take a dump.

For reasons I couldn't pinpoint, my nerves were shot. I'd already taken a couple swigs of whiskey to try to settle my ass down, but it was no use.

I stared at my wrist, hoping whatever ominous feeling I had was just a false alarm. As I started to tell Toto to hurry up because it was fucking cold outside, he hunched over and did his business.

"It's about time, little man!" I said, scooping him up and walking inside.

"Just called the florist. Well, florists. The first one didn't have enough," Shepley said.

I smiled. "The girls are going to shit. Did you make sure they would deliver before they get home?"

"Yeah."

"What if they come home early?"

"They'll be here in plenty of time."

I nodded.

"Hey," Shepley said with a half smile. "You nervous about tonight?"

"No," I said, frowning.

"You are, too, you pussy! You're nervous about date night!"

"Don't be a dick," I said, retreating to my room.

My black shirt was already pressed and waiting on its hanger. It wasn't anything special—one of two button-down shirts that I owned.

The date party would be my first, yes, and I was going with my girlfriend for the first time, but the knot in my stomach was from something else. Something I couldn't quite put my finger on. As if something terrible was lurking in the immediate future.

On edge, I went back into the kitchen and poured another shot of whiskey. The doorbell rang, and I looked up from the counter to see Shepley jogging across the living room from his room, a towel around his waist.

"I could've gotten it."

"Yeah, but then you would have had to stop crying in your Jim Beam," he grumbled, pulling on the door. A small man carrying two mammoth bouquets bigger than he was stood in the doorway.

"Uh, yeah . . . this way, buddy," Shepley said, opening the door wider.

Ten minutes later, the apartment was beginning to look the way I'd imagined. The thought of getting Abby flowers before the date party had come to mind, but one bouquet wasn't enough.

Just as one delivery guy left, another arrived, and then another. Once every surface in the apartment proudly displayed at least two or three ostentatious bouquets of red, pink, yellow, and white roses, Shepley and I were satisfied.

I took a quick shower, shaved, and was slipping on a pair of jeans as the Honda's engine whirred loudly in the parking lot. A few moments after it shut off, America pushed through the front door, and then Abby. Their reaction to the flowers was immediate, and Shepley and I were grinning like idiots as they squealed in delight.

Shepley looked around the room, standing proud. "We went to buy you two flowers, but neither of us thought just one bouquet would do it."

Abby wrapped her arms around my neck. "You guys are . . . you're amazing. Thank you."

I smacked her ass, letting my palm linger on the gentle curve just above her upper thigh. "Thirty minutes until the party, Pidge."

The girls dressed in Shepley's room while we waited. It took me all of five minutes to button up my shirt, find a belt, and slip on socks and shoes. The girls, however, took for fucking ever.

Shepley, impatient, knocked on the door. The party had started fifteen minutes earlier.

"Time to go, ladies," Shepley said.

America walked out in a dress that looked like a second skin, and Shepley whistled, sparking an instant smile on her face.

"Where is she?" I asked.

"Abby's having some trouble with her shoe. She'll be out in just a sec," America explained.

"The suspense is killin' me, Pigeon!" I called.

The door squeaked, and out walked Abby, fidgeting with her short, white dress. Her hair was swept to one side, and even though her tits were carefully hidden, they were accentuated by the tight-fitting fabric.

America elbowed me, and I blinked. "Holy shit."

"Are you ready to be freaked out?" America asked.

"I'm not freaked out—she looks amazing."

Abby smiled with mischief in her eyes, and then slowly turned around to show the steep dip of the fabric in the back.

"Okay, now I'm freakin' out," I said, walking over to her and turning her away from Shepley's eyes.

"You don't like it?" she asked.

"You need a jacket." I jogged to the rack and hastily draped Abby's coat over her shoulders.

"She can't wear that all night, Trav." America chuckled.

"You look beautiful, Abby," Shepley said, trying to apologize for my behavior.

"You do," I said, desperate to be heard and understood without causing a fight. "You look incredible . . . but you can't wear that. Your skirt is . . . wow, your legs are . . . your skirt is too short and it's only half a dress! It doesn't even have a back on it!"

"That's the way it's made, Travis." Abby smiled. At least she wasn't pissed.

"Do you two live to torture each other?" Shepley frowned.

"Do you have a longer dress?" I asked.

Abby looked down. "It's actually pretty modest in the front. It's just the back that shows off a lot of skin."

"Pigeon," I said, wincing, "I don't want you to be mad, but I can't take you to my frat house looking like that. I'll get in a fight the first five minutes."

She leaned up and kissed my lips. "I have faith in you."

"This night is gonna suck," I groaned.

"This night is going to be fantastic," America said, offended.

"Just think of how easy it will be to get it off later," Abby said. She pushed up on the balls of her feet to kiss my neck.

I stared up at the ceiling, trying not to let her lips, sticky from her lip gloss, weaken my case. "That's the problem. Every other guy there will be thinking the same thing."

"But you're the only one that gets to find out," she lilted. When I didn't respond, she leaned back to look me in the eyes. "Do you really want me to change?"

I scanned her face, and every other part of her, and then exhaled. "No matter what you wear, you're gorgeous. I should just get used to it, now, right?" Abby shrugged, and I shook my head. "All right, we're already late. Let's go."

I KEPT MY ARMS AROUND ABBY AS WE WALKED ACROSS the lawn to the Sigma Tau house. Abby was shivering, so I walked quickly and awkwardly with her in tow, trying to get her out of the cold as fast as her high heels would allow. The second we pushed through the thick, double doors, I immediately popped a cigarette in my mouth to add to the typical frat party haze. The bass from the speakers downstairs buzzed like a heartbeat under our feet.

After Shepley and I took care of the girls' coats, I led Abby to the kitchen, with Shepley and America just behind. We stood there, beers in hand, listening to Jay Gruber and Brad Pierce discuss my last fight. Lexie pawed at Brad's shirt, clearly bored with the man talk.

"Dude, you got your girl's name on your wrist? What in the hell possessed you to do that?" Brad said.

I turned over my hand to reveal Abby's nickname. "I'm crazy about her," I said, looking down at Abby.

"You barely know her," Lexie scoffed.

"I know her."

In my peripheral vision, I saw Shepley pull America toward the stairs, so I took Abby's hand and followed. Unfortunately, Brad and Lexie did the same. In a line, we descended the stairs to the basement, the music growing louder with each step.

The second my feet hit the last stair, the DJ played a slow song. Without hesitation, I pulled Abby onto the concrete dance floor, lined with furniture that had been pushed to the side for the party.

Abby's head fit perfectly in the crook of my neck. "I'm glad I never went to one of these things before," I said in her ear. "It's right that I've only brought you."

Abby pressed her cheek against my chest, and her fingers pressed into my shoulders.

"Everyone's staring at you in this dress," I said. "I guess it's kinda cool . . . being with the girl everyone wants."

Abby leaned back to make a show of rolling her eyes. "They don't want me. They're curious why *you* want me. And anyway, I feel sorry for anyone that thinks they have a chance. I am hopelessly and completely in love with you."

How could she even wonder? "You know why I want you? I didn't know I was lost until you found me. I didn't know what alone was until the first night I spent without you in my bed. You're the one thing I've got right. You're what I've been waiting for, Pigeon."

Abby reached up to take my face between her hands, and I wrapped my arms around her, lifting her off the floor. Our lips pressed together gently, and as she worked her lips against mine, I made sure to silently communicate how much I loved her in that kiss, because I could never get it right with just words.

After a few songs and one hostile, yet entertaining moment between Lexie and America, I decided it was a good time to head upstairs. "C'mon, Pidge. I need a smoke."

Abby followed me up the stairs. I made sure to grab her coat before continuing to the balcony. The second we stepped outside, I paused, as did Abby, and Parker, and the makeup-spackled girl he was fingering.

The first move was made by Parker, who pulled his hand from underneath the girl's skirt.

"Abby," he said, surprised and breathless.

"Hey, Parker," Abby replied, choking back a laugh.

"How, uh . . . how have you been?"

She smiled politely. "I've been great, you?"

"Uh"—he looked at his date—"Abby this is Amber. Amber . . . Abby."

"*Abby* Abby?" she asked.

Parker gave one quick, uncomfortable nod. Amber shook Abby's hand with a disgusted look on her face, and then eyed me as if she had just encountered the enemy. "Nice to meet you . . . I guess."

"Amber," Parker warned.

I laughed once, and then opened the doors for them to walk through. Parker grabbed Amber's hand and retreated into the house.

"That was . . . awkward," Abby said, shaking her head and folding arms around her. She looked over the edge at the few couples braving the winter wind.

"At least he's moved on from trying his damndest to get you back," I said, smiling.

"I don't think he was trying to get me back so much as trying to keep me away from you."

"He took *one* girl home for me *once*. Now he acts like he's made a habit of swooping in and saving every freshman I bagged."

Abby shot me a wry look from the corner of her eye. "Did I ever tell you how much I *loathe* that word?"

"Sorry," I said, pulling her into my side. I lit a cigarette and took a deep breath, turning over my hand. The delicate but thick black lines of ink weaved together to form *Pigeon*. "How weird is it that this tat isn't just my new favorite, but it makes me feel at ease to know it's there?"

"Pretty weird," Abby said. I shot her a look, and she laughed. "I'm kidding. I can't say I understand it, but it's sweet . . . in a Travis Maddox sort of way."

"If it feels this good to have this on my arm, I can't imagine how it's going to feel to get a ring on your finger."

"Travis . . ."

"In four, or maybe five years," I said, inwardly cringing that I went that far.

Abby took a breath. "We need to slow down. Way, way down."

"Don't start this, Pidge."

"If we keep going at this pace, I'm going to be barefoot and pregnant before I graduate. I'm not ready to move in with you, I'm not ready for a ring, and I'm certainly not ready to settle down."

I gently cupped her shoulders. "This isn't the 'I wanna see other people' speech, is it? Because I'm not sharing you. No fucking way."

"I don't want anyone else," she said, exasperated.

I relaxed and released her shoulders, turning to grip the railing. "What are you saying, then?" I asked, terrified of her answer.

"I'm saying we need to slow down. That's *all* I'm saying."

I nodded, unhappy.

Abby reached for my arm. "Don't be mad."

"It seems like we take one step forward and two steps back, Pidge. Every time I think we're on the same page, you put up a wall. I don't get it . . . most girls are hounding their boyfriends to get serious, to talk about their feelings, to take the next step . . ."

"I thought we established that I'm not *most girls*?"

I dropped my head, frustrated. "I'm tired of guessing. Where do you see this going, Abby?"

She pressed her lips against my shirt. "When I think about my future, I see you."

I hugged her to my side, every muscle in my body immediately relaxing with her words. We both watched the night clouds move across the starless, black sky. The laughter and humming of the voices below sparked a smile across Abby's face. I watched the same partygoers she did, huddling together and rushing into the house from the street.

For the first time that day, the ominous feeling hovering over me began to fade away.

"Abby! There you are! I've been looking all over for you!" America said, bursting through the door. She held up her cell phone. "I just got off the phone with my dad. Mick called them last night."

Abby's nose wrinkled. "Mick? Why would he call them?"

America raised her eyebrows. "Your mother kept hanging up on him."

"What did he want?"

America pressed her lips together. "To know where you were."

"They didn't tell him, did they?"

America's face fell. "He's your father, Abby. Dad felt he had a right to know."

"He's going to come here," Abby said, her voice swelling with panic. "He's going to come here, Mare!"

"I know! I'm sorry!" America said, trying to comfort her friend. Abby pulled away from her and covered her face with her hands.

I wasn't sure what the hell was going on, but I touched Abby's shoulders. "He won't hurt you, Pigeon," I said. "I won't let him."

"He'll find a way," America said, watching Abby with heavy eyes. "He always does."

"I have to get out of here." Abby pulled her coat tight, and then pulled at the handles of the French doors. She was too upset to slow down long enough to first push down the handles before pulling the doors. As tears fell down her cheeks, I covered her hands with mine. After helping her open the doors, Abby looked at me. I wasn't sure if her cheeks were flush with embarrassment or from the cold, but all I wanted was to make it go away.

I took Abby under my arm, and together we went through

the house, down the stairs and through the crowd to the front door. Abby moved quickly, desperate to get to the safety of the apartment. I had only heard about Mick Abernathy's accolades as a poker player from my father. Watching Abby run like a frightened little girl made me hate any time my family wasted being in awe of him.

Midstep, America's hand shot out and grabbed Abby's coat. "Abby!" she whispered, pointing to a small group of people.

They were crowded around an older, slovenly man, unshaven and dirty to the point where he looked like he smelled. He was pointing to the house, holding a small picture. The couples were nodding, discussing the photo among themselves.

Abby stormed over to the man and pulled the photo from his hands. "*What* in the *hell* are you doing here?"

I looked down at the picture in her hand. She couldn't have been more than fifteen, scrawny, with mousy hair and sunken eyes. She must have been miserable. No wonder she wanted to get away.

The three couples around him backed away. I glanced back at their stunned faces, and then waited for the man to answer. It was Mick fucking Abernathy. I recognized him by the unmistakable sharp eyes nestled in that dirty face.

Shepley and America stood on each side of Abby. I cupped her shoulders from behind.

Mick looked at Abby's dress and clicked his tongue in disapproval. "Well, well, Cookie. You can take the girl out of Vegas—"

"Shut up. Shut up, Mick. Just turn around," she pointed behind him, "and go back to wherever you came from. I don't want you here."

"I can't, Cookie. I need your help."

"What else is new?" America sneered.

Mick narrowed his eyes at America, and then returned his attention to his daughter. "You look awful pretty. You've grown up. I wouldn't've recognized you on the street."

Abby sighed. "What do you want?"

He held up his hands and shrugged. "I seemed to have gotten myself in a pickle, kiddo. Old Dad needs some money."

Abby's entire body tensed. "How much?"

"I was doing good, I really was. I just had to borrow a bit to get ahead and . . . you know."

"I know," she snapped. "How much do you need?"

"Twenty-five."

"Well, shit, Mick, twenty-five hundred? If you'll get the hell outta here . . . I'll give that to you now," I said, pulling out my wallet.

"He means twenty-five thousand," Abby said, her voice cold.

Mick's eyes rolled over me, from my face to my shoes. "Who's this clown?"

My eyebrows shot up from my wallet, and instinctively, I leaned in toward my prey. The only thing stopping me was feeling Abby's small frame between us, and knowing that this skeevy little man was her father. "I can see, now, why a smart guy like yourself has been reduced to asking your teenage daughter for an allowance."

Before Mick could speak, Abby pulled out her cell phone. "Who do you owe this time, Mick?"

Mick scratched his greasy, graying hair. "Well, it's a funny story, Cookie—"

"*Who?*" Abby shouted.

"Benny."

Abby leaned into me. "Benny? You owe *Benny?* What in the

hell were you . . ." She paused. "I don't have that kind of money, Mick."

He smiled. "Something tells me you do."

"Well, I don't! You've really done it this time, haven't you? I knew you wouldn't stop until you got yourself killed!"

He shifted; the smug grin on his face had vanished. "How much ya got?"

"Eleven thousand. I was saving for a car."

America's eyes darted in Abby's direction. "Where did you get eleven thousand dollars, Abby?"

"Travis's fights."

I tugged on her shoulders until she looked at me. "You made *eleven thousand* off my fights? When were you betting?"

"Adam and I had an understanding," she said casually.

Mick's eyes were suddenly animated. "You can double that in a weekend, Cookie. You could get me the twenty-five by Sunday, and Benny won't send his thugs for me."

"It'll clean me out, Mick. I have to pay for school," Abby said, a tinge of sadness in her voice.

"Oh, you can make it back in no time," he said, waving his hand dismissively.

"When is your deadline?" Abby asked.

"Monday mornin'. Midnight," he said, unapologetically.

"You don't have to give him a fucking dime, Pigeon," I said.

Mick grabbed Abby's wrist. "It's the least you could do! I wouldn't be in this mess if it weren't for you!"

America slapped his hand away and then shoved him. "Don't you dare start that shit again, Mick! She didn't make you borrow money from Benny!"

Mick glared at Abby. The light of hatred in his eyes made any connection with her as his daughter disappear. "If it weren't for her, I woulda had my own money. You took everything from me, Abby. I have nothin'!"

Abby choked back a cry. "I'll get your money to Benny by Sunday. But when I do, I want you to leave me the *hell* alone. I won't do this again, Mick. From now on, you're on your own, do you hear me? Stay. Away."

He pressed his lips together and then nodded. "Have it your way, Cookie."

Abby turned around and headed for the car.

America sighed. "Pack your bags, boys. We're going to Vegas." She walked toward the Charger, and Shepley and I stood, frozen.

"Wait. What?" He looked to me. "Like Las Vegas, Vegas? As in Nevada?"

"Looks that way," I said, shoving my hands in my pockets.

"We're just going to book a flight to Vegas," Shepley said, still trying to process the situation.

"Yep."

Shepley walked over to open America's door to let her and Abby in on the passenger side, and then slammed it shut, blank faced. "I've never been to Vegas."

An impish grin pulled one side of my mouth to the side. "Looks like it's time to pop that cherry."

CHAPTER TWENTY

You Win Some,
You Lose Some

Abby barely spoke while we packed, and even less on the way to the airport. She stared off into space most of the time unless one of us asked her a question. I wasn't sure if she was drowning in despair, or just focused on the looming challenge ahead.

Checking in to the hotel, America did all the talking, flashing her fake ID, as if she had done it a thousand times before.

It occurred to me, then, that she probably *had* done it before. Vegas was where they had procured such flawless IDs, and why America never seemed to worry about what Abby could handle. They'd seen it all before, in the bowels of the city of sin.

Shepley was an unmistakable tourist, his head leaned back, gawking at the ostentatious ceiling. We pulled our luggage into the elevator, and I pulled Abby to my side.

"You okay?" I asked, touching my lips to her temple.

"I don't want to be here," she choked out.

The doors opened, revealing the intricate pattern of the rug that lined the hallway. America and Shepley went one way, Abby and I the other. Our room was at the end of the hall.

Abby shoved the card key into the slot, and then pushed open the door. The room was large, dwarfing the king-size bed in the middle of the room.

I left the suitcase against the wall, pressing all the switches until the thicker curtain separated to reveal the busy, blinking lights and traffic of the Las Vegas Strip. Another button pulled away a second set of sheer curtains.

Abby didn't pay attention to the window. She didn't even bother to look up. The glitter and gold had lost its luster for her years before.

I set our carry-on bags on the floor and looked around the room. "This is nice, right?" Abby glared at me. "What?"

She opened her suitcase in one motion, and shook her head. "This isn't a vacation, Travis. You shouldn't be here."

In two steps, I was behind her, crossing my arms around her middle. She was different here, but I wasn't. I could still be someone she could count on, someone who could protect her from the ghosts of her past.

"I go where you go," I said against her ear.

She leaned her head back against my chest and sighed. "I have to get on the floor. You can stay here or check out the Strip. I'll see you later, okay?"

"I'm going with you."

She turned to face me. "I don't want you there, Trav."

I didn't expect that from her, especially not the cold tone of her voice.

Abby touched my arm. "If I'm going to win fourteen thousand dollars in one weekend, I have to concentrate. I don't like who I'm going to be while I'm at those tables, and I don't want you to see it, okay?"

I brushed her hair from her eyes, and then kissed her cheek. "Okay, Pidge." I couldn't pretend to understand what she meant, but I would respect it.

America knocked on the door and then traipsed in wearing the same nude number she wore to the date party. Her heels were sky high, and she had put on two extra layers of makeup. She looked ten years older.

I waved to America, and then grabbed the extra card key off the table. America was already building Abby up for her night, reminding me of a trainer offering a pep talk to his fighter before a big boxing match.

Shepley was standing in the hall, staring at three trays of half-eaten food on the floor left there by guests across the hall.

"What do you want to do first?" I asked.

"I'm definitely not marrying you."

"You're fucking hilarious. Let's go downstairs."

The elevator door opened, and the hotel came alive. It was like the hallways were the veins, and the people were its lifeblood. Groups of women dressed like porn stars, families, foreigners, the occasional bachelor party, and hotel employees followed each other in organized chaos.

It took a while to get past the stores that lined the exits and reach the boulevard, but we broke out onto the street and walked until we saw a crowd gathered in front of one of the casinos. The fountains were on, performing to some patriotic song. Shepley was mesmerized, seemingly unable to move while he watched the water dance and spray.

We must have caught the last the two minutes, because the lights soon dimmed, the water fizzled, and the crowd immediately dispersed.

"What was that about?" I asked.

Shepley still stared at the now calm pond. "I don't know, but it was cool."

The streets were lined with Elvis, Michael Jackson, showgirls, and cartoon characters, all readily available to take a picture for a price. At one point, I kept hearing a flapping noise, and then I pinpointed where it was coming from. Men were standing on the sidewalk, snapping a stack of cards in their hands. They handed one to Shepley. It was a picture of a ridiculously big-breasted woman in a seductive pose. They were selling hookers and strip clubs. Shepley tossed the card to the ground. The sidewalk was covered in them.

A girl walked past, eyeing me with a drunken smile. She carried her heels in her hand. As she ambled by, I noticed her blackened feet. The ground was filthy, the foundation for the glitz and glamour above.

"We're saved," Shepley said, walking over to a street vendor selling Red Bull and whatever liquor you could imagine. Shepley ordered two with vodka, and smiled when he took his first sip. "I may never wanna leave."

I checked the time on my cell phone. "It's been an hour. Let's head back."

"Do you remember where we were? Because I don't."

"Yeah. This way."

We retraced our steps. I was glad when we finally ended up

at our hotel, because in truth I wasn't exactly sure how to get back, either. The Strip wasn't hard to navigate, but there were a lot of distractions along the way, and Shepley was definitely in vacation mode.

I searched the poker tables for Abby, knowing that's where she would be. I caught a glimpse of her caramel hair; she sat upright and confident at a table full of old men, and America; the girls were a stark contrast from the rest of those camped out in the poker area.

Shepley waved me over to a blackjack table, and we played a while to pass the time.

Half an hour later, Shepley nudged my arm. Abby was standing, talking to a guy with olive skin and dark hair, in a suit and tie. He had her by the arm, and I immediately stood.

Shepley grabbed my shirt. "Hold up, Travis. He works here. Just give it a minute. You might get us all kicked out if you don't keep your head."

I watched them. He was smiling, but Abby was all business. He acknowledged America, then.

"They know him," I said, trying to read their lips to figure out the distant conversation. The only thing I could make out was *have dinner with me* from the douche in the suit, and Abby saying *I'm here with someone.*

Shepley couldn't hold me back this time, but I stopped a few feet away when I saw the suit kiss Abby's cheek.

"It was good to see you again. See you tomorrow . . . five o'clock all right? I'm on the floor at eight," he said.

My stomach sank, and my face felt like it was on fire. America tugged on Abby's arm, noting my presence.

"Who was that?" I asked.

Abby nodded in the suit's direction. "That is Jesse Viveros. I've known him a long time."

"How long?"

She glanced back at her empty chair at the poker table. "Travis, I don't have time for this."

"I guess he chucked the youth minister idea," America said, sending a flirtatious grin in Jesse's direction.

"That's your ex-boyfriend?" I asked, instantly angry. "I thought you said he was from Kansas?"

Abby shot America an impatient glare, and then took my chin in her hand. "He knows I'm not old enough to be in here, Trav. He gave me until midnight. I will explain everything later, but for now I have to get back to the game, all right?"

My teeth clenched, and I closed my eyes. My girlfriend had just agreed to go out with her ex-boyfriend. Everything inside me wanted to throw a typical Maddox tantrum, but Abby needed me to man up for the moment. Acting against my instincts, I decided to let it go, and leaned down to kiss her. "All right. I'll see you at midnight. Good luck."

I turned, pushing my way through the crowd, hearing Abby's voice surge at least two octaves. "Gentlemen?"

It reminded me of those girls who would talk like children when they tried to get my attention, hoping to come across as innocent.

"I don't understand why she had to make any deals with that Jesse guy," I growled.

"So she could stay, I guess?" Shepley asked, staring up at the ceiling again.

"There are other casinos. We can just go to another one."

"She knows people here, Travis. She probably came here because she knew if she got caught, they wouldn't rat her out to the cops. She has a fake ID, but I bet it wouldn't take long for security to recognize her. These casinos pay high dollar for people to point out the hustlers, right?"

"I guess," I said, frowning.

We met Abby and America at the table, watching as America gathered Abby's winnings.

Abby looked at her watch. "I need more time."

"Wanna try the blackjack tables?"

"I can't lose money, Trav."

I smiled. "You can't lose, Pidge."

America shook her head. "Blackjack's not her game."

"I won a little," I said, digging in my pockets. "I'm up six hundred. You can have it."

Shepley handed Abby his chips. "I only made three. It's yours."

Abby sighed. "Thanks, guys, but I'm still short five grand." She looked at her watch again and then looked up to see Jesse approaching.

"How did you do?" he asked, smiling.

"I'm five K short, Jess. I need more time."

"I've done all I can, Abby."

"Thanks for letting me stay."

Jesse offered an uncomfortable smile. He was obviously just as scared of these people as Abby. "Maybe I can get my dad to talk to Benny for you?"

"It's Mick's mess. I'm going to ask him for an extension."

Jesse shook his head. "You know that's not going to happen, Cookie, no matter how much you come up with. If it's less than what he owes, Benny's going to send someone. You stay as far away from him as you can."

"I have to try," Abby said, her voice broken.

Jesse took a step forward, leaning in to keep his voice low. "Get on a plane, Abby. You hear me?"

"I hear you," she snapped.

Jesse sighed, and his eyes grew heavy with sympathy. He wrapped his arms around Abby and then kissed her hair. "I'm sorry. If my job wasn't at stake, you know I'd try to figure something out."

The hairs on the back of my neck stood on end, something that only happened when I felt threatened and was about to unleash my full wrath on someone.

Just before I tackled him, Abby pulled away.

"I know," she said. "You did what you could."

Jesse lifted her chin with his finger. "I'll see you tomorrow at five." He bent down to kiss the corner of her mouth, and then walked away.

It was then that I noticed my body was leaning forward, and Shepley was once again gripping my shirt, his knuckles white.

Abby's eyes were stuck to the floor.

"What's at five?" I seethed.

"She agreed to dinner if Jesse would let her stay. She didn't have a choice, Trav," America said.

Abby peered up at me with her big, apologetic eyes.

"You had a choice," I said.

"Have you ever dealt with the Mob, Travis? I'm sorry if your feelings are hurt, but a free meal with an old friend isn't a high price to pay to keep Mick alive."

I clamped my jaw closed, refusing to let it open for words to spill out that I would regret later.

"C'mon, you guys, we have to find Benny," America said, pulling Abby by the arm.

Shepley walked beside me as we followed the girls down the Strip to Benny's building. It was one block away from the bright lights, but it was somewhere the gold had never touched—and wasn't meant to. Abby paused, and then walked up a few steps to a large, green door. She knocked, and I held her other hand to keep it from trembling.

The doorman appeared in the open doorway. He was enormous—black, intimidating, and as wide as he was tall—with the stereotypical Vegas sleazeball standing next to him. Gold chains, suspicious eyes, and a gut from eating too much of his mother's cooking.

"Benny," Abby breathed.

"My, my . . . you're not Lucky Thirteen anymore, now, are ya? Mick didn't tell me what a looker you've grown into. I've been waiting for you, Cookie. I hear you have a payment for me."

Abby nodded, and Benny gestured to the rest of us. "They're with me," she said, her voice surprisingly strong.

"I'm afraid your companions will have to wait outside," the doorman said in an abnormally deep bass tone.

I took Abby by the arm, turning my shoulder in a protective stance. "She's not going in there alone. I'm coming with her."

Benny eyed me for a moment, and then smiled to his doorman. "Fair enough. Mick will be glad to know you have such a good friend with you."

We followed him inside. I kept a firm grip on Abby's arm, making sure to stand between her and the biggest threat—the

doorman. We walked behind Benny, followed him into an elevator, and then traveled up four floors.

When the doors opened, a large mahogany desk came into
view. Benny hobbled to his plush chair and sat down, gesturing for us to take the two empty seats facing his desk. I sat, but
adrenaline was streaming through my veins, making me twitch
and fidget. I could hear and see everything in the room, including the two thugs standing in the shadows behind Benny's desk.

Abby reached over to grab my hand, and I gave her a reassuring squeeze.

"Mick owes me twenty-five thousand. I trust you have the full
amount," Benny said, scribbling something on a notepad.

"Actually," Abby paused, clearing her throat, "I'm five K
short, Benny. But I have all day tomorrow to get that. And five
thousand is no problem, right? You know I'm good for it."

"Abigail," Benny said, frowning, "You disappoint me. You
know my rules better than that."

"P-please, Benny. I'm asking you to take the nineteen-nine,
and I'll have the rest for you tomorrow."

Benny's beady eyes darted from Abby to me, and then back
again. The thugs stepped out of their dark corners, and the hairs
on the back of my neck were standing on end again.

"You know I don't take anything but the full amount. The
fact that you're trying to hand me less tells me something. You
know what it tells me? That you're not sure if you can get the full
amount."

The thugs took another step forward. I took stock of their
pockets and any shape under their clothing that screamed
weapon. They both had some sort of knife, but I didn't see any

guns. That didn't mean they didn't have one stuffed in a boot, but I doubted either one was as fast as me. If I needed to, I could get it away from them and get us the hell out of there.

"I can get your money, Benny," Abby giggled nervously. "I won eighty-nine hundred in six hours."

"So are you saying you'll bring me eighty-nine hundred in six more hours?" Benny smiled his devilish grin.

"The deadline isn't until midnight tomorrow," I said, glancing behind us and watching the approaching shadow men.

"W-what are you doing, Benny?" Abby asked, her posture rigid.

"Mick called me tonight. He said you're taking care of his debt."

"I'm doing him a favor. I don't owe you any money," she said sternly.

Benny leaned both of his fat, stubby elbows onto his desk. "I'm considering teaching Mick a lesson, and I'm curious just how lucky you are, kiddo."

Instinctively, I shot out of my chair, pulling Abby with me. I jerked her behind me, backing up toward the door.

"Josiah is outside the door, young man. Where exactly do you think you're going to escape to?"

"Travis," Abby warned.

There would be no more talking. If I let either of these goons past me, they would hurt Abby. I moved her behind me.

"I hope you know, Benny, that when I take out your men, I mean no disrespect. But I'm in love with this girl, and I can't let you hurt her."

Benny burst into a loud cackle. "I gotta hand it to you, son.

You've got the biggest balls of anyone that's come through those doors. I'll prepare you for what you're about to get. The rather large fella to your right is David, and if he can't take you out with his fists, he's going to use that knife in his holster. The man to your left is Dane, and he's my best fighter. He's got a fight tomorrow, as a matter of fact, and he's never lost. Mind you don't hurt your hands, Dane. I've got a lot of money riding on you."

Dane smiled at me with wild, amused eyes. "Yes, sir."

"Benny, stop! I can get you the money!" Abby cried.

"Oh no . . . this is going to get interesting very fast." Benny chuckled, settling back into his seat.

David rushed me. He was clumsy and slow, and before he even had a chance to reach for his knife, I incapacitated him, shoving his nose straight down into my knee. I then threw two punches into his rat face. Knowing this wasn't a basement fight, and that I was fighting to get me and Abby out alive, I put everything I had into each swing. It felt good, as if every bit of pent-up rage inside me was finally allowed an outlet. Two more punches and an elbow later, David was lying on the floor in a bloody heap.

Benny's head fell back, laughing hysterically and pounding his desk with the delight of a child watching Saturday morning cartoons. "Well, go on, Dane. He didn't scare you, did he?"

Dane approached me more carefully, with the focus and precision of a professional fighter. His fist flew at my face, but I stepped to the side, ramming my shoulder into him at full force. We stumbled back together, and fell onto Benny's desk.

Dane grabbed me with both arms, hurling me to the ground. He was faster than I had anticipated, but not fast enough. We scuffled on the floor for a moment while I bought time to get a good grip, but then Dane gained ground, positioning himself to get in a few punches on me while I was trapped beneath him on the floor.

I grabbed Dane's nuts and twisted. It shocked him and he cried out, pausing just long enough for me to get the upper hand. I kneeled over him, holding him by his long hair, loading punch after punch into the side of his head. Dane's face rammed into the front of Benny's desk with each blow, and then he scrambled to his feet, disoriented and bleeding.

I watched him for a moment, and then attacked again, letting my rage flow through me with every strike. Dane dodged once and landed his knuckles to my jaw.

He may have been a fighter, but Thomas hit a lot harder than he did. This was going to be cake.

I smiled and held up my index finger. "That's your one."

Benny's unrestrained laughter filled the room while I finished his goon off. My elbow landed in the center of Dane's face, knocking him out before he hit the ground.

"Amazing young man! Simply amazing!" Benny said, clapping with delight.

Immediately I grabbed for Abby, pulling her behind me when Josiah filled the doorway with his massive frame.

"Should I take care of this, sir?" Josiah asked. His voice was deep but innocent, as if he was just doing the only job he was good at, and didn't truly desire to hurt either of us.

"No! No, no . . . ," Benny said, still giddy with the impromptu performance. "What is your name?"

"Travis Maddox," I said between breaths. I wiped Dane's and David's blood off of my hands and onto my jeans.

"Travis Maddox, I believe you can help your little girlfriend out."

"How's that?" I puffed.

"Dane was supposed to fight tomorrow night. I had a lot of cash riding on him, and it doesn't look like Dane will be fit to win a fight anytime soon. I suggest you take his place, make my bankroll for me, and I'll forgive the remaining fifty-one hundred of Mick's debt."

I turned to Abby. "Pigeon?"

"Are you all right?" she asked, wiping the blood from my face. She bit her lip, her face crumpling around her mouth. Her eyes filled with tears.

"It's not my blood, baby. Don't cry."

Benny stood. "I'm a busy man, son. Pass or play?"

"I'll do it," I said. "Give me the when and where and I'll be there."

"You'll be fighting Brock McMann. He's no wallflower. He was barred from the UFC last year."

I knew the name. "Just tell me where I need to be."

Benny gave me the information, then a shark's grin spread across his face. "I like you, Travis. I think we'll be good friends."

"I doubt it," I said. I opened the door for Abby and sustained a protective stance beside her until we cleared the front door.

"Jesus Christ!" America cried upon seeing the splattered blood covering my clothing. "Are you guys okay?" She grabbed Abby's shoulders and scanned her face.

"I'm okay. Just another day at the office. For both of us," Abby said, wiping her eyes.

With her hand in mine, we rushed to the hotel, with Shepley and America close behind.

The only people that seemed to notice my blood-spattered clothes was the kid in the elevator.

Once we were all back in my and Abby's room, I stripped down and went into the bathroom to wash the sleaze off me.

"What in the hell happened in there?" Shepley finally asked.

I could hear their voices murmuring as I stood under the water, recalling the last hour. As scary as it was for Abby to be in such real danger, it felt fucking amazing to unleash on Benny's two goons David and Dane. It was like the best drug in existence.

I wondered if they had come to yet, or if Benny just had them dragged outside and left in the alley.

A strange calm came over me. Pummeling Benny's men was an outlet for every bit of anger and frustration that had accumulated over the years, and now I almost felt normal.

"I'm gonna kill him! I'm going to kill that sorry son of a bitch!" America shouted.

I shut off the shower and wrapped a towel around my waist.

"One of the guys I knocked out had a fight tomorrow night," I said to Shepley. "I'm taking his place and in return Benny will forgive the last five K Mick owes."

America stood up. "This is ridiculous! Why are we helping Mick, Abby? He threw you to the wolves! I'm going to *kill* him!"

"Not if I kill him first," I seethed.

"Get in line," Abby said.

Shepley shifted nervously. "So you're fighting tomorrow?"

I nodded once. "At a place called Zero's. Six o'clock. It's Brock McMann, Shep."

Shepley shook his head. "No way. No fucking way, Trav. The guy's a maniac!"

"Yeah," I said, "but he's not fighting for his girl, is he?" I took Abby in my arms, kissing the top of her hair. She was still trembling. "You okay, Pigeon?"

"This is wrong. This is wrong on so many levels. I don't know which one to talk you out of first."

"Did you not see me tonight? I'm going to be fine. I've seen Brock fight before. He's tough, but not unbeatable."

"I don't want you to do this, Trav."

"Well, I don't want you to go to dinner with your ex-boyfriend tomorrow night. I guess we both have to do something unpleasant to save your good-for-nothing father."

CHAPTER TWENTY-ONE
Slow Death

SHEPLEY SAT BESIDE ME ON A BENCH IN A SMALL BUT well-lit room. It was the first time I wouldn't walk out into a basement for a staged fight. The audience would consist of the shadow people of Vegas: locals, mobsters, drug dealers, and their arm candy. The crowd outside was a dark army, exponentially louder, and far more thirsty for blood. I would be surrounded by a cage instead of people.

"I still don't think you should do this," America said from the other side of the room.

"Not now, baby," Shepley said. He was helping me wrap tape around my hands.

"Are you nervous?" she asked, uncharacteristically quiet.

"No. I'd be better if Pidge was here, though. Have you heard from her?"

"I'll text her. She'll be here."

"Did she love him?" I asked, wondering what their dinner conversation consisted of. He was obviously no preacher man now, and I wasn't sure what he expected in return for his favor.

"No," America said. "She never said so, anyway. They grew up together, Travis. He was the only person she could count on for a long time."

I wasn't sure if that made me feel better or worse. "Did she text you back yet?"

"Hey," Shepley said, smacking my cheek. "Hey! You have Brock McMann waiting for you. Your head needs to be in this one hundred percent. Quit being a pussy and focus!"

I nodded, trying to remember the few times I'd seen Brock fight. He'd been banned from the UFC for sucker punches and a rumor that he'd accosted the UFC president. It had been a while, but he was a notoriously dirty fighter and pulled blatantly illegal shit just out of sight of the ref. The key would be to not get in that position. If he locked his legs around me, it could go downhill pretty fast.

"You're gonna play this safe, Trav. Let him attack first. Kind of the same way you fought the night you were trying to win your bet with Abby. You're not fighting some varsity wrestling reject. This isn't the Circle, and you're not trying to create a show for the crowd."

"The hell if I'm not."

"You've gotta win, Travis. You're fighting for Abby, don't forget that."

I nodded. Shepley was right. If I lost, Benny wouldn't get his money, and Abby would still be in danger.

A tall, large man in a suit and greasy hair walked in. "You're up. Your trainer can join you on the outside of the cage, but the girls . . . where's the other girl?"

A lined formed between my eyebrows. "She's coming."

"... they have reserved seats on the end of the second row on your corner."

Shepley turned back to America. "I'll walk you there." He looked to the suit. "Nobody touches her. I will fucking kill the first person that does."

The suit offered a ghost of a smile. "Benny already said no distractions. We'll have eyes on her at all times."

Shepley nodded, and then held out his hand for America. She took it, and they quietly followed me through the door.

The announcers amplified voice echoed through huge speakers placed at each corner of the vast room. It looked like a small concert hall, easily seating a thousand people, and they were all on their feet, either cheering or eyeing me suspiciously as I walked out.

The gate to the cage opened, and I stepped inside.

Shepley watched the suit seat America, and once he was satisfied that she was okay, turned to me. "Remember: play it smart. Let him attack first, and the goal is to win for Abby."

I nodded.

Seconds later, music blared from the speakers, and both the motion and volume from the stands exploded into a frenzy. Brock McMann emerged from a hallway as a spotlight in the rafters illuminated the severe expression on his face. He had an entourage that kept the spectators at bay while he bounced up and down to stay loose. I figured he'd probably been training for this fight for weeks if not months.

That was okay. I'd been beat up by my brothers my whole life. I'd had plenty of training.

I turned to check in with America. She shrugged, and I

frowned. The biggest fight of my life was minutes away, and Abby wasn't there. Just when I turned to watch Brock enter the cage, I heard Shepley's voice.

"Travis! Travis! She's here!"

I turned, desperately searching for Abby, to see her running down the steps at full speed. She stopped just short of the cage, slamming her hands into the chain-link to stop herself.

"I'm here! I'm here," she breathed.

We kissed through the space between the fence, and she held my face in her hands with the few fingers she could fit through. "I love you." She shook her head. "You don't have to do this, you know."

I smiled. "Yeah, I do."

"Let's do this, Romeo. I don't have all night," Brock called from the other side.

I didn't turn around, but Abby glanced over my shoulder. When she caught sight of Brock, her cheeks flushed with anger, and her expression turned cold. Less than a second later, her eyes returned to mine, warming again. She smiled an impish grin.

"Teach that asshole some manners."

I winked at her and smiled. "Anything for you, baby."

Brock met me in the center of the ring, toe to toe.

"Be smart!" Shepley yelled.

I leaned over to whisper in Brock's ear. "I just want you to know I'm a big fan, even though you're kind of a prick and a cheat. So don't take it personally when you get KTFO'd tonight."

Brock's square jaws worked violently under the skin, and his eyes lit up—not with anger, but with stunned confusion.

"Be *smart*, Travis!" Shepley yelled again, seeing the look in my eyes.

The bell sounded, and I immediately attacked. Using every bit of force, I let the same fury free that I'd unleashed on Benny's goons.

Brock stumbled backward, trying to position himself to guard or kick me, but I gave him no time, using both of my fists to run him into the ground.

It was an extraordinary release not to hold back. Relishing the pure adrenaline ripping through me, I forgot myself, and Brock dodged my blow, coming back with a right hook. His throws had a lot more bite than the amateurs I went up against at school—and it was fucking awesome. Fighting Brock brought back memories of some of the more serious disagreements I'd had with my brothers, when words escalated to an ass whipping.

I felt right at home trading punches with Brock; in that moment, my rage had a purpose and a place.

Each time Brock's fists landed a blow, it only served to amp up my adrenaline, and I could feel my already powerful punches picking up more steam.

He tried to wrestled me to the ground, but I planted my feet in a squatlike position, stabilizing myself against his desperate movements to throw me off balance. While he thrashed around, my clenched hand made contact with his head, ears, and temple numerous times.

The once white tape around my knuckles was now crimson, but I felt no pain, only the sheer pleasure of unleashing every negative emotion that had weighed me down for so long. I remembered how relaxing it felt to beat the hell out of Benny's men. Win or lose, I looked forward to what kind of person I would be after this fight.

The referee, Shepley, and Brock's trainer surrounded me, pulling me off of my opponent.

"Bell, Travis! Stop!" Shepley said.

Shepley dragged me to one corner, and Brock was pulled to the other. I turned to look at Abby. She was wringing her hands together, but her wide smile told me she was okay. I winked at her, and she blew me a kiss. The gesture reenergized me, and I returned to the middle of the cage with renewed determination.

Once the bell rang, I attacked again, this time taking more care to dodge just as many times as I threw a punch. Once or twice, Brock wrapped his arms around me, breathing hard, and tried to bite me or knee me in the balls. I'd just push him off and hit him harder.

In the third round, Brock stumbled, swung or kicked and missed. He was running out of steam fast. Feeling winded myself, I was taking more breaks between swings. The adrenaline that had once surged through my body felt tapped out, and my head was beginning to pound.

Brock landed a punch, and then another. I blocked a third, and then, ready for it to end, went in for the kill. With my remaining strength, I dodged Brock's knee and then swung around, planting my elbow straight into his nose. His head flew back, looking straight upward, he took a few steps, and then fell to the ground.

The noise from the crowd was deafening, but I could only hear one voice.

"Oh my God! Yes! Yay, baby!" Abby screamed.

The referee checked Brock, and then walked over to me, lifting my hand. Shepley, America, and Abby were all let into the cage, and they swarmed me. I picked up Abby and planted my lips on hers.

"You did it," she said, cupping my face in her hands.

The celebration was cut short when Benny and a fresh batch of bodyguards entered the cage. I set Abby on her feet, and took a defensive stance in front of her.

Benny was all smiles. "Well done, Maddox. You saved the day. If you have a minute, I'd like to talk to you."

I looked back at Abby, who grabbed my hand. "It's okay. I'll meet you at that door," I said, nodding to the closest door, "in ten minutes."

"Ten?" she asked with worry in her eyes.

"Ten," I said, kissing her forehead. I looked to Shepley. "Keep an eye on the girls."

"I think maybe I should go with you."

I leaned into Shepley's ear. "If they want to kill us, Shepley, there's not much we can do about it. I think Benny has something else in mind." I leaned back and slapped his arm. "I'll see you in ten."

"Not eleven. Not fifteen. Ten," Shepley said, pulling a reluctant Abby away.

I followed Benny to the same room I had waited in before the fight. To my surprise, he made his men wait outside.

He held out his hands, gesturing to the room. "I thought this would be better. So you could see that I'm not always this . . . bad man that maybe I'm made out to be."

His body language and tone were relaxed, but I kept my ears and eyes open for any surprises.

Benny smiled. "I have a proposition for you, son."

"I'm not your son."

"True," he conceded. "But after I offer you a hundred and fifty grand a fight, I think you might want to be."

"What fights?" I asked. I figured he would try to say that Abby still owed him. I had no clue he'd try to offer me a job.

"You are obviously a very vicious, very talented young man. You belong in that cage. I can make that happen . . . and I can also make you a very rich man."

"I'm listening."

Benny grinned wider. "I'll schedule one fight a month."

"I'm still in college."

He shrugged. "We'll schedule around it. I'll fly you out, and Abby if you wish, first class, on weekends, if that's what you want. Making money like this, though, you might want to put a hold on the college education."

"Six figures a fight?" I did the math, trying not to let my surprise show. "To fight and what else?"

"That's it, kid. Just fight. Make me money."

"Just fight . . . and I can quit when I want."

He smiled. "Well, sure, but I don't see that happening anytime soon. You love it. I saw you. You were drunk with it, in that cage."

I stood there for a moment, mulling over his offer. "I'll think about it. Let me talk to Abby."

"Fair enough."

I SET OUR SUITCASES ON THE BED AND COLLAPSED BESIDE them. I'd mentioned Benny's offer to Abby, but she wasn't receptive at all. Then the plane ride home was a little tense, so I decided to leave it alone until we got home.

Abby was drying off Toto after giving him a bath. He'd been staying with Brazil, and she was revolted with the way he smelled.

"Oh! You smell so much better!" She giggled as he shook, spraying water all over her and the floor. He stood up on his hind legs, covering her face with tiny puppy kisses. "I missed you, too, little man."

"Pigeon?" I asked, nervously knotting my fingers together.

"Yeah?" she said, rubbing Toto with the yellow towel in her hands.

"I wanna do this. I want to fight in Vegas."

"No," she said, smiling at Toto's happy face.

"You're not listening. I'm gonna do it. You'll see in a few months that it was the right decision."

She looked up at me. "You're going to work for Benny."

I nodded nervously and then smiled. "I just wanna take care of you, Pidge."

Tears glossed her eyes. "I don't want anything bought with that money, Travis. I don't want anything to do with Benny or Vegas or anything that goes along with it."

"You didn't have a problem with the thought of buying a car with the money from my fights here."

"That's different, and you know it."

I frowned. "It's gonna be okay, Pidge. You'll see."

She watched me for a moment, and then her cheeks flushed. "Why did you even ask me, Travis? You were going to work for Benny no matter what I said."

"I want your support on this, but it's too much money to turn down. I would be crazy to say no."

She paused for a long time, her shoulders fell, and then nodded. "Okay, then. You've made your decision."

My mouth stretched into a wide smile. "You'll see, Pigeon. It's going to be great." I pushed off the bed, walked over to Abby and kissed her fingers. "I'm starved. You hungry?"

She shook her head.

I kissed her hairline before making my way to the kitchen. My lips hummed a chipper tune from a random song while I grabbed two slices of bread and some salami and cheese. *Man, she's missing out,* I thought, squeezing spicy mustard onto the bread slices.

It took about three bites for me to finish, and then I washed it down with a beer, wondering what else there was to eat. I didn't realize how spread thin my body felt until we'd gotten home. Aside from the fight, nerves probably also had something to do with it. Now that Abby knew my plans and it was settled, the nerves went away just enough for me to have an appetite again.

Abby padded down the hall and then rounded the corner, suitcase in hand. She didn't look at me when she crossed the living room to the door.

"Pigeon?" I called.

I walked to the still-open door, seeing Abby approaching America's Honda.

When she didn't answer, I jogged down the stairs and across the grass to where Shepley, America, and Abby stood.

"What are you doing?" I asked, gesturing to the suitcase.

Abby smiled awkwardly. It was immediately obvious something wasn't right.

"Pidge?"

"I'm taking my stuff to Morgan. They have all those washers and dryers and I have a ridiculous amount of laundry to do."

I frowned. "You were going to leave without telling me?"

"She was coming back in, Trav. You're so freakin' paranoid," America said.

"Oh," I said, still unsure. "You staying here tonight?"

"I don't know. I guess it depends on when my laundry gets done."

Although I knew she was probably still uneasy with my decision about Benny, I let it go, smiled, and pulled her against me. "In three weeks, I'll pay someone to do your laundry. Or you can just throw away your dirty clothes and buy new ones."

"You're fighting for Benny again?" America asked, shocked.

"He made me an offer I couldn't refuse."

"Travis," Shepley began.

"Don't you guys start on me, too. If I'm not changing my mind for Pidge, I'm not changing my mind for you."

America traded glances with Abby. "Well, we better get you back, Abby. That pile of clothes is gonna take you forever."

I leaned down to kiss Abby's lips. She pulled me close and kissed me hard, making me feel a little better about her unease. "See you later," I said, holding the door open while she sat in the passenger seat. "Love you."

Shepley lifted Abby's suitcase into the hatchback of the Honda, and America slid into her seat, reaching over to pull across her seat belt.

I shut Abby's door, and then folded my arms across my chest.

Shepley stood beside me. "You're not really going to fight for Benny, are you?"

"It's a lot of money, Shepley. Six figures a fight."

"*Six* figures?"

"Could you say no?"

"I would if I thought America would dump my ass over it."

I laughed once. "Abby's not going to *dump* me over this."

America backed out of the parking lot, and I noticed tears spilling down Abby's cheeks.

I jogged to her window, tapping on the glass. "What's wrong, Pidge?"

"Go, Mare," she mouthed, wiping her eyes.

I jogged alongside the car, slamming my palm against the glass. Abby wouldn't look at me, and absolute terror sunk into my bones. "Pigeon? America! Stop the fucking car! Abby, don't do this!"

America turned onto the main road and pressed on the gas.

I sprinted after them, but when the Honda was nearly out of sight, I turned and ran for my Harley. I dug my hand in my pocket for my keys as I ran, and leaped onto the seat.

"Travis, don't," Shepley warned.

"She's fucking leaving me, Shep!" I yelled, barely starting the bike before revving the throttle into a 180, and flying down the street.

America had just shut her door when I made it into Morgan Hall's parking lot. I nearly laid my bike over coming to a halt and failing to root the kickstand on the first try. I ran over to the Honda and jerked open the passenger door. America's teeth were clenched, ready for whatever I might throw at her.

I looked to Morgan's brick and mortar, knowing Abby was somewhere inside. "You gotta let me in, Mare," I begged.

"I'm sorry," she said. She put the car in reverse and backed out of the parking space.

Just as I raced up the steps, taking two at a time, a girl I hadn't seen before was walking out. I grabbed the door, but she blocked my way.

"You can't come in without an escort."

I pulled out my bike keys and jingled them in her face. "My girlfriend, Abby Abernathy, left her car keys at my apartment. I'm just bringing them by."

The girl nodded, unsure, and then moved out of my way.

Leaping up several steps at a time in the stairwell, I finally reached Abby's floor and her dorm room door. I took a few deep breaths. "Pidge?" I said, trying to be quiet. "You gotta let me in, baby. We've got to talk about this."

She didn't answer.

"Pigeon, please. You're right. I didn't listen to you. We can sit down and discuss this some more, okay? I just . . . please answer the door. You're scarin' me to death."

"Go away, Travis," Kara said from the other side.

I pounded on the door with the side of my fist. "Pidge? Open the fucking door, dammit! I'm not leaving until you talk to me! Pigeon!"

"What?" Kara growled, opening the door. She pushed her glasses up, and sniffed. For such a tiny girl, she had a very severe expression.

I sighed, relieved that at least I would be able to see Abby. Looking over Kara's shoulder, Abby wasn't in my direct line of sight.

"Kara," I said, trying to stay calm. "Tell Abby I need to see her. Please."

"She's not here."

"She's here," I said, quickly losing my patience.

Kara's weight shifted. "I haven't seen her tonight. I haven't seen her in several days, actually."

"I know she's here!" I yelled. "Pigeon?"

"She's not . . . Hey!" Kara said, shrieking when I shouldered past her.

The door cracked against the wall. I pulled the knob and looked behind it, and then in the closets, even under the bed. "Pigeon! Where is she?"

"I haven't seen her!" Kara shouted.

I walked into the hall, looking in both directions, and Kara slammed the door shut behind me, followed by the click of the bolt lock.

The wall felt cold against my back, and I suddenly realized I didn't have a coat on. Slowly sliding down the concrete block wall to my ass, I covered my face with my hands. She might have hated me at the moment, but she had to come home sometime.

After twenty minutes, I pulled out my phone and shot her a text.

Pidge, please. i know ur pissed, but we can still talk about this

And then another.

Please come home.

And another.

Please? i love you.

She didn't respond. I waited another half hour, and then sent her more.

im @ Morgan would u @ least call me to let me know if ur coming home 2nite?

Pigeon I'm so fuckin sorry. Please come home. I need 2 c u.

U know im not the 1 being unreasonable here. U could @ least answer me.

i don't fucking deserve this ok so im an asshat 4 thinking i could solve all our problems with money but @least i don't run away every time we have 1

im sorry i didn't mean that

what do u want me 2 do? i will do whatever u want me 2 ok? just please talk 2 me.

this is bullshit

im in love with u. i don't understand how u can just walk away

Just before sunrise, when I was sure I'd officially made a total ass of myself and Abby was probably certain that I was insane, I picked myself up off the floor. The fact that security had never showed to escort me out was amazing in itself, but if I was still sitting in the hallway when the girls started leaving for class, that luck would more than likely run out.

After trudging down the stairs in defeat, I sat on my bike, and even though a T-shirt was the only thing between my skin and the frigid winter air, I ignored it. Hoping to see Abby in history class, I went straight home to thaw my skin under a hot shower.

Shepley stood at the doorway of my bedroom while I got dressed.

"What do you want, Shep?"

"Did you talk to her?"

"No."

"At all? Text? Anything?"

"I said no," I snapped.

"Trav." Shepley sighed. "She's probably not going to be in class today. I don't want me and America in the middle of this, but that's what she said."

"Maybe she will," I said, buckling my belt. I put on Abby's favorite cologne, and then slipped on my coat before grabbing my backpack.

"Hold up, I'll drive you."

"No, I'll take the bike."

"Why?"

"In case she agrees to come back to the apartment with me so we can talk."

"Travis, I think it's time you consider the fact that she might not—"

"Shut the fuck up, Shep," I said, glancing over to him. "Just this one time, don't be reasonable. Don't try to save me. Just be my friend, okay?"

Shepley nodded once. "You got it."

America came out of Shepley's room, still in her pj's. "Travis, it's time to let her go. She was done the second you made it clear you were working for Benny."

When I didn't reply, she continued, "Travis . . ."

"Don't. No offense, Mare, but I can't even look at you right now."

Without waiting for a response, I slammed the door behind me. Theatrics were worth it just to vent a little of the anxiety I felt about seeing Abby. Better than getting on my hands and knees in a panic to beg her back in the middle of class. Not that I wouldn't go that far if that was what it would take to change her mind.

Walking slowly to class and even taking the stairs didn't keep me from being a half hour early. I hoped Abby would show up, and we'd have time to talk before, but when the previous class let out, she still wasn't there.

I sat down, next to her empty seat, and picked at my leather bracelet while the other students filtered into the classrooms and took their seats. It was just another day for them. Watching their world continue while mine was coming to an end was disturbing.

Except for a few stragglers sneaking in behind Mr. Chaney, everyone was accounted for—everyone but Abby. Mr. Chaney flipped open his book, greeted the classroom, and then started his lecture. His words blurred together as my heart knocked against my chest, swelling more with each breath. My teeth clenched and my eyes watered as thoughts of Abby being some-where else, relieved to be away from me, amplified my anger.

I stood and stared at Abby's empty desk.

"Er . . . Mr. Maddox? Are you feeling well?" Mr. Chaney asked.

I kicked over her desk and then mine, barely registering the gasps and shrieks of the students watching.

"GOD DAMMIT!" I screamed, kicking my desk again.

"Mr. Maddox," Mr. Chaney said in a strangely calm voice. "I think it's best you get some fresh air."

I stood over the toppled desks, breathing hard.

"Leave my classroom, Travis. Now," Chaney said, this time his voice more firm.

I jerked my backpack from the floor and shoved open the door, hearing the wood crash against the wall behind it.

"Travis!"

The only detail that registered about the voice was that it was female. I flipped around, for half a second hopeful that it was Abby.

Megan sauntered down the hall, stopping next to me. "I thought you had class?" She smiled. "Doing anyone exciting this weekend?"

"What do you need?"

She raised an eyebrow, her eyes bright with recognition. "I know you. You're pissed. Things didn't work out with the nun?"

I didn't answer.

"I could have told you that." She shrugged, and then took a step closer, whispering in my ear so close her full lips brushed against my ear. "We're the same, Travis: not good for anybody."

My eyes darted to hers, traveled down to her lips, and then back. She leaned in with her trademark small, sexy smile.

"Fuck off, Megan."

Her smile vanished, and I walked away.

CHAPTER TWENTY-TWO

Not Good for Anybody

THE NEXT WEEK SEEMED ENDLESS. AMERICA AND I decided it would be best if she stayed at Morgan for a while. Shepley reluctantly agreed. Abby missed all three days of history and found somewhere else other than the cafeteria to eat. I tried to catch up with her after a few of her classes, but she either never went to them or had left early. She wouldn't answer her phone.

Shepley assured me that she was okay, and nothing had happened to her. As agonizing as it was to know I was two degrees from Abby, it would have been worse to be cut off from her completely and have no idea if she was dead or alive. Even though it seemed she wanted nothing to do with me, I couldn't stop hoping that at some point soon she would forgive me or start missing me as much as I missed her and show up at the apartment. Thinking about never seeing her again was too painful, so I decided to keep waiting.

On Friday, Shepley knocked on my door.

"Come in," I said from the bed, staring up at the ceiling.

"You going out tonight, buddy?"

"No."

"Maybe you should call Trent. Go get a couple of drinks and get your mind off things for a while."

"No."

Shepley sighed. "Listen, America's coming over, but . . . and I hate to do this to you . . . but you can't bug her about Abby. I barely talked her into coming. She just wants to stay in my room. Okay?"

"Yeah."

"Call Trent. And you need to eat something and take a shower. You look like shit."

With that, Shepley shut the door. It still didn't shut right from the time I had kicked it down. Every time someone closed it, the time I destroyed the apartment over Abby leaving came to mind, and the fact that she came back to me not long after, leading to our first time.

I closed my eyes, but like every other night that week, couldn't sleep. How people like Shepley went through this torment over and over with different girls was insane. Meeting someone after Abby, even if that girl were to somehow measure up, I couldn't imagine putting my heart out there again. Not just so I could feel like this all over again. Like a slow death. Turns out I'd had it right all along.

Twenty minutes later, I could hear America's voice in the living room. The sounds of them talking quietly as they hid from me in Shepley's room echoed throughout the apartment.

Even America's voice was too much to take. Knowing she had probably just spoken to Abby was excruciating.

I forced myself to stand up and make my way to the bathroom to take care of showering and other basic hygiene rituals I'd neglected over the last week. America's voice was drowned out by the water, but the second I turned the lever off, I could hear her again.

I got dressed, and grabbed my bike keys, set to take a long ride. I'd probably end up at Dad's to break the news.

Just as I passed Shepley's bedroom door, America's phone rang. It was the ringtone she'd assigned to Abby. My stomach sank.

"I can come pick you up and take you somewhere for dinner," she said.

Abby was hungry. She might go to the cafeteria.

I jogged out to the Harley and raced out of the parking lot, speeding and running red lights and stop signs all the way to campus.

When I got to the cafeteria, Abby wasn't there. I waited a few more minutes, but she never showed. My shoulders sagged, and I trudged in darkness toward the parking lot. It was a quiet night. Cold. Opposite of the night I walked Abby to Morgan after I won our bet, reminding me of how empty it felt not having her beside me.

A small figure some yards away appeared, walking toward the cafeteria alone. It was Abby.

Her hair was pulled up into a bun, and when she got closer, I noticed she wasn't wearing any makeup. Her arms crossed against her chest, she didn't have a coat on, only a thick, gray cardigan to ward off the cold.

"Pigeon?" I said, walking into the light from the shadows.

Abby jerked to a stop, and then relaxed a bit when she recognized me.

"Jesus, Travis! You scared the hell out of me!"

"If you would answer your phone when I call I wouldn't have to sneak around in the dark."

"You look like hell," she said.

"I've been through there once or twice this week."

She pulled her arms tighter around her, and I had to stop myself from hugging her to keep her warm.

Abby sighed. "I'm actually on my way to grab something to eat. I'll call you later, okay?"

"No. We have to talk."

"Trav—"

"I turned Benny down. I called him Wednesday and told him no."

I was hoping she would smile, or at least show some sign that she approved.

Her face remained blank. "I don't know what you want me to say, Travis."

"Say you forgive me. Say you'll take me back."

"I can't."

My face crumpled.

Abby tried to walk around. Instinctively, I stepped in front of her. If she walked away this time, I would lose her. "I haven't slept, or ate . . . I can't concentrate. I *know* you love me. Everything will be the way it used to be if you'd just take me back."

She closed her eyes. "We are dysfunctional, Travis. I think you're just obsessed with the thought of owning me more than anything else."

"That's not true. I love you more than my life, Pigeon."

"That's exactly what I mean. That's crazy talk."

"It's not crazy. It's the truth."

"Okay . . . so what exactly is the order for you? Is it money, me, your life . . . or is there something that comes before money?"

"I realize what I've done, okay? I see where you'd think that, but if I'd known that you were gonna leave me, I would have never . . . I just wanted to take care of you."

"You've said that."

"Please don't do this. I can't stand feeling like this . . . it's . . . it's killin' me," I said, on the verge of panic. The wall Abby kept around her when we were just friends was back up, stronger than before. She wasn't listening. I couldn't get through to her.

"I'm done, Travis."

I winced. "Don't say that."

"It's *over*. Go home."

My eyebrows pulled in. "*You're* my home."

Abby paused, and for a moment I felt like I'd actually gotten through to her, but her eyes lost focus, and the wall was up again. "You made your choice, Trav. I've made mine."

"I'm going to stay the hell out of Vegas, and away from Benny . . . I'm going to finish school. But I need you. I *need* you. You're my best friend."

For the first time since I was a little kid, hot tears burned in my eyes and dripped down one of my cheeks. Unable to restrain myself, I reached out for Abby, wrapped her small frame in my arms, and planted my lips on hers. Her mouth was cold and stiff, so I cradled her face in my hands, kissing her harder, desperate to get a reaction.

"Kiss me," I begged.

Abby's kept her mouth taut, but her body was lifeless. If I let her go, she would have fallen. "Kiss me!" I pleaded. "Please, Pigeon! I told him no!"

Abby shoved me away. "Leave me *alone*, Travis!"

She shouldered passed me, but I grabbed her wrist. She kept her arm straight, outstretched behind her, but she didn't turn around.

"I am *begging* you." I fell to my knees, her hand still in mine. My breath puffed out in white steam as I spoke, reminding me of the cold. "I'm begging you, Abby. Don't do this."

Abby glanced back, and then her eyes drifted down her arm to mine, seeing the tattoo on my wrist. The tattoo that bared her name.

She looked away, toward the cafeteria. "Let me go, Travis."

The air knocked out of me, and with all hope obliterated, I relaxed my hand, and let her slip out of my fingers.

Abby didn't look back as she walked away from me, and my palms fell flat on the sidewalk. She wasn't coming back. She didn't want me anymore, and there was nothing I could do or say to change it.

Several minutes passed before I could gain the strength to stand. My feet didn't want to move, but somehow I forced them to cooperate long enough to get me to the Harley. I sat on the seat, and let my tears fall. Loss was something I'd only experienced once before in my life, but this felt more real. Losing Abby wasn't a story I remembered from early childhood—it was in my face, debilitating me like a sickness, robbing me of my senses and physically, excruciatingly painful.

My mother's words echoed in my ear. Abby was the girl I had to fight for, and I went down fighting. None of it was ever going to be enough.

A red Dodge Intrepid pulled up next to my bike. I didn't have to look up to see who it was.

Trenton killed the engine, resting an arm out of the open window. "Hey."

"Hey," I said, wiping my eyes with my jacket sleeve.

"Rough night?"

"Yeah," I nodded, staring at the Harley's fuel tank.

"I just got off work. I need a fuckin' drink. Ride with me to the Dutch."

I took a long, faltering breath. Trenton, like Dad and the rest of my brothers, always knew how to handle me. We both knew I shouldn't drive in my condition.

"Yeah."

"Yeah?" Trenton said with a small, surprised smile.

I swung my leg backward over the seat, and then walked around to the passenger side of Trenton's car. The heat from the vents made my skin burn, and for the first time that night I felt how biting cold the air was, and recognized that I didn't have nearly enough clothes on for the temperature.

"Shepley called you?"

"Yep." He backed out from the parking space and slowly weaved through the lot, finding the street at a turtle's pace. He looked over at me. "I guess a guy named French called his girl? Said you and Abby were fighting outside the cafeteria."

"We weren't fighting. I was just . . . trying to get her back."

Trenton nodded once, pulling into the street. "That's what I figured."

We didn't speak again until we took our stools at the bar of

the Dutch. The crowd was rough, but Bill, the owner and bartender, knew Dad well from when we were kids, and most of the
regulars watched us grow up.

"Good to see you boys. It's been a while," Bill said, wiping
down the counter before setting a beer and a shot on the bar in
front of each of us.

"Hey, Bill," Trenton said, immediately tossing back his shot.

"You feeling okay, Travis?" Bill asked.

Trenton answered for me. "He'll feel better after a few
rounds."

I was grateful. In that moment, if I spoke, I might have broken
down.

Trenton continued buying me whiskey until my teeth were
numb and I was on the verge of passing out. I must have done so
sometime between the bar and the apartment, because I woke
up the next morning on the couch in my clothes, unsure of how
in the hell I got there.

Shepley closed the door, and I heard the familiar sound of
America's Honda rev up and pull away.

I sat up and closed one eye. "Did you guys have a good night."

"Yeah. Did you?"

"I guess so. Did you hear me come in?"

"Yeah, Trent carried your ass upstairs and threw you on the
couch. You were laughing, so I'd say it was a successful night."

"Trent can be a dick, but he's a good brother."

"That he is. You hungry?"

"Fuck no," I groaned.

"Alrighty, then. I'm gonna make me some cereal."

I sat on the couch, going over the night before in my mind.
The last hours were hazy, but when I backed up to the moment

I saw Abby on campus, I winced.

"I told Mare we had plans today. I thought we'd go to the lumber place to replace your creaky ass door."

"You don't have to babysit me, Shep."

"I'm not. We're leaving in half an hour. Wash the stank off you, first," he said, sitting in the recliner with his bowl of Mini Wheats. "And then we're going to come home and study. Finals."

"Fuck," I said with a sigh.

"I'll order pizza for lunch, and we can just eat leftovers for dinner."

"Thanksgiving is coming up, remember? I'll be eating pizza three meals a day for two days straight. No, thank you."

"Okay, Chinese, then."

"You're micromanaging," I said.

"I know. Trust me, it helps."

I nodded slowly, hoping he was right.

THE DAYS PASSED SLOWLY. BUT STAYING UP LATE TO study with Shepley, and sometimes America, helped to shorten the sleepless nights. Trenton promised not to tell Dad or the rest of the Maddox boys about Abby until after Thanksgiving, but I still dreaded it, knowing I'd already told them all she would come. They would ask about her, and then see right through me when I lied.

After my last class on Friday, I called Shepley. "Hey, I know this is supposed to be off-limits, but I need you to find out where Abby is going for break."

"Well, that's easy. She'll be with us. She spends the holidays at America's."

"Really?"

"Yeah, why?"

"Nothing," I said, abruptly hanging up the phone.

I walked around campus in the light rain, waiting for Abby's class to let out. Outside the Hoover building, I saw a few people from Abby's calculus class congregated outside. The back of Parker's head came into view, and then Abby.

She was huddled inside her winter coat, seeming uncomfortable as Parker babbled on.

I pulled down my red ball cap and jogged in their direction. Abby's eyes drifted to mine; recognition made her eyebrows raise infinitesimally.

The same mantra played on repeat in my head. *No matter what smart-ass comment Parker makes, play it cool. Don't fuck this up. Don't. Fuck. This. Up.*

To my surprise, Parker left without saying a word to me.

I shoved my hands into the front pockets of my hoodie. "Shepley said you're going with him and Mare to Wichita tomorrow."

"Yeah?"

"You're spending the whole break at America's?"

She shrugged, trying too hard to be unaffected by my presence. "I'm really close with her parents."

"What about your mom?"

"She's a drunk, Travis. She won't know it's Thanksgiving."

My stomach lurched, knowing the answer to my next question was going to be my last chance. Thunder rolled above us and I looked up, squinting as the large drops fell against my face.

"I need to ask you for a favor," I said, ducking from the hard rain. "C'mere." I pulled Abby under the closest awning so she wouldn't get soaked from the sudden downpour.

"What kind of favor?" she asked, clearly suspicious. It was hard to hear her over the rain.

"My uh . . ." I shifted my weight, my nerves attempting to get the best of me. My mind screamed *abort!*, but I was determined to at least try. "Dad and the guys are still expecting you on Thursday."

"Travis!" Abby whined.

I looked to my feet. "You said you would come."

"I know, but . . . it's a little inappropriate now, don't you think?"

"You said you would come," I said again, trying to keep my voice calm.

"We were still together when I agreed to go home with you. You *knew* I wasn't going to come."

"I *didn't* know, and it's too late, anyway. Thomas is flying in, and Tyler took off work. Everyone's looking forward to seeing you."

Abby cringed, twirling a piece of her wet hair around her finger. "They were going to come anyway, weren't they?"

"Not everyone. We haven't had all of us there for Thanksgiving in years. They all made an effort to be there, since I promised them a real meal. We haven't had a woman in the kitchen since Mom died and . . ."

"That's not sexist or anything."

"That's not what I meant, Pidge, c'mon. We all want you there. That's all I'm sayin'."

"You haven't told them about us, have you?"

"Dad would ask why, and I'm not ready to talk to him about it. I'd never hear the end of how stupid I am. Please come, Pidge."

"I have to put the turkey in at six in the morning. We'd have to leave here by five . . ."

"Or we could stay there."

Her eyebrows shot up. "No way! It's bad enough that I'm going to have to lie to your family and pretend we're still together."

Her reaction, although anticipated, still stung my ego a little. "You act like I'm asking you to light yourself on fire."

"You should have told them!"

"I will. After Thanksgiving . . . I'll tell them."

She sighed and then looked away. Waiting for her answer was like pulling out my fingernails one by one.

"If you promise me that this isn't some stunt to try and get back together, I'll do it."

I nodded, trying not to be too eager. "I promise."

Her lips formed a hard line, but there was the tiniest hint of a smile in her eyes. "I'll see you at five."

I leaned down to kiss her cheek. I'd just meant to give her a quick peck, but my lips had missed her skin, and it was hard to pull away. "Thanks, Pigeon."

After Shepley and America headed out for Wichita in the Honda, I cleaned the apartment, folded the last load of laundry, smoked half a pack of cigarettes, packed an overnight bag, and then cussed the clock for being so slow. When four thirty finally rolled around, I jogged down the steps to Shepley's Charger, trying not to speed all the way to Morgan.

When I arrived at Abby's door, her confused expression took me by surprise.

"Travis," she breathed.

"Are you ready?"

Abby raised an eyebrow. "Ready for what?"

"You said pick you up at five."

She folded her arms across my chest. "I meant five in the *morning!*"

"Oh. I guess I should call Dad and let him know we won't be staying after all."

"Travis!" she wailed.

"I brought Shep's car so we didn't have to deal with our bags on the bike. There's a spare bedroom you can crash in. We can watch a movie or—"

"I'm *not* staying at your dad's!"

My face fell. "Okay. I'll uh . . . I'll see you in the morning."

I took a step back, and Abby shut the door. She would still come, but my family would definitely know something was up if she didn't show up tonight like I'd said she would. I walked down the hall slowly as I punched in Dad's number. He was going to ask why, and I didn't want to outright lie to him.

"Travis, wait."

I flipped around to see Abby standing in the hallway.

"Give me a minute to pack a few things."

I smiled, nearly overwhelmed with relief. We walked together back to her room, and I waited in the doorway while she shoved a few things in a bag. The scene reminded me of the night I'd won the bet, and I realized that I wouldn't have traded a single second we spent together.

"I still love you, Pidge."

She didn't look up. "Don't. I'm not doing this for you."

I sucked in a breath, physical pain shooting in all directions in my chest. "I know."

CHAPTER TWENTY-THREE

Acceptance Speech

THE EASY CONVERSATIONS WE USED TO HAVE WERE lost on me. Nothing that came to mind seemed appropriate, and I was worried about pissing her off before we got to Dad's.

The plan was for her to play the part, start to miss me, and then maybe I would get another chance to beg her back. It was a long shot, but the only thing I had going for me.

I pulled into the wet gravel drive, and carried our bags to the front porch.

Dad answered the door with a smile.

"Good to see ya, son." His smiled broadened when he looked at the damp but beautiful girl standing beside me. "Abby Abernathy. We're looking forward to dinner tomorrow. It's been a long time since . . . Well. It's been a long time."

Inside the house, Dad rested his hand on his protruding belly and grinned. "I set you two up in the guest bedroom, Trav. I didn't figure you would wanna fight with the twin bed in your room."

Abby looked to me. "Abby's uh . . . she's going to uh . . . going to take the guest room. I'm going to crash in mine."

Trenton walked up, his face screwed into disgust. "*Why?* She's been staying at your apartment, hasn't she?"

"Not lately," I said, trying not to lunge at him. He knew exactly why.

Dad and Trenton traded glances.

"Thomas's room has been storage for years now, so I was going to let him take your room. I guess he can sleep on the couch," Dad said, looking at its ratty, discolored cushions.

"Don't worry about it, Jim. We were just trying to be respectful," Abby said, touching my arm.

Dad's laughter bellowed throughout the house, and he patted her hand. "You've met my sons, Abby. You should know it's damn near impossible to offend me."

I nodded toward the stairs, and Abby followed. I gently pushed open the door with my foot and sat our bags on the floor, looking at the bed and then turning to Abby. Her gray eyes were big as they scanned the room, stopping on a picture of my parents that hung from the wall.

"I'm sorry, Pidge. I'll sleep on the floor."

"Damn straight you will," she said, pulling her hair up into a ponytail. "I can't believe I let you talk me into this."

I sat on the bed, realizing just how unhappy she was about the situation. I guess part of me hoped she'd be as relieved as I was to be together. "This is going to be a fucking mess. I don't know what I was thinking."

"I know exactly what you were thinking. I'm not stupid, Travis."

I looked up and offered a tired smile. "But you still came."

"I have to get everything ready for tomorrow," she said, opening the door.

I stood. "I'll help you."

As Abby prepared the potatoes, pies, and turkey, I was busy fetching and handing her things, and completed the small cooking tasks she assigned to me. The first hour was awkward, but when the twins arrived, everyone seemed to congregate in the kitchen, helping Abby to relax. Dad told Abby stories about us boys, and we laughed about tales of previous disastrous Thanksgivings when we attempted to do something other than order pizza.

"Diane was a hell of a cook," Dad mused. "Trav doesn't remember, but there was no sense trying after she passed."

"No pressure, Abby," Trenton said. He chuckled, and then grabbed a beer from the fridge. "Let's get out the cards. I want to try to make back some of my money that Abby took."

Dad waved his finger. "No poker this weekend, Trent. I brought down the dominoes; go set those up. No betting, dammit. I mean it."

Trenton shook his head. "All right, old man, all right." My brothers meandered from the kitchen, and Trenton followed, stopping to look back. "C'mon, Trav."

"I'm helping Pidge."

"There's not much more to do, baby," Abby said. "Go ahead."

I knew she had only said it for show, but it didn't change the way it made me feel. I reached for her hip. "You sure?"

She nodded and I leaned over to kiss her cheek, squeezing her hip with my fingers before following Trenton into the game room.

We sat down in the card room, settling in for a friendly game of dominoes.

Trenton broke out the box, cursing the cardboard for slicing the underside of his fingernail before dealing out the bones.

Taylor snorted. "You're such a fucking baby, Trent, just deal."

"You can't count anyway, douche. What are you so eager about?"

I laughed at Trenton's comeback, drawing his attention to me.

"You and Abby are getting along well," he said. "How did this all work out?"

I knew what he meant, and I shot him a glare for broaching the subject in front of the twins. "With much persuasion."

Dad arrived and sat down. "She's a good girl, Travis. I'm happy for you, son."

"She is," I said trying not to let the sadness show on my face.

Abby was busy cleaning in the kitchen, and it seemed I spent every second fighting the urge to join her. It may have been a family holiday, but I wanted to spend every spare moment with her that I could.

A half hour later, grinding noises alerted me to the fact that the dishwasher had been started. Abby walked by to wave quickly before making her way to the stairs. I jumped up and took her hand.

"It's early, Pidge. You're not going to bed, are ya?"

"It's been a long day. I'm tired."

"We were getting ready to watch a movie. Why don't you come back down and hang out?"

She looked up the stairs and then down to me. "Okay."

I led her by the hand to the couch, and we sat together as the opening credits rolled.

"Shut off that light, Taylor," Dad ordered.

I reached behind Abby, resting my arm on the back of the couch. I fought wrapping both my arms around her. I was wary about her reaction, and I didn't want to take advantage of the situation when she was doing me a favor.

Halfway through the movie, the front door flew open, and Thomas rounded the corner, bags in hand.

"Happy Thanksgiving!" he said, setting his luggage on the floor.

Dad stood up and hugged him, and everyone but me stood to greet him.

"You're not going to say hi to Thomas?" Abby whispered.

I watched my dad and brothers hug and laugh. "I got one night with you. I'm not going to waste a second of it."

"Hi there, Abby. It's good to see you again." Thomas smiled.

I touched Abby's knee. She looked down, and then back to me. Noticing her expression, I took my hand off her leg and interlocked my fingers in my lap.

"Uh-oh. Trouble in paradise?" Thomas asked.

"Shut up, Tommy," I grumbled.

The mood in the room shifted, and all eyes fell on Abby, waiting for an explanation. She smiled nervously, and then took my hand into both of hers.

"We're just tired," she said, smiling. "We've been working all evening on the food." Her cheek pressed into my shoulder.

I looked down at our hands and then squeezed, wishing there was some way I could say then how much I appreciated what she'd done.

"Speaking of tired, I'm exhausted." Abby breathed. "I'm gonna head to bed, baby." She looked to everyone else. "Good night, guys."

"Night, sis," Dad said.

My brothers all said good night, and watched Abby make her way up the stairs.

"I'm gonna turn in, too," I said.

"I bet you are," Trenton teased.

"Lucky bastard," Tyler grumbled.

"Hey. We're not going to talk about your sister like that," Dad warned.

Ignoring my brothers, I jogged up the stairs, catching the bedroom door just before it closed. Realizing she might want to get dressed, and wouldn't be comfortable doing it in front of me anymore, I froze. "Did you want me to wait in the hall while you dressed for bed?"

"I'm going to hop in the shower. I'll just get dressed in the bathroom."

I rubbed the back of my neck. "All right. I'll make a pallet, then."

Her big eyes were solid steel as she nodded, her wall obviously impenetrable. She picked out a few things from her bag before making her way to the bathroom.

Digging in the closet for sheets and a blanket, I spread out the linens on the floor beside the bed, thankful we'd at least have some time alone to talk. Abby emerged from the bathroom, and I dropped a pillow on the floor at the head of the pallet, and then took my turn in the shower.

I wasted no time, quickly scrubbing the soap all over my body, letting the water rinse away the suds as soon as they lathered. Within ten minutes, I was already dried off and dressed, walking back into the bedroom.

Abby lay in bed when I returned, the sheets as high on her

chest as she could get them. The pallet wasn't nearly as inviting as a bed with Abby snuggled up inside. I realized my last night with her was going to be spent awake, listening to her breathe just inches away, unable to touch her.

I turned off the light, and situated myself on the floor. "This is our last night together, isn't it?"

"I don't wanna fight, Trav. Just go to sleep."

I turned over to face her, propping up my head with my hand. Abby turned over, too, and our eyes met.

"I love you."

She watched me for a moment. "You promised."

"I promised this wasn't a stunt to get back together. It wasn't." I reached up a hand to touch hers. "But if it meant being with you again, I can't say I wouldn't consider it."

"I care about you. I don't want you to hurt, but I should have followed my gut in the first place. It would've never worked."

"You did love me, though, right?"

She pressed her lips together. "I still do."

Every emotion washed over me in waves, so strong that I couldn't tell one from the other. "Can I ask you for a favor?"

"I'm sort of in the middle of the last thing you asked me to do," she said with a smirk.

"If this is really it . . . if you're really done with me . . . will you let me hold you tonight?"

"I don't think it's a good idea, Trav."

My hand gripped tight over hers. "Please? I can't sleep knowing you're just a foot away, and I'm never gonna get the chance again."

Abby stared at me for a few seconds, and then frowned. "I'm not having sex with you."

"That's not what I'm asking."

Abby's eyes darted around the floor for a bit as she contemplated her answer. Finally shutting her eyes tight, she scooted from the edge of the bed, and turned down the covers.

I crawled into the bed beside her, hastily pulling her tight into my arms. It felt so incredible that coupled with the tension in the room, I struggled not to break down.

"I'm going to miss this," I said.

I kissed her hair and pulled her closer, burying my face into her neck. She rested her hand on my back, and I sucked in another breath, trying to breathe her in, to let that moment of time burn into my brain.

"I . . . I don't think I can do this, Travis," she said, trying to wriggle free.

I didn't mean to restrain her, but if holding on meant avoiding that deep burning pain I'd felt for days on end, it just made sense to hang on.

"I can't do this," she said again.

I knew what she meant. Being together like that was heartbreaking, but I didn't want it to end.

"Then don't," I said against her skin. "Give me another chance."

After one last attempt to break free, Abby covered her face with both hands and cried in my arms. I looked up at her, tears burning my eyes.

I pulled one hand gently away and kissed her palm. Abby took a staggered breath as I looked at her lips, and then back to her eyes. "I'll never love anyone the way I love you, Pigeon."

She sniffed and touched my face, offering an apologetic expression. "I can't."

"I know," I said, my voice breaking. "I never once convinced myself that I was good enough for you."

Abby's face crumpled and she shook her head. "It's not just you, Trav. We're not good for each other."

I shook my head, wanting to disagree, but she was half right. She deserved better, what she'd wanted all along. Who the fuck was I to take that from her?

With that recognition, I took a deep breath, and then rested my head against her chest.

I AWOKE, HEARING COMMOTION DOWNSTAIRS.

"Ow!" Abby yelped from the kitchen.

I jogged down the stairs, pulling a T-shirt over my head.

"You okay, Pidge?" The cold floor sent shock waves through my body, starting with my feet. "Shit! The floor's fucking freezing!" I jumped on one foot, and then the other, causing Abby to stifle a giggle.

It was still early, probably five or six, and everyone else was asleep. Abby bent over to push the turkey into the oven, and my morning tendency to protrude through my shorts had even more of a reason to do so.

"You can go back to bed. I just had to put the turkey in," she said.

"Are you coming?"

"Yeah."

"Lead the way," I said, sweeping my hand toward the stairs.

I yanked my shirt off as we both shoved our legs under the

covers, pulling the blanket up to our necks. I tightened my arms around her as we shivered, waiting for our body heat to warm the small space between our skin and the covers.

I looked out the windows, seeing large snowflakes fall from the gray sky. I kissed Abby's hair, and she seemed to melt against me. In that embrace, it felt like nothing had changed.

"Look, Pidge. It's snowing."

She turned to face the window. "It kind of feels like Christmas," she said, lightly pressing her cheek against my skin. A sigh from my throat prompted her to look at me. "What?"

"You won't be here for Christmas."

"I'm here, now."

I pulled my mouth into a half smile, and then leaned down to kiss her lips. Abby pulled back and shook her head.

"Trav . . ."

I held on tight and lowered my chin. "I've got less than twenty-four hours with you, Pidge. I'm gonna kiss you. I'm gonna kiss you a lot today. *All* day. Every chance I get. If you want me to stop, just say the word, but until you do, I'm going to make every second of my last day with you count."

"Travis—" Abby began, but after a few seconds of thought, her line of sight lowered from my eyes to my lips.

Not wanting to hesitate, I immediately bent down to kiss her. She kissed me back, and although I'd just meant for it to be short and sweet, my lips parted, making her body react. Her tongue slipped into my mouth, and every part of me that was warm-blooded male screamed for me to go full steam ahead. I pulled her against me, and Abby let her leg fall to one side, welcoming my hips to fit tightly between her thighs.

Within moments, she was naked beneath me, and it took just two quick motions for me to remove my clothes. Pressing my mouth against hers, hard, I gripped the iron vines of the headboard with both hands, and in one quick movement, pushed myself inside her. My body instantly felt hot, and I couldn't stop moving or rocking against her, unable to control myself. I moaned into Abby's mouth when she arched her back to move her hips against mine. At one point she flattened her feet on the bed so she could raise up to let me slip inside of her fully.

With one hand on the iron, and the other on the nape of Abby's neck, I rocked into her over and over, everything that had happened between us, all the pain I'd felt, forgotten. The light from the window poured in as beads of sweat began to form on our skin, making it a little easier to slide back and forth.

I was just about to finish when Abby's legs began to quiver, and her nails dug into my back. I held my breath and thrust into her one last time, groaning with the intense spasms throughout my body.

Abby relaxed against the mattress, her hairline damp, and her limbs limp.

I breathed as if I'd just finished a marathon, sweat dripping from the hair above my ear and down the side of my face.

Abby's eyes lit up when she heard voices murmuring downstairs. I turned on my side, scanning her face with pure adoration.

"You said you were just going to kiss me." She looked at me the way she used to, making it easy to pretend.

"Why don't we just stay in bed all day?"

"I came here to cook, remember?"

"No, you came here to help *me* cook, and I don't report for duty for another eight hours."

She touched my face, her expression preparing me for what she might say. "Travis, I think we—"

"Don't say it, okay? I don't want to think about it until I have to." I stood up and pulled on my boxers, walking over to Abby's bag. I tossed her clothes to the bed, and then yanked my T-shirt over my head. "I want to remember this as a good day."

It seemed not long after we awoke, it was lunchtime. The day raced by, far too fucking fast. I dreaded every minute, cursing the clock as it approached the evening.

Admittedly, I was all over Abby. It didn't even matter that she was putting on a show, I refused to even consider the truth while she was next to me.

When we sat down for dinner, Dad insisted that I carve the turkey, and Abby smiled with pride as I stood up to do the honors.

The Maddox clan annihilated Abby's hard work, and showered her with compliments.

"Did I make enough?" She laughed.

Dad smiled, pulling his fork through his lips to get it clean for dessert. "You made plenty, Abby. We just wanted to tide ourselves over until next year . . . unless you'd like to do this all over again at Christmas. You're a Maddox, now. I expect you at every holiday, and not to cook."

With Dad's words, the truth seeped in, and my smile faded.

"Thanks, Jim."

"Don't tell her that, Dad," Trenton said. "She's gotta cook. I haven't had a meal like this since I was five!" He shoveled half a slice of pecan pie into his mouth, humming with satisfaction.

While my brothers cleared the table and washed the dishes, I sat with Abby on the couch, trying not to hold her too tight.

Dad had already turned in, his belly full, making him too tired
to attempt to stay awake.

I pulled Abby's legs onto my lap, and slipped off her shoes,
massaging the soles of her feet with my thumbs. She loved that,
and I knew it. I might have been trying to subtly remind her
about how good we were together, even though I knew deep
down that it was time for her to move on.

Abby did love me, but she also cared about me too much to
send me packing when she should. Even though I'd told her before that I couldn't walk away from her, I finally realized that I
loved her too much to fuck up her life by staying, or to lose her
completely by forcing us both to hang on until we hated each
other.

"This was the best Thanksgiving we've had since Mom died,"
I said.

"I'm glad I was here to see it."

I took a deep breath. "I'm different," I said, conflicted about
what I would say next. "I don't know what happened to me in
Vegas. That wasn't me. I was thinking about everything we could
buy with that money, and that was *all* I was thinking about. I
didn't see how much it hurt you for me to want to take you back
there, but deep down, I think I knew. I deserved for you to leave
me. I deserved all the sleep I lost and the pain I've felt. I needed
all that to realize how much I need you, and what I'm willing to
do to keep you in my life.

"You said you're done with me, and I accept that. I'm a different person since I met you. I've changed . . . for the better. But no
matter how hard I try, I can't seem to do right by you. We were
friends first, and I can't lose you, Pigeon. I will always love you,
but if I can't make you happy, it doesn't make much sense for me

to try to get you back. I can't imagine being with anyone else, but I'll be happy as long as we're friends."

"You want to be friends?"

"I want you to be happy. Whatever that takes."

She smiled, breaking the part of my heart that wanted to take back everything I'd just said. Part of me hoped she would tell me to shut the fuck up because we belonged together.

"Fifty bucks says you'll be thanking me for this when you meet your future wife."

"That's an easy bet," I said. I couldn't imagine a life without her, and she was already thinking about our separate futures. "The only woman I'd ever wanna marry just broke my heart."

Abby wiped her eyes and then stood up. "I think it's time you took me home."

"C'mon, Pigeon. I'm sorry, that wasn't funny."

"It's not that, Trav. I'm just tired, and I'm ready to go home."

I sucked in a breath and nodded, standing up. Abby hugged my brothers goodbye, and asked Trenton to say goodbye to Dad. I stood at the door with our bags, watching them all agree to come home for Christmas.

When I slowed to a stop at Morgan Hall, I felt the tiniest bit of closure, but it didn't stop my heart from shattering.

I leaned over to kiss her cheek, and then held the door open, watching as she walked inside. "Thanks for today. You don't know how happy you made my family."

Abby stopped at the bottom of the stairs and turned. "You're going to tell them tomorrow, aren't you?"

I glanced at the Charger, trying to hold back the tears. "I'm pretty sure they already know. You're not the only one with a poker face, Pidge."

I left her on the steps alone, refusing to look back. From now on, the love of my life was only an acquaintance. I wasn't sure what expression I had on my face, but I didn't want her to see it.

The Charger whined as I drove far beyond the speed limit back to my father's. I stumbled into the living room, and Thomas handed me a bottle of whiskey. They all had some in a glass.

"You told them?" I asked Trenton, my voice broken.

Trenton nodded.

I collapsed to my knees, and my brothers surrounded me, placing their hands on my head and shoulders for support.

CHAPTER TWENTY-FOUR
Forget

"TRENT'S CALLING AGAIN! ANSWER YOUR DAMN PHONE!" Shepley yelled from the living room.

I kept my cell on top of the television. The farthest point from my bedroom in the apartment.

The first torturous days without Abby, I locked it in the glove box of the Charger. Shepley brought it back in, arguing that it should be in the apartment in case my dad called. Unable to deny that logic, I agreed, but only if it stayed on the TV.

The urge to pick it up and call Abby was maddening otherwise.

"Travis! Your phone!"

I stared up at the white ceiling, thankful that my other brothers had gotten the hint, and felt annoyed that Trenton hadn't. He'd kept me busy or drunk at night, but was under the impression he had to also call me during every break while he was at work. I felt I was on some sort of Maddox suicide watch.

Two and a half weeks into winter break, the urge to call Abby had turned into need. Any access at all to my phone seemed like a bad idea.

Shepley pushed open the door and threw the small, black rectangle into the air. It landed on my chest.

"Jesus, Shep. I told you . . ."

"I know what you said. You have eighteen missed calls."

"All Trent?"

"One is from Panty Wearers Anonymous."

I picked up the phone from my stomach, straightened my arm, and then opened my hand, letting the hard plastic fall to the floor. "I need a drink."

"You need a shower. You smell like shit. You also need to brush your damn teeth, shave, and put deodorant on."

I sat up. "You talk a lot of shit, Shep, but I seem to remember doing your laundry and making you soup for three entire months after Anya."

He sneered. "At least I brushed my teeth."

"I need you to schedule another fight," I said, falling back onto the mattress.

"You just had one two nights ago, and another a week before that. Numbers were down because of break. Adam won't schedule another until classes resume."

"Then bring in the locals."

"Too risky."

"Call Adam, Shepley."

Shepley walked over to my bed, picked up my cell phone, clicked a few buttons, and then threw the phone back onto my stomach. "Call him yourself."

I held up the phone to my ear.

"Asshat! What've you been doing? Why haven't you answered your phone? I wanna go out tonight!" Trenton said.

I narrowed my eyes at the back of my cousin's head, but he left my room without looking back.

"I don't feel like it, Trent. Call Cami."

"She's a bartender. It's New Year's Eve. We can go see her though! Unless you have other plans . . ."

"No. I don't have other plans."

"You just wanna lay there and die?"

"Pretty much." I sighed.

"Travis, I love you little brother, but you are being a huge pussy. She was the love of your life. I get it. It sucks. I know. But like it or not, life's gotta go on."

"Thank you, Mr. Rogers."

"You aren't old enough to know who that even is."

"Thomas made us watch reruns, remember?"

"No. Listen. I get off at nine. I'm gonna pick you up at ten. If you aren't dressed and ready, and I mean *showered and shaved* ready, I'm going to call a bunch of people and tell them you're having a party at your house with six free kegs and hookers."

"Damn it, Trenton, don't."

"You know I will. Last warning. Ten o'clock, or by eleven you'll have guests. Ugly ones."

I groaned. "I fucking hate you."

"No you don't. See you in ninety minutes."

The phone grated in my ear before it hung up. Knowing Trenton, he was probably calling from his boss's office, kicked back with his feet on the desk.

I sat up, looking around the room. The walls were empty, devoid of the pictures of Abby that had once crowded the white paint. The sombrero hung above my bed again, proudly displayed after the shame of being replaced by the framed black-and-white photo of Abby and me.

Trenton was really going to make me do this. I imagined myself sitting at the bar, the world celebrating around me, ignoring the fact that I was miserable and—according to Shepley and Trenton—being a pussy.

Last year I danced with Megan and ended up taking home Kassie Beck, who would've been a good one to keep on the list had she not thrown up in the hall closet.

I wondered what plans Abby had for the night but tried not to allow my mind to wander too far into the realm of who she might be meeting. Shepley hadn't mentioned America having plans. Unsure if that was being kept from me on purpose, pushing the issue just seemed too masochistic, even for me.

The night table drawer squeaked when I pulled it open. My fingers padded across the bottom and paused at the corners of a small box. Carefully I pulled it out, holding it in my hands against my chest. My chest rose and fell with a sigh, and then I opened the box, wincing at the sight of the sparkling diamond ring inside. There was only one finger that belonged inside that white gold circle, and with each passing day, that dream seemed less and less possible.

I knew when I bought the ring that it would be years before I gave it to Abby, but it made sense to keep it just in case the perfect moment happened to arise. Knowing it was there gave me something to look forward to, even now. Inside that box was the little bit of hope I had left.

After putting away the diamond, and giving myself a long mental pep talk, I finally trudged down the hall to the bathroom, intentionally keeping my eyes from my reflection in the mirror. The shower and shave didn't improve my mood, and neither (I would later point out to Shepley) did brushing my teeth. I put on a buttoned-up black shirt and blue jeans, and then slipped on my black boots.

Shepley knocked on my door and walked in, dressed and ready to go as well.

"You're going?" I asked, buckling my belt. I'm not sure why I was surprised. Without America there, he wouldn't have plans with anyone other than us.

"Is that okay?"

"Yeah. Yeah, I just . . . I guess you and Trent worked this out before."

"Well, yeah," he said, skeptical and maybe a little amused that I had just figured it out.

The Intrepid's horn honked outside, and Shepley pointed to the hallway with his thumb. "Let's roll."

I nodded once and followed him out. Trenton's car smelled like cologne and cigarettes. I popped a Marlboro in my mouth and lifted up my ass so I could get into my pocket for a lighter.

"So, the Red's packed, but Cami told the door guy to let us in. They've got a live band, I guess, and pretty much everyone is home. Should be a good one."

"Hanging out with our drunken, loser high school classmates in a dead college town. Score," I grumbled.

Trenton smiled. "I got a friend coming. You'll see."

My eyebrows pulled in. "Tell me you didn't."

A few people were huddled outside the door, waiting for people to leave so they could enter. We slipped past them, ignoring their complaints while we paid and walked straight in.

A table sat by the entrance, once full of New Year's Eve party hats, glasses, Glow Sticks, and kazoos. The freebies had been mostly picked through, but it didn't stop Trenton from finding a ridiculous pair of glasses that were shaped into the numbers of the new year. Glitter was all over the floor, and the band was playing "Hungry Like the Wolf."

I glowered at Trenton, who pretended not to notice. Shepley and I followed my older brother to the bar, where Cami was de-capping bottles and shaking drinks at full speed, pausing only momentarily to type in numbers into the register or write down an addition to someone's tab. Her tip jars were overflowing, and she had to shove down the greenbacks into the glass every time someone added a bill.

When she saw Trenton, her eyes lit up. "You made it!" Cami grabbed three bottles of beer, popped the tops, and sat them on the bar in front of him.

"I said I would." He smiled, leaning over the counter to peck her lips.

That was the end of their conversation, as she quickly turned to slide another beer bottle down the bar and strained to hear another order.

"She's good," Shepley said, watching her.

Trenton smiled. "She damn sure is."

"Are you . . . ?" I began.

"No," Trent said, shaking his head. "Not yet. I'm working on it. She's got some asshole college boy in Cali. He just needs to piss her off one last time and she's going to figure out what a pecker head he is."

"Good luck with that," Shepley said, taking a swig of his beer.

Trenton and I intimidated a small group enough for them to

leave their table, so we nonchalantly commandeered it to start
our night of drinking and people watching.

Cami took care of Trenton from afar, sending over a waitress
regularly with full shot glasses of tequila and beer bottles. I was
glad it was my fourth shot of Cuervo when the second 1980s
ballad of the night began.

"This band sucks ass, Trent," I yelled over the noise.

"You just don't appreciate the legacy of hair bands!" he yelled
back. "Hey. Looky there," he said, pointing to the dance floor.

A redhead sauntered across the crowded space, a glossed
smile brightening her pale face.

Trenton stood up to hug her, and her smile grew wider.
"Hey, T! How've you been?"

"Good! Good! Working. You?"

"Great! I'm living in Dallas, now. Working at a PR firm." Her
eyes scanned our table, to Shepley and then to me. "Oh my God!
Is this your baby brother? I used to babysit you!"

My eyebrows pulled together. She had double Ds and curves
like a 1940s pinup model. I was sure if I had spent any time with
her in my formative years, I would have remembered.

Trent smiled. "Travis, you remember Carissa, don't you? She
graduated with Tyler and Taylor."

Carissa held out her hand, and I shook it once. I put the filter
end of a cigarette between my front teeth, and flicked the lighter.
"I don't think I do," I said, sticking the nearly empty pack in my
front shirt pocket.

"You weren't very old." She smiled.

Trenton gestured to Carissa. "She just went through a bad
divorce with Seth Jacobs. You remember Seth?"

I shook my head, already tired of the game Trenton was playing.

Carissa took the full shot glass that was in front of me and slurped it dry, and then she sidestepped until she was next to me. "I heard you've gone through a rough time lately, too. Maybe we could keep each other company tonight?"

By the look in her eyes, I could see she was drunk . . . and lonely. "Not looking for a babysitter," I said, taking a drag.

"Well, maybe just a friend? It's been a long night. I came here alone because all of my girlfriends are married now, ya know?" She giggled nervously.

"Not really."

Carissa looked down, and I felt a small bit of guilt. I was being a dick, and she hadn't done anything to deserve that from me.

"Hey, I'm sorry," I said. "I don't really wanna be here."

Carissa shrugged. "Me, either. But I didn't want to be alone."

The band stopped playing, and the lead singer began counting down from ten. Carissa looked around, and then back to me, her eyes glossing over. Her line of sight fell to my lips, and then in unison the crowd screamed, "HAPPY NEW YEAR!"

The band played a rough version of "Auld Lang Syne," and then Carissa's lips smashed into mine. My mouth moved against hers for a moment, but her lips were so foreign, so different from what I was used to, it only made Abby's memory more vivid, and the realization that she was gone more painful.

I pulled away and wiped my mouth with my sleeve.

"I'm so sorry," Carissa said, watching me leave the table.

I pushed through the crowd to the men's bathroom and locked myself in the only stall. I pulled out my phone and held it in my hands, my vision blurry and the rotten twang of tequila on my tongue.

Abby's probably drunk, too, I thought. *She wouldn't care if I called. It's New Year's Eve. She might even be waiting for my call.*

I scrolled over the names in my address book, stopping on Pigeon. I turned over my wrist, seeing the same inked into my skin. If Abby wanted to talk to me, she would have called. My chance had come and gone, and I told her at Dad's I would let her move on. Drunk or not, calling her was selfish.

Someone knocked on the stall door. "Trav?" Shepley asked. "You okay?"

I unlocked the door and stepped outside, my phone still in my hand.

"Did you call her?"

I shook my head, and then looked to the tile wall across the room. I reared back, and then launched my phone, watching it shatter into a million pieces and scatter on the floor. Some poor bastard standing at the urinal jumped, his shoulders flying up to his ears.

"No," I said. "And I'm not going to."

Shepley followed me back to the table without a word. Carissa was gone, and three new shots were waiting for us.

"I thought she might get your mind off things, Trav, I'm sorry. It always makes me feel better to bag a really hot chick when I've been where you're at," Trenton said.

"Then you haven't been where I'm at," I said, slamming the tequila to the back of my throat. I stood up quickly, grabbing the edge of the table for stability. "Time for me to go home and pass out, boys."

"You sure?" Trenton asked, looking mildly disappointed.

After Trenton got Cami's attention long enough to say goodbye, we made our way to the Intrepid. Before he started the car, he looked over at me.

"You think she'll ever take you back?"

"No."

"Then maybe it's time you accept that. Unless you don't want her in your life at all."

"I'm trying."

"I mean when classes start. Pretend it's like it was before you saw her naked."

"Shut up, Trent."

Trenton turned over the engine and put the car in reverse. "I was just thinking," he said, turning the wheel, and then shoving the shifter into drive, "that you were happy when you guys were friends, too. Maybe you could go back to that. Maybe you thinking you can't is why you're so miserable."

"Maybe," I said, staring out the window.

THE FIRST DAY OF SPRING SEMESTER FINALLY ARRIVED. I hadn't slept all night, tossing and turning, both dreading and eagerly anticipating seeing Abby again. Regardless of my sleepless night, I was determined to be all smiles, never letting on how much I'd suffered, to Abby or anyone else.

At lunch, my heart nearly exploded out of my chest when I saw her. She looked different, but the same. The difference was that she seemed like a stranger. I couldn't just walk up to her and kiss her or touch her like before. Abby's big eyes blinked once when she saw me, and I smiled and winked back, sitting at the end of our usual table. The football players were busy bitching about their loss to State, so I tried to relieve their angst by telling them some of my more colorful experiences over break, like watching Trenton salivate over Cami, and the time that his Intrepid broke down and we were almost arrested for public intoxication while walking home.

From the corner of my eye, I saw Finch hug Abby to his side, and for a moment I wondered if she wished I would go away, or if she might be upset.

Either way, I hated not knowing.

Throwing the last bite of something deep-fried and disgusting into my mouth, I tossed my tray and walked up behind Abby, resting my hands on her shoulders.

"How's your classes, Shep?" I asked, willing my voice not to sound anything but casual.

Shepley's face pinched. "First day sucks. Hours of syllabi and class rules. I don't even know why I show up the first week. How about you?"

"Eh . . . it's all part of the game. How 'bout you, Pidge?" I tried not to let the tension in my shoulders affect my hands.

"The same." Her voice was small, distant.

"Did you have a good break?" I asked, playfully swaying her from side to side.

"Pretty good."

Yeah. This was awkward as fuck.

"Sweet. I've got another class. Later." I walked out of the cafeteria quickly, reaching for the Marlboro box in my pocket before I even shouldered through the metal doors.

The next two classes were torture. The only place that felt like a safe haven was my bedroom, away from campus, away from ev-

erything that reminded me that I was alone, and away from the
rest of the world, which was continuing on, not giving a shit that
I was in so much pain it was palpable. Shepley kept telling me it
wouldn't be so bad after a while, but it didn't seem to be letting up.

I met my cousin in the parking lot in front of Morgan Hall,
trying hard not to stare at the entrance. Shepley seemed on edge
and didn't talk much on the ride to the apartment.

When he pulled into his parking spot, he sighed. I debated
whether or not to ask him if he and America were having problems, but I didn't think I could handle his shit *and* mine.

I grabbed my backpack from the backseat and pushed the
door open, stopping only long enough to unlock the door.

"Hey," Shepley said, shutting the door behind him. "You all
right?"

"Yeah," I said from the hallway, not turning around.

"That was kind of awkward in the cafeteria."

"I guess," I said, taking another step.

"So, uh . . . I should probably tell you something I overheard.
I mean . . . hell, Trav, I don't know if I should tell you or not. I
don't know if it'll make it worse or better."

I turned around. "Overheard from who?"

"Mare and Abby were talking. It was . . . mentioned that Abby's been miserable all break."

I stood in silence, trying to keep my breathing even.

"Did you hear what I said?" Shepley asked, his brows pulling
together.

"What does that mean?" I asked, throwing my hands up.
"She's been miserable without me? Because we're not friends
anymore? What?"

Shepley nodded. "Definitely a bad idea."

"Tell me!" I yelled, feeling myself shake. "I can't . . . I can't keep feeling like this!" I threw my keys down the hall, hearing a loud crack when they made contact with the wall. "She barely acknowledged me today, and you're telling me she wants me back? As a friend? The way it was before Vegas? Or is she just miserable in general?"

"I don't know."

I let my bag fall to the floor and kicked it in Shepley's general direction. "Wh-why are you doing this to me, man? Do you think I'm not suffering enough, because I promise you, it's too much."

"I'm sorry, Trav. I just thought I'd wanna know . . . if it were me."

"You're not me! Just fucking . . . leave it alone, Shep. Leave it the hell alone." I slammed my door and sat on my bed, my head resting on my hands.

Shepley cracked open the door. "I'm not trying to make it worse, if that's what you think. But I knew if you found out later, you would have kicked my ass for not telling you. That's all I'm sayin'."

I nodded once. "Okay."

"You think . . . you think if maybe you focused on all the bullshit you had to endure with her, that'd make it easier?"

I sighed. "I've tried. I keep coming back to the same thought."

"What's that?"

"Now that it's over, I wish I could have all the bad stuff back . . . just so I could have the good."

Shepley's eyes bounced around the room, trying to think of something else comforting to say, but he was clearly all out of advice. His cell phone beeped.

"It's Trent," Shepley said, reading the display screen. His eyes lit up. "You want to grab some drinks with him at the Red? He gets off at five today. His car broke down and he wants you to take him to see Cami. You should go, man. Take my car."

"All right. Let him know I'm comin'." I sniffed, and wiped my nose before standing up.

Sometime between me leaving the apartment and pulling into the gravel lot of the tattoo parlor Trenton worked at, Shepley had alerted Trenton to my shitty day. Trenton gave it away when he insisted on going straight to the Red Door as soon as he slid into the passenger seat of the Charger, instead of wanting to go home to change first.

When we arrived, we were alone except for Cami, the owner, and some guy stocking Cami's bar, but it was the middle of the week—prime college bar time and coin beer night. It didn't take long for the room to fill with people.

I was already lit by the time Lexi and some of her friends had made a drive-by, but it wasn't until Megan stopped by that I even bothered to look up.

"Looking pretty sloppy, Maddox."

"Nah," I said, trying to get my numb lips to form around my words.

"Let's dance," she whined, tugging on my arm.

"I don't think I can," I said, swaying.

"I don't think you should," Trenton said, amused.

Megan bought me a beer and took the stool next to mine. Within ten minutes, she was pawing at my shirt, and not so subtly touching my arms, and then my hands. Just before closing, she had given up her stool to stand next to me—or more like straddle my thigh.

"So I didn't see the bike outside. Did Trenton drive you?"

"Nope. I brought Shepley's car."

"I love that car," she cooed. "You should let me drive you home."

"You wanna drive the Charger?" I asked, slurring.

I glanced over to Trenton, who was stifling a laugh. "Probably not a bad idea, little brother. Be safe . . . in every way."

Megan pulled me off the stool, and then out of the bar into the parking lot. She wore a sequined tube top with a jean skirt and boots, but she didn't seem to mind the cold—if it was cold. I couldn't tell.

She giggled as I threw my arm around her shoulders to help steady myself as I walked. When we reached the passenger side of Shepley's car, she stopped giggling.

"Some things never change, huh, Travis?"

"Guess not," I said, staring at her lips.

Megan wrapped her arms around my neck and pulled me in, not even hesitating to stick her tongue into my mouth. It was wet and soft, and vaguely familiar.

After a few minutes of playing grab ass and trading spit, she hiked her leg up, wrapping it around me. I grabbed her thigh, and rammed my pelvis into hers. Her ass slammed against the car door, and she moaned into my mouth.

Megan always liked it rough.

Her tongue made a trail down my neck, and it was then that I noticed the cold, feeling the warmth left behind by her mouth cool quickly from the winter air.

Megan's hand reached between us, and she grabbed my dick, smiling that I was right where she wanted me to be. "Mmmmm, Travis," she hummed, biting my lip.

"Pigeon." The word came out muffled as I crashed my mouth against hers. At that stage of the night, it was easy enough to pretend.

Megan giggled. "What?" In true Megan fashion, she didn't demand an explanation when I didn't respond. "Let's go to your apartment," she said, grabbing the keys from my hand. "My roommate is sick."

"Yeah?" I asked, pulling on the door handle. "You really wanna drive the Charger?"

"Better me than you," she said, kissing me one last time before leaving me for the driver's side.

While Megan drove, she laughed and talked about her break all while opening my jeans and reaching inside. It was a good thing I was drunk, because I hadn't been laid since Thanksgiving. Otherwise, by the time we reached the apartment, Megan would have had to catch a cab and call it a night.

Halfway home, the empty fishbowl flashed in my mind. "Wait a sec. Wait a sec," I said, pointing down the street. "Stop at the Swift Mart. We gotta pick up some . . ."

Megan reached into her purse and pulled out a small box of condoms. "Gotcha covered."

I leaned back and smiled. She really was my kind of girl.

Megan pulled up into Shepley's parking spot, having been to the apartment enough times to know. She jogged around in tiny steps, trying to hurry along in her stilettos.

I leaned on her to walk up the stairs, and she laughed against my mouth when I finally figured out the door was already unlocked and shoved through it.

Midkiss, I froze. Abby was standing in the front room, holding Toto.

"Pigeon," I said, stunned.

"Found it!" America said, jogging out of Shepley's room.

"What are you doing here?" I asked.

Abby's expression morphed from surprise to anger. "It's good to see you're feeling like your old self, Trav."

"We were just leaving," America snarled. She grabbed Abby's hand as they slid past me and Megan.

It took me a moment to react, but I made my way down the steps, for the first time noticing America's Honda. A string of expletives ran through my mind.

Without thinking, I grabbed a fistful of Abby's coat. "Where are you going?"

"Home," she snapped, straightening her coat in a huff.

"What are you doing here?"

The packed snow crunched under America's feet as she walked up behind Abby, and suddenly Shepley was beside me, his wary eyes fixed on his girlfriend.

Abby lifted her chin. "I'm sorry. If I knew you were going to be here, I wouldn't have come."

I shoved my hands in my coat pockets. "You can come here anytime you want, Pidge. I never wanted you to stay away."

"I don't want to *interrupt*." She looked to the top of the stairs, where Megan of course stood to watch the show. "Enjoy your evening," she said, turning away.

I grabbed her arm. "Wait. You're *mad*?"

She yanked her coat from my grip. "You know"—she laughed once—"I don't even know why I'm surprised."

She might have laughed, but she had hatred in her eyes. No matter what I did—moving on without her, or lying in my bed agonizing over her—she would have hated me. "I can't win amie McGuire

with you. I can't *win* with you! You say you're done . . . I'm fucking miserable over here! I had to break my phone into a million pieces to keep from calling you every minute of the damn day—I've had to play it off like everything is just fine at school so you can be happy . . . and you're fucking *mad* at me? You *broke* my *fuckin'* heart!" I screamed.

"Travis, you're drunk. Let Abby go home," Shepley said.

I grabbed Abby's shoulders and pulled her closer, looking into her eyes. "Do you want me or not? You can't keep doing this to me, Pidge!"

"I didn't come here to see you."

"I don't want her," I said, staring at her lips. "I'm just so fucking unhappy, Pigeon." I leaned in to kiss her, but she grabbed my chin and held me away.

"You've got her lipstick on your mouth, Travis," she said, disgusted.

I took a step back and lifted my shirt, wiping my mouth. Red streaks left behind made it impossible to deny. "I just wanted to forget. Just for one fuckin' night."

One tear spilled over onto Abby's cheek, but she quickly wiped it away. "Then don't let me stop you."

She turned to walk away, but I grabbed her arm again.

A blond blur was suddenly in my face, lashing out and striking at me with small but vicious fists.

"Leave her alone, you bastard!"

Shepley grabbed America, but she pushed him away, turning to slap my face. The sound of her hand against my cheek was quick and loud, and I flinched with the noise. Everyone froze for a moment, shocked at America's sudden rage.

Shepley grabbed his girlfriend again, holding her wrists, and pulling her to the Honda while she thrashed about.

She fought him violently, her blond hair whipping around as she attempted to get away.

"How *could* you? She deserved better from you, Travis!"

"America, STOP!" Shepley yelled, louder than I'd ever heard him.

Her arms fell to her side as she glared at Shepley in disgust. "You're *defending* him?"

Although he was scared as hell, he stood his ground. "Abby broke up with *him*. He's just trying to move on."

America's eyes narrowed, and she pulled her arm from his grip. "Well then, why don't you go find a random WHORE"— she looked at Megan—"from the Red and bring her home to fuck, and then let me know if it helps you get over me."

"Mare." Shepley grabbed for her, but she evaded him, slamming the door as she sat behind the wheel. Abby opened the passenger door and sat next to her.

"Baby, don't leave," Shepley begged, leaning down into the window.

America started the car. "There is a right side and a wrong side here, Shep. And *you* are on the *wrong* side."

"I'm on your side," he said, his eyes desperate.

"Not anymore, you're not," she said, backing out.

"America? America!" Shepley yelled.

When the Honda was out of sight, Shepley turned around, breathing hard.

"Shepley, I'm—"

Before I could get a word out, Shepley reared back and launched his fist into my jaw.

I took the blow, touched my face, and then nodded. I deserved that.

"Travis?" Megan called from the stairs.

"I'll take her home," Shepley said.

I watched the taillights of the Honda get smaller as it took Abby farther away, feeling a lump form in my throat. "Thanks."

CHAPTER TWENTY-FIVE
Possession

S HE'S GOING TO BE THERE.

Showing up would be a mistake.

It would be awkward.

She's going to be there.

What if someone asks her to dance?

What if she meets her future husband and I'm there to witness it?

She doesn't want to see me.

I might get drunk and do something to piss her off.

She might get drunk and do something to piss me off.

I shouldn't go.

I had to go. She was going to be there.

I mentally listed the pros and cons for going to the Valentine's party but kept coming back to the same conclusion: I needed to see Abby, and that's where she would be.

Shepley was getting ready in his room, barely speaking to me since he and America had finally gotten back together. In part because they stayed holed up in his room making up for lost time, and he still blamed me for the five weeks they'd spent apart.

America never missed a moment to let me know she hated my guts, especially after the most recent time I'd broken Abby's heart. I had talked Abby into leaving her date with Parker to come with me to a fight. Of course I wanted her there, but I made the mistake of admitting it was also that I had primarily asked her so I could win a pissing contest. I wanted Parker to know he had no hold on her. Abby felt I'd taken advantage of her feelings for me, and she was right.

All of those things were enough to feel guilty about, but the fact that Abby had been attacked in a place where I'd taken her made it nearly impossible to look anyone in the eye. Adding to all of that our close call with the law totaled up to me being a gigantic fuckup.

Regardless of my constant apologies, America spent her days in the apartment shooting dirty looks in my direction, and snapping unwarranted shitty remarks. Even after all that, I was glad Shepley and America had reconciled. If she wouldn't have taken him back, Shepley might have never forgiven me.

"I'm going," Shepley said. He walked into my room, where I sat in my boxers, still conflicted about what to do. "Picking up Mare at the dorm."

I nodded once. "Abby's still going?"

"Yeah. With Finch."

I managed a half smile. "Should that make me feel better?"

Shepley shrugged. "It would me." He looked around my walls and nodded. "You put the pictures back up."

I looked around, nodding once. "I don't know. It didn't feel right to just have them sitting in a bottom drawer."

"I guess I'll see you later."

"Hey, Shep?"

"Yeah," he said, not turning around.

"I really am sorry, cousin."

Shepley sighed. "I know."

The second he left, I walked into the kitchen to pour the last of the whiskey. The liquid amber sat still in the glass, waiting to offer comfort.

I shot it back and closed my eyes, considering a trip to the liquor store. But there wasn't enough whiskey in the universe to help me make my decision.

"Fuck it," I said, grabbing my bike keys.

After a stop at Ugly Fixer Liquor's, I drove the Harley over the curb and parked in the front yard of the fraternity house, opening the half-pint I'd just bought.

Finding courage at the bottom of the bottle, I walked into Sig Tau. The entire house was covered in pink and red; cheap decorations were hung from the ceiling, and glitter covered the floor. The bass from the speakers downstairs hummed throughout the house, muffling the laughter and constant drone of conversation.

Standing room only, I had to turn and maneuver my way through the crowd of couples, keeping an eye out for Shepley, America, Finch, or Abby. Mostly Abby. She wasn't standing in the kitchen, or in any of the other rooms. She wasn't on the balcony, either, so I made my way downstairs. My breath caught when I saw her.

The beat of the music slowed, and her angel's smile was noticeable even across the dim basement. Her arms wrapped around Finch's neck, and he awkwardly moved with her to the music.

My feet propelled me forward, and before I knew what I was doing, or stopped to think about the consequences, I found myself standing inches away from them.

"Mind if I cut in, Finch?"

Abby froze, her eyes flashing with recognition.

Finch's eyes bounced between me and Abby. "Sure."

"Finch," she hissed as he walked away.

I pulled her against me and took a step.

Abby kept dancing but kept as much space between us as possible. "I thought you weren't coming."

"I wasn't, but I knew you were here. I had to come."

With each passing minute, I expected her to walk away, and every minute she stayed in my arms felt like a miracle. "You look beautiful, Pidge."

"Don't."

"Don't what? Tell you you're beautiful?"

"Just . . . don't."

"I didn't mean it."

"Thanks," she snapped.

"No . . . you look beautiful. I meant that. I was talking about what I said in my room. I'm not going to lie. I enjoyed pulling you from your date with Parker . . ."

"It wasn't a date, Travis. We were just eating. He won't speak to me now, thanks to you."

"I heard. I'm sorry."

"No you're not."

"Y-you're right," I said, stuttering when I noticed she was getting angry. "But I . . . that wasn't the only reason I took you to the fight. I wanted you there with me, Pidge. You're my good luck charm."

"I'm not your anything." She glared up at me.

My eyebrows pulled in and I stopped midstep. "You're my *everything*."

Abby's lips formed a hard line, but her eyes softened.

"You don't really hate me . . . do you?" I asked.

Abby turned away, putting more distance between us. "Sometimes I wish that I did. It would make everything a whole hell of a lot easier."

A cautious, small smile spread across my lips. "So what pisses you off more? What I did to make you wanna hate me? Or knowing that you can't?"

In a flash, Abby's anger returned. She shoved past me, running up the stairs to the kitchen. I stood alone in the middle of the floor, both dumbfounded and disgusted that I'd somehow managed to reignite her hatred for me all over again. Trying to speak to her at all seemed futile, now. Every interaction just added to the growing snowball of clusterfucks that was our relationship.

I walked up the stairs and made a beeline for the keg, cursing my greediness and the empty bottle of whiskey lying somewhere in Sig Tau's front lawn.

After an hour of beer and monotonous, drunken conversation with frat brothers and their dates, I glanced over at Abby, hoping to catch her eye. She was already looking at me, but looked away. America seemed to be in the middle of an attempt to cheer her up, and then Finch touched her arm. He was obviously ready to leave.

She drank the remainder of her beer in a quick swig, and then took Finch's hand. She walked two steps, and then froze when the same song that we had danced to at her birthday party floated up the stairs. She reached out and grabbed Finch's bottle, taking another swig.

I wasn't sure if it was the whiskey talking, but something

about the look in her eyes told me the memories the song triggered were just as painful for her as they were for me.

She still cared about me. She had to.

One of my frat brothers leaned against the counter beside Abby and smiled. "Wanna dance?"

It was Brad, and although I knew he had probably just noticed the forlorn look on her face and was trying to cheer her up, the hairs on the back of my neck stood on end. Just as she shook her head to say no, I was next to her, and my stupid fucking mouth was moving before my brain could tell it to stop.

"Dance with me."

America, Shepley, and Finch were all staring at Abby, waiting for her answer as anxiously as I was.

"Leave me alone, Travis," she said, crossing her arms.

"This is our song, Pidge."

"We don't have a song."

"Pigeon . . ."

"No."

She looked to Brad and forced a smile. "I would love to dance, Brad."

Brad's freckles stretched across his cheeks as he smiled, gesturing with his hand for Abby to lead the way to the stairs.

I staggered backward, feeling like I'd just been punched in the gut. A combination of anger, jealousy, and sadness boiled in my blood.

"A toast!" I yelled, climbing onto a chair. On my way to the top, I stole someone's beer and held it out in front of me. "To douche bags!" I said, gesturing to Brad. "And to girls that break your heart." I bowed to Abby. My throat tightened. "And to the absolute fucking horror of losing your best friend because you were stupid enough to fall in love with her."

I tilted back the beer, finishing what was left, and then tossed it to the floor. The room was silent except for the music playing in the basement, and everyone stared at me in mass confusion.

Abby's quick movement drew my attention when she grabbed Brad's hand, leading him downstairs to the dance floor.

I jumped off the chair and started for the basement, but Shepley put the side of his fist against my chest, leaning into me. "You need to stop," he said in a hushed voice. "This is only going to end badly."

"If it ends, what does it matter?" I shoved past Shepley and down the stairs to where Abby was dancing with Brad. The snowball was too big to stop, so I decided just to roll with it. There was no shame in going balls out. We couldn't go back to being friends, so making one of us hate the other seemed like a good idea.

I pushed my way through the couples on the dance floor, stopping beside Abby and Brad. "I'm cutting in."

"No, you're not. Jesus!" Abby said, ducking her head with embarrassment.

My eyes bore into Brad's. "If you don't back away from my girl, I'll rip out your fucking throat. Right here on the dance floor."

Brad seemed conflicted, his eyes nervously darting from me to his dance partner. "Sorry, Abby," he said, slowly pulling his arms away. He retreated to the stairs.

"How I feel about you right now, Travis . . . it very closely resembles hate."

"Dance with me," I pleaded, shifting to keep my balance.

The song ended and Abby sighed. "Go drink another bottle of whiskey, Trav." She turned to dance with the only single guy on the dance floor.

The tempo was faster, and with every beat, Abby moved closer and closer to her new dance partner. David, my least favorite Sig Tau brother, danced behind her, grabbing her hips. They smiled as they two-timed her, putting their hands all over her body. David grabbed her hips and dug his pelvis into her ass. Everyone stared. Instead of feeling jealous, guilt washed over me. This is what I had reduced her to.

In two steps, I bent down and wrapped my arm around Abby's legs, throwing her over my shoulder, shoving David to the ground for being such an opportunistic dick.

"Put me down!" Abby said, pounding her fists into my back.

"I'm not going to let you embarrass yourself over me," I growled, taking the stairs two at a time.

Every pair of eyes we passed watched Abby kick and scream as I carried her across the room. "You don't think," she said while she struggled, "this is embarrassing? Travis!"

"Shepley! Is Donnie outside?" I yelled, ducking from her flailing limbs.

"Uh . . . yeah?" he said.

"Put her down!" America said, taking a step toward us.

"America," Abby said, squirming, "don't just stand there! *Help* me!"

America's mouth turned up and she laughed once. "You two look ridiculous."

"Thanks a lot, *friend*!" she said, incredulous. Once we were outside, Abby only fought harder. "Put me down, dammit!"

I walked over to Donnie's waiting car, opened the back door, and tossed Abby inside. "Donnie, you're the DD tonight?"

Donnie turned around, nervously watching the chaos from the driver's seat. "Yeah."

"I need you to take us to my apartment," I said as I got in beside her.

"Travis . . . I don't think . . ."

"Do it, Donnie, or I'll shove my fist through the back of your head, I swear to God."

Donnie immediately put the car into gear and pulled away from the curb. Abby lunged for the door handle. "I'm not going to your apartment!"

I grabbed one of her wrists, and then the other. She leaned down, sinking her teeth into my forearm. It hurt like hell, but I just closed my eyes. When I was sure she'd broken the skin and it felt like fire was shooting up my arm, I growled to offset the pain.

"Do your worst, Pidge. I'm tired of your shit."

She released me and then thrashed around again, trying to hit me, more for being insulted than trying to get away. "*My shit?* Let me out of this fucking car!"

I pulled her wrists close to my face. "I love you, dammit! You're not going anywhere until you sober up and we figure this out!"

"You're the only one that hasn't figured it out, Travis!"

I released her wrists, and she crossed her arms, pouting the rest of the way to the apartment.

When the car slowed to a stop, Abby leaned forward. "Can you take me home, Donnie?"

I opened the door, and then pulled Abby out by the arm,

swinging her over my shoulder again. "Night, Donnie," I said, carrying her up the stairs.

"I'm calling your dad!" Abby cried.

I couldn't help but laugh. "And he'd probably pat me on the shoulder and tell me that it's about damn time!"

Abby's body writhed while I pulled the keys from my pocket. "Knock it off, Pidge, or we're going to fall down the stairs!"

Finally the door opened, and I stomped straight into Shepley's room.

"Put. Me. *Down!*" Abby screamed.

"Fine," I said, dropping her onto Shepley's bed. "Sleep it off. We'll talk in the morning."

I imagined how pissed she must have been, but even though my back was throbbing from being lambasted by Abby's fists for the last twenty minutes, it was a relief to have her in the apartment again.

"You can't tell me what to do anymore, Travis! I don't belong to you!"

Her words ignited a deep anger inside me. I stomped to the bed, planted my hands on the mattress on each side of her thighs, and leaned into her face.

"Well, I belong to you!" I screamed. I put so much force behind my words, I could feel all the blood rush to my face. Abby met my glare, refusing to even flinch. I looked at her lips, panting. "I belong to you," I whispered, my anger fading as desire took over.

Abby reached out, but instead of slapping my face, she grabbed each of my cheeks and slammed her mouth into mine. Without hesitation, I lifted her into my arms and carried her into my bedroom, letting us both fall into my mattress.

Abby grabbed at my clothes, desperate to remove them. I unzipped her dress with one smooth movement, and then watched as she pulled it quickly over her head, tossing it to the floor. Our eyes met, and then I kissed her, moaning into her mouth when she kissed me back.

Before I'd even had the chance to think, we were both naked. Abby grabbed my ass, anxious to pull me inside of her, but I resisted, the adrenaline burning through the whiskey and beer. My senses returned, and thoughts of permanent consequences began flashing though my mind. I had been an ass, I had pissed her off, but I never wanted Abby to wonder if I'd taken advantage of this moment.

"We're both drunk," I said, breathing hard.

"Please."

Her thighs squeezed my hips, and I could feel the muscles under her soft skin quiver in anticipation.

"This isn't right." I fought against the alcohol haze that told me that the next few hours with her was worth whatever was on the other side of that moment.

I pressed my forehead against hers. As much as I wanted her, the painful thought of making Abby take the walk of shame in the morning was stronger than what my hormones were telling me to do. If she really wanted to go through with this, I needed solid proof.

"I want you," she whispered against my mouth.

"I need you to say it."

"I'll say whatever you want."

"Then say that you belong to me. Say that you'll take me back. I won't do this unless we're together."

"We've never really been apart, have we?"

I shook my head, sweeping my lips across hers. Not good enough. "I need to hear you say it. I need to know you're mine."

"I've been yours since the second we met," she said, begging.

I stared into her eyes for a few seconds, and then felt my mouth turn up into a half smile, hoping her words were true and not just spoken in the moment. I leaned down and kissed her tenderly, and then she slowly pulled me into her. My entire body felt like it was melting inside of her.

"Say it again." Part of me couldn't believe it was all really happening.

"I'm yours." She breathed. "I don't ever want to be apart from you again."

"Promise me," I said, groaning with another thrust.

"I love you. I'll love you forever." She looked straight into my eyes when she spoke, and it finally clicked that her words weren't just an empty promise.

I sealed my mouth over hers, the rhythm of our movements picking up momentum. Nothing else needed to be said, and for the first time in months, my world wasn't upside down. Abby's back arched, and her legs wrapped around my back, hooked at the ankles. I tasted every part of her skin I could reach as if I'd been starving for it. A part of me was. An hour passed, and then another. Even when I was exhausted, I kept going, afraid if we stopped I would wake up, and it would all be just a dream.

I SQUINTED AGAINST THE LIGHT POURING INTO THE room. I couldn't sleep all night, knowing when the sun came up, it would all be over. Abby stirred, and my teeth clenched. The few hours we spent together wasn't enough. I wasn't ready.

Abby nuzzled her cheek against my chest. I kissed her hair, and then her forehead, and then her cheeks, neck, shoulders, and then I brought her hand to my mouth and tenderly kissed her wrist, palm, and fingers. I wanted to squeeze her but restrained myself. My eyes filled with hot tears for the third time since I'd brought her to my apartment. When she woke, she was going to be mortified, angry, and then leave me forever.

I'd never been so afraid to see the different shades of gray in her irises.

Her eyes still closed, Abby smiled, and I brought my mouth back to hers, terrified for the realization to hit.

"Good morning," she said against my mouth.

I moved halfway above her and then continued to touch my lips to various spots on her skin. My arms dug beneath her, between her back and the mattress, and I buried my face in her neck, taking in her scent before she bolted out the door.

"You're quiet this morning," she said, running her hands over the bare skin of my back. She slid her palms over my ass, and then hooked her leg over my hip.

I shook my head. "I just want to be like this."

"Did I miss something?"

"I didn't mean to wake you up. Why don't you just go back to sleep?"

Abby leaned back against the pillow, pulling up my chin to face her.

"What in the hell is wrong with you?" she asked, her body suddenly tense.

"Just go back to sleep, Pigeon. Please?"

"Did something happen? Is it America?" With the last question, she sat up.

I sat up with her, wiping my eyes.

"No . . . America's fine. They got home around four this morning. They're still in bed. It's early, let's just go back to sleep."

Her eyes bounced around to different points of my room as she remembered the night before. Knowing any moment she would recall the fact that I'd dragged her out of the party and made a spectacle, I put both hands on each side of her face and kissed her one last time.

"Have you slept?" she asked, wrapping her arms around my middle.

"I . . . couldn't. I didn't wanna . . ."

She kissed my forehead. "Whatever it is, we'll get through it, okay? Why don't you get some sleep? We'll figure it out when you wake up."

That was not what I expected. My head popped up and I scanned her face. "What do you mean? That *we'll* get through it?"

Her eyebrows pulled in. "I don't know what's going on, but I'm here."

"You're here? As in you're staying? With me?"

Her expression scattered in different directions. "Yes. I thought we discussed this last night?"

"We did." I probably looked like a total tool, but I nodded emphatically.

Abby's eyes narrowed. "You thought I was going to wake up pissed at you, didn't you? You thought I was going to leave?"

"That *is* what you're famous for."

"Is that what you're so upset about? You stayed up all night worrying about what would happen when I woke up?"

I shifted. "I didn't mean for last night to happen like that. I was a little drunk, and I followed you around the party like some fucking stalker, and then I dragged you out of there, against your will ... and then we ..." I shook my head, disgusted with myself.

"Had the best sex of my life?" Abby said, smiling and squeezing my hand.

I laughed once, astounded at how well the conversation was going. "So we're okay?"

Abby held my face and kissed me tenderly. "Yes, dummy. I promised, didn't I? I told you everything you wanted to hear, we're back together, and you're still not happy?"

My breath faltered, and I choked back tears. It still didn't seem real.

"Travis, stop. I love you," she said, using her thin fingers to smooth lines around my eyes. "This absurd standoff could have been over at Thanksgiving, but ..."

"Wait ... what?" I interrupted, leaning back.

"I was fully prepared to give in on Thanksgiving, but you said you were done trying to make me happy, and I was too proud to tell you that I wanted you back."

"Are you fucking kidding me? I was just trying to make it easier on you! Do you know how *miserable* I've been?"

Abby frowned. "You looked just fine after break."

"That was for you! I was afraid I'd lose you if I didn't pretend to be okay with being friends. I could have been with you this whole time? What the *fuck*, Pigeon?"

"I ... I'm sorry."

"You're *sorry*? I damn near drank myself to death, I could

barely get out of bed, I shattered my phone into a million pieces on New Year's Eve to keep from calling you . . . and you're *sorry?*"

Abby bit her bottom lip and nodded, ashamed. "I'm so . . . *so* sorry."

"You're forgiven," I said without hesitation. "Don't ever do it again."

"I won't. I promise."

I shook my head, grinning like an idiot. "I fucking love you."

CHAPTER TWENTY-SIX
Panic

LIFE HAD RETURNED TO NORMAL—MAYBE MORE FOR Abby than for me. On the surface we were happy, but I could feel a wall of caution building around me. Not a second with Abby was taken for granted. If I looked over at her and wanted to touch her, I did. If she wasn't at the apartment and I missed her, I went to Morgan. If we were at the apartment, she was in my arms.

Returning to school as a couple for the first time since the fall had the expected effect. As we walked around together, holding hands, laughing, and occasionally kissing—okay, more than occasionally—the gossip spiked to an all-time high. As always at this school, whispers and tabloid-worthy stories continued until another scandal rocked the campus.

On top of the unrest I already felt about my and Abby's relationship, Shepley was growing increasingly irritable about the last fight of the year. I wasn't far behind. We both depended on the winnings from that fight to fund our living expenses for the summer, not to mention part of the fall. Since I'd decided the last fight of the year was also my last fight for good, we would need it.

Spring break inched closer, but still no word from Adam. Shepley had finally heard through multiple lines of communication that Adam was lying low after the arrests following the most recent fight.

On the Friday before break, the campus mood felt lighter, even with the fresh batch of snow that had been dumped onto the state overnight. On our way to the cafeteria for lunch, Abby and I had barely escaped a public snowball fight; America, not so much.

We all chatted and laughed, waiting in line for trays of God-knows-what, and then sat at our regular seats. Shepley comforted America while I amused Brazil with the story of how Abby hustled my brothers on poker night. My phone buzzed, but it didn't register until Abby pointed it out.

"Trav?" she said.

I turned, tuning everything out the second she said my name.

"You might want to get that."

I looked down at the cell phone and sighed. "Or not." Part of me needed that last fight, but part of me knew it would be time spent away from Abby. After she was attacked at the last one, there was no way I could concentrate if she came to this one without protection—and I couldn't concentrate fully if she wasn't there, either. The last fight of the year was always the biggest, and I couldn't afford to have my head somewhere else.

"It could be important," Abby said.

I held the phone to my ear. "What's up, Adam?"

"Mad Dog! You're gonna love this. It's done. I got John fucking Savage! He's planning to go pro next year! Chance of a goddamn lifetime, my friend! Five figures. You'll be set for a while."

"This is my last fight, Adam."

The other end of the line was quiet. I could imagine his jaw working under the skin. More than once he'd accused Abby of threatening his cash flow, and I was sure he would blame her for my decision.

"Are you bringing her?"

"I'm not sure yet."

"You should probably leave her at home, Travis. If this really is your last fight, I need you all in."

"I won't go without her, and Shep's leaving town."

"No fucking around this time. I mean it."

"I know. I heard you."

Adam sighed. "If you really won't consider leaving her at home, maybe you could call Trent. That would probably set your mind at ease, and then you could concentrate."

"Hmmm . . . that's not a bad idea, actually," I said.

"Think about it. Let me know," Adam said, hanging up the phone.

Abby stared at me expectantly.

"It's enough to pay rent for the next eight months. Adam got John Savage. He's trying to go pro."

"I haven't seen him fight, have you?" Shepley asked, leaning forward.

"Just once in Springfield. He's good."

"Not good enough," Abby said. I leaned in and kissed her forehead. "I can stay home, Trav."

"No," I said, shaking my head.

"I don't want you to get hit like you did last time because you're worried about me."

"No, Pidge."

"I'll wait up for you." She smiled, but it was obviously forced, making me even more determined.

"I'm going to ask Trent to come. He's the only one I'd trust so I can concentrate on the fight."

"Thanks a lot, asshole," Shepley grumbled.

"Hey, you had your chance," I said, only half teasing.

Shepley's mouth pulled to the side. He could pout all day long, but he dropped the ball at Hellerton, letting Abby get away from him like that. If he'd been paying attention, it would have never happened, and we all knew it.

America and Abby swore that it was a fluke accident, but I didn't hesitate to tell him otherwise. He was watching the fight instead of Abby, and if Ethan had finished what he started, I would be in jail for murder. Shepley apologized to Abby for weeks, but then I took him aside and told him to knock it off. None of us liked reliving it every time his guilt got the best of him.

"Shepley, it wasn't your fault. You pulled him off of me, remember?" Abby said, reaching around America to pat his arm. She turned to me. "When is the fight?"

"Next week sometime. I want you there. I need you there." If I'd been any less of an asshole, I would have insisted she stay home, but it had already been established on numerous occasions that I wasn't. My need to be around Abby Abernathy overruled any rational thought. It had always been that way, and I imagined it always would.

Abby smiled, resting her chin on my shoulder. "Then I'll be there."

I dropped Abby off at her final class, kissing her goodbye before meeting Shepley and America at Morgan. The campus was quickly emptying, and I finally resorted to smoking my cigarettes around the corner so I wouldn't have to dodge a coed carrying luggage or laundry every three minutes.

I pulled my cell phone from my pocket and dialed Trenton's number, listening to each ring with increasing impatience. Finally, his voice mail picked up. "Trent, it's me. I need a huge favor. It's time sensitive, so call me back ASAP. Later."

I hung up, seeing Shepley and America pushing through the glass doors of the dorm, each holding two of her bags.

"Looks like you're all set."

Shepley smiled; America didn't.

"They're really not that bad," I said, nudging her with my elbow. Her scowl didn't disappear.

"She'll feel better once we get there," Shepley said, more to encourage his girlfriend than to convince me.

I helped them pack the trunk of the Charger, and then we waited for Abby to finish her midterm and find us in the parking lot.

I pulled my beanie over my ears and lit a cigarette, waiting. Trenton still hadn't called back, and I was getting nervous that he wouldn't be able to come. The twins were halfway to Colorado with some of their fellow Sig Tau alums, and I didn't trust anyone else to keep Abby safe.

I took several drags, working out the different scenarios in my head if Trenton didn't call back, and how fucking selfish I was being, requiring her presence in a place where I knew she could be in danger. Complete concentration was needed to win this fight, and that depended on two things: Abby's presence, and Abby's safety. If Trenton had to work or didn't call me back, I'd have to call off the fight. That was the only option.

I took a final drag off the last cigarette in the pack. I'd been so wrapped up in worry, I hadn't realized how much I'd been smoking. I looked down at my watch. Abby should have gotten out of class by now.

Just then, she called my name.

"Hey, Pigeon."

"Everything okay?"

"It is now," I said, pulling her against me.

"Okay. What's up?"

"Just have a lot on my mind." I sighed. When she made it known that my answer wasn't good enough, I continued, "This week, the fight, you being there . . ."

"I told you I would stay home."

"I need you there, Pidge," I said, flicking my cigarette to the ground. I watched it disappear into a deep footprint in the snow, and then took Abby's hand.

"Have you talked to Trent?" she asked.

"I'm waiting for him to call me back."

America rolled down the window and poked her head out of Shepley's Charger. "Hurry up! It's freaking freezing!"

I smiled and opened the door for Abby. While I stared out the window Shepley and America repeated the same conversation they'd had since she learned she would be meeting his parents. Just as we pulled into the parking lot of the apartment, my phone rang.

"What the fuck, Trent?" I asked, seeing his name on the display. "I called you hours ago. It's not like you're productive at work or anything."

"It hasn't been *hours*, and I'm sorry. I've been at Cami's."

"Whatever. Listen, I need a favor. I've got a fight next week. I need you to go. I don't know when it is, but when I call you, I need you there within an hour. Can you do that for me?"

"I don't know. What's in it for me?" he teased.

"Can you do it or not, douche bag? Because I need you to keep an eye on Pigeon. Some asshole put his hands on her last time and—"

"What the fuck, Chuck? Are you serious?"

"Yeah."

"Who did it?" Trenton asked, his tone immediately grave.

"I took care of it. So if I call . . . ?"

"Yeah. I mean, of course, little brother, I'll be there."

"Thanks, Trent." I clicked my phone shut and leaned my head against the back of the seat.

"Relieved?" Shepley asked, watching my anxiety unwind inside the rearview mirror.

"Yeah. I wasn't sure how I was going to do it without him there."

"I told you—" Abby began, but I stopped her.

"Pidge, how many times do I have to say it?"

She shook her head at my impatient tone. "I don't understand it, though. You didn't need me there before."

I turned to her, my finger touching her cheek. She clearly had no idea how deep my feelings ran. "I didn't know you before. When you're not there, I can't concentrate. I'm wondering where you are, what you're doing . . . if you're there and I can see you, I can focus. I know it's crazy, but that's how it is."

"And crazy is exactly the way I like it," she said, leaning up to kiss my lips.

"Obviously," America muttered under breath.

Before the sun set too far into the horizon, America and Shepley took the Charger south.

Abby shook the Honda keys and smiled. "At least we don't have to freeze on the Harley."

I smiled.

Abby shrugged. "Maybe we should, I don't know, consider getting our own car?"

"After the fight, we'll go shopping for one. How about that?"

She jumped up, wrapped her arms and legs around me, and covered my cheeks, mouth, and neck with kisses.

I walked up the stairs to the apartment, making a beeline to the bedroom.

Abby and I spent the next four days snuggled up either in the bed, or on the couch with Toto, watching old movies. It made waiting on Adam's call tolerable.

Finally on Tuesday night, between *Boy Meets World* reruns, Adam's number lit up my cell phone's display. My eyes met Abby's.

"Yeah?"

"Mad Dog. You're up in an hour. Keaton Hall. Bring your game face, sweet pea, he's Hulk Hogan on steroids."

"See you then." I stood up, bringing Abby with me. "Change into something warm, baby. Keaton is an old building, and they've probably shut off the heaters for break."

Abby did a little happy dance before jogging down the hall to the bedroom. The corners of my mouth turned up. What other woman would be that excited to see her boyfriend trade punches? No wonder I fell in love with her.

I slipped on a hoodie and my boots, and waited for Abby by the front door.

"Coming!" she called, strutting around the corner. She gripped each side of the door jamb and shifted her hip to the side.

"What do you think?" she asked, pouting her lips attempting to imitate a model . . . or a duck. I wasn't sure which.

My eyes traveled down from her long, heather gray cardigan, white T, and tight blue jeans tucked inside tall black boots. She meant it as a joke, thinking she looked frumpy, but my breath caught at the sight of her.

Her body relaxed, and she let her hands fall to her thighs. "That bad?"

"No," I said, trying to find the words. "Not bad at all."

With one hand I opened the door, and held out the other. With a bounce in her walk, Abby crossed the living room and intertwined her fingers in mine.

The Honda was slow to start, but we made it to Keaton in plenty of time. I called Trenton on the way, hoping to God he would come through for me like he'd promised.

Abby stood with me, waiting for Trenton beside the tall, seasoned north wall of Keaton. The east and west walls were protected with steel scaffolding. The university was preparing to give their oldest building a face-lift.

I lit a cigarette and took a drag, blowing smoke out of my nose.

Abby squeezed my hand. "He'll be here."

People were already filtering in from every direction, parking blocks away in different lots. The closer it came to fight time, the more people could be seen scaling the south fire escape.

I frowned. The building choice hadn't been thought through. The last fight of the year always brought the more serious punters out, and they always came early so they could place their bets and secure a good view. The size of the pot also brought out the less experienced spectators, who showed up late and ended up flattened against the walls. This year's was exceptionally large. Keaton was on the outskirts of campus, which was preferred, but its basement was one of the smallest.

"This is one of the worst ideas Adam has had yet," I grumbled.

"It's too late to change it now," Abby said, her eyes traveling up the concrete blocks.

I popped open my cell and shot a sixth text to Trenton, and then snapped the phone shut.

"You seem nervous tonight," Abby whispered.

"I'll feel better when Trent gets his punk ass here."

"I'm here, you whiny little girl," Trenton said in a hushed voice.

I sighed with relief.

"How ya been, sis?" Trenton asked Abby, hugging her with one arm, and then playfully shoving me with the other.

"I'm good, Trent," she said, amused.

I led Abby by the hand to the back of the building, glancing back to Trenton as we walked. "If the cops show and we get separated, meet me at Morgan Hall, okay?"

Trenton nodded just as I stopped next to an open window low to the ground.

"You're fuckin' with me," Trenton said, staring down at the window. "Abby's barely gonna fit through there."

"You'll fit," I assured him, crawling down into the blackness inside.

Now accustomed to breaking and entering, Abby didn't hesitate to crawl on the frozen ground and inch backward through the window, falling into my arms.

We waited for a few moments, and then Trenton grunted as he pushed off the ledge and landed on the floor, nearly losing his balance as his feet hit the concrete.

"You're lucky I love Abby. I wouldn't do this shit for just any-one," he grumbled, brushing off his shirt.

I jumped up, shutting the window with one quick pull. "This way," I said, leading Abby and my brother through the dark.

We weaved farther into the building until a small flicker of light could be seen ahead. A low hum of voices came from the same point, as our three pairs of feet grated against the loose concrete on the floor.

Trenton sighed after the third turn. "We're never gonna find our way out of here."

"Just follow me out. It'll be fine," I said.

It was easy to discern how close we were by the growing vol-ume of the crowd waiting in the main room. Adam's voice came over the bullhorn, yelling names and numbers.

I stopped in the next room, glancing around at the desks and chairs covered in white sheets. A sick feeling came over me. The venue was a mistake. Almost as big as bringing Abby somewhere so dangerous. If a fight broke out, Abby would be protected by Trenton, but the usual safe haven away from the crowd was full of furniture and equipment.

"So how you're gonna play this?" Trenton asked.

"Divide and conquer."

"Divide what?"

"His head from the rest of his body."

Trenton nodded quickly. "Good plan."

"Pigeon, I want you to stand by this doorway, okay?" Abby looked into the main room, her eyes wide as she took in the chaos. "Pigeon, did you hear me?" I asked, touching her arm.

"What?" she asked, blinking.

"I want you to stand by this doorway, okay? Keep hold of Trent's arm at all times."

"I won't move," she said. "I promise."

I smiled at her sweet, overwhelmed expression. "Now *you* look nervous."

She glanced to the doorway, and then back at me. "I don't have a good feeling about this, Trav. Not about the fight, but . . . something. This place gives me the creeps."

I couldn't disagree. "We won't be here long."

Adam's voice came over the horn, starting his opening announcement.

I touched each side of Abby's face, and looked into her eyes. "I love you." A ghost of a smile touched her lips, and I pulled her into me, holding her tight against my chest.

". . . so don't use your hos to scam the system, boys!" Adam's voice said, amplified by the bullhorn.

I hooked Abby's arm around Trenton's. "Don't take your eyes off her. Even for a second. This place'll get crazy once the fight starts."

". . . so let's welcome tonight's contender—JOHN SAVAGE!"

"I'll guard her with my life, little brother," Trenton said, lightly tugging Abby's arm for emphasis. "Now go kick this guy's ass and let's get out of here."

"Shake in your boots, boys, and drop your panties, ladies! I give you: TRAVIS 'MAD DOG' MADDOX!"

At Adam's introduction, I stepped into the main room.

Arms flailed, and the voices of many boomed in unison. The sea
of people parted before me, and I slowly made my way out to the
Circle.

The room was lit only with lanterns hanging from the ceiling. Still trying to keep a low profile from nearly getting busted
before, Adam didn't want bright lights tipping anyone off.

Even in the dim light, I could see the severity of John Savage's expression. He towered over me, his eyes wild and eager.
He bounced from one foot to the other a few times, and then
stood still, glowering down at me with murder in mind.

Savage was no amateur, but there were only three ways to
win: knockout, submission, and decision. The reason the advantage had always been in my favor was because I had four brothers, who all fought different ways.

If John Savage fought like Trenton, he would rely on offense,
speed, and surprise attacks—which I had trained for my entire
life.

If he fought like the twins—with combinations of punches
and kicks, or switching up his tactics to land blows—I had
trained for that all my life.

Thomas was the most lethal. If Savage fought smart, and he
probably did, judging by the way he was sizing me up, he would
fight with the perfect balance of strength, speed, and strategy.
I'd only traded blows with my eldest brother a handful of times
in my life, but by the time I was sixteen, he couldn't defeat me
without help from my other brothers.

No matter how hard John Savage had trained, or what
advantage he thought he had, I had fought him before. I had
fought everyone that could fight worth a damn before . . . and
I had won.

Adam blew the bullhorn, and Savage took a short step back before powering a blow in my direction.

I dodged. He would definitely fight like Thomas.

Savage got too close, so I pulled up my boot and launched him back into the crowd. They pushed him back into the circle, and he approached me with renewed purpose.

He landed two punches in a row, and then I grabbed him, shoving his face down into my knee. John stumbled backward, got his wits about him, and then charged again.

I swung and missed, and then he tried to wrap his arms around my middle. Already sweaty, it was easy to slip from his grasp. When I turned, his elbow met with my jaw, and the world stopped for less than a second before I shook it off and answered him with a left and right hook, landing one right after the other.

Savage's bottom lip split and splattered. Drawing first blood heightened the volume in the room to a deafening decibel.

My elbow reared back, and my fist followed all the way through, making a short pit stop at Savage's nose. I didn't hold back, purposefully stunning him so I would have time to look back and check on Abby. She stood where I'd asked her to, her arm still hooked around Trenton's.

Satisfied she was okay, I focused on the fight again, dodging quickly when Savage threw a wobbly punch, and then threw his arms around me, yanking us both to the ground.

John landed under me, and without even trying, my elbow rammed into his face. He put my body in a vise grip with his legs, locking them together at the ankles.

"I'm going to end you, you fucking punk!" John growled.

I smiled, and then pushed off the ground, lifting both of us.

Savage struggled to take me off balance, but it was time to get Abby home.

Trenton's voice erupted over the rest of the crowd. "Slam his ass, Travis!"

I fell forward and slightly to the side, slamming John's back and head against the concrete in a devastating blow. My opponent now dazed, I reared back my elbow and shoved my fists into his face and the sides of his head over and over until a pair of arms hooked under my mine and pulled me away.

Adam threw a red square on Savage's chest, and the room exploded as Adam grabbed my wrist and raised my hand in the air.

I looked to Abby, who was bobbing up and down, heads above the rest of the crowd, held up by my brother.

Trenton was yelling something, a huge smile on his face.

Just as the crowd began to disperse, I caught a horrified look on Abby's face, and seconds later, a collective cry from the crowd sparked panic. A hanging lantern in the corner of the main room had fallen, catching a white sheet on fire. The blaze spread quickly to the sheet beside it, starting a chain reaction.

The screaming crowd rushed to the mouth of the stairs as smoke quickly filled the room. Frightened faces, both male and female, were highlighted by flames.

"Abby!" I screamed, realizing just how far away she was, and just how many people were between us. If I couldn't get to her, she and Trenton would have to find their way back to the window through the maze of dark hallways. Terror dug into my core, spurring me to wildly push through whoever got in my way.

The room darkened, and a loud popping noise sounded from the other side of the room. The other lanterns were igniting and adding to the blaze in small explosions. I caught a glimpse of

Trenton, who was grabbing at Abby's arm, pulling her behind him as he tried to force his way through the crowd.

Abby shook her head, pulling back.

Trenton looked around, forming a plan of escape while they stood in the center of the confusion. If they tried to go out the fire escape, they would be the last ones out. The fire was growing fast. They wouldn't make it through the crowd to get to the exit in time.

Any attempt I made to get to Abby was thwarted as the crowd surged and pushed me farther away. The excited cheering that filled the room before was replaced by horrified shrieks of fear and desperation as everyone fought to reach the exits.

Trenton pulled Abby to the doorway, but she struggled against him to look back. "Travis!" she yelled, reaching out for me.

I took a breath to yell back, but smoke filled my lungs. I coughed, waving the smoke away.

"This way, Trav!" Trenton yelled.

"Just get her out of here, Trent! Get Pigeon out!"

Abby's eyes widened, and she shook her head. "Travis!"

"Just go!" I said. "I'll catch up to you outside!"

Abby paused for a moment before her lips formed a hard line. Relief came over me. Abby Abernathy had a strong survival instinct, and it had just kicked in. She grabbed Trenton's sleeve and pulled him back into the darkness, away from the fire.

I turned, looking for my own way out. Dozens of spectators were clawing their way to the narrow access to the stairs, screaming and fighting one another to get to the exit.

The room was nearly black with smoke, and I felt my lungs struggling for air. I kneeled to the ground, trying to remember the different doors that lined the main room. I turned back to the stairway. That was the way I wanted to go, away from the fire, but I refused to panic. There was a second exit that led to the fire escape, one only a few people would think to go through. I crouched and ran toward where I remembered it being, but I stopped.

Thoughts of Abby and Trenton getting lost flashed in my mind, pulling me away from the exit.

I heard my name, and squinted toward the sound.

"Travis! Travis! This way!" Adam stood in the doorway, waving me toward him.

I shook my head. "I'm going to get Pigeon!"

The path to the smaller room where Trenton and Abby escaped through was almost clear, so I sprinted across the room, hitting someone head-on. It was a girl, a freshman by the looks of her, her face covered with black streaks. She was terrified and scrambled to her feet.

"H-help me! I can't . . . I don't know the way out!" she said, coughing.

"Adam!" I yelled. I pushed her toward the direction of the exit. "Help her out of here!"

The girl raced for Adam, and he grabbed her hand before they disappeared through the exit before the smoke totally obscured it from view.

I pushed off the floor and ran toward Abby. Others were running around in the dark mazes too, crying and panting as they tried to find a way out.

"Abby!" I yelled into the darkness. I was terrified they had taken a wrong turn.

A small group of girls stood in the end of a hallway, crying. "Have you seen a guy and a girl go through here? Trenton's about this tall, looks like me?" I said, holding a hand to my forehead.

They shook their heads.

My stomach sank. Abby and Trenton had gone the wrong way.

I pointed past the frightened group. "Follow that hall until you get to the end. There is a stairwell with a door at the top. Take it, and then turn left. There's a window you can get out of."

One of the girls nodded, wiped her eyes, and then barked at her friends to follow.

Instead of backtracking down the halls from where we came, I turned left, running through the blackness, hoping that I would get lucky and run into them somehow.

I could hear screaming from the main room as I pushed on, determined to make sure Abby and Trenton had found their way out. I wouldn't leave until I knew for sure.

After running through several hallways, I felt panic weighing down my chest. The smell of smoke had caught up to me, and I knew that with the construction, the aged building, the furniture, and the sheets that covered them feeding the fire, the entire basement level would be swallowed by the flames in minutes.

"Abby!" I yelled again. "Trent!"

Nothing.

CHAPTER TWENTY-SEVEN
Fire and Ice

THE SMOKE HAD BECOME INESCAPABLE. NO MATTER what room I found myself in, every breath was shallow and hot, burning my lungs.

I leaned down and grabbed my knees, panting. My sense of direction was weakened, both by the darkness, and the real possibility of not being able to find my girlfriend or brother before it was too late. I wasn't even sure if I could find my *own* way out.

Between bouts of coughing, I heard a knocking sound coming from the adjacent room.

"Help me! Somebody help me!"

It was Abby. Renewed resolve came over me, and I scrambled toward her voice, feeling through the blackness. My hands touched a wall, and then I stopped when I felt a door. It was locked. "Pidge?" I yelled, yanking on the door.

Abby's voice became more shrill, spurring me to take a step back and kick at the door until it flew open.

Abby stood on a desk just under a window, banging her hands against the glass so desperately, she didn't even realize I'd broken into the room.

"Pigeon?" I said, coughing.

"Travis!" she cried, scrambling down from the desk and into my arms.

I cupped her cheeks. "Where's Trent?"

"He followed them!" she bawled, tears streaming down her face. "I tried to get him to come with me, but he wouldn't come!"

I looked down the hall. The fire was barreling toward us, feeding on the covered furniture that lined the walls.

Abby gasped at the sight, and then coughed. My eyebrows pulled in, wondering where in the hell he was. If he was at the end of that hallway, he couldn't have made it. A sob welled up in my throat, but the look of terror in Abby's eyes forced it away.

"I'm gonna get us outta here, Pidge." I pressed my lips against hers in one quick, firm movement, and then climbed on top of her makeshift ladder.

I pushed at the window, the muscles of my arms quivering as I used all of my remaining strength against the glass.

"Get back, Abby! I'm gonna break the glass!"

Abby took one step away, her entire body shaking. My elbow bent as I reared back my fist, and I let out a grunt as I rammed it into the window. Glass shattered, and I reached out my hand.

"Come on!" I yelled.

The heat from the fire took over the room. Motivated by pure fear, I lifted Abby from the floor with one arm, and pushed her outside.

She waited on her knees as I climbed out, and then helped me to my feet. Sirens blared from the other side of the building, and red and blue lights from fire engines and police cruisers danced across the brick on the adjacent buildings.

I pulled Abby with me, sprinting to where a crowd of people

stood in front of the building. We scanned the soot-covered faces for Trenton while I yelled his name. Each time I called out, my voice became more broken. He wasn't there. I checked my phone, hoping he'd called. Seeing that he hadn't, I slammed it shut.

Nearing hopelessness, I covered my mouth, unsure of what to do next. My brother had gotten lost in the burning building. He wasn't outside, leading to only one conclusion.

"TRENT!" I screamed, stretching my neck as I searched the crowd.

Those that had escaped were hugging and whimpering behind the emergency vehicles, watching in horror as the pumper trucks shot water through the windows. Firefighters ran inside, pulling hoses behind them.

"He didn't get out," I whispered. "He didn't get out, Pidge." Tears streamed down my cheeks, and I fell to my knees.

Abby followed me to the ground, holding me in her arms.

"Trent's smart, Trav. He got out. He had to have found a different way."

I fell forward into Abby's lap, gripping her shirt with both fists.

An hour passed. The cries and wailing from the survivors and spectators outside the building had softened to an eerie quiet. Firefighters brought out just two survivors, and then continuously came out empty-handed. Each time someone emerged from the building, I held my breath, part of me hoping it was Trenton, the other fearing that it was.

Half an hour later, the bodies they returned with were lifeless. Instead of performing CPR, they simply laid them next to the other victims and covered their bodies. The ground was lined with casualties, far outnumbering those of us that had escaped.

"Travis?"

Adam stood beside us. I got up, pulling Abby along with me.

"I'm glad to see you guys made it out," Adam said, looking stunned and bewildered. "Where's Trent?"

I didn't answer.

Our eyes returned to the charred remains of Keaton Hall, the thick black smoke still billowing from the windows. Abby buried her face into my chest and gripped my shirt in her small fists.

It was a nightmarish scene, and all I could do was stare.

"I have to uh . . . I have to call my dad," I said, furrowing my brow.

"Maybe you should wait, Travis. We don't know anything, yet," Abby said.

My lungs burned, just like my eyes. The numbers blurred together as tears overflowed and poured down my cheeks. "This ain't fucking right. He shoulda never been there."

"It was an accident, Travis. You couldn't have known something like this was going to happen," Abby said, touching my cheek.

My face compressed, and I clenched my eyes shut. I was going to have to call my father and tell him that Trenton was still inside a burning building, and that it was my fault. I didn't know if my family could handle another loss. Trenton had lived with my dad while trying to get back on his feet, and they were a little closer than the rest of us.

My breath caught as I punched in the numbers, imagining my father's reaction. The phone felt cold in my hand, and so I pulled Abby against me. Even if she didn't know it yet, she had to be freezing.

The numbers turned into a name, and my eyes widened. I was getting another call.

"Trent?"

"Are you okay?" Trent yelled in my ear, his voice thick with panic.

A surprised laugh escaped my lips as I looked at Abby. "It's Trent!"

Abby gasped and squeezed my arm.

"Where are you?" I asked, desperate to find him.

"I'm at Morgan Hall, you dumb fuck! Where you told me to meet you! Why aren't you here?"

"What do you mean you're at Morgan? I'll be there in a second, don't you fucking move!"

I took off in a sprint, dragging Abby behind me. When we reached Morgan, we were both coughing and gasping for breath. Trenton ran down the steps, crashing into both of us.

"Jesus H. Christ, brother! I thought you were toast!" Trenton said, squeezing us tight.

"You asshole!" I screamed, shoving him away. "I thought you were fucking dead! I've been waiting for the firefighters to carry your charred body from Keaton!"

I frowned at Trenton for a moment, and then pulled him back into a hug. My arm shot out, fumbling around until I felt Abby's sweater, and then pulled her back into a hug as well. After several moments, I let Trenton go.

Trenton looked at Abby with an apologetic frown. "I'm sorry, Abby. I panicked."

She shook her head. "I'm just glad you're okay."

"*Me?* I would have been better off dead if Travis had seen me come out of that building without you. I tried to find you after you ran off, but then I got lost and had to find another way. I walked along the outside wall looking for that window, but I ran into some cops and they made me leave. I've been flippin' the fuck out over here!" he said, running his hand over his head.

I wiped Abby's cheeks with my thumbs, and then pulled up my shirt, using it to wipe the soot from my face. "Let's get out of here. The cops are going to be crawling all over the place soon."

After hugging my brother again, he headed to his car, and we walked to America's Honda. I watched Abby buckle her seat belt, and then frowned when she coughed.

"Maybe I should take you to the hospital. Get you checked out."

"I'm fine," she said, interlacing her fingers in mine. She looked down, seeing a deep cut across my knuckles. "Is that from the fight or the window?"

"The window," I answered, frowning at her bloodied nails.

Her eyes turned soft. "You saved my life, you know."

My eyebrows pushed together. "I wasn't leaving without you."

"I knew you'd come."

I kept Abby's hand in mine until we arrived at the apartment. Abby took a long shower, and with shaky hands, I poured us both a glass of bourbon.

She padded down the hallway, and then collapsed onto the bed in a daze.

"Here," I said, handing her a full glass of amber liquid. "It'll help you relax."

"I'm not tired."

I held out the glass again. She might have grown up around mobsters in Vegas, but we'd just seen death—a lot of it—and barely escaped it ourselves. "Just try to get some rest, Pidge."

"I'm almost afraid to close my eyes," she said, taking the glass and gulping the liquid down.

I took the empty glass and sat it on the nightstand, then sat beside her on the bed. We sat in silence, reflecting on the last few hours. It didn't seem real.

"A lot of people died tonight," I said.

"I know."

"We won't find out until tomorrow just how many."

"Trent and I passed a group of kids on the way out. I wonder if they made it. They looked so scared . . ."

Abby's hands began to tremble, so I comforted her the only way I knew how. I held her.

She relaxed against my chest and sighed. Her breathing evened out, and she nuzzled her cheek deeper into my skin. For the first time since we'd gotten back together, I felt completely at ease with her, as if we'd returned to the way things were before Vegas.

"Travis?"

I lowered my chin and whispered into her hair. "What, baby?"

Our phones rang in unison, and she simultaneously answered hers while she handed me mine.

"Hello?"

"Travis? You all right, man?"

"Yeah, buddy. We're okay."

"I'm okay, Mare. We're all okay," Abby said, reassuring America on the other line.

"Mom and Dad are freaking out. We're watching it on the news right now. I didn't tell them you would be there. What?" Shepley pulled his face away from the phone to answer his parents. "No, Mom. Yeah, I'm talking to him! He's fine! They're at the apartment! So," he continued, "what the hell happened?"

"Fucking lanterns. Adam didn't want any bright lights drawing attention and getting us busted. One caught the whole fucking place on fire . . . it's bad, Shep. A lot of people died."

Shepley breathed deep. "Anyone we know?"

"I don't know, yet."

"I'm glad you're okay, brother. I'm . . . Jesus, I'm glad you're okay."

Abby described the horrific moments when she was stumbling through the dark, trying to find her way out.

I winced when she recounted how she dug her fingers into the window when she tried to get it open.

"Mare, don't leave early. We're fine," Abby said. "We're fine," she said again, this time with emphasis. "You can hug me on Friday. I love you, too. Have a good time."

I pressed my cell phone tight against my ear. "Better hug your girl, Shep. She sounds upset."

Shepley sighed. "I just . . ." He sighed again.

"I know, man."

"I love you. You're as much a brother as I could ever have."

"Me, too. See you soon."

After Abby and I hung up our phones, we sat in silence, still processing what had happened. I leaned back against the pillow, and then pulled Abby against my chest.

"America all right?"

"She's upset. She'll be okay."

"I'm glad they weren't there."

I could feel Abby's jaw working against my skin, and I inwardly cursed myself for giving her more gruesome thoughts.

"Me, too," she said with a shiver.

"I'm sorry. You've been through a lot tonight. I don't need to add anything else to your plate."

"You were there, too, Trav."

I thought about what it was like, searching for Abby in the dark, not knowing if I would find her, and then finally kicking through that door and seeing her face.

"I don't get scared very often," I said. "I was scared the first morning I woke up and you weren't here. I was scared when you left me after Vegas. I was scared when I thought I was going to have to tell my dad that Trent had died in that building. But when I saw you across the flames in that basement . . . I was terrified. I made it to the door, was a few feet from the exit, and I couldn't leave."

"What do you mean? Are you *crazy*?" she asked, her head jerking up to look into my eyes.

"I've never been so clear about anything in my life. I turned around, made my way to that room you were in, and there you were. Nothing else mattered. I didn't even know if we would make it out or not, I just wanted to be where you were, whatever that meant. The only thing I'm afraid of is a life without you, Pigeon."

Abby leaned forward, softly kissing my lips. When our mouths parted, she smiled. "Then you have nothing to be afraid of. We're forever."

I sighed. "I'd do it all over again, you know. I wouldn't trade one second if it meant we were right here, in this moment."

She took in a deep breath, and I gently kissed her forehead.

"This is it," I whispered.

"What?"

"The moment. When I watch you sleeping . . . that peace on

your face? This is it. I haven't had it since before my mom died, but I can feel it again." I took another deep breath and pulled her closer. "I knew the second I met you that there was something about you I needed. Turns out it wasn't something about you at all. It was just you."

Abby offered a tired smile as she buried her face into my chest. "It's *us*, Trav. Nothing makes sense unless we're together. Have you noticed that?"

"*Noticed?* I've been telling you that all year!" I teased. "It's official. Bimbos, fights, leaving, Parker, Vegas . . . even fires . . . our relationship can withstand anything."

She lifted her head, her eyes fixed on mine. I could see a plan forming behind her irises. For the first time, I didn't worry what her next step would be, because I knew in my core whatever path she chose, it would be a path we walked together.

"Vegas?" she asked.

I frowned, forming a line between my brows. "Yeah?"

"Have you thought about going back?"

My eyebrows shot up in disbelief. "I don't think that's a good idea for me."

"What if we just went for a night?"

I glanced around the dark room, confused. "A night?"

"Marry me," she blurted out. I heard the words, but it took a second for them to register.

My mouth widened into a ridiculous grin. She was full of shit, but if that was what helped get her mind off what we'd just gone through, I was happy to play along.

"When?"

She shrugged. "We can book a flight tomorrow. It's spring break. I don't have anything going on tomorrow, do you?"

"I'm callin' your bluff," I said, reaching for my phone. Abby lifted her chin, making a show of her stubborn side. "American Airlines," I said, watching her reaction closely. She didn't flinch.

"American Airlines, how can I help you?"

"I need two tickets to Vegas, please. Tomorrow."

The woman looked up a flight time, and then asked how long we were going to stay.

"Hmmmm . . ." I waited for Abby to give in, but she didn't. "Two days, round-trip. Whatever you have."

She rested her chin on my chest with a big smile, waiting for me to finish the call.

The woman asked for my payment information, so I asked Abby for my wallet. That was the point I thought she would laugh and tell me to hang up the phone, but she happily pulled out the card from my wallet and handed it to me.

I gave my credit card numbers to the agent, glancing up at Abby after each set. She just listened, amused. I said the expiration date, and it crossed my mind that I was about to pay for two plane tickets we probably wouldn't use. Abby did have a hell of a poker face, after all. "Er, yes ma'am. We'll just pick them up at the desk. Thank you."

I handed Abby the phone, and she placed it on the night stand.

"You just asked me to marry you," I said, still waiting for her to admit she wasn't serious.

"I know."

"That was the real deal, you know. I just booked two tickets to Vegas for noon tomorrow. So that means we're getting married tomorrow night."

"Thank you."

My eyes narrowed. "You're going to be Mrs. Maddox when you start classes on Monday."

"Oh," she said, looking around.

I raised an eyebrow. "Second thoughts?"

"I'm going to have some serious paperwork to change next week."

I nodded slowly, cautiously hopeful. "You're going to marry me tomorrow?"

She grinned. "Uh-huh."

"You're serious?"

"Yep."

"I fucking *love* you!" I grabbed each side of her face, slamming my lips against hers. "I love you so much, Pigeon," I said, kissing her over and over. Her lips had trouble keeping up.

"Just remember that in fifty years when I'm still kicking your ass in poker." She giggled.

"If it means sixty or seventy years with you, baby . . . you have my full permission to do your worst."

She raised one eyebrow. "You're gonna regret that."

"I bet I won't."

Her sweet grin turned into the expression of the confident Abby Abernathy I saw hustling pros at the poker table in Vegas. "Are you confident enough to bet that shiny bike outside?"

"I'll put in everything I have. I don't regret a single second with you, Pidge, and I never will."

She held out her hand and I took it without hesitation, shaking it once, and then bringing it to my mouth, pressing my lips tenderly against her knuckles.

"Abby Maddox . . . ," I said, unable to stop smiling.

She hugged me, tensing her shoulders as she squeezed. "Travis and Abby Maddox. Has a nice ring to it."

"Ring?" I said, frowning.

"We'll worry about rings later. I sort of sprung this on you."

"Uh . . ." I trailed off, remembering the box in the drawer. I wondered if giving it to her was even a good idea. A few weeks ago, maybe even a few days ago, Abby might have freaked out, but we were past that now. I hoped.

"What?"

"Don't freak out," I said. "I kind of . . . already took care of that part."

"What part?"

I stared up at the ceiling and sighed, realizing my mistake too late. "You're going to freak out."

"Travis . . ."

I reached for the drawer of the nightstand, and felt around for a moment.

Abby frowned, and then blew her damp hair from her eyes. "What? You bought condoms?"

I laughed once. "No, Pidge," I said, reaching farther into the drawer. My hand finally touched the familiar corners, and I watched Abby's expression as I pulled the small box from its hiding place.

Abby looked down as I placed the small velvet square on my chest, reaching behind me to rest my head on my arm.

"What's that?" she asked.

"What does it look like?"

"Okay. Let me rephrase the question: When did you get that?"

I inhaled. "A while ago."

"Trav—"

"I just happened to see it one day, and I knew there was only one place it could belong . . . on your perfect little finger."

"One day when?"

"Does it matter?"

"Can I see it?" she smiled, her gray irises shining.

Her unexpected reaction caused another wide smile to stretch across my face. "Open it."

Abby lightly touched the box with one finger, and then grasped the golden seal with both hands, slowly pulling the lid open. Her eyes widened, and then she slammed the lid shut.

"Travis!" she wailed.

"I knew you'd freak out!" I said, sitting up and cupping my hands over hers.

"Are you *insane*?"

"I know. I know what you're thinking, but I had to. It was The One. And I was right! I haven't seen one since that was as perfect as this one!" I inwardly cringed, hoping she didn't pick up on the fact that I'd just admitted how often I actually looked at rings.

Her eyes popped open, and then she slowly peeled her hands from the case. Trying again, she pulled open the lid, and then plucked the ring from the slit that held it in place.

"It's . . . my God, it's amazing," she whispered as I took her left hand in mine.

"Can I put it on your finger?" I asked, peering up at her. When she nodded, I pressed my lips together, and then slid the silver band over her knuckle, holding it in place for just a second or two before letting go. "*Now* it's amazing."

We both stared at her hand for a moment. It was finally where it belonged.

"You could have put a down payment on a car for this," she said quietly, as if she had to whisper in the ring's presence.

I touched her ring finger to my lips, kissing the skin just ahead of her knuckle. "I've imagined what this would look like on your hand a million times. Now that it's there . . ."

"What?" She smiled, hoping for me to finish.

"I thought I was going to have to sweat five years before I'd feel like this."

"I wanted it as much as you did. I've just got a hell of a poker face," she said, pressing her lips against mine.

As much as I wanted to undress her until the only thing she had on was my ring, I nestled back against the pillow, and let her rest her body against mine. If there was a way to focus on something other than the horror of that night, we'd managed it.

CHAPTER TWENTY-EIGHT
Mr. and Mrs.

Abby stood on the curb, her hand holding the only two fingers I had free. The rest were gripping bags or trying to flag down America.

We had driven the Honda to the airport two days prior, so Shepley had to drop his girlfriend off at her car. America insisted on being the one to pick us up, and everyone knew why. When she pulled up to the curb, she looked straight ahead. She didn't even get out to help with the bags.

Abby hobbled to the passenger seat and got in, babying the side she'd just inked with my last name.

I tossed the bags in the hatchback, and then pulled on the handle of the backseat. "Uh . . . ," I said, pulling on it again. "Open the door, Mare."

"I don't think I will," she said, whipping her head around to glare at me.

She pulled forward a bit, and Abby tensed. "Mare, stop."

America slammed on the brakes, and raised an eyebrow. "You nearly get my best friend killed at one of your stupid fights, then you bring her to Vegas and marry her when I'm out of town, so not only can I not be the maid of honor, but I can't even *witness* it?"

I pulled on the handle again. "C'mon, Mare. I wish I could say I'm sorry, but I'm married to the love of my life."

"The love of your life is a Harley!" America seethed. She pulled forward again.

"Not anymore!" I begged.

"America Mason . . . ," Abby began. She tried to sound intimidating, but America shot a glare in her direction so severe, it left Abby cowering against the door.

The cars behind us honked, but America was too enraged to pay attention.

"Okay!" I said, holding up one hand. "Okay. What if we uh . . . what if we have another wedding this summer? The dress, the invites, the flowers, everything. You can help her plan it. You can stand next to her, throw her a bachelorette party, whatever you want."

"It's not the same!" America growled, but then the tension in her face relaxed a bit. "But it's a start." She reached behind her and pulled up the lock.

I yanked on the handle and slid into the seat, careful not to speak again until we reached the apartment.

Shepley was wiping down his Charger when we pulled into the apartment parking lot. "Hey!" He smiled and hugged me first, and then Abby. "Congratulations, you two."

"Thanks," Abby said, still feeling uneasy from America's temper tantrum.

"I guess it's a good thing America and I were already discussing getting our own place."

"Oh, you were," Abby said, cocking her head at her friend.

"Looks like we weren't the only ones making decisions on our own."

"We were going to talk about it with you," America said defensively.

"No hurry," I said. "But I would like some help today getting the rest of Abby's stuff moved over."

"Yeah, sure. Brazil just got home. I'll tell him we need his truck."

Abby's eyes darted between the three of us. "Are we going to tell him?"

America couldn't contain her smug smile. "It'll be hard to deny with that big-ass rock on your finger."

I frowned. "You don't want anyone to know?"

"Well, no, it's not that. But, we eloped, baby. People are going to freak out."

"You're Mrs. Travis Maddox, now. Fuck 'em," I said without hesitation.

Abby smiled at me, and then looked down at her ring. "That I am. Guess I better represent the family appropriately."

"Oh, shit," I said. "We gotta tell Dad."

Abby's face turned white. "We do?"

America laughed. "You sure are expecting a lot from her already. Baby steps, Trav, Jesus."

I sneered at her, still irritated that she wouldn't let me in the car at the airport.

Abby waited for an answer.

I shrugged. "We don't have to do it today, but pretty soon, okay? I don't want him hearing it from anyone else."

She nodded. "I understand. Let's just take the weekend and

enjoy our first few days as newlyweds without inviting everyone into our marriage just yet."

I smiled, pulling our luggage from the hatchback of the Honda. "Deal. Except one thing."

"What's that?"

"Can we spend the first few days looking for a car? I'm pretty sure I promised you a car."

"Really?" She smiled.

"Pick a color, baby."

Abby jumped on me again, wrapping her legs and arms around me and covering my face with kisses.

"Oh, stop it, you two," America said.

Abby dropped to her feet, and America pulled on her wrist. "Let's go in. I wanna see your tat!"

The girls rushed up the stairs, leaving me and Shepley to the luggage. I helped him with America's numerous, heavy bags, grabbing mine and Abby's as well.

We heaved the luggage up the stairs and were grateful that the door had been left open.

Abby was lying on the couch, her jeans unbuttoned and folded over, looking down as America inspected the delicate, black curves along Abby's skin.

America looked up at Shepley, who was red-faced and sweating. "I'm so glad we're not crazy, baby."

"Me, too," Shepley said. "I hope you wanted these in here, because I'm not taking them back out to the car."

"I did, thank you." She smiled sweetly, returning to Abby's ink.

Shepley puffed as he disappeared into his bedroom, bringing out a bottle of wine in each hand.

"What's that?" Abby said.

"Your reception," Shepley said with a wide grin.

ABBY PULLED SLOWLY INTO AN EMPTY PARKING SPACE, carefully checking each side. She had chosen a brand-new, silver Toyota Camry the day before, and the few times I could get her behind the wheel, she drove it as if she were secretly borrowing someone's Lamborghini.

After two stops, she finally put the gearshift in Park, and turned off the engine.

"We'll have to get a parking sticker," she said, checking the space on her side again.

"Yes, Pidge. I'll take care of it," I said for the fourth time.

I wondered to myself if I should have waited another week or so before adding the stress of a new car. We both knew by the end of the day that the school's rumor mill would be spreading the news of our marriage, along with a fictional scandal or two. Abby purposefully wore skinny jeans and a tight-fitting sweater to ward off the inevitable questions about a pregnancy. We might have gotten married on the fly, but kids were a whole new level, and we were both content to wait.

A few drops fell from the gray, spring sky as we started our trek to our classes across campus. I pulled my red ball cap low on my forehead, and Abby opened her umbrella. We both stared at Keaton Hall as we passed, noting the yellow tape and blackened brick above each window. Abby grabbed at my coat, and I held her, trying not to think about what had happened.

Shepley heard that Adam had been arrested. I hadn't said anything to Abby, afraid that I was next, and that it would cause her needless worry.

Part of me thought that the news about the fire would keep unwanted attention from Abby's ring finger, but I knew that the news of our marriage would be a welcome distraction from the grim reality of losing classmates in such a horrific way.

Like I expected, when we arrived at the cafeteria, my frat brothers and the football team were congratulating us on our wedding and our impending son.

"I'm not pregnant," Abby said, shaking her head.

"But . . . you guys are married, right?" Lexi said, dubious.

"Yes," Abby said simply.

Lexi raised an eyebrow. "I'll guess we'll find out the truth soon enough."

I jerked my head to the side. "Beat it, Lex."

She ignored me. "I guess you both heard about the fire?"

"A little bit," Abby said, clearly uncomfortable.

"I heard students were having a party down there. That they've been sneaking into basements all year."

"Is that so?" I asked. From the corner of my eye I could see Abby looking up at me, but I tried not to look too relieved. If that was true, maybe I'd be off the hook.

The rest of the day was spent either being stared at or congratulated. For the first time, I wasn't stopped between classes by different girls wanting to know my plans for the weekend. They just watched as I walked by, hesitant to approach someone else's husband. It was actually kinda nice.

My day was going pretty well, and I wondered if Abby could

say the same. Even my psych professor offered me a small smile
and nod when she overhead my answer to questions about
whether the rumor was true.

After our last class, I met Abby at the Camry, and tossed our
bags into the backseat. "Was it as bad as you thought?"

"Yes." She breathed.

"I guess today wouldn't be a good day to break it to my dad,
then, huh?"

"No, but we'd better. You're right, I don't want him hearing
the news somewhere else."

Her answer surprised me, but I didn't question it. Abby tried
to get me to drive, but I refused, insisting she get comfortable
behind the wheel.

The drive to Dad's from campus didn't take long—but longer than if I'd driven. Abby obeyed all traffic laws, mostly because she was nervous about getting pulled over and accidentally
handing the cop the fake ID.

Our little town seemed different as it passed by, or maybe
it was me that wasn't the same. I wasn't sure if it was being a
married man that made me feel a little more relaxed—laid-back,
even—or if I had finally settled into my own skin. I was now in
a situation where I didn't have to prove myself, because the one
person that fully accepted me, my best friend, was now a permanent fixture in my life.

It seemed like I had completed a task, overcome an obstacle.
I thought about my mother, and the words she said to me almost
a lifetime ago. That's when it clicked: she had asked me not to
settle, to fight for the person I loved, and for the first time, I
did what she expected of me. I had finally lived up to who she
wanted me to be.

I took a deep, cleansing breath, and reached over to rest my hand on Abby's knee.

"What is it?" she asked.

"What is what?"

"The look on your face."

Her eyes shifted between me and the road, extremely curious. I imagined it was a new expression, but I couldn't begin to explain what it might look like.

"I'm just happy, baby."

Abby half hummed, half laughed. "Me, too."

Admittedly I was a little nervous about telling my dad about our eventful getaway to Vegas, but not because he would be mad. I couldn't quite put my finger on it, but the butterflies in my stomach swirled faster and harder with every block closer that we came to Dad's house.

Abby pulled into the gravel driveway, soggy from the rain, and stopped beside the house.

"What do you think he'll say?" she asked.

"I don't know. He'll be happy, I know that."

"You think so?" Abby asked, reaching for my hand.

I squeezed her fingers between mine. "I know so."

Before we could make it to the front door, Dad stepped out onto the porch.

"Well, hello there, kids" he said, smiling. His eyes scrunched as his cheeks pushed up the puffy bags under his eyes. "I wasn't sure who was out here. Did you get a new car, Abby? It's nice."

"Hey, Jim." Abby smiled. "Travis did."

"It's ours," I said, pulling off my ball cap. "We thought we'd stop by."

"I'm glad you did . . . glad you did. We're getting some rain, I guess."

"I guess," I said, my nerves stifling any ability I had for small talk. What I thought were nerves was really just excitement to share the news with my father.

Dad knew something was amiss. "You had a good spring break?"

"It was . . . interesting," Abby said, leaning into my side.

"Oh?"

"We took a trip, Dad. We skipped on over to Vegas for a couple of days. We decided to uh . . . we decided to get married."

Dad paused for a few seconds, and then his eyes quickly searched for Abby's left hand. When he found the validation he was looking for, he looked to Abby, and then to me.

"Dad?" I said, surprised by the blank expression on his face.

My father's eyes glossed a bit, and then the corners of his mouth slowly turned up. He outstretched his arms, and enveloped me and Abby at the same time.

Smiling, Abby peeked over at me. I winked back at her.

"I wonder what Mom would say if she were here," I said.

Dad pulled back, his eyes wet with happy tears. "She'd say you did good, son." He looked at Abby. "She'd say thank you for giving her boy back something that left him when she did."

"I don't know about that," Abby said, wiping her eyes. She was clearly overwhelmed by Dad's sentiment.

He hugged us again, laughing and squeezing at the same time. "You wanna bet?"

EPILOGUE

The walls dripped with rainwater from the streets above. The droplets plopped down into deepening puddles, as if they were crying for him, the bastard lying in the middle of the basement in a pool of his own blood.

I breathed hard, looking down at him, but not for long. Both of my Glocks were pointed in opposite directions, holding Benny's men in place until the rest of my team arrived.

The earpiece buried deep in my ear buzzed. "ETA ten seconds, Maddox. Good work." The head of my team, Henry Givens, spoke quietly, knowing as well as I did that with Benny dead, it was all over.

A dozen men with automatic rifles and dressed in black from head to toe rushed in, and I lowered my weapons. "They're just bag men. Get 'em the hell out of here."

After holstering my pistols, I pulled the remaining tape from my wrists and trudged up the basement stairs. Thomas waited for me at the top, his khaki coat and hair drenched from the storm.

"You did what you had to do," he said, following me to the

car. "You all right?" he said, reaching for the cut on my eyebrow.

I'd been sitting in that wooden chair for two hours, getting my ass kicked while Benny questioned me. They'd figured me out that morning—all part of the plan, of course—but the end of his interrogation was supposed to result in his arrest, not his death.

My jaws worked violently under the skin. I had come a long way from losing my temper and beating the hell out of anyone that sparked my rage. But in just a few seconds, all of my training had been rendered worthless, and it just took Benny speaking her name for that to happen.

"I've gotta get home, Tommy. I've been away for weeks, and it's our anniversary . . . or what's left of it."

I yanked open the car door, but Thomas grabbed my wrist. "You need to be debriefed, first. You've spent years on this case."

"Wasted. I've wasted years."

Thomas sighed. "You don't wanna bring this home with you, do you?"

I sighed. "No, but I have to go. I promised her."

"I'll call her. I'll explain."

"You'll lie."

"It's what we do."

The truth was always ugly. Thomas was right. He practically raised me, but I didn't truly know him until I was recruited by the FBI. When Thomas left for college, I thought he was studying advertising, and later he told us he was an advertising executive in California. He was so far away, it was easy for him to keep his cover.

Looking back, it made sense, now, why Thomas had decided

to come home for once without needing a special occasion—the night he met Abby. Back then, when he'd first started investigating Benny and his numerous illegal activities, it was just blind luck that his little brother met and fell in love with the daughter of one of Benny's borrowers. Even better that we ended up entangled in his business.

The second I graduated with a degree in criminal justice, it just made sense for the FBI to contact me. The honor was lost on me. It never occurred to me or Abby that they had thousands of applications a year, and didn't make a habit of recruiting. But I was a built-in undercover operative, already having connections to Benny.

Years of training and time away from home had culminated to Benny lying on the floor, his dead eyes staring up at the ceiling of the underground. The entire magazine of my Glock was buried deep in his torso.

I lit a cigarette. "Call Sarah at the office. Tell her to book me the next flight. I want to be home before midnight."

"He threatened your family, Travis. We all know what Benny is capable of. No one blames you."

"He knew he was caught, Tommy. He knew he had nowhere to go. He baited me. He baited me, and I fell for it."

"Maybe. But detailing the torture and death of the wife of his most lethal acquaintance wasn't exactly good business. He had to know he couldn't intimidate you."

"Yeah," I said through clenched teeth, remembering the vivid picture Benny painted of kidnapping Abby and stripping the flesh away from her bones piece by piece. "I bet he wishes he wasn't such a good storyteller, now."

"And there is always Mick. He's next on the list."

"I told you, Tommy. I can consult on that one. Not a good idea for me to participate."

Thomas only smiled, willing to wait another time for that discussion.

I slid into the backseat of the car that was waiting to take me to the airport. Once the door closed behind me, and the driver pulled away from the curb, I dialed Abby's number.

"Hi, baby," Abby lilted.

Immediately, I took a deep, cleansing breath. Her voice was all the debriefing I needed.

"Happy anniversary, Pigeon. I'm on my way home."

"You are?" she asked, her voice rising an octave. "Best present, ever."

"How's everything?"

"We're over at Dad's. James just won another hand of poker. I'm starting to worry."

"He's your son, Pidge. Does it surprise you that he's good at cards?"

"He beat *me*, Trav. He's good."

I paused. "He beat you?"

"Yes."

"I thought you had a rule about that."

"I know." She sighed. "I know. I don't play anymore, but he had a bad day, and it was a good way to get him to talk about it."

"How's that?"

"There's a kid at school. Made a comment about me today."

"Not the first time a boy made a pass at the hot math teacher."

"No, but I guess it was particularly crude. Jay told him to shut up. There was a scuffle."

"Did Jay beat his ass?"

"Travis!"

I laughed. "Just asking!"

"I saw it from my classroom. Jessica got there before I did. She might have . . . humiliated her brother. A little. Not on purpose."

I closed my eyes. Jessica, with her big honey-brown eyes, long dark hair, and ninety pounds of mean, was my mini-me. She had an equally bad temper and never wasted time with words. Her first fight was in kindergarten, defending her twin brother, James, against a poor, unsuspecting girl who was teasing him. We tried to explain to her that the little girl probably just had a crush, but Jessie wouldn't have any of it. No matter how many times James begged her to let him fight his own battles, she was fiercely protective, even if he was eight minutes older.

I puffed. "Let me talk to her."

"Jess! Dad's on the phone!"

A sweet, small voice came over the line. It was amazing to me that she could be as savage as I ever was, and still sound—and look—like an angel.

"Hi, Daddy."

"Baby . . . did you find some trouble today?"

"It wasn't my fault, Daddy."

"It never is."

"Jay was bleeding. He was pinned down."

My blood boiled, but steering my kids in the right direction came first. "What did Papa say?"

"He said, 'It's about time someone humbled Steven Matese.'"

I was glad she couldn't see me smile at her spot-on Jim Maddox impression.

"I don't blame you for wanting to defend your brother, Jess, but you have to let him fight some battles on his own."

"I will. Just not when he's on the ground."

I choked back another swell of laughter. "Let me talk to Mom. I'll be home in a few hours. Love you bunches, baby."

"Love you, too, Daddy!"

The phone scratched a bit as it made the transition from Jessica to Abby, and then my wife's smooth voice was back on the line.

"You didn't help at all, did you?" she asked, already knowing the answer.

"Probably not. She had a good argument."

"She always does."

"True. Listen, we're pulling up to the airport. I'll see you soon. Love you."

When the driver parked next to the curb in the terminal, I rushed to pull out my bag from the trunk. Sarah, Thomas's assistant, just sent through an email with my itinerary, and my flight was leaving in half an hour. I rushed through check-in and security, and made it to the gate just as they were calling the first group.

The flight home seemed to last an eternity, as they always did. Even though I used a quarter of it to freshen up and change clothes in the bathroom—which was always a challenge—the time left over still dragged by.

Knowing my family was waiting for me was brutal, but the fact that it was my and Abby's eleventh anniversary made it even worse. I just wanted to hold my wife. It was all I had ever wanted to do. I was just as in love with her in our eleventh year as I was in the first.

Every anniversary was a victory, a middle finger to everyone

who thought we wouldn't last. Abby tamed me, marriage settled me down, and when I became a father, my entire outlook
changed.

I stared down at my wrist and pulled back my cuff. Abby's
nickname was still there, and it still made me feel better knowing it was there.

The plane landed, and I had to keep myself from sprinting
through the terminal. Once I got to my car, my patience had
expired. For the first time in years, I ran stoplights and weaved
in and out of traffic. It was actually kind of fun, reminding me
of my college days.

I pulled into the drive and turned off the headlights. The
front porch light flipped on as I approached.

Abby opened the door, her caramel hair just barely graz-
ing her shoulders, and her big gray eyes, although a little tired,
showed how relieved she was to see me. I pulled her into my
arms, trying not to squeeze her too tightly.

"Oh my God," I sighed, burying my face in her hair. "I missed
you so much."

Abby pulled away, touching the cut on my brow. "Did you
take a fall?"

"It was a rough day at work. I might have run into the car
door when I was leaving for the airport."

Abby pulled me against her again, digging her fingers into
my back. "I'm so glad you're home. The kids are in bed, but they
refuse to go to sleep until you tuck them in."

I pulled back and nodded, and then bent at the waist, cupping Abby's round stomach. "How about you?" I asked my third
child. I kissed Abby's protruding belly button, and then stood
up again.

Abby rubbed her middle in a circular motion. "He's still cooking."

"Good." I pulled a small box from my carry-on and held it in front of me. "Eleven years today, we were in Vegas. It's still the best day of my life."

Abby took the box, and then tugged on my hand until we were in the entryway. It smelled like a combination of cleaner, candles, and kids. It smelled like home.

"I got you something, too."

"Oh, yeah?"

"Yeah." She smiled. She left me for a moment, disappearing into the office, and then came out with a manila envelope. "Open it."

"You got me mail? Best wife, ever," I teased.

Abby simply smiled.

I opened the lip, and pulled out the small stack of papers inside. Dates, times, transactions, even emails. To and from Benny, to Abby's father, Mick. He'd been working for Benny for years. He'd borrowed more money from him, and then had to work off his debt so he wouldn't get killed when Abby refused to pay it off.

There was only one problem: Abby knew I worked with Thomas . . . but as far as I knew, she thought I worked in advertising.

"What's this?" I asked, feigning confusion.

Abby still had a flawless poker face. "It's the connection you need to tie Mick to Benny. This one right here," she said, pulling the second paper from the pile, "is the nail in the coffin."

"Okay . . . but what am I supposed to do with it?"

Abby's expression morphed into a dubious grin. "Whatever you do with these things, honey. I just thought if I did a little digging, you could stay home a little longer this time."

My mind raced, trying to figure a way out of this. I had somehow blown my cover. "How long have you known?"

"Does it matter?"

"Are you mad?"

Abby shrugged. "I was a little hurt at first. You have quite a few white lies under your belt."

I hugged her to me, the papers and envelope still in my hand. "I'm so sorry, Pidge. I'm so, so sorry." I pulled away. "You haven't told anyone, have you?"

She shook her head.

"Not even America or Shepley? Not even Dad or the kids?"

She shook her head again. "I'm smart enough to figure it out, Travis. You think I'm not smart enough to keep it to myself? Your safety is at stake."

I cupped her cheeks in my hand. "What does this mean?"

She smiled. "It means you can stop saying you have yet another convention to go to. Some of your cover stories are downright insulting."

I kissed her again, tenderly touching my lips to hers. "Now what?"

"Kiss the kids, and then you and I can celebrate eleven years of in-your-face-we-made-it. How about that?"

My mouth stretched into a wide grin, and then looked down at the papers. "Are you going to be okay with this? Helping take down your dad?"

Abby frowned. "He's said it a million times. I was the end of him. At least I can make him proud about being right. And the kids are safer this way."

I laid the papers on the end of the entryway table. "We'll talk about this later."

I walked down the hall, pulling Abby by the hand behind me. Jessica's room was the closest, so I ducked in and kissed her cheek, careful not to wake her, and then I crossed the hall to James's room. He was still awake, lying there quietly.

"Hey, buddy," I whispered.

"Hey, Dad."

"I hear you had a rough day. You all right?" He nodded. "You sure?"

"Steven Matese is a douche bag."

I nodded. "You're right, but you could probably find a more appropriate way to describe him."

James pulled his mouth to the side.

"So. You beat Mom at poker today, huh?"

James smiled. "Twice."

"She didn't tell me that part," I said, turning to Abby. Her dark, curvy silhouette graced the lit doorway. "You can give me the play-by-play tomorrow."

"Yes, sir."

"I love ya."

"Love you, too, Dad."

I kissed my son's nose and then followed his mom down the hall to our room. The walls were full of family and school portraits, and framed artwork.

Abby stood in the middle of the room, her belly full with our third child, dizzyingly beautiful, and happy to see me, even after she learned what I'd been keeping from her for the better part of our marriage.

I had never been in love before Abby, and no one had even piqued my interest since. My life was the woman standing before me, and the family we'd made together.

Abby opened the box, and looked up at me, tears in her eyes. "You always know just what to get. It's perfect," she said, her graceful fingers touching the three birthstones of our children. She slipped it on her right ring finger, holding out her hand to admire her new bauble.

"Not as good as you getting me a promotion. They're going to know what you did, you know, and it's going to get complicated."

"It always seems to with us," she said, unaffected.

I took a deep breath, and shut the bedroom door behind me. Even though we'd put each other through hell, we'd found heaven. Maybe that was more than a couple of sinners deserved, but I wasn't going to complain.

ACKNOWLEDGMENTS

I HAVE TO START BY THANKING MY INCREDIBLE HUSBAND, Jeff. Without fail he has offered his support and encouragement, and has kept the children happy and busy so mommy can work. I wouldn't be able to do this without him, and I truly mean that. He takes care of me so completely, I literally just have to sit in my office and write. My husband possesses seemingly endless patience and understanding that I wish I had just a fraction of. He loves me on my worst days, and refuses to let me believe there is anything I can't do. Jeff, thank you for loving me so perfectly that I can funnel that into my writing to let others experience a little bit of what you've given me. I'm so lucky to have you.

My two sweet girls, who let mommy work for hours into the night without complaining so that I could meet my first real deadline on time, and to the most handsome man in the world, my son, for waiting until I typed "The End" to make his appearance into the world.

Beth Petrie, my most treasured friend, who is the closest thing to a sister I could have. Three years ago she said I could finish a novel during X-ray school with two kids and a job. She said

I would accomplish everything I wanted to, and she's still saying it. I've said this a million times, but I'll say it again: if it weren't for Beth, not a single word of *Beautiful Disaster*, or *Providence*, or any of my other novels, would have been written. It did not occur to me to write a novel until she said, "Do it. Go sit down at your computer right now and start typing!" She is the sole reason I have traveled down this magical path that has freed me in so many ways. She has saved me in even more ways than that. Thank you, Bethy. Thank you, thank you, thank you.

Rebecca Watson, my film and literary agent, for her hard work and dedication this year, for taking me on when I was still an up-and-coming author, and to E L James for introducing us.

Abbi Glines, my sweet friend and fellow writer, who took a look at *Walking Disaster* in its infancy and assured me that yes, I was doing the male point-of-view right.

Colleen Hoover, Tammara Webber, and Elizabeth Reinhardt, for making my editor's job a bit easier. You teach me something almost every day, whether it's writing, my career, or life lessons.

The women of FP, my writers group, and on some days my rock and salvation. I cannot say enough how much your friendship means to me. You have been with me through every up and down, disappointment, and celebration in the last year. Your advice is invaluable, and your encouragement has gotten me through so many rough days.

Nicole Williams, my friend and fellow writer. Thank you for being so gracious and kind. The way you handle every aspect of your career is an inspiration to me, and I can't wait to see what life has in store for you.

Karly Lane, fellow writer, friend, and lifesaver! Thank you for the encouragement and humor, and for stepping in to help me (brilliantly) when I was stuck.

Tina Bridges, RN and former hospice angel. When I needed answers to some very tough questions, she didn't hesitate to let me dig as deep and dark as I needed to get to the unpleasant truth about death and dying. Tina, you are an amazing person for helping so many children get through unimaginable loss. I applaud you for your courage and compassion.

Foreign literary agents and staff of the Intercontinental Literary Agency. Everything you've accomplished this year had been so far beyond the spectrum of what I could have done for myself. Thank you so much for bringing my book to over twenty countries in as many languages!

Maryse Black, book blogger, genius, supermodel, and friend. You have brought Travis to so many wonderful people who love him almost as much as you do. No wonder he loves you so much. I've watched your blog grow from something fun to a force of nature, and I'm so glad we began our journeys around the same time. It's amazing to see where we've been, where we are, and where we'll go!

I'd also like to thank my editor Amy Tannenbaum for not only loving and believing in this unconventional love story as much as I do, but for being such a joy to work with, and making the entire transition to traditional publishing so positive.

My publicist Ariele Fredman, who has walked me through an unknown (to me) jungle of press and interviews, and for taking such great care of me.

Judith Curr, my publisher, for her constant words of encouragement and validation that I was a part of the Atria family not only by her words, but by her actions.

Julia Scribner and the rest of the Atria staff for working so hard on production, marketing, sales, and everything else that goes into getting this novel from my computer to the readers' hands. I'm not sure what I expected from traditional publishing, but I'm so glad my path led me to Atria Books!

Beautiful
DISASTER

Beautiful DISASTER

A NOVEL

JAMIE McGUIRE

ATRIA PAPERBACK

New York   London   Toronto   Sydney   New Delhi

ATRIA PAPERBACK
A Division of Simon & Schuster, Inc.
1230 Avenue of the Americas
New York, NY 10020

First Atria Paperback edition August 2012

ATRIA PAPERBACK and colophon are trademarks of Simon & Schuster, Inc.

For information about special discounts for bulk purchases, please contact Simon & Schuster Special Sales at 1-866-506-1949 or business@simonandschuster.com.

The Simon & Schuster Speakers Bureau can bring authors to your live event. For more information or to book an event, contact the Simon & Schuster Speakers Bureau at 1-866-248-3049 or visit our website at www.simonspeakers.com.

Designed by Rhea Braunstein

Manufactured in the United States of America

40 39 38 37 36 35 34

Library of Congress Cataloging-in-Publication Data

McGuire, Jamie.
Beautiful disaster : a novel / Jamie McGuire.—1st Atria Books trade paperback ed.
   p. cm.
1. Man-woman relationships—Fiction. 2. College stories. I. Title.
PS3613.C4994B43 2012
813'.6—dc23   2012027866

ISBN 978-1-4767-1204-8
ISBN 978-1-4767-1205-5 (ebook)

For the fans
whose love for a story
turned a wish
into the book in your hand

Beautiful
DISASTER

Chapter One
Red Flag

EVERYTHING IN THE ROOM SCREAMED THAT I DIDN'T belong. The stairs were crumbling, the rowdy patrons were shoulder to shoulder, and the air was a medley of sweat, blood, and mold. Voices blurred as they yelled numbers and names back and forth, and arms flailed about, exchanging money and gestures to communicate over the noise. I squeezed through the crowd, following close behind my best friend.

"Keep your cash in your wallet, Abby!" America called to me. Her broad smile gleamed even in the dim light.

"Stay close! It'll get worse once it starts!" Shepley yelled over the noise. America grabbed his hand and then mine as Shepley led us through the sea of people.

The sharp bleating of a bullhorn cut through the smoky air. The noise startled me, and I jumped in reaction, looking for the source of the blast. A man stood on a wooden chair, holding a wad of cash in one hand, the horn in the other. He held the plastic to his lips.

"Welcome to the bloodbath! If you are looking for Economics 101 . . . you are in the wrong fucking place, my friend! If you seek the Circle, this is Mecca! My name is Adam. I make the rules and I call the fight. Betting ends once the opponents are on the floor. No touching the fighters, no assistance, no bet switching, and no encroachment of the ring. If you break these rules, you will get the piss beat out of you and you will be thrown out on your ass without your money! That includes you, ladies! So don't use your hos to scam the system, boys!"

Shepley shook his head. "Jesus, Adam!" he yelled to the emcee over the noise, clearly disapproving of his friend's choice of words.

My heart pounded in my chest. With a pink cashmere cardigan and pearl earrings, I felt like a schoolmarm on the beaches of Normandy. I promised America that I could handle whatever we happened upon, but at ground zero I felt the urge to grip her toothpick of an arm with both hands. She wouldn't put me in any danger, but being in a basement with fifty or so drunken college boys intent on bloodshed and capital, I wasn't exactly confident of our chances to leave unscathed.

After America met Shepley at freshman orientation, she frequently accompanied him to the secret fights held in different basements of Eastern University. Each event was hosted in a different spot, and kept secret until just an hour before the fight.

Because I ran in somewhat tamer circles, I was surprised to learn of an underground world at Eastern; but Shepley knew about it before he had ever enrolled. Travis, Shepley's roommate and cousin, entered his first fight seven months before. As a freshman, he was rumored to be the most lethal competitor Adam had seen in the three years since creating the Circle. Beginning his sophomore year, Travis was unbeatable. Together,

Travis and Shepley easily paid their rent and bills with the winnings.

Adam brought the bullhorn to his mouth once again, and the yelling and movement escalated to a feverish pace.

"Tonight we have a new challenger! Eastern's star varsity wrestler, Marek Young!"

Cheering ensued, and the crowd parted like the Red Sea when Marek entered the room. A circular space cleared, and the mob whistled, booed, and taunted the contender. He bounced up and down and rocked his neck back and forth, his face severe and focused. The crowd quieted to a dull roar, and my hands shot to my ears when music blared through the large speakers on the other side of the room.

"Our next fighter doesn't need an introduction, but because he scares the shit outta me, I'll give him one, anyway! Shake in your boots, boys, and drop your panties, ladies! I give you: Travis 'Mad Dog' Maddox!"

The volume exploded when Travis appeared in a doorway across the room. He made his entrance, shirtless, relaxed, and unaffected. He strolled into the center of the circle as if he were showing up to another day at work. Lean muscles stretched under his tattooed skin as he popped his fists against Marek's knuckles. Travis leaned in and whispered something in Marek's ear, and the wrestler struggled to keep his stern expression. Marek stood toe-to-toe with Travis, and they looked directly into each other's eyes. Marek's expression was murderous; Travis looked mildly amused.

The men took a few steps back, and Adam sounded the horn. Marek took a defensive stance, and Travis attacked.

I stood on my tiptoes when I lost my line of sight, leaning from side to side to get a better view. I inched up, sliding through the screaming crowd. Elbows jabbed into my sides, and shoulders rammed into me, bouncing me back and forth like a pinball. The tops of the fighters' heads became visible, so I continued to push my way forward.

When I finally reached the front, Marek grabbed Travis with his thick arms and tried to throw him to the ground. When Marek leaned down with the motion, Travis rammed his knee into Marek's face. Before Marek could shake off the blow, Travis lit into him, his fists making contact with Marek's bloodied face over and over.

Five fingers sank into my arm and I jerked back.

"What the hell are you doing, Abby?" Shepley said.

"I can't see from back there!" I called to him.

I turned just in time to see Marek land a solid punch. Travis turned, and for a moment I thought he had dodged another blow, but he made a complete circle, crashing his elbow straight into the center of Marek's nose. Blood sprayed my face, and splattered down the front of my cardigan. Marek fell to the concrete floor with a thud, and for a brief moment the room was completely silent.

Adam threw a scarlet square of fabric onto Marek's limp body, and the mob detonated. Cash changed hands once again, and the expressions divided into the smug and the frustrated.

I was pushed around with the movement of those coming and going. America called my name from somewhere in the back, but I was mesmerized by the trail of red from my chest to my waist.

A pair of heavy black boots stepped in front of me, diverting my attention to the floor. My eyes traveled upward; jeans spattered with blood, a set of finely chiseled abs, a bare, tattooed chest drenched in sweat, and finally a pair of warm, brown eyes. I was shoved from behind, and Travis caught me by the arm before I fell forward.

"Hey! Back up off her!" Travis frowned, shoving anyone who came near me. His stern expression melted into a smile at the sight of my shirt, and then he dabbed my face with a towel. "Sorry about that, Pigeon."

Adam patted the back of Travis's head. "C'mon, Mad Dog! You have some dough waitin' on ya!"

Travis's eyes didn't stray from mine. "It's a damn shame about the sweater. It looks good on you." In the next moment he was engulfed by fans, disappearing the way he came.

"What were you thinking, you idiot?" America yelled, yanking my arm.

"I came here to see a fight, didn't I?" I said, smiling.

"You aren't even supposed to be here, Abby," Shepley scolded.

"Neither is America," I said.

"She doesn't try to jump in the circle!" He frowned. "Let's go."

America smiled at me and wiped my face. "You are such a pain in the ass, Abby. God, I love you!" She hooked her arm around my neck, and we made our way up the stairs and into the night.

America followed me into my dorm room and then sneered at my roommate, Kara. I immediately peeled off the bloody cardigan, throwing it into the hamper.

"Gross. Where have you been?" Kara asked from her bed.

I looked to America, who shrugged. "Nosebleed. You haven't seen one of Abby's famous nosebleeds?"

Kara pushed up her glasses and shook her head.

"Oh, you will." She winked at me and then shut the door behind her. Less than a minute later, my cell phone chimed. Per her usual, America texted me seconds after we had said goodbye.

staying w shep c u 2morrow ring queen

I peeked at Kara, who watched me as if my nose would gush at any moment.

"She was kidding," I said.

Kara nodded with indifference and then looked down to the mess of books on her bedspread.

"I guess I'll get a shower," I said, grabbing a towel and my shower bag.

"I'll alert the media," Kara deadpanned, keeping her head down.

THE NEXT DAY, SHEPLEY AND AMERICA JOINED ME FOR lunch. I had intended to sit alone, but as students filtered into the cafeteria, the chairs around me were filled by either Shepley's frat brothers or members of the football team. Some of them had been at the fight, but no one mentioned my ringside experience.

"Shep," a passing voice called.

Shepley nodded, and America and I both turned to see Travis take a seat at the end of the table. He was followed by two voluptuous bottle blondes wearing Sigma Kappa Ts. One of them sat on Travis's lap; the other sat beside him, pawing at his shirt.

"I think I just threw up a little bit in my mouth," America muttered.

The blonde on Travis's lap turned to America. "I heard that, skank."

America grabbed her roll and threw it down the table, narrowly missing the girl's face. Before the girl could say another word, Travis let his knees give way, sending her tumbling to the floor.

"Ouch!" she squealed, looking up at Travis.

"America's a friend of mine. You need to find another lap, Lex."

"Travis!" she whined, scrambling to her feet.

Travis turned his attention to his plate, ignoring her. She looked at her sister and huffed, and they left hand in hand.

Travis winked at America, and, as if nothing had happened, shoveled another bite into his mouth. It was then that I noticed a small cut on his eyebrow. He traded glances with Shepley and then began a conversation with one of the football guys across from him.

Although the crowd at the lunch table had thinned, America, Shepley, and I lingered to discuss our weekend plans. Travis stood up to leave but stopped at our end of the table.

"What?" Shepley asked loudly, holding his hand to his ear.

I tried to ignore him for as long as possible, but when I looked up, Travis was staring at me.

"You know her, Trav. America's best friend? She was with us the other night," Shepley said.

Travis smiled at me in what I assumed was his most charming expression. He oozed sex and rebelliousness with his buzzed brown hair and tattooed forearms, and I rolled my eyes at his attempt to lure me in.

"Since when do you have a best friend, Mare?" Travis asked.

"Since junior year," she answered, pressing her lips together as she smiled in my direction. "Don't you remember, Travis? You ruined her sweater."

Travis smiled. "I ruin a lot of sweaters."

"Gross," I muttered.

Travis spun the empty chair beside me and sat, resting his arms in front of him. "So you're the Pigeon, huh?"

"No," I snapped. "I have a name."

He seemed amused at the way I regarded him, which only served to make me angrier.

"Well? What is it?" he asked.

I took a bite of the last apple spear on my plate, ignoring him.

"Pigeon it is, then," he said, shrugging.

I glanced up at America and then turned to Travis. "I'm trying to eat here."

Travis settled in for the challenge I presented. "My name's Travis. Travis Maddox."

I rolled my eyes. "I know who you are."

"You do, huh?" Travis said, raising his wounded eyebrow.

"Don't flatter yourself. It's hard not to notice when fifty drunks are chanting your name."

Travis sat up a bit taller. "I get that a lot." I rolled my eyes again, and Travis chuckled. "Do you have a twitch?"

"A what?"

"A twitch. Your eyes keep wiggling around." He laughed

again when I glared at him. "Those are some amazing eyes, though," he said, leaning just inches from my face. "What color is that, anyway? Gray?"

I looked down to my plate, letting the long strands of my caramel hair create a curtain between us. I didn't like the way it made me feel when he was so close. I didn't want to be like the scores of other girls at Eastern that blushed in his presence. I didn't want him to affect me in that way at all.

"Don't even think about it, Travis. She's like my sister," America warned.

"Baby," Shepley said, "you just told him no. He's never gonna stop, now."

"You're not her type," she hedged.

Travis feigned offense. "I'm everyone's type!"

I peeked over at him and smiled.

"Ah! A smile. I'm not a rotten bastard after all," he winked. "It was nice to meet you, Pidge." He walked around the table and leaned into America's ear.

Shepley threw a french fry at his cousin. "Get your lips outta my girl's ear, Trav!"

"Networking! I'm networking!" Travis walked backward with his hands up in an innocent gesture.

A few more girls followed behind him, giggling and running their fingers through their hair to get his attention. He opened the door for them, and they nearly squealed in delight.

America laughed. "Oh, no. You're in trouble, Abby."

"What did he say?" I asked, wary.

"He wants you to bring her to the apartment, doesn't he?" Shepley said. America nodded, and he shook his head. "You're a smart girl, Abby. I'm telling you now, if you fall for his shit and then end up getting mad at him, you can't take it out on me and America, all right?"

I smiled. "I won't fall for it, Shep. Do I look like one of the Barbie twins to you?"

"She won't fall for it," America assured him, touching his arm.

"This isn't my first rodeo, Mare. Do you know how many times he's screwed things up for me because he one-nights the best friend? All of a sudden it's a conflict of interest to date me because it's fraternizing with the enemy! I'm tellin' ya, Abby," he looked at me, "don't tell Mare she can't come over or date me because you fall for Trav's line of BS. Consider yourself warned."

"Unnecessary, but appreciated," I said. I tried to reassure Shepley with a smile, but his pessimism was driven by years of being burned by Travis's endeavors.

America waved, leaving with Shepley as I walked to my afternoon class. I squinted in the bright sun, gripping my backpack straps. Eastern was exactly what I hoped it would be, from the smaller classrooms to the unfamiliar faces. It was a new start for me; I could finally walk somewhere without the whispers of those who knew—or thought they knew—anything about my past. I was as indistinguishable as any other wide-eyed, overachieving freshman on her way to class; no staring, no rumors, no pity or judgment. Only the illusion of what I wanted them to see: cashmered, no-nonsense Abby Abernathy.

I sat my backpack on the floor and collapsed into the chair, bending down to fish my laptop from my bag. When I popped up to set it on my desk, Travis slid into the next desk.

"Good. You can take notes for me," he said. He chewed

on the pen in his mouth and smiled, undoubtedly at his most charming.

I shot a disgusted look at him. "You're not even in this class."

"The hell if I'm not. I usually sit up there," he said, nodding to the top row. A small group of girls was staring at me, and I noticed an empty chair in the center.

"I'm not taking notes for you," I said, booting up my computer.

Travis leaned so close that I could feel his breath on my cheek. "I'm sorry . . . did I offend you in some way?"

I sighed and shook my head.

"Then what is your problem?"

I kept my voice low. "I'm not sleeping with you. You should give up, now."

A slow smile crept across his face before he spoke. "I haven't asked you to sleep with me." His eyes drifted to the ceiling in thought. "Have I?"

"I'm not a Barbie twin or one of your little groupies up there," I said, glancing at the girls behind us. "I'm not impressed with your tattoos or your boyish charm or your forced indifference, so you can stop the antics, okay?"

"Okay, Pigeon." He was infuriatingly impervious to my rudeness. "Why don't you come over with America tonight?" I sneered at his request, but he leaned closer. "I'm not trying to bag you. I just wanna hang out."

"Bag me? How do you ever get laid talking like that?"

Travis burst into laughter, shaking his head. "Just come over. I won't even flirt with you, I swear."

"I'll think about it."

Professor Chaney strolled in, and Travis turned his attention to the front of the room. A residual smile lingered on his face, making the dimple in his cheek sink in. The more he smiled, the more I wanted to hate him, and yet it was the very thing that made hating him impossible.

"Who can tell me which president had a cross-eyed wife with a bad case of the uglies?" Chaney asked.

"Make sure you get that down," Travis whispered. "I'm gonna need to know that for job interviews."

"Shhh," I said, typing Chaney's every word.

Travis grinned and relaxed into his chair. As the hour progressed, he alternated between yawning and leaning against my arm to look at my monitor. I made a concentrated effort to ignore him, but his proximity and the muscles bulging from his arm made it difficult. He picked at the black leather band around his wrist until Chaney dismissed us.

I hurried out the door and down the hall. Just when I felt sure I was at a safe distance, Travis Maddox was at my side.

"Have you thought about it?" he asked, slipping on his sunglasses.

A petite brunette stepped in front of us, wide-eyed and hopeful. "Hey, Travis," she lilted, playing with her hair.

I paused, recoiling from her sugary tone, and then walked around her. I'd seen her before, talking normally in the commons area of the girls' dorm, Morgan Hall. Her tone sounded much more mature then, and I wondered what it was about a toddler's voice she thought Travis would find appealing. She babbled in a higher octave for a bit longer until he was next to me once again.

Pulling a lighter from his pocket, he lit a cigarette and blew out a thick cloud of smoke. "Where was I? Oh yeah . . . you were thinking."

I grimaced. "What are you talking about?"

"Have you thought about coming over?"

"If I say yes, will you quit following me?"

He considered my stipulation and then nodded. "Yes."

"Then I'll come over."

"When?"

I sighed. "Tonight. I'll come over tonight."

Travis smiled and stopped in his tracks. "Sweet. See you then, Pidge," he called after me.

I rounded the corner to see America standing with Finch outside our dormitory. The three of us ended up at the same table at freshman orientation, and I knew he would be the welcome third wheel to our well-oiled machine. He wasn't excessively tall, but still he towered over my five feet four inches. His round eyes offset his long, lean features, and his bleached hair was usually fashioned into a spike at the front.

"Travis Maddox? Jesus, Abby, since when did you start fishing in the deep end?" Finch said with disapproving eyes.

America pulled the gum from her mouth in a long string. "You're only making it worse by brushing him off. He's not used to that."

"What do you suggest I do? Sleep with him?"

America shrugged. "It'll save time."

"I told him I'd come over tonight."

Finch and America traded glances.

"What? He promised to quit bugging me if I said yes. You're going over there tonight, right?"

"Well, yeah," America said. "You're really coming?"

I smiled and walked past them into the dorms, wondering if Travis would make good on his promise not to flirt. He wasn't hard to figure out; he either saw me as a challenge, or safely unattractive enough to be a good friend. I wasn't sure which bothered me more.

FOUR HOURS LATER, AMERICA KNOCKED ON MY DOOR TO take me to Shepley and Travis's. She didn't hold back when I walked into the hall.

"Yuck, Abby! You look homeless!"

"Good," I said, smiling at my ensemble. My hair was piled on top of my head in a messy bun. I had scrubbed the makeup from my face and replaced my contacts with rectangular black-rimmed glasses. Sporting a ratty T-shirt and sweatpants, I shuffled along in a pair of flip-flops. The idea had come to me hours before that either way, unattractive was the best plan. Ideally, Travis would be instantly turned off and stop his ridiculous persistence. If he was looking for a buddy, I was aiming for too homely to be seen with.

America rolled down her window and spit out her gum. "You're so obvious. Why didn't you just roll in dog shit to make your outfit complete?"

"I'm not trying to impress anyone," I said.

"Obviously."

We pulled into the parking lot of Shepley's apartment complex, and I followed America to the stairs. Shepley opened the door, laughing as I walked in. "What happened to you?"

"She's trying to be unimpressive," America said.

America followed Shepley into his room. The door closed and I stood alone, feeling out of place. I sat in the recliner closest to the door and kicked off my flip-flops.

Their apartment was more aesthetically pleasing than the typical bachelor pad. The predictable posters of half-naked women and stolen street signs were on the walls, but it was clean, the furniture was new, and the smell of stale beer and dirty clothes was notably absent.

"It's about time you showed up," Travis said, collapsing onto the couch.

I smiled and pushed my glasses up the bridge of my nose, waiting for him to recoil at my appearance. "America had a paper to finish."

"Speaking of papers, have you started the one for History yet?"

He didn't bat an eye at my messy hair, and I frowned at his reaction. "Have you?"

"I finished it this afternoon."

"It's not due until next Wednesday," I said, surprised.

"I just plugged it out. How hard can a two-page essay on Grant be?"

"I'm a procrastinator, I guess," I shrugged. "I probably won't start on it until this weekend."

"Well, if you need help, just let me know."

I waited for him to laugh, or to show some sign that he was joking, but his expression was sincere. I raised an eyebrow. "You're going to help me with my paper?"

"I have an A in that class," he said, a bit miffed at my disbelief.

"He has As in all his classes. He's a freakin' genius. I hate him," Shepley said as he led America into the living room by the hand.

I watched Travis with a dubious expression and his eyebrows shot up. "What? You don't think a guy covered in tats and that trades punches for a living can get the grades? I'm not in school because I have nothing better to do."

"Why do you have to fight at all, then? Why didn't you try for scholarships?" I asked.

"I did. I was awarded half my tuition. But there are books, living expenses, and I gotta come up with the other half sometime. I'm serious, Pidge. If you need help with anything, just ask."

"I don't need your help. I can write a paper." I wanted to leave it at that. I should have left it at that, but this new side of him he'd revealed gnawed at my curiosity. "You can't find something else to do for a living? Less—I don't know—sadistic?"

Travis shrugged. "It's an easy way to make a buck. I can't make that much working at the mall."

"I wouldn't say it's easy if you're getting hit in the face."

"What? You're worried about me?" he winked. I made a face, and he chuckled. "I don't get hit that often. If they swing, I move. It's not that hard."

I laughed once. "You act as if no one else has come to that conclusion."

"When I throw a punch, they take it and try to reciprocate. That's not gonna win a fight."

I rolled my eyes. "What are you, the Karate Kid? Where did you learn to fight?"

Shepley and America glanced at each other, and then their eyes wandered to the floor. It didn't take long to recognize I had said something wrong.

Travis didn't seem affected. "I had a dad with a drinking problem and a bad temper, and four older brothers that carried the asshole gene."

"Oh." My ears smoldered.

"Don't be embarrassed, Pidge. Dad quit drinking, the brothers grew up."

"I'm not embarrassed." I fidgeted with the falling strands of my hair and then decided to pull it down and smooth it into another bun, trying to ignore the awkward silence.

"I like the au naturel thing you have going on. Girls don't come over here like that."

"I was coerced into coming here. It didn't occur to me to impress you," I said, irritated that my plan had failed.

He smiled his boyish, amused grin, and I turned up my anger a notch, hoping it would cover my unease. I didn't know how most girls felt around him, but I'd seen how they behaved. I was experiencing more of a disoriented, nauseated feeling than giggly infatuation, and the harder he worked to make me smile, the more unsettled I felt.

"I'm already impressed. I don't normally have to beg girls to come to my apartment."

"I'm sure," I said, screwing my face into disgust.

He was the worst kind of confident. Not only was he shamelessly aware of his appeal, he was so used to women throwing themselves at him that he regarded my cool demeanor as refreshing instead of an insult. I would have to change my strategy.

America pointed the remote at the television and switched it on. "There's a good movie on tonight. Anyone want to find out where Baby Jane is?"

Travis stood up. "I was just heading out for dinner. You hungry, Pidge?"

"I already ate," I shrugged.

"No you haven't," America said, before realizing her mistake. "Oh . . . er . . . that's right, I forgot you grabbed a . . . pizza? Before we left."

I grimaced at her miserable attempt to fix her blunder, and then waited for Travis's reaction.

He walked across the room and opened the door. "C'mon. You've gotta be hungry."

"Where are you going?"

"Wherever you want. We can hit a pizza place."

I looked down at my clothes. "I'm not really dressed."

He appraised me for a moment and then grinned. "You look fine. Let's go, I'm starvin'."

I stood up and waved to America, passing Travis to walk down the stairs. I stopped in the parking lot, watching in horror as he straddled a matte black motorcycle.

"Uh . . ." I trailed off, scrunching my exposed toes.

He shot an impatient glare in my direction. "Oh, get on. I'll go slow."

"What is that?" I asked, reading the writing on the gas tank too late.

"It's a Harley Night Rod. She's the love of my life, so don't scratch the paint when you get on."

"I'm wearing flip-flops!"

Travis stared at me as if I'd spoken a foreign language. "I'm wearing boots. Get on."

He slipped on his sunglasses, and the engine snarled when

he brought it to life. I climbed on and reached behind me for something to grab on to, but my fingers slipped from leather to the plastic cover of the taillight.

Travis grabbed my wrists and wrapped them around his middle. "There's nothing to hold on to but me, Pidge. Don't let go," he said, pushing the bike backward with his feet. With a flick of his wrist, he pulled onto the street, and we took off like a rocket. The pieces of my hair that hung loose beat against my face, and I ducked behind Travis, knowing I would end up with bug guts on my glasses if I looked over his shoulder.

He gunned the throttle when we pulled into the driveway of the restaurant, and once he slowed to a stop, I wasted no time scrambling to the safety of the concrete.

"You're a lunatic!"

Travis chuckled, leaning his bike onto its kickstand before dismounting. "I went the speed limit."

"Yeah, if we were on the autobahn!" I said, pulling out my bun to separate the rats with my fingers.

Travis watched me pull hair away from my face and then walked to the door, holding it open. "I wouldn't let anything happen to you, Pigeon."

I stormed past him into the restaurant, my head not quite in sync with my feet. Grease and herbs filled the air as I followed him across the red, breadcrumb-speckled carpet. He chose a booth in the corner, away from the patches of students and families, and then ordered two beers. I scanned the room, watching the parents coaxing their boisterous children to eat, and looking away from the inquisitive glances of Eastern students.

"Sure, Travis," the waitress said, writing down our drink

orders. She looked a bit high from his presence as she returned to the kitchen.

I tucked the windblown hair behind my ears, suddenly embarrassed by my appearance. "Come here often?" I asked acerbically.

Travis leaned on the table with his elbows, his brown eyes fixated on mine. "So what's your story, Pidge? Are you a man-hater in general, or do you just hate me?"

"I think it's just you," I grumbled.

He laughed once, amused at my mood. "I can't figure you out. You're the first girl that's ever been disgusted with me before sex. You don't get all flustered when you talk to me, and you don't try to get my attention."

"It's not a ploy. I just don't like you."

"You wouldn't be here if you didn't like me."

My frown involuntarily smoothed and I sighed. "I didn't say you're a bad person. I just don't like being a foregone conclusion for the sole reason of having a vagina." I focused on the grains of salt on the table until I heard a choking noise from Travis's direction.

His eyes widened and he quivered with howling laughter. "Oh my God! You're killing me! That's it. We have to be friends. I won't take no for an answer."

"I don't mind being friends, but that doesn't mean you have to try to get in my panties every five seconds."

"You're not sleeping with me. I get it."

I tried not to smile, but failed.

His eyes brightened. "You have my word. I won't even think about your panties . . . unless you want me to."

I rested my elbows on the table and leaned into them. "And that won't happen, so we can be friends."

An impish grin sharpened his features as he leaned in a bit closer. "Never say never."

"So what's your story?" I asked. "Have you always been Travis 'Mad Dog' Maddox, or is that just since you came here?" I used two fingers on each hand as quotation marks when I said his nickname, and for the first time his confidence waned. He looked a bit embarrassed.

"No. Adam started that after my first fight."

His short answers were beginning to bug me. "That's it? You're not going to tell me anything about yourself?"

"What do you wanna know?"

"The normal stuff. Where you're from, what you want to be when you grow up . . . things like that."

"I'm from here, born and raised, and I'm a Criminal Justice major."

With a sigh, he unrolled his silverware and straightened them beside his plate. He looked over his shoulder, his jaw tense. Two tables seating the Eastern soccer team erupted in laughter, and Travis seemed to be annoyed at what they were laughing about.

"You're joking," I said in disbelief.

"No, I'm a local," he said, distracted.

"I meant about your major. You don't look like the criminal justice type."

His eyebrows pulled together, suddenly focused on our conversation. "Why?"

I scanned the tattoos covering his arm. "I'll just say that you seem more criminal and less justice."

"I don't get in any trouble . . . for the most part. Dad was pretty strict."

"Where was your mom?"

"She died when I was a kid," he said, matter-of-fact.

"I'm ... I'm sorry," I said, shaking my head. His answer caught me off guard.

He dismissed my sympathy. "I don't remember her. My brothers do, but I was just three when she died."

"Four brothers, huh? How did you keep them straight?" I teased.

"I kept them straight by who hit the hardest, which also happened to be oldest to youngest. Thomas; the twins, Taylor and Tyler; and then Trenton. You never, ever got caught alone in a room with Taylor and Ty. I learned half of what I do in the Circle from them. Trenton was the smallest, but he's fast. He's the only one that can land a punch on me now."

I shook my head, dumbfounded at the thought of five Travises running around in one household. "Do they all have tattoos?"

"Pretty much. Except Thomas. He's an ad exec in California."

"And your dad? Where's he?"

"Around," he said. His jaws were working again, increasingly irritated with the soccer team.

"What are they laughing about?" I asked, gesturing to the rowdy table. He shook his head, clearly not wanting to share. I crossed my arms and squirmed in my seat, nervous about what they were saying that caused him so much aggravation. "Tell me."

"They're laughing about me having to take you to dinner, first. It's not usually ... my thing."

"First?" When the realization settled on my face, Travis

winced at my expression. I spoke before I thought. "And I was afraid they were laughing about you being seen with me dressed like this, and they think I'm going to sleep with you," I grumbled.

"Why wouldn't I be seen with you?"

"What were we talking about?" I asked, warding off the heat rising in my cheeks.

"You. What's your major?" he asked.

"Oh, er . . . General Ed, for now. I'm still undecided, but I'm leaning toward Accounting."

"You're not a local, though. You must be a transplant."

"Wichita. Same as America."

"How did you end up here from Kansas?"

I picked at the label of my beer bottle. "We just had to get away."

"From what?"

"My parents."

"Oh. What about America? She has parent issues, too?"

"No, Mark and Pam are great. They practically raised me. She sort of tagged along; she didn't want me to come alone."

Travis nodded. "So, why Eastern?"

"What's with the third degree?" I said. The questions were drifting from small talk to personal, and I was beginning to get uncomfortable.

Several chairs knocked together as the soccer team left their seats. They traded one last joke before they meandered toward the door. Their pace quickened when Travis stood up. Those in the back of the group pushed those in front to escape before Travis made his way across the room. He sat down, forcing the frustration and anger away.

I raised an eyebrow.

"You were going to say why you chose Eastern," he prompted.

"It's hard to explain," I said, shrugging. "I guess it just felt right."

He smiled as he opened his menu. "I know what you mean."

Chapter Two
Pig

FAMILIAR FACES FILLED THE SEATS OF OUR FAVORITE lunch table. America sat on one side of me, Finch on the other, and the rest of the spaces were picked off by Shepley and his Sigma Tau brothers. It was hard to hear with the low roar inside the cafeteria, and the air conditioner seemed to be on the fritz again. The air was thick with the smells of fried foods and sweaty skin, but somehow everyone seemed to be more energetic than usual.

"Hey, Brazil," Shepley said, greeting the man sitting in front of me. His olive skin and chocolate eyes offset the white Eastern Football hat pulled low on his forehead.

"Missed you after the game Saturday, Shep. I drank a beer or six for ya," he said with a broad white grin.

"I appreciate it. I took Mare out to dinner," he said, leaning over to kiss the top of America's long blond hair.

"You're sittin' in my chair, Brazil."

Brazil turned to see Travis standing behind him, and then looked to me, surprised. "Oh, is she one of your girls, Trav?"

"Absolutely not," I said, shaking my head.

Brazil looked to Travis, who stared at him expectantly. Brazil shrugged and then took his tray to the end of the table.

Travis smiled at me as he settled into the seat. "What's up, Pidge?"

"What is that?" I asked, unable to look away from his tray. The mystery food on his plate looked like a wax display.

Travis laughed and took a drink from his water glass. "The cafeteria ladies scare me. I'm not about to critique their cooking skills."

I didn't miss the appraising eyes of those sitting at the table. Travis's behavior piqued their curiosity, and I subdued a smile at being the only girl they had seen him insist on sitting with.

"Ugh . . . that Bio test is after lunch," America groaned.

"Did you study?" I asked.

"God, no. I spent the night reassuring my boyfriend that you weren't going to sleep with Travis."

The football players seated at the end of our table stopped their obnoxious laughter to listen more closely, making the other students take notice. I glared at America, but she was unconcerned with any blame, nudging Shepley with her shoulder.

"Jesus, Shep. You've got it that bad, huh?" Travis asked, throwing a packet of ketchup at his cousin. Shepley didn't answer, but I smiled appreciatively at Travis for the diversion.

America rubbed his back. "He's going to be okay. It's just going to take him a while to believe Abby is resistant to your charms."

"I haven't tried to charm her," Travis sniffed, seeming offended. "She's my friend."

I looked to Shepley. "I told you. You have nothing to worry about."

Shepley finally met my eyes, and upon seeing my sincere expression, his eyes brightened a bit.

"Did you study?" Travis asked me.

I frowned. "No amount of studying is going to help me with Biology. It's just not something I can wrap my head around."

Travis stood up. "C'mon."

"What?"

"Let's go get your notes. I'm going to help you study."

"Travis . . ."

"Get your ass up, Pidge. You're gonna ace that test."

I tugged on one of America's long yellow braids as I passed. "See you in class, Mare."

She smiled. "I'll save you a seat. I'll need all the help I can get."

Travis followed me to my room, and I pulled out my study guide while he popped open my book. He quizzed me relentlessly, and then clarified a few things I didn't understand. In the way that he explained it, the concepts went from being confusing to obvious.

". . . and somatic cells use mitosis to reproduce. That's when you have the phases. They sound sort of like a woman's name: Prometa Anatela."

I laughed. "Prometa Anatela?"

"Prophase, metaphase, anaphase, and telophase."

"Prometa Anatela," I repeated, nodding.

He smacked the top of my head with the papers. "You got this. You know this study guide backward and forward."

I sighed. "Well . . . we'll see."

"I'm going to walk you to class. I'll quiz you on the way."

I locked the door behind us. "You're not going to be mad if I flunk this test, are you?"

"You're not going to flunk, Pidge. We need to start earlier for the next one, though," he said, keeping in step with me to the science building.

"How are you going to tutor me, do your homework, study, and train for your fights?"

Travis chuckled. "I don't train for my fights. Adam calls me, tells me where the fight is, and I go."

I shook my head in disbelief as he held the paper in front of him to ask the first question. We had nearly finished a second round of the study guide when we reached my class.

"Kick ass," he smiled, handing me the notes and leaning against the doorjamb.

"Hey, Trav."

I turned to see a tall, somewhat lanky man smile at Travis on his way into the classroom.

"Parker," Travis nodded.

Parker's eyes brightened a bit when he looked to me, and he smiled. "Hi, Abby."

"Hi," I said, surprised that he knew my name. I had seen him in class, but we'd never met.

Parker continued to his seat, joking with those sitting beside him. "Who's that?" I asked.

Travis shrugged, but the skin around his eyes seemed tenser than before. "Parker Hayes. He's one of my Sig Tau brothers."

"You're in a frat?" I asked, doubtful.

"Sigma Tau, same as Shep. I thought you knew that," he said, looking beyond me to Parker.

"Well . . . you don't seem the . . . fraternity type," I said, eyeing the tattoos on his forearms.

Travis turned his attention to me and grinned. "My dad is an alumnus, and my brothers are all Sig Tau. It's a family thing."

"And they expected you to pledge?" I asked, skeptical.

"Not really. They're just good guys," he said, flicking my papers. "Better get to class."

"Thanks for helping me," I said, nudging him with my elbow. America passed, and I followed her to our seats.

"How did it go?" she asked.

I shrugged. "He's a good tutor."

"Just a tutor?"

"He's a good friend, too."

She seemed disappointed, and I giggled at the fallen expression on her face.

It had always been a dream of America's for us to date friends, and roommates-slash-cousins, for her, was hitting the jackpot. She wanted us to room together when she decided to come with me to Eastern, but I vetoed her idea, hoping to spread my wings a bit. Once she finished pouting, she focused on finding a friend of Shepley's to introduce me to.

Travis's healthy interest in me had surpassed her ideas.

I breezed through the test and sat on the steps outside the building, waiting for America. When she slumped down beside me in defeat, I waited for her to speak.

"That was awful!" she cried.

"You should study with us. Travis explains it really well."

America groaned and leaned her head on my shoulder. "You were no help at all! Couldn't you have given me a courtesy nod or something?" I hooked my arm around her neck and walked her to our dorm.

* * *

OVER THE NEXT WEEK, TRAVIS HELPED WITH MY HIS-
tory paper and tutored me in Biology. We stood together scanning the grade board outside Professor Campbell's office. My
student number was three spots from the top.

"Third-highest test grade in the class! Nice, Pidge!" he
said, squeezing me. His eyes were bright with excitement and
pride, and an awkward feeling made me take a step back.

"Thanks, Trav. Couldn't have done it without you," I said,
pulling on his T-shirt.

He tossed me over his shoulder, making his way through the
crowd behind us. "Make way! Move it, people! Let's make room
for this poor woman's hideously disfigured, ginormous brain!
She's a fucking genius!"

I giggled at the amused and curious expressions of my classmates.

AS THE DAYS WENT BY, WE FIELDED THE PERSISTENT RU-
mors about a relationship. Travis's reputation helped to quiet
the gossip. He had never been known to stay with one girl longer than a night, so the more times we were seen together, the
more people understood our platonic relationship for what it
was. Even with the constant questions about our involvement, the
stream of attention Travis received from his coeds didn't recede.

He continued to sit next to me in History and eat with me at
lunch. It didn't take long to realize I had been wrong about him,
even finding myself defensive toward those who didn't know
Travis the way that I did.

In the cafeteria, Travis set a can of orange juice in front
of me.

"You didn't have to do that. I was going to grab one," I said, peeling off my jacket.

"Well, now you don't have to," he said, flashing the dimple on his left cheek.

Brazil snorted. "Did she turn you into a cabana boy, Travis? What's next, fanning her with a palm tree leaf, wearing a Speedo?"

Travis shot him a murderous glare, and I jumped to his defense. "You couldn't fill a Speedo, Brazil. Shut the hell up."

"Easy, Abby! I was kidding!" Brazil said, holding up his hands.

"Just . . . don't talk about him like that," I said, frowning.

Travis's expression was a mixture of surprise and gratitude. "Now I've seen it all. I was just defended by a girl," he said, standing up. Before he left with his tray, he offered one more warning glare to Brazil, and then walked outside to stand with a small group of fellow smokers outside the building.

I tried not to watch him while he laughed and talked. Every girl in the group subtly competed for the space next to him, and America shoved her elbow into my ribs when she noticed my attention was elsewhere.

"Whatcha lookin' at, Abby?"

"Nothing. I'm not looking at anything."

She rested her chin on her hand and shook her head. "They're so obvious. Look at the redhead. She's run her fingers through her hair as many times as she's blinked. I wonder if Travis gets tired of that."

Shepley nodded. "He does. Everyone thinks he's this asshole, but if they only knew how much patience he has dealing with every girl that thinks she can tame him . . . He can't go anywhere without them bugging him. Trust me; he's much more polite than I would be."

"Oh, like you wouldn't love it," America said, kissing his cheek.

Travis was finishing his cigarette outside the cafeteria when I passed. "Wait up, Pidge. I'll walk you."

"You don't have to walk me to every class, Travis. I know how to get there on my own."

Travis was easily sidetracked by a girl with long black hair and a short skirt. She walked by, smiling at him. He followed her with his eyes and nodded in the girl's direction, throwing down his cigarette.

"I'll catch up with you later, Pidge."

"Yeah," I said, rolling my eyes as he jogged to the girl's side.

Travis's seat remained empty during class, and I found myself a bit irritated with him for missing over a girl he didn't know. Professor Chaney dismissed early, and I hurried across the lawn, aware that I was to meet Finch at three to give him Sherri Cassidy's Music Appreciation notes. I looked at my watch and quickened my pace.

"Abby?"

Parker jogged across the grass to walk beside me. "I don't think we've officially met," he said, holding out his hand. "Parker Hayes."

I took his hand and smiled. "Abby Abernathy."

"I was behind you when you got your Bio test grade. Congratulations," he smiled, shoving his hands in his pockets.

"Thanks. Travis helped, or I would've been at the bottom of that list, trust me."

"Oh, are you guys . . . ?"

"Friends."

Parker nodded and smiled. "Did he tell you there's a party at the House this weekend?"

"We mostly just talk about Biology and food."

Parker laughed. "That sounds like Travis."

At the door of Morgan Hall, Parker scanned my face with his big green eyes. "You should come. It'll be fun."

"I'll talk to America. I don't think we have any plans."

"Are you a package deal?"

"We made a pact this summer. No parties solo."

"Smart." He nodded in approval.

"She met Shep at orientation, so I haven't really had to tag along with her much. This will be the first time I've needed to ask her, so I'm sure she'll be happy to come." I inwardly cringed. Not only was I babbling, I'd made it obvious that I didn't get asked to parties.

"Great. I'll see you there," he said. He flashed his perfect Banana Republic–model smile with his square jaw and naturally tan skin, turning to walk across campus.

I watched him walk away; he was tall, clean-shaven, with a pressed pin-striped dress shirt and jeans. His wavy dark-blond hair bounced when he walked.

I bit my lip, flattered by his invitation.

"Now, he's more your speed," Finch said in my ear.

"He's cute, huh?" I asked, unable to stop smiling.

"Hell, yes. In that preppy, missionary-position kind of way."

"Finch!" I cried, smacking him on the shoulder.

"Did you get Sherri's notes?"

"I did," I said, pulling them from my bag. He lit a cigarette, held it between his lips, and squinted at the papers.

"Fucking brilliant," he said, scanning the pages. He folded them away in his pocket, and then took another drag. "Good thing Morgan's boilers are out. You'll need a cold shower after getting ogled by that tall drink of water."

"The dorm doesn't have hot water?" I wailed.

"That's the word," Finch said, sliding his backpack over his shoulder. "I'm off to Algebra. Tell Mare I said not to forget me this weekend."

"I'll tell her," I grumbled, glaring up at the antique brick walls of our dormitory. I stomped up to my room, pushed through the door, and let my backpack fall to the floor.

"No hot water," Kara mumbled from her side of the desk.

"I heard."

My cell phone buzzed and I clicked it open, reading a text message from America cursing the boilers. A few moments later there was a knock on the door.

America walked in and plopped onto my bed, arms crossed. "Can you believe this shit? How much are we paying and we can't even take a hot shower?"

Kara sighed. "Stop whining. Why don't you just stay with your boyfriend? Haven't you been staying with him, anyway?"

America's eyes darted in Kara's direction. "Good idea, Kara. The fact that you're a total bitch comes in handy sometimes."

Kara kept her eyes on her computer monitor, unfazed by America's jab.

America pulled out her cell phone and clicked out a text message with amazing precision and speed. Her phone chirped, and she smiled at me. "We're staying with Shep and Travis until they fix the boilers."

"What? I'm not!" I cried.

"Oh, yes you are. There's no reason for you to be stuck here freezing in the shower when Travis and Shep have two bathrooms at their place."

"I wasn't invited."

"I'm inviting you. Shep already said it was fine. You can sleep on the couch . . . if Travis isn't using it."

"And if he's using it?"

America shrugged. "Then you can sleep in Travis's bed."

"No way!"

She rolled her eyes. "Don't be such a baby, Abby. You guys are friends, right? If he hasn't tried anything by now, I don't think he will."

Her words made my open mouth snap shut. Travis had been around me in one way or another every night for weeks. I had been so occupied with making sure everyone knew we were just friends, it hadn't occurred to me that he really was interested only in friendship. I wasn't sure why, but I felt insulted.

Kara looked at us with disbelief. "Travis Maddox hasn't tried to sleep with you?"

"We're friends!" I said in a defensive tone.

"I know, but he hasn't even tried? He's slept with everyone."

"Except us," America said, looking her over. "And you."

Kara shrugged. "Well, I've never met him. I've just heard."

"Exactly," I snapped. "You don't even know him."

Kara returned to her monitor, oblivious to our presence.

I sighed. "All right, Mare. I need to pack."

"Make sure you pack for a few days; who knows how long it will take them to fix the boilers?" she said, entirely too excited.

Dread settled over me as if I were about to sneak into enemy territory. "Ugh . . . all right."

Jamie McGuire

America bounced when she hugged me. "This is going to be so fun!"

Half an hour later we loaded down her Honda and headed for the apartment. America hardly took a breath between ramblings as she drove. She honked her horn as she slowed to a stop in her usual parking space. Shepley jogged down the steps and pulled both of our suitcases from the trunk, following us up the stairs.

"It's open," he puffed.

America pushed the door and held it open. Shepley grunted when he dropped our luggage to the floor. "Christ, baby! Your suitcase is twenty more pounds than Abby's!"

America and I froze when a woman emerged from the bathroom, buttoning her blouse.

"Hi," she said, surprised. Her mascara-smeared eyes examined us before settling on our luggage. I recognized her as the leggy brunette Travis had followed from the cafeteria.

America glared at Shepley.

He held up his hands. "She's with Travis!"

Travis rounded the corner in a pair of boxer shorts and yawned. He looked at his guest and then patted her backside. "My company's here. You'd better go."

She smiled and wrapped her arms around him, kissing his neck. "I'll leave my number on the counter."

"Eh . . . don't worry about it," Travis said in a casual tone.

"What?" she asked, leaning back to look in his eyes.

"Every time!" America said. She looked at the woman. "How are you surprised by this? He's Travis Fucking Maddox! He is famous for this very thing, and every time they're surprised!" she said, turning to Shepley. He put his arm around her, gesturing for her to calm down.

The girl narrowed her eyes at Travis and then grabbed her purse and stormed out, slamming the door behind her.

Travis walked into the kitchen and opened the fridge as if nothing had happened.

America shook her head and walked down the hall. Shepley followed her, angling his body to compensate for the weight of her suitcase as he trailed behind.

I collapsed against the recliner and sighed, wondering if I was crazy for agreeing to come. I didn't realize Shepley's apartment was a revolving door for clueless bimbos.

Travis stood behind the breakfast bar, crossed his arms over his chest, and smiled. "What's wrong, Pidge? Hard day?"

"No, I'm thoroughly disgusted."

"With me?" He was smiling. I should have known that he expected the conversation. It only made me less inclined to hold back.

"Yes, you. How can you just use someone like that and treat them that way?"

"How did I treat her? She offered her number, I declined."

My mouth fell open at his lack of remorse. "You'll have sex with her, but you won't take her number?"

Travis leaned on the counter with his elbows. "Why would I want her number if I'm not going to call her?"

"Why would you sleep with her if you're not going to call her?"

"I don't promise anyone anything, Pidge. She didn't stipulate a relationship before she spread-eagled on my couch."

I stared at the couch with revulsion. "She's someone's daughter, Travis. What if, down the line, someone treats your daughter like that?"

"My daughter better not drop her panties for some jackass she just met, let's put it that way."

I crossed my arms, angry that he made sense. "So, besides admitting that you're a jackass, you're saying that because she slept with you, she deserved to be tossed out like a stray cat?"

"I'm saying that I was honest with her. She's an adult, it was consensual . . . she was a little too eager about it, if you want to know the truth. You act like I committed a crime."

"She didn't seem as clear about your intentions, Travis."

"Women usually justify their actions with whatever they make up in their heads. She didn't tell me up front that she expected a relationship any more than I told her I expected sex with no strings. How is it any different?"

"You're a pig."

Travis shrugged. "I've been called worse."

I stared at the couch, the cushions still askew and bunched up from its recent use. I recoiled at the thought of how many women had given themselves away against the fabric. Itchy fabric at that.

"I guess I'm sleeping on the recliner," I grumbled.

"Why?"

I glared at him, furious over his confused expression. "I'm not sleeping on that thing! God knows what I'd be lying in!"

He lifted my luggage off the floor. "You're not sleeping on the couch or the recliner. You're sleeping in my bed."

"Which is more unsanitary than the couch, I'm sure."

"There's never been anyone in my bed but me."

I rolled my eyes. "Give me a break!"

"I'm absolutely serious. I bag 'em on the couch. I don't let them in my room."

"Then why am I allowed in your bed?"

One corner of his mouth pulled up into an impish grin. "Are you planning on having sex with me tonight?"

"No!"

"That's why. Now get your cranky ass up, take your hot shower, and then we can study some Bio."

I glared at him for a moment and then grudgingly did as he commanded. I stood under the shower entirely too long, letting the water wash away my aggravation. Massaging the shampoo through my hair, I sighed at how wonderful it was to shower in a noncommunal bathroom again—no flip-flops, no toiletry bag, just the relaxing blend of water and steam.

The door opened, and I jumped. "Mare?"

"No, it's me," Travis said.

I automatically wrapped my arms over the parts I didn't want him to see. "What are you doing in here? Get out!"

"You forgot a towel, and I brought your clothes, and your toothbrush, and some weird face cream I found in your bag."

"You went through my stuff?" I shrieked. He didn't answer. Instead, I heard the faucet turn on and the sound of his toothbrush against his teeth.

I peeked out of the plastic curtain, holding it against my chest. "Get out, Travis."

He looked up at me, his lips covered in suds from his toothpaste. "I can't go to bed without brushing my teeth."

"If you come within two feet of this curtain, I will poke out your eyes while you sleep."

"I won't peek, Pidge," he chuckled.

I waited under the water with my arms wrapped tightly across my chest. He spit, gurgled, and spit again, and then the door closed. I rinsed the soap from my skin, dried as quickly as possible, and then pulled my T-shirt and shorts on, slipping on my glasses and raking a comb through my hair. The night moisturizer Travis had brought caught my eye, and I couldn't help but smile. He was thoughtful and almost nice when he wanted to be.

Travis opened the door again. "C'mon, Pidge! I'm gettin' old, here!"

I threw my comb at him and he ducked, shutting the door and laughing to himself all the way to his room. I brushed my teeth and then shuffled down the hall, passing Shepley's bedroom on the way.

"Night, Abby," America called from the darkness.

"Night, Mare."

I hesitated before landing two soft knocks on Travis's door.

"Come in, Pidge. You don't have to knock."

He pulled the door open and I walked in, seeing his black iron-rod bed parallel to the line of windows on the far side of the room. The walls were bare except for a lone sombrero above his headboard. I half expected his room to be covered in posters of barely clothed women, but I didn't even see an advertisement for a beer brand. His bed was black, his carpet gray; everything else in the room was white. It looked as if he'd just moved in.

"Nice PJs," Travis said, noting my yellow-and-navy plaid shorts and gray Eastern T. He sat on his bed and patted the pillow beside him. "Well, come on. I'm not going to bite you."

"I'm not afraid of you," I said, walking over to the bed and dropping my Biology book beside him. "Do you have a pen?"

He nodded to his night table. "Top drawer."

I reached across the bed and pulled open the drawer, finding three pens, a pencil, a tube of K-Y Jelly, and a clear glass bowl overflowing with packages of different brands of condoms. Revolted, I grabbed a pen and shoved the drawer shut.

"What?" he asked, turning a page of my book.

"Did you rob the health clinic?"

"No. Why?"

I pulled the cap off the pen, unable to keep the sickened expression from my face. "Your lifetime supply of condoms."

"Better safe than sorry, right?"

I rolled my eyes. Travis returned to the pages, a wry smile breaking across his lips. He read the notes to me, highlighting the main points while he asked me questions and patiently explained what I didn't comprehend.

After an hour, I pulled off my glasses and rubbed my eyes. "I'm beat. I can't memorize one more macromolecule."

Travis smiled, closing my book. "All right."

I paused, unsure of our sleeping arrangements. Travis left the room and walked down the hall, mumbling something into Shepley's room before turning on the shower. I turned back the covers and then pulled them up to my neck, listening to the high-pitched whine of the water running through the pipes.

Ten minutes later, the water shut off, and the floor creaked under Travis's steps. He strolled across the room with a towel wrapped around his hips. He had tattoos on opposite sides of his chest, and black tribal art covering each of his bulging shoulders.

On his right arm, the black lines and symbols spanned from
his shoulder to his wrist; on the left, the tattoos stopped at his
elbow, with one single line of script on the underside of his forearm. I intentionally kept my back to him while he stood in front
of his dresser and dropped his towel to slip on a pair of boxers.

After flipping off the light, he crawled into the bed beside me.

"You're sleeping here, too?" I asked, turning to look at him.
The full moon outside the windows cast shadows across his face.
"Well, yeah. This is my bed."

"I know, but I . . ." I paused. My only other options were the
couch or the recliner.

Travis grinned and shook his head. "Don't you trust me by
now? I'll be on my best behavior, I swear," he said, holding up
fingers that I was sure the Boy Scouts of America had never
considered using.

I didn't argue, I simply turned away and rested my head on
the pillow, tucking the covers behind me to create a clear barrier
between his body and mine.

"Goodnight, Pigeon," he whispered into my ear. I could feel
his minty breath on my cheek, giving rise to goose bumps on
every inch of my flesh. Thank God it was dark enough that he
couldn't see my embarrassing reaction or the flush of my cheeks
that followed.

IT SEEMED LIKE I HAD JUST CLOSED MY EYES WHEN
I heard the alarm. I reached over to turn it off, but wrenched
back my hand in horror when I felt warm skin beneath my fingers. I tried to recall where I was. When the answer hit, it mortified me that Travis might think I'd done it on purpose.

"Travis? Your alarm," I whispered. He still didn't move. "Travis!" I said, nudging him. When he still didn't stir, I reached across him, fumbling in the dim light until I felt the top of the clock. Unsure of how to turn it off, I smacked the top of it until I hit the snooze button, and then fell against my pillow with a huff.

Travis chuckled.

"You were awake?"

"I promised I'd behave. I didn't say anything about letting you lay on me."

"I didn't lie on you," I protested. "I couldn't reach the clock. That has to be the most annoying alarm I've ever heard. It sounds like a dying animal."

He reached over and flipped a button. "You want breakfast?"

I glared at him, and then shook my head. "I'm not hungry."

"Well, I am. Why don't you ride with me down the street to the café?"

"I don't think I can handle your lack of driving skills this early in the morning," I said. I swung my feet over the side of the bed and shoved them into my slippers, shuffling to the door.

"Where are you going?" he asked.

"To get dressed and go to class. Do you need an itinerary while I'm here?"

Travis stretched, and then walked over to me, still in his boxers. "Are you always so temperamental, or will that taper off once you believe I'm not just creating some elaborate scheme to get into your pants?" His hands cupped my shoulders, and I felt his thumbs caress my skin in unison.

"I'm not temperamental."

He leaned in close and whispered in my ear. "I don't want to sleep with you, Pidge. I like you too much."

He walked past me to the bathroom, and I stood, stunned. Kara's words replayed in my mind. Travis Maddox slept with everyone; I couldn't help but feel deficient in some way, knowing he had no desire to even try to sleep with me.

The door opened again, and America walked through. "Wakey, wakey, eggs 'n' bakey!" she smiled, yawning.

"You're turning into your mother, Mare," I grumbled, rifling through my suitcase.

"Oooh . . . did someone miss some sleep last night?"

"He barely breathed in my direction," I said acerbically.

A knowing smile brightened America's face. "Oh."

"Oh, what?"

"Nothing," she said, returning to Shepley's room.

Travis was in the kitchen, humming a random tune while scrambling eggs. "You sure you don't want some?" he asked.

"I'm sure. Thanks, though."

Shepley and America walked in, and Shepley pulled two plates from the cabinet, holding them out as Travis shoveled a pile of steaming eggs onto each one. Shepley set the plates on the bar, and he and America sat together, satisfying the appetite they more than likely worked up the night before.

"Don't look at me like that, Shep. I'm sorry, I just don't want to go," America said.

"Baby, the House has a date party twice a year," Shepley spoke as he chewed. "It's a month away. You'll have plenty of time to find a dress and do all that girl stuff."

"I would, Shep . . . that's really sweet . . . but I'm not gonna know anyone there."

"A lot of the girls that come don't know a lot of people there," he said, surprised at the rejection.

She slumped in her chair. "The sorority bitches get invited to those things. They'll all know each other . . . it'll be weird."

"C'mon, Mare. Don't make me go alone."

"Well . . . maybe you could find someone to take Abby?" she said, looking at me, and then at Travis.

Travis raised an eyebrow, and Shepley shook his head. "Trav doesn't go to the date parties. It's something you take your girlfriend to . . . and Travis doesn't . . . you know."

America shrugged. "We could set her up with someone."

I narrowed my eyes at her. "I can hear you, you know."

America used the face she knew I couldn't say no to. "Please, Abby? We'll find you a nice guy that's funny and witty, and you know I'll make sure he's hot. I promise you'll have a good time! And who knows? Maybe you'll hit it off."

Travis threw the pan in the sink. "I didn't say I wouldn't take her."

I rolled my eyes. "Don't do me any favors, Travis."

"That's not what I meant, Pidge. Date parties are for the guys with girlfriends, and it's common knowledge that I don't do the girlfriend thing. But I won't have to worry about you expecting an engagement ring afterward."

America jutted her lip out. "Pretty please, Abby?"

"Don't look at me like that!" I complained. "Travis doesn't want to go, I don't want to go . . . we won't be much fun."

Travis crossed his arms and leaned against the sink. "I didn't say I didn't want to go. I think it'd be fun if the four of us went," he shrugged.

Everyone's eyes focused on me, and I recoiled. "Why don't we hang out here?"

America pouted and Shepley leaned forward. "Because I

have to go, Abby. I'm a freshman. I have to make sure everything's moving smoothly, everyone has a beer in their hand, things like that."

Travis walked across the kitchen and wrapped his arm around my shoulders, pulling me to his side. "C'mon, Pidge. Will you go with me?"

I looked at America, then at Shepley, and finally to Travis. "Yes," I sighed.

America squealed and hugged me, and then I felt Shepley's hand on my back. "Thanks, Abby," Shepley said.

Chapter Three
Cheap Shot

FINCH TOOK ANOTHER DRAG. THE SMOKE FLOWED FROM his nose in two thick streams. I angled my face toward the sun as he regaled me with his recent weekend of dancing, booze, and a very persistent new friend.

"If he's stalking you, then why do you let him buy you drinks?" I laughed.

"It's simple, Abby. I'm broke."

I laughed again, and Finch jabbed his elbow into my side when he caught sight of Travis walking toward us.

"Hey, Travis," Finch lilted, winking at me.

"Finch," Travis said with a nod. He dangled his keys. "I'm headed home, Pidge. You need a ride?"

"I was just going in," I said, grinning up at him through my sunglasses.

"You're not staying with me tonight?" he asked. His face was a combination of surprise and disappointment.

"No, I am. I just had to grab a few things that I forgot."

"Like what?"

"Well, my razor for one. What do you care?"

"It's about time you shaved your legs. They've been tearing the hell outta mine," he said with an impish grin.

Finch's eyes bulged as he gave me a quick once-over, and I made a face at Travis. "That's how rumors get started!" I looked at Finch and shook my head. "I'm sleeping in his bed . . . just sleeping."

"Right," Finch said with a smug smile.

I smacked Finch's arm before yanking the door open and climbing the stairs. By the time I reached the second floor, Travis was beside me.

"Oh, don't be mad. I was just kidding."

"Everyone already assumes we're having sex. You're making it worse."

"Who cares what they think?"

"I do, Travis! I do!" I pushed open my door, shoved random items into a small tote, and then stormed out, with Travis trailing behind. He chuckled as he took the bag from my hand, and I glared at him. "It's not funny. Do you want the whole school to think I'm one of your sluts?"

Travis frowned. "No one thinks that. And if they do, they better hope I don't hear about it."

He held the door open for me, and after walking through, I stopped abruptly in front of him.

"Whoa!" he said, slamming into me.

I flipped around. "Oh my God! People probably think we're together and you're shamelessly continuing your . . . lifestyle. I must look pathetic!" I said, coming to the realization as I spoke. "I don't think I should stay with you anymore. We should just stay away from each other in general for a while."

I took my bag from him, and he snatched it back.

"No one thinks we're together, Pidge. You don't have to quit talking to me to prove a point."

We engaged in a tug-of-war with the tote, and when he refused to let go, I growled loudly in frustration. "Have you ever had a girl—that's a friend—stay with you? Have you ever given girls rides to and from school? Have you eaten lunch with them every day? No one knows what to think about us, even when we tell them!"

He walked to the parking lot, holding my effects hostage. "I'll fix this, okay? I don't want anyone thinking less of you because of me," he said with a troubled expression. His eyes brightened and he smiled. "Let me make it up to you. Why don't we go to the Dutch tonight?"

"That's a biker bar," I sneered, watching him fasten my tote to his bike.

"Okay, then let's go to the club. I'll take you to dinner and then we can go to the Red Door. My treat."

"How will going out to dinner and then to a club fix the problem? When people see us out together it will make it worse."

He straddled his bike. "Think about it. Me, drunk, in a room full of scantily clad women? It won't take long for people to figure out we're not a couple."

"So what am I supposed to do? Take a guy home from the bar to drive the point home?"

"I didn't say that. No need to get carried away," he said with a frown.

I rolled my eyes and climbed onto the seat, wrapping my arms around his middle. "Some random girl is going to follow us home from the bar? That's how you're going to make it up to me?"

"You're not jealous, are you, Pigeon?"

"Jealous of what? The STD-infested imbecile you're going to piss off in the morning?"

Travis laughed, and then started his Harley. He flew toward his apartment at twice the speed limit, and I closed my eyes to block out the trees and cars we left behind.

After climbing off his bike, I smacked his shoulder. "Did you forget I was with you? Are you trying to get me killed?"

"It's hard to forget you're behind me when your thighs are squeezing the life out of me." A smirk came with his next thought. "I couldn't think of a better way to die, actually."

"There is something very wrong with you."

We had barely made it inside when America shuffled out of Shepley's bedroom. "We were thinking about going out tonight. You guys in?"

I looked at Travis and grinned. "We're going to swing by the sushi place before we go to Red."

America's smile spanned from one side of her face to the other. "Shep!" she cried, scampering into the bathroom. "We're going out tonight!"

I was the last one in the shower, so Shepley, America, and Travis were impatiently standing by the door when I stepped out of the bathroom in a black dress and hot pink heels.

America whistled. "Hot damn, Mama!"

I smiled in appreciation, and Travis held out his hand. "Nice legs."

"Did I mention that it's a magic razor?"

"I don't think it's the razor," he smiled, pulling me out the door.

We were far too loud and obnoxious in the sushi bar, and had already had a night's worth to drink before we stepped foot in the Red Door. Shepley pulled into the parking lot, taking time to find a space.

"Sometime tonight, Shep," America muttered.

"Hey, I have to find a wide space. I don't want some drunken idiot dinging the paint."

Once we parked, Travis leaned the seat forward and helped me out. "I meant to ask you about your IDs. They're flawless. You didn't get them around here."

"Yeah, we've had them for a while. It was necessary . . . in Wichita," I said.

"'Necessary?'" Travis asked.

"It's a good thing you have connections," America said. She hiccupped and covered her mouth, giggling.

"Dear God, woman," Shepley said, holding America's arm as she awkwardly stepped along the gravel. "I think you're already done for the night."

Travis made a face. "What are you talking about, Mare? What connections?"

"Abby has some old friends that—"

"They're fake IDs, Trav," I interrupted. "You have to know the right people if you want them done right, right?"

America purposefully looked away from Travis, and I waited.

"Right," he said, extending his hand for mine.

I grabbed three of his fingers and smiled, knowing by his expression that he wasn't satisfied with my answer.

"I need another drink!" I said as a second attempt to change the subject.

"Shots!" America yelled.

Shepley rolled his eyes. "Oh, yeah. That's what you need, another shot."

Once inside, America immediately pulled me onto the dance floor. Her blond hair was everywhere, and I laughed at the duck face she made when she moved to the music. When the song was over, we joined the boys at the bar. An excessively voluptuous platinum blonde was already at Travis's side, and America's face screwed into revulsion.

"It's going to be like this all night, Mare. Just ignore them," Shepley said, nodding to a small group of girls standing a few feet away. They eyed the blonde, waiting for their turn.

"It looks like Vegas threw up on a flock of vultures," America sneered.

Travis lit a cigarette as he ordered two more beers, and the blonde bit her puffy, glossed lip and smiled. The bartender popped the tops open and slid the bottles to Travis. The blonde picked up one of the beers, but Travis pulled it from her hand.

"Uh . . . not yours," he said to her, handing it to me.

My initial thought was to toss the bottle in the trash, but the woman looked so offended, I smiled and took a drink. She walked off in a huff, and I chuckled that Travis didn't seem to notice.

"Like I would buy a beer for some chick at a bar," he said, shaking his head. I held up my beer, and he pulled up one side of his mouth into a half smile. "You're different."

I clinked my bottle against his. "To being the only girl a guy with no standards doesn't want to sleep with," I said, taking a swig.

"Are you serious?" he asked, pulling the bottle from my mouth. When I didn't recant, he leaned toward me. "First of all ... I have standards. I've never been with an ugly woman. Ever. Second of all, I wanted to sleep with you. I thought about throwing you over my couch fifty different ways, but I haven't because I don't see you that way anymore. It's not that I'm not attracted to you, I just think you're better than that."

I couldn't hold back the smug smile that crept across my face. "You think I'm too good for you."

He sneered at my second insult. "I can't think of a single guy I know that's good enough for you."

The smugness melted away, replaced with a touched, appreciative smile. "Thanks, Trav," I said, setting my empty bottle on the bar.

Travis pulled on my hand. "C'mon," he said, tugging me through the crowd to the dance floor.

"I've had a lot to drink! I'm going to fall!"

Travis smiled and pulled me to him, grabbing my hips. "Shut up and dance."

America and Shepley appeared beside us. Shepley moved like he'd been watching too many Usher videos. Travis had me near panic with the way he pressed against me. If he used any of those moves on the couch, I could see why so many girls chanced humiliation in the morning.

He cinched his hands around my hips, and I noticed that his expression was different, almost serious. I ran my hands over his flawless chest and six-pack as they stretched and tensed under his tight shirt to the music. I turned my back to him, smiling when he wrapped his arms around my waist. Coupled with the alcohol in my system, when he pulled my body against his, things came to mind that were anything but friendly.

The next song bled into the one we were dancing to, and Travis showed no signs of wanting to return to the bar. The sweat beaded on the back of my neck, and the multicolored strobe lights made me feel a bit dizzy. I closed my eyes and leaned my head against his shoulder. He grabbed my hands and pulled them up and around his neck. His hands ran down my arms and down my ribs, finally returning to my hips. When I felt his lips and then his tongue against my neck, I pulled away from him.

He chuckled, looking a bit surprised. "What, Pidge?"

My temper flared, making the sharp words I wanted to say stick in my throat. I retreated to the bar and ordered another Corona. Travis took the stool beside me, holding up his finger to order one for himself. As soon as the bartender set the bottle in front of me, I tipped it up and drank half the contents before slamming it to the bar.

"You think that is going to change anyone's mind about us?" I said, pulling my hair to the side, covering the spot he kissed.

He laughed once. "I don't give a damn what they think about us."

I shot him a dirty look and then turned to face forward.

"Pigeon," he said, touching my arm.

I pulled away from him. "Don't. I could never get drunk enough to let you get me on that couch."

His face twisted in anger, but before he could say anything, a dark-haired stunner with pouty lips, enormous blue eyes, and far too much cleavage approached him.

"Well, if it isn't Travis Maddox," she said, bouncing in all the right places.

He took a drink, and then his eyes locked on mine. "Hey, Megan."

"Introduce me to your girlfriend," she smiled. I rolled my eyes.

Travis tipped his head back to finish his beer, and then slid his empty bottle down the bar. Everyone waiting to order watched it until it fell into the trash can at the end. "She's not my girlfriend."

He grabbed Megan's hand, and she happily traipsed behind him to the dance floor. He all but mauled her for one song, and then another, and another. They were causing a scene with the way she let him grope her, and when he bent her over I turned my back to them.

"You look pissed," a man said as he sat next to me. "Is that your boyfriend out there?"

"No, he's just a friend," I grumbled.

"Well, that's good. That could have been pretty awkward for you if he was." He faced the dance floor, shaking his head at the spectacle.

"Tell me about it," I said, drinking the last of my beer. I barely tasted the last two I had put away, and my teeth were numb.

"Would you like another one?" he asked. I looked over at him and he smiled. "I'm Ethan."

"Abby," I said, taking his outstretched hand.

He held up two fingers to the bartender, and I smiled. "Thanks."

"So, you live here?" he asked.

"In Morgan Hall at Eastern."

"I have an apartment in Hinley."

"You go to State?" I asked. "What is that . . . like, an hour away? What are you doing over here?"

"I graduated last May. My little sister goes to Eastern. I'm staying with her this week while I apply for jobs."

"Uh-oh . . . living in the real world, huh?"

Ethan laughed. "And it's everything they say it is."

I pulled the gloss out of my pocket and smeared it across my lips, using the mirror lining the wall behind the bar.

"That's a nice shade," he said, watching me press my lips together.

I smiled, feeling the anger at Travis and the heaviness of the alcohol. "Maybe you can try it on later."

Ethan's eyes brightened as I leaned in closer, and I smiled when he touched my knee. He pulled back his hand when Travis stepped between us.

"You ready, Pidge?"

"I'm talking, Travis," I said, moving him back. His shirt was damp from the circus on the dance floor, and I made a show of wiping my hand on my skirt.

Travis made a face. "Do you even know this guy?"

"This is Ethan," I said, sending my new friend the best flirty smile I could manage.

He winked at me, and then looked at Travis, extending his hand. "Nice to meet you."

Travis watched me expectantly until I finally gave in, waving my hand in his general direction. "Ethan, this is Travis," I muttered.

"Travis Maddox," he said, staring at Ethan's hand as if he wanted to rip it off.

Ethan's eyes grew wide, and he awkwardly pulled back his hand. "Travis Maddox? Eastern's Travis Maddox?"

I rested my cheek on my fist, dreading the inevitable testosterone-fueled story swapping that would soon ensue.

Travis stretched his arm behind me to grip the bar. "Yeah, what of it?"

"I saw you fight Shawn Smith last year, man. I thought I was about to witness someone's death!"

Travis glowered down at him. "You wanna see it again?"

Ethan laughed once, his eyes darting back and forth between us. When he realized Travis was serious, he smiled at me apologetically and left.

"Are you ready, now?" he snapped.

"You are a complete asshole, you know that?"

"I've been called worse," he said, helping me off the stool.

We followed America and Shepley to the car, and when Travis tried to grab my hand to lead me across the parking lot, I yanked it away. He wheeled around and I jerked to a stop, leaning back when he came within a few inches of my face.

"I should just kiss you and get it over with!" he yelled. "You're being ridiculous! I kissed your neck, so what?"

I could smell the beer and cigarettes on his breath and pushed him away. "I'm not your fuck buddy, Travis."

He shook his head in disbelief. "I never said you were! You're around me 24-7, you sleep in my bed, but half the time you act like you don't wanna be seen with me!"

"I came here with you!"

"I have never treated you with anything but respect, Pidge."

I stood my ground. "No, you just treat me like your property. You had no right to run Ethan off like that!"

"Do you know who Ethan is?" he asked. When I shook my head, he leaned in closer. "I do. He was arrested last year for sexual battery, but the charges were dropped."

I crossed my arms. "Oh, so you have something in common?"

Travis's eyes narrowed, and the muscles in his jaws twitched under his skin. "Are you calling me a rapist?" he said in a cold, low tone.

I pressed my lips together, even angrier that he was right. I had taken it too far. "No, I'm just pissed at you!"

"I've been drinking, all right? Your skin was three inches from my face, and you're beautiful, and you smell fucking awesome when you sweat. I kissed you! I'm sorry! Get over yourself!"

His excuse made the corners of my mouth turn up. "You think I'm beautiful?"

He frowned with disgust. "You're gorgeous and you know it. What are you smiling about?"

I tried to quell my amusement, to no avail. "Nothing. Let's go."

Travis laughed once and shook his head. "Wha . . . ? You . . . ? You're a pain in my ass!" he yelled, glaring at me. I couldn't stop smiling, and after a few seconds, Travis's mouth turned up. He shook his head again, and then hooked his arm around my neck. "You're making me crazy. You know that, right?"

At the apartment, we all stumbled through the door. I made a beeline for the bathroom to wash the smoke out of my hair.

When I stepped out of the shower, I saw that Travis had brought me one of his T-shirts and a pair of his boxers to change into.

The shirt swallowed me, and the boxers disappeared under the shirt. I crashed into the bed and sighed, still smiling at what he'd said in the parking lot.

Travis stared at me for a moment, and I felt a twinge in my chest. I had an almost ravenous urge to grab his face and plant my mouth on his, but I fought against the alcohol and hormones raging through my bloodstream.

"Night, Pidge," he whispered, turning over.

I fidgeted, not yet ready to sleep. "Trav?" I said, leaning up to rest my chin on his shoulder.

"Yeah?"

"I know I'm drunk, and we just got into a ginormous fight over this, but . . ."

"I'm not having sex with you, so quit asking," he said, his back still turned to me.

"What? No!" I cried.

Travis laughed and turned, looking at me with a soft expression. "What, Pigeon?"

I sighed. "This," I said, laying my head on his chest and stretching my arm across his middle, snuggling as close to him as I could.

He stiffened and held his hands up, as if he didn't know how to react. "You are drunk."

"I know," I said, too intoxicated to be embarrassed.

He relaxed one hand against my back, and the other on my wet hair, and then pressed his lips to my forehead. "You are the most confusing woman I've ever met."

"It's the least you can do after scaring off the only guy that approached me tonight."

"You mean Ethan the rapist? Yeah, I owe you for that one."

"Never mind," I said, feeling the beginning of a rejection coming on.

He grabbed my arm and held it on his stomach to keep me from pulling away. "No, I'm serious. You need to be more careful. If I wasn't there . . . I don't even want to think about it. And now you expect me to apologize for running him off?"

"I don't want you to apologize. It's not even about that."

"Then what's it about?" he asked, searching my eyes for something. His face was just a few inches from mine, and I could feel his breath on my lips.

I frowned. "I'm drunk, Travis. It's the only excuse I have."

"You just want me to hold you until you fall asleep?"

I didn't answer.

He shifted to look straight into my eyes. "I should say no to prove a point," he said, his eyebrows pulling together. "But I would hate myself later if I said no and you never asked me again."

I nestled my cheek against his chest, and he tightened his arms, sighing. "You don't need an excuse, Pigeon. All you have to do is ask."

I CRINGED AT THE SUNLIGHT POURING THROUGH THE window and the alarm blaring into my ear. Travis was still asleep, surrounding me with both his arms and his legs. I maneuvered an arm free to reach over and pound the snooze button. Wiping my face, I looked over at him, sleeping soundly two inches from me.

"Oh my God," I whispered, wondering how we'd managed to become so tangled. I took a deep breath and held it as I worked to free myself from his grip.

"Stop it, Pidge, I'm sleepin'," he mumbled, squeezing me against him.

After several attempts, I finally slid from his grip and sat on the edge of the bed, looking back at his half-naked body draped in covers. I watched him for a moment and sighed. The lines were becoming blurred, and it was my fault.

His hand slid across the sheets and touched my fingers. "What's wrong, Pigeon?" he said, his eyes barely open.

"I'm going to get a glass of water, you want anything?" Travis shook his head and closed his eyes, his cheek flat against the mattress.

"Morning, Abby," Shepley said from the recliner when I rounded the corner.

"Where's Mare?"

"Still sleeping. What are you doing up so early?" he asked, looking at the clock.

"The alarm went off, but I always wake up early after I drink. It's a curse."

"Me, too," he nodded.

"You better get Mare up. We have class in an hour," I said, turning on the tap, and leaning over to take a sip.

Shepley nodded. "I was just going to let her sleep."

"Don't do that. She'll be mad if she misses."

"Oh," he said, standing up. "Better wake her, then." He wheeled around. "Hey, Abby?"

"Yeah?"

"I don't know what's going on with you and Travis, but

I know that he's going to do something stupid to piss you off. It's a tic he has. He doesn't get close with anyone very often, and for whatever reason he's let you in. But you have to overlook his demons. It's the only way he'll know."

"Know what?" I asked, raising an eyebrow at his melodramatic speech.

"If you'll climb over the wall," he answered simply.

I shook my head and chuckled. "Whatever you say, Shep."

Shepley shrugged, and then disappeared into his bedroom. I heard soft murmurs, a protesting groan, and then America's sweet giggling.

I swirled the oatmeal around in my bowl, and squeezed the chocolate syrup in as I stirred.

"That's sick, Pidge," Travis said, wearing only a pair of green plaid boxers. He rubbed his eyes and pulled a box of cereal from the cabinet.

"Good morning to you, too," I said, snapping the cap on the bottle.

"I hear your birthday is coming up. Last stand of your teenage years," he grinned, his eyes puffy and red.

"Yeah . . . I'm not a big birthday person. I think Mare is going to take me to dinner or something." I smiled. "You can come if you want."

"All right," he shrugged. "It's a week from Sunday?"

"Yes. When's your birthday?"

He poured the milk, dunking the flakes with his spoon, "Not 'til April. April first."

"Shut up."

"No, I'm serious," he said, chewing.

"Your birthday is on April Fools'?" I asked again, raising an eyebrow.

He laughed. "Yes! You're gonna be late. I better get dressed."

"I'm riding with Mare."

I could tell he was being intentionally cool when he shrugged. "Whatever," he said, turning his back to me to finish his cereal.

Chapter Four
The Bet

"HE'S DEFINITELY STARING AT YOU," AMERICA WHISpered, leaning back to peek across the room.

"Stop looking, dummy, he's going to see you."

America smiled and waved. "He's already seen me. He's still staring."

I hesitated for a moment and then finally worked up enough courage to look in his direction. Parker was looking right at me, grinning.

I returned his smile and then pretended to type something on my laptop.

"Is he still staring?" I murmured.

"Yep," she giggled.

After class, Parker stopped me in the hall.

"Don't forget about the party this weekend."

"I won't," I said, trying not to bat my eyes or do anything else ridiculous.

America and I made our way across the lawn to the cafeteria to meet Travis and Shepley for lunch. She was still laughing about Parker's behavior when they approached.

"Hey, baby," America said, kissing her boyfriend square on the mouth.

"What's so funny?" Shepley asked.

"Oh, a guy in class was staring at Abby all hour. It was adorable."

"As long as he was staring at Abby," Shepley winked.

"Who was it?" Travis grimaced.

I adjusted my backpack, prompting Travis to slide it off my arms and hold it. I shook my head. "Mare's imagining things."

"Abby! You big fat liar! It was Parker Hayes, and he was being so obvious. The guy was practically drooling."

Travis's expression twisted into disgust. "Parker Hayes?"

Shepley pulled on America's hand. "We're headed to lunch. Will you be enjoying the fine cafeteria cuisine this afternoon?"

America kissed him again in answer, and Travis and I followed behind. I sat my tray between America and Finch, but Travis didn't sit in his normal seat across from me. Instead, he sat a few seats down. It was then that I realized he hadn't said much during our walk to the cafeteria.

"Are you okay, Trav?" I asked.

"Me? Fine, why?" he said, smoothing the features of his face.

"You've just been quiet."

Several members of the football team approached the table and sat down, laughing loudly. Travis looked a bit annoyed as he rolled his food around on his plate.

Chris Jenks tossed a french fry onto Travis's tray. "What's up, Trav? I heard you bagged Tina Martin. She's been raking your name through the mud today."

"Shut up, Jenks," Travis said, keeping his eyes on his food.

I leaned forward so the brawny giant sitting in front of Travis could experience the full force of my glare. "Knock it off, Chris."

Travis's eyes bored into mine. "I can take care of myself, Abby."

"I'm sorry, I . . ."

"I don't want you to be sorry. I don't want you to be anything," he snapped, shoving away from the table and storming out the door.

Finch looked over at me with raised eyebrows. "Whoa. What was that about?"

I stabbed a Tater Tot with my fork and puffed. "I don't know."

Shepley patted my back. "It's nothing you did, Abby."

"He just has stuff going on," America added.

"What kind of stuff?" I asked.

Shepley shrugged and turned his attention to his plate. "You should know by now that it takes patience and a forgiving attitude to be friends with Travis. He's his own universe."

I shook my head. "That's the Travis everyone else sees . . . not the Travis I know."

Shepley leaned forward. "There's no difference. You just have to ride the wave."

After class, I rode with America to the apartment to find Travis's motorcycle gone. I went into his room and curled into a ball on his bed, resting my head on my arm. Travis had been fine that morning. As much time as we had spent together, I couldn't believe I didn't see that something had been bothering him. Not only that, it disturbed me that America seemed to know what was going on and I didn't.

My breathing evened out and my eyes grew heavy; it wasn't long before I fell asleep. When my eyes opened again, the night sky had darkened the window. Muffled voices filtered down the hall from the living room, including Travis's deep tone. I crept down the hall, and then froze when I heard my name.

"Abby gets it, Trav. Don't beat yourself up," Shepley said.

"You're already going to the date party. What's the harm in asking her out?" America asked.

I stiffened, waiting for his response. "I don't want to date her; I just want to be around her. She's . . . different."

"Different how?" America asked, sounding irritated.

"She doesn't put up with my bullshit, it's refreshing. You said it yourself, Mare: I'm not her type. It's just not . . . like that with us."

"You're closer to her type than you know," America said.

I backed up as quietly as I could, and when the wooden boards creaked beneath my bare feet, I reached over to pull Travis's bedroom door shut and then walked down the hall.

"Hey, Abby," America said with a grin. "How was your nap?"

"I was out for five hours. That's closer to a coma than a nap."

Travis stared at me for a moment, and when I smiled at him, he walked straight toward me, grabbed my hand, and pulled me down the hall to his bedroom. He shut the door, and I felt my heart pounding in my chest, bracing for him to say something else to crush my ego.

His eyebrows pulled in. "I'm so sorry, Pidge. I was an asshole to you earlier."

I relaxed a bit, seeing the remorse in his eyes. "I didn't know you were mad at me."

"I wasn't mad at you. I just have a bad habit of lashing out at those I care about. It's a piss-poor excuse, I know, but I am sorry," he said, enveloping me in his arms.

I nestled my cheek against his chest, settling in. "What were you mad about?"

"It's not important. The only thing I'm worried about is you."

I leaned back to look up at him. "I can handle your temper tantrums."

His eyes scanned my face for several moments before a small smile spread across his lips. "I don't know why you put up with me, and I don't know what I'd do if you didn't."

I could smell the mixture of cigarettes and mint on his breath, and I looked at his lips, my body reacting to how close we were. Travis's expression changed and his breathing staggered—he had noticed, too.

He leaned in infinitesimally, and then we both jumped when his cell phone rang. He sighed, pulling it from his pocket.

"Yeah. Hoffman? Jesus . . . all right. That'll be an easy grand. Jefferson?" He looked at me and winked. "We'll be there." He hung up and took my hand. "Come with me." He pulled me down the hall. "That was Adam," he said to Shepley. "Brady Hoffman will be at Jefferson in ninety minutes."

Shepley nodded and stood up, digging his cell phone from his pocket. He quickly tapped in the information, sending exclusive text invitations to those who knew about the Circle. Those ten or so members would text ten members on their list, and so on, until every member knew exactly where the floating fight ring would be held.

"Here we go," America said, smiling. "We'd better freshen up!"

The air in the apartment was tense and buoyant at the same time. Travis seemed the least affected, slipping on his boots and a white tank top as if he were leaving to run an errand.

America led me down the hall to Travis's bedroom and frowned. "You have to change, Abby. You can't wear that to the fight."

"I wore a freaking cardigan last time and you didn't say anything!" I protested.

"I didn't think you'd go last time. Here," she threw clothes at me, "put this on."

"I am not wearing this!"

"Let's go!" Shepley called from the living room.

"Hurry up!" America snapped, running into Shepley's room.

I pulled on the deep-cut yellow halter top and tight low-rise jeans America had thrown at me, and then slipped on a pair of heels, raking a brush through my hair as I shuffled down the hall. America came out of her room with a short green baby-doll dress and matching heels, and when we rounded the corner, Travis and Shepley were standing at the door.

Travis's mouth fell open. "Oh, hell no. Are you trying to get me killed? You've gotta change, Pidge."

"What?" I asked, looking down.

America grabbed her hips. "She looks cute, Trav, leave her alone!"

Travis took my hand and led me down the hall. "Get a T-shirt on . . . and some sneakers. Something comfortable."

"What? Why?"

"Because I'll be more worried about who's looking at your tits in that shirt instead of Hoffman," he said, stopping at his door.

"I thought you said you didn't give a damn what anyone else thought?"

"That's a different scenario, Pigeon." Travis looked down at my chest and then up at me. "You can't wear this to the fight, so please . . . just . . . please just change," he stuttered, shoving me into the room and shutting me in.

"Travis!" I yelled. I kicked off my heels, and shoved my feet into my Converses. Then I wiggled out of my halter top, throwing it across the room. The first cotton shirt that touched my hands I yanked over my head, and then ran down the hall, standing in the doorway.

"Better?" I huffed, pulling my hair into a ponytail.

"Yes!" Travis said, relieved. "Let's go!"

We raced to the parking lot. I jumped on the back of Travis's motorcycle as he ripped the engine and peeled out, flying down the road to the college. I squeezed his middle in anticipation; the rushing to get out the door sent adrenaline surging through my veins.

Travis drove over the curb, parking his motorcycle in the shadows behind the Jefferson Liberal Arts building. He pushed his sunglasses to the top of his head and then grabbed my hand, smiling as we snuck to the back of the building. He stopped at an open window near the ground.

My eyes widened with realization. "You're joking."

Travis smiled. "This is the VIP entrance. You should see how everyone else gets in."

I shook my head as he worked his legs through, and then disappeared. I leaned down and called into oblivion, "Travis!"

"Down here, Pidge. Just come in feet first, I'll catch you."

"You're out of your damn mind if you think I'm jumping into the dark!"

"I'll catch you! I promise! Now get your ass in here!"

I sighed, touching my forehead with my hand. "This is insane!"

I sat down, and then scooted forward until half of my body was dangling in the dark. I turned onto my stomach and pointed my toes, feeling for the floor. I waited for my feet to touch Travis's hand, but I lost my grip, squealing when I fell backward. A pair of hands grabbed me, and I heard Travis's voice in the darkness.

"You fall like a girl," he chuckled.

He lowered my feet to the ground and then pulled me deeper into the blackness. After a dozen steps, I could hear the familiar yelling of numbers and names, and then the room was illuminated. A lantern sat in the corner, lighting the room just enough that I could make out Travis's face.

"What are we doing?"

"Waiting. Adam has to run through his spiel before I go in."

I fidgeted. "Should I wait here, or should I go in? Where do I go when the fight starts? Where's Shep and Mare?"

"They went in the other way. Just follow me out; I'm not sending you into that shark pit without me. Stay by Adam; he'll keep you from getting crushed. I can't look out for you and throw punches at the same time."

"Crushed?"

"There's going to be more people here tonight. Brady Hoffman is from State. They have their own Circle there. It will be our crowd and their crowd, so the room's gonna get crazy."

"Are you nervous?" I asked.

He smiled, looking down at me. "No. You look a little nervous, though."

"Maybe," I admitted.

"If it'll make you feel better, I won't let him touch me. I won't even let him get one in for his fans."

"How are you going to manage that?"

He shrugged. "I usually let them get one in—to make it look fair."

"You . . . ? You let people hit you?"

"How much fun would it be if I just massacred someone and they never got a punch in? It's not good for business, no one would bet against me."

"What a load of crap," I said, crossing my arms.

Travis raised an eyebrow. "You think I'm yankin' your chain?"

"I find it hard to believe that you only get hit when you let them hit you."

"Would you like to make a wager on that, Abby Abernathy?" he smiled, his eyes animated.

I smiled. "I'll take that bet. I think he'll get one in on you."

"And if he doesn't? What do I win?" he asked. I shrugged as the yelling on the other side of the wall grew to a roar. Adam greeted the crowd, and then went over the rules.

Travis's mouth stretched into a wide grin. "If you win, I'll go without sex for a month." I raised an eyebrow, and he smiled again. "But if I win, you have to stay with me for a month."

"What? I'm staying with you anyway! What kind of bet is that?" I shrieked over the noise.

"They fixed the boilers at Morgan today," Travis said with a smile and a wink.

A smirk softened my expression as Adam called Travis's name. "Anything is worth watching you try abstinence for a change."

Travis kissed my cheek, and then walked out, standing tall. I followed behind, and when we crossed into the next room, I was startled by the number of people packed together in the small space. It was standing room only, but the shoving and shouting only amplified once we entered the room. Travis nodded in my direction, and then Adam's hand was on my shoulder, pulling me to his side.

I leaned into Adam's ear. "I've got two on Travis," I said.

Adam's eyebrows shot up as he watched me pull two Benjamins from my pocket. He held out his palm, and I slapped the bills into his hand.

"You're not the Goody Two-shoes I thought you were," he said, giving me a once-over.

Brady was at least a head taller than Travis, and I gulped when I saw them stand toe-to-toe. Brady was massive, twice Travis's size and solid muscle. I couldn't see Travis's expression, but it was obvious that Brady was out for blood.

Adam pressed his lips against my ear. "You might want to plug your ears, kiddo."

I cupped my hands on each side of my head, and Adam sounded the horn. Instead of attacking, Travis took a few steps back. Brady swung, and Travis dodged to the right. Brady swung again, and Travis ducked and sidestepped to the other side.

"What the hell? This ain't a boxing match, Travis!" Adam yelled.

Travis landed a punch to Brady's nose. The volume in the basement was deafening then. Travis sank a left hook into Brady's jaw, and my hands flew over my mouth when Brady attempted a few more punches, each one catching air. Brady fell against his entourage when Travis elbowed him in the face. Just when I thought it was almost over, Brady came out swinging again. Throw after throw, Brady couldn't seem to keep up. Both men were covered in sweat, and I gasped when Brady missed another punch, slamming his hand into a cement pillar. When he folded over, cradling his fist beneath him, Travis went in for the kill.

He was relentless, first bringing his knee to Brady's face and then pummeling him over and over until Brady stumbled and hit the ground. The noise level boomed as Adam left my side to throw the red square on Brady's bloodied face.

Travis disappeared behind his fans, and I pressed my back against the wall, feeling my way to the doorway we came in. Reaching the lantern was a huge relief. I worried about being knocked down and trampled.

My eyes focused on the doorway, waiting for the crowd to spill into the small room. After several minutes and no sign of Travis, I prepared to retrace my steps to the window. With the number of people trying to leave at once, it wasn't safe enough to chance wandering around.

Just as I stepped into the darkness, footsteps crunched against the loose concrete on the floor. Travis was looking for me in a panic.

"Pigeon!"

"I'm here!" I called out, running into his arms.

Travis looked down and frowned. "You scared the shit out of me! I almost had to start another fight just to get to you . . . I finally get here and you're gone!"

"I'm glad you're back. I wasn't looking forward to trying to find my way in the dark."

All worry left his face, and he smiled widely. "I believe you lost the bet."

Adam stomped in, looked at me, and then glowered at Travis. "We need to talk."

Travis winked at me. "Stay put. I'll be right back."

They disappeared into the darkness. Adam raised his voice a few times, but I couldn't make out what he was saying. Travis returned, shoving a wad of cash into his pocket, and then he offered a half smile. "You're going to need more clothes."

"You're really going to make me stay with you for a month?"

"Would you have made me go without sex for a month?"

I laughed, knowing I would. "We better stop at Morgan."

Travis beamed. "This should be interesting."

As Adam passed, he slammed my winnings into my palm, and then merged into the dissipating mob.

Travis raised an eyebrow. "You put in?"

I smiled and shrugged. "I thought I should get the full experience."

He led me to the window and then crawled out, turning to help me up and out into the fresh night air. The crickets were chirping in the shadows, stopping just long enough to let us pass. The monkey grass that lined the sidewalk waved in the gentle breeze, reminding me of the sound the ocean makes when I wasn't quite close enough to hear the waves breaking. It wasn't too hot or too cold; it was the perfect night.

"Why on earth would you want me to stay with you, anyway?" I asked.

Travis shrugged, shoving his hands in his pockets. "I don't know. Everything's better when you're around."

The warm and fuzzies I felt from his words quickly faded with the sight of the red blotchy mess on his shirt. "Ew. You have blood all over you."

Travis looked down with indifference and then opened the door, gesturing for me to walk in. I breezed by Kara, who studied on her bed, held captive by the textbooks that surrounded her.

"The boilers were fixed this morning," she said.

"I heard," I said, rifling through my closet.

"Hi," Travis said to Kara.

Kara's face twisted as she scanned Travis's sweaty, bloody form.

"Travis, this is my roommate, Kara Lin. Kara, Travis Maddox."

"Nice to meet you," Kara said, pushing her glasses up the bridge of her nose. She glanced at my bulging bags. "Are you moving out?"

"Nope. Lost a bet."

Travis burst into laughter, grabbing my bags. "Ready?"

"Yeah. How am I going to get all of this to your apartment? We're on your bike."

Travis smiled and pulled out his cell phone. He carried my luggage to the street, and minutes later, Shepley's black vintage Charger pulled up.

The passenger-side window rolled down, and America poked her head out. "Hey, chickie!"

"Hey yourself. The boilers are working again at Morgan. Are you still staying with Shep?"

She winked. "Yeah, I thought I'd stay tonight. I heard you lost a bet."

Before I could speak, Travis shut the trunk and Shep sped off, with America squealing as she fell back into the car.

We walked to his Harley, and he waited for me to settle into my seat. When I wrapped my arms around him, he rested his hand on mine.

"I'm glad you were there tonight, Pidge. I've never had so much fun at a fight in my life."

I perched my chin on his shoulder and smiled. "That was because you were trying to win our bet."

He angled his neck to face me. "Damn right I was." There was no amusement in his eyes; he was serious, and he wanted me to see it.

My eyebrows shot up. "Is that why you were in such a bad mood today? Because you knew they'd fixed the boilers, and I would be leaving tonight?"

Travis didn't answer; he only smiled as he started his motorcycle. The drive to the apartment was uncharacteristically slow. At every stoplight, Travis would either cover my hands with his, or he would rest his hand on my knee. The lines were blurring again, and I wondered how we would spend a month together and not ruin everything. The loose ends of our friendship were tangling in a way I never imagined.

When we arrived in the apartment parking lot, Shepley's Charger sat in its usual spot.

I stood in front of the steps. "I always hate it when they've been home for a while. I feel like we're going to interrupt them."

"Get used to it. This is your place for the next four weeks," Travis smiled and turned his back to me. "Get on."

"What?" I smiled.

"C'mon, I'll carry you up."

I giggled and hopped onto his back, interlacing my fingers on his chest as he ran up the stairs. America opened the door before we made it to the top and smiled.

"Look at you two. If I didn't know better . . ."

"Knock it off, Mare," Shepley said from the couch.

America smiled as if she'd said too much, and then opened the door wide so we could both fit through. Travis collapsed against the recliner. I squealed when he leaned against me.

"You're awfully cheerful this evening, Trav. What gives?" America prompted.

I leaned over to see his face. I'd never seen him so pleased.

"I just won a shitload of money, Mare. Twice as much as I thought I would. What's not to be happy about?"

America grinned. "No, it's something else," she said, watching Travis's hand as he patted my thigh. She was right; he was different. There was an air of peace around him, almost as if some kind of new contentment had settled into his soul.

"Mare," Shepley warned.

"Fine, I'll talk about something else. Didn't Parker invite you to the Sig Tau party this weekend, Abby?"

Travis's smile vanished and he turned to me, waiting for an answer.

"Er . . . yeah? Aren't we all going?"

"I'll be there," Shepley said, distracted by the television.

"And that means I'm going," America said, looking expectantly at Travis.

Travis watched me for a moment, and then nudged my leg. "Is he picking you up or something?"

"No, he just told me about the party."

America's mouth spread into a mischievous grin, almost bobbing in anticipation. "He said he'd see you there, though. He's really cute."

Travis shot an irritated glance in America's direction and then looked to me. "Are you going?"

"I told him I would," I shrugged. "Are you going?"

"Yeah," he said without hesitation.

Shepley's attention turned to Travis then. "You said last week you weren't."

"I changed my mind, Shep. What's the problem?"

"Nothing," he grumbled, retreating to his bedroom.

America frowned at Travis. "You know what the problem is," she said. "Why don't you quit driving him crazy and just get it over with." She joined Shepley in his room, and their voices were reduced to murmuring behind the closed door.

"Well, I'm glad everyone else knows," I said.

Travis stood up. "I'm going to take a quick shower."

"Is there something going on with them?" I asked.

"No, he's just paranoid."

"It's because of us," I guessed. Travis's eyes lit up and he nodded.

"What?" I asked, eyeing him suspiciously.

"You're right. It's because of us. Don't fall asleep, okay? I wanna talk to you about something."

He walked backward a few steps, and then disappeared

behind the bathroom door. I twisted my hair around my finger, mulling over the way he emphasized the word "us," and the look on his face when he'd said it. I wondered if there had ever been lines at all, and if I was the only one who considered Travis and I just friends anymore.

Shepley burst out of his room, and America ran after him. "Shep, don't!" she pleaded.

He looked back to the bathroom door, and then to me. His voice was low, but angry. "You promised, Abby. When I told you to spare judgment, I didn't mean for you two to get involved! I thought you were just friends!"

"We are," I said, shaken by his surprise attack.

"No, you're not!" he fumed.

America touched his shoulder. "Baby, I told you it will be fine."

He pulled away from her grip. "Why are you pushing this, Mare? I told you what's going to happen!"

She grabbed his face with both hands. "And I told you it won't! Don't you trust me?"

Shepley sighed, looked at her, at me, and then stomped into his room.

America fell into the recliner beside me, and puffed. "I just can't get it into his head that whether you and Travis work out or not, it won't affect us. But he's been burned too many times. He doesn't believe me."

"What are you talking about, Mare? Travis and I aren't together. We are just friends. You heard him earlier . . . he's not interested in me that way."

"You heard that?"

"Well, yeah."

"And you believe it?"

I shrugged. "It doesn't matter. It'll never happen. He told me he doesn't see me like that, anyway. Besides, he's a total commitmentphobe, I'd be hard pressed to find a girlfriend outside of you that he hasn't slept with, and I can't keep up with his mood swings. I can't believe Shep thinks otherwise."

"Because not only does he know Travis . . . he's talked to Travis, Abby."

"What do you mean?"

"Mare?" Shepley called from the bedroom.

America sighed. "You're my best friend. I think I know you better than you know yourself sometimes. I see you two together, and the only difference between me and Shep and you and Travis is that we're having sex. Other than that? No difference."

"There is a huge, huge difference. Is Shep bringing home different girls every night? Are you going to the party tomorrow to hang out with a guy with definite dating potential? You know I can't get involved with Travis, Mare. I don't even know why we're discussing it."

America's expression turned to disappointment. "I'm not seeing things, Abby. You have spent almost every moment with him for the last month. Admit it, you have feelings for him."

"Let it go, Mare," Travis said, tightening his towel around his waist.

America and I jumped at the sound of Travis's voice, and when my eyes met his, I could see the happiness was gone. He walked down the hall without another word, and America looked at me with a sad expression.

"I think you're making a mistake," she whispered. "You don't need to go to that party to meet a guy, you've got one that's crazy about you right here," she said, leaving me alone.

I rocked in the recliner, letting everything that had happened in the last week replay in my mind. Shepley was angry with me, America was disappointed in me, and Travis . . . he went from being happier than I'd ever seen him to so offended that he was speechless. Too nervous to crawl into bed with him, I watched the clock change from minute to minute.

An hour had passed when Travis came out of his room and down the hall. When he rounded the corner, I expected him to ask me to come to bed, but he was dressed and had his bike keys in his hand. His sunglasses were hiding his eyes, and he popped a cigarette in his mouth before grabbing the knob of the door.

"You're leaving?" I asked, sitting up. "Where are you going?"

"Out," he said, yanking the door open, and then slamming it closed behind him.

I fell back in the recliner and huffed. I had somehow become the villain and had no idea how I'd managed to get there.

When the clock above the television read two a.m., I finally resigned myself to going to bed. The mattress was lonely without him, and the idea of calling his cell kept creeping into my mind. I had nearly fallen asleep when Travis's motorcycle pulled into the parking lot. Two car doors shut shortly after, and then several pairs of footsteps climbed the stairs. Travis fumbled with the lock, and then the door opened. He laughed and mumbled, and then I heard not one, but two female voices. Their giggling was interrupted by the distinct sounds of kissing and moaning. My heart sank, and I was instantly angry that I felt that way. My eyes clenched shut when one of the girls squealed, and then

I was sure the next sound was the three of them collapsing onto the couch.

I considered asking America for her keys, but Shepley's door was directly in view of the couch, and I couldn't stomach witnessing the picture that went along with the noises in the living room. I buried my head under the pillow, and then shut my eyes when the door popped open. Travis walked across the room, opened the top night-table drawer, picked through his bowl of condoms, and then shut the drawer, jogging down the hall. The girls giggled for what seemed like half an hour, and then it was quiet.

Seconds later, moans, humming, and shouting filled the apartment. It sounded as if a pornographic movie were being filmed in the living room. I covered my face with my hands, and shook my head. Whatever lines had blurred or disappeared in the last week, an impenetrable stone wall had gone up in their place. I shook off my ridiculous emotions, forcing myself to relax. Travis was Travis, and we were, without a doubt, friends, and only friends.

The shouting and other nauseating noises quieted down after an hour, followed by whining, and then grumbling by the women after being dismissed. Travis showered and then collapsed onto his side of the bed, turning his back to me. Even after his shower, he smelled like he'd drunk enough whiskey to sedate a horse, and I was livid that he'd driven his motorcycle home in such a state.

After the awkwardness faded and the anger weakened, I still couldn't sleep. When Travis's breaths were deep and even, I sat up to look at the clock. The sun was going to rise in less than an hour. I ripped the covers off of me, walked down the hall, and took a blanket from the hall cabinet. The only evidence of Travis's threesome was two empty condom packages on the floor. I stepped over them and fell into the recliner.

I closed my eyes. When I opened them again, America and Shepley were sitting quietly on the couch, watching a muted television. The sun lit the apartment, and I cringed when my back complained at any attempted movement.

America's attention darted to me. "Abby?" she said, rushing to my side. She watched me with wary eyes. She was waiting for anger, or tears, or another emotionally charged outburst.

Shepley looked miserable. "I'm sorry about last night, Abby. This is my fault."

I smiled. "It's okay, Shep. You don't have to apologize."

America and Shepley traded glances, and then she grabbed my hand. "Travis went to the store. He is . . . ugh, it doesn't matter what he is. I packed your stuff, and I'll take you to the dorms before he gets home so you don't have to deal with him."

It wasn't until that moment that I felt like crying; I had been kicked out. I worked to keep my voice smooth before I spoke. "Do I have time to take a shower?"

America shook her head. "Let's just go, Abby, I don't want you to have to see him. He doesn't deserve to—"

The door flew open, and Travis walked in, his arms laden with grocery sacks. He walked straight into the kitchen, furiously working to get the cans and boxes into the cabinets.

"When Pidge wakes up, let me know, okay?" he said in a soft voice. "I got spaghetti, and pancakes, and strawberries, and that oatmeal shit with the chocolate packets, and she likes Fruity Pebbles cereal, right, Mare?" he asked, turning.

When he saw me, he froze. After an awkward pause, his expression melted, and his voice was smooth and sweet. "Hey, Pigeon."

I couldn't have been more confused if I had woken up in a foreign country. Nothing made sense. At first I thought I had been evicted, and then Travis comes home with bags full of my favorite foods.

He took a few steps into the living room, nervously shoving his hands in his pockets. "You hungry, Pidge? I'll make you some pancakes. Or there's, uh... there's some oatmeal. And I got you some of that pink foamy shit that girls shave with, and a hair dryer, and a... a... just a sec, it's in here," he said, rushing to the bedroom.

The door opened and shut, and then he rounded the corner, the color gone from his face. He took a deep breath, and his eyebrows pulled in. "Your stuff's packed."

"I know," I said.

"You're leaving," he said, defeated.

I looked to America, who glowered at Travis as if she could kill him. "You actually expected her to stay?"

"Baby," Shepley whispered.

"Don't fucking start with me, Shep. Don't you dare defend him to me," America seethed.

Travis looked desperate. "I am so sorry, Pidge. I don't even know what to say."

"Come on, Abby," America said. She stood and pulled on my arm.

Travis took a step, but America pointed her finger at him. "So help me God, Travis! If you try to stop her, I will douse you with gasoline and light you on fire while you sleep!"

"America," Shepley said, sounding a bit desperate himself. I could see that he was torn between his cousin and the woman he loved, and I felt terrible for him. The situation was exactly what he had tried to avoid all along.

"I'm fine," I said, exasperated by the tension in the room.

"What do you mean, you're fine?" Shepley asked, almost hopeful.

I rolled my eyes. "Travis brought women home from the bar last night, so what?"

America looked worried. "Huh-uh, Abby. Are you saying you're okay with what happened?"

I looked to all of them. "Travis can bring home whoever he wants. It's his apartment."

America stared at me as if I'd lost my mind, Shepley was on the verge of a smile, and Travis looked worse than before.

"You didn't pack your things?" Travis asked.

I shook my head and looked at the clock; it was after two in the afternoon. "No, and now I'm going to have to unpack it all. I still have to eat, and shower, and get dressed . . ." I said, walking into the bathroom. Once the door closed behind me, I leaned against it and slid down to the floor. I was sure I had pissed off America beyond repair, but I'd made Shepley a promise, and I intended to keep my word.

A soft knock tapped on the door above me. "Pidge?" Travis said.

"Yeah?" I said, trying to sound normal.

"You're staying?"

"I can go if you want me to, but a bet's a bet."

The door vibrated with the soft bump of Travis's forehead

against it. "I don't want you leave, but I wouldn't blame you if you did."

"Are you saying I'm released from the bet?"

There was a long pause. "If I say yes, will you leave?"

"Well, yeah. I don't live here, silly," I said, forcing a small laugh.

"Then no, the bet's still in effect."

I looked up and shook my head, feeling tears burn my eyes. I had no idea why I was crying, but I couldn't stop. "Can I take a shower, now?"

"Yeah . . ." he sighed.

I heard America's shoes enter the hall and stomp by Travis. "You're a selfish bastard," she growled, slamming Shepley's door behind her.

I pushed myself up from the floor, turned on the shower, and then undressed, pulling the curtain closed behind me.

After another knock on the door, Travis cleared his throat. "Pigeon? I brought some of your stuff."

"Just set it on the sink. I'll get it."

Travis walked in and shut the door behind him. "I was mad. I heard you spitting out everything that's wrong with me to America and it pissed me off. I just meant to go out and have a few drinks and try to figure some things out, but before I knew it, I was piss drunk, and those girls . . ." He paused. "I woke up this morning and you weren't in bed, and when I found you on the recliner and saw the wrappers on the floor, I felt sick."

"You could have just asked me instead of spending all that money at the grocery store just to bribe me to stay."

"I don't care about the money, Pidge. I was afraid you'd leave and never speak to me again."

I cringed at his explanation. I hadn't stopped to think how it would make him feel to hear me talk about how wrong for me he was, and now the situation was too messed up to salvage.

"I didn't mean to hurt your feelings," I said, standing under the water.

"I know you didn't. And I know it doesn't matter what I say now, because I fucked things up . . . just like I always do."

"Trav?"

"Yeah?"

"Don't drive drunk on your bike anymore, okay?"

I waited for a full minute until he finally took a deep breath and spoke. "Yeah, okay," he said, shutting the door behind him.

Chapter Five
Parker Hayes

"COME IN," I CALLED, HEARING A KNOCK ON THE DOOR.
Travis froze in the doorway. "Wow."

I smiled and looked down at my dress. A bustier that elongated into a short skirt, it was admittedly more daring than what I had worn in the past. The material was thin, black, and see-through over a nude shell. Parker would be at that party, and I had every intention of being noticed.

"You look amazing," he said as I slid on my heels.

I gave his white dress shirt and jeans an approving nod. "You look nice, too."

His sleeves were bunched above his elbows, revealing the intricate tattoos on his forearms. I noticed that his favorite black leather cuff was around his wrist when he shoved his hands in his pockets.

America and Shepley waited for us in the living room.

"Parker is going to piss himself when he sees you," America giggled as Shepley led the way to the car.

Travis opened the door, and I slid into the backseat of Shepley's Charger. Although we had occupied that seat countless times before, it was suddenly awkward to sit next to him.

Cars lined the street; some even parked on the front lawn. The house was bursting at the seams, and people were still walking down the street from the dorms. Shepley pulled into the grass lot in the back, and America and I followed the boys inside.

Travis brought me a red plastic cup full of beer and then leaned in to whisper in my ear. "Don't take these from anyone but me or Shep. I don't want anyone slipping anything into your drink."

I rolled my eyes. "No one is going to put anything in my drink, Travis."

"Just don't drink anything that doesn't come from me, okay? You're not in Kansas anymore, Pigeon."

"I haven't heard that one before," I said sarcastically, taking a drink.

An hour had passed, and Parker was still a no-show. America and Shepley were dancing to a slow song in the living room when Travis tugged on my hand. "Wanna dance?"

"No, thanks," I said.

His face fell.

I touched his shoulder. "I'm just tired, Trav."

He put his hand on mine and began to speak, but when I looked beyond him I saw Parker. Travis noticed my expression and turned.

"Hey, Abby! You made it!" Parker smiled.

"Yeah, we've been here for an hour or so," I said, pulling my hand from under Travis's.

"You look incredible!" he yelled over the music.

"'Thanks!" I grinned, glancing over to Travis. His lips were pressed together, and a line had formed between his eyebrows.

Parker nodded toward the living room and smiled. "You wanna dance?"

I wrinkled my nose and shook my head. "Nah, I'm kinda tired."

Parker looked at Travis then. "I thought you weren't coming."

"I changed my mind," Travis said, irritated that he had to explain.

"I see that," Parker said, looking to me. "You wanna get some air?"

I nodded and then followed Parker up the stairs. He paused, reaching to take my hand as we climbed to the second floor. When we reached the top, he pushed open a pair of French doors to the balcony.

"Are you cold?" he asked.

"A little chilly," I said, smiling when he pulled off his jacket and covered my shoulders. "Thanks."

"You're here with Travis?"

"We rode together."

Parker's mouth stretched across his face in a broad grin, and then he looked out onto the lawn. A group of girls were in a huddle, arms hooked together to fight the cold. Crepe paper and beer cans littered the grass along with empty bottles of liquor. Amid the clutter, Sig Tau brothers were standing around their masterpiece: a pyramid of kegs decorated with white lights.

Parker shook his head. "This place is going to be destroyed in the morning. The cleanup crew is going to be busy."

"You have a cleanup crew?"

"Yeah," he smiled, "we call them freshmen."

"Poor Shep."

"He's not on it. He gets a pass because he's Travis's cousin, and he doesn't live in the House."

"Do you live in the House?"

Parker nodded. "The last two years. I need to get an apartment, though. I need a quieter place to study."

"Let me guess . . . Business major?"

"Biology, with a minor in Anatomy. I've got one more year left, take the MCAT, and then hopefully I'm off to Harvard Med."

"You already know you're in?"

"My dad went to Harvard. I mean, I don't know for sure, but he's a generous alumnus, if you know what I mean. I carry a 4.0, got a 2200 on my SATs, thirty-six on my ACTs. I'm in a good position for a spot."

"Your dad's a doctor?"

Parker confirmed it with a good-natured smile. "Orthopedic surgeon."

"Impressive."

"How about you?" he asked.

"Undecided."

"Typical freshman answer."

I sighed in dramatic fashion. "I guess I just blew my chances at being exceptional."

"Oh, you don't have to worry about that. I noticed you the first day of class. What are you doing in Calculus Three as a freshman?"

I smiled and twisted my hair around my finger. "Math is sort of easy for me. I packed on the classes in high school and took two summer courses at Wichita State."

"Now that's impressive," he said.

We stood on the balcony for over an hour, talking about everything from local eateries to how I became such good friends with Travis.

"I wouldn't mention it, but the two of you seem to be the topic of conversation."

"Great," I murmured.

"It's just unusual for Travis. He doesn't befriend women. He tends to make enemies of them more often than not."

"Oh, I don't know. I've seen more than a few who either have short-term memory loss or are all too forgiving when it comes to him."

Parker laughed. His white teeth gleamed against his golden tan. "People just don't understand your relationship. You have to admit, it's a bit ambiguous."

"Are you asking if I'm sleeping with him?"

He smiled. "You wouldn't be here with him if you were. I've known him since I was fourteen, and I'm well aware of how he operates. I'm curious about your friendship, though."

"It is what it is," I shrugged. "We hang out, eat, watch TV, study, and argue. That's about it."

Parker laughed out loud, shaking his head at my honesty. "I've heard you're the only person who's allowed to put Travis in his place. That's an honorable title."

"Whatever that means. He's not as bad as everyone makes him out to be."

The sky turned purple and then pink as the sun broke above the horizon. Parker looked at his watch, glancing over the railing to the thinning crowd on the lawn. "Looks like the party's over."

"I better track down Shep and Mare."

"Would you mind if I drove you home?" he asked.

I tried to subdue my excitement. "Not at all. I'll let America know." I walked through the door, and then cringed before turning around. "Do you know where Travis lives?"

Parker's thick brown eyebrows pulled in. "Yes, why?"

"That's where I'm staying," I said, bracing for his reaction.

"You're staying with Travis?"

"I sort of lost a bet, so I'm there for a month."

"A month?"

"It's a long story," I said, shrugging sheepishly.

"But you two are just friends?"

"Yes."

"Then I'll take you to Travis's," he smiled.

I trotted down the stairs to find America and passed a sullen Travis, who seemed annoyed with the drunken girl speaking to him. He followed me into the hall as I tugged on America's dress.

"You guys can go ahead. Parker offered me a ride home."

"What?" America said with excitement in her eyes.

"What?" Travis asked, angry.

"Is there a problem?" America asked him.

He glared at America, and then pulled me around the corner, his jaw flitting under his skin. "You don't even know the guy."

I pulled my arm from his grip. "This is none of your business, Travis."

"The hell if it's not. I'm not letting you ride home with a complete stranger. What if he tries something on you?"

"Good! He's cute!"

Travis's expression contorted from surprise to anger, and

I braced myself for what he might say next. "Parker Hayes, Pidge? Really? Parker Hayes," he repeated with disdain. "What kind of name is that, anyway?"

I crossed my arms. "Stop it, Trav. You're being a jerk."

He leaned in, seeming flustered. "I'll kill him if he touches you."

"I like him," I said, emphasizing every word.

He seemed stunned at my confession, and then his features turned severe. "Fine. If he ends up holding you down in the backseat of his car, don't come crying to me."

My mouth popped open; I was offended and instantly furious. "Don't worry, I won't," I said, shouldering past him.

Travis grabbed my arm and sighed, peering at me over his shoulder. "I didn't mean it, Pidge. If he hurts you—if he even makes you feel uncomfortable—you let me know."

The anger subsided, and my shoulders fell. "I know you didn't. But you have got to curb this overprotective big-brother thing you've got going on."

Travis laughed once. "I'm not playing the big brother, Pigeon. Not even close."

Parker rounded the corner and pushed his hands inside his pockets, offering his elbow to me. "All set?"

Travis clenched his jaw, and I stepped to the other side of Parker to distract him from Travis's expression. "Yeah, let's go." I took Parker's arm and walked with him a few steps before turning to say goodbye to Travis, but he was glowering at the back of Parker's head. His eyes darted to me, and then his features smoothed.

"Stop it," I said through my teeth, following Parker through the remnants of the crowd to his car.

"I'm the silver one." The headlights of his car blinked twice when he hit the keyless entry.

He opened the passenger side door, and I laughed. "You drive a Porsche?"

"She's not just a Porsche. She's a Porsche 911 GT3. There's a difference."

"Let me guess, it's the love of your life?" I said, quoting Travis's statement about his motorcycle.

"No, it's a car. The love of my life will be a woman with my last name."

I allowed a small smile, trying not to be overly affected by his sentiment. He held my hand to help me into the car, and when he slid behind the wheel, he leaned his head against his seat and smiled at me.

"What are you doing tonight?"

"Tonight?" I asked.

"It's morning. I want to ask you to dinner before someone else beats me to it."

A grin extended across my face. "I don't have any plans."

"I'll pick you up at six?"

"Okay," I said, watching him slink his fingers between mine.

Parker took me straight to Travis's, keeping to the speed limit, my hand in his. He pulled behind the Harley, and like before, opened my door. Once we reached the landing, he leaned down to kiss my cheek.

"Get some rest. I'll see you tonight," he whispered in my ear.

"'Bye," I said, turning the knob. When I pushed, the door gave way and I surged forward.

Travis grabbed my arm before I fell. "Easy there, Grace."

I turned to see Parker staring at us with an uncomfortable

expression. He leaned over to peer into the apartment. "Any humiliated, stranded girls in there I need to give a ride?"

Travis glared at Parker. "Don't start with me."

Parker smiled and winked. "I'm always giving him a hard time. I don't get to quite as often since he realized it's easier if he can get them to drive their own cars."

"I guess that does simplify things," I said, teasing Travis.

"Not funny, Pidge."

"Pidge?" Parker asked.

"It's, uh . . . short for Pigeon. It's just a nickname, I don't even know where he came up with it," I said. It was the first time I'd felt awkward about the name Travis had bestowed on me the night we met.

"You're going to have to fill me in when you find out. Sounds like a good story," Parker smiled. "Night, Abby."

"Don't you mean good morning?" I said, watching him trot down the stairs.

"That, too," he called back with a sweet smile.

Travis slammed the door, and I had to jerk my head back before it caught me in the face. "What?" I snapped.

Travis shook his head and walked to his bedroom. I followed him and then hopped on one foot to pull off my heel. "He's nice, Trav."

He sighed and walked over to me. "You're gonna hurt yourself," he said, hooking his arm around my waist with one hand and pulling off my heels with the other. He tossed them into the closet and then pulled off his shirt, making his way to the bed.

I unzipped my dress and shimmied it over my hips, kicking it into the corner. I yanked a T-shirt over my head and then unsnapped my bra, pulling it through the sleeve of my shirt. When

I wrapped my hair into a bun on top of my head, I noticed him staring.

"I'm sure there's nothing I have that you haven't seen before," I said, rolling my eyes. I slid under the covers and settled against my pillow, curling into a ball. He unbuckled his belt and pulled his jeans down, stepping out of them.

I waited while he stood quietly for a moment. I had my back to him, so I wondered what he was doing, standing beside the bed in silence. The bed concaved when he finally crawled onto the mattress beside me, and I stiffened when his hand rested on my hip.

"I missed a fight tonight," he said. "Adam called. I didn't go."

"Why?" I said, turning to face him.

"I wanted to make sure you got home."

I wrinkled my nose. "You didn't have to babysit me."

He traced the length of my arm with his finger, sending shivers up my spine. "I know. I guess I still feel bad about the other night."

"I told you I didn't care."

He sat up on his elbow, a dubious frown on his face. "Is that why you slept on the recliner? Because you didn't care?"

"I couldn't fall asleep after your . . . friends left."

"You slept just fine in the recliner. Why couldn't you sleep with me?"

"You mean next to a guy who still smelled like the pair of barflies he had just sent home? I don't know! How selfish of me!"

Travis winced. "I said I was sorry."

"And I said I didn't care. Good night," I said, turning over.

Several moments of silence passed. He slid his hand across

the top of my pillow, resting his hand on mine. He caressed the delicate pieces of skin between my fingers, and then he pressed his lips against my hair. "As worried as I was that you'd never speak to me again . . . I think it's worse that you're indifferent."

My eyes closed. "What do you want from me, Travis? You don't want me to be upset about what you did, but you want me to care. You tell America that you don't want to date me, but you get so pissed off when I say the same thing that you storm out and get ridiculously drunk. You don't make any sense."

"Is that why you said those things to America? Because I said I wouldn't date you?"

My teeth clenched. He had just insinuated that I was playing games with him. I formed the most direct answer I could think of. "No, I meant what I said. I just didn't mean it as an insult."

"I just said that because," he scratched his short hair nervously, "I don't want to ruin anything. I wouldn't even know how to go about being who you deserve. I was just trying to get it worked out in my head."

"Whatever that means. I have to get some sleep. I have a date tonight."

"With Parker?" he asked, anger seeping through his tone.

"Yes. Can I please go to sleep?"

"Sure," he said, shoving himself off the bed and then slamming the door behind him. The recliner squeaked under his weight, and then muffled voices from the television drifted down the hall. I forced my eyes shut and tried to calm down enough to doze off, even if it was just for a few hours.

The clock read three p.m. when I peeled my eyes open. I grabbed a towel and my robe, and then trudged into the bathroom. As soon as I closed the shower curtain, the door opened and shut. I waited for someone to speak, but the only sound was the toilet lid smacking against porcelain.

"Travis?"

"Nope, it's me," America said.

"Do you have to pee in here? You have your own bathroom."

"Shep has been in there for half an hour with the beer shits. Not going in there."

"Nice."

"I hear you have a date tonight. Travis is pissed!" she lilted.

"At six! He is so sweet, America. He's just . . ." I trailed off, sighing. I was gushing, and it wasn't like me to gush. I kept thinking about how perfect he had been since the moment we'd met. He was exactly what I needed: the polar opposite of Travis.

"Rendered you speechless?" she giggled.

I poked my head from the curtain. "I didn't want to come home! I could have talked to him forever!"

"Sounds promising. Isn't it kind of weird that you're here, though?"

I ducked under the water, rinsing away the suds. "I explained it to him."

The toilet flushed, and the faucet turned on, making the water flash cold for a moment. I cried out and the door flew open.

"Pidge?" Travis said.

America laughed. "I just flushed the toilet, Trav, calm down."

"Oh. You all right, Pigeon?"

"I'm great. Get out." The door shut again and I sighed. "Is it too much to ask for locks on the doors?" America didn't answer. "Mare?"

"It's really too bad you two couldn't get on the same page. You're the only girl who could have . . ." She sighed. "Never mind. It doesn't matter, now."

I turned off the water and wrapped myself in a towel. "You're as bad as he is. It's a sickness . . . no one here makes sense. You're pissed at him, remember?"

"I know," she nodded.

I turned on my new hair dryer and began the process of primping for my date with Parker. I curled my hair and painted my nails and lips a deep shade of red. It was a bit much for a first date. I frowned at myself in the mirror. It wasn't Parker I was trying to impress. I wasn't in a position to be insulted when Travis accused me of playing games, after all.

As I took one last glance at myself in the mirror, guilt washed over me. Travis was trying so hard, and I was being a stubborn brat. I walked out into the living room and Travis smiled, not the reaction I had expected at all.

"You . . . are beautiful."

"Thank you," I said, rattled by the absence of irritation or jealousy in his voice.

Shepley whistled. "Nice choice, Abby. Guys dig red."

"And the curls are gorgeous," America added.

The doorbell chimed and America smiled, waving with exaggerated excitement. "Have fun!"

I opened the door. Parker held a small bouquet of flowers, wearing slacks and a tie. His eyes did a quick once-over from my dress to my shoes and then back up.

"You are the most beautiful creature I've ever seen," he said, enamored.

I looked behind me to wave to America, whose smile was so wide I could see every one of her teeth. Shepley wore the expression of a proud father, and Travis kept his eyes on the television.

Parker held out his hand, leading me to his shiny Porsche. Once we were inside, he let out a puff of air.

"What?" I asked.

"I have to say, I was a bit nervous about picking up the woman Travis Maddox is in love with . . . from his apartment. You don't know how many people have accused me of insanity today."

"Travis is not in love with me. He can barely stand to be near me sometimes."

"Then it's a love-hate relationship? Because when I broke it to my brothers that I was taking you out tonight, they all said the same thing. He's been behaving so erratically—even more than usual—that they've all come to the same conclusion."

"They're wrong," I insisted.

Parker shook his head as if I were utterly clueless. He rested his hand on mine. "We'd better go. I have a table waiting."

"Where?"

"Biasetti's. I took a chance . . . I hope you like Italian."

I raised one eyebrow. "Wasn't it short notice for reservations? That place is always packed."

"Well . . . it's our restaurant. Half, anyway."

"I like Italian."

Parker drove to the restaurant at exactly the speed limit, using his turn signal appropriately and slowing at a reasonable rate for each yellow light. When he spoke, he barely took his eyes from the road. When we arrived at the restaurant, I giggled.

"What?" he asked.

"You're just . . . a very cautious driver. It's a good thing."

"Different from the back of Travis's motorcycle?" he smiled.

I should have laughed, but the difference didn't feel like a good thing. "Let's not talk about Travis tonight. Okay?"

"Fair enough," he said, leaving his seat to open my door.

We were seated right away at a table by a large bay window. Although I was in a dress, I looked impoverished compared to the other women in the restaurant. They were dripping with diamonds and wearing cocktail dresses. I'd never eaten anywhere so swanky.

We ordered, and Parker closed his menu, smiling at the waiter. "And bring us a bottle of the Allegrini Amarone, please."

"Yes, sir," the waiter said, taking our menus.

"This place is unbelievable," I whispered, leaning against the table.

His green eyes softened. "Thank you, I'll let my father know you think so."

A woman approached our table. Her blond hair was pulled into a tight French bun, a gray streak interrupting the smooth wave of her bangs. I tried not to stare at the sparkling jewels resting around her neck, or those swaying back and forth on her ears, but they were made to be noticed. Her squinty blue eyes targeted me.

She quickly turned away to look at my date. "Who's your friend, Parker?"

"Mother, this is Abby Abernathy. Abby, this is my mother, Vivienne Hayes."

I extended my hand and she shook it once. In a well-practiced move, interest lit the sharp features of her face, and she looked to Parker. "Abernathy?"

I gulped, worried that she had recognized the name.

Parker's expression turned impatient. "She's from Wichita, Mom. You don't know her family. She goes to Eastern."

"Oh?" Vivienne eyed me again. "Parker is leaving next year for Harvard."

"That's what he said. I think that's great. You must be very proud."

The tension around her eyes smoothed a bit, and the corners of her mouth turned up in a smug grin. "We are. Thank you."

I was amazed at how her words were so polite, and yet they dripped with insult. It wasn't a talent she had developed overnight. Mrs. Hayes must have spent years impressing her superiority upon others.

"It's good to see you, Mom. Good night." She kissed his cheek, rubbed the lipstick off with her thumb, and then returned to her table. "Sorry about that, I didn't know she would be here."

"It's fine. She seems . . . nice."

Parker laughed. "Yes, for a piranha." I stifled a giggle, and he offered an apologetic smile. "She'll warm up. It just takes her a while."

"Hopefully by the time you leave for Harvard."

We talked endlessly about the food, Eastern, calculus, and even the Circle. Parker was charming and funny and said all the right things. Various people approached Parker to greet him, and he always introduced me with a proud smile. He was regarded as a celebrity within the walls of the restaurant, and when we left, I felt the appraising eyes of everyone in the room.

"Now what?" I asked.

"I'm afraid I have a midterm in Comparative Vertebrate

Anatomy first thing Monday morning. I have some studying to do," he said, covering my hand with his.

"Better you than me," I said, trying not to seem too disappointed.

He drove to the apartment, and then led me up the stairs by the hand.

"Thank you, Parker." I was aware of the ridiculous grin on my face. "I had a fantastic time."

"Is it too early to ask for a second date?"

"Not at all," I beamed.

"I'll call you tomorrow?"

"Sounds perfect."

Then came the moment of awkward silence. The element of dates I dread. To kiss or not to kiss, I hated that question.

Before I had a chance to wonder whether he would kiss me or not, he touched each side of my face and pulled me to him, pressing his lips against mine. They were soft and warm and wonderful. He pulled back once and then kissed me again.

"Talk to you tomorrow, Abs."

I waved, watching him walk down the steps to his car. "'Bye."

Once again, when I turned the knob, the door yanked away and I fell forward. Travis caught me, and I regained my footing.

"Would you stop that?" I said, closing the door behind me.

"'Abs'? What are you, a workout video?" he sneered.

"'Pigeon'?" I said with the same amount of disdain. "An annoying bird that craps all over the sidewalk?"

"You like Pigeon," he said defensively. "It's a dove, an attractive girl, a winning card in poker, take your pick. You're my Pigeon."

I grabbed his arm to remove my heels and then walked to

his room. As I changed into my pajamas, I tried my best to stay mad at him.

Travis sat on the bed and crossed his arms. "Did you have a good time?"

"I had," sigh, "a fantastic time. A perfect time. He's . . ." I couldn't think of an adequate word to describe him, so I just shook my head.

"He kissed you?"

I pressed my lips together and nodded. "He's got really soft lips."

Travis recoiled. "I don't care what kind of lips he has."

"Trust me, it's important. I get so nervous with first kisses, too, but this one wasn't so bad."

"You get nervous about a kiss?" he asked, amused.

"Just first kisses. I loathe them."

"I'd loathe them, too, if I had to kiss Parker Hayes."

I giggled and left for the bathroom to scrub the makeup from my face. Travis followed, leaning against the doorjamb. "So you're going out again?"

"Yep. He's calling me tomorrow." I dried my face and scampered down the hall, hopping into the bed.

Travis stripped down to his boxers, and sat down with his back to me. A bit slumped over, he looked exhausted. The lean muscles of his back stretched as he did, and he glanced back at me for a moment. "If you had such a good time, why are you home so early?"

"He has a big test on Monday."

Travis wrinkled his nose. "Who cares?"

"He's trying to get into Harvard. He has to study."

He huffed, crawling onto his stomach. I watched him shove

his hands under his pillow, seeming irritated. "Yeah, that's what he keeps telling everyone."

"Don't be an ass. He has priorities . . . I think it's responsible."

"Shouldn't his girl top his priorities?"

"I'm not his girl. We've been on one date, Trav," I scolded.

"So what did you guys do?" I shot him a dirty look and he laughed. "What? I'm curious!"

Seeing that he was sincere, I described everything, from the restaurant to the food to the sweet and funny things Parker said. I knew my mouth was frozen in a ridiculous grin, but I couldn't stop smiling while describing my perfect evening.

Travis watched me with an amused smile while I blathered on, even asking questions. Although he seemed frustrated with the situation regarding Parker, I had the distinct feeling that he enjoyed seeing me so happy.

Travis settled in on his side of the bed, and I yawned. We stared at each other for a moment before he sighed. "I'm glad you had a good time, Pidge. You deserve it."

"Thanks," I grinned. The ringtone of my cell phone reverberated from the night table, and I jerked up to look at the display.

"Hello?"

"It's tomorrow," Parker said.

I looked at the clock and laughed. It was 12:01. "It is."

"So what about Monday night?" he asked.

I covered my mouth for a moment and then took a deep breath. "Uh, yeah. Monday night is great."

"Good. I'll see you Monday," he said. I could hear the smile in his voice.

I hung up and glanced at Travis, who watched with mild annoyance. I turned away from him and curled into a ball, tensing with excitement.

"You're such a girl," Travis said, turning his back to me.

I rolled my eyes.

He turned over, pulling me to face him. "You really like Parker?"

"Don't ruin this for me, Travis!"

He stared at me for a moment, and then shook his head, turning away once again. "Parker Hayes."

Chapter Six
Turning Point

MONDAY NIGHT'S DATE MET MY EVERY EXPECTATION. We ate Chinese food while I giggled at Parker's skills with chopsticks. When he brought me home, Travis opened the door before he could kiss me. When we went out the following Wednesday night, Parker made sure to kiss me in the car.

Thursday at lunch, Parker met me in the cafeteria and surprised everyone when he sat in Travis's spot. When Travis finished his cigarette and came inside, he walked past Parker with indifference, sitting at the end of the table. Megan approached him but was instantly disappointed when he waved her off. Everyone at the table was quiet after that, and I found it difficult to focus on anything Parker talked about.

"I'm assuming I just wasn't invited," Parker said, catching my attention.

"What?"

"I heard your birthday party is on Sunday. I wasn't invited?"

America peeked at Travis, who glared at Parker as if he were seconds away from mowing him down.

"It was a surprise party, Parker," America said softly.

"Oh," Parker said, cringing.

"You're throwing me a surprise party?" I asked America.

She shrugged. "It was Trav's idea. It's at Brazil's on Sunday. Six o'clock."

Parker's cheeks flushed a faint red. "I suppose I'm really not invited, now."

"No! Of course you are!" I said, holding his hand on top of the table. Twelve pairs of eyes zeroed in on our hands. I could see that Parker was just as uncomfortable with the attention as I was, so I let go and pulled my hands onto my lap.

Parker stood up. "I have a few things I need to do before class. I'll call you later."

"Okay," I said, offering an apologetic smile.

Parker leaned over the table and kissed my lips. The silence was cafeteria-wide, and America elbowed me after Parker walked out.

"Isn't it creepy how everyone watches you?" she whispered. She glanced around the room with a frown. "What?" America yelled. "Mind your business, perverts!" One by one, heads turned away, and murmuring ensued.

I covered my eyes with my hands. "You know, before I was pathetic because I was thought to be Travis's poor clueless girl-friend. Now I'm evil because everyone thinks I'm bouncing back and forth between Travis and Parker like a Ping-Pong ball." When America didn't comment, I looked up. "What? Don't tell me you're buying into that crap, too!"

"I didn't say anything!" she said.

I stared at her in disbelief. "But that's what you think?"

America shook her head, but she didn't speak. The icy stares from the other students were suddenly apparent, and I stood up, walking to the end of the table.

"We need to talk," I said, tapping Travis's shoulder. I tried to sound polite, but the anger bubbling inside me put an edge to my words. The entire student populace, including my best friend, thought I was juggling two men. There was only one solution.

"So talk," Travis said, popping something breaded and fried into his mouth.

I fidgeted, noticing the curious eyes of everyone within earshot. When Travis still didn't move, I grabbed his arm and gave it a good tug. He stood up and followed me outside with a grin on his face.

"What, Pidge?" he said, looking at my hand on his arm and then at me.

"You've got to let me out of the bet," I begged.

His face fell. "You want to leave? Why? What'd I do?"

"You didn't do anything, Trav. Haven't you noticed everyone staring? I am quickly becoming the pariah of Eastern U."

Travis shook his head and lit a cigarette. "Not my problem."

"Yes, it is. Parker said everyone thinks he has a death wish because you're in love with me."

Travis's eyebrows shot up and he choked on the puff of smoke he'd just inhaled. "People are saying that?" he said between coughs.

I nodded. He looked away with wide eyes, taking another drag.

"Travis! You have to release me from the bet! I can't date Parker and live with you at the same time. It looks terrible!"

"So quit dating Parker."

I glared at him. "That's not the problem and you know it."

"Is that the only reason you want to leave? Because of what people are saying?"

"At least before I was clueless and you were the bad guy," I grumbled.

"Answer the question, Pidge."

"Yes!"

Travis looked beyond me to the students entering and leaving the cafeteria. He was deliberating, and I grew impatient while he took his time making his decision.

Finally, he stood tall, resolved. "No."

I shook my head, sure that I had misunderstood. "Excuse me?"

"No. You said so yourself: A bet's a bet. After the month's up, you'll be off with Parker, he'll become a doctor, you'll get married and have your 2.5 children, and I'll never see you again." He grimaced at his own words. "I still have three weeks. I'm not giving that up for lunchroom gossip."

I looked through the glass window to see the entire cafeteria watching us. The unwelcome attention made my eyes burn. I shouldered past him to walk to my next class.

"Pigeon," Travis called after me.

I didn't turn around.

That night, America sat on the tile floor of the bathroom, babbling about the boys while I stood in front of the mirror and pulled my hair into a ponytail. I was only half listening, thinking about how patient Travis had been—for Travis—knowing he didn't like the idea of Parker picking me up from his apartment every other night.

The expression on Travis's face when I asked him to let me out of the bet, and again when I told him people were saying he was in love with me, flashed in my mind. I couldn't stop wondering why he didn't deny it.

"Well, Shep thinks you're being too hard on him. He's never had anyone he's cared enough to—"

Travis poked his head in and smiled as he watched me fuss with my hair. "Wanna grab dinner?" he asked.

America stood up to look at herself in the mirror, combing her fingers through her golden hair. "Shep wants to check out that new Mexican place downtown if you guys wanna go."

Travis shook his head. "I thought me and Pidge could go alone tonight."

"I'm going out with Parker."

"Again?" he said, annoyed.

"Again," I said in a singsong voice.

The doorbell rang, and I hurried past Travis to open the door. Parker stood in front of me, his naturally wavy blond hair framing his clean-shaven face.

"Do you ever look less than gorgeous?" Parker asked.

"Based on the first time she came over here, I'm going to say yes," Travis said from behind me.

I rolled my eyes and smiled, holding up a finger to Parker to signal him to wait. I turned and threw my arms around Travis. He stiffened with surprise and then relaxed, pulling me tight against him.

I looked into his eyes and smiled. "Thanks for organizing my birthday party. Can I take a rain check on dinner?"

A dozen emotions scrolled across Travis's face, and then the corners of his mouth turned up. "Tomorrow?"

I squeezed him and grinned. "Absolutely." I waved to him as Parker grabbed my hand.

"What was that about?" Parker asked.

"We haven't been getting along lately. That was my version of an olive branch."

"Should I be worried?" he asked, opening my door.

"No." I kissed his cheek.

At dinner, Parker talked about Harvard, and the House, and his plans to search for an apartment. His eyebrows pulled in. "Will Travis be escorting you to your birthday party?"

"I'm not really sure. He hasn't said anything about it."

"If he doesn't mind, I'd like to take you." He took my hand in his and kissed my fingers.

"I'll ask him. The party was his idea, so . . ."

"I understand. If not, I'll just see you there," he smiled.

Parker took me to the apartment, slowing to a stop in the parking lot. When he kissed me goodbye, his lips lingered on mine. He yanked up the parking brake as his lips traveled along the ridge of my jaw to my ear and then halfway down my neck. It took me off guard, and I let out a quiet sigh in response.

"You are so beautiful," he whispered. "I've been distracted all night, with your hair pulled away from your neck." He peppered my neck with kisses and I exhaled, a hum escaping with my breath.

"What took you so long?" I smiled, lifting my chin to give him better access.

Parker focused on my lips. He grabbed each side of my face, kissing me a bit firmer than usual. We didn't have much room in the car, but we made the space available work to our advantage. He leaned against me, and I bent my knee as I fell against the window. His tongue slipped inside my mouth, and his hand grabbed my ankle and then slid up my leg to my thigh. The windows fogged within minutes with our labored breath sticking to the cool windows. His lips grazed my collarbone, and then his head jerked up when the glass vibrated with several loud thumps.

Parker sat up, and I righted myself, adjusting my dress. I jumped when the door flew open. Travis and America stood beside the car. America wore a sympathetic frown, and Travis seemed just short of flying into a blind rage.

"What the hell, Travis?" Parker yelled.

The situation suddenly felt dangerous. I'd never heard Parker raise his voice, Travis's knuckles were white as he balled them into fists at his sides—and I was in the way. America's hand seemed tiny when she placed it on Travis's bulky arm, shaking her head at Parker in silent warning.

"C'mon, Abby. I need to talk to you," she said.

"About what?"

"Just come on!" she snapped.

I looked to Parker, seeing the irritation in his eyes. "I'm sorry, I have to go."

"No, it's fine. Go ahead."

Travis helped me from the Porsche and then kicked the door shut. I flipped around and stood between him and the car, shoving his shoulder. "What is wrong with you? Knock it off!"

America seemed nervous. It didn't take long to figure out why. Travis reeked of whiskey; she had insisted on accompanying him, or he'd asked her to come. Either way she was a deterrent to violence.

The wheels of Parker's shiny Porsche squealed out of the

parking lot, and Travis lit a cigarette. "You can go in, now, Mare."

She tugged on my skirt. "C'mon, Abby."

"Why don't you stay, Abs," he seethed.

I nodded for America to go ahead and she reluctantly complied. I crossed my arms, ready for a fight, preparing myself to lash out at him after the inevitable lecture. Travis took several drags from his cigarette, and when it was obvious that he wasn't going to explain, my patience ran out.

"Why did you do that?" I asked.

"Why? Because he was mauling you in front of my apartment!" he yelled. His eyes were unfocused, and I could see that he was incapable of rational conversation.

I kept my voice calm. "I may be staying with you, but what I do and who I do it with is my business."

He flicked his cigarette to the ground. "You're so much better than that, Pidge. Don't let him fuck you in a car like a cheap prom date."

"I wasn't going to have sex with him!"

He gestured to the empty space where Parker's car sat. "What were you doing, then?"

"Haven't you ever made out with someone, Travis? Haven't you just messed around without letting it get that far?"

He frowned and shook his head as if I were speaking gibberish. "What's the point in that?"

"The concept exists for a lot of people . . . especially those that date."

"The windows were all fogged up, the car was bouncing . . . how was I supposed to know?" he said, waving his arms in the direction of the empty parking slot.

"Maybe you shouldn't spy on me!"

He rubbed his face and shook his head. "I can't stand this, Pigeon. I feel like I'm going crazy."

I threw out my hands and let them hit my thighs. "You can't stand what?"

"If you sleep with him, I don't wanna know about it. I'll go to prison for a long time if I find out he . . . just don't tell me."

"Travis," I seethed. "I can't believe you just said that! That's a big step for me!"

"That's what all girls say!"

"I don't mean the sluts you deal with! I mean me!" I said, holding my hand to my chest. "I haven't . . . ugh! Never mind." I walked away from him, but he grabbed my arm, twirling me around to face him.

"You haven't what?" he asked, weaving a bit. I didn't answer—I didn't have to. I could see the recognition light up his face and he laughed once. "You're a virgin?"

"So what?" I said, the blood under my cheeks igniting.

His eyes drifted from mine, in and out of focus as he tried to think through the whiskey. "That's why America was so sure it wouldn't get too far."

"I had the same boyfriend all four years of high school. He was an aspiring Baptist youth minister! It never came up!"

Travis's anger vanished, and relief was apparent in his eyes. "A youth minister? What happened after all that hard-earned abstinence?"

"He wanted to get married and stay in . . . Kansas. I didn't." I was desperate to change the subject. The amusement in Travis's eyes was humiliating enough. I didn't want him digging further into my past.

He took a step toward me and held each side of my face. "A virgin," he said, shaking his head. "I would have never guessed with the way you danced at the Red."

"Very funny," I said, stomping up the stairs.

Travis attempted to follow me but tripped and fell, rolling onto his back and laughing hysterically.

"What are you doing? Get up!" I said, helping him to his feet.

He hooked his arm around my neck, and I helped him up the stairs. Shepley and America were already in bed, so with no help in sight, I kicked off my heels to avoid breaking my ankles while walking Travis to the bedroom. He fell on his back to the bed, pulling me with him.

When we landed, my face was just inches from his. His expression was suddenly serious. He leaned up, nearly kissing me, but I pushed him away. Travis's eyebrows pulled in.

"Knock it off, Trav," I said.

He held me tight against him until I quit struggling, and then he flicked the strap of my dress, causing it to hang off my shoulder. "Since the word virgin came out of those beautiful lips of yours . . . I have a sudden urge to help you out of that dress."

"Well, that's too bad. You were ready to kill Parker for the same thing twenty minutes ago, so don't be a hypocrite."

"Fuck Parker. He doesn't know you like I do."

"Trav, c'mon. Let's get your clothes off and get you in bed."

"That's what I'm talkin' about," he chuckled.

"How much did you drink?" I asked, finally getting my footing between his legs.

"Enough," he smiled, pulling at the hem of my dress.

"You probably surpassed enough a gallon ago," I said, slapping his hand away. I planted my knee on the mattress beside him and pulled his shirt over his head. He reached for me again and I grabbed his wrist, sniffing at the pungent stench in the air. "God, Trav, you reek of Jack Daniel's."

"Jim Beam," he corrected with a drunken nod.

"It smells like burned wood and chemicals."

"It tastes like it, too," he laughed. I pulled open his belt buckle and yanked it from the loops. He laughed with the jerking motion and then lifted his head to look at me. "Better guard your virginity, Pidge. You know I like it rough."

"Shut up," I said, unbuttoning his jeans, slipping them down over his hips and then off his legs. I threw the denim to the floor and stood with my hands on my hips, breathing hard. His legs were hanging off the end of the bed, his eyes closed, his breathing deep and heavy. He had passed out.

I walked to the closet, shaking my head as I rifled through our clothes. I unzipped my dress and shoved it down over my hips, letting it fall to my ankles. Kicking it into the corner, I pulled off my ponytail holder and shook out my hair.

The closet was bursting with his clothes and mine, and I puffed, blowing my hair from my face as I searched through the mess for a T-shirt. As I pulled one off the hanger, Travis slammed into my back, wrapping his arms around my waist.

"You scared the shit outta me!" I complained.

He ran his hands over my skin. They felt different, slow and deliberate. I closed my eyes when he pulled me against him and buried his face in my hair, nuzzling my neck. As I felt his bare skin against mine, it took me a moment to protest.

"Travis . . ."

He pulled my hair to one side and grazed his lips along my

back from one shoulder to the other, unsnapping the clasp of my bra. He kissed the bare skin at the base of my neck and I closed my eyes; the warm softness of his mouth felt too good to make him stop. A quiet moan escaped from his throat when he pressed his pelvis against mine, and I could feel how much he wanted me through his boxers. I held my breath, knowing the only thing keeping us from that big step I was so opposed to a few moments before was two thin pieces of fabric.

Travis turned me to face him, and then pressed against me, leaning my back against the wall. Our eyes met, and I could see the ache in his expression as he scanned the bare pieces of my skin. I had seen him peruse women before, but this was different. He didn't want to conquer me; he wanted me to say yes.

He leaned in to kiss me, stopping just an inch away. I could feel the heat from his skin radiating against my lips, and I had to stop myself from drawing him in the rest of the way. His fingers were digging into my skin as he deliberated, and then his hands slid from my back to the hem of my panties. His index fingers slid down my hips in between my skin and the lacy fabric, and in the same moment that he was about to slip the delicate threads down my legs, he hesitated. Just when I opened my mouth to say yes, he clenched his eyes shut.

"Not like this," he whispered, brushing his lips across mine. "I want you, but not like this."

He stumbled, falling backward against the bed, and I stood for a moment with my arms crossed across my stomach. When his breathing evened out, I shoved my arms through the shirt I still had in my hand and yanked it over my head. Travis didn't move, and I blew out a slow breath of air, knowing I couldn't restrain either of us if I crawled in bed and he woke up with a less honorable perspective.

I hurried to the recliner and collapsed into it, covering my face with my hands. I felt the layers of frustration dancing and crashing into each other inside of me. Parker had left feeling slighted, Travis waited until I was seeing someone—someone I truly liked—to show an interest in me, and I seemed to be the only girl he couldn't bring himself to sleep with, even when he was wasted.

The next morning, I poured orange juice into a tall glass and took a sip as I bobbed my head to the music playing from my iPod. I had awakened before the sun and then squirmed in the recliner until eight. After that, I decided to clean up the kitchen to pass the time until my less ambitious roommates awoke. I loaded the dishwasher and swept and mopped, and then wiped the counters down. When the kitchen was sparkling, I grabbed the basket of clean clothes and sat on the couch, folding until there were a dozen or more piles surrounding me.

Murmuring came from Shepley's room. America giggled and then it was quiet for a few minutes more, followed by noises that made me feel a bit uncomfortable sitting alone in the living room.

I stacked the piles of folded clothes in the basket and carried it to Travis's room, smiling when I saw that he hadn't moved from where he had fallen the night before. I set the basket down and pulled the blanket over him, stifling a laugh when he turned over.

"View, Pigeon," he said, mumbling something inaudible before his breathing returned to slow and deep.

I couldn't help but watch him sleep; knowing he was dreaming about me sent a thrill through my veins that I couldn't explain. Travis seemed to settle back into a quiet sleep, so I decided to take a shower, hoping the sound of someone up and around would quiet Shepley and America's moans and the creaking and banging of the bed against the wall. When I turned off the water, I realized they weren't worried about who could hear.

I combed my hair, rolling my eyes at America's high-pitched yelps, more closely resembling a poodle than a porn star. The doorbell rang, and I grabbed my blue terry-cloth robe and tightened the belt, jogging across the living room floor. The noises from Shepley's bedroom immediately cut off, and I opened the door to Parker's smiling face.

"Good morning," he said.

I raked my wet hair back with my fingers. "What are you doing here?"

"I didn't like the way we said goodbye last night. I went out this morning to get your birthday present, and I couldn't wait to give it to you. So," he said, pulling a shiny box from his jacket pocket, "Happy Birthday, Abs."

He set the silver package in my hand, and I leaned in to kiss his cheek. "Thank you."

"Go ahead. I want to see your face when you open it."

I slipped my finger under the tape on the underside of the box, and then pulled the paper off, handing it to him. A rope of shimmering diamonds sat snugly in a white gold bracelet.

"Parker," I whispered.

He beamed. "You like it?"

"I do," I said, holding it in front of my face in awe, "but it's too much. I couldn't accept this if we'd been dating a year, much less a week."

Parker grimaced. "I thought you might say that. I searched high and low all morning for the perfect birthday present, and when I saw this, I knew there was only one place it could ever belong," he said, taking it from my fingers and clasping it around my wrist. "And I was right. It looks incredible on you."

I held up my wrist and shook my head, hypnotized by the brilliance of colors reacting to the sunlight. "It's the most beautiful thing I've ever seen. No one's ever given me anything so . . ." *expensive* came to mind, but I didn't want to say that, "elaborate. I don't know what to say."

Parker laughed, and then kissed my cheek. "Say that you'll wear it tomorrow."

I grinned from ear to ear. "I'll wear it tomorrow," I said, looking to my wrist.

"I'm glad you like it. The look on your face was worth the seven stores I went to."

I sighed. "You went to seven stores?" He nodded, and I took his face in my hands. "Thank you. It's perfect," I said, kissing him quickly.

He hugged me tight. "I have to get back. I'm having lunch with my parents, but I'll call you later, okay?"

"Okay. Thank you!" I called after him, watching him trot down the stairs.

I hurried into the apartment, unable to take my eyes off of my wrist.

"Holy shit, Abby!" America said, grabbing my hand. "Where did you get this?"

"Parker brought it. It's my birthday present," I said.

America gawked at me, and then down at the bracelet. "He bought you a diamond tennis bracelet? After a week? If I didn't know better, I'd say you have a magic crotch!"

I laughed out loud, beginning a ridiculous giggle-fest in the living room.

Shepley emerged from his bedroom, looking tired and satisfied. "What are you fruitcakes shrieking about in here?"

America held up my wrist. "Look! Her birthday present from Parker!"

Shepley squinted, and then his eyes popped open. "Whoa."

"I know, right?" America said, nodding.

Travis stumbled around the corner, looking a bit beat up. "You guys are loud as fuck," he groaned, buttoning his jeans.

"Sorry," I said, pulling my hand from America's grip. Our almost moment crept into my mind, and I couldn't seem to look him in the eyes.

He downed the rest of my orange juice, and then wiped his mouth. "Who in the hell let me drink that much last night?"

America sneered, "You did. You went out and bought a fifth after Abby left with Parker and killed the whole thing by the time she got back."

"Damn," he said, shaking his head. "Did you have fun?" he asked, looking to me.

"Are you serious?" I asked, showing my anger before thinking. "What?"

America laughed. "You pulled her out of Parker's car, seeing red when you caught them making out like high schoolers. They fogged up the windows and everything!"

Travis's eyes unfocused, scanning his memories of the night before. I worked to stifle my temper. If he didn't remember pulling me from the car, he wouldn't remember how close I came to handing my virginity to him on a silver platter.

"How pissed are you?" he asked, wincing.

"Pretty pissed." I was angrier that my feelings had nothing to do with Parker. I tightened my robe and stomped down the hall. Travis's footsteps were right behind me.

"Pidge," he said, catching the door when I shut it in his face. He slowly pushed it open and stood before me, waiting to suffer my wrath.

"Do you remember anything you said to me last night?" I asked.

"No. Why? Was I mean to you?" His bloodshot eyes were heavy with worry, which only served to amplify my anger.

"No, you weren't mean to me! You . . . we . . ." I covered my eyes with my hands and then froze when I felt Travis's hand on my wrist.

"Where'd this come from?" he said, glaring at the bracelet.

"It's mine," I said, pulling away from him.

He didn't take his eyes from my wrist. "I've never seen it before. It looks new."

"It is."

"Where'd you get it?"

"Parker gave it to me about fifteen minutes ago," I said, watching his face morph from confusion to rage.

"What the fuck was that douchebag doing here? Did he stay the night?" he asked, his voice rising with each question.

I crossed my arms. "He went shopping for my birthday present this morning and brought it by."

"It's not your birthday yet." His face turned a deep shade of red as he worked to keep his temper under control.

"He couldn't wait," I said, lifting my chin with stubborn pride.

"No wonder I had to drag your ass out of his car, sounds like you were . . ." he trailed off, pressing his lips together.

I narrowed my eyes. "What? Sounds like I was what?"

His jaws tensed and he took a deep breath, blowing it out from his nose. "Nothing. I'm just pissed off, and I was going to say something shitty that I didn't mean."

"It's never stopped you before."

"I know. I'm working on it," he said, walking to the door. "I'll let you get dressed."

When he reached for the knob, he paused, rubbing his arm. As soon as his fingers touched the tender splatter of purple pooling under his skin, he pulled up his elbow and noticed the bruise. He stared at it for a moment and then turned to me.

"I fell on the stairs last night. And you helped me to bed . . ." he said, sifting through the blurry images in his mind.

My heart was pounding, and I swallowed hard as I watched realization strike. His eyes narrowed. "We," he began, taking a step toward me, looking at the closet and then to the bed.

"No, we didn't. Nothing happened," I said, shaking my head.

He cringed, the memory obviously replaying in his mind. "You fog up Parker's windows, I pull you out of the car, and then I try to . . ." he said, shaking his head. He turned for the door and grabbed the knob, his knuckles white. "You're turning me into a fucking psycho, Pigeon," he growled over his shoulder. "I don't think straight when I'm around you."

"So it's my fault?"

He turned. His eyes fell from my face to my robe, to my

legs, and then my feet, returning to my eyes. "I don't know. My memory is a little hazy . . . but I don't recall you saying no."

I took a step forward, ready to argue that irrelevant little fact, but I couldn't. He was right. "What do you want me to say, Travis?"

He looked at the bracelet and then back at me with accusing eyes. "You were hoping I wouldn't remember?"

"No! I was pissed that you forgot!"

His brown eyes bored into mine. "Why?"

"Because if I would have . . . if we would have . . . and you didn't . . . I don't know why! I just was!"

He stormed across the room, stopping inches from me. His hands touched my cheeks, his breathing quick as he scanned my face. "What are we doin', Pidge?"

My eyes began at his belt and then rose over the muscles and tattoos of his stomach and chest, finally settling on the warm brown of his irises. "You tell me."

Chapter Seven
Nineteen

"Abby?" Shepley said, knocking on the door. "Mare was going to run some errands; she wanted me to let you know in case you needed to go."

Travis hadn't taken his eyes from mine. "Pidge?"

"Yeah," I called to Shepley. "I have some stuff I need to take care of."

"All right, she's ready to go when you are," Shepley said, his footsteps disappearing down the hall.

"Pidge?"

I pulled a few things from the closet and slid past him. "Can we talk about this later? I have a lot to do today."

"Sure," he said with a contrived smile.

It was a relief to escape to the bathroom. I quickly closed the door behind me. Two weeks left in the apartment and no way to put off the conversation—at least, not for that long. The logical part of my brain insisted that Parker was my type: attractive, smart, and interested in me. Why I bothered with Travis was something I would never understand.

Whatever the reason, it was making us both insane. I had

been divided into two separate people: the docile, polite person I was with Parker, and the angry, confused, frustrated person I turned into around Travis. The entire school had witnessed Travis going from unpredictable before to damn near volatile now.

I dressed quickly, leaving Travis and Shepley to go downtown with America. She giggled about her morning sexcapade with Shepley, and I listened with dutiful nods in all the right places. It was hard to focus on the topic at hand with the diamonds of my bracelet creating tiny dots of light on the ceiling of the car, reminding me of the choice I was suddenly faced with. Travis wanted an answer, and I didn't have one.

"Okay, Abby. What's going on? You've been quiet."

"This thing with Travis . . . it's just a mess."

"Why?" she said, her sunglasses pushing up when she wrinkled her nose.

"He asked me what we were doing."

"What are you doing? Are you with Parker or what?"

"I like him, but it's been a week. We're not serious or anything."

"You have feelings for Travis, don't you?"

I shook my head. "I don't know how I feel about him. I just don't see it happening, Mare. He's too much of a bad thing."

"Neither one of you will just come out and say it, that's the problem. You're both so scared of what might happen that you're fighting it tooth and nail. I know for a fact that if you looked Travis in the eye and told him you wanted him, he would never look at another woman again."

"You know that for a fact?"

"Yes. I have the inside track, remember?"

I paused in thought for a moment. Travis had been talking to Shepley about me, but Shepley wouldn't encourage a relationship by telling America. He knew she would tell me. This led me to the only conclusion: America had overheard them. I wanted to ask her what was said, but thought better of it.

"That situation is a broken heart just waiting to happen," I said, shaking my head. "I don't think he's capable of being faithful."

"He wasn't capable of carrying on a friendship with a female, either, but you two sure shocked the whole of Eastern."

I fingered my bracelet and sighed. "I don't know. I don't mind how things are. We can just be friends."

America shook her head. "Except that you're not just friends," she sighed. "You know what? I'm over this conversation. Let's go get our hair and makeup done. I'll buy you a new outfit for your birthday."

"I think that's exactly what I need," I said.

After hours of manicures, pedicures, being brushed, waxed, and powdered, I stepped into my shiny yellow high heels and tugged on my new gray dress.

"Now that's the Abby I know and love!" America laughed, shaking her head at my ensemble. "You have to wear that to your party tomorrow."

"Wasn't that the plan all along?" I said, smirking. My cell phone buzzed in my purse, and I held it to my ear. "Hello?"

"It's dinner time! Where the hell did you two run off to?" Travis said.

"We indulged in a little pampering. You and Shep knew how to eat before we came along. I'm sure you can manage."

"Well, no shit. We worry about you, ya know."

I looked at America and smiled. "We're fine."

"Tell him I'll have you back in no time. I have to stop by Brazil's to pick up some notes for Shep, and then we'll be home."

"Did you get that?" I asked.

"Yeah. See you then, Pidge."

We drove to Brazil's in silence. America turned off the ignition, staring at the apartment building ahead. Shepley asking America to drive over surprised me; we were just a block from Shepley and Travis's apartment.

"What's wrong, Mare?"

"Brazil just gives me the creeps. The last time I was here with Shep, he was being all flirty."

"Well, I'll go in with you. If he so much as winks at you, I'll stab him in the eye with my new heels, okay?"

America smiled and hugged me. "Thanks, Abby!"

We walked to the back of the building, and America took a deep breath before knocking on the door. We waited, but no one came.

"I guess he's not here?" I asked.

"He's here," she said, irritated. She banged on the wood with the side of her fist and then the door swung open.

"HAPPY BIRTHDAY!" the crowd inside yelled.

The ceiling was pink-and-black bubbles, every inch covered by helium balloons with long silver strings hanging down in the faces of the guests. The crowd separated, and Travis approached me with a broad smile, touching each side of my face and kissing my forehead.

"Happy birthday, Pigeon."

"It's not 'til tomorrow," I said. Still in shock, I tried smiling at everyone around us.

Travis shrugged. "Well, since you were tipped off, we had to make some last minute changes to surprise you. Surprised?"

"Very!" I said as Finch hugged me.

"Happy birthday, baby!" Finch said, kissing my lips.

America nudged me with her elbow. "Good thing I got you to run errands with me today or you would have shown up looking like ass!"

"You look great," Travis said, scanning my dress.

Brazil hugged me, pressing his cheek to mine. "And I hope you know America's Brazil-is-creepy story was just a line to get you in here."

I looked at America and she laughed. "It worked, didn't it?"

Once everyone took turns hugging me and wishing me a happy birthday, I leaned into America's ear. "Where's Parker?"

"He'll be here later," she whispered. "Shepley couldn't get him on the phone to let him know until this afternoon."

Brazil cranked up the volume on the stereo, and everyone screamed. "Come here, Abby!" he said, walking to the kitchen. He lined up shot glasses along the counter and pulled a bottle of tequila from the bar. "Happy birthday from the football team, baby girl," he smiled, pouring each shot glass full of Patrón. "This is the way we do birthdays: You turn nineteen, you have nineteen shots. You can drink 'em or give 'em away, but the more you drink, the more of these you get," he said, fanning out a handful of twenties.

"Oh my God!" I squealed.

"Drink 'em up, Pidge!" Travis said.

I looked to Brazil, suspicious. "I get a twenty for every shot I drink?"

"That's right, lightweight. Gauging by the size of you, I'm

going to say we'll get away with losing sixty bucks by the end of the night."

"Think again, Brazil," I said, grabbing the first shot glass, rolling it across my lip, tipping my head back to empty the glass and then rolling it the rest of the way, dropping it into my other hand.

"Holy shit!" Travis exclaimed.

"This is really a waste, Brazil," I said, wiping the corners of my mouth. "You shoot Cuervo, not Patrón."

The smug smile on Brazil's face faded, and he shook his head and shrugged. "Get after it, then. I've got the wallets of twelve football players that say you can't finish ten."

I narrowed my eyes. "Double or nothing says I can drink fifteen."

"Whoa!" Shepley cried. "You're not allowed to hospitalize yourself on your birthday, Abby!"

"She can do it," America said, staring at Brazil.

"Forty bucks a shot?" Brazil said, looking unsure.

"Are you scared?" I asked.

"Hell no! I'll give you twenty a shot, and when you make it to fifteen, I'll double your total."

"That's how Kansans do birthdays," I said, popping back another shot.

An hour and three shots later, I was in the living room dancing with Travis. The song was a rock ballad, and Travis mouthed the words to me as we danced. He dipped me at the end of the first chorus, and I let my arms fall behind me. He popped me back up, and I sighed.

"You can't do that when I start getting into the double-digit shots," I giggled.

"Did I tell you how incredible you look tonight?"

I shook my head and hugged him, laying my head on his shoulder. He tightened his grip, and buried his face in my neck, making me forget about decisions or bracelets or my separate personalities; I was exactly where I wanted to be.

When the music changed to a faster beat, the door opened.

"Parker!" I said, running over to hug him. "You made it!"

"Sorry I'm late, Abs," he said, pressing his lips against mine. "Happy birthday."

"Thanks," I said, seeing Travis stare at us from the corner of my eye.

Parker lifted my wrist. "You wore it."

"I said I would. Wanna dance?"

He shook his head. "Uh . . . I don't dance."

"Oh. Well, you wanna witness my sixth shot of Patrón?" I smiled, holding up my five twenties. "I make double if I get to fifteen."

"That's a bit dangerous, isn't it?"

I leaned into his ear. "I am totally hustling them. I've played this game with my dad since I was sixteen."

"Oh," he said, frowning with disapproval. "You drank tequila with your dad?"

I shrugged. "It was his way of bonding."

Parker seemed unimpressed as his eyes left mine, scanning the crowd. "I can't stay long. I'm leaving early for a hunting trip with my father."

"It's a good thing my party was tonight, or you wouldn't have made it tomorrow," I said, surprised to hear of his plans.

He smiled and took my hand. "I would have made it back in time."

I pulled him to the kitchen, picked up another shot glass, and killed it, slamming it on the counter upside down like I had the previous five. Brazil handed me another twenty, and I danced into the living room. Travis grabbed me, and we danced with America and Shepley.

Shepley slapped me on the butt. "One!"

America added a second swat on my backside, and then the entire party joined in, sans Parker.

At number nineteen, Travis rubbed his hands together. "My turn!"

I rubbed my sore posterior. "Be easy! My ass hurts!"

With an evil smirk, he reared his hand far above his shoulder. I closed my eyes tight. After a few moments, I peeked back. Just before his hand made contact, he stopped and gave me a gentle pat.

"Nineteen!" he exclaimed.

The guests cheered, and America started a drunken rendition of "Happy Birthday." I laughed when the part came to say my name and the entire room sang "Pigeon."

Another slow song came over the stereo, and Parker pulled me to the makeshift dance floor. It didn't take me long to figure out why he didn't dance.

"Sorry," he said after stepping on my toes for the third time.

I leaned my head on his shoulder. "You're doing just fine," I lied.

He pressed his lips against my temple. "What are you doing Monday night?"

"Going to dinner with you?"

"Yes. In my new apartment."

"You found one!"

He laughed and nodded. "We'll order in, though. My cooking isn't exactly edible."

"I'd eat it, anyway," I said, smiling up at him.

Parker glanced around the room and then led me to a hallway. He gently pressed me against the wall, kissing me with his soft lips. His hands were everywhere. At first I played along, but after his tongue infiltrated my lips, I got the distinct feeling that I was doing something wrong.

"Okay, Parker," I said, maneuvering away.

"Everything all right?"

"I just think it's rude of me to make out with you in a dark corner when I have guests out there."

He smiled and kissed me again. "You're right, I'm sorry. I just wanted to give you a memorable birthday kiss before I left."

"You're leaving?"

He touched my cheek. "I have to wake up in four hours, Abs."

I pressed my lips together. "Okay. I'll see you Monday?"

"You'll see me tomorrow. I'll stop by when I get back."

He led me to the door and then kissed my cheek before he left. I noticed that Shepley, America, and Travis were all staring at me.

"Daddy's gone!" Travis yelled when the door closed. "Time to get the party started!"

Everyone cheered, and Travis pulled me to the center of the floor.

"Hang on . . . I'm on a schedule," I said, leading him by the hand to the counter. I knocked back another shot, and laughed when Travis took one from the end, sucking it down. I grabbed another and swallowed, and he did the same.

"Seven more, Abby," Brazil said, handing me two more twenty-dollar bills.

I wiped my mouth as Travis pulled me to the living room again. I danced with America and then Shepley, but when Chris Jenks from the football team tried to dance with me, Travis pulled him back by the shirt and shook his head. Chris shrugged and turned, dancing with the first girl he saw.

The tenth shot hit hard, and I felt a little dizzy standing on Brazil's couch with America, dancing like clumsy grade-schoolers. We giggled over nothing, waving our arms around to the beat.

I stumbled, nearly falling off the couch backward, but Travis's hands were instantly on my hips to steady me.

"You've made your point," he said. "You've drunk more than any girl we've ever seen. I'm cutting you off."

"The hell you are," I slurred. "I have six hundred bucks waiting on me at the bottom of that shot glass, and you of all people aren't going to tell me I can't do something extreme for cash."

"If you're that hard up for money, Pidge . . ."

"I'm not borrowing money from you," I sneered.

"I was gonna suggest pawning that bracelet," he smiled.

I smacked him on the arm just as America started the count-down to midnight. When the hands of the clock superimposed on the twelve, we all celebrated.

I was nineteen.

America and Shepley kissed each of my cheeks, and then Travis lifted me off the ground, twirling me around.

"Happy birthday, Pigeon," he said with a soft expression.

I stared into his warm brown eyes for a moment, feeling lost inside of them. The room was frozen in time as we stared at each other, so close I could feel his breath on my skin.

"Shots!" I said, stumbling to the counter.

"You look torn up, Abby. I think it's time to call it a night," Brazil said.

"I'm not a quitter," I said. "I wanna see my money."

Brazil placed a twenty under the last two glasses, and then he yelled at his teammates, "She's gonna drink 'em! I need fifteen!"

They all groaned and rolled their eyes, pulling out their wallets to form a stack of twenties behind the last shot glass. Travis had emptied the other four shots on the other side of my fifteen.

"I would have never believed that I could lose fifty bucks on a fifteen-shot bet with a girl," Chris complained.

"Believe it, Jenks," I said, picking up a glass in each hand.

I knocked back each of the glasses and waited for the vomit rising in my throat to settle.

"Pigeon?" Travis asked, taking a step in my direction.

I raised a finger and Brazil smiled. "She's going to lose it," he said.

"No, she won't," America shook her head. "Deep breath, Abby."

I closed my eyes and inhaled, picking up the last shot.

"Holy God, Abby! You're going to die of alcohol poisoning!" Shepley cried.

"She's got this," America assured him.

I tipped my head and let the tequila flow down my throat. My teeth and lips had been numb since shot number eight, and the kick of the eighty proof had long since lost its edge. The entire party erupted into whistles and yells as Brazil handed me the stack of money.

"Thank you," I said with pride, tucking the money away in my bra.

"You are incredibly sexy right now," Travis said in my ear as we walked to the living room.

We danced into the morning, and the tequila running through my veins eased me into oblivion.

Chapter Eight
Rumors

WHEN MY EYES FINALLY PEELED OPEN, I SAW THAT MY pillow consisted of denim and legs. Travis sat with his back against the tub; his head leaned against the wall, passed out cold. He looked as rough as I felt. I pulled the blanket off of me and stood up, gasping at my horrifying reflection in the mirror above the sink.

I looked like death.

Mascara smeared, black tearstains down my cheek, lipstick smudged across my mouth, and my hair had balls of rats on each side.

Sheets, towels, and blankets surrounded Travis. He had fashioned a soft pallet to sleep on while I expelled the fifteen shots of tequila I'd consumed the night before. Travis had held my hair out of the toilet, and sat with me all night.

I turned on the faucet, holding my hand under the water until it was the temperature I wanted. Scrubbing the mess from my face, I heard a moan from the floor. Travis stirred, rubbed his eyes, and stretched, and then looked beside him, jerking in a panic.

"I'm right here," I said. "Why don't you go to bed? Get some sleep?"

"You okay?" he said, wiping his eyes once more.

"Yeah, I'm good. Well, good as I can be. I'll feel better once I get a shower."

He stood up. "You took my crazy title last night, just so you know. I don't know where that came from, but I don't want you to do it again."

"It's pretty much what I grew up around, Trav. Not a big deal."

He took my chin in his hands and wiped the remaining smeared mascara from under my eyes with his thumbs. "It was a big deal to me."

"Fine, I won't do it again. Happy?"

"Yes. But I have something to tell you, if you promise not to freak out."

"Oh, God, what did I do?"

"Nothing, but you need to call America."

"Where is she?"

"At Morgan. She got into it with Shep last night."

I rushed through my shower and yanked on the clothes Travis had set on the sink. When I emerged from the bathroom, Shepley and Travis were sitting in the living room.

"What did you do to her?" I demanded.

Shepley's face fell. "She's really pissed at me."

"What happened?"

"I was mad that she encouraged you to drink so much. I thought we were going to end up taking you to the hospital. One thing led to another, and the next thing I know, we're screaming at each other. We were both drunk, Abby. I said some things I can't take back," he shook his head, looking to the floor.

"Like what?" I said, angry.

"I called her a few names I'm not proud of and then told her to leave."

"You let her leave here drunk? Are you some kind of idiot?" I said, grabbing at my purse.

"Easy, Pidge. He feels bad enough," Travis said.

I fished my cell phone out of my purse, dialing America's number.

"Hello?" she answered. She sounded awful.

"I just heard," I sighed. "Are you okay?" I walked down the hall for privacy, glancing back once to shoot a dirty look at Shepley.

"I'm fine. He's an asshole." Her words were abrupt, but I could hear the hurt in her voice. America had mastered the art of hiding her emotions, and she could have hidden it from anyone but me.

"I'm sorry I didn't go with you."

"You were out of it, Abby," she said dismissively.

"Why don't you come get me? We can talk about it."

She breathed into the phone. "I don't know. I don't really feel like seeing him."

"I'll tell him to stay inside, then."

After a long pause, I heard keys clink in the background. "All right. I'll be there in a minute."

I walked into the living room, pulling my purse over my shoulder. They watched me open the door to wait for America, and Shepley scooted forward on the couch.

"She's coming here?"

"She doesn't want to see you, Shep. I told her you'd stay inside."

He sighed and fell against the cushion. "She hates me."

"I'll talk to her. You better get one amazing apology together, though."

Ten minutes later, a car horn beeped twice outside, and I closed the door behind me. When I reached the bottom of the stairs, Shepley rushed past me to America's red Honda, and hunched over to see her through the window. I stopped in my tracks, watching America snub him as she looked straight ahead. She rolled down her window, and Shepley seemed to be explaining, and then they began to argue. I went inside to give them their privacy.

"Pigeon?" Travis said, trotting down the stairs.

"It doesn't look good."

"Let them figure it out. Come inside," he said, intertwining his fingers in mine to lead me up the stairs.

"Was it that bad?" I asked.

He nodded. "It was pretty bad. They're just getting out of the honeymoon stage, though. They'll work it out."

"For someone that's never had a girlfriend, you seem to know about relationships."

"I have four brothers and a lot of friends," he said, grinning to himself.

Shepley stomped into the apartment and slammed the door behind him. "She's fucking impossible!"

I kissed Travis on the cheek. "That's my cue."

"Good luck," Travis said.

I slid in beside America, and she huffed. "He's fucking impossible!"

I giggled, but she shot a glare in my direction. "Sorry," I said, forcing my smile to fade.

We set out for a drive and America yelled and cried and yelled some more. At times she broke into rants that seemed to be directed at Shepley, as if he were sitting in my place. I sat quietly, letting her work it out in a way only America can.

"He called me irresponsible! Me! As if I don't know you! As if I haven't seen you rob your dad of hundreds of dollars drinking twice as much. He doesn't know what the hell he's talking about! He doesn't know what your life was like! He doesn't know what I know, and he acts like I'm his child instead of his girlfriend!" I rested my hand on hers, but she pulled it away. "He thought you would be the reason we wouldn't work out, and then he ended up doing the job on his own. And speaking of you, what the hell was that last night with Parker?"

The sudden change of topic took me by surprise. "What do you mean?"

"Travis threw you that party, Abby, and you go off and make out with Parker. And you wonder why everyone is talking about you!"

"Hold on a minute! I told Parker we shouldn't be back there. What does it matter if Travis threw me that party or not? I'm not with him!"

America looked straight ahead, blowing a puff of air from her nose.

"All right, Mare. What is it? You're mad at me now?"

"I'm not mad at you. I just don't associate with complete idiots."

I shook my head and then looked out the window before I said something I couldn't take back. America had always been able to make me feel like shit on command.

"Do you even see what's going on?" she asked. "Travis quit

fighting. He doesn't go out without you. He hasn't brought any girls home since the bimbo twins, has yet to murder Parker, and you're worried that people are saying you're playing them both. You know why that is, Abby? Because it's the truth!"

I turned, slowly craning my neck in her direction, trying to give her the dirtiest look I knew how. "What the hell is wrong with you?

"You're dating Parker now, and you're so happy," she said in a mocking tone. "Then why aren't you at Morgan?"

"Because I lost the bet, you know that!"

"Give me a break, Abby! You talk about how perfect Parker is, you go on these amazing dates with him, talk to him for hours on the phone, and then you lie next to Travis every night. Do you see what's wrong with this situation? If you really liked Parker, your stuff would be at Morgan right now."

I clenched my teeth. "You know I've never welshed on a bet, Mare."

"That's what I thought," she said, twisting her hands around the steering wheel. "Travis is what you want, and Parker is what you think you need."

"I know it looks that way, but—"

"It looks that way to everyone. So if you don't like the way people are talking about you—change. It's not Travis's fault. He's done a 180 for you. You're reaping the rewards, and Parker's getting the benefits."

"A week ago you wanted to pack me up and never let Travis come near me again! Now you're defending him?"

"Abigail! I'm not defending him, stupid! I'm looking out for you! You're both crazy about each other! Do something about it!"

"How could you possibly think I should be with him?" I wailed. "You are supposed to be keeping me away from people like him!"

She pressed her lips together, clearly losing her patience. "You have worked so hard to separate yourself from your father. That's the only reason you're even considering Parker! He's the complete opposite of Mick, and you think Travis is going to land you right back where you were. He's not like your dad, Abby."

"I didn't say he was, but it's putting me in a prime position to follow in his footsteps."

"Travis wouldn't do that to you. I think you underestimate just how much you mean to him. If you'd just tell him—"

"No. We didn't leave everything behind to have everyone here look at me the way they did in Wichita. Let's focus on the problem at hand. Shep is waiting for you."

"I don't want to talk about Shep," she said, slowing to a stop at the light.

"He's miserable, Mare. He loves you."

Her eyes filled with tears and her bottom lip quivered. "I don't care."

"Yes, you do."

"I know," she whimpered, leaning against my shoulder.

She cried until the light changed, and then I kissed her head. "Green light."

She sat up, wiping her nose. "I was pretty mean to him earlier. I don't think he'll talk to me now."

"He'll talk to you. He knew you were mad."

America wiped her face and then made a slow U-turn. I was worried it would take a lot of coaxing on my part to get her to come in with me, but Shepley ran down the stairs before she turned off the ignition.

He yanked open her car door, pulling her to her feet. "I'm so sorry, baby. I should have minded my own business, I . . . please don't leave. I don't know what I'd do without you."

America took his face in her hands and smiled. "You're an arrogant ass, but I still love you."

Shepley kissed her over and over like he hadn't seen her in months, and I smiled at a job well done. Travis stood in the doorway, grinning as I made my way into the apartment.

"And they lived happily ever after," Travis said, shutting the door behind me.

I collapsed on the couch, and he sat next to me, pulling my legs onto his lap.

"What do you wanna do today, Pidge?"

"Sleep. Or rest . . . or sleep."

"Can I give you your present first?"

I pushed his shoulder. "Shut up. You got me a present?"

His mouth curved into a nervous smile. "It's not a diamond bracelet, but I thought you'd like it."

"I'll love it, sight unseen."

He lifted my legs off of his lap and then disappeared into Shepley's bedroom. I raised an eyebrow when I heard him murmuring, and then he emerged with a box. He sat it on the floor at my feet, crouching behind it.

"Hurry, I want you to be surprised," he smiled.

"Hurry?" I asked, lifting the lid.

My mouth fell open when a pair of big, dark eyes looked up at me.

"A puppy?" I shrieked, reaching into the box. I lifted the

dark, wiry-haired baby to my face, and it covered my mouth in warm, wet kisses.

Travis beamed, triumphant. "You like him?"

"Him? I love him! You got me a puppy!"

"It's a cairn terrier. I had to drive three hours to pick him up Thursday after class."

"So when you said you were going with Shepley to take his car to the shop . . ."

"We went to get your present," he nodded.

"He's wiggly!" I laughed.

"Every girl from Kansas needs a Toto," Travis said, helping me hang on to the tiny fuzz ball in my lap.

"He does look like Toto! That's what I'm going to call him," I said, wrinkling my nose at the squirmy pup.

"You can keep him here. I'll take care of him for you when you're back at Morgan," his mouth pulled up into a half smile, "and it's my security that you'll visit when your month is up."

I pressed my lips together. "I would have come back anyway, Trav."

"I'd do anything for that smile that's on your face right now."

"I think you need a nap, Toto. Yes, you do," I cooed to the puppy.

Travis nodded, pulled me onto his lap, and then stood up. "Come on, then."

He carried me into his bedroom, pulled back the covers, and then lowered me to the mattress. Crawling over me, he reached over to pull the curtains closed and then fell onto his pillow.

"Thanks for staying with me last night," I said, stroking Toto's soft fur. "You didn't have to sleep on the bathroom floor."

"Last night was one of the best nights of my life."

I turned to see his expression. When I saw that he was serious, I shot him a dubious look. "Sleeping in between the toilet and the tub on a cold, hard tile floor with a vomiting idiot was one of your best nights? That's sad, Trav."

"No, sitting up with you when you're sick and you falling asleep in my lap was one of my best nights. It wasn't comfortable, I didn't sleep worth a shit, but I brought in your nineteenth birthday with you, and you're actually pretty sweet when you're drunk."

"I'm sure between the heaving and purging I was very charming."

He pulled me close, patting Toto, who was snuggled up to my neck. "You're the only woman I know that still looks incredible with your head in the toilet. That's saying something."

"Thanks, Trav. I won't make you babysit me again."

He leaned against his pillow. "Whatever. No one can hold your hair back like I can."

I giggled and closed my eyes, letting myself sink into the darkness.

"GET UP, ABBY!" AMERICA YELLED, SHAKING ME.

Toto licked my cheek. "I'm up! I'm up!"

"We have class in half an hour!"

I jumped from the bed. "I've been asleep for . . . fourteen hours? What the hell?"

"Just get in the shower! If you're not ready in ten minutes, I'm leaving your ass here!"

"I don't have time to take a shower!" I said, changing out of the clothes I fell asleep in.

Travis propped his head on his hand and chuckled. "You

girls are ridiculous. It's not the end of the world if you're late for one class."

"It is if you're America. She doesn't miss and she hates being late," I said, pulling a shirt over my head and stepping into my jeans.

"Let Mare go ahead. I'll take you."

I hopped on one foot and then the other, pulling my boots on. "My bag is in her car, Trav."

"Whatever," he shrugged, "just don't hurt yourself getting to class." He lifted Toto, cradling him with one arm like a tiny football, taking him down the hall.

America rushed me out the door and into the car. "I can't believe he got you that puppy," she said, looking behind her as she backed out from the parking spot.

Travis stood in the morning sun in his boxers and bare feet, clutching his arms around him from the cold. He watched Toto sniff a small patch of grass, coaxing him like a proud father.

"I've never had a dog before," I said. "This should be interesting."

America glanced at Travis before shoving the Honda into gear. "Look at him," she said, shaking her head. "Travis Maddox: Mr. Mom."

"Toto is adorable. Even you will be putty in his paws."

"You can't take it back to the dorm with you, you know. I don't think Travis thought this out."

"Travis said he'd keep him at the apartment."

She raised one eyebrow. "Of course he will. Travis thinks ahead, I'll give him that," she said, shaking her head as she slammed on the gas.

I puffed, sliding into my seat with one minute to spare. Once the adrenaline absorbed into my system, the heaviness from my postbirthday coma settled over my body. America elbowed me when class was dismissed, and I followed her to the cafeteria.

Shepley met us at the door, and I noticed right away that something was wrong.

"Mare," Shepley said, grabbing her arm.

Travis jogged to where we stood and grabbed his hips, puffing until he caught his breath.

"Is there a mob of angry women chasing you?" I teased.

He shook his head. "I was trying to catch you ... before you ... went in," he breathed.

"What's going on?" America asked Shepley.

"There's a rumor," Shepley began. "Everyone's saying that Travis took Abby home and ... the details are different, but it's pretty bad."

"What? Are you serious?" I cried.

America rolled her eyes. "Who cares, Abby? People have been speculating about you and Trav for weeks. It's not the first time someone has accused you two of sleeping together."

Travis and Shepley traded glances.

"What?" I said. "There's something else, isn't there?"

Shepley winced. "They're saying you slept with Parker at Brazil's, and then you let Travis ... take you home, if you know what I mean."

My mouth fell open. "Great! So I'm the school slut now?"

Travis's eyes darkened and his jaws tensed. "This is my fault. If it was anyone else, they wouldn't be saying that about you." He walked into the cafeteria, his hands in fists at his sides.

America and Shepley followed behind him. "Let's just hope no one is stupid enough to say anything to him," America said.

"Or her," Shepley added.

Travis sat a few seats across and down from me, brooding over his Reuben. I waited for him to look at me, wanting to offer a comforting smile. Travis had a reputation, but I let Parker take me into the hall.

Shepley elbowed me while I stared at his cousin. "He just feels bad. He's probably trying to deflect the rumor."

"You don't have to sit down there, Trav. Come on, come sit," I said, patting the empty surface in front of me.

"I heard you had quite a birthday, Abby," Chris Jenks said, throwing a piece of lettuce on Travis's plate.

"Don't start with her, Jenks," Travis warned, glowering.

Chris smiled, pushing up his round, pink cheeks. "I heard Parker is furious. He said he came by your apartment yesterday, and you and Travis were still in bed."

"They were taking a nap, Chris," America sneered.

My eyes darted to Travis. "Parker came by?"

He shifted uncomfortably in his chair. "I was gonna tell you."

"When?" I snapped.

America leaned into my ear. "Parker heard the rumor, and came by to confront you. I tried to stop him, but he walked down the hall and . . . totally got the wrong idea."

I planted my elbows on the table, covering my face with my hands. "This just keeps getting better."

"So you guys really didn't do the deed?" Chris asked. "Damn, that sucks. Here I thought Abby was right for you after all, Trav."

"You better stop now, Chris," Shepley warned.

"If you didn't sleep with her, mind if I take a shot?" Chris said, chuckling to his teammates.

My face burned with the initial embarrassment, but then America screamed in my ear, reacting to Travis jumping from his seat. He reached over the table and grabbed Chris by the throat with one hand and a fistful of T-shirt in the other. The linebacker slid across the table, and dozens of chairs grated across the floor as people stood to watch. Travis punched him repeatedly in the face, his elbow spiking high in the air before he landed each blow. The only thing Chris could do was to cover his face with his hands.

No one touched Travis. He was out of control, and his reputation left everyone afraid to get in his way. The football players ducked and winced as they watched their teammate being assaulted without mercy on the tile floor.

"Travis!" I screamed, running around the table.

In midpunch, Travis withheld his fist and then released Chris's shirt, letting him fall to the floor. He was panting when he turned to look at me; I'd never seen him look so frightening. I swallowed and took a step back as he shouldered past me.

I took a step to follow him, but America grabbed my arm. Shepley kissed her quickly and then followed his cousin out the door.

"Jesus," America whispered.

We turned to watch Chris's teammates pick him off the floor, and I cringed at his red and puffy face. Blood trickled from his nose, and Brazil handed him a napkin from the table.

"That crazy son of a bitch!" Chris groaned, sitting on the chair and holding his hand to his face. He looked at me. "I'm sorry, Abby. I was just kidding."

I had no words to reply. I couldn't explain what had just happened any more than he could.

"She didn't sleep with either of them," America said.

"You never know when to shut up, Jenks," Brazil said, disgusted.

America pulled on my arm. "C'mon. Let's go."

She didn't waste time tugging me to her car. When she put the gear in drive, I grabbed her wrist. "Wait! Where are we going?"

"We're going to Shep's. I don't want him to be alone with Travis. Did you see him? Dude's gone off the deep end!"

"Well, I don't want to be around him, either!"

America stared at me in disbelief. "There's obviously something going on with him. Don't you want to know what it is?"

"My sense of self-preservation is outweighing my curiosity at this point, Mare."

"The only thing that stopped him was your voice, Abby. He'll listen to you. You need to talk to him."

I sighed and released her wrist, falling against the back of my seat. "All right. Let's go."

We pulled into the parking lot, and America slowed to a stop between Shepley's Charger and Travis's Harley. She walked to the stairs, putting her hands on her hips with a touch of her own dramatic flair.

"C'mon, Abby!" America called, motioning for me to follow.

Hesitant, I finally followed, stopping when I saw Shepley hurry down the stairs to speak quietly in America's ear. He looked at me, shook his head, and then whispered to her once again.

"What?" I asked.

"Shep doesn't . . ." she fidgeted. "Shep doesn't think it's a good idea that we go in. Travis is still pretty mad."

"You mean he doesn't think I should go in," I said. America shrugged sheepishly and then looked to Shepley.

Shepley touched my shoulder. "You didn't do anything wrong, Abby. He just doesn't . . . he doesn't want to see you right now."

"If I didn't do anything wrong, then why doesn't he want to see me?"

"I'm not sure; he won't talk to me about it. I think he's embarrassed that he lost his temper in front of you."

"He lost his temper in front of the entire cafeteria! What do I have to do with it?"

"More than you think," Shepley said, dodging my eyes.

I watched them for a moment, and then pushed past them, running up the stairs. I burst through the doors to find an empty living room. The door to Travis's room was closed, so I knocked.

"Travis? It's me, open up."

"Walk away, Pidge," he called from the other side of the door.

I peeked in to see him sitting on the edge of his bed, facing the window. Toto pawed at his back, unhappy about being ignored.

"What is going on with you, Trav?" I asked. He didn't answer, so I stood beside him, crossing my arms. His jaw tensed, but he no longer wore the frightening expression he had in the cafeteria. He seemed sad. The deep, hopeless kind.

"You're not going to talk to me about this?"

I waited, but he remained quiet. I turned for the door, and he finally sighed. "You know the other day when Brazil mouthed off to me and you rushed to my defense? Well . . . that's what happened. I just got a little carried away."

"You were angry before Chris said anything," I said, returning to sit beside him on the bed.

He continued to stare out the window. "I meant what I said before. You need to walk away, Pidge. God knows I can't walk away from you."

I touched his arm. "You don't want me to leave."

Travis's jaws tensed again, and then he took me under his arm. He paused for a moment and then kissed my forehead, pressing his cheek against my temple. "It doesn't matter how hard I try. You're going to hate me when it's all said and done."

I wrapped my arms around him. "We have to be friends. I won't take no for an answer," I quoted.

His eyebrows pulled in, and then he cradled me to him with both arms, still staring out the window. "I watch you sleeping a lot. You always look so peaceful. I don't have that kind of quiet. I have all this anger and rage boiling inside of me—except when I watch you sleep.

"That's what I was doing when Parker walked in," he continued. "I was awake, and he walked in and just stood there with this shocked look on his face. I knew what he thought, but I didn't set him straight. I didn't explain because I wanted him to think something happened. Now the whole school thinks you were with us both in the same night."

Toto nuzzled his way onto my lap, and I rubbed his ears. Travis reached over to pet him once and then rested his hand on mine. "I'm sorry."

I shrugged. "If he believes the gossip, it's his own fault."

"It's hard to think anything else when he sees us in bed together."

"He knows I'm staying with you. I was fully clothed, for Christ's sake."

Travis sighed. "He was probably too pissed to notice. I know you like him, Pidge. I should have explained. I owe you that much."

"It doesn't matter."

"You're not mad?" he asked, surprised.

"Is that what you're so upset about? You thought I'd be mad at you when you told me the truth?"

"You should be. If someone single-handedly sunk my reputation, I'd be a little pissed."

"You don't care about reputations. What happened to the Travis that doesn't give a shit what anyone thinks?" I teased, nudging him.

"That was before I saw the look on your face when you heard what everyone's saying. I don't want you to get hurt because of me."

"You would never do anything to hurt me."

"I'd rather cut off my arm," he sighed.

He relaxed his cheek against my hair. I didn't have a reply, and Travis seemed to have said everything he needed to, so we sat in silence. Once in a while, Travis would squeeze me tighter to his side. I gripped his shirt, not knowing how else to make him feel better other than to just let him hold me.

When the sun began to set, I heard a faint knock at the door. "Abby?" America's voice sounded small on the other side of the wood.

"Come in, Mare," Travis answered.

America walked in with Shepley, and she smiled at the sight

of us tangled in each other's arms. "We were going to grab a bite to eat. You two feel like making a Pei Wei run?"

"Ugh . . . Asian again, Mare? Really?" Travis asked.

I smiled. He sounded like himself again.

America noticed as well. "Yes, really. You guys coming or not?"

"I'm starving," I said.

"Of course you are, you didn't get to eat lunch," he said, frowning. He stood up, bringing me with him. "Come on. Let's get you some food."

He kept his arm around me and didn't let go until we were in the booth at Pei Wei.

As soon as Travis left for the bathroom, America leaned in. "So? What did he say?"

"Nothing," I shrugged.

She raised an eyebrow. "You were in his room for two hours. He didn't say anything?"

"He usually doesn't when he's that mad," Shepley said.

"He had to have said something," America prodded.

"He said he got a little carried away taking up for me, and that he didn't tell Parker the truth when he walked in. That's it," I said, straightening the salt and pepper.

Shepley shook his head, closing his eyes.

"What, baby?" America asked, sitting taller.

"Travis is," he sighed, rolling his eyes. "Forget it."

America wore a stubborn expression. "Oh, hell no, you can't just—"

She cut off when Travis sat down and swung his arm behind me. "Damn it! The food's not here yet?"

We laughed and joked until the restaurant closed, and then

filed into the car for the ride home. Shepley carried America up the stairs on his back, but Travis stayed behind, tugging on my arm to keep me from following. He looked up at our friends until they disappeared behind the door and then offered a regretful smile. "I owe you an apology for today, so I'm sorry."

"You've already apologized. It's fine."

"No, I apologized for Parker. I don't want you thinking I'm some psycho that goes around attacking people over the tiniest thing," he said, "but I owe you an apology because I didn't defend you for the right reason."

"And that would be . . ." I prompted.

"I lunged at him because he said he wanted to be next in line, not because he was teasing you."

"Insinuating there is a line is plenty reason for you to defend me, Trav."

"That's my point. I was pissed because I took that as him wanting to sleep with you."

After processing what Travis meant, I grabbed the sides of his shirt and pressed my forehead against his chest. "You know what? I don't care," I said, looking up at him. "I don't care what people are saying or that you lost your temper or why you messed up Chris's face. The last thing I want is a bad reputation, but I'm tired of explaining our friendship to everyone. To hell with 'em."

Travis's eyes turned soft, and the corners of his mouth turned up. "Our friendship? Sometimes I wonder if you listen to me at all."

"What do you mean?"

"Let's go in. I'm tired."

I nodded, and he held me against his side until we were

inside the apartment. America and Shepley had already shut themselves in their bedroom, and I slipped in and out of the shower. Travis sat with Toto outside while I dressed in my pajamas, and within half an hour, we were both in bed.

I rested my head on my arm, breathing out a long, relaxing puff of air. "Just two weeks left. What are you going to do for drama when I move back to Morgan?"

"I don't know," he said. I could see his tormented frown, even in the darkness.

"Hey," I touched his arm. "I was kidding."

I watched him for a long time, breathing, blinking, and trying to relax. He fidgeted a bit and then looked over at me. "Do you trust me, Pidge?"

"Yeah, why?"

"C'mere," he said, pulling me against him. I stiffened for a second or two before resting my head on his chest. Whatever was going on with him, he needed me near him, and I couldn't have objected even if I'd wanted to. It felt right lying next to him.

Chapter Nine
Promise

FINCH SHOOK HIS HEAD. "OKAY, SO YOU'RE WITH Parker, or with Travis? I'm confused."

"Parker's not talking to me, so that's sort of up in the air right now," I said, bouncing to readjust my backpack.

He blew out a puff of smoke and then picked a piece of tobacco from his tongue. "So are you with Travis?"

"We're friends, Finch."

"You realize everyone thinks you two are having some sort of freaky friends-with-benefits thing going on that you're not admitting to, right?"

"I don't care. They can think what they want."

"Since when? What happened to the nervous, mysterious, guarded Abby I know and love?"

"She died from the stress of all the rumors and assumptions."

"That's too bad. I'm going to miss pointing and laughing at her."

I smacked Finch's arm, and he laughed. "Good. It's about time you quit pretending," he said.

"What do you mean?"

"Honey, you're talking to someone who's lived most of his life pretending. I spotted you a mile away."

"What are you trying to say, Finch? That I'm a closet lesbian?"

"No, that you're hiding something. The cardigans, the demure sophisticate that goes to fancy restaurants with Parker Hayes . . . that's not you. Either you were a small-town stripper or you've been to rehab. The latter's my guess."

I laughed out loud. "You are a terrible guesser!"

"So what's your secret?"

"If I told you, it wouldn't be a secret, now would it?"

His features sharpened with an impish grin. "I've shown you mine, now show me yours."

"I hate to be the bearer of bad news, but your sexual orientation isn't exactly a secret, Finch."

"Fuck! And I thought I had the mysterious sex-kitten thing going for me," he said, taking another drag.

I cringed before I spoke. "Did you have a good home life, Finch?"

"My mom's great . . . my dad and I had a lot of issues to work out, but we're good, now."

"I had Mick Abernathy for a father."

"Who's that?"

I giggled. "See? It's not a big deal if you don't know who he is."

"Who is he?"

"A mess. The gambling, the drinking, the bad temper . . . it's hereditary in my family. America and I came here so I could start fresh, without the stigma of being the daughter of a drunken has-been."

"A gambling has-been from Wichita?"

"I was born in Nevada. Everything Mick touched turned to gold back then. When I turned thirteen, his luck changed."

"And he blamed you."

"America gave up a lot to come here with me so I could get away, but I get here and walk face-first into Travis."

"And when you look at Travis . . ."

"It's all too familiar."

Finch nodded, flicking his cigarette to the ground. "Shit, Abby. That sucks."

I narrowed my eyes. "If you tell anyone what I just told you, I'll call the Mob. I know some of them, you know."

"Bullshit."

I shrugged. "Believe what you want."

Finch eyed me suspiciously, and then smiled. "You are officially the coolest person I know."

"That's sad, Finch. You should get out more," I said, stopping at the cafeteria entrance.

He pulled my chin up. "It'll all work out. I'm a firm believer in the whole things-happening-for-a-reason adage. You came here, America met Shep, you found your way to the Circle, something about you turned Travis Maddox's world upside down. Think about it," he said, planting a quick kiss on my lips.

"Hey now!" Travis said. He grabbed me by the waist, lifted me off my feet, returning me to the ground behind him. "You're the last person I'd have to worry about that shit from, Finch! Throw me a bone, here!" he teased.

Finch leaned to the side of Travis and winked. "Later, Cookie."

When Travis turned to face me, his smile faded. "What's the frown for?"

I shook my head, trying to let the adrenaline run its course. "I just don't like that nickname. It has some bad memories attached to it."

"Term of endearment from the youth minister?"

"No," I grumbled.

Travis punched his palm. "Do you want me to go beat the piss out of Finch? Teach him a lesson? I'll take him out."

I couldn't help but smile. "If I wanted to take Finch out, I'd just tell him Prada went out of business, and he'd finish the job for me."

Travis laughed, nudging toward the door. "Let's go! I'm wasting away, here!"

We sat at the lunch table together picking on each other with pinches and elbows to the ribs. Travis's mood was as optimistic as on the night I lost the bet. Everyone at the table noticed, and when he instigated a mini–food fight with me, it garnered the attention of those sitting at the tables around us.

I rolled my eyes. "I feel like a zoo animal."

Travis watched me for a moment, noted those staring, and then stood up. "I CAN'T!" he yelled. I stared in awe as the entire room jerked their heads in his direction. Travis bobbed his head a couple of times to a beat in his head.

Shepley closed his eyes. "Oh, no."

Travis smiled. "Get no . . . sa . . . tis . . . faction," he sang. He kept belting out the lyrics as he climbed onto the table as everyone stared.

He pointed to the football players at the end of the table and they smiled and yelled the lyrics back in unison. The whole room clapped to the beat.

Travis sang into his fist and danced past me.

The whole room chanted in harmony.

Travis jerked his hips, and a few whistles and squeals from the girls in the room fired off. He walked by me again, singing the chorus to the other side of the room, the football players his backup singers.

He pointed to his clapping audience. Some people stood and danced with him, but most just watched with amused amazement.

He jumped to the adjacent table and America squealed and clapped, elbowing me. I shook my head; I had died and woken up in *High School Musical*.

The football players were humming the base line, "Na, na, nanana! Na, na, na! Na na, nanana!"

Travis held his fist-microphone high, then jumped down, leaned across the table, and sang into my face.

The room clapped to the beat, and as he hit the final note, he stood smiling and breathless.

The entire room exploded into applause, even a few whistles. I shook my head after he kissed my forehead, and then stood up to take a bow. When he returned to his seat in front of me, he chuckled.

"They're not looking at you, now, are they?" he panted.

"Thanks. You really shouldn't have," I said.

"Abs?"

I looked up to see Parker standing at the end of the table. All eyes were on me once again.

"We need to talk," Parker said, seeming nervous. I looked at America, Travis, and then to Parker. "Please?" he asked, shoving his hands in his pockets.

I nodded, following him outside. He walked past the windows to the privacy of the side of the building. "I didn't mean to draw attention to you again. I know how you hate that."

"Then you might have just called if you wanted to talk," I said.

He nodded, looking to the ground. "It wasn't my intention to find you in the cafeteria. I saw the commotion, and then you, and I just went in. I'm sorry."

I waited, and he spoke again, "I don't know what happened with you and Travis. It's none of my business . . . you and I have only been on a handful of dates. I was upset at first, but then I realized that it wouldn't have bothered me if I didn't have feelings for you."

"I didn't sleep with him, Parker. He held my hair while I hurled a pint of Patrón in his toilet. That's as romantic as it got."

He laughed once. "I don't think we've really gotten a fair shot . . . not with you living with Travis. The truth is, Abby, I like you. I don't know what it is, but I can't seem to stop thinking about you." I smiled and he took my hand, running his finger over my bracelet. "I probably scared you off with this ridiculous present, but I've never been in this situation before. I feel like I'm constantly competing with Travis for your attention."

"You didn't scare me off with the bracelet."

He pressed his lips together. "I'd like to take you out again in a couple of weeks, after your month is up with Travis. Then we can concentrate on getting to know each other without the distraction."

"Fair enough."

He leaned down and closed his eyes, pressing his lips against mine. "I'll call you soon."

I waved goodbye, and then returned to the cafeteria, passing Travis.

He grabbed me, pulling me onto his lap. "Breakin' up is hard to do?"

"He wants to try again when I'm back at Morgan."

"Shit, I'm going to have to think of another bet," he said, pulling my plate in front of me.

The next two weeks flew by. Other than class, I spent every waking moment with Travis, and most of that time we spent alone. He took me to dinner, for drinks and dancing at the Red, bowling; and he was called out to two fights. When we weren't laughing ourselves silly, we were play-wrestling, or snuggling on the couch with Toto, watching a movie. He made a point to ignore every girl that batted an eyelash at him, and everyone talked about the new Travis.

My last night in the apartment, America and Shepley were inexplicably absent, and Travis labored over a special Last Night dinner. He bought wine, set out napkins, and even brought home new silverware for the occasion. He sat our plates on the breakfast bar and pulled his stool to the other side to sit across from me. For the first time, I got the distinct feeling we were on a date.

"This is really good, Trav. You've been holding out on me," I said as I chewed the Cajun chicken pasta he had prepared.

He forced a smile, and I could see he was working hard to keep the conversation light. "If I told you before, you would have expected it every night." His smile faded, and his eyes fell to the table.

I rolled my food around on my plate. "I'm going to miss you, too, Trav."

"You're still gonna come over, right?"

"You know I will. And you'll be at Morgan's, helping me study just like you did before."

"But it won't be the same," he sighed. "You'll be dating Parker, we're going to get busy . . . go in different directions."

"It's not going to change that much."

He managed a single laugh. "Who would have thought from the first time we met that we'd be sitting here? You couldn't have told me three months ago that I'd be this miserable over saying goodbye to a girl."

My stomach sank. "I don't want you to be miserable."

"Then don't go," he said. His expression was so desperate that the guilt formed a lump in my throat.

"I can't move in here, Travis. That's crazy."

"Says who? I just had the best two weeks of my life."

"Me, too."

"Then why do I feel like I'm never gonna see you again?"

I didn't have a reply. His jaws tensed, but he wasn't angry. The urge to go to him grew insistent, so I stood up and walked around the bar, sitting on his lap. He didn't look at me, so I hugged his neck, pressing my cheek against his.

"You're going to realize what a pain in the ass I was, and then you'll forget all about missing me," I said into his ear.

He puffed a breath of air as he rubbed my back. "Promise?"

I leaned back and looked into his eyes, touching each side of his face with my hands. I caressed his jaw with my thumb; his expression was heartbreaking. I closed my eyes and leaned down to kiss the corner of his mouth, but he turned so that I caught more of his lips than I'd intended.

Even though the kiss surprised me, I didn't pull back right away.

Travis kept his lips on mine, but he didn't take it any further.

I finally pulled away, playing it off with a smile. "I have a big day tomorrow. I'm going to clean up the kitchen, and then I'm going to head to bed."

"I'll help you," he said.

We did the dishes together in silence, with Toto asleep at our feet. He dried the last dish and set it in the rack and then led me down the hall, holding my hand a bit too tight. The distance from the mouth of the hallway to his bedroom door seemed to take twice as long. We both knew that goodbye was just a few hours away.

He didn't even try to pretend not to watch this time as I changed into one of his T-shirts for bed. He stripped down to his boxers and climbed under the blanket, waiting for me to join him.

Once I did, Travis flipped off the lamp, and then pulled me against him without permission or apology. He tensed his arms and sighed, and I nestled my face into his neck. I shut my eyes tight, trying to savor the moment. I knew I would wish for that moment back every day of my life, so I lived it with everything I had.

He looked out the window. The trees cast a shadow across his face. Travis clenched his eyes shut, and a sinking feeling settled over me. It was agonizing to see him suffer, knowing that not only was I the cause of it . . . I was the only one that could take it away.

"Trav? Are you okay?" I asked.

There was a long pause before he finally spoke. "I've never been less okay in my life."

I pressed my forehead against his neck, and he squeezed me tighter. "This is silly," I said. "We're going to see each other every day."

"You know that's not true."

The weight of the grief we both felt was crushing, and an irrepressible need came over me to save us both. I lifted my chin, but hesitated; what I was about to do would change everything. I reasoned that Travis didn't see intimacy as anything but a way to pass the time, and I shut my eyes again and swallowed back my fears. I had to do something, knowing we would both lie awake, dreading every passing minute until morning.

My heart pounded as I touched his neck with my lips and then tasted his flesh in a slow, tender kiss. He looked down with surprise, and then his eyes softened with the realization of what I wanted.

He leaned down, pressing his lips against mine with a delicate sweetness. The warmth from his lips traveled all the way to my toes, and I pulled him closer to me. Now that we had taken the first step, I had no intention of stopping there.

I parted my lips, letting Travis's tongue find its way to mine. "I want you," I said.

Suddenly, the kiss slowed, and he tried to pull away. Determined to finish what I had started, my mouth worked against his more anxiously. In reaction, Travis backed away until he was on his knees. I rose with him, keeping our mouths melded together.

He gripped each of my shoulders to hold me at bay. "Wait a

sec," he whispered with an amused smile, breathing hard. "You don't have to do this, Pidge. This isn't what tonight is about."

He was holding back, but I could see it in his eyes that his self-control wouldn't last long.

I leaned in again, and this time his arms gave way just enough for me to brush my lips against his. I looked up at him from under my brows, resolute. It took me a moment to say the words, but I would say them. "Don't make me beg," I whispered against his mouth.

With those four words, his reservations vanished. He kissed me, hard and eager. My fingers ran down the length of his back and settled on the elastic of his boxers, nervously running along the gather of the fabric. His lips grew impatient then, and I fell against the mattress when he crashed into me. His tongue found its way to mine once again, and when I gained the courage to slide my hand between his skin and the boxers, he groaned.

Travis yanked the T-shirt over my head, and then his hand impatiently traveled down my side, gripping my panties and slipping them down my legs with one hand. His mouth returned to mine once more as his hand slid up the inside of my thigh, and I let out a long, faltering breath when his fingers wandered where no man had touched me before. My knees arched and twitched with each movement of his hand, and when I dug my fingers into his flesh, he positioned himself above me.

"Pigeon," he said, panting, "it doesn't have to be tonight. I'll wait until you're ready."

I reached for the top drawer of his nightstand, pulling it open. Feeling the plastic between my fingers, I touched the corner to my mouth, tearing the package open with my teeth.

His free hand left my back, and then he pulled his boxers down, kicking them off as if he couldn't stand them between us.

The package crackled in his fingertips, and after a few moments, I felt him between my thighs. I closed my eyes.

"Look at me, Pigeon."

I peered up at him, and his eyes were intent and soft at the same time. He tilted his head, leaning down to kiss me tenderly, and then his body tensed, pushing himself inside of me in a small, slow movement. When he pulled back, I bit my lip with the discomfort; when he rocked into me again, I clenched my eyes shut with the pain. My thighs tightened around his hips, and he kissed me again.

"Look at me," he whispered.

When I opened my eyes, he pressed inside me again, and I cried out with the wonderful burning it caused. Once I relaxed, the motion of his body against mine was more rhythmic. The nervousness I had felt in the beginning had disappeared, and Travis grabbed at my flesh as if he couldn't get enough. I pulled him into me, and he moaned when the way it felt became too much.

"I've wanted you for so long, Abby. You're all I want," he breathed against my mouth.

He grabbed my thigh with one hand and propped himself up with his elbow, just inches above me. A thin sheet of sweat began to bead on our skin, and I arched my back as his lips traced my jaw and then followed a single line down my neck.

"Travis," I sighed.

When I said his name, he pressed his cheek against mine, and his movements became more rigid. The noises from his throat grew louder, and he finally pressed inside me one last time, groaning and quivering above me.

After a few moments, he relaxed and let his breathing slow.

"That was some first kiss," I said with a tired, content expression.

He scanned my face and smiled. "Your last first kiss."

I was too shocked to reply.

He collapsed beside me on his stomach, stretching one arm across my middle, and resting his forehead against my cheek. I ran my fingers along the bare skin of his back until I heard his breathing even out.

I lay awake for hours, listening to Travis's deep breaths and the wind weaving through the trees outside. America and Shepley came in the front door quietly, and I heard them tiptoe down the hall, murmuring to each other.

We had packed my things earlier in the day, and I flinched at how uncomfortable the morning would be. I had thought once Travis slept with me his curiosity would be satiated, but instead he was talking about forever. My eyes snapped shut with the thought of his expression when he learned that what had happened between us wasn't a beginning, it was closure. I couldn't go down that road, and he would hate me when I told him.

I maneuvered out from under his arm and got dressed, carrying my shoes with me down the hall to Shepley's room. America sat on the bed, and Shepley was pulling off his shirt in front of the closet.

"Everything okay, Abby?" Shepley asked.

"Mare?" I said, signaling for her to join me in the hall.

She nodded, watching me with cautious eyes. "What's going on?"

"I need you to take me to Morgan now. I can't wait 'til tomorrow."

One side of her mouth turned up with a knowing smile. "You never could handle goodbyes."

Shepley and America helped me with my bags, and I stared out the window of America's car on my journey back to Morgan Hall. When we set down the last of the bags in my room, America grabbed me.

"It's going to be so different in the apartment, now."

"Thanks for bringing me home. The sun will be up in a few hours. You better go," I said, squeezing once before letting go.

America didn't look back when she left my room, and I chewed my lip nervously, knowing how angry she would be when she realized what I'd done.

My shirt crackled as I pulled it over my head; the static in the air had intensified with the coming winter. Feeling a bit lost, I curled into a ball underneath my thick comforter and inhaled through my nose; Travis's scent still lingered on my skin.

The bed felt cold and foreign, a sharp contrast to the warmth of Travis's mattress. I had spent thirty days in a cramped apartment with Eastern's most infamous tramp, and after all the bickering and late-night houseguests, it was the only place I wanted to be.

THE PHONE CALLS BEGAN AT EIGHT IN THE MORNING, and then every five minutes for an hour.

"Abby!" Kara groaned. "Answer your stupid phone!"

I reached over and turned it off. It wasn't until I heard the banging on the door that I realized I wouldn't be allowed to spend the day holed up in my room as planned.

Kara yanked on the knob. "What?"

America pushed past her, and stood beside my bed. "What in the hell is going on?" she yelled. Her eyes were red and puffy, and she was still in her pajamas.

I sat up. "What, Mare?"

"Travis is a fucking wreck! He won't talk to us, he's trashed the apartment, threw the stereo across the room . . . Shep can't talk any sense into him!"

I rubbed my eyes with the heels of my hand and blinked. "I don't know."

"Bullshit! You're going to tell me what in the hell is going on, and you're going to tell me now!"

Kara grabbed her shower bag and fled. She slammed the door behind her, and I frowned, afraid she would tell the resident adviser, or worse, the dean of students.

"Keep it down, America, Jesus," I whispered.

She clenched her teeth. "What did you do?"

I assumed he would be upset with me; I didn't know he'd fly into a rage. "I . . . don't know," I swallowed.

"He took a swing at Shep when he found out we helped you leave. Abby! Please tell me!" she pleaded, her eyes glossing over. "It's scaring me!"

The fear in her eyes forced only the partial truth. "I just couldn't say goodbye. You know it's hard for me."

"It's something else, Abby. He's gone fucking nuts! I heard him call your name, and then he stomped all over the apartment looking for you. He barged into Shep's room, demanding to know where you were. Then he tried to call you. Over and over and over," she sighed. "His face was . . . Jesus, Abby. I've never seen him like that.

"He ripped his sheets off the bed, and threw them away, threw his pillows away, shattered his mirror with his fist, kicked his door . . . broke it from the hinges! It was the scariest thing I've ever seen in my life!"

I closed my eyes, forcing the tears that had pooled in my eyes down my cheeks.

America thrust her cell phone at me. "You have to call him. You have to at least tell him you're okay."

"Okay, I'll call him."

She shoved her phone at me again. "No, you're calling him now."

I took her phone in my hand and fingered the buttons, trying to imagine what I could possibly say to him. She snatched it out of my hand, dialed, and then handed it to me. I held the phone to my ear and took a deep breath.

"Mare?" Travis answered, his voice thick with worry.

"It's me."

The line was quiet for several moments before he finally spoke. "What the fuck happened to you last night? I wake up this morning, and you're gone and you . . . you just leave and don't say goodbye? Why?"

"I'm sorry. I—"

"You're sorry? I've been going crazy! You don't answer your phone, you sneak out and—wh-why? I thought we finally had everything figured out!"

"I just needed some time to think."

"About what?" He paused. "Did I . . . did I hurt you?"

"No! It's nothing like that! I'm really, really sorry. I'm sure America told you. I don't do goodbyes."

"I need to see you," he said, his voice desperate.

I sighed. "I have a lot to do today, Trav. I have to unpack and I have piles of laundry."

"You regret it," he said, his voice breaking.

"It's not . . . that's not what it is. We're friends. That's not going to change."

"Friends? Then what the fuck was last night?" he said, anger bleeding through his voice.

I closed my eyes tight. "I know what you want. I just can't . . . do that right now."

"So you just need some time?" he asked in a calmer voice. "You could have told me that. You didn't have to run out on me."

"It just seemed like the easiest way."

"Easier for who?"

"I couldn't sleep. I kept thinking about what it would be like in the morning, loading Mare's car and . . . I couldn't do it, Trav," I said.

"It's bad enough that you aren't going to be here anymore. You can't just drop out of my life."

I forced a smile. "I'll see you tomorrow. I don't want anything to be weird, okay? I just need to sort some stuff out. That's all."

"Okay," he said. "I can do that."

I hung up the phone, and America glared at me. "You slept with him? You bitch! You weren't even going to tell me?"

I rolled my eyes and fell against the pillow. "This isn't about you, Mare. This has just become one convoluted clusterfuck."

"What's so difficult about it? You two should be deliriously happy, not breaking doors and hiding in your room!"

"I can't be with him," I whispered, keeping my eyes on the ceiling.

Her hand covered mine, and she spoke softly. "Travis needs

work. Trust me, I understand any and all reservations you have about him, but look how much he's already changed for you. Think about the last two weeks, Abby. He's not Mick."

"I'm Mick! I get involved with Travis and everything we've worked for . . . poof!" I snapped my fingers. "Just like that!"

"Travis wouldn't let that happen."

"It's not up to him, now is it?"

"You're going to break his heart, Abby. You're going to break his heart! The one girl he trusts enough to fall for, and you're going to nail him to the wall!"

I turned away from her, unable to see the expression that went with the pleading tone in her voice. "I need the happy ending. That's why we came here."

"You don't have to do this. It could work."

"Until my luck runs out."

America threw up her hands, letting them fall into her lap. "Jesus, Abby, not this shit again. We talked about this."

My phone rang, and I looked at the display. "It's Parker."

She shook her head. "We're still talking."

"Hello?" I answered, avoiding America's glare.

"Abs! Day one of freedom! How does it feel?" he said.

"It feels . . . free," I said, unable to muster up any enthusiasm.

"Dinner tomorrow night? I've missed you."

"Yeah," I wiped my nose with my sleeve. "Tomorrow's great."

After I hung up the phone, America frowned. "He's going to ask me when I get back," she said. "He's going to want to know what we talked about. What am I supposed to tell him?"

"Tell him that I'll keep my promise. By this time tomorrow, he won't miss me."

Chapter Ten
Poker Face

TWO TABLES OVER, ONE TABLE BACK. AMERICA AND Shepley were barely visible from my seat, and I hunched over, watching Travis stare at the empty chair I usually occupied, before sitting at the end of the lunch table. I felt ridiculous for hiding, but I wasn't prepared to sit across from him for an entire hour. When I finished my meal, I took a deep breath and walked outside to where Travis was finishing his cigarette.

I had spent most of the night trying to form a plan to get us to where we were before. If I treated our encounter the way he regarded sex in general, I would have a better chance. The plan risked losing him altogether, but I hoped his enormous male ego would force him to play it off the same way.

"Hey," I said.

He grimaced. "Hey. I thought you'd be at lunch."

"I had to run in and out; I have to study," I shrugged, doing my best impression of casual.

"Need some help?"

"It's Calculus. I think I've got it handled."

"I can just hang out for moral support." He smiled, digging

his hand into his pocket. The solid muscles in his arm tensed with the movement, and the thought of them flexing as he thrust himself inside me replayed with vivid detail in my head.

"Er . . . what?" I asked, disoriented from the sudden erotic thought that had flashed in my mind.

"Are we supposed to pretend the other night never happened?"

"No, why?" I feigned confusion and he sighed, frustrated with my behavior.

"I don't know . . . because I took your virginity?" He leaned toward me, saying the words in a hushed voice.

I rolled my eyes. "I'm sure it's not the first time you've deflowered a virgin, Trav."

Just as I had feared, my casual demeanor made him angry. "As a matter of fact, it was."

"C'mon . . . I said I didn't want any weirdness between us."

Travis took one last drag of his cigarette and flicked it to the ground. "Well, if I've learned anything in the last few days, it's that you don't always get what you want."

"Hey, Abs," Parker said, kissing my cheek.

Travis gave Parker a murderous expression.

"I'll pick you up around six?" Parker said.

I nodded. "Six."

"See you in a bit," he said, continuing to class. I watched him walk away, afraid to endure the consequences of the last ten seconds.

"You're going out with him tonight?" Travis seethed. His jaw was clenched, and I could see it working under his skin.

"I told you he was going to ask me out after I got back to Morgan. He called me yesterday."

"Things have changed a little bit since that conversation, don't you think?"

"Why?"

He walked away from me, and I swallowed, trying to keep the tears at bay. Travis stopped and came back, leaning into my face. "That's why you said I wouldn't miss you after today! You knew I'd find out about you and Parker, and you thought I'd just . . . what? Get over you? Do you not trust me, or am I just not good enough? Tell me, damn it! Tell me what the fuck I did to you to make you do this!"

I stood my ground, staring straight into his eyes. "You didn't do anything to me. Since when is sex so life or death to you?"

"Since it was with you!"

I glanced around, seeing that we were making a scene. People were walking by slowly, staring and whispering to each other. I felt my ears burn, and it spread across my face, making my eyes water.

He closed his eyes, trying to compose himself before he spoke again. "Is that it? You don't think it meant anything to me?"

"You are Travis Maddox."

He shook his head, disgusted. "If I didn't know any better, I'd think you were shoving my past in my face."

"I don't think four weeks ago constitutes the past." His face contorted and I laughed. "I'm kidding! Travis, it's fine. I'm fine, you're fine. There's no need to make a big deal of it."

All emotion disappeared from his face and he took a deep breath through his nose. "I know what you're trying to do." His eyes unfocused for a moment, lost in thought. "I'll just have to prove it to you, then." His eyes narrowed as he looked into mine, as determined as he was before one of his fights. "If you think I'm just going to go back to fucking around, you're wrong. I don't want anyone else. You wanna be friends? Fine, we're friends. But you and I both know that what happened wasn't just sex."

He stormed past me and I closed my eyes, exhaling the breath I didn't know I'd been holding. Travis glanced back at me and then continued to his next class. An escaping tear fell down my cheek and I quickly wiped it away. The curious stares of my classmates targeted my back as I plodded to class.

Parker was on the second row, and I slid into the desk next to him.

A grin stretched across his face. "I'm looking forward to tonight."

I took a breath and smiled, trying to change gears from my conversation with Travis. "What's the plan?"

"Well, I'm all settled in my apartment. I thought we'd have dinner there."

"I'm looking forward to tonight, too," I said, trying to convince myself.

With America's refusal to help, Kara was a reluctant assistant to aid me in choosing a dress for my date with Parker. As soon as I pulled it on over my head, I yanked it off and slipped on a pair of jeans instead. After brooding about my failed plan all afternoon, I couldn't talk myself into dressing up. Keeping the cool weather in mind, I pulled on a thin ivory cashmere sweater over a brown tank top, and waited by the door. When Parker's shiny Porsche pulled in front of Morgan, I pushed my way out the door before he had time to make it up the walk.

"I was going to come get you," he said, disappointed as he held open the door.

"Then I saved you a trip," I said, buckling my seat belt.

He slid in beside me and leaned over, touching each side of my face, kissing me with his plush, soft lips. "Wow," he breathed, "I've missed your mouth."

His breath was minty, his cologne smelled incredible, his hands were warm and soft, and he looked fantastic in his jeans and green dress shirt, but I couldn't shake the feeling that something was missing. That excitement I had in the beginning was noticeably absent, and I silently cursed Travis for taking that away.

I forced a smile. "I'm going to take that as a compliment."

His apartment was exactly as I had imagined: immaculate, with expensive electronics in every corner, and most likely decorated by his mother.

"So? What do you think?" he said, grinning like a child showing off a new toy.

"It's great," I nodded.

His expression changed from playful to intimate, and he pulled me into his arms, kissing my neck. Every muscle in my body tensed. I wanted to be anywhere but in that apartment.

My cell phone rang, and I offered him an apologetic smile before answering.

"How's the date goin', Pidge?"

I turned my back to Parker and whispered into the phone. "What do you need, Travis?" I tried to make my tone sharp, but it was softened by my relief to hear his voice.

"I wanna go bowling tomorrow. I need my partner."

"Bowling? You couldn't have called me later?" I felt like a hypocrite for saying the words, knowing I had hoped for an excuse to keep Parker's lips off of me.

"How am I supposed to know when you're gonna get done? Oh. That didn't come out right..." he trailed off, sounding amused with himself.

"I'll call you tomorrow and we can talk about it then, okay?"

"No, it's not okay. You said you wanna be friends, but we can't hang out?" I rolled my eyes, and Travis huffed. "Don't roll your eyes at me. Are you coming or not?"

"How did you know I rolled my eyes? Are you stalking me?" I asked, noting the drawn curtains.

"You always roll your eyes. Yes? No? You're wasting precious date time."

He knew me so well. I fought the urge to ask him to pick me up right then. I couldn't help but smile at the thought.

"Yes!" I said in a hushed voice, trying not to laugh. "I'll go."

"I'll pick you up at seven."

I turned to Parker, grinning like the Cheshire Cat.

"Travis?" he asked with a knowing expression.

"Yes," I frowned, caught.

"You're still just friends?"

"Still just friends," I nodded once.

We sat at the table, eating Chinese takeout. I warmed up to him after a while, and he reminded me of how charming he was. I felt lighter, almost giggly, a marked change from earlier. As hard as I tried to push the thought from my head, I couldn't deny that it was my plans with Travis that had brightened my mood.

After dinner, we sat on the couch to watch a movie, but before the beginning credits were over, Parker had me on my back. I was glad I had chosen to wear jeans; I wouldn't have been able to fend him off as easily in a dress. His lips traveled down to my collarbone, and his hand stopped at my belt. He clumsily worked to pull it open, and once it popped, I slid out from under him to stand up.

"Okay! I think a single is all you'll be hitting tonight," I said, buckling my belt.

"What?"

"First base . . . second base? Never mind. It's late, I better go."

He sat up and gripped my legs. "Don't go, Abs. I don't want you to think that's why I brought you here."

"Isn't it?"

"Of course not," he said, pulling me onto his lap. "You're all I've thought about for two weeks. I apologize for being impatient."

He kissed my cheek, and I leaned into him, smiling when his breath tickled my neck. I turned to him and pressed my lips against his, trying my hardest to feel something—but I didn't. I pulled away from him and sighed.

Parker furrowed his brow. "I said I was sorry."

"I said it was late."

We drove to Morgan, and Parker squeezed my hand after he kissed me goodnight. "Let's try again. Biasetti's tomorrow?"

I pressed my lips together. "I'm bowling with Travis tomorrow."

"Wednesday, then?"

"Wednesday's great," I said, offering a contrived smile.

Parker shifted in his seat. He was working up to something. "Abby? There's a date party in a couple weekends at the House . . ."

I inwardly cringed, dreading the discussion we would inevitably have.

"What?" he asked, chuckling nervously.

"I can't go with you," I said, letting myself out of the car.

He followed, meeting me at the Morgan entrance. "You have plans?"

I winced. "Travis already asked me."

"Travis asked you what?"

"To the date party," I explained, a bit frustrated.

Parker's face flushed, and he shifted his weight. "You're going to the date party with Travis? He doesn't go to those things. And you're just friends. It doesn't make sense for you to go with him."

"America wouldn't go with Shep unless I went."

He relaxed. "Then you can go with me," he smiled, intertwining his fingers in mine.

I grimaced at his solution. "I can't cancel with Travis and then go with you."

"I don't see the problem," he shrugged. "You can be there for America, and Travis will get out of having to go. He is a staunch advocate for doing away with date parties. He thinks it's a platform for our girlfriends to force us to declare a relationship."

"It was me that didn't want to go. He talked me into it."

"Now you have an excuse," he shrugged. He was maddeningly confident that I was going to change my mind.

"I didn't want to go at all."

Parker's patience had run out. "I just want to be clear; you don't want to go to the date party. Travis wants to go, he asked you, and you won't cancel with him to go with me, even though you didn't want to go in the first place?"

I had a hard time meeting his glare. "I can't do that to him, Parker, I'm sorry."

"Do you understand what a date party is? It's something you go to with your boyfriend."

His patronizing tone made any empathy I'd felt for him disappear. "Well, I don't have a boyfriend, so technically I shouldn't go at all."

"I thought we were going to try again. I thought we had something."

"I am trying."

"What do you expect me to do? Sit at home alone while you're at my fraternity's date party with someone else? Should I ask another girl?"

"You can do what you want," I said, irritated with his threat.

He looked up and shook his head. "I don't want to ask another girl."

"I don't expect you not to go to your own party. I'll see you there."

"You want me to ask someone else? And you're going with Travis. Do you not see how completely absurd that is?"

I crossed my arms, ready for a fight. "I told him I would go before you and I ever went out, Parker. I can't cancel on him."

"You can't, or you don't want to?"

"Same difference. I'm sorry that you don't understand." I pulled the door open to Morgan, and Parker put his hand on mine.

"All right," he sighed in resignation. "This is obviously an issue I'm going to have to work through. Travis is one of your best friends; I do understand that. I don't want it to affect our relationship. Okay?"

"Okay," I said, nodding.

He opened the door and gestured to me to walk through,

kissing my cheek before I walked inside. "See you Wednesday at six?"

"Six," I said, waving as I walked up the stairs.

America was walking out of the shower room when I turned the corner, and her eyes brightened when she recognized me. "Hey, chickie! How'd it go?"

"It went," I said, deflated.

"Uh-oh."

"Don't tell Travis, okay?"

She huffed. "I won't. What happened?"

"Parker asked me to the date party."

America tightened her towel. "You're not bailing on Trav, are you?"

"No, and Parker's not happy about it."

"Understandable," she said, nodding. "It's also too damn bad."

America pulled the strands of her long, wet hair over one shoulder, and drops of water trickled down her bare skin. She was a walking contradiction. She applied to Eastern so we could move together. She was my self-proclaimed conscience, intent on stepping in when I gave in to my imbedded tendencies to fly off track. It went against everything we talked about for me to get involved with Travis, and she had become his overly enthusiastic cheerleader.

I leaned against the wall. "Would you be mad if I didn't go at all?"

"No, I would be unbelievably and irrevocably pissed off. That's grounds for a full-blown cat fight, Abby."

"Then I guess I'm going," I said, shoving my key in the lock. My cell phone rang, and a picture of Travis making a funny face appeared on the display. "Hello?"

"You home yet?"

"Yeah, he dropped me off about five minutes ago."

"I'll be there in five more."

"Wait! Travis?" I said after he'd hung up.

America laughed. "You just had a disappointing date with Parker, and you smiled when Travis called. Are you really that dense?"

"I didn't smile," I protested. "He's coming here. Will you meet him outside and tell him I went to bed?"

"You did, too, and no . . . go tell him yourself."

"Yes, Mare, me going out there to tell him I'm in bed is so gonna work." She turned her back to me, walking to her room. I threw up my hands, letting them fall to my thighs. "Mare! Please?"

"Have fun, Abby," she smiled, disappearing into her room.

I walked down the stairs to see Travis on his motorcycle, parked at the front steps. He wore a white T-shirt with black artwork, setting off the tattoos on his arms.

"Aren't you cold?" I asked, tugging my jacket tighter.

"You look nice. Did you have a good time?"

"Uh . . . yeah, thanks," I said, distracted. "What are you doing here?"

He pulled back the throttle, and the engine snarled. "I was going to take a ride to clear my head. I want you to come with me."

"It's cold, Trav."

"You want me to go get Shep's car?"

"We're going bowling tomorrow. Can't you wait until then?"

"I went from being with you every second of the day to seeing you for ten minutes if I'm lucky."

I smiled and shook my head. "It's only been two days, Trav."

"I miss you. Get your ass on the seat and let's go."

I couldn't argue. I missed him, too. More than I would ever admit to him. I zipped up my jacket and climbed on behind him, slipping my fingers through the belt loops of his jeans. He pulled my wrists to his chest and then folded them across one another. Once he was satisfied that I was holding him tightly enough, he took off, racing down the road.

I rested my cheek against his back and closed my eyes, breathing in his scent. It reminded me of his apartment and his sheets and the way he smelled when he walked around with a towel around his waist. The city blurred past us, and I didn't care how fast he was driving or how cold the wind was as it whipped across my skin; I wasn't even paying attention to where we were. The only thing I could think about was his body against mine. We had no destination or time frame, and we drove the streets long after they had been abandoned by everyone but us.

Travis pulled into a gas station and parked. "You want anything?" he asked.

I shook my head, climbing off the bike to stretch my legs. He watched me rake my fingers through the tangles in my hair and smiled.

"Quit it. You're fucking beautiful."

"Just point me to the nearest eighties rock video," I said.

He laughed and then yawned, swatting at the moths that buzzed around him. The nozzle clicked, sounding louder than it should in the quiet night. We seemed to be the only two people on earth.

I pulled out my cell phone to check the time. "Oh my God, Trav. It's three in the morning."

"You wanna go back?" he asked, his face shadowed with disappointment.

I pressed my lips together. "We better."

"We're still going bowling tonight?"

"I told you I would."

"And you're still going to Sig Tau with me in a couple weeks, right?"

"Are you insinuating that I don't follow through? I find that a little insulting."

He pulled the nozzle from his tank and hooked it on its base. "I just never know what you're going to do anymore."

He sat on his bike and helped me to climb on behind him. I hooked my fingers in his belt loops and then thought better of it, wrapping my arms around him.

He sighed and leaned the bike upright, reluctant to start the engine. His knuckles turned white as he gripped the handlebars. He took a breath, beginning to speak, and then shook his head.

"You're important to me, you know," I said, squeezing him.

"I don't understand you, Pigeon. I thought I knew women, but you're so fucking confusing I don't know which way is up."

"I don't understand you, either. You're supposed to be Eastern's ladies' man. I'm not getting the full freshmen experience they promised in the brochure," I teased.

"Well, that's a first. I've never had a girl sleep with me to get me to leave her alone," he said, keeping his back to me.

"That's not what it was, Travis," I lied, ashamed that he had guessed my intentions without realizing how right he was.

He shook his head and started the engine, pulling out onto the street. He drove uncharacteristically slow, stopping at all the yellow lights, taking the long way to campus.

When we pulled in front of the entrance to Morgan Hall, the same sadness I felt the night I left the apartment consumed me. It was ridiculous to be so emotional, but each time I did something to push him away, I was terrified it would work.

He walked me to the door, and I pulled out my keys, avoiding his eyes. As I fumbled with the metal in my hand, his hand was suddenly at my chin, his thumb softly touching my lips.

"Did he kiss you?" he asked.

I pulled away, surprised that his fingers caused a burning feeling that seared every nerve from my mouth to my toes. "You really know how to screw up a perfect night, don't you?"

"You thought it was perfect, huh? Does that mean you had a good time?"

"I always do when I'm with you."

He looked to the ground and his eyebrows pulled together. "Did he kiss you?"

"Yes," I sighed, irritated.

His eyes closed tight. "Is that all?"

"That is none of your business!" I said, yanking open the door.

Travis pushed it closed and stood in my way, his expression apologetic. "I need to know."

"No you don't! Move, Travis!"

"Pigeon . . ."

"You think because I'm no longer a virgin, I'll screw anyone that'll have me? Thanks!" I said, shoving him.

"I didn't say that, damn it! Is it too much to ask for a little peace of mind?"

"Why would it give you peace of mind to know if I'm sleeping with Parker?"

"How can you not know? It's obvious to everyone else but you!" he said, exasperated.

"I guess I'm just an idiot, then. You're on a roll tonight, Trav," I said, reaching for the door handle.

He gripped my shoulders. "The way I feel about you . . . it's crazy."

"You got the crazy part right," I snapped, pulling away from him.

"I practiced this in my head the whole time we were on the bike, so just hear me out," he said.

"Travis—"

"I know we're fucked up, all right? I'm impulsive and hot-tempered, and you get under my skin like no one else. You act like you hate me one minute, and then you need me the next. I never get anything right, and I don't deserve you . . . but I fucking love you, Abby. I love you more than I've loved anyone or anything, ever. When you're around, I don't need booze or money or the fighting or the one-night stands . . . all I need is you. You're all I think about. You're all I dream about. You're all I want."

My plan to feign ignorance was an epic fail. I couldn't pretend to be impervious when he had laid all of his cards on the table. When we met, something inside both of us had changed, and whatever that was, it made us need each other. For reasons unknown to me, I was his exception, and as much as I had tried to fight my feelings, he was mine.

He shook his head, cupped each side of my face, and looked into my eyes. "Did you sleep with him?"

Hot tears filled my eyes as I shook my head no. He slammed his lips against mine, and his tongue entered my mouth without hesitation. Unable to control myself, I gripped his shirt in my fists, and pulled him to me. He hummed in his amazing deep voice and gripped me so tight that it was difficult to breathe.

He pulled back, breathless. "Call Parker. Tell him you don't wanna see him anymore. Tell him you're with me."

I closed my eyes. "I can't be with you, Travis."

"Why the hell not?" he said, letting go.

I shook my head, afraid of his reaction to the truth.

He laughed once. "Unbelievable. The one girl I want, and she doesn't want me."

I swallowed, knowing I would have to get closer to the truth than I had in months. "When America and I moved out here, it was with the understanding that my life was going to turn out a certain way. Or that it wouldn't turn out a certain way. The fighting, the gambling, the drinking . . . it's what I left behind. When I'm around you . . . it's all right there for me in an irresistible, tattooed package. I didn't move hundreds of miles away to live it all over again."

He pulled my chin up so that I would face him. "I know you deserve better than me. You think I don't know that? But if there was any woman made for me . . . it's you. I'll do whatever I have to do, Pidge. Do you hear me? I'll do anything."

I turned away from his grip, ashamed that I couldn't tell him the truth. I was the one that wasn't good enough. I would be the one to ruin everything, to ruin him. He would hate me one day, and I couldn't see the look in his eye when he came to that conclusion.

He held the door shut with his hand. "I'll stop fighting the second I graduate. I won't drink a single drop again. I'll give you the happy ever after, Pigeon. If you just believe in me, I can do it."

"I don't want you to change."

"Then tell me what to do. Tell me and I'll do it," he pleaded.

Any thoughts of being with Parker were long gone, and I knew it was because of my feelings for Travis. I thought about the different paths my life would take from that moment—trusting Travis with a leap of faith and risking the unknown, or pushing him away and knowing exactly where I would end up, which included a life without him—either decision terrified me.

"Can I borrow your phone?" I asked.

Travis pulled his brows together, confused. "Sure," he said, pulling his phone from his pocket, handing it to me.

I dialed, and then closed my eyes as it rang in my ear.

"Travis? What the hell? Do you know what time it is?" Parker answered. His voice was deep and raspy, and I instantly felt my heart vibrating in my chest. It hadn't occurred to me that he would know I had called from Travis's phone.

My next words somehow found their way to my trembling lips. "I'm sorry for calling you so early, but this couldn't wait. I . . . can't go to dinner with you on Wednesday."

"It's almost four in the morning, Abby. What's going on?"

"I can't see you at all, actually."

"Abs . . ."

"I'm . . . pretty sure I'm in love with Travis," I said, bracing for his reaction.

After a few moments of shocked silence, he hung up in my ear.

My eyes still focused on the pavement, I handed Travis his

phone and then reluctantly peered up at his expression. A combination of confusion, shock, and adoration scrolled across his face.

"He hung up," I grimaced.

He scanned my face with careful hope in his eyes. "You love me?"

"It's the tattoos," I shrugged.

A wide smile stretched across his face, making his dimple sink into his cheek. "Come home with me," he said, enveloping me in his arms.

My eyebrows shot up. "You said all that to get me in bed? I must have made quite an impression."

"The only thing I'm thinking about right now is holding you in my arms all night."

"Let's go," I said.

Despite the excessive speed and the shortcuts, the ride to the apartment seemed endless. When we finally arrived, Travis carried me up the stairs. I giggled against his lips as he fumbled to unlock the door. When he set me on my feet and closed the door behind us, he let out a long, relieved sigh.

"It hasn't seemed like home since you left," he said, kissing my lips.

Toto scampered down the hall and wagged his tiny tail, pawing at my legs. I cooed at him as I lifted him off the floor.

Shepley's bed squeaked, and then his feet stomped across the floor. His door flew open as he squinted from the light. "Fuck no, Trav, you're not pulling this shit! You're in love with Ab . . ."—his eyes focused and he recognized his mistake—". . . by. Hey, Abby."

"Hey, Shep," I said, setting Toto on the floor.

Travis pulled me past his still-shocked cousin and kicked the door shut behind us, pulling me into his arms and kissing me without a second thought, as if we had done it a million times before. I pulled his shirt over his head, and he slipped my jacket off my shoulders. I stopped kissing him long enough to remove my sweater and tank top and then crashed into him again. We undressed each other, and within seconds he lowered me to his mattress. I reached above my head to pull open the drawer and plunged my hand inside, searching for anything that crackled.

"Shit," he said, panting and frustrated. "I got rid of them."

"What? All of them?" I breathed.

"I thought you didn't . . . if I wasn't with you, I wasn't going to need them."

"You're kidding me!" I said, letting my head fall against the headboard.

His forehead fell against my chest. "Consider yourself the opposite of a foregone conclusion."

I smiled and kissed him. "You've never been with anyone without one?"

He shook his head. "Never." I looked around for a moment, lost in thought. He laughed once at my expression. "What are you doing?

"Ssh, I'm counting." Travis watched me for a moment and then leaned down to kiss my neck. "I can't concentrate while you're doing tha . . ."—I sighed—"the twenty-fifth and two days . . ." I breathed.

Travis chuckled. "What the hell are you talkin' about?"

"We're good," I said, sliding down so I was directly beneath him.

He pressed his chest against mine, and kissed me tenderly. "Are you sure?"

I let my hands glide from his shoulders to his backside and pulled him against me. He closed his eyes and let out a long, deep groan.

"Oh my God, Abby," he breathed. He rocked into me again, another hum emanating from his throat. "Holy shit, you feel amazing."

"Is it different?"

He looked into my eyes. "It's different with you, anyway, but"—he took in a deep breath and tensed again, closing his eyes for a moment—"I'm never going to be the same after this."

His lips searched every inch of my neck, and when he found his way to my mouth, I sunk my fingertips into the muscles of his shoulders, losing myself in the intensity of the kiss.

Travis brought my hands above my head and intertwined his fingers with mine, squeezing my hands with each thrust. His movements became a bit rougher, and I dug my nails into his hands, my insides tensing with incredible force.

I cried out, biting my lip and clenching my eyes shut.

"Abby," he whispered, sounding conflicted, "I need a . . . I need to . . ."

"Don't stop," I begged.

He rocked into me again, groaning so loudly that I covered his mouth. After a few labored breaths, he looked into my eyes and then kissed me over and over. His hands cupped each side of my face and then he kissed me again, slower, more tender. He touched his lips to mine, and then my cheeks, my forehead, my nose, and then finally returned to my lips.

I smiled and sighed, exhaustion setting in. Travis pulled me next to him, situating the covers over us. I rested my cheek against his chest, and he kissed my forehead once more, locking his fingers together behind me.

"Don't leave this time, okay? I wanna wake up just like this in the morning."

I kissed his chest, feeling guilty that he had to ask. "I'm not going anywhere."

Chapter Eleven
Jealousy

I AWOKE ON MY STOMACH, NAKED AND TANGLED IN TRA-
vis Maddox's sheets. I kept my eyes closed, feeling his fingers
caressing my arm and back.

He exhaled with a deep, contented sigh, speaking in a
hushed voice. "I love you, Abby. I'm going to make you happy,
I swear it."

The bed concaved as he shifted, and then his lips were on
my back in slow, small kisses. I remained still, and just as he
had made his way up to the skin just below my ear, he left me
to walk across the room. His footsteps leisurely plodded down
the hall, and the pipes whined with the water pressure of the
shower.

I opened my eyes and sat up, stretching. Every muscle in my
body ached, muscles that I never knew I had. I held the sheet to
my chest, looking out the window, watching the yellow and red
leaves spiral from their branches to the ground.

His cell phone vibrated somewhere on the floor, and after
clumsily searching the crumpled clothes next to the bed, I found

it in his jeans pocket. The display was lit with only a number, no name.

"Hello?"

"Is uh . . . is Travis there?" a woman asked.

"He's in the shower, can I take a message?"

"Of course he is. Tell him that Megan called, would ya?"

Travis walked in, tightening his towel around his water-splotched waist, and smiled as I held out his phone.

"It's for you," I said.

He kissed me before looking at the display, and then shook his head. "Yeah? It was my girlfriend. What do you need, Megan?" He listened for a moment and then smiled, "Well, Pigeon's special, what can I say?" After a long pause, he rolled his eyes. I could only imagine what she was saying. "Don't be a bitch, Megan. Listen, you can't call my phone anymore . . . Well, love'll do that to ya," he said, looking at me with a soft expression. "Yes, with Abby. I mean it, Meg, no more phone calls . . . Later."

He tossed his phone on the bed, and then sat beside me. "She was a little pissy. Did she say anything to you?"

"No, she just asked for you."

"I erased the few numbers I had on my phone, but I guess that doesn't stop them from calling me. If they don't figure it out on their own, I'll set them straight."

He watched me expectantly, and I couldn't help but smile. I had never seen this side of him. "I trust you, you know."

He pressed his lips to mine. "I wouldn't blame you if you expected me to earn it."

"I've got to get in the shower. I've already missed one class."

"See? I'm a good influence already."

I stood up, and he tugged on the sheet. "Megan said there's a Halloween party this weekend at the Red Door. I went with her last year, it was pretty fun."

"I'm sure it was," I said, raising an eyebrow.

"I just mean a lot of people come out. They have a pool tournament and cheap drinks . . . wanna go?"

"I'm not really . . . I don't do the dress-up thing. I never have."

"I don't, either. I just go," he shrugged.

"Are we still going bowling tonight?" I asked, wondering if the invitation was just to get some alone time with me that he no longer needed.

"Well, hell yeah! I'm gonna kick your ass, too!"

I narrowed my eyes at him. "Not this time you're not. I have a new superpower."

He laughed. "And what's that? Harsh language?"

I leaned over to kiss his neck once, and then ran my tongue up to his ear, kissing his earlobe. He froze in place.

"Distraction," I breathed into his ear.

He grabbed my arms and flipped me onto my back. "You're going to miss another class."

AFTER FINALLY TALKING HIM INTO LEAVING THE APART-ment long enough to attend history class, we raced to campus and slid into our seats just before Professor Chaney began. Travis turned his red baseball cap backward to plant a kiss on my lips in full view of everyone in the classroom.

On our way to the cafeteria, he took my hand in his, intertwining our fingers as we walked. He seemed so proud to be holding my hand, announcing to the world that we were finally together. Finch noticed, looking at our hands and then to me with a ridiculous grin. He wasn't the only one; our simple display of affection generated stares and murmuring from everyone we passed.

At the door of the cafeteria, Travis blew out his last puff of smoke, looking to me when I hesitated. America and Shepley were already inside, and Finch had lit another cigarette, leaving me to go in with Travis alone. I was certain the gossip had soared to a new level since Travis had kissed me in full view of everyone in our history class, and I dreaded walking out onto the stage the cafeteria presented.

"What, Pigeon?" he said, tugging on my hand.

"Everyone is watching us."

He pulled my hand to his mouth and kissed my fingers. "They'll get over it. It's just the initial shock. Remember when we first started hanging out? Their curiosity died down after a while and they got used to seeing us together. C'mon," he said, pulling me through the door.

One of the reasons I had chosen Eastern U was its modest population, but the exaggerated interest in scandal that came with it was at times exhausting. It was a running joke; everyone was aware of how ridiculous the rumor mill was, and yet they all shamelessly participated in it.

We sat down in our usual spots with our food. America smiled at me with a knowing expression. She chatted as if everything was normal, but the football players at the other end of the table were staring at me like I was on fire.

Travis tapped my apple with his fork. "You gonna eat that, Pidge?"

"No, you can have it, baby."

Heat consumed my ears when America's head jerked to look at me.

"It just came out," I said, shaking my head. I peeked up at Travis, whose expression was a mixture of amusement and adoration.

We had exchanged the term a few times that morning, and it hadn't occurred to me that it was new to everyone else until it tumbled from my mouth.

"You two have just reached the level of annoyingly cute," America grinned.

Shepley tapped my shoulder. "You staying over tonight?" he asked, his words garbled amid the bread in his mouth. "I promise I won't come out of my room cussing at you."

"You were defending my honor, Shep. You're forgiven," I said.

Travis took a bite of the apple and chewed, looking as happy as I'd ever seen him. The peace in his eyes had returned, and even as the dozens of people watched our every move, everything felt . . . right.

I thought of all the times I had insisted being with Travis was the wrong decision and how much time I had wasted fighting my feelings for him. Looking across the table at his soft brown eyes and the dimple dancing in his cheek as he chewed, I couldn't remember what I was so worried about.

"He looks awful happy. Did you finally give it up, Abby?" Chris said, elbowing his teammates.

"You're not very smart, are ya, Jenks?" Shepley said, frowning.

The blood instantly rose to my cheeks, and I looked to Travis who had murder in his eyes. My embarrassment took a backseat to Travis's anger, and I shook my head dismissively. "Just ignore him."

After another tense moment, his shoulders relaxed a bit, and he nodded once, taking a deep breath. After a few seconds, he winked at me.

I reached my hand across the table, sliding my fingers into his. "You meant what you said last night, didn't you?"

He began to speak, but Chris's laughter filled the cafeteria. "Holy God! Travis Maddox is whipped?"

"Did you mean it when you said you didn't want me to change?" he asked, squeezing my hand.

I looked down at Chris laughing to his teammates and then turned to Travis. "Absolutely. Teach that asshole some manners."

A mischievous grin spread across his face, and he walked down to the end of the table where Chris sat. Silence spread across the room, and Chris swallowed back his laughter.

"Hey, I was just givin' you a hard time, Travis," he said, looking up at him.

"Apologize to Pidge," Travis said, glowering down at him.

Chris looked down at me with a nervous grin. "I . . . I was just kidding, Abby. I'm sorry."

I glared at him as he looked up to Travis for approval. When Travis walked away, Chris snickered and then whispered something to Brazil. My heart began to pound when I saw Travis stop in his tracks and ball his hands into fists at his side.

Brazil shook his head and huffed in an exasperated sigh. "Just remember when you wake up, Chris . . . that you bring it on yourself."

Travis lifted Finch's tray off the table and swung it into Chris's face, knocking him off his chair. Chris tried to scramble under the table, but Travis pulled him out by his legs and then began to whale on him.

Chris curled into a ball, and then Travis kicked him in the back. Chris arched and turned, holding his hands out, allowing Travis to land several punches to his face. The blood began to flow, and Travis stood up, winded.

"If you even look at her, you piece of shit, I'll break your fuckin' jaw!" Travis yelled. I winced when he kicked Chris in the leg one last time.

The women working in the cafeteria scampered out, shocked at the bloody mess on the floor.

"Sorry," Travis said, wiping Chris's blood from his cheek.

Some of the students stood up to get a better look; others remained seated, watching with mild amusement. The football team simply stared at Chris's limp body on the floor, shaking their heads.

Travis turned, and Shepley stood, grabbing both my arm and America's hand, and pulled us out the door behind his cousin. We walked the short distance to Morgan Hall, and America and I sat on the front steps, watching Travis pace back and forth.

"You okay, Trav?" Shepley asked.

"Just . . . give me a minute," he said, putting his hands low on his hips as he walked.

Shepley shoved his hands into his pockets. "I'm surprised you stopped."

"Pidge said to teach him some manners, Shep, not kill him. It took everything I had to quit when I did."

America slipped on her large, square sunglasses to look up at Travis. "What did Chris say that set you off, anyway?"

"Something he'll never say again," Travis seethed.

America looked to Shepley, who shrugged. "I didn't hear it."

Travis's hands balled into fists again. "I'm goin' back in there."

Shepley touched Travis's shoulder. "Your girl's out here. You don't need to go back in there."

Travis looked at me, forcing himself to stay calm. "He said . . . everyone thinks Pidge has . . . Jesus, I can't even say it."

"Just say it already," America muttered, picking at her nails.

Finch walked up behind Travis, clearly thrilled by all the excitement. "Every straight guy at Eastern wants to try her out because she landed the unattainable Travis Maddox," he shrugged. "That's what they're saying in there now, at least."

Travis shouldered past Finch, heading for the cafeteria. Shepley bolted after him, grabbing his arm. My hands flew to my mouth when Travis swung, and Shepley ducked. My eyes darted to America who was unaffected, accustomed to their routine.

I could think of only one thing to do to stop him. I scrambled off the steps, wheeling around, directly in his path. I jumped on him, wrapping my legs around his waist, and he gripped my thighs as I grabbed each side of his face, planting a long, deep kiss on his mouth. I could feel his anger melt away as he kissed me, and when I pulled away, I knew I had won.

"We don't care what they think, remember? You can't start now," I said, smiling with confidence. I had more of an effect on him than I ever thought possible.

"I can't let them talk about you like that, Pigeon," he said with a frustrated frown, lowering me to my feet.

I slid my arms under his, interlocking my fingers behind his back. "Like what? They think I have something special because you've never settled down before. Do you disagree?"

"Hell no, I just can't stand the thought of every guy in this school wanting to bag you because of it." He pressed his forehead against mine. "This is going to make me crazy. I can already tell."

"Don't let them get to you, Travis," Shepley said. "You can't fight everybody."

Travis sighed. "Everybody. How would you feel if everybody thought about America like that?"

"Who says they don't?" America said, offended. We all laughed, and America made a face. "I wasn't kidding."

Shepley pulled her to her feet by her hands and kissed her cheek. "We know, baby. I gave up being jealous a long time ago. I'd never have time to do anything else."

America smiled in appreciation, and then hugged him. Shepley had an uncanny ability to make everyone around him feel at ease, no doubt the result from growing up around Travis and his brothers. It was probably more of a defense mechanism than anything.

Travis nuzzled my ear, and I giggled until I saw Parker approach. The same sense of urgency I'd felt when Travis wanted to return to the cafeteria overcame me, and I instantly let go of Travis to quickly walk the ten or so feet to intercept Parker.

"I need to talk to you," he said.

I glanced behind me, and then shook my head as a warning.

"Now is not a good time, Parker. It's a really, really bad time, actually. Travis and Chris got into it at lunch, and he's still a little raw. You need to go."

Parker eyed Travis, and then returned his attention to me, determined. "I just heard what happened in the cafeteria. I don't think you realize what you're getting yourself into. Travis is bad news, Abby. Everyone knows it. No one is talking about how great it is that you've turned him around . . . they're all waiting for him to do what he does best. I don't know what he's told you, but you have no clue what kind of person he is."

I felt Travis's hands on my shoulders. "Why don't you tell her, then?"

Parker shifted nervously. "Do you know how many humiliated girls I've taken home from parties after they've spent a few hours alone in a room with him? He's going to hurt you."

Travis's fingers tightened in reaction, and I rested my hand on his until he relaxed. "You should go, Parker."

"You should listen to what I'm saying, Abs."

"Don't fucking call her that," Travis growled.

Parker didn't take his eyes from mine. "I'm worried about you."

"I appreciate it, but it's unnecessary."

Parker shook his head. "He saw you as a long-term challenge, Abby. He has you thinking you're different from the other girls so he could get you in the sack. He's going to get tired of you. He has the attention span of a toddler."

Travis stepped around me, standing so close to Parker that their noses nearly touched. "I let you have your say. My patience has run out." Parker tried to look at me, but Travis leaned in his way. "Don't you fucking look at her. Look at me, you spoiled shit stain." Parker focused on Travis's eyes and waited. "If you so much as breathe in her direction, I'll make sure you'll be limping through med school."

Parker took a few steps back until I was in his line of sight. "I thought you were smarter than that," he said, shaking his head before turning away.

Travis watched him leave, and then turned around, his eyes searching mine. "You know that's a bunch of bullshit, right? It's not true."

"I'm sure that's what everyone is thinking," I grumbled, noting the interest of those walking by.

"Then I'll prove them wrong."

AS THE WEEK WORE ON, TRAVIS TOOK HIS PROMISE VERY seriously. He no longer humored the girls that stopped him on his way to and from class, and at times he was rude about it. By the time we walked into the Red for the Halloween party, I was a little nervous about how he planned to keep the intoxicated coeds away.

America, Finch, and I sat at a nearby table while watching Shepley and Travis play pool against two of their Sig Tau brothers.

"Go, baby!" America called, standing up on the rungs of her stool.

Shepley winked at her and then took his shot, sinking it into the far right pocket.

"Wooo!" she squealed.

A trio of women dressed as Charlie's Angels approached Travis while he waited his turn, and I smiled as he tried his best to ignore them. When one of them traced the line of one of his tattoos, Travis pulled his arm away. He waved her off so he could make a shot, and she pouted to her friends.

"Can you believe how ridiculous they are? The girls here are shameless," America said.

Finch shook his head in awe. "It's Travis. I think it's the bad-boy thing. They either want to save him or think they're immune to his wicked ways. I'm not sure which."

"It's probably both," I laughed, giggling at the girls waiting for Travis to pay them attention. "Can you imagine hoping you're the one he'll pick? Knowing you'll be used for sex?"

"Daddy issues," America said, taking a sip of her drink.

Finch put out his cigarette and tugged on our dresses. "Come on, girls! The Finch wants to dance!"

"Only if you promise not to call yourself that ever again," America said.

Finch jutted out his bottom lip, and America smiled. "Come on, Abby. You don't wanna make Finch cry, do you?"

We joined the policemen and vampires on the dance floor, and Finch broke out his Timberlake moves. I glanced at Travis over my shoulder and caught him watching me from the corner of his eye, pretending to watch Shepley sink the eight ball for the game. Shepley collected their winnings, and Travis walked to the long, shallow table that bordered the dance floor, taking a drink. Finch flailed about on the dance floor, finally sandwiching himself between America and me. Travis rolled his eyes, chuckling as he returned to our table with Shepley.

"I'm going to get another drink. Want anything?" America shouted over the music.

"I'll go with you," I said, looking to Finch and pointing at the bar.

Finch shook his head and continued to dance. America and I shouldered through the crowd to the bar. The bartenders were overwhelmed, so we settled in for a long wait.

"The boys are making a killing tonight," America said.

I leaned into her ear. "Why anyone bets against Shep I'll never understand."

"For the same reason they bet against Travis. They're idiots," she smiled.

A man in a toga leaned against the bar beside America and smiled. "What are you ladies drinking this evening?"

"We buy our own beverages, thanks," America said, facing forward.

"I'm Mike," he said, and then pointed to his friend, "This is Logan."

I smiled politely, looking to America, who made her best go-away expression. The bartender took our order and then nodded to the men behind us, turning to make America's drink. She brought over a square glass full of pink, frothy liquid and three beers. Mike handed her some money, and she nodded.

"This is something else," Mike said, scanning the crowd.

"Yeah," America said, annoyed.

"I saw you dancing out there," Logan said to me, nodding to the dance floor. "You looked good."

"Uh . . . thanks," I said, trying to remain polite, wary that Travis was just a few yards away.

"You wanna dance?" he asked.

I shook my head. "No, thanks. I'm here with my—"

"Boyfriend," Travis said, appearing out of nowhere. He

glared at the men standing in front of us, and they backed away a bit, clearly intimidated.

America couldn't contain her smug smile as Shepley wrapped his arm around her. Travis nodded across the room. "Run along, now."

The men glanced at America and me and then took a few cautious steps backward before retreating behind the safety of the crowd.

Shepley kissed America. "I can't take you anywhere!" She giggled, and I smiled at Travis, who was glowering down at me.

"What?"

"Why did you let him buy your drink?"

America let go of Shepley, noticing Travis's mood. "We didn't, Travis. I told them not to."

Travis took the bottle from my hand. "Then what's this?"

"Are you serious?" I asked.

"Yes, I'm fucking serious," he said, tossing the beer in the trash can by the bar. "I've told you a hundred times . . . you can't be taking drinks from random guys. What if he put something in it?"

America held up her glass. "The drinks were never out of our sight, Trav. You're overreacting."

"I'm not talking to you," Travis said, his eyes boring into mine.

"Hey!" I said, instantly angry. "Don't talk to her like that."

"Travis," Shepley warned, "let it go."

"I don't like you letting other guys buy you drinks," Travis said.

I raised an eyebrow. "Are you trying to pick a fight?"

"Would it bother you to walk up to the bar and see me sharing a drink with some chick?"

I nodded once. "Okay. You're oblivious to all women, now. I get it. I should be making the same effort."

"It would be nice." He was clearly trying to subdue his temper, and it was a bit unnerving to be on the wrong side of his wrath. His eyes were still bright with anger, and an innate urge to go on the offensive bubbled to the surface.

"You're going to have to tone down the jealous-boyfriend thing, Travis. I didn't do anything wrong."

Travis shot me an incredulous look. "I walk up here, and some guy is buying you a drink!"

"Don't yell at her!" America said.

Shepley put his hand on Travis's shoulder. "We've all had a lot to drink. Let's just get out of here." Shepley's usually calming effect was lost on Travis, and I was instantly annoyed that his tantrum had ended our night.

"I have to tell Finch we're leaving," I grumbled, shouldering past Travis to the dance floor.

A warm hand encapsulated my wrist. I wheeled around, seeing Travis's fingers locked without regret. "I'll go with you."

I twisted my arm from his grip. "I am fully capable of walking a few feet by myself, Travis. What is wrong with you?"

I spied Finch in the middle and pushed my way out to him. "We're leaving!"

"What?" Finch yelled over the music.

"Travis is in a pissy mood! We're leaving!"

Finch rolled his eyes and shook his head, waving as I left the dance floor. Just as I spotted America and Shepley, I was tugged backward by a man in a pirate costume.

"Where do you think you're going?" he smiled, bumping up against me.

I laughed and shook my head at the silly face he was making. Just as I turned to walk away, he grabbed my arm. It didn't take long for me to realize he wasn't grabbing at me, he was grabbing for me—for protection.

"Whoa!" he cried, looking beyond me with wide eyes.

Travis barreled his way onto the dance floor, and plunged his fist straight into the pirate's face, the force sending both of us to the ground. With my palms flat on the wooden floor, I blinked my eyes in stunned disbelief. Feeling something warm and wet on my hand, I turned it over and recoiled. It was covered in blood from the man's nose. His hand was cupped over his face, but the bright red liquid poured down his forearm as he writhed on the floor.

Travis scrambled to pick me up, seeming as shocked as I was. "Oh shit! Are you all right, Pidge?"

When I got to my feet, I yanked my arm from his grip. "Are you insane?"

America grabbed my wrist and pulled me through the crowd to the parking lot. Shepley unlocked his doors and after I slid into my seat, Travis turned to me.

"I'm sorry, Pigeon, I didn't know he had a hold of you."

"Your fist was two inches from my face!" I said, catching the oil-stained towel Shepley had thrown at me. I wiped the blood from my hand, revolted.

The seriousness of the situation darkened his face and he

winced. "I wouldn't have swung if I thought I could have hit you. You know that, right?"

"Shut up, Travis. Just shut up," I said, staring at the back of Shepley's head.

"Pidge . . ." Travis began.

Shepley hit his steering wheel with the heel of his hand. "Shut up, Travis! You said you're sorry, now shut the fuck up!"

The trip home was made in complete silence. Shepley pulled his seat forward to let me out of the car, and I looked to America, who nodded with understanding.

She kissed her boyfriend good night. "I'll see you tomorrow, baby."

Shep nodded in resignation and kissed her. "Love you."

I walked past Travis to America's Honda, and he jogged to my side. "C'mon. Don't leave mad."

"Oh, I'm not leaving mad. I'm furious."

"She needs some time to cool off, Travis," America warned, unlocking her door.

When the passenger side lock popped, Travis held his hand against the door. "Don't leave, Pigeon. I was out of line. I'm sorry."

I held up my hand, showing him the remnants of dried blood on my palm. "Call me when you grow up."

He leaned against the door with his hip. "You can't leave."

I raised an eyebrow, and Shepley jogged around the car beside us. "Travis, you're drunk. You're about to make a huge mistake. Just let her go home, cool off . . . you can both talk tomorrow when you're sober."

Travis's expression turned desperate. "She can't leave," he said, staring into my eyes.

"It's not going to work, Travis," I said, tugging on the door. "Move!"

"What do you mean it's not gonna work?" Travis asked, grabbing my arm.

"I mean the sad face. I'm not falling for it," I said, pulling away.

Shepley watched Travis for a moment, and then turned to me. "Abby . . . this is the moment I was talking about. Maybe you should . . ."

"Stay out of it, Shep," America snapped, starting the car.

"I'm gonna fuck up. I'm gonna fuck up a lot, Pidge, but you have to forgive me."

"I'm going to have a huge bruise on my ass in the morning! You hit that guy because you were pissed at me! What should that tell me? Because red flags are going up all over the place right now!"

"I've never hit a girl in my life," he said, surprised at my words.

"And I'm not about to be the first one!" I said, tugging on the door. "Move, damn it!"

Travis nodded, and then took a step back. I sat beside America, slamming the door. She put the car in reverse, and Travis leaned down to look at me through the window.

"You're going to call me tomorrow, right?" he said, touching the windshield.

"Just go, Mare," I said, refusing to meet his eyes.

The night was long. I kept looking at the clock and cringed when I saw that another hour had passed. I couldn't stop thinking about Travis and whether or not I would call him, wondering if he was awake as well. I finally resorted to sticking the earbuds of my iPod in my ear and listening to every loud, obnoxious song on my playlist.

The last time I looked at the clock, it was after four. The birds were already chirping outside my window, and I smiled when my eyes began to feel heavy. It seemed like just a few moments later when I heard a knock at the door, and America burst through it. She pulled the earbuds from my ears and then fell into my desk chair.

"Mornin', sunshine. You look like hell," she said, blowing a pink bubble from her mouth and then letting it smack loudly as it popped.

"Shut UP, America!" Kara said from under her covers.

"You realize people like you and Trav are going to fight, right?" America said, filing her nails as she chewed the huge wad of gum in her mouth.

I turned over on the bed. "You are officially fired. You are a terrible conscience."

She laughed. "I just know you. If I handed you my keys right now, you'd drive straight over there."

"I would not!"

"Whatever," she lilted.

"It's eight o'clock in the morning, Mare. They're probably still passed out cold."

Just then, I heard a faint knock on the door. Kara's arm shot out from under her comforter and turned the knob. The door slowly opened, revealing Travis in the doorway.

"Can I come in?" he asked in a low, raspy voice. The purple circles under his eyes announced his lack of sleep, if he'd had any at all.

I sat up in bed, startled by his exhausted appearance. "Are you okay?"

He walked in and fell to his knees in front of me. "I'm so sorry, Abby. I'm sorry," he said, wrapping his arms around my waist and burying his head in my lap.

I cradled his head in my arms and peered up at America.

"I'm uh ... I'm gonna go," she said, awkwardly fumbling for the door handle.

Kara rubbed her eyes and sighed and then grabbed her shower bag. "I'm always very clean when you're around, Abby," she grumbled, slamming the door behind her.

Travis looked up at me. "I know I get crazy when it comes to you, but God knows I'm tryin', Pidge. I don't wanna screw this up."

"Then don't."

"This is hard for me, ya know. I feel like any second you're going to figure out what a piece of shit I am and leave me. When you were dancing last night, I saw a dozen different guys watching you. You go to the bar, and I see you thank that guy for your drink. Then that douchebag on the dance floor grabs you."

"You don't see me throwing punches every time a girl talks to you. I can't stay locked up in the apartment all the time. You're going to have to get a handle on your temper."

"I will. I've never wanted a girlfriend before, Pigeon. I'm not used to feeling this way about someone ... about anyone. If you'll be patient with me, I swear I'll get it figured out."

"Let's get something straight; you're not a piece of shit, you're amazing. It doesn't matter who buys me drinks or who asks me to dance or who flirts with me. I'm going home with you. You've asked me to trust you, and you don't seem to trust me."

He frowned. "That's not true."

"If you think I'm going to leave you for the next guy that comes along, then you don't have much faith in me."

He tightened his grip. "I'm not good enough for you, Pidge. That doesn't mean I don't trust you, I'm just bracing for the inevitable."

"Don't say that. When we're alone, you're perfect. We're perfect. But then you let everyone else ruin it. I don't expect a 180, but you have to pick your battles. You can't come out swinging every time someone looks at me."

He nodded. "I'll do anything you want. Just . . . tell me you love me."

"You know I do."

"I need to hear you say it," he said, his brows pulling together.

"I love you," I said, touching my lips to his. "Now quit being such a baby."

He laughed, crawling into the bed with me. We spent the next hour in the same spot under the covers, giggling and kissing, barely noticing when Kara returned from the shower.

"Could you get out? I have to get dressed," Kara said to Travis, tightening her robe.

Travis kissed my cheek, and then stepped into the hall. "See ya in a sec."

I fell against my pillow as Kara rummaged through her closet. "What are you so happy about?" she grumbled.

"Nothing," I sighed.

"Do you know what codependency is, Abby? Your boyfriend is a prime example, which is creepy considering he went from having no respect for women at all to thinking he needs you to breathe."

"Maybe he does," I said, refusing to let her spoil my mood.

"Don't you wonder why that is? I mean . . . he's been through half the girls at this school. Why you?"

"He says I'm different."

"Sure he does. But why?"

"Why do you care?" I snapped.

"It's dangerous to need someone that much. You're trying to save him, and he's hoping you can. You two are a disaster."

I smiled at the ceiling. "It doesn't matter what or why it is. When it's good, Kara . . . it's beautiful."

She rolled her eyes. "You're hopeless."

Travis knocked on the door, and Kara let him in.

"I'm going to the commons to study. Good luck," she said in the most insincere voice she could muster.

"What was that about?" Travis asked.

"She said we're a disaster."

"Tell me something I don't know," he smiled. His eyes were suddenly focused, and he kissed the tender skin behind my ear. "Why don't you come home with me?"

I rested my hand on the back of his neck and sighed at the feeling of his soft lips against my skin. "I think I'm going to stay here. I'm constantly at your apartment."

His head popped up. "So? You don't like it there?"

I touched his cheek and sighed. He was so quick to worry. "Of course I do, but I don't live there."

He ran the tip of his nose up my neck. "I want you there. I want you there every night."

"I'm not moving in with you," I said, shaking my head.

"I didn't ask you to move in with me. I said I want you there."

"Same thing!" I laughed.

Travis frowned. "You're really not staying with me tonight?"

I shook my head, and his eyes traveled up my wall to the ceiling. I could almost see the wheels spinning inside his head. "What are you up to?" I asked, narrowing my eyes.

"I'm trying to think of another bet."

Chapter Twelve
Two of a Kind

I FLIPPED A TINY WHITE PILL IN MY MOUTH AND SWAL-
lowed, chasing it with a large glass of water. I was standing in
the middle of Travis's bedroom in a bra and panties, getting
ready to slip into my pajamas.

"What's that?" Travis asked from the bed.

"Uh . . . my pill?"

He frowned. "What pill?"

"The pill, Travis. You have yet to replenish your top drawer
and the last thing I need is to worry about whether or not I'm
going to get my period."

"Oh."

"One of us has to be responsible," I said, raising an eyebrow.

"My God, you're sexy," Travis said, propping his head up
with his hand. "The most beautiful woman at Eastern is my
girlfriend. That's insanity."

I rolled my eyes and slipped the purple silk over my head,
crawling in bed beside him. I straddled his lap and kissed his
neck, giggling when he let his head fall against the headboard.
"Again? You're gonna kill me, Pidge."

"You can't die," I said, covering his face with kisses. "You're too damn mean."

"No, I can't die because there are too many jackasses falling over themselves to take my place! I may live forever just to spite them!"

I giggled against his mouth and he flipped me onto my back. His finger slid under the delicate purple ribbon tied at the crest of my shoulder and slid it down my arm, kissing the skin it left behind.

"Why me, Trav?"

He leaned back, searching my eyes. "What do you mean?"

"You've been with all these women, refused to settle down, refuse to even take a phone number . . . so why me?"

"Where is this coming from?" he said, his thumb caressing my cheek.

I shrugged. "I'm just curious."

"Why me? You have half the men at Eastern just waiting for me to screw up."

I wrinkled my nose. "That's not true. Don't change the subject."

"It is true. If I hadn't been chasing you from the beginning of school, you'd have more than Parker Hayes following you around. He's just too self-absorbed to be scared of me."

"You're avoiding my question! And poorly, I might add."

"Okay! Why you?" A smile spread across his face and he leaned down to touch his lips to mine. "I had a thing for you since the night of that first fight."

"What?" I said with a dubious expression.

"It's true. You in that cardigan with blood all over you? You looked absolutely ridiculous," he chuckled.

"Thanks."

His smiled faded. "It was when you looked up at me. That was the moment. You had this wide-eyed, innocent look . . . no pretenses. You didn't look at me like I was Travis Maddox," he said, rolling his eyes at his own words, "you looked at me like I was . . . I don't know, a person, I guess."

"News flash, Trav. You are a person."

He brushed my bangs from my face. "No, before you came, Shepley was the only one that treated me like anyone else. You didn't get all awkward or flirt or run your fingers through your hair. You saw me."

"I was a complete bitch to you."

He kissed my neck. "That's what sealed the deal."

I slipped my hands down his back and into his boxers. "I hope this gets old soon. I don't see myself ever getting tired of you."

"Promise?" he asked, smiling.

His phone buzzed on the night table and he smiled again, holding it to his ear. "Yeah? . . . Oh, hell no, I got Pidge here with me. We're just gettin' ready to go to bed . . . Shut the fuck up, Trent, that's not funny . . . Seriously? What's he doin' in town?" He looked at me and sighed. "All right. We'll be there in half an hour . . . You heard me, douchebag. Because I don't go anywhere without her, that's why. Do you want me to pound your face when I get there?" Travis hung up and shook his head.

I raised an eyebrow. "That is the weirdest conversation I've ever heard."

"That was Trent. Thomas is in town and it's poker night at my dad's."

"Poker night?" I swallowed.

"Yeah, they usually take all of my money. Cheatin' bastards."

"I'm going to meet your family in thirty minutes?"

He looked at his watch. "Twenty-seven minutes to be exact."

"Oh my God, Travis!" I wailed, jumping out of bed.

"What are you doing?" he sighed.

I rummaged through the closet and yanked on a pair of jeans, hopping up and down to pull them up, and then pulled the nightgown over my head, throwing it into Travis's face. "I can't believe you gave me twenty minutes' notice to meet your family! I could kill you right now!"

He pulled my nightgown from his eyes and laughed at my desperate attempt to look presentable. I grabbed a black V-neck shirt and tugged it to its proper position and then ran to the bathroom, brushing my teeth and ripping a brush through my hair. Travis walked up behind me, fully dressed and ready, and wrapped his arms around my waist.

"I'm a mess!" I said, frowning in the mirror.

"Do you even realize how beautiful you are?" he asked, kissing my neck.

I huffed, scampering into his room to slip on a pair of heels, and then took Travis's hand as he led me to the door. I stopped, zipping up my black leather jacket and pulling my hair up into a tight bun in preparation for the blustery ride to his father's house.

"Calm down, Pigeon. It's just a bunch of guys sitting around a table."

"This is the first time I'm meeting your dad and your

brothers ... all at the same time ... and you want me to calm down?" I said, climbing onto his bike behind him.

He angled his neck, touching my cheek as he kissed me. "They're going to love you, just like I do."

When we arrived, I let my hair fall down my back and ran my fingers through it a few times before Travis led me through the door.

"Holy Christ! It's the asshat!" one of the boys called.

Travis nodded once. He tried to look annoyed, but I could see that he was excited to see his brothers. The house was dated, with yellow-and-brown faded wallpaper and shag carpet in different shades of brown. We walked down a hall to a room straight ahead with the door wide open. Smoke wafted into the hallway, and his brothers and father were seated at a round wooden table with mismatched chairs.

"Hey, hey ... watch the language around the young lady," his dad said, the cigar in his mouth bobbing while he talked.

"Pidge, this is my dad, Jim Maddox. Dad, this is Pigeon."

"Pigeon?" Jim asked, an amused expression on his face.

"Abby," I said, shaking his hand.

Travis pointed to his brothers. "Trenton, Taylor, Tyler, and Thomas."

They all nodded, and all but Thomas looked like older versions of Travis: buzz cuts, brown eyes, their T-shirts stretched over their bulging muscles, and covered in tattoos. Thomas wore a dress shirt and loosened tie, his eyes were hazel green, and his dark blond hair was longer by about an inch.

"Does Abby have a last name?" Jim asked.

"Abernathy," I nodded.

"It's nice to meet you, Abby," Thomas said, smiling.

"Really nice," Trenton said, giving me an impish once-over. Jim slapped the back of his head and he yelped. "What'd I say?" he said, rubbing the back of his head.

"Have a seat, Abby. Watch us take Trav's money," one of the twins said. I couldn't tell which was which; they were carbon copies of each other, even their tattoos matched.

The room was peppered with vintage pictures of poker games, pictures of poker legends posing with Jim and someone I assumed to be Travis's grandfather, and antique playing cards along the shelves.

"You knew Stu Ungar?" I asked, pointing to a dusty photo.

Jim's squinty eyes brightened. "You know who Stu Ungar is?"

I nodded. "My dad's a fan, too."

He stood up, pointing to the picture beside it. "And that's Doyle Brunson, there."

I smiled. "My dad saw him play, once. He's unbelievable."

"Trav's granddaddy was a professional . . . we take poker very seriously around here," Jim smiled.

I sat between Travis and one of the twins while Trenton shuffled the deck with moderate skill. The boys put in their cash and Jim divvied out the chips.

Trenton raised an eyebrow. "You wanna play, Abby?"

I smiled politely and shook my head. "I don't think I should."

"You don't know how?" Jim asked.

I couldn't hold back a smile. Jim looked so serious, almost paternal. I knew what answer he expected, and I hated to disappoint him.

Travis kissed my forehead. "Play . . . I'll teach you."

"You should just kiss your money goodbye, now, Abby," Thomas laughed.

I pressed my lips together and dug into my purse, pulling out two fifties. I held them out to Jim and waited patiently as he traded them for chips. Trenton's mouth tightened into a smug smile, but I ignored him.

"I have faith in Travis's teaching skills," I said.

One of the twins clapped his hands together. "Hells yeah! I'm going to get rich tonight!"

"Let's start small this time," Jim said, throwing in a five-dollar chip.

Trenton dealt, and Travis fanned out my hand for me. "Have you ever played cards?"

"It's been a while," I nodded.

"Go Fish doesn't count, Pollyanna," Trenton said, looking at his cards.

"Shut your hole, Trent," Travis said, glancing up at his brother before looking back down to my hand. "You're shooting for higher cards, consecutive numbers, and if you're really lucky, in the same suit."

The first hand, Travis looked at my cards and I looked at his. I mainly nodded and smiled, playing when I was told. Both Travis and I lost, and my chips had dwindled by the end of the first round.

After Thomas dealt to begin the second round, I wouldn't let Travis see my cards. "I think I've got this," I said.

"You sure?" he asked.

"I'm sure, baby," I said.

Three hands later, I had won back my chips and annihilated

the stacked chips of the others with a pair of aces, a straight, and the high card.

"Bullshit!" Trenton whined. "Beginner's luck sucks!"

"You've got a fast learner, Trav," Jim said, moving his mouth around his cigar.

Travis swigged his beer. "You're makin' me proud, Pigeon!" His eyes were bright with excitement, and his smile was different than I'd ever seen before.

"Thanks."

"Those that cannot do, teach," Thomas said, smirking.

"Very funny, asshole," Travis murmured.

Four hands later, I tipped back the last of my beer and narrowed my eyes at the only man at the table who hadn't folded. "The action's on you, Taylor. You gonna be a baby or you going to put in like a man?"

"Fuck it," he said, throwing the last of his chips in.

Travis looked at me, his eyes animated. It reminded me of the expressions of those watching his fights.

"Whatdya got, Pigeon?"

"Taylor?" I prompted.

A wide grin spread across his face. "Flush!" he smiled, spreading his cards faceup on the table.

Five pairs of eyes turned to me. I scanned the table and then slammed my cards down. "Read 'em and weep, boys! Aces and eights!" I said, giggling.

"A full house? What the fuck?" Trenton cried.

"Sorry. I've always wanted to say that," I said, pulling in my chips.

Thomas's eyes narrowed. "This isn't just beginner's luck. She plays."

Travis eyed Thomas for a moment and then looked to me. "Have you played before, Pidge?"

I pressed my lips together and shrugged, displaying my best innocent smile. Travis's head fell back, bursting into a barrage of laughter. He tried to speak but couldn't and then hit the table with his fist.

"Your girlfriend just fucking hustled us!" Taylor said, pointing in my direction.

"NO FUCKING WAY!" Trenton wailed, standing up.

"Good plan, Travis. Bring a card shark to poker night," Jim said, winking at me.

"I didn't know!" he said, shaking his head.

"Bullshit," Thomas said, eyeing me.

"I didn't!" he said through his laughter.

"I hate to say it, bro. But I think I just fell in love with your girl," Tyler said.

"Hey, now," Travis said, his smile quickly fading into a grimace.

"That's it. I was going easy on you, Abby, but I'm winning my money back, now," Trenton warned.

Travis sat out for the last few rounds, watching his brothers try their hardest to regain their money. Hand after hand, I pulled in their chips, and hand after hand, Thomas watched me more closely. Every time I laid my cards down, Travis and Jim laughed, Taylor cursed, Tyler proclaimed his undying love for me, and Trenton threw a full-blown tantrum.

I cashed in my chips and gave them each one hundred dollars once we settled into the living room. Jim refused, but the brothers accepted with gratitude. Travis grabbed my hand and we walked to the door.

I could see he was unhappy, so I squeezed his fingers in mine. "What's wrong?"

"You just gave away four hundred bucks, Pidge!" Travis frowned.

"If this was poker night at Sig Tau, I would have kept it. I can't rob your brothers the first time I meet them."

"They would have kept your money!" he said.

"And I wouldn't have lost a second of sleep over it, either," Taylor said.

Thomas stared at me in silence from the corner of the room.

"Why do you keep starin' at my girl, Tommy?"

"What did you say your last name was?" Thomas asked.

I shifted my weight nervously. My mind raced for something witty or sarcastic to say to deflect the question. I picked at my nails instead, silently cursing myself. I should have known better than to win all those hands. Thomas knew. I could see it in his eyes.

Travis, noticing my unease, turned to his brother and put his arm around my waist. I wasn't sure if he was doing it in protective reaction, or if he was bracing himself for what his brother might say.

Travis shifted, visibly uncomfortable with his brother's questioning. "It's Abernathy. What of it?"

"I can see why you didn't put it together before tonight, Trav, but now you don't have an excuse," Thomas said, smug.

"What the fuck are you talking about?" Travis asked.

"Are you related to Mick Abernathy by any chance?" Thomas asked.

All heads turned in my direction, and I nervously raked my hair back with my fingers. "How do you know Mick?"

Travis angled his head to look into my eyes. "He's only one of the best poker players that ever lived. Do you know him?"

I winced, knowing I had finally been cornered into telling the truth. "He's my father."

The entire room exploded.

"NO FUCKING WAY!"

"I KNEW IT!"

"WE JUST PLAYED MICK ABERNATHY'S DAUGHTER!"

"MICK ABERNATHY? HOLY SHIT!"

Thomas, Jim, and Travis were the only ones not shouting. "I told you guys I shouldn't play," I said.

"If you would have mentioned you were Mick Abernathy's daughter, I think we would have taken you more seriously," Thomas said.

I peered over at Travis, who stared at me in awe. "You're Lucky Thirteen?" he asked, his eyes a bit hazy.

Trenton stood and pointed at me, his mouth opened wide. "Lucky Thirteen is in our house! No way! I don't fucking believe it!"

"That was the nickname the papers gave me. And the story wasn't exactly accurate," I said, fidgeting.

"I need to get Abby home, guys," Travis said, still staring at me.

Jim peered at me over his glasses. "Why wasn't it accurate?"

"I didn't take my dad's luck. I mean, how ridiculous," I chuckled, twisting my hair nervously around my finger.

Thomas shook his head. "No, Mick gave that interview. He said at midnight on your thirteenth birthday his luck ran dry."

"And yours picked up," Travis added.

"You were raised by mobsters!" Trenton said, smiling with excitement.

"Uh . . . no." I laughed once. "They didn't raise me. They were just . . . around a lot."

"That was a damn shame, Mick running your name through the mud like that in all the papers. You were just a kid," Jim said, shaking his head.

"If anything it was beginner's luck," I said, desperately trying to hide my humiliation.

"You were taught by Mick Abernathy," Jim said, shaking his head in awe. "You were playing pros, and winning, at thirteen years old, for Christ's sakes." He looked at Travis and smiled. "Don't bet against her, son. She doesn't lose."

Travis looked at me, then, his expression still shocked and disoriented. "Uh . . . we gotta go, Dad. Bye, guys."

The deep, excited chatter of Travis's family faded as he pulled me out the door and to his bike. I twisted my hair into a bun and zipped up my coat, waiting for him to speak. He climbed onto his bike without a word, and I straddled the seat behind him.

I was sure he felt that I hadn't been honest with him, and he was probably embarrassed that he found out about such an important part of my life the same time his family had. I expected a huge argument when we returned to his apartment, and I went over a dozen different apologies in my head before we reached the front door.

He led me down the hall by my hand, and then helped me with my coat.

I pulled at the caramel knot on the crown of my head, and

my hair fell past my shoulders in thick waves. "I know you're mad," I said, unable to look him in the eye. "I'm sorry I didn't tell you, but it's not something I talk about."

"Mad at you?" he said. "I am so turned on I can't see straight. You just robbed my asshole brothers of their money without batting an eyelash, you have achieved legend status with my father, and I know for a fact that you purposely lost that bet we made before my fight."

"I wouldn't say that . . ."

He lifted his chin. "Did you think you were going to win?"

"Well . . . no, not exactly," I said, pulling off my heels.

Travis smiled. "So you wanted to be here with me. I think I just fell in love with you all over again."

"How are you not mad right now?" I asked, tossing my shoes to the closet.

He sighed and nodded. "That's pretty big, Pidge. You should have told me. But I understand why you didn't. You came here to get away from all of that. It's like the sky opened up . . . everything makes sense, now."

"Well, that's a relief."

"Lucky Thirteen," he said, shaking his head and pulling my shirt over my head.

"Don't call me that, Travis. It's not a good thing."

"You're fucking famous, Pigeon!" he said, surprised at my words. He unbuttoned my jeans and pulled them down around my ankles, helping me to step out of them.

"My father hated me after that. He still blames me for all his problems."

Travis yanked off his shirt and hugged me to him. "I still

can't believe the daughter of Mick Abernathy is standing in front of me, and I've been with you this whole time and had no idea."

I pushed away from him. "I'm not Mick Abernathy's daughter, Travis! That's what I left behind. I'm Abby. Just Abby!" I said, walking over to the closet. I yanked a T-shirt off its hanger and pulled it over my head.

He sighed. "I'm sorry. I'm a little starstruck."

"It's just me!" I held the palm of my hand to my chest, desperate for him to understand.

"Yeah, but . . ."

"But nothing. The way you're looking at me right now? This is exactly why I didn't tell you." I closed my eyes. "I won't live like that anymore, Trav. Not even with you."

"Whoa! Calm down, Pigeon. Let's not get carried away." His eyes focused and he walked over to wrap me in his arms. "I don't care what you were or what you're not anymore. I just want you."

"I guess we have that in common, then."

He led me to the bed, smiling down at me. "It's just you and me against the world, Pidge."

I curled up beside him, settling into the mattress. I had never planned on anyone besides myself and America knowing about Mick, and I never expected that my boyfriend would belong to a family of poker buffs. I heaved a heavy sigh, pressing my cheek against his chest.

"What's wrong?" he asked.

"I don't want anyone to know, Trav. I didn't want you to know."

"I love you, Abby. I won't mention it again, okay? Your secret's safe with me," he said, kissing my forehead.

• ◆ •

"MR. MADDOX, THINK YOU COULD TONE IT DOWN UNTIL after class?" Professor Chaney said, reacting to my giggling as Travis nuzzled my neck.

I cleared my throat, feeling my cheeks radiate with embarrassment.

"I don't think so, Dr. Chaney. Have you gotten a good look at my girl?" Travis said, gesturing to me.

Laughter echoed throughout the room, and my face caught fire. Professor Chaney glanced at me with a half-amused, half-awkward expression and then shook his head at Travis.

"Just do your best," Chaney said.

The class laughed again, and I sunk into my seat. Travis rested his arm on the back of my chair, and the lecture continued. After class had been dismissed, Travis walked me to my next class.

"Sorry if I embarrassed you. I can't help myself."

"Try."

Parker walked by, and when I returned his nod with a polite smile, his eyes brightened. "Hey, Abby. See you inside." He walked into the classroom, and Travis glowered at him for a few tense moments.

"Hey," I tugged on his hand until he looked at me. "Forget about him."

"He's been telling the guys at the House that you're still calling him."

"That's not true," I said, unaffected.

"I know that, but they don't. He said he's just biding his time. He told Brad that you're just waiting for the right time to dump me, and how you call him to say how unhappy you are. He's starting to piss me off."

"He has quite an imagination." I glanced at Parker, and when he met my eyes and smiled, I glared at him.

"Would you get mad if I embarrassed you one more time?"

I shrugged and Travis wasted no time leading me into the classroom. He stopped at my desk, setting my bag on the floor. He looked over at Parker and then pulled me to him, one hand on the nape of my neck, one hand on my backside, and then kissed me, deep and determined. He worked his lips against mine in the way he usually reserved for his bedroom, and I couldn't help but grab his shirt with both fists.

The murmuring and giggles grew louder after it became clear that Travis wasn't going to let go anytime soon.

"I think he just got her pregnant!" someone from the back of the room said, laughing.

I pulled away with my eyes closed, trying to regain my composure. When I looked at Travis, he was staring at me with the same forced restraint.

"I was just trying to make a point," he whispered.

"Good point," I nodded.

Travis smiled, kissed my cheek, and then looked to Parker, who was fuming in his seat.

"I'll see you at lunch," he winked.

I fell against my seat and sighed, trying to shake off the tingling between my thighs.

I labored through Calculus, and when class was over I noticed Parker standing against the wall by the door.

"Parker," I nodded, determined not to give him the reaction he was hoping for.

"I know you're with him. He doesn't have to violate you in front of an entire class on my account."

I stopped in my tracks and poised to attack. "Then maybe you should stop telling your frat brothers that I'm calling you. You're going to push him too far, and I'm not going to feel sorry for you when he puts his boot in your ass."

He wrinkled his nose. "Listen to you. You've been around Travis too much."

"No, this is me. It's just a side of me you know nothing about."

"You didn't exactly give me a chance, did you?"

I sighed. "I don't want to fight with you, Parker. It just didn't work out, okay?"

"No, it's not okay. You think I enjoy being the laughingstock of Eastern? Travis Maddox is the one we all appreciate because he makes us look good. He uses girls, tosses them aside, and even the biggest jerks at Eastern look like Prince Charming after Travis."

"When are you going to open your eyes and realize that he's different now?"

"He doesn't love you, Abby. You're a shiny new toy. Although, after the scene he made in class, I'm assuming you're not all that shiny anymore."

I slapped his face with a loud smack before I realized what I'd done.

"If you would have waited two seconds, I could have saved you the effort, Pidge," Travis said, pulling me behind him.

I grabbed his arm. "Travis, don't."

Parker looked a bit nervous as a perfect red outline of my hand appeared on his cheek.

"I warned you," Travis said, shoving Parker violently against the wall.

Parker's jaws tensed and he glared at me. "Consider this closure, Travis. I can see now that you two are made for each other."

"Thanks," Travis said, hooking his arm around my shoulders.

Parker pushed himself from the wall and quickly rounded the corner to descend the stairs with a quick glance to make sure Travis didn't follow.

"Are you okay?" Travis asked.

"My hand stings."

He smiled. "That was badass, Pidge. I'm impressed."

"He'll probably sue me and I'll end up paying his way into Harvard. What are you doing here? I thought we were meeting in the cafeteria?"

One side of his mouth pulled up in an impish grin. "I couldn't concentrate in class. I'm still feelin' that kiss."

I looked down the hall and then to him. "Come with me."

His eyebrows pulled together over his smile. "What?"

I walked backward, pulling him along until I felt the knob of the Physics lab. The door swung open, and I glanced behind me, seeing that it was empty and dark. I tugged on his hand, giggling at his confused expression, and then locked the door, pushing him against it.

I kissed him and he chuckled. "What are you doin'?"

"I don't want you to be unable to concentrate in class," I said, kissing him again. He lifted me up and I wrapped my legs around him.

"I'm not sure what I ever did without you," he said, holding me up with one hand and unbuckling his belt with the other, "but I don't ever want to find out. You're everything I've ever wanted, Pigeon."

"Just remember that when I take all of your money in the next poker game," I said, pulling off my shirt.

Chapter ~~Thirteen~~ Fourteen
Full House

I TWIRLED AROUND, SCRUTINIZING MY REFLECTION with a skeptical eye. The dress was white, backless, and dangerously short, the bodice held up by a short string of rhinestones that formed a halter around my neck.

"Wow! Travis is going to piss himself when he sees you in that!" America said.

I rolled my eyes. "How romantic."

"You're getting that one. Don't try any more on, that's the one," she said, clapping with excitement.

"You don't think it's too short? Mariah Carey shows less skin."

America shook her head. "I insist."

I took a turn on the bench while America tried on one dress after another, more indecisive when it came to choosing one for herself. She settled on an extremely short, tight, flesh-colored number that left one of her shoulders bare.

We rode in her Honda to the apartment to find the Charger gone and Toto alone. America pulled out her phone and dialed, smiling when Shepley answered.

"Where'd you go, baby?" She nodded and then looked at me. "Why would I be mad? What kind of surprise?" she said. She looked at me again and then walked into Shepley's bedroom, closing the door.

I rubbed Toto's black pointy ears while America murmured in the bedroom. When she emerged, she tried to subdue the smile on her face.

"What are they up to now?" I asked.

"They're on their way home. I'll let Travis tell you," she said, grinning from ear to ear.

"Oh, God . . . what?" I asked.

"I just said I can't tell you. It's a surprise."

I fidgeted with my hair and picked at my nails, unable to sit still while I waited for Travis to unveil his latest surprise. A birthday party, a puppy—I couldn't imagine what could be next.

The loud engine of Shepley's Charger announced their arrival. The boys laughed as they walked up the stairs.

"They're in a good mood," I said. "That's a good sign."

Shepley walked in first. "I just didn't want you to think there was a reason that he got one and I didn't."

America stood up to greet her boyfriend and threw her arms around him. "You're so silly, Shep. If I wanted an insane boyfriend, I'd date Travis."

"It doesn't have anything to do with how I feel about you," Shepley added.

Travis walked through the door with a square gauze bandage on his wrist. He smiled at me and then collapsed on the couch, resting his head on my lap.

I couldn't look away from the bandage. "Okay . . . what did you do?"

Travis smiled and pulled me down to kiss him. I could feel
the nervousness radiating from him. Outwardly he was smiling,
but I had the distinct feeling he wasn't sure how I would react to
what he had done.

"I got a few things today."

"Like what?" I asked, suspicious.

Travis laughed. "Calm down, Pidge. It's nothing bad."

"What happened to your wrist?" I said, pulling his hand up
by his fingers.

A thunderous diesel motor pulled up outside and Travis
hopped up from the couch, opening the door. "It's about fucking time! I've been home for at least five minutes!" he said with
a smile.

One man walked in backward, carrying a plastic-covered
gray sofa, followed by another man bringing in the rear. Shepley
and Travis moved the couch—with me and Toto still on it—
forward, and then the men sat the new one in its place. Travis
pulled off the plastic and then lifted me in his arms, setting me
on the soft cushions.

"You got a new one?" I asked, grinning from ear to ear.

"Yep, and a couple of other things, too. Thanks, guys," he
said as the movers lifted the old couch and left the way they
came.

"There goes a lot of memories," I smirked.

"None that I want to hold on to." He sat beside me and
sighed, watching me for a moment before he pulled off the tape
that held the gauze on his arm. "Don't freak out."

My mind raced with what could be under that bandage.
I imagined a burn or stitches or something equally gruesome.

He pulled the bandage back and I gasped at the black script

tattooed across the underside of his wrist, the skin around it red and shiny from the antibiotic he had smeared on. I shook my head in disbelief as I read the word.

Pigeon

"Do you like it?" he asked.

"You had my name tattooed on your wrist?" I said the words, but it didn't sound like my voice. My mind stretched in every direction, and yet I managed to speak in a calm, even tone.

"Yeah." He kissed my cheek as I stared in disbelief at the permanent ink in his skin.

"I tried to talk him out of it, Abby. He hasn't done anything crazy in a while. I think he was having withdrawal," Shepley said, shaking his head.

"What do you think?" Travis prompted.

"I don't know what to think," I said.

"You should have asked her first, Trav," America said, shaking her head and covering her mouth with her fingers.

"Asked her what? If I could get a tattoo?" he frowned, turning to me. "I love you. I want everyone to know I'm yours."

I shifted nervously. "That's permanent, Travis."

"So are we," he said, touching my cheek.

"Show her the rest," Shepley said.

"The rest?" I said, looking down to his other wrist.

Travis stood, pulling up his shirt. His impressive six-pack stretched and tightened with the movement. Travis turned, and on his side was another fresh tattoo spanning the length of his ribs.

"What is that?" I asked, squinting at the vertical symbols.

"It's Hebrew," Travis said with a nervous grin.

"What does it mean?"

"It says, 'I belong to my beloved, and my beloved is mine.'"

My eyes darted to his. "You weren't happy with just one tattoo, you had to get two?"

"It's something I always said I would do when I met The One. I met you . . . I went and got the tats." His smile faded when he saw my expression. "You're pissed, aren't you?" he said, pulling his shirt down.

"I'm not mad. I'm just . . . it's a little overwhelming."

Shepley squeezed America to his side with one arm. "Get used to it now, Abby. Travis is impulsive and goes balls to the wall on everything. This'll tide him over until he can get a ring on your finger."

America's eyebrows shot up, first to me, and then to Shepley. "What? They just started dating!"

"I . . . think I need a drink," I said, walking into the kitchen.

Travis chuckled, watching me rifle the cabinets. "He was kidding, Pidge."

"I was?" Shepley asked.

"He wasn't talking about anytime soon," Travis hedged. He turned to Shepley and grumbled, "Thanks a lot, asshole."

"Maybe you'll quit talking about it, now," Shepley grinned.

I poured a shot of whiskey into a glass and jerked my head back, swallowing it all at once. My face compressed as the liquid burned down my throat.

Travis gently wrapped his arms around my middle from behind. "I'm not proposing, Pidge. They're tattoos."

"I know," I said, nodding my head as I poured another drink.

Travis pulled the bottle from my hand and twisted the cap

on, shoving it back into the cabinet. When I didn't turn around, he pivoted my hips so that I would face him.

"Okay. I should have talked to you about it first, but I decided to buy the couch, and then one thing led to another. I got excited."

"This is very fast for me, Travis. You've mentioned moving in together, you just branded yourself with my name, you're telling me you love me . . . this is all very . . . fast."

Travis frowned. "You're freakin' out. I told you not to freak out."

"It's hard not to! You found out about my dad and everything you felt before has suddenly been amplified!"

"Who's your dad?" Shepley asked, clearly unhappy about being out of the loop. When I didn't acknowledge his question, he sighed. "Who's her dad?" he asked America. America shook her head dismissively.

Travis's expression twisted with disgust. "My feelings for you have nothing to do with your dad."

"We're going to this date party tomorrow. It's supposed to be this big deal where we're announcing our relationship or something, and now you have my name on your arm and this proverb talking about how we belong to each other! It's freaky, okay? I'm freaked out!"

Travis grabbed my face and planted his mouth on mine, and then he lifted me off the floor, setting me on the counter. His tongue begged entrance into my mouth, and when I let him in, he moaned.

His fingers dug into my hips, pulling me closer. "You are so fucking hot when you're mad," he said against my lips.

"Okay," I breathed, "I'm calm."

He smiled, pleased that his plan of distraction had worked. "Everything's still the same, Pidge. It's still just you and me."

"You two are nuts," Shepley said, shaking his head.

America playfully smacked Shepley's shoulder. "Abby bought something for Travis today, too."

"America!" I scolded.

"You found a dress?" he asked, smiling.

"Yeah." I wrapped my legs and arms around him. "Tomorrow it's going to be your turn to be freaked out."

"I'm looking forward to it," he said, pulling me off the counter. I waved to America as Travis carried me down the hall.

FRIDAY AFTER CLASS, AMERICA AND I SPENT THE AFTERnoon downtown, primping and indulging. We had our nails and toes done, errant hairs waxed, skin bronzed, and hair highlighted. When we returned to the apartment, every surface had been covered with bouquets of roses. Reds, pinks, yellows, and whites—it looked like a floral shop.

"Oh my God!" America squealed when she walked through the door.

Shepley looked around him, standing proud. "We went to buy you two flowers, but neither of us thought just one bouquet would do it."

I hugged Travis. "You guys are . . . you're amazing. Thank you."

He smacked my backside. "Thirty minutes until the party, Pidge."

The boys dressed in Travis's room while we slipped on our dresses in Shepley's. Just as I fastened my silver heels, there was a knock on the door.

"Time to go, ladies," Shepley said.

America walked out, and Shepley whistled.

"Where is she?" Travis asked.

"Abby's having some trouble with her shoe. She'll be out in just a sec," America explained.

"The suspense is killin' me, Pigeon!" Travis called.

I walked out, fidgeting with my dress while Travis stood in front of me, blank-faced.

America elbowed him and he blinked. "Holy shit."

"Are you ready to be freaked out?" America asked.

"I'm not freaked out—she looks amazing," Travis said.

I smiled and then slowly turned around to show him the steep dip of the fabric in the back of the dress.

"Okay, now I'm freakin' out," he said, walking over to me and turning me around.

"You don't like it?" I asked.

"You need a jacket." He jogged to the rack and then hastily draped my coat over my shoulders.

"She can't wear that all night, Trav," America chuckled.

"You look beautiful, Abby," Shepley said as an apology for Travis's behavior.

Travis's expression was pained as he spoke. "You do. You look incredible . . . but you can't wear that. Your skirt is . . . wow, your legs are . . . your skirt is too short and it's only half a dress! It doesn't even have a back on it!"

I couldn't help but smile. "That's the way it's made, Travis."

"Do you two live to torture each other?" Shepley frowned.

"Do you have a longer dress?" Travis asked.

I looked down. "It's actually pretty modest in the front. It's just the back that shows off a lot of skin."

"Pigeon," he winced with his next words, "I don't want you to be mad, but I can't take you to my frat house looking like that. I'll get in a fight the first five minutes."

I leaned up on the balls of my feet and kissed his lips. "I have faith in you."

"This night is gonna suck," he groaned.

"This night is going to be fantastic," America said, offended.

"Just think of how easy it will be to get it off later," I said, kissing his neck.

"That's the problem. Every other guy there will be thinking the same thing."

"But you're the only one that gets to find out," I lilted. He didn't respond, and I leaned back to assess his expression. "Do you really want me to change?"

Travis scanned my face, my dress, my legs, and then exhaled. "No matter what you wear, you're gorgeous. I should just get used to it, now, right?" I shrugged and he shook his head. "All right, we're already late. Let's go."

I huddled next to Travis for warmth as we walked from the car to the Sigma Tau house. The air was smoky but warm. Music boomed from the basement, and Travis bobbed his head to the beat. Everyone seemed to turn at once. I wasn't sure if they were staring because Travis was at a date party or because he was wearing slacks or because of my dress, but they were all staring.

America leaned over to whisper in my ear. "I'm so glad you're here, Abby. I feel like I just walked into a Molly Ringwald movie."

"Glad I could help," I grumbled.

Travis and Shepley took our coats and then led us across the room to the kitchen. Shepley took four beers out of the fridge and handed one to America and then one to me. We stood in the kitchen, listening to Travis's frat brothers discuss his last fight. The sorority sisters accompanying them happened to be the same busty blondes who followed Travis into the cafeteria the first time we spoke.

Lexie was easy to recognize. I couldn't forget the look on her face when Travis pushed her from his lap for insulting America. She watched me with curiosity, seeming to study my every word. I knew she was curious why Travis Maddox apparently found me irresistible, and I found myself making an effort to show her. I kept my hands on Travis, inserting clever quips at precise moments of conversation, and joked with him about his new tattoos.

"Dude, you got your girl's name on your wrist? What in the hell possessed you to do that?" Brad said.

Travis proudly turned over his hand to reveal my name. "I'm crazy about her," he said, looking down at me with soft eyes.

"You barely know her," Lexie scoffed.

He didn't take his eyes from mine. "I know her." He furrowed his brow. "I thought the tat freaked you out. Now you're bragging about it?"

I leaned up to kiss his cheek and shrugged. "It's growing on me."

Shepley and America made their way downstairs, and we followed hand in hand. Furniture had been pushed along the walls for a makeshift dance floor. Just as we descended the stairs, a slow song began to play.

Travis didn't hesitate to pull me into the middle, holding me close and pulling my hand to his chest. "I'm glad I've never gone to one of these things before. It's right that I've only brought you."

I smiled and pressed my cheek against his chest. He held his hand against my lower back, warm and soft against my bare skin.

"Everyone's staring at you in this dress," he said. I looked up, expecting to see a tense expression, but he was smiling. "I guess it's kinda cool . . . being with the girl everyone wants."

I rolled my eyes. "They don't want me. They're curious why you want me. And anyway, I feel sorry for anyone that thinks they have a chance. I am hopelessly and completely in love with you."

A pained look shadowed his face. "You know why I want you? I didn't know I was lost until you found me. I didn't know what alone was until the first night I spent without you in my bed. You're the one thing I've got right. You're what I've been waiting for, Pigeon."

I reached up to take his face between my hands and he wrapped his arms around me, lifting me off the floor. I pressed my lips against his, and he kissed me with the emotion of everything he'd just said. It was in that moment that I realized why he'd gotten the tattoo, why he had chosen me, and why I was different. It wasn't just me, and it wasn't just him, it was what we were together that was the exception.

A faster beat vibrated the speakers, and Travis lowered me to my feet. "Still wanna dance?"

America and Shepley appeared beside us and I raised an eyebrow. "If you think you can keep up with me."

Travis smirked. "Try me."

I moved my hips against his and ran my hand up his shirt,

unfastening his top two buttons, Travis chuckled and shook his head, and I turned around, moving against him to the beat. He grabbed my hips and I reached around, grabbing his backside. I leaned forward and his fingers dug into my skin. When I stood up, he touched his lips to my ear.

"Keep that up and we'll be leaving early."

I turned around and smiled, throwing my arms around his neck. He pressed himself against me and I untucked his shirt, slipping my hands up his back, pressing my fingers into his lean muscles, and then smiling at the noise he made when I tasted his neck.

"Jesus, Pigeon, you're killin' me," he said, gripping the hem of my skirt, pulling it up just enough to graze my thighs with his fingertips.

"I guess we know what the appeal is," Lexie sneered from behind us.

America spun, stomping toward Lexie on the warpath. Shepley grabbed her just in time.

"Say it again!" America said. "I dare you, bitch!"

Lexie cowered behind her boyfriend, shocked at America's threat.

"Better get a muzzle on your date, Brad," Travis warned.

Two songs later, the hair on the back of my neck was heavy and damp. Travis kissed the skin just below my ear. "C'mon, Pidge. I need a smoke."

He led me up the stairs, and then grabbed my coat before leading me up to the second floor. We walked out onto the balcony to find Parker and his date. She was taller than I, her short, dark hair pinned back with a single bobby pin. I noticed her pointy stilettos immediately, with her leg hooked around

Parker's hip. She stood with her back against the brick, and when Parker noticed us walk out, he pulled his hand from underneath her skirt.

"Abby," he said, surprised and breathless.

"Hey, Parker," I said, stifling a laugh.

"How, uh . . . how have you been?"

I smiled politely. "I've been great. You?"

"Uh," he looked at his date, "Abby, this is Amber. Amber . . . Abby."

"Abby Abby?" she asked.

Parker gave one quick, uncomfortable nod. Amber shook my hand with a disgusted look on her face, and then eyed Travis as if she had just encountered the enemy. "Nice to meet you . . . I guess."

"Amber," Parker warned.

Travis laughed once and then opened the doors for them to walk through. Parker grabbed Amber's hand and retreated into the house.

"That was . . . awkward," I said, shaking my head as I folded my arms, leaning against the railing. It was cold, and there were only a handful of couples outside.

Travis was all smiles. Not even Parker could dampen his mood. "At least he's moved on from trying his damnedest to get you back."

"I don't think he was trying to get me back so much as trying to keep me away from you."

Travis wrinkled his nose. "He took one girl home for me once. Now he acts like he's made a habit of swooping in and saving every freshman I bagged."

I gave him a wry look from the corner of my eye. "Did I ever tell you how much I loathe that word?"

"Sorry," he said, pulling me to his side. He lit his cigarette and took a deep breath. The smoke he blew out was thicker than usual, mixing with the winter air. He turned his hand over and took a long look at his wrist. "How weird is it that this tat isn't just my new favorite, but it makes me feel at ease to know it's there?"

"Pretty weird." Travis raised an eyebrow and I laughed. "I'm kidding. I can't say I understand it, but it's sweet . . . in a Travis Maddox sort of way."

"If it feels this good to have this on my arm, I can't imagine how it's going to feel to get a ring on your finger."

"Travis . . ."

"In four or maybe five years," he added.

I took a breath. "We need to slow down. Way, way down."

"Don't start this, Pidge."

"If we keep going at this pace, I'm going to be barefoot and pregnant before I graduate. I'm not ready to move in with you, I'm not ready for a ring, and I'm certainly not ready to settle down."

Travis gripped my shoulders and turned me to face him. "This isn't the 'I wanna see other people' speech, is it? Because I'm not sharing you. No fucking way."

"I don't want anyone else," I said, exasperated. He relaxed and released my shoulders, gripping the railing.

"What are you saying, then?" he asked, staring across the horizon.

"I'm saying we need to slow down. That's all I'm saying." He nodded, clearly unhappy. I touched his arm. "Don't be mad."

"It seems like we take one step forward and two steps back, Pidge. Every time I think we're on the same page, you put up a wall. I don't get it . . . most girls are hounding their boyfriends to get serious, to talk about their feelings, to take the next step . . ."

"I thought we established that I'm not most girls?"

He let his head drop, frustrated. "I'm tired of guessing. Where do you see this going, Abby?"

I pressed my lips against his shirt. "When I think about my future, I see you."

Travis relaxed, pulling me close. We both watched the night clouds move across the sky. The lights of the school dotted the darkened block, and partygoers folded their arms against thick coats, scurrying to the warmth of the fraternity house.

I saw the same peace in Travis's eyes that I had witnessed only a handful of times. And it hit me that just like on the other nights, his content expression was a direct result of reassurance from me.

I had experienced insecurity: those living one stroke of bad luck to another, men who were afraid of their own shadow. It was easy to be afraid of the dark side of Vegas, the side the neon and glitter never seemed to touch. But Travis Maddox wasn't afraid to fight or to defend someone he cared about or to look into the humiliated and angry eyes of a scorned woman. He could walk into a room and stare down someone twice his size, believing that no one could touch him—that he was invincible to anything that tried to make him fall.

He was afraid of nothing. Until he'd met me.

I was the one part of his life that was unknown, the wild card, the variable he couldn't control. Regardless of the moments of peace I had given him, in every other moment of every other day, the turmoil he felt without me was made ten times worse in my presence. The anger that took hold of him before was only harder for him to manage. Being the exception was no longer a mysterious, special thing. I had become his weakness.

Just as I was to my father.

"Abby! There you are! I've been looking all over for you!" America said, bursting through the door. She held up her cell phone. "I just got off the phone with my dad. Mick called them last night."

"Mick?" My face screwed into disgust. "Why would he call them?"

America raised her eyebrows as if I should know the answer. "Your mother kept hanging up on him."

"What did he want?" I said, feeling sick.

She pressed her lips together. "To know where you were."

"They didn't tell him, did they?"

America's face fell. "He's your father, Abby. Dad felt he had a right to know."

"He's going to come here," I said, feeling my eyes burn. "He's going to come here, Mare!"

"I know! I'm sorry!" she said, trying to hug me. I pulled away from her and covered my face with my hands.

A familiar pair of strong, protective hands rested on my shoulders. "He won't hurt you, Pigeon," Travis said. "I won't let him."

"He'll find a way," America said, watching me with heavy eyes. "He always does."

"I have to get out of here." I pulled my coat around me and pulled at the handles of the French doors. I was too upset to slow down long enough to coordinate pushing down the

handles while pulling at the doors at the same time. Just as frustrated tears fell down my frozen cheeks, Travis's hand covered
mine. He pressed down, helping me to push the handles, and
then with his other hand he pulled open the doors. I looked at
him, conscious of the ridiculous scene I was making, expecting
to see a confused or disapproving look on his face, but he looked
down at me only with understanding.

Travis took me under his arm and together we went through
the house, down the stairs and through the crowd to the front
door. The three of them struggled to keep up with me as I made
a beeline for the Charger.

America's hand shot out and grabbed my coat, stopping me
in my tracks. "Abby!" she whispered, pointing to a small group
of people.

They were crowded around an older, disheveled man who
pointed frantically to the house, holding up a picture. The
couples were nodding, discussing the photo among one another.

I stormed over to the man and pulled the photo from his
hands. "What in the hell are you doing here?"

The crowd dispersed, walking into the house, and Shepley
and America stood on each side of me. Travis cupped my shoulders from behind.

Mick looked at my dress and clicked his tongue in disapproval. "Well, well, Cookie. You can take the girl out of
Vegas . . ."

"Shut up. Shut up, Mick. Just turn around," I pointed behind him, "and go back to wherever you came from. I don't want
you here."

"I can't, Cookie. I need your help."

"What else is new?" America sneered.

Mick narrowed his eyes at America and then looked to me. "You look awful pretty. You've grown up. I wouldn't've recognized you on the street."

I sighed, impatient with the small talk. "What do you want?"

He held up his hands and shrugged. "I seemed to have gotten myself in a pickle, kiddo. Old Dad needs some money."

I closed my eyes. "How much?"

"I was doing good, I really was. I just had to borrow a bit to get ahead and . . . you know."

"I know," I snapped. "How much do you need?"

"Twenty-five."

"Well, shit, Mick, twenty-five hundred? If you'll get the hell outta here . . . I'll give that to you now," Travis said, pulling out his wallet.

"He means twenty-five thousand," I said, glaring at my father.

Mick's eyes scanned over Travis. "Who's this clown?"

Travis's eyebrows shot up from his wallet and I felt his weight lean into my back. "I can see, now, why a smart guy like yourself has been reduced to asking your teenage daughter for an allowance."

Before Mick could speak, I pulled out my cell phone. "Who do you owe this time, Mick?"

Mick scratched his greasy, graying hair. "Well, it's a funny story, Cookie—"

"Who?" I shouted.

"Benny."

My mouth fell open and I took a step back, into Travis. "Benny? You owe Benny? What in the hell were you . . ." I took a breath; there was no point. "I don't have that kind of money, Mick."

He smiled. "Something tells me you do."

"Well, I don't! You've really done it, this time, haven't you? I knew you wouldn't stop until you got yourself killed!"

He shifted; the smug grin on his face had vanished. "How much ya got?"

I clenched my jaw. "Eleven thousand. I was saving for a car."

America's eyes darted in my direction. "Where did you get eleven thousand dollars, Abby?"

"Travis's fights," I said, my eyes boring into Mick's.

Travis pulled on my shoulders to look into my eyes. "You made eleven thousand off my fights? When were you betting?"

"Adam and I had an understanding," I said, unconcerned with Travis's surprise.

Mick's eyes were suddenly animated. "You can double that in a weekend, Cookie. You could get me the twenty-five by Sunday, and Benny won't send his thugs for me."

My throat felt dry and tight. "It'll clean me out, Mick. I have to pay for school."

"Oh, you can make it back in no time," he said, waving his hand dismissively.

"When is your deadline?" I asked.

"Monday mornin'. Midnight," he said, unapologetic.

"You don't have to give him a fucking dime, Pigeon," Travis said, tugging on my arm.

Mick grabbed my wrist. "It's the least you could do! I wouldn't be in this mess if it weren't for you!"

America slapped his hand away and then shoved him. "Don't

you dare start that shit again, Mick! She didn't make you borrow money from Benny!"

Mick looked at me with loathing in his eyes. "If it weren't for her, I woulda had my own money. You took everything from me, Abby. I have nothin'!"

I thought time away from Mick would lessen the pain that came with being his daughter, but the tears flowing from my eyes said otherwise. "I'll get your money to Benny by Sunday. But when I do, I want you to leave me the hell alone. I won't do this again, Mick. From now on, you're on your own, do you hear me? Stay. Away."

He pressed his lips together and then nodded. "Have it your way, Cookie."

I turned around and headed for the car, hearing America behind me. "Pack your bags, boys. We're going to Vegas."

Chapter Fifteen
City of Sin

Travis set down our bags and looked around the room. "This is nice, right?"

I glared at him and he raised his brow. "What?"

The zipper of my suitcase whined as I pulled it around its borders, and I shook my head. Different strategies and the lack of time crowded my head. "This isn't a vacation. You shouldn't be here, Travis."

In the next moment he was behind me, crossing his arms around my middle. "I go where you go."

I leaned my head against his chest and sighed. "I have to get on the floor. You can stay here or check out the Strip. I'll see you later, okay?"

"I'm going with you."

"I don't want you there, Trav." A hurt expression weighted his face, and I touched his arm. "If I'm going to win fourteen thousand dollars in one weekend, I have to concentrate. I don't like who I'm going to be while I'm at those tables, and I don't want you see it, okay?"

He brushed my hair from my eyes and kissed my cheek. "Okay, Pidge."

Travis waved to America as he left the room, and she approached me in the same dress she had worn to the date party. I changed into a short gold number and slipped on a pair of heels, grimacing at the mirror. America pulled back my hair and then handed me a black tube.

"You need about five more coats of mascara, and they're going to toss your ID on sight if you don't slather on some more blush. Have you forgotten how this game is played?"

I snatched the mascara from her hand and spent another ten minutes on my makeup. Once I finished, my eyes began to gloss over. "Dammit, Abby, don't cry," I said, looking up and dabbing under my eyes with a tissue.

"You don't have to do this. You don't owe him anything." America cupped my shoulders as I stood in front of the mirror one last time.

"He owes Benny money, Mare. If I don't, they'll kill him."

Her expression was one of pity. I had seen her look at me that way many times before, but this time she was desperate. She'd seen him ruin my life more times than either of us could count. "What about the next time? And the next time? You can't keep doing this."

"He agreed to stay away. Mick Abernathy is a lot of things, but he's no welsher."

We walked down the hall and stepped into an empty elevator. "You have everything you need?" I asked, keeping the cameras in mind.

America clicked her fake driver's license with her nails and smiled. "The name's Candy. Candy Crawford," she said in her flawless southern accent.

I held out my hand. "Jessica James. Nice to meet you, Candy."

We both slipped on our sunglasses and stood stone-faced as the elevator opened, revealing the neon lights and bustle of the casino floor. People moved in all directions from all walks of life. Vegas was heavenly hell, the one place you could find dancers in ostentatious feathers and stage makeup, prostitutes with insufficient yet acceptable attire, businessmen in luxurious suits, and wholesome families in the same building. We strutted down an aisle lined with red ropes and handed a man in a red jacket our IDs. He eyed me for a moment and I pulled down my glasses.

"Anytime today would be great," I said, bored.

He returned our IDs and stood aside, letting us pass. We passed aisle after aisle of slot machines and the blackjack tables and then stopped at the roulette wheel. I scanned the room, watching the various poker tables, settling on the one with older gentlemen in the seats.

"That one," I said, nodding across the way.

"Start off aggressive, Abby. They won't know what hit 'em."

"No. They're old Vegas. I have to play it smart this time."

I walked over to the table, using my most charming smile. Locals could smell a hustler from a mile away, but I had two things in my favor that covered the scent of any con: youth . . . and tits.

"Good evening, gentlemen. Mind if I join you?"

They didn't look up. "Sure, sweet cheeks. Grab a seat and look pretty. Just don't talk."

"I want in," I said, handing America my sunglasses. "There's not enough action at the blackjack tables."

One of the men chewed on his cigar. "This is a poker table, Princess. Five-card draw. Try your luck on the slot machines."

I sat in the only empty seat, making a show of crossing my legs. "I've always wanted to play poker in Vegas. And I have all these chips," I said, setting my rack of chips on the table, "and I'm really good online."

All five men looked at my chips and then at me. "There's a minimum ante, Sugar," the dealer said.

"How much?"

"Five hundred, Peach. Listen . . . I don't want to make you cry. Do yourself a favor and pick out a shiny slot machine."

I pushed forward my chips, shrugging my shoulders in the way a reckless and overly confident girl might before realizing she'd just lost her college fund. The men looked at each other. The dealer shrugged and tossed in his own.

"Jimmy," one of the players said, offering his hand. When I took it, he pointed at the other men. "Mel, Pauli, Joe, and that's Winks." I looked over to the skinny man chewing on a toothpick, and as predicted, he winked at me.

I nodded and waited with fake anticipation as the first hand was dealt. I purposely lost the first two, but by the fourth hand, I was up. It didn't take as long for the Vegas veterans to figure me out as it did Thomas.

"You said you played online?" Pauli asked.

"And with my dad."

"You from here?" Jimmy asked.

"Wichita," I said.

"She's no online player, I'll tell you that," Mel grumbled.

An hour later, I had taken twenty-seven hundred dollars from my opponents, and they were beginning to sweat.

"Fold," Jimmy said, throwing down his cards with a frown.

"If I didn't see it with my own eyes, I would have never believed," I heard behind me.

America and I turned at the same time, and my lips stretched across my face in a wide smile. "Jesse." I shook my head. "What are you doing here?"

"This is my place you're scamming, Cookie. What are you doing here?"

I rolled my eyes and turned to my suspicious new friends. "You know I hate that, Jess."

"Excuse us," Jesse said, pulling me by the arm to my feet. America eyed me warily as I was ushered a few feet away.

Jesse's father ran the casino, and it was more than just a surprise that he had joined the family business. We used to chase each other down the halls of the hotel upstairs, and I always beat him when we raced elevators. He had grown up since I'd seen him last. I remembered him as a gangly prepubescent teenager; the man before me was a sharply dressed pit boss, not at all gangly and certainly all man. He still had the silky brown skin and green eyes I remembered, but the rest of him was a pleasant surprise.

His emerald irises sparkled in the bright lights. "This is surreal. I thought it was you when I walked by, but I couldn't convince myself that you would come back here. When I saw this Tinker Bell cleaning up at the vets' table, I knew it was you."

"It's me," I said.

"You look . . . different."

"So do you. How's your dad?"

"Retired," he smiled. "How long are you here?"

"Just until Sunday. I have to get back to school."

"Hey, Jess," America said, taking my arm.

"America," he chuckled. "I should have known. You are each other's shadows."

"If her parents ever knew that I brought her here, all that would have come to an end a long time ago."

"It's good to see you, Abby. Why don't you let me buy you dinner?" he asked, scanning my dress.

"I'd love to catch up, but I'm not here for fun, Jess."

He held out his hand and smiled. "Neither am I. Hand over your ID."

My face fell, knowing I had a fight on my hands. Jesse wouldn't give in to my charms so easily. I knew I would have to tell him the truth. "I'm here for Mick. He's in trouble."

Jesse shifted. "What kind of trouble?"

"The usual."

"I wish I could help. We go way back, and you know I respect your dad, but you know I can't let you stay."

I grabbed his arm and squeezed. "He owes Benny money."

Jesse closed his eyes and shook his head. "Jesus."

"I have until tomorrow. I'm calling in a solid IOU, Jesse. Just give me until then."

He touched his palm to my cheek. "I'll tell you what . . . if you have dinner with me tomorrow, I'll give you until midnight."

I looked at America and then to Jesse. "I'm here with someone."

He shrugged. "Take it or leave it, Abby. You know how things are done here. You can't have something for nothing."

I sighed, defeated. "Fine. I'll meet you tomorrow night at Ferraro's if you give me until midnight."

He leaned down and kissed my cheek. "It was good to see

you again. See you tomorrow . . . five o'clock, all right? I'm on the floor at eight."

I smiled as he walked away, but it quickly faded when I saw Travis staring at me from the roulette table.

"Oh shit," America said, tugging on my arm.

Travis glared at Jesse as he passed, and then made his way to me. He shoved his hands in his pockets and glanced at Jesse, who was watching us from the corner of his eye.

"Who was that?"

I nodded in Jesse's direction. "That is Jesse Viveros. I've known him a long time."

"How long?"

I looked back at the vet table. "Travis, I don't have time for this."

"I guess he chucked the youth minister idea," America said, sending a flirtatious grin in Jesse's direction.

"That's your ex-boyfriend?" Travis asked, instantly angry. "I thought you said he was from Kansas?"

I shot America an impatient glare and then took Travis's chin in my hand, insisting on his full attention. "He knows I'm not old enough to be in here, Trav. He gave me until midnight. I will explain everything later, but for now I have to get back to the game, all right?"

Travis's jaws fluttered under his skin, and then he closed his eyes, taking a deep breath. "All right. I'll see you at midnight." He bent down to kiss me, but his lips were cold and distant. "Good luck."

I smiled as he melted into the crowd, and then I turned my attention to the men. "Gentlemen?"

"Have a seat, Shirley Temple," Jimmy said. "We'll be making our money back now. We don't appreciate being hustled."

"Do your worst." I smiled.

"You have ten minutes," America whispered.

"I know," I said.

I tried to block out the time and America's knee bobbing nervously under the table. The pot was at sixteen thousand dollars—the night's all-time high, and it was all or nothing.

"I've never seen anything like you, kid. You've had almost a perfect game. And she's got no tell, Winks. You notice?" Pauli said.

Winks nodded; his cheerful demeanor had evaporated a bit more with every hand. "I noticed. Not a rub or a smile, even her eyes stay the same. It's not natural. Everybody's got a tell."

"Not everybody," America said, smug.

I felt a familiar pair of hands touch my shoulders. I knew it was Travis, but I didn't dare turn around, not with three thousand dollars sitting in the middle of the table.

"Call," Jimmy said.

Those who had crowded around us applauded when I laid down my hand. Jimmy was the only one close enough to touch me with three of a kind. Nothing my straight couldn't handle.

"Unbelievable!" Pauli said, throwing his two deuces to the table.

"I'm out," Joe grumbled, standing up and stomping away from the table.

Jimmy was a bit more gracious. "I can die tonight and feel I've played a truly worthy opponent, kiddo. It's been a pleasure, Abby."

I froze. "You knew?"

Jimmy smiled. The years of cigar smoke and coffee stained his large teeth. "I've played you before. Six years ago. I've wanted a rematch for a long time."

Jimmy extended his hand. "Take care, kid. Tell your dad Jimmy Pescelli says hello."

America helped gather my winnings, and I turned to Travis, looking at my watch. "I need more time."

"Wanna try the blackjack tables?"

"I can't lose money, Trav."

He smiled. "You can't lose, Pidge."

America shook her head. "Blackjack's not her game."

Travis nodded. "I won a little. I'm up six hundred. You can have it."

Shepley handed me his chips. "I only made three. It's yours."

I sighed. "Thanks, guys, but I'm still short five grand."

I looked at my watch again and then looked up to see Jesse approaching. "How did you do?" he asked, smiling.

"I'm five K short, Jess. I need more time."

"I've done all I can, Abby."

I nodded, knowing I had already asked too much. "Thanks for letting me stay."

"Maybe I can get my dad to talk to Benny for you?"

"It's Mick's mess. I'm going to ask him for an extension."

Jesse shook his head. "You know that's not going to happen, Cookie, no matter how much you come up with. If it's less than what he owes, Benny's going to send someone. You stay as far away from him as you can."

I felt my eyes burn. "I have to try."

Jesse took a step forward, leaning in to keep his voice low. "Get on a plane, Abby. You hear me?"

"I hear you," I snapped.

Jesse sighed, and his eyes grew heavy with sympathy. He wrapped his arms around me and kissed my hair. "I'm sorry. If it wasn't my job at stake, you know I'd try to figure something out."

I nodded, pulling away from him. "I know. You did what you could."

He lifted my chin with his finger. "I'll see you tomorrow at five." He bent down to kiss the corner of my mouth and then walked past me without another word.

I glanced to America, who watched Travis. I didn't dare meet his eyes; I couldn't imagine what angry expression was on his face.

"What's at five?" Travis said, his voice dripping with subdued anger.

"She agreed to dinner if Jesse would let her stay. She didn't have a choice, Trav," America said. I could tell by the cautious tone of her voice that Travis was beyond angry.

I peered up at him, and he glowered at me with the same betrayed expression Mick had on his face the night he realized I'd taken his luck.

"You had a choice."

"Have you ever dealt with the Mob, Travis? I'm sorry if your feelings are hurt, but a free meal with an old friend isn't a high price to pay to keep Mick alive."

I could see that Travis wanted to lash out at me, but there was nothing he could say.

"C'mon, you guys, we have to find Benny," America said, pulling me by the arm.

Travis and Shepley followed behind in silence as we walked down the Strip to Benny's building. The traffic—both cars and people on the thoroughfare—were just beginning to concentrate. With each step, I felt a sick, hollow feeling in my stomach, my mind racing to think of a compelling argument to make Benny see reason. By the time we knocked on the large green door I had seen so many times before, I had come up as short as my bankroll.

It wasn't a surprise to see the enormous doorman—black, frightening, and as wide as he was tall—but I was stunned to see Benny standing beside him.

"Benny," I breathed.

"My, my . . . you're not Lucky Thirteen anymore, now, are ya? Mick didn't tell me what a looker you've grown into. I've been waiting for you, Cookie. I hear you have a payment for me."

I nodded and Benny gestured to my friends. I lifted my chin to feign confidence. "They're with me."

"I'm afraid your companions will have to wait outside," the doorman said in an abnormally deep bass tone.

Travis immediately took me by the arm. "She's not going in there alone. I'm coming with her."

Benny eyed Travis and I swallowed. When Benny looked up to his doorman and the corners of his mouth turned up, I relaxed a bit.

"Fair enough," Benny said. "Mick will be glad to know you have such a good friend with you."

I followed him inside, turning to see the worried look on America's face. Travis kept a firm grip on my arm, purposefully standing between me and the doorman. We followed Benny into an elevator and traveled up four floors in silence, and then the doors opened.

A large mahogany desk sat in the middle of a vast room. Benny hobbled to his plush chair and sat down, gesturing for us to take the two empty seats facing his desk. When I sat down, the leather felt cold beneath me, and I wondered how many people had sat in that same chair, moments from their death. I reached over to grab Travis's hand, and he gave me a reassuring squeeze.

"Mick owes me twenty-five thousand. I trust you have the full amount," Benny said, scribbling something on a notepad.

"Actually," I paused, clearing my throat, "I'm five K short, Benny. But I have all day tomorrow to get that. And five thousand is no problem, right? You know I'm good for it."

"Abigail," Benny said, frowning, "You disappoint me. You know my rules better than that."

"P-please, Benny. I'm asking you to take the 19,900 and I'll have the rest for you tomorrow."

Benny's beady eyes darted from me to Travis and then back again. It was then that I noticed two men taking a step forward from the shadowed corners of the room. Travis's grip on my hand grew tighter, and I held my breath.

"You know I don't take anything but the full amount. The fact that you're trying to hand me less tells me something. You know what it tells me? That you're not sure if you can get the full amount."

The men from the corners took another step forward.

"I can get your money, Benny," I giggled nervously. "I won eighty-nine hundred in six hours."

"So are you saying you'll bring me eighty-nine hundred in six more hours?" Benny smiled his devilish grin.

"The deadline isn't until midnight tomorrow," Travis said, glancing behind us and then watching the approaching shadow men.

"W-what are you doing, Benny?" I asked, my posture rigid.

"Mick called me tonight. He said you're taking care of his debt."

"I'm doing him a favor. I don't owe you any money," I said sternly, my survival instincts kicking in.

Benny leaned both of his fat, stubby elbows onto his desk. "I'm considering teaching Mick a lesson, and I'm curious just how lucky you are, kiddo."

Travis shot out of his chair, pulling me with him. He jerked me behind him, backing up toward the door.

"Josiah is outside the door, young man. Where exactly do you think you're going to escape to?"

I was wrong. When I was thinking about persuading Benny to see reason, I should have anticipated Mick's will to survive and Benny's penchant for retribution.

"Travis," I warned, watching Benny's henchmen approach us.

Travis pushed me behind him a few feet and stood tall. "I hope you know, Benny, that when I take out your men, I mean no disrespect. But I'm in love with this girl, and I can't let you hurt her."

Benny burst into a loud cackle. "I gotta hand it to you, son. You've got the biggest balls of anyone that's come through those doors. I'll prepare you for what you're about to get. The rather large fella to your right is David, and if he can't take you out with his fists, he's going to use that knife in his holster. The man to your left is Dane, and he's my best fighter. He's got a fight tomorrow, as a matter of fact, and he's never lost. Mind you don't hurt your hands, Dane. I've got a lot of money riding on you."

Dane smiled at Travis with wild, amused eyes. "Yes, sir."

"Benny, stop! I can get you the money!" I cried.

"Oh no . . . this is going to get interesting very fast," Benny chuckled, settling back into his seat.

David rushed Travis and my hands flew up to my mouth. The man was strong but clumsy and slow. Before David could swing or reach for his knife, Travis incapacitated him, shoving David's face straight down into his knee. When Travis threw a punch, he wasted no time, throwing every bit of strength he had into the man's face. Two punches and an elbow later, David was lying on the floor in a bloody heap.

Benny's head fell back, laughing hysterically and pounding his desk with the delight of a child watching Saturday morning cartoons. "Well, go on, Dane. He didn't scare you, did he?"

Dane approached Travis more carefully, with the focus and precision of a professional fighter. His fist flew at Travis's face with incredible speed, but Travis dodged, ramming his shoulder into Dane at full force. They fell against Benny's desk, and then Dane grabbed Travis with both arms, hurling him to the ground. They scuffled on the floor for a moment, and then Dane gained ground, positioning himself to get in a few punches on Travis while he was trapped beneath him on the floor. I covered my face, unable to watch.

I heard a cry of pain, and then I looked up to see Travis hovering over Dane, holding him by his shaggy hair, jabbing punch after punch into the side of his head. Dane's face rammed into the front of Benny's desk with each blow, and then he scrambled to his feet, disoriented and bleeding.

Travis watched him for a moment, and then attacked again, grunting with every strike, once again using the full force of his strength. Dane dodged once and landed his knuckles on Travis's jaw.

Travis smiled and held up his finger. "That's your one."

I couldn't believe my ears. Travis had let Benny's thug hit him. He was enjoying himself. I had never seen Travis fight without constraint; it was a bit frightening to see him unleash everything he had on these trained killers and have the upper hand. Until that moment, I hadn't realized just what Travis was capable of.

With Benny's disturbing laughter in the background, Travis finished Dane off, landing his elbow in the center of Dane's face, knocking him out before he hit the ground. I followed his body as it bounced once on Benny's imported rug.

"Amazing, young man! Simply amazing!" Benny said, clapping with delight.

Travis pulled me behind him as Josiah filled the doorway with his massive frame.

"Should I take care of this, sir?"

"No! No, no . . ." Benny said, still giddy with the impromptu performance. "What is your name?"

Travis was still breathing hard. "Travis Maddox," he said, wiping Dane's and David's blood off his hands and onto his jeans.

"Travis Maddox, I believe you can help your little girlfriend out."

"How's that?" Travis puffed.

"Dane was supposed to fight tomorrow night. I had a lot of cash riding on him, and it doesn't look like Dane will be fit to win a fight anytime soon. I suggest you take his place, make my bankroll for me, and I'll forgive the remaining fifty-one hundred of Mick's debt."

Travis turned to me. "Pigeon?"

"Are you all right?" I asked, wiping the blood from his face. I bit my lip, feeling my face crumple with a combination of fear and relief.

Travis smiled. "It's not my blood, baby. Don't cry."

Benny stood. "I'm a busy man, son. Pass or play?"

"I'll do it," Travis said. "Give me the when and where and I'll be there."

"You'll be fighting Brock McMann. He's no wallflower. He was barred from the UFC last year."

Travis was unaffected. "Just tell me where I need to be."

Benny's shark's grin spread across his face. "I like you, Travis. I think we'll be good friends."

"I doubt it," Travis said. He opened the door for me and sustained a protective stance until we cleared the front door.

"Jesus Christ!" America cried upon seeing the splattered blood covering Travis's clothing. "Are you guys okay?" She grabbed my shoulders and scanned my face.

"I'm okay. Just another day at the office. For both of us," I said, wiping my eyes.

Travis grabbed my hand and we rushed to the hotel with Shepley and America close behind. Not many paid attention to Travis's appearance. He was covered in blood, and only the occasional out-of-towner seemed to notice.

"What in the hell happened in there?" Shepley finally asked.

Travis stripped down to his Skivvies and disappeared into the bathroom. The shower turned on and America handed me a box of tissues.

"I'm fine, Mare."

She sighed and pushed the box at me once again. "You're not fine."

"This is not my first rodeo with Benny," I said. My muscles were sore from twenty-four hours of stress-induced tension.

"It's your first time to watch Travis go apeshit on someone," Shepley said. "I've seen it once before. It's not pretty."

"What happened?" America insisted.

"Mick called Benny. Passed accountability on to me."

"I'm gonna kill him! I'm going to kill that sorry son of a bitch!" America shouted.

"He's not holding me responsible, but he was going to teach Mick a lesson for sending his daughter to pay off his debt. He called two of his damned dogs on us, and Travis took them out. Both of them. In under five minutes."

"So Benny let you go?" America asked.

Travis appeared from the bathroom with a towel around his waist, the only evidence of his scuffle a small red mark on his cheekbone below his right eye. "One of the guys I knocked out had a fight tomorrow night. I'm taking his place and in return Benny will forgive the last five K Mick owes."

America stood up. "This is ridiculous! Why are we helping Mick, Abby? He threw you to the wolves! I'm going to kill him!"

"Not if I kill him first," Travis seethed.

"Get in line," I said.

"So you're fighting tomorrow?" Shepley asked.

"At a place called Zero's. Six o'clock. It's Brock McMann, Shep."

Shepley shook his head. "No way. No fucking way, Trav. The guy's a maniac!"

"Yeah," Travis said, "but he's not fighting for his girl, is he?" Travis cradled me in his arms, kissing the top of my hair. "You okay, Pigeon?"

"This is wrong. This is wrong on so many levels. I don't know which one to talk you out of first."

"Did you not see me tonight? I'm going to be fine. I've seen Brock fight before. He's tough, but not unbeatable."

"I don't want you to do this, Trav."

"Well, I don't want you to go to dinner with your ex-boyfriend tomorrow night. I guess we both have to do something unpleasant to save your good-for-nothing father."

I had seen it before. Vegas changed people, creating monsters and broken men. It was easy to let the lights and stolen dreams seep into your blood. I had seen the energized, invincible look on Travis's face many times growing up, and the only cure was a plane ride home.

JESSE FROWNED WHEN I LOOKED AT MY WATCH AGAIN.

"You have somewhere to be, Cookie?" Jesse asked.

"Please stop calling me that, Jesse. I hate it."

"I hated it when you left, too. Didn't stop you."

"This is a tired, worn-out conversation. Let's just have dinner, okay?"

"Okay, let's talk about your new man. What's his name? Travis?" I nodded. "What are you doing with that tattooed psychopath? He looks like a reject from the Manson Family."

"Be nice, Jesse, or I'm walking out of here."

"I can't get over how different you look. I can't get over that you're sitting in front of me."

I rolled my eyes. "Get over it."

"There she is," Jesse said. "The girl I remember."

I looked down at my watch. "Travis's fight is in twenty minutes. I better go."

"We still have dessert coming."

"I can't, Jess. I don't want him worrying if I'm going to show up. It's important."

His shoulders fell. "I know. I miss the days when I was important."

I rested my hand on his. "We were just kids. That was a lifetime ago."

"When did we grow up? You being here is a sign, Abby. I thought I'd never see you again and here you sit. Stay with me."

I shook my head slowly, hesitant to hurt my oldest friend. "I love him, Jess."

His disappointment shadowed the small grin on his face. "Then you'd better go."

I kissed his cheek and fled the restaurant, catching a taxi.

"Where you headed?" The cab driver asked.

"Zero's."

The cabby turned to look at me, giving me a once-over. "You sure?"

"I'm sure! Go!" I said, tossing cash over the seat.

Chapter Sixteen
Home

Travis finally broke through the crowd with Benny's hand on his shoulder, whispering in his ear. Travis nodded and replied. My blood ran cold as I watched him be so friendly to the man who had threatened us less than twenty-four hours before. Travis basked in the applause and congratulations of his triumph as the crowd roared. He walked taller, his smile was wider, and when he reached me, he planted a quick kiss on my mouth.

I could taste the salty sweat mixed with the coppery taste of blood on his lips. He had won the fight, but not without a few battle wounds of his own.

"What was that about?" I asked, watching Benny laugh with his cohorts.

"I'll tell you later. We have a lot to talk about," he said with a broad grin.

A man patted Travis on the back.

"Thanks," Travis said, turning to him and shaking his outstretched hand.

"Looking forward to seeing another match of yours, son," the man said, handing him a bottle of beer. "That was incredible."

"C'mon, Pidge." He took a sip of his beer, swished it around in his mouth, and then spit, the amber liquid on the ground tinged with blood. He weaved through the crowd, taking in a deep breath when we made it to the sidewalk outside. He kissed me once and then led me down the Strip, his steps quick and purposeful.

In the elevator of our hotel, he pushed me against the mirrored wall, grabbed my leg, and pulled it up in a quick motion against his hip. His mouth crashed into mine, and I felt the hand under my knee slide up my thigh and pull up my skirt.

"Travis, there's a camera in here," I said against his lips.

"I don't give a fuck," he chuckled. "I'm celebrating."

I pushed him away. "We can celebrate in the room," I said, wiping my mouth and looking down at my hand, seeing streaks of crimson.

"What's wrong with you, Pigeon? You won, I won, we paid off Mick's debt, and I just got the offer of a lifetime."

The elevator opened and I stood in place as Travis stepped out into the hall. "What kind of offer?" I asked.

Travis reached out his hand, but I ignored it. My eyes narrowed, already knowing what he would say.

He sighed. "I told you, we'll talk about it later."

"Let's talk about it now."

He leaned in and pulled me by the wrist into the hallway and then lifted me off the floor into his arms.

"I am going to make enough money to replace what Mick took from you, to pay for the rest of your tuition, pay off my bike, and buy you a new car," he said, sliding the card key in and out of its slot. He pushed open the door and set me on my feet. "And that's just the beginning!"

"And how exactly are you going to do that?" My chest tightened and my hands began to tremble.

He took my face in his hands, ecstatic. "Benny is going to let me fight here in Vegas. Six figures a fight, Pidge. Six figures a fight!"

I closed my eyes and shook my head, blocking out the excitement in his eyes. "What did you say to Benny?" Travis lifted my chin, and I opened my eyes, afraid he had already signed a contract.

He chuckled. "I told him I'd think about it."

I exhaled the breath I'd been holding. "Oh, thank God. Don't scare me like that, Trav. I thought you were serious."

Travis grimaced and steadied himself before he spoke. "I am serious, Pigeon. I told him I needed to talk to you first, but I thought you'd be happy. He's scheduling one fight a month. Do you have any idea how much money that is? Cash!"

"I can add, Travis. I can also keep my senses when I'm in Vegas, which you obviously can't. I have to get you out of here before you do something stupid." I walked over to the closet and ripped our clothes from the hangers, furiously stuffing them into our suitcases.

Travis gently grabbed my arms and spun me around. "I can do this. I can fight for Benny for a year and then we'll be set for a long, long time."

"What are you going to do? Drop out of school and move here?"

"Benny's going to fly me out, work around my schedule."

I laughed once, incredulous. "You can't be that gullible,

Travis. When you're on Benny's payroll, you aren't just going to fight once a month for him. Did you forget about Dane? You'll end up being one of his thugs!"

He shook his head. "We already discussed that, Pidge. He doesn't want me to do anything but fight."

"And you trust him? You know they call him Slick Benny around here!"

"I wanted to buy you a car, Pigeon. A nice one. Both of our tuitions will be paid in full."

"Oh? The mob is handing out scholarships, now?"

Travis's jaws clenched. He was irritated at having to convince me. "This is good for us. I can sock it away until it's time for us to buy a house. I can't make this kind of money anywhere else."

"What about your Criminal Justice degree? You're going to be seeing your old classmates quite a bit working for Benny, I promise you."

"Baby, I understand your reservations, I do. But I'm being smart about this. I'll do it for a year and then we'll get out and do whatever the hell we want."

"You don't just quit Benny, Trav. He's the only one that can tell you when you're done. You have no idea what you're dealing with! I can't believe you're even considering this! Working for a man that would have beat the hell out of the both of us last night if you hadn't stopped him?"

"Exactly. I stopped him."

"You stopped two of his lightweight goons, Travis. What are you going to do if there are a dozen of them? What are you going to do if they come after me during one of your fights?"

"It wouldn't make sense for him to do that. I'll be making him lots of money."

"The moment you decide you're not going to do that anymore, you're expendable. That's how these people work."

Travis walked away from me and looked out the window, the blinking lights coloring his conflicted features. He had made his decision before he'd ever come to me about it.

"It's going to be all right, Pigeon. I'll make sure it is. And then we'll be set."

I shook my head and turned around, shoving our clothes into our suitcases. When we set down on the tarmac at home, he would be his old self again. Vegas did strange things to people, and I couldn't reason with him while he was intoxicated with the flow of cash and whiskey.

I refused to discuss it further until we were on the plane, afraid Travis would let me leave without him. I buckled my seat belt and clenched my teeth, watching him stare longingly out the window as we climbed into the night sky. He was already missing the wickedness and limitless temptations Vegas had to offer.

"That's a lot of money, Pidge."

"No."

His head jerked in my direction. "This is my decision. I don't think you're looking at the big picture."

"I think you've lost your damn mind."

"You're not even going to consider it?"

"No, and neither are you. You're not going to work for a murderous criminal in Las Vegas, Travis. It's completely ridiculous for you to think I could consider it."

Travis sighed and looked out the window. "My first fight is in three weeks."

My mouth dropped open. "You already agreed to it?"

He winked. "Not yet."

"But you're going to?"

He smiled. "You'll quit being mad when I buy you a Lexus."

"I don't want a Lexus," I seethed.

"You can have anything you want, baby. Imagine how it's going to feel driving into any dealership you want, and all you have to do is pick your favorite color."

"You're not doing this for me. Stop pretending you are."

He leaned over, kissing my hair. "No, I'm doing it for us. You just can't see how great it's going to be."

A cold shiver radiated from my chest, traveling down my spine into my legs. He wouldn't see reason until we were in the apartment, and I was terrified that Benny had made him an offer he couldn't refuse. I shook off my fears; I had to believe Travis loved me enough to forget the dollar signs and false promises Benny had made.

"Pidge? Do you know how to cook a turkey?"

"A turkey?" I said, taken off guard by the sudden change of conversation.

He squeezed my hand. "Well, Thanksgiving break is coming up, and you know my dad loves you. He wants you to come for Thanksgiving, but we always end up ordering pizza and watching the game. I thought maybe me and you could try cooking a bird together. You know, have a real turkey dinner for once in the Maddox house."

I pressed my lips together, trying not to laugh. "You just thaw the turkey and put it in a pan and cook it in the oven all day. There's not much to it."

"So you'll come? You'll help me?"

I shrugged. "Sure."

His attention was diverted from the intoxicating lights below, and I allowed myself to hope that he would see how wrong he was about Benny after all.

TRAVIS SET OUR SUITCASES ON THE BED AND COLLAPSED beside them. He hadn't pushed the Benny issue, and I was hopeful that Vegas had begun to filter out of his system. I bathed Toto, disgusted that he reeked of smoke and dirty socks from being in Brazil's apartment all weekend, and then towel-dried him in the bedroom.

"Oh! You smell so much better!" I giggled as he shook, spraying me with tiny droplets of water. He stood up on his hind legs, covering my face with tiny puppy kisses. "I missed you, too, little man."

"Pigeon?" Travis asked, nervously knotting his fingers together.

"Yeah?" I said, rubbing Toto with the fluffy yellow towel in my hands.

"I wanna do this. I want to fight in Vegas."

"No," I said, smiling at Toto's happy face.

He sighed. "You're not listening. I'm gonna do it. You'll see in a few months that it was the right decision."

I looked up at him. "You're going to work for Benny."

He nodded nervously and then smiled. "I just wanna take care of you, Pidge."

Tears glossed my eyes, knowing he was resolved. "I don't want anything bought with that money, Travis. I don't want anything to do with Benny or Vegas or anything that goes along with it."

"You didn't have a problem with the thought of buying a car with the money from my fights here."

"'That's different and you know it."

He frowned. "It's gonna be okay, Pidge. You'll see."

I watched him for a moment, hoping for a glimmer of amusement in his eyes, waiting for him to tell me that he was joking. But all I could see was uncertainty and greed.

"Why did you even ask me, Travis? You were going to work for Benny no matter what I said."

"I want your support on this, but it's too much money to turn down. I would be crazy to say no."

I sat for a moment, stunned. Once it had all sunk in, I nodded. "Okay, then. You've made your decision."

Travis beamed. "You'll see, Pigeon. It's going to be great." He pushed off the bed, walked over to me, and kissed my fingers. "I'm starved. You hungry?"

I shook my head and he kissed my forehead before making his way to the kitchen. Once his footsteps left the hall, I pulled my clothes from their hangers, grateful that I had room in my suitcase for most of my belongings. Angry tears fell down my cheeks. I knew better than to take Travis to that place. I had fought tooth and nail to keep him from the dark edges of my life, and the moment the opportunity presented itself, I dragged him to the core of everything I hated without a second thought.

Travis was going to be a part of that, and if he wouldn't let me save him, I had to save myself.

The suitcase was filled to its limit, and I stretched the zipper over the bulging contents. I yanked it off the bed and down the hall, passing the kitchen without glancing in its direction. I hurried down the steps, relieved that America and Shepley were still kissing and laughing in the parking lot, transferring her things from his Charger to her Honda.

"Pigeon?" Travis called from the doorway of the apartment.

I touched America's wrist. "I need you to take me to Morgan, Mare."

"What's going on?" she said, noting the seriousness of the situation by my expression.

I glanced behind me to see Travis jogging down the stairs and across the grass to where we stood.

"What are you doing?" he said, gesturing to my suitcase.

If I'd told him in that moment, all hope of separating myself from Mick, and Vegas, and Benny, and everything I didn't want would be lost. Travis wouldn't let me leave, and by morning I would have convinced myself to accept his decision.

I scratched my head and smiled, trying to buy some time to think of an excuse.

"Pidge?"

"I'm taking my stuff to Morgan. They have all those washers and dryers and I have a ridiculous amount of laundry to do."

He frowned. "You were going to leave without telling me?"

I glanced to America and then to Travis, struggling for the most believable lie.

"She was coming back in, Trav. You're so freakin' paranoid," America said with the dismissive smile she had used to deceive her parents so many times.

"Oh," he said, still unsure. "You staying here tonight?" he asked me, pinching the fabric of my coat.

"I don't know. I guess it depends on when my laundry gets done."

Travis smiled, pulling me against him. "In three weeks, I'll pay someone to do your laundry. Or you can just throw away your dirty clothes and buy new ones."

"You're fighting for Benny again?" America asked, shocked.

"He made me an offer I couldn't refuse."

"Travis," Shepley began.

"Don't you guys start on me, too. If I'm not changing my mind for Pidge, I'm not changing my mind for you."

America met my eyes with understanding, "Well, we better get you back, Abby. That pile of clothes is gonna take you forever."

I nodded and Travis leaned down to kiss me. I pulled him closer, knowing it would be the last time I felt his lips against mine. "See you later," he said. "Love you."

Shepley lifted my suitcase into the hatchback of the Honda, and America slid into her seat beside me. Travis folded his arms across his chest, chatting with Shepley as America switched on the ignition.

"You can't stay in your room tonight, Abby. He's going to come straight there when he figures it out," America said as she slowly backed away from the parking block.

Tears filled my eyes and spilled over, falling down my cheeks. "I know."

Travis's cheerful expression changed when he saw the look on my face. He wasted no time jogging to my window. "What's wrong, Pidge?" he said, tapping on the glass.

"Go, Mare," I said, wiping my eyes. I focused on the road ahead as Travis jogged alongside the car.

"Pigeon? America! Stop the fucking car!" he yelled, slamming his palm against the glass. "Abby, don't do this!" he said, realization and fear distorting his expression.

America turned onto the main road and pressed on the gas. "I'm never going to hear the end of this—just so you know."

"I'm so, so sorry, Mare."

She glanced into the rearview mirror and pushed her foot to the floor. "Jesus Christ, Travis," she muttered under her breath.

I turned to see him running at full speed behind us, vanishing and reappearing between the lights and shadows of the street lamps. After he reached the end of the block, he turned in the opposite direction, sprinting to the apartment.

"He's going back to get his bike. He's gonna follow us to Morgan and cause a huge scene."

I closed my eyes. "Just . . . hurry. I'll sleep in your room tonight. Think Vanessa will mind?"

"She's never there. He's really going to work for Benny?"

The word was stuck in my throat, so I simply nodded.

America grabbed my hand and squeezed. "You're making the right decision, Abby. You can't go through that again. If he won't listen to you, he's not going to listen to anyone."

My cell phone rang. I looked down to see Travis's silly face and then pressed ignore. Less than five seconds later, it rang again. I turned it off and shoved it into my purse.

"This is going to be a god-awful fucking mess," I said, shaking my head and wiping my eyes.

"I don't envy your life for the next week or so. I can't imagine breaking up with someone that refuses to stay away. You know that's how it's going to be, right?"

We pulled into the parking lot at Morgan, and America held open the door as I lugged my suitcase in. We rushed to her room and I puffed, waiting for her to unlock her door. She held it open and then tossed me the key.

"He's going to end up getting arrested or something," she said.

She ran down the hall and I watched her rush across the parking lot from the window, getting in her car just as Travis pulled up on his bike beside her. He ran around to the passenger side and yanked open the door, looking to Morgan's doors when he realized I wasn't in the car. America backed out while Travis ran into the building, and I turned, watching the door.

Down the hall, Travis pounded on my door, calling my name. I had no idea if Kara was there, but if she was, I felt bad for what she would have to endure for the next few minutes until Travis accepted that I wasn't in my room.

"Pidge? Open the fucking door, dammit! I'm not leaving until you talk to me! Pigeon!" he yelled, banging on the door so loudly the entire building could have heard.

I cringed when I heard Kara's mousy voice.

"What?" she growled.

I pressed my ear against the door, struggling to hear Travis's low murmurs. I didn't have to strain for long.

"I know she's here!" he yelled. "Pigeon?"

"She's not . . . Hey!" Kara squealed.

The door cracked against the cement block wall of our room and I knew that Travis had forced his way in. After a full minute of silence, I heard Travis yell down the hall. "Pigeon! Where is she?"

"I haven't seen her!" Kara shouted, angrier than I'd ever heard her. The door slammed shut, and sudden nausea overwhelmed me as I waited for what Travis would do next.

After several minutes of quiet, I cracked open the door, peering down the wide hallway. Travis sat with his back against the wall with his hands covering his face. I shut the door as quietly as I could, worrying that the campus police had been called.

After an hour, I glanced down the hall again. Travis hadn't moved.

I checked twice more during the night, finally falling asleep around four. I purposefully overslept, knowing I would skip classes that day. I turned on my phone to check my messages, seeing that Travis had flooded my inbox. The endless texts he'd sent me through the night varied from apologies to rants.

I called America in the afternoon, hoping Travis hadn't confiscated her cell phone. When she answered, I sighed.

"Hey."

America kept her voice low. "I haven't told Shepley where you are. I don't want him in the middle of this. Travis is crazy pissed at me right now. I'm probably staying at Morgan tonight."

"If Travis hasn't calmed down . . . good luck getting any sleep here. He made an Oscar-worthy performance in the hall last night. I'm surprised no one called security."

"He was kicked out of History today. When you didn't show, he kicked over both of your desks. Shep heard that he waited for you after all of your classes. He's losin' it, Abby. I told him you were done the second he made the decision to work for Benny. I can't believe he thought for a single second you would be okay with that."

"I guess I'll see you when you get here. I don't think I can go to my room, yet."

America and I were roommates over the next week, and she made sure to keep Shepley away so he wouldn't be tempted to tell Travis of my whereabouts. It was a full-time job avoiding a run-in with him. I avoided the cafeteria at all costs, as well as History class, and I played it safe by leaving my classes early. I knew that I would have to talk to Travis sometime, but

I couldn't until he had calmed down enough to accept my decision.

I sat alone Friday night, lying in bed, holding the phone to my ear. I rolled my eyes when my stomach growled.

"I can come pick you up and take you somewhere for dinner," America said.

I flipped through my History book, skipping over where Travis had doodled and scribbled love notes in the margins. "No, it's your first night with Shep in almost a week, Mare. I'm just going to pop over to the cafeteria."

"You sure?"

"Yeah. Tell Shep I said hi."

I walked slowly to the cafeteria, in no hurry to suffer the stares of those at the tables. The entire school was abuzz with the breakup, and Travis's volatile behavior didn't help. Just when the lights of the cafeteria came into view, I saw a dark figure approach.

"Pigeon?"

Startled, I jerked to a stop. Travis walked into the light, unshaven and pale. "Jesus, Travis! You scared the hell out of me!"

"If you would answer your phone when I call I wouldn't have to sneak around in the dark."

"You look like hell," I said.

"I've been through there once or twice this week."

I tightened my arms around me. "I'm actually on my way to grab something to eat. I'll call you later, okay?"

"No. We have to talk."

"Trav . . ."

"I turned Benny down. I called him Wednesday and told

him no." There was a hopeful glimmer in his eyes, but it disappeared when he registered my expression.

"I don't know what you want me to say, Travis."

"Say you forgive me. Say you'll take me back."

I clenched my teeth together, forbidding myself to cry. "I can't."

Travis's face crumpled. I took the opportunity to walk around him, but he sidestepped to stand in my way. "I haven't slept, or ate . . . I can't concentrate. I know you love me. Everything will be the way it used to be if you'd just take me back."

I closed my eyes. "We are dysfunctional, Travis. I think you're just obsessed with the thought of owning me more than anything else."

"That's not true. I love you more than my life, Pigeon," he said, hurt.

"That's exactly what I mean. That's crazy talk."

"It's not crazy. It's the truth."

"Okay . . . so what exactly is the order for you? Is it money, me, your life . . . or is there something that comes before money?"

"I realize what I've done, okay? I see where you'd think that, but if I'd known that you were gonna leave me, I would have never . . . I just wanted to take care of you."

"You've said that."

"Please don't do this. I can't stand feeling like this . . . it's . . . it's killin' me," he said, exhaling as if the air had been knocked out of him.

"I'm done, Travis."

He winced. "Don't say that."

"It's over. Go home."

His eyebrows pulled in. "You're my home."

His words cut me, and my chest tightened so much that it was hard to breathe. "You made your choice, Trav. I've made mine," I said, inwardly cursing the quivering in my voice.

"I'm going to stay the hell out of Vegas and away from Benny . . . I'm going to finish school. But I need you. I *need* you. You're my best friend." His voice was desperate and broken, matching his expression.

In the dim light I could see a tear fall from his eye, and in the next moment he reached out for me and I was in his arms, his lips on mine. He squeezed me tight against his chest as he kissed me, and then cradled my face in his hands, pressing his lips harder against my mouth, desperate to get a reaction.

"Kiss me," he whispered, sealing his mouth on mine. I kept my eyes and mouth closed, relaxing in his arms. It took everything I had not to move my mouth with his, having longed for his lips all week. "Kiss me!" he begged. "Please, Pigeon! I told him no!"

When I felt hot tears searing down my cold face, I shoved him away. "Leave me alone, Travis!"

I had only made it a few feet when he grabbed my wrist. My arm was straight, outstretched behind me. I didn't turn around.

"I am begging you." My arm lowered and tugged as he fell to his knees. "I'm begging you, Abby. Don't do this."

I turned to see his agonized expression, and then my eyes drifted down my arm to his, seeing my nickname in thick black letters on his flexed wrist. I looked away, toward the cafeteria. He had proven to me what I had been afraid of all along. As much as he loved me, when money was involved, I would be second. Just as I was with Mick.

If I gave in, either he would change his mind about Benny, or he would resent me every time money could have made his life easier. I imagined him in a blue-collar job, coming home with the same look in his eyes that Mick had when he returned after a night of bad luck. It would be my fault that his life wasn't what he wanted it to be, and I couldn't let my future be plagued with the bitterness and regret that I left behind.

"Let me go, Travis."

After several moments he finally released my arm. I ran to the glass door, yanking it open without looking back. Everyone in the room stared at me as I walked toward the buffet, and just as I reached my destination, heads angled to see outside the windows where Travis was on his knees, palms flat on the pavement.

The sight of him on the ground made the tears I'd been holding back rush down my face. I passed the stacks of plates and trays, dashing down the hall to the bathrooms. It was bad enough that everyone had witnessed the scene between me and Travis. I couldn't let them see me cry.

I cowered in the stall for an hour, bawling uncontrollably until I heard a tiny knock on the door.

"Abby?"

I sniffed. "What are you doing in here, Finch? You're in the girls' bathroom."

"Kara saw you come in and came to the dorms to get me. Let me in," he said in a soft voice.

I shook my head. I knew he couldn't see me, but I couldn't

speak another word. I heard him sigh and then his palms slapped on the floor as he crawled under the stall.

"I can't believe you're making me do this," he said, pulling himself under with his hands. "You're going to be sorry you didn't open the door, because I just crawled along that piss-covered floor and now I'm going to hug you."

I laughed once, and then my face compressed around my smile as Finch pulled me into his arms. My knees went out from under me, and Finch carefully lowered me to the floor, pulling me into his lap.

"Ssshh," he said, rocking me in his arms. He sighed and shook his head. "Damn, girl. What am I gonna do with you?"

Chapter Seventeen
No, Thanks

I DOODLED ON THE FRONT OF MY NOTEBOOK, MAKING squares in squares, connecting them to each other to form rudimentary 3-D boxes. Ten minutes before class was to begin, the classroom was still empty. Life was in the beginning stages of normal, but it still took me a few minutes to psych myself up to be around anyone other than Finch and America.

"Just because we're not dating anymore doesn't mean you can't wear the bracelet I bought you," Parker said as he slid into the desk beside me.

"I've been meaning to ask you if you wanted it back."

He smiled, leaning over to add a bow to the top of one of the boxes on the paper. "It was a gift, Abs. I don't give gifts with conditions."

Dr. Ballard flipped on her overhead as she took her seat at the head of the class and then rummaged through papers on her cluttered desk. The room was suddenly abuzz with chatter echoing against the large rain-spattered windows.

"I heard that you and Travis broke up a couple of weeks ago." Parker held up a hand seeing my impatient expression. "It's none of my business. You've just looked so sad, and I wanted to tell you that I'm sorry."

"Thanks," I muttered, turning to a fresh page in my notebook.

"And I also wanted to apologize for my behavior before. What I said was . . . unkind. I was just angry, and I lashed out at you. It wasn't fair, and I'm sorry."

"I'm not interested in dating, Parker," I warned.

He chuckled. "I'm not trying to take advantage. We're still friends, and I want to make sure that you're okay."

"I'm okay."

"Are you going home for Thanksgiving break?"

"I'm going home with America. I usually have Thanksgiving at her house."

Parker began to speak but Dr. Ballard began her lecture. The subject of Thanksgiving made me think of my previous plans to help Travis with a turkey. I thought about what that would have been like, and I found myself worrying that they would be ordering pizza yet again. A sinking feeling came over me. I instantly pushed it from my mind, trying my best to concentrate on Dr. Ballard's every word.

After class, my face flushed when I saw Travis jogging toward me from the parking lot. He was clean-shaven again, wearing a hooded sweatshirt and his favorite red baseball cap, ducking his head away from the rain.

"I'll see you after break, Abs," Parker said, touching my back.

I expected an angry glare from Travis, but he didn't seem to notice Parker as he approached. "Hey, Pidge."

I offered an awkward smile, and he shoved his hands into the front pocket of his sweatshirt. "Shepley said you're going with him and Mare to Wichita tomorrow."

"Yeah?"

"You're spending the whole break at America's?"

I shrugged, trying to seem casual. "I'm really close with her parents."

"What about your mom?"

"She's a drunk, Travis. She won't know it's Thanksgiving."

He was suddenly nervous, and my stomach wrenched with the possibility of a second public breakup. Thunder rolled above us and Travis looked up, squinting as the large drops fell against his face.

"I need to ask you for a favor," he said. "C'mere." He pulled me under the closest awning and I complied, trying to avoid another scene.

"What kind of favor?" I asked, suspicious.

"My uh . . ." He shifted his weight. "Dad and the guys are still expecting you on Thursday."

"Travis!" I whined.

He looked at his feet. "You said you would come."

"I know, but . . . it's a little inappropriate now, don't you think?"

He seemed unaffected. "You said you would come."

"We were still together when I agreed to go home with you. You knew I wasn't going to come."

"I didn't know, and it's too late, anyway. Thomas is flying in, and Tyler took off work. Everyone's looking forward to seeing you."

I cringed, twirling the damp strands of my hair around my finger. "They were going to come anyway, weren't they?"

"Not everyone. We haven't had all of us there for Thanksgiving in years. They all made an effort to be there since I promised them a real meal. We haven't had a woman in the kitchen since Mom died and . . ."

"That's not sexist or anything,"

He tilted his head. "That's not what I meant, Pidge, c'mon. We all want you there. That's all I'm sayin'."

"You haven't told them about us, have you?" I said the words in the most accusatory tone I could manage.

He fidgeted for a moment, and then shook his head. "Dad would ask why, and I'm not ready to talk to him about it. I'd never hear the end of how stupid I am. Please come, Pidge."

"I have to put the turkey in at six in the morning. We'd have to leave here by five . . ."

"Or we could stay there."

My eyebrows shot up. "No way! It's bad enough that I'm going to have to lie to your family and pretend we're still together."

"You act like I'm asking you to light yourself on fire."

"You should have told them!"

"I will. After Thanksgiving . . . I'll tell them."

I sighed, looking away. "If you promise me that this isn't some stunt to try and get back together, I'll do it."

He nodded. "I promise."

Although he was trying to hide it, I could see a spark in his eyes. I pressed my lips together, trying not to smile. "I'll see you at five."

Travis leaned down to kiss my cheek, his lips lingering on my skin. "Thanks, Pigeon."

America and Shepley met me at the door of the cafeteria and we walked in together. I yanked the silverware from its holder and then dropped my plate onto the tray.

"What's with you, Abby?" America asked.

"I'm not coming with you guys tomorrow."

Shepley's mouth fell open. "You're going to the Maddoxes?"

America's eyes darted to mine. "You're what?"

I sighed and shoved my campus ID at the cashier. "I promised Trav I'd go when we were on the plane, and he told them all I'd be there."

"In his defense," Shepley began, "he really didn't think you guys were gonna break up. He thought you'd come around. It was too late by the time he figured out that you were serious."

"That's bullshit, Shep, and you know it," America seethed. "You don't have to go if you don't want to, Abby."

She was right. It wasn't as if I didn't have a choice. But I couldn't do that to Travis. Not even if I hated him. And I didn't.

"If I don't go, he'll have to explain to them why I didn't show, and I don't want to ruin his Thanksgiving. They're all coming home thinking I'm going to be there."

Shepley smiled. "They all really like you, Abby. Jim was just talking to my dad about you the other day."

"Great," I muttered.

"Abby's right," Shepley said. "If she doesn't go, Jim will spend the day bitching at Trav. There's no sense in ruining their day."

America put her arm around my shoulders. "You can still come with us. You're not with him anymore. You don't have to keep saving him."

"I know, Mare. But it's the right thing to do."

THE SUN MELTED INTO THE BUILDINGS OUTSIDE THE window, and I stood in front of my mirror, brushing my hair while trying to decide how I was going to go about pretending with Travis. "It's just one day, Abby. You can handle one day," I said to the mirror.

Pretending had never been a problem for me; it was what was going to happen while we were pretending that I was worried about. When Travis dropped me off after dinner, I was going to have to make a decision. A decision that would be skewed by a false sense of happiness we would portray for his family.

Knock, knock.

I turned, looking at the door. Kara hadn't been back to our room all evening, and I knew that America and Shepley were already on the road. I couldn't imagine who it could be. I set my brush on the table and pulled open the door.

"Travis," I breathed.

"Are you ready?"

I raised an eyebrow. "Ready for what?"

"You said pick you up at five."

I folded my arms across my chest. "I meant five in the morning!"

"Oh. I guess I should call Dad and let him know we won't be staying after all."

"Travis!" I wailed.

"I brought Shep's car so we didn't have to deal with our bags on the bike. There's a spare bedroom you can crash in. We can watch a movie or—"

"I'm not staying at your dad's!"

His face fell. "Okay. I'll uh . . . I'll see you in the morning."

He took a step back and I shut the door, leaning against it. Every emotion I had weaved in and out of my insides, and I heaved an exasperated sigh. With Travis's disappointed expression fresh on my mind, I pulled open the door and stepped out, seeing that he was slowly walking down the hall, dialing his phone.

"Travis, wait." He flipped around and the hopeful look in his eyes made my chest ache. "Give me a minute to pack a few things."

A relieved, appreciative smile spread across his face and he followed me to my room, watching me shove a few things in a bag from the doorway.

"I still love you, Pidge."

I didn't look up. "Don't. I'm not doing this for you."

He sucked in a breath. "I know."

We rode in silence to his dad's house. The car felt charged with nervous energy, and it was hard to sit still against the cold leather seats. Once we arrived, Trenton and Jim walked out onto the porch, all smiles. Travis carried our bags from the car, and Jim patted his back.

"Good to see ya, son." His smiled broadened when he looked at me. "Abby Abernathy. We're looking forward to dinner tomorrow. It's been a long time since . . . Well. It's been a long time."

I nodded and followed Travis into the house. Jim rested his hand on his protruding belly and grinned. "I set you two up in the guest bedroom, Trav. I didn't figure you would wanna fight with the twin beds in your room."

I looked to Travis. It was difficult watching him struggle to speak. "Abby's uh . . . she's going to uh . . . going to take the guest room. I'm going to crash in mine."

Trenton made a face. "Why? She's been staying at your apartment, hasn't she?"

"Not lately," he said, desperately trying to avoid the truth.

Jim and Trenton traded glances. "Thomas's room has been storage for years now, so I was going to let him take your room. I guess he can sleep on the couch," Jim said, looking at the ratty, discolored cushions in the living room.

"Don't worry about it, Jim. We were just trying to be respectful," I said, touching his arm.

His laughter bellowed throughout the house, and he patted my hand. "You've met my sons, Abby. You should know it's damn near impossible to offend me."

Travis nodded toward the stairs, and I followed him. He pushed open the door with his foot and sat our bags on the floor, looking at the bed and then turning to me. The room was lined in brown paneling, the brown carpet beyond normal wear and tear. The walls were a dirty white, the paint peeling in places. I saw only one frame on the wall; enclosed was a picture of Jim and Travis's mother. The background was a generic portrait-studio blue; the couple sported feathered hair and young, smiling faces. It must have been taken before they had the boys; neither of them could have been older than twenty.

"I'm sorry, Pidge. I'll sleep on the floor."

"Damn straight you will," I said, pulling my hair into a ponytail. "I can't believe I let you talk me into this."

He sat on the bed and rubbed his face in frustration. "This is going to be a fucking mess. I don't know what I was thinking."

"I know exactly what you were thinking. I'm not stupid, Travis."

He looked up at me and smiled. "But you still came."

"I have to get everything ready for tomorrow," I said, opening the door.

Travis stood up. "I'll help you."

We peeled a mountain of potatoes, cut up vegetables, set out the turkey to thaw, and started the piecrusts. The first hour was more than uncomfortable, but when the twins arrived, everyone seemed to congregate in the kitchen. Jim told stories about each of his boys, and we laughed about tales of earlier disastrous Thanksgivings when they attempted to do something other than order pizza.

"Diane was a hell of a cook," Jim mused. "Trav doesn't remember, but there was no sense trying after she passed."

"No pressure, Abby," Trenton said. He chuckled, and then grabbed a beer from the fridge. "Let's get out the cards. I want to try to make back some of my money that Abby took."

Jim waved his finger at his son. "No poker this weekend, Trent. I brought down the dominoes; go set those up. No betting, dammit. I mean it."

Trenton shook his head. "All right, old man, all right." Travis's brothers meandered from the kitchen, and Trenton followed, stopping to look back. "C'mon, Trav."

"I'm helping Pidge."

"There's not much more to do, baby," I said. "Go ahead."

His eyes softened at my words, and he touched my hip. "You sure?"

I nodded and he leaned over to kiss my cheek, squeezing my hip with his fingers before following Trenton into the game room.

Jim watched his sons file out of the doorway, shaking his head and smiling. "This is incredible what you're doing, Abby. I don't think you realize how much we all appreciate it."

"It was Trav's idea. I'm glad I could help."

His large frame settled against the counter, taking a swig of his beer while he pondered his next words. "You and Travis haven't talked much. You having problems?"

I squeezed the dish soap into the sink as it filled with hot water, trying to think of something to say that wasn't a bald-faced lie. "Things are a little different, I guess."

"That's what I thought. You have to be patient with him. Travis doesn't remember much about it, but he was close to his mom, and after we lost her he was never the same. I thought he'd grow out of it, you know, with him being so young. It was hard on all of us, but Trav . . . he quit trying to love people after that. I was surprised that he brought you here. The way he acts around you, the way he looks at you . . . I knew you were somethin' special."

I smiled, but kept my eyes on the dishes I was scrubbing.

"Travis'll have a hard time. He's going to make a lot of mistakes. He grew up around a bunch of motherless boys and a lonely, grouchy old man for a father. We were all a little lost after Diane died, and I guess I didn't help the boys cope the way I should have.

"I know it's hard not to blame him, but you have to love him, anyway, Abby. You're the only woman he's loved besides his mother. I don't know what it'll do to him if you leave him, too."

I swallowed back the tears and nodded, unable to reply. Jim rested his hand on my shoulder and squeezed. "I've never seen him smile the way he does when he's with you. I hope all my boys have an Abby one day."

His footsteps faded down the hallway and I gripped the edge of the sink, trying to catch my breath. I knew spending the holiday with Travis and his family would be difficult, but I didn't think my heart would be broken all over again. The men joked and laughed in the next room as I washed and dried the dishes, putting them away. I cleaned the kitchen and then washed my hands, making my way to the stairs for the night.

Travis grabbed my hand. "It's early, Pidge. You're not going to bed, are ya?"

"It's been a long day. I'm tired."

"We were getting ready to watch a movie. Why don't you come back down and hang out?"

I looked up the stairs and then down to his hopeful smile. "Okay."

He led me by the hand to the couch, and we sat together as the opening credits rolled.

"Shut off that light, Taylor," Jim ordered.

Travis reached his arm behind me, resting his arm on the back of the couch. He was trying to keep up pretenses while appeasing me. He had been careful not to take advantage of the situation, and I found myself conflicted, both grateful and disappointed. Sitting so close to him, smelling the mixture of tobacco and his cologne, it was very difficult for me to keep my distance, both physically and emotionally. Just as I had feared, my resolve was wavering. I struggled to block out everything Jim had said in the kitchen.

Halfway through the movie, the front door flew open and Thomas rounded the corner, bags in hand.

"Happy Thanksgiving!" he said, setting his luggage on the floor.

Jim stood up and hugged his oldest son, and everyone but Travis stood to greet him.

"You're not going to say hi to Thomas?" I whispered.

He didn't look at me when he spoke, watching his family hug and laugh. "I got one night with you. I'm not going to waste a second of it."

"Hi there, Abby. It's good to see you again," Thomas smiled.

Travis touched my knee with his hand and I looked down and then to Travis. Noticing my expression, Travis took his hand off my leg and interlocked his fingers in his lap.

"Uh-oh. Trouble in paradise?" Thomas asked.

"Shut up, Tommy," Travis grumbled.

The mood in the room shifted, and I felt all eyes on me, waiting for an explanation. I smiled nervously and took Travis's hand into both of mine.

"We're just tired. We've been working all evening on the food," I said, leaning my head against Travis's shoulder.

He looked down at our hands and then squeezed, his eyebrows pulling in a bit.

"Speaking of tired, I'm exhausted," I breathed. "I'm gonna head to bed, baby." I looked to everyone else. "Good night, guys."

"Night, sis," Jim said.

Travis's brothers all bade me good night, and I headed up the stairs.

"I'm gonna turn in, too," I heard Travis say.

"I bet you are," Trenton teased.

"Lucky bastard," Tyler grumbled.

"Hey. We're not going to talk about your sister like that," Jim warned.

My stomach sank. The only real family I'd had in years was America's parents, and although Mark and Pam had always looked out for me with true kindness, they were borrowed. The six unruly, foul-mouthed, loveable men downstairs had welcomed me with open arms, and tomorrow I would tell them goodbye for the last time.

Travis caught the bedroom door before it closed and then froze. "Did you want me to wait in the hall while you dressed for bed?"

"I'm going to hop in the shower. I'll just get dressed in the bathroom."

He rubbed the back of his neck. "All right. I'll make a pallet, then."

I nodded, making my way to the bathroom. I scrubbed myself raw in the dilapidated shower, focusing on the water stains and soap scum to fight the overwhelming dread I felt for both the night and the morning. When I returned to the bedroom, Travis dropped a pillow on the floor on his makeshift bed. He offered a weak smile before leaving me to take a turn in the shower.

I crawled into bed, pulling the covers to my chest, trying to ignore the blankets on the floor. When Travis returned, he stared at the pallet with the same sadness that I did, and then turned off the light, situating himself on his pillow.

It was quiet for a few minutes, and then I heard Travis heave a miserable sigh. "This is our last night together, isn't it?"

I waited a moment, trying to think of the right thing to say. "I don't wanna fight, Trav. Just go to sleep."

Hearing him shift, I turned onto my side to look down at him, pressing my cheek into the pillow. He supported his head with his hand and stared into my eyes.

"I love you."

I watched him for a moment. "You promised."

"I promised this wasn't a stunt to get back together. It

wasn't." He reached up his hand to touch mine. "But if it meant being with you again, I can't say I wouldn't consider it."

"I care about you. I don't want you to hurt, but I should have followed my gut in the first place. It would've never worked."

"You did love me, though, right?"

I pressed my lips together. "I still do."

His eyes glossed over, and he squeezed my hand. "Can I ask you for a favor?"

"I'm sort of in the middle of the last thing you asked me to do," I said with a smirk.

His features were taut, unaffected by my expression. "If this is really it . . . if you're really done with me . . . will you let me hold you tonight?"

"I don't think it's a good idea, Trav."

His hand gripped tight over mine. "Please? I can't sleep knowing you're just a foot away, and I'm never gonna get the chance again."

I stared into his desperate eyes for a moment and then frowned. "I'm not having sex with you."

He shook his head. "That's not what I'm asking."

I searched the dimly lit room with my eyes, thinking about the consequences, wondering if I could tell Travis no if he changed his mind. I shut my eyes tight and then pushed away from the edge of the bed, turning down the blanket. He crawled into bed beside me, hastily pulling me tight into his arms. His bare chest rose and fell with uneven breaths, and I cursed myself for feeling so peaceful against his skin.

"I'm going to miss this," I said.

He kissed my hair and pulled me to him. He seemed unable to get close enough to me. He buried his face in my neck and

I rested my hand on his back in comfort, although I was just as heartbroken as he was. He sucked in a breath and pressed his forehead against my neck, pressing his fingers into the skin of my back. As miserable as we were the last night of the bet, this was much, much worse.

"I . . . I don't think I can do this, Travis."

He pulled me tighter and I felt the first tear fall from my eye down my temple. "I can't do this," I said, clenching my eyes shut.

"Then don't," he said against my skin. "Give me another chance."

I tried to push myself out from under him, but his grip was too solid for any possibility of escape. I covered my face with both hands as my quiet sobs shook us both. Travis looked up at me, his eyes heavy and wet.

With his large, gentle fingers, he pulled my hand away from my eyes and kissed my palm. I took a faltering breath as he looked at my lips and then back to my eyes. "I'll never love anyone the way I love you, Pigeon."

I sniffed and touched his face. "I can't."

"I know," he said, his voice broken. "I never once convinced myself that I was good enough for you."

My face crumpled and I shook my head. "It's not just you, Trav. We're not good for each other."

He shook his head, wanting to say something but thinking better of it. After a long, deep breath, he rested his head against my chest. When the green numbers on the clock across the room read eleven o'clock, Travis's breaths finally slowed and evened out. My eyes grew heavy, and I blinked a few times before slipping out of consciousness.

◆ ◆ ◆

"OW!" I YELPED, PULLING MY HAND FROM THE STOVE AND automatically nursing the burn with my mouth.

"You okay, Pidge?" Travis asked, shuffling across the floor and slipping a T-shirt over his head. "Shit! The floor's fucking freezing!" I stifled a giggle as I watched him hop on one foot and then the other until the soles of his feet acclimated to the frigid tile.

The sun had barely peeked through the blinds, and all but one of the Maddoxes were sleeping soundly in their beds. I pushed the antique tin pan further into the oven and then closed the door, turning to cool my fingers under the sink.

"You can go back to bed. I just had to put the turkey in."

"Are you coming?" he asked, wrapping his arms around his chest to ward off the chill in the air.

"Yeah."

"Lead the way," he said, sweeping his hand toward the stairs.

Travis yanked his shirt off as we both shoved our legs under the covers, pulling the blanket up to our necks. He tightened his arms around me as we shivered, waiting for our body heat to warm the small space between our skin and the covers.

I felt his lips against my hair, and then his throat moved when he spoke. "Look, Pidge. It's snowing."

I turned to face the window. The white flakes were only visible in the glow of the street lamp. "It kind of feels like Christmas," I said, my skin finally warming up against his. He sighed and I turned to see his expression. "What?"

"You won't be here for Christmas."

"I'm here, now." He pulled his mouth up on one side and leaned down to kiss my lips. I leaned back and shook my head. "Trav . . ."

His grip tightened and he lowered his chin, his chestnut eyes determined. "I've got less than twenty-four hours with you, Pidge. I'm gonna kiss you. I'm gonna kiss you a lot today. All day. Every chance I get. If you want me to stop, just say the word, but until you do, I'm going to make every second of my last day with you count."

"Travis—" I thought about it for a moment, and I reasoned that he was under no illusions about what would happen when he took me home. I had come there to pretend, and as hard as it would be for us both later, I didn't want to tell him no.

When he noticed me staring at his lips, the corner of his mouth turned up again, and he leaned down to press his soft mouth against mine. It began sweet and innocent, but the moment his lips parted, I caressed his tongue with mine. His body instantly tensed, and he took a deep breath in through his nose, pressing his body against me. I let my knee fall to the side and he moved above me, never taking his mouth from mine.

He wasted no time undressing me, and when there was no more fabric between us, he gripped the iron vines of the headboard with both hands, and in one quick movement, he was inside me. I bit my lip hard, stifling the cry that was clawing its way up my throat. Travis moaned against my mouth, and I pressed my feet against the mattress, anchoring myself so I could raise my hips to meet his.

One hand on the iron and the other on the nape of my neck, he rocked against me over and over, and my legs quivered with his firm, determined movements. His tongue searched my mouth, and I could feel the vibration of his deep groans against my chest as he kept to his promise to make our last day together memorable. I could spend a thousand years trying to block that moment from my memory, and it would still be burned into my mind.

An hour had passed when I clenched my eyes shut, my every nerve focused on the shuddering of my insides. Travis held his breath as he thrust inside me one last time. I collapsed against the mattress, completely spent. Travis heaved with deep breaths, speechless and dripping with sweat.

I could hear voices downstairs and I covered my mouth, giggling at our misbehavior. Travis turned on his side, scanning my face with his soft, brown eyes.

"You said you were just going to kiss me." I grinned.

As I lay next to his bare skin, seeing the unconditional love in his eyes, I let go of my disappointment and my anger and my stubborn resolve. I loved him, and no matter what my reasons were to live without him, I knew it wasn't what I wanted. Even if I hadn't changed my mind, it was impossible for us to stay away from each other.

"Why don't we just stay in bed all day?" he smiled.

"I came here to cook, remember?"

"No, you came here to help me cook, and I don't report for duty for another eight hours."

I touched his face; the urge to end our suffering had become unbearable. When I told him I had changed my mind and that things were back to normal, we wouldn't have to spend the day pretending. We could spend it celebrating instead.

"Travis, I think we . . ."

"Don't say it, okay? I don't want to think about it until I have to." He stood up and pulled on his boxers, walking over to my bag. He tossed my clothes on the bed and then yanked his shirt over his head. "I want to remember this as a good day."

I made eggs for breakfast and sandwiches for lunch, and when the game began, I started dinner. Travis stood behind me at every opportunity, his arms wrapped around my waist, his lips on my neck. I caught myself glancing at the clock, eager to find a moment alone with him to tell him my decision. I was anxious to see the look on his face and to get back to where we were.

The day was filled with laughter, conversation, and a steady stream of complaints from Tyler about Travis's constant display of affection.

"Get a room, Travis! Jesus!" Tyler groaned.

"You are turning a hideous shade of green," Thomas teased.

"It's because they're making me sick. I'm not jealous, douche-bag," Tyler sneered.

"Leave 'em alone, Ty," Jim warned.

When we sat down for dinner, Jim insisted on Travis carving the turkey, and I smiled as he proudly stood up to comply. I was a bit nervous until the compliments washed in. By the time I served the pie, there wasn't a morsel of food left on the table.

"Did I make enough?" I laughed.

Jim smiled, pulling his fork through his lips to get ready for dessert. "You made plenty, Abby. We just wanted to tide our-selves over until next year . . . unless you'd like to do this all over again at Christmas. You're a Maddox, now. I expect you at every holiday, and not to cook."

I glanced over at Travis, whose smiled had faded, and my heart sank. I had to tell him soon. "Thanks, Jim."

"Don't tell her that, Dad," Trenton said. "She's gotta cook. I haven't had a meal like this since I was five!" He shoveled half a slice of pecan pie into his mouth, humming with satisfaction.

I felt at home, sitting at a table full of men who were leaning back in their chairs, rubbing their full bellies. Emotion overwhelmed me when I fantasized about Christmas and Easter and every other holiday I would spend at that table. I wanted nothing more than to be a part of this broken, loud family that I adored.

When the pies were gone, Travis's brothers began to clear the table and the twins manned the sink.

"I'll do that," I said, standing.

Jim shook his head. "No, you don't. The boys can take care of it. You just take Travis to the couch and relax. You've worked hard, sis."

The twins splashed each other with dishwater and Trenton cussed when he slipped on a puddle and dropped a plate. Thomas chastised his brothers, getting the broom and dustpan to sweep up the glass. Jim patted his sons on the shoulders and then hugged me before retreating to his room for the night.

Travis pulled my legs onto his lap and slipped off my shoes, massaging the soles of my feet with his thumbs. I leaned my head back and sighed.

"This was the best Thanksgiving we've had since Mom died."

I pulled my head up to see his expression. He was smiling, but it was tinged with sadness.

"I'm glad I was here to see it."

Travis's expression changed and I braced myself for what he was about to say. My heart pounded against my chest, hoping he would ask me back so I could say yes. Las Vegas seemed like a lifetime ago, sitting in the home of my new family.

"I'm different. I don't know what happened to me in Vegas. That wasn't me. I was thinking about everything we could buy with that money, and that was all I was thinking about. I didn't see how much it hurt you for me to want to take you back there, but deep down, I think I knew. I deserved for you to leave me. I deserved all the sleep I lost and the pain I've felt. I needed all that to realize how much I need you and what I'm willing to do to keep you in my life."

I chewed on my lip, impatient to get to the part where I said yes. I wanted him to take me back to the apartment and spend the rest of the night celebrating. I couldn't wait to relax on the new couch with Toto, watching movies and laughing like we used to.

"You said you're done with me, and I accept that. I'm a different person since I met you. I've changed . . . for the better. But no matter how hard I try, I can't seem to do right by you. We were friends first, and I can't lose you, Pigeon. I will always love you, but if I can't make you happy, it doesn't make much sense for me to try to get you back. I can't imagine being with anyone else, but I'll be happy as long as we're friends."

"You want to be friends?" I asked, the words burning in my mouth.

"I want you to be happy. Whatever that takes."

My insides wrenched at his words, and I was surprised at the overpowering pain I felt. He was giving me an out, and it was exactly when I didn't want it. I could have told him that I had changed my mind, and he would take back everything he'd just said, but I knew that it wasn't fair to either of us to hold on just when he had let go.

I smiled to fight the tears. "Fifty bucks says you'll be thanking me for this when you meet your future wife."

Travis's eyebrows pulled together as his face fell. "That's an easy bet. The only woman I'd ever wanna marry just broke my heart."

I couldn't fake a smile after that. I wiped my eyes and then stood up. "I think it's time you took me home."

"C'mon, Pigeon. I'm sorry, that wasn't funny."

"It's not that, Trav. I'm just tired, and I'm ready to go home."

He sucked in a breath and nodded, standing up. I hugged his brothers goodbye, and asked Trenton to say goodbye to Jim for me. Travis stood at the door with our bags as they all agreed to come home for Christmas, and I held my smile long enough to get out the door.

WHEN TRAVIS WALKED ME TO MORGAN, HIS FACE WAS still sad, but the torment was gone. The weekend wasn't a stunt to get me back after all. It was closure.

He leaned over to kiss my cheek and held the door open for me, watching as I walked inside. "Thanks for today. You don't know how happy you made my family."

I stopped at the bottom of the stairs. "You're going to tell them tomorrow, aren't you?"

He looked out to the parking lot and then at me. "I'm pretty sure they already know. You're not the only one with a poker face, Pidge."

I stared at him, stunned, and for the first time since I'd met him, he walked away from me without looking back.

Chapter Eighteen
The Box

FINALS WERE A CURSE FOR EVERYONE BUT ME. I KEPT busy, studying with Kara and America in my room and at the library. I only saw Travis in passing when the schedules changed for tests. I went home with America for winter break, thankful that Shepley had stayed with Travis so I wouldn't suffer their constant displays of affection.

The last four days of break I caught a cold, giving me a good reason to stay in bed. Travis said he wanted to be friends, but he hadn't called. It was a relief to have a few days to wallow in self-pity. I wanted to get it out of my system before returning to school.

The return trip to Eastern seemed to take years. I was eager to start the spring semester, but I was far more eager to see Travis again.

The first day of classes, a fresh energy had swept over the campus along with a blanket of snow. New courses meant new friends and a new beginning. I didn't have a single class with Travis, Parker, Shepley, or America, but Finch was in all but one of mine.

I anxiously waited for Travis at lunch, but when he came in he simply winked at me and then sat at the end of the table with the rest of his frat brothers. I tried to concentrate on America and Finch's conversation about the last football game of the season, but Travis's voice kept catching my attention. He was regaling tales of his adventures and brushes with the law he'd had over break, and news of Trenton's new girlfriend they'd met one night while they were at the Red Door. I braced myself for mention of any girl he'd brought home or met, but if he had, he wasn't sharing it with his friends.

Red and gold metallic balls still hung from the ceiling of the cafeteria, blowing with the current of the heaters. I pulled my cardigan around me, and Finch noticed, hugging me to him and rubbing my arm. I knew that I was paying far too much attention to Travis's general direction, waiting for him to look up at me, but he seemed to have forgotten that I was sitting at the table.

He seemed impervious to the hordes of girls that approached him after news of our breakup, but he was also content with our relationship returning to its platonic state, however strained. We had spent almost a month apart, leaving me nervous and unsure about how to act around him.

Once he finished his lunch, my heart fluttered when he walked up behind me and rested his hands on my shoulders.

"How's your classes, Shep?" he asked.

Shepley's face pinched. "First day sucks. Hours of syllabi and class rules. I don't even know why I show up the first week. How about you?"

"Eh . . . it's all part of the game. How 'bout you, Pidge?" he asked.

"The same," I said, trying to keep my voice casual.

"Did you have a good break?" he asked, playfully swaying me from side to side.

"Pretty good," I said. I tried my best to sound convincing.

"Sweet. I've got another class. Later."

I watched him make a beeline for the doors, shoving them both open and then lighting a cigarette as he walked.

"Huh," America said in a high-pitched tone. She watched Travis cut across the greens through the snow and then shook her head.

"What?" Shepley asked.

America rested her chin on the heel of her hand, seeming vexed. "That was kind of weird, wasn't it?"

"How so?" Shepley asked, flicking America's blond braid back to brush his lips across her neck.

America smiled and leaned into his kiss. "He's almost normal . . . as normal as Trav can be. What's up with him?"

Shepley shook his head and shrugged. "I don't know. He's been that way for a while."

"How backward is that, Abby? He's fine and you're miserable," America said, unconcerned with listening ears.

"You're miserable?" Shepley asked with a surprised expression.

My mouth fell open and my face flamed with instant embarrassment. "I am not!"

She pushed her salad around in the bowl. "Well, he's damn near ecstatic."

"Drop it, Mare," I warned.

She shrugged and took another bite. "I think he's faking it."

Shepley nudged her. "America? You goin' to the Valentine's Day date party with me or what?"

"Can't you ask me like a normal boyfriend? Nicely?"

"I have asked you . . . repeatedly. You keep telling me to ask you later."

She slumped in her chair, pouting. "I don't wanna go without Abby."

Shepley's face screwed with frustration. "She was with Trav the whole time last time. You barely saw her."

"Quit being a baby, Mare," I said, throwing a stick of celery at her.

Finch elbowed me. "I'd take you, Cupcake, but I'm not into the frat-boy thing, sorry."

"That's actually a damn good idea," Shepley said, his eyes bright.

Finch grimaced at the thought. "I'm not Sig Tau, Shep. I'm not anything. Fraternities are against my religion."

"Please, Finch?" America asked.

"Déjà vu," I grumbled.

Finch looked at me from the corner of his eye and then sighed. "It's nothing personal, Abby. I can't say I've ever been on a date . . . with a girl."

"I know." I shook my head dismissively, waving away my deep embarrassment. "It's fine. Really."

"I need you there," America said. "We made a pact, remember? No parties alone."

"You'll hardly be alone, Mare. Quit being so dramatic," I said, already annoyed with the conversation.

"You want dramatic? I pulled a trash can beside your bed, held a box of Kleenex for you all night, and got up to get you cough medicine twice when you were sick over break! You owe me!"

I wrinkled my nose. "I have kept your hair vomit free so many times, America Mason!"

"You sneezed in my face!" she said, pointing to her nose.

I blew my bangs from my eyes. I could never argue with America when she was determined to get her way. "Fine," I said through my teeth.

"Finch?" I asked him with my best fake smile. "Will you go to the stupid Sig Tau Valentine's date party with me?"

Finch hugged me to his side. "Yes. But only because you called it stupid."

I walked with Finch to class after lunch, discussing the date party and how much we were both dreading it. We picked out a pair of desks in our Physiology class, and I shook my head when the professor began my fourth syllabus of the day. The snow began to fall again, drifting against the windows, politely begging entrance and then falling with disappointment to the ground.

After class was dismissed, a boy I'd met only once at the Sig Tau house knocked on my desk as he walked by, winking. I offered a polite smile and then glanced over to Finch. He shot me a wry grin, and I gathered my book and laptop, shoving them into my backpack with little effort.

I lugged my bag over my shoulders and trudged to Morgan along the salted sidewalk. A small group of students had started a snowball fight on the greens, and Finch shuddered at the sight of them, covered in white powder.

I wobbled my knee, keeping Finch company as he finished his cigarette. America scurried beside us, rubbing her bright green mittens together.

"Where's Shep?" I asked.

"He went home. Travis needed help with something, I guess."

"You didn't go with him?"

"I don't live there, Abby."

"Only in theory," Finch winked at her.

America rolled her eyes. "I enjoy spending time with my boyfriend, so sue me."

Finch flicked his cigarette into the snow. "I'm heading out, ladies. I'll see you at dinner?"

America and I nodded, smiling when Finch first kissed my cheek and then America's. He stayed on the wet sidewalk, careful to stay in the middle so that he wouldn't miss and step into the snow.

America shook her head at his efforts. "He is ridiculous."

"He's a Floridian, Mare. He's not used to the snow."

She giggled and pulled me toward the door.

"Abby!"

I turned to see Parker jogging past Finch. He stopped, catching his breath a moment before he spoke. His puffy gray coat heaved with each breath, and I chuckled at America's curious stare as she watched him.

"I was . . . whew! I was going to ask you if you wanted to grab a bite to eat tonight."

"Oh. I uh . . . I already told Finch I'd eat with him."

"All right, it's no big deal. I was just going to try that new burger place downtown. Everyone's saying it's really good."

"Maybe next time," I said, realizing my mistake. I hoped that he wouldn't take my flippant reply as a postponement. He nodded and shoved his hands into his pockets, quickly walking back the way he came.

Kara was reading ahead in her brand-new books, grimacing at America and me when we walked in. Her demeanor hadn't improved since we'd returned from break.

Before, I had spent so much time at Travis's that Kara's insufferable comments and attitude were tolerable. Spending every evening and night with her during the two weeks before the semester ended made my decision not to room with America more than just regrettable.

"Oh, Kara. How I've missed you," America said.

"The feeling is mutual," Kara grumbled, keeping her eyes on her book.

America chatted about her day and plans with Shepley for the weekend. We scoured the Internet for funny videos, laughing so hard we were wiping away tears. Kara huffed a few times at our disruption, but we ignored her.

I was grateful for America's visit. The hours passed so quickly that I didn't spend a moment wondering if Travis had called until she decided to call it a night.

America yawned and looked at her watch. "I'm going to bed, Ab . . . aw, shit!" she said, snapping her fingers. "I left my makeup bag at Shep's."

"That's not a tragedy, Mare," I said, still giggling from the latest video we'd watched.

"It wouldn't be if I didn't have my birth control in there. C'mon. I have to go get it."

"Can't you just get Shepley to bring them?"

"Travis has his car. He's at the Red with Trent."

I felt sick. "Again? Why is he hanging out with Trent so much, anyway?"

America shrugged. "Does it matter? C'mon!"

"I don't want to run into Travis. It'll be weird."

"Do you ever listen to me? He's not there, he's at the Red. Come on!" she whined, tugging on my arm.

I stood up with mild resistance as she pulled me from the room.

"Finally," Kara said.

We pulled up to Travis's apartment, and I noted that the Harley was parked under the stairs and that Shepley's Charger was missing. I breathed a sigh of relief and followed America up the icy steps.

"Careful," she warned.

If I'd known how unsettling it would be to set foot in the apartment again, I wouldn't have let America talk me into going there. Toto scampered around the corner at full speed, crashing into my legs when his tiny paws failed to get traction on the entryway tile. I picked him up, letting him greet me with his baby kisses. At least he hadn't forgotten me.

I carried him around the apartment, waiting while America searched for her bag.

"I know I left it here!" she said from the bathroom, stomping down the hall to Shepley's room.

"Did you look in the cabinet under the sink?" Shepley asked.

I looked at my watch. "Hurry, Mare. We need to get going."

America sighed in frustration from the bedroom.

I looked down at my watch again, and then jumped when the front door burst open behind me. Travis stumbled in, his arms wrapped around Megan, who was giggling against his mouth. A box in her hand caught my eye, and I felt sick when I realized what it was: condoms. Her other hand was on the back of his neck, and I couldn't tell whose arms were tangled around who.

Travis did a double take when he saw me standing alone in the middle of the living room, and when he froze, Megan looked up with a residual smile still on her face.

"Pigeon," Travis said, stunned.

"Found it!" America said, jogging out of Shepley's room.

"What are you doing here?" he asked. The stench of whiskey blew in with the flurry of snowflakes, and my uncontrollable anger overcame any need to feign indifference.

"It's good to see you're feeling like your old self, Trav," I said. The heat that radiated from my face burned my eyes and blurred my vision.

"We were just leaving," America snarled. She grabbed my hand as we slid past Travis.

We flew down the steps toward her car, and I was thankful that it was just a few steps further, feeling the tears well up in my eyes. I almost fell backward when my coat snagged on something midstep. America's hand slipped from mine and she flipped around the same time I did.

Travis had a fistful of my coat, and my ears caught fire, stinging in the cold night air. His lips and collar were a ridiculous shade of deep red.

"Where are you going?" he said, a half-drunk, half-confused look in his eyes.

"Home," I snapped, straightening my coat when he released me.

"What are you doing here?"

I could hear the packed snow crunch under America's feet as

she walked up behind me, and Shepley flew down the stairs to stand behind Travis, his wary eyes fixed on his girlfriend.

"I'm sorry. If I'd known you were going to be here, I wouldn't have come."

He shoved his hands in his coat pockets. "You can come here anytime you want, Pidge. I never wanted you to stay away."

I couldn't manage the acidity in my voice. "I don't want to interrupt." I looked to the top of the stairs, where Megan stood with a smug expression. "Enjoy your evening," I said, turning away.

He grabbed my arm. "Wait. You're mad?"

I yanked my coat from his grip. "You know . . . I don't even know why I'm surprised."

His eyebrows pulled in. "I can't win with you. I can't win with you! You say you're done . . . I'm fucking miserable over here! I had to break my phone into a million pieces to keep from calling you every minute of the damn day—I've had to play it off like everything is just fine at school so you can be happy . . . and you're fucking mad at me? You broke my fuckin' heart!" His last words echoed into the night.

"Travis, you're drunk. Let Abby go home," Shepley said.

Travis grabbed my shoulders and pulled me to him. "Do you want me or not? You can't keep doing this to me, Pidge!"

"I didn't come here to see you." I said, glaring up at him.

"I don't want her," he said, staring at my lips. "I'm just so fucking unhappy, Pigeon." His eyes glossed over and he leaned in, tilting his head to kiss me.

I grabbed him by the chin, holding him back. "You've got her lipstick on your mouth, Travis," I said, disgusted.

He took a step back and lifted his shirt, wiping his mouth. He stared at the red streaks on the white fabric and shook his head. "I just wanted to forget. Just for one fuckin' night."

I wiped an escaped tear. "Then don't let me stop you."

I tried to retreat to the Honda, but Travis grabbed my arm again. In the next moment, America was wildly hitting his arm with her fists. He looked at her, blinking for a moment in stunned disbelief. She balled up her fists and pounded them against his chest until he released me.

"Leave her alone, you bastard!"

Shepley grabbed her and she pushed him away, turning to slap Travis's face. The sound of her hand against his cheek was quick and loud, and I flinched with the noise. Everyone froze for a moment, shocked at America's sudden rage.

Travis frowned, but he didn't defend himself. Shepley grabbed her again, holding her wrists and pulling her to the Honda while she thrashed about.

She fought him violently, her blond hair whipping around with her attempts to get away. I was amazed at her determination to get at Travis. Pure hate glowed in her usually sweet, carefree eyes.

"How could you? She deserved better from you, Travis!"

"America, STOP!" Shepley yelled, louder than I'd ever heard him.

Her arms fell to her side as she glared at Shepley with incredulity. "You're defending him?"

Although he seemed nervous, he stood his ground. "Abby broke up with him. He's just trying to move on."

Her eyes narrowed and she pulled her arm from his grip.

"Well then, why don't you go find a random WHORE—" she looked at Megan—"from the Red and bring her home to fuck and then let me know if it helps you get over me."

"Mare," Shepley grabbed for her but she evaded him, slamming the door as she sat behind the wheel. I sat beside her, trying not to look at Travis.

"Baby, don't leave," Shepley begged, leaning down into the window.

She started the car. "There is a right side and a wrong side here, Shep. And you are on the wrong side."

"I'm on your side," he said, his eyes desperate.

"Not anymore you're not," she said, backing out.

"America? America!" Shepley called after her as she raced to the road, leaving him behind.

I sighed. "Mare, you can't break up with him over this. He's right."

America put her hand on mine and squeezed. "No he's not. Nothing about what just happened was right."

When we pulled into the parking lot beside Morgan, America's phone rang. She rolled her eyes as she answered. "I don't want you calling me anymore. I mean it, Shep," she said. "No, you're not . . . because I don't want you to, that's why. You can't defend what he's done; you can't condone him hurting Abby like that and be with me . . . that's exactly what I mean, Shepley! It doesn't matter! You don't see Abby screwing the first guy she sees! It's not Travis that's the problem, Shepley. He didn't ask you to defend him! Ugh . . . I'm done talking about this. Don't call me again. Goodbye."

She shoved her way out of the car and stomped across the

road and up the steps. I tried to keep in step with her, waiting to hear his side of their conversation.

When her phone rang again, she turned it off. "Travis made Shep take Megan home. He wanted to come by on his way back."

"You should let him, Mare."

"No. You're my best friend. I can't stomach what I saw tonight, and I can't be with someone that will defend it. End of conversation, Abby, I mean it."

I nodded and she hugged my shoulders, pulling me against her side as we walked up the stairs to our rooms. Kara was already asleep, and I skipped the shower, crawling into bed fully dressed, coat and all. I couldn't stop thinking about Travis stumbling in the door with Megan or the red lipstick smeared across his face. I tried to block out the sickening images of what would have happened had I not been there, and I crossed over several emotions, settling on despair.

Shepley was right. I had no right to be angry, but it didn't help me to ignore the pain.

FINCH SHOOK HIS HEAD WHEN I SAT IN THE DESK BESIDE him. I knew that I looked awful; I barely had the energy to change clothes and brush my teeth. I had only slept an hour the night before, unable to shake the sight of the red lipstick on Travis's mouth or the guilt over Shepley and America's breakup.

America chose to stay in bed, knowing once the anger subsided, depression would set in. She loved Shepley, and although she was determined to end things because he had picked the wrong side, she was prepared to suffer the backlash of her decision.

After class, Finch walked with me to the cafeteria. As I had feared, Shepley was waiting at the door for America. When he saw me, he didn't hesitate.

"Where's Mare?"

"She didn't go to class this morning."

"She's in her room?" he said, turning for Morgan.

"I'm sorry, Shepley," I called after him.

He froze and wheeled around with the face of a man who had reached his limit. "I wish you and Travis would just get your shit together! You're a goddamn tornado! When you're happy, it's love and peace and butterflies. When you're pissed, you take the whole fucking world down with you!"

He stomped away, and I exhaled the breath I was holding. "That went well."

Finch pulled me into the cafeteria. "The whole world. Wow. Think you could work your voodoo before the test on Friday?"

"I'll see what I can do."

Finch chose a different table, and I was more than happy to follow him there. Travis sat with his frat brothers, but he didn't get a tray and he didn't stay long. He noticed me just as he was leaving, but he didn't stop.

"So America and Shepley broke up, too, huh?" Finch asked while he chewed.

"We were at Shep's last night and Travis came home with Megan and . . . it was a mess. They took sides."

"Ouch."

"Exactly. I feel terrible."

Finch patted my back. "You can't control the decisions they make, Abby. So I guess this means we get to skip the Valentine's thing at Sig Tau?"

"Looks that way."

Finch smiled. "I'll still take you out. I'll take you and Mare both out. It'll be fun."

I leaned on his shoulder. "You're the best, Finch."

I hadn't thought about Valentine's, but I was glad I had plans. I couldn't imagine how miserable I would feel spending it with America alone, hearing her rant about Shepley and Travis all night. She would still do that—she wouldn't be America if she didn't—but at least it would be a limited tirade if we were in public.

THE WEEKS OF JANUARY PASSED, AND AFTER A COM-mendable but failed attempt by Shepley to get America back, I saw less and less of both him and Travis. By February, they stopped coming to the cafeteria altogether, and I only saw Travis a handful of times on my way to class.

The weekend before Valentine's Day, America and Finch talked me into going to the Red, and on the entire drive to the club, I dreaded seeing Travis there. We walked in, and I sighed with relief to see no sign of him.

"First round's on me," Finch said, pointing out a table and sliding through the crowd to the bar.

We sat down and watched as the dance floor went from being empty to overflowing with drunken college students. After our fifth round, Finch pulled us to the dance floor, and I finally felt relaxed enough to have a good time. We giggled and bumped against each other, laughing hysterically when a man swung his dance partner around and she missed his hand, sliding across the floor on her side.

America raised her hands above her head, shaking her curls

to the music. I laughed at her signature dance face and then stopped abruptly when I saw Shepley walk up behind her. He whispered something in her ear and she flipped around. They traded words and then America grabbed my hand, leading me to our table.

"Of course. The one night we go out, and he shows up," she grumbled.

Finch brought each one of us two more drinks, including a shot each. "I thought you might need them."

"You thought right." America tilted her head back before we could toast, and I shook my head, clinking my glass to Finch's. I tried to keep my eyes on my friends' faces, worried that with Shepley being there, Travis wouldn't be far behind.

Another song came over the speakers and America stood up. "Fuck it. I'm not sitting at this table the rest of the night."

"Atta girl!" Finch smiled, following her to the dance floor.

I followed them, glancing around for Shepley. He had disappeared. I relaxed again, trying to shake off the feeling that Travis would show up on the dance floor with Megan. A boy I'd seen around campus danced behind America, and she smiled, welcoming the distraction. I had a suspicion that she was making a show of enjoying herself in hopes that Shepley would see. I looked away for a second, and when I looked back to America, her dance partner was gone. She shrugged, continuing to shake her hips to the beat.

The next song began to play and a different boy appeared behind America, his friend dancing next to me. After a few moments, my new dance partner maneuvered behind me, and I felt a bit unsure when I felt his hands on my hips. As if he'd read my mind, his hands left my waist. I looked behind me, and he was gone. I looked up at America, and the man behind her was gone as well.

Finch seemed a bit nervous, but when America raised an eyebrow at his expression, he shook his head and continued dancing.

By the third song, I was sweaty and tired. I retreated to our table, resting my heavy head on my hand, and laughed as I watched yet another hopeful ask America to dance. She winked at me from the dance floor, and then I stiffened when I saw him yanked backward, disappearing through the crowd.

I stood up and walked around the dance floor, keeping my eye on the hole he was pulled through, and felt the adrenaline burn through the alcohol in my veins when I saw Shepley holding the surprised man by his collar. Travis was beside him, laughing hysterically until he looked up and saw me watching them. He hit Shepley's arm, and when Shepley looked in my direction, he shoved his victim backward onto the floor.

It didn't take me long to figure out what was going on: they had been yanking the guys who were dancing with us off the dance floor and threatening them to get them to stay away from us.

I narrowed my eyes at them both and then made my way to America. The crowd was thick, and I had to shove a few people out of my way. Shepley grabbed my hand before I made it to the dance floor.

"Don't tell her!" he said, trying to subdue his smile.

"What the hell do you think you're doing, Shep?"

He shrugged, still proud of himself. "I love her. I can't let other guys dance with her."

"Then what's your excuse for yanking the guy that was danc-ing with me?" I said, crossing my arms.

"That wasn't me," Shepley said, quickly glancing at Travis. "Sorry, Abby. We were just having fun."

"Not funny."

"What's not funny?" America said, glaring at Shepley.

He swallowed, shooting a pleading look in my direction. I owed him a favor, so I kept my mouth shut.

He sighed in relief when he realized I wouldn't rat him out, and then he looked at America with sweet adoration. "Wanna dance?"

"No, I don't wanna dance," she said, walking back to the table. He followed her, leaving Travis and me standing together.

Travis shrugged. "Wanna dance?"

"What? Megan's not here?"

He shook his head. "You used to be a sweet drunk."

"Happy to disappoint you," I said, turning toward the bar.

He followed, pulling two guys from their seats. I glared at him for a moment, but he ignored me, sitting down and then watching me with an expectant expression.

"Are you gonna sit? I'll buy you a beer."

"I thought you didn't buy drinks for girls at the bar."

He tilted his head in my direction with an impatient frown. "You're different."

"That's what you keep telling me."

"C'mon, Pidge. What happened to us being friends?"

"We can't be friends, Travis. Obviously."

"Why not?"

"Because I don't want to watch you maul a different girl every night, and you won't let anyone dance with me."

He smiled. "I love you. I can't let other guys dance with you."

"Oh yeah? How much did you love me when you were buying that box of condoms?"

Travis winced and I stood up, making my way to the table. Shepley and America were in a tight embrace and making a scene while they kissed passionately.

"I think we're going to the Sig Tau Valentine's date party again," Finch said with a frown.

I sighed. "Shit."

Chapter Nineteen
Hellerton

AMERICA HADN'T BEEN BACK TO MORGAN HALL SINCE her reunion with Shepley. She was consistently absent at lunch, and her phone calls were few and far between. I didn't begrudge them the time to make up for the time they'd spent apart. Truthfully, I was happy that America was too busy to call me from Shepley and Travis's apartment. It was awkward hearing Travis in the background, and I felt a little jealous that she was spending time with him and I wasn't.

Finch and I were seeing more of each other, and I was selfishly thankful that he was just as alone as I was. We went to class, ate together, and studied together, and even Kara grew accustomed to having him around.

My fingers were beginning to get numb from the frigid air as I stood outside Morgan while he smoked.

"Would you consider quitting before I get hypothermia from standing here for moral support?" I asked.

Finch laughed. "I love you, Abby. I really do, but no. Not quitting."

"Abby?"

I turned to see Parker walking down the sidewalk with his hands shoved into his pockets. His full lips were dry under his red nose, and I laughed when he put an imaginary cigarette to his mouth and blew out a puff of misty air.

"You could save a lot of money this way, Finch," he smiled.

"Why is everyone trashing on my smoking habit today?" he asked, annoyed.

"What's up, Parker?" I asked.

He fished two tickets from his pocket. "That new Vietnam movie is out. You said you wanted to see it the other day, so I thought I would grab us some tickets for tonight."

"No pressure," Finch said.

"I can go with Brad if you have plans," he said with a shrug.

"So it's not a date?" I asked.

"Nope, just friends."

"And we've seen how that works out for you," Finch teased.

"Shut up!" I giggled. "That sounds fun, Parker, thanks."

His eyes brightened. "Would you like to get some pizza or something before? I'm not a big fan of theater food, myself."

"Pizza's great," I nodded.

"The movie's at nine, so I'll pick you up at six thirty or so?"

I nodded again and Parker waved goodbye.

"Oh, Jesus," Finch said. "You're a glutton, Abby. You know that's not going to fly with Travis when he gets wind of it."

"You heard him. It's not a date. And I can't make plans based on what is okay with Travis. He didn't clear it with me before he brought Megan home."

"You're never going to let that go, are you?"

"Probably not, no."

*   *   *

WE SAT IN A CORNER BOOTH, AND I RUBBED MY MITTENS together, trying to get warm. I couldn't help but notice we were in the same booth Travis and I sat in when we first met, and I smiled at the memory of that day.

"What's funny?" Parker asked.

"I just like this place. Good times."

"I noticed the bracelet," he said.

I looked down at the sparkling diamonds on my wrist. "I told you I liked it."

The waitress handed us menus and took our drink orders. Parker updated me on his spring schedule, and talked about the progress in his studies for the MCAT. By the time the waitress served our beers, Parker had barely taken a breath. He seemed nervous, and I wondered if he wasn't under the impression that we were on a date, regardless of what he'd said.

He cleared his throat. "I'm sorry. I think I've monopolized the conversation long enough." He tipped his beer bottle and shook his head. "I just haven't talked to you for any length of time in so long that I suppose I had a lot to say."

"It's fine. It has been a long time."

Just then, the door chimed. I turned to see Travis and Shepley walk in. It took Travis less than a second to meet my stare, but he didn't look surprised.

"Jesus," I muttered under my breath.

"What?" Parker asked, turning to see them sit in a booth across the room.

"There's a burger place down the street we can go to," Parker said in a hushed voice. As nervous as he was before, it had been taken to a whole new level now.

"I think it would be more awkward to leave at this point," I grumbled.

His face fell, defeated. "You're probably right."

We tried to continue our conversation, but it was noticeably forced and uncomfortable. The waitress spent an extended period of time at Travis's table, raking her fingers through her hair and shifting her weight from one foot to the other. She finally remembered to take our order when Travis answered his cell phone.

"I'll have the tortellini," Parker said, looking to me.

"And I'll have . . ." I trailed off. I was distracted when Travis and Shepley stood up.

Travis followed Shepley to the door, but he hesitated, stopped, and turned around. When he saw me watching him, he walked straight across the room. The waitress had an expectant smile, as if she thought he had come to say goodbye. She was quickly disappointed when he stood beside me without so much as blinking in her direction.

"I've got a fight in forty-five minutes, Pidge. I want you there."

"Trav . . ."

His face was stoic, but I could see the tension around his eyes. I wasn't sure if he didn't want to leave my dinner with Parker to fate or if he truly wanted me there with him, but I had made my decision the second he'd asked.

"I need you there. It's a rematch with Brady Hoffman, the guy from State. It's a big crowd, lots of money floating around . . . and Adam says Brady's been training."

"You've fought him before, Travis, you know it's an easy win."

"Abby," Parker said quietly.

"I need you there," Travis said.

I looked at Parker with an apologetic smile. "I'm sorry."

"Are you serious?" he said, his eyebrows shooting up. "You're just going to leave in the middle of dinner?"

"You can still call Brad, right?" I asked, standing up.

The corners of Travis's mouth turned up infinitesimally as he tossed a twenty on the table. "That should cover it."

"I don't care about the money . . . Abby . . ."

I shrugged. "He's my best friend, Parker. If he needs me there, I have to go."

I felt Travis's hand encapsulate mine as he led me away. Parker watched with a stunned look on his face. Shepley was already on the phone in his Charger, spreading the word. Travis sat in the back with me, keeping my hand firmly in his.

"I just got off the phone with Adam, Trav. He said the State guys all showed up drunk and padded with cash. They're already riled up, so you might wanna keep Abby out of the way."

Travis nodded. "You can keep an eye on her."

"Where's America?" I asked.

"Studying for her Physics test."

"That's a nice lab," Travis said. I laughed once and then looked to Travis, who had a small grin on his face.

"When did you see the lab? You haven't had Physics," Shepley said.

Travis chuckled and I elbowed him. He pressed his lips together until the urge to laugh subsided, and then he winked at me, squeezing my hand once again. His fingers intertwined in mine, and I heard a small sigh escape his lips. I knew what he was thinking because I felt the same. In that sliver of time, it was as if nothing had changed.

We pulled into a dark patch of the parking lot, and Travis refused to let go of my hand until we crawled into the window of the basement of the Hellerton Science Building. It had been built just the year before, so it didn't suffer from stagnant air and dust like the other basements we'd snuck into.

Just as we entered the hallway, the roar of the crowd reached our ears. I poked my head out to see an ocean of faces, many of them unfamiliar. Everyone had a bottle of beer in their hand, but the State students were easy to pick out of the crowd. They were the ones that swayed with their eyes half closed.

"Stay close to Shepley, Pigeon. It's going to get crazy in here," he said from behind me. He scanned the crowd, shaking his head at the sheer numbers.

Hellerton's basement was the most spacious on campus, so Adam liked to schedule fights there when he expected a larger crowd. Even with the addition of space, people were being rubbed against the walls and shoving one another to get a good spot.

Adam rounded the corner and didn't try to hide his dissatisfaction with my presence. "I thought I told you that you couldn't bring your girl to the fights anymore, Travis."

Travis shrugged. "She's not my girl anymore."

I kept my features smooth, but he had said the words so matter-of-factly that I felt a stabbing sensation in my chest.

Adam looked down at our intertwined fingers and then up at Travis. "I'm never gonna figure you two out." He shook his head and then glanced to the mob. People were still streaming in from the stairs, and those on the floor were already packed together. "We've got an insane pot tonight, Travis, so no fuckin' off, okay?"

"I'll make sure it's entertaining, Adam."

"That's not what I'm worried about. Brady's been training."

"So have I."

"Bullshit," Shepley laughed.

Travis shrugged. "I got in a fight with Trent last weekend. That little shit is fast."

I chuckled and Adam glared at me. "You better take this seriously, Travis," he said, staring into his eyes. "I have a lot of money riding on this fight."

"And I don't?" Travis said, irritated with Adam's lecture.

Adam turned, holding the bullhorn to his lips as he stood upon a chair above the multitude of drunken spectators. Travis pulled me against his side as Adam greeted the crowd and then went over the rules.

"Good luck," I said, touching his chest. I hadn't felt nervous watching his fights other than the one he'd had with Brock McMann in Vegas, but I couldn't shake the ominous feeling I'd had since we stepped foot in Hellerton. Something was off, and Travis felt it, too.

Travis grabbed my shoulders and planted a kiss on my lips. He pulled away quickly, nodding once. "That's all the luck I need."

I was still stunned from the warmth of Travis's lips when Shepley pulled me to the wall beside Adam. I was bumped and elbowed, reminding me of the first night I watched Travis fight, but the crowd was less focused, and some of the State students were getting hostile. Easterners cheered and whistled for Travis when he broke into the Circle, and State's crowd alternated between booing Travis and cheering for Brady.

I was in prime position to see Brady tower over Travis, twitching impatiently for the bullhorn to sound. As usual, Travis had a slight grin on his face, unaffected by the madness around him. When Adam began the fight, Travis intentionally let Brady get in the first punch. I was surprised when his face jerked hard to the side with the blow. Brady had been training.

Travis smiled, his teeth a bright red, and then he focused on matching every punch Brady dealt.

"Why is he letting him hit him so much?" I asked Shepley.

"I don't think he's letting him anymore," Shepley said, shaking his head. "Don't worry, Abby. He's getting ready to take it up a notch."

After ten minutes Brady was winded, but he still landed solid blows into Travis's sides and jaw. Travis caught Brady's shoe when he tried to kick him, and held his leg high with one hand, punching him in the nose with incredible force and then lifting Brady's leg higher, causing him to lose his balance. The crowd exploded when Brady fell, but he wasn't on the floor for long. He stood, but with the addition of two lines of dark red streaming from his nose. In the next moment, he landed two more punches to Travis's face. Blood rose from a cut on Travis's eyebrow and dripped down his cheek.

I closed my eyes and turned away, hoping Travis would end the fight soon. The small shift of my body caught me in the current of onlookers, and before I could right myself, I was several feet from a preoccupied Shepley. Efforts to fight against the crowd were ineffective, and before long I was being rubbed against the back wall.

The nearest exit was on the other side of the room, an equal distance to the door we'd come in. My back slammed against the concrete wall, knocking the wind out of me.

"Shep!" I yelled, waving my hand above me to get his attention. The fight was at its peak. No one could hear me.

A man lost his footing and used my shirt to right himself, spilling his beer down my front. I was soaked from neck to waist, reeking with the bitter stench of cheap beer. The man still had my shirt bunched in his fist as he tried to pull himself from the floor, and I ripped his fingers open two at time until he released me. He didn't look twice at me, pushing his way forward through the crowd.

"Hey! I know you!" Another man yelled into my ear.

I leaned away, recognizing him right away. It was Ethan, the man Travis threatened at the bar—the man that had somehow escaped sexual assault charges.

"Yeah," I said, looking for a hole in the crowd as I straightened my shirt.

"That's a nice bracelet," he said, running his hand down my arm and grabbing my wrist.

"Hey," I warned, pulling my hand away.

He rubbed my arm, swaying and grinning. "We were rudely interrupted last time I tried to talk to you."

I stood on my tiptoes, seeing Travis land two blows into Brady's face. He scanned the crowd between each one. He was looking for me instead of focusing on the fight. I had to get back to my spot before he was too distracted.

I had barely made headway into the crowd when Ethan's fingers dug into the back of my jeans. My back slammed into the wall once more.

"I wasn't finished talking to you," Ethan said, scanning my wet shirt.

I pulled his hand from the back of my jeans, digging in my nails. "Let go!" I yelled when he resisted.

Ethan laughed and pulled me against him. "I don't wanna let go."

I scanned the crowd for a familiar face, trying to push Ethan away at the same time. His arms were heavy, and his grip was tight. In a panic, I couldn't distinguish State students from Easterners. No one seemed to notice my scuffle with Ethan, and it was so loud no one could hear me protest, either. He leaned in, reaching his hand around to my backside.

"I always thought you'd be a nice piece of ass," he said, breathing stale beer in my face.

"Get OFF!" I screamed, pushing him.

I looked for Shepley, and saw that Travis had finally picked me out of the crowd. He instantly pushed against the packed bodies surrounding him.

"Travis!" I screamed, but it was muffled against the cheering. I pushed Ethan with one hand and reached for Travis with the other.

Travis made little progress before being shoved back into the Circle. Brady took advantage of Travis's distraction and rammed an elbow in the side of his head.

The crowd quieted down a bit when Travis punched someone in the crowd, trying once again to get to me.

"Get the fuck off her!" Travis yelled.

In a line between where I stood and Travis's desperate attempt to reach me, heads turned in my direction. Ethan was oblivious, trying to keep me still long enough to kiss me.

He ran his nose across my cheekbone and then down my neck.

"You smell really good," he slurred.

I pushed his face away, but he grabbed my wrist, unfazed.

Wide-eyed, I searched for Travis again. He desperately pointed me out to Shepley. "Get her! Shep! Get Abby!" he said, still trying to push through the crowd. Brady pulled him back into the circle and punched him again.

"You're fucking hot, you know that?" Ethan said.

I closed my eyes when I felt his mouth on my neck. Anger welled up within me and I pushed him again. "I said get OFF!" I yelled, ramming my knee into his groin.

He doubled over, one hand automatically flying to the source of the pain, the other still gripping my shirt, refusing to let go.

"You bitch!" he cried.

In the next moment, I was free. Shepley's eyes were wild, staring into Ethan's as he gripped him by the collar of his shirt. He held Ethan against the wall while he nailed him with his fist repeatedly in the face, stopping only when the blood poured from Ethan's mouth and nose.

Shepley pulled me to the stairs, shoving anyone who stood in his path. He helped me through an open window, and then down a fire escape, catching me when I leapt the few feet to the ground.

"You okay, Abby? Did he hurt you?" Shepley asked.

One sleeve of my white sweater hung only by a few threads; otherwise I had escaped unscathed. I shook my head, still stunned.

Shepley gently took my cheeks in his hands, looking into my eyes. "Abby, answer me. Are you all right?"

I nodded. As the adrenaline absorbed into my blood stream, the tears began to flow. "I'm okay."

He hugged me, pressing his cheek against my forehead, and then stiffened. "Over here, Trav!"

Travis ran at us full speed, slowing only when he had me in his arms. He was covered in blood, his eye dripping and his mouth spattered with red.

"Jesus Christ . . . is she hurt?" he asked.

Shepley's hand was still on my back. "She said she's okay."

Travis held me at arm's length by my shoulders and frowned. "Are you hurt, Pidge?"

Just as I shook my head, I saw the first of the mob from the basement trickling down from the fire escape. Travis kept me tight in his arms, silently scanning the faces. A short, squat man hopped down from the ladder and froze when he noticed us standing on the sidewalk.

"You," Travis snarled.

He let me go, running across the grass, tackling the man to the ground.

I looked to Shepley, confused and horrified.

"That's the guy that kept shoving Travis back in the Circle," Shepley said.

A small crowd gathered around them as they scuffled on the ground. Travis pounded his fist into the man's face over and over. Shepley pulled me into his chest, still panting. The man stopped fighting back, and Travis left him on the ground in a bloody heap. Those gathered around him fanned out, giving Travis a wide berth, seeing the rage in his eyes.

"Travis!" Shepley yelled, pointing to the other side of the building.

Ethan hobbled in the shadows, using the brick wall of
Hellerton to hold himself up. When he heard Shepley yell
for Travis, he turned just in time to see his assailant charge.
Ethan limped across the lawn, throwing down the beer bottle
in his hands and moving as fast as his legs could carry him to
the street. Just as he reached his car, Travis grabbed him and
slammed him against it.

Ethan pleaded with Travis, even as Travis gripped his shirt
and rammed his head into the car door. The begging was cut
off with the loud thud of his skull against the windshield, and
then Travis pulled him to the front of the car and shattered the
headlight with Ethan's face. Travis launched him onto the hood,
pressing his face into the metal while shouting obscenities.

"Shit," Shepley said. I turned to see Hellerton glow blue
and red from the lights of a quickly approaching police cruiser.
Droves of people jumped from the landing, forming a human
waterfall down the fire escape, and a flurry of running students
burst into every direction.

"Travis!" I screamed.

Travis left Ethan's limp body on the hood of the car to sprint
toward us. Shepley pulled me to the parking lot, ripping open
his door. I jumped into the backseat, anxiously waiting for them
both to get in. Cars flew from their spots and out of the driveway, screeching to a halt when a second police car blocked the
drive.

Travis and Shepley jumped into their seats, and Shepley
cursed when he saw the trapped cars backing from the only
exit. He slammed the car into drive, and the Charger bounced
as it jumped the curb. He spun out over the grass, and we flew

between two buildings, bouncing again when he hit the road behind the school.

The tires squealed and the engine snarled when Shepley slammed his foot on the accelerator. I slid across the seat into the wall of the cab when we took a turn, bumping my already sore elbow. The streetlights streaked across the window as we raced to the apartment, but it seemed like an hour had passed by the time we pulled into the parking lot.

Shepley threw the Charger into park, and turned off the ignition. The boys opened their doors in silence, and Travis reached into the backseat, lifting me into his arms.

"What happened? Holy shit, Trav, what happened to your face?" America said, running down the stairs.

"I'll tell you inside," Shepley said, guiding her to the door.

Travis carried me up the stairs, through the living room and down the hall without a word, setting me on his bed. Toto pawed at my legs, jumping onto the bed to lick my face.

"Not now, buddy," Travis said in a hushed voice, taking the puppy to the hall and shutting the door.

He knelt in front of me, touching the frayed edges of my sleeve. His eye was in the beginning stages of a bruise, red and swollen. The angry skin above it was cut and wet with blood. His lips were smeared with scarlet, and the hide had been ripped away from some of his knuckles. His once-white T-shirt was now soiled with a combination of blood, grass, and dirt.

I touched his eye and he winced, pulling away from my hand. "I'm so sorry, Pigeon. I tried to get to you. I tried . . ." He cleared his throat of the anger and worry that choked him. "I couldn't get to you."

"Will you ask America to take me back to Morgan?" I said.

"You can't go back there tonight. The place is crawling with cops. Just stay here. I'll sleep on the couch."

I sucked in a faltering breath, trying to ward off any more tears. He felt bad enough.

Travis stood up and opened the door.

"Where are you going?" I asked.

"I've gotta get a shower. I'll be right back."

America shoved past him, sitting beside me on the bed, pulling me into her chest. "I'm so sorry I wasn't there!" she cried.

"I'm fine," I said, wiping my tearstained face.

Shepley knocked on the door as he entered, bringing me a short glass half full of whiskey.

"Here," he said, handing it to America. She cupped my hands around it and nudged me.

I tipped back my head, letting the liquid flow down my throat. My face compressed as the whiskey burned its way to my stomach. "Thanks," I said, handing the glass back to Shepley.

"I should have gotten to her sooner. I didn't even realize she was gone. I'm sorry, Abby. I should've . . ."

"It's not your fault, Shep. It's not anyone's fault."

"It's Ethan's fault," he seethed. "That sick bastard was dry-fucking her against the wall."

"Baby!" America said, appalled. She pulled me to her side.

"I need another drink," I said, shoving my empty glass at Shepley.

"Me, too," Shepley said, returning to the kitchen.

Travis walked in with a towel around his waist, holding a cold can of beer against his eye. America turned her back to us as Travis slipped on his boxers, and then he grabbed his pillow.

Shepley brought four glasses this time, all full to the brim with amber liquor. We all knocked back the whiskey without hesitation.

"I'll see you in the morning," America said, kissing my cheek.

Travis took my glass, setting it on the nightstand. He watched me for a moment and then walked over to his closet, pulling a T-shirt off the hanger and tossing it to the bed.

"I'm sorry I'm such a fuckup," he said, holding the beer to his eye.

"You look awful. You're going to feel like shit tomorrow."

He shook his head, disgusted. "Abby, you were attacked tonight. Don't worry about me."

"It's hard not to when your eye is swelling shut," I said, situating his shirt on my lap.

His jaw tensed. "It wouldn't've happened if I'd just let you stay with Parker. But I knew if I asked you, you'd come. I wanted to show him that you were still mine, and then you get hurt."

The words took me off guard, as if I hadn't heard him right. "That's why you ask me to come tonight? To prove a point to Parker?"

"It was part of it," he said, ashamed.

The blood drained from my face. For the first time since we'd met, Travis had fooled me. I had gone to Hellerton with him thinking he needed me, thinking that despite everything, we were back to where we were before. I was nothing more than a water hydrant; he had marked his territory, and I had allowed him to do it.

My eyes filled with tears. "Get out."

"Pigeon," he said, taking a step toward me.

"Get OUT!" I said, grabbing the glass from the nightstand and throwing it at him. He ducked, and it shattered against the wall in hundreds of tiny, glistening shards. "I hate you!"

Travis heaved as if the air had been knocked out of him, and with a pained expression, he left me alone.

I yanked off my clothes and pulled the T-shirt on. The noise that burst from my throat surprised me. It had been a long time since I had sobbed uncontrollably. Within moments, America rushed into the room.

She crawled into the bed and wrapped her arms around me. She didn't ask questions or try to console me; she only held me as I let the tears drench the pillowcase.

Chapter Twenty
Last Dance

JUST BEFORE THE SUN BREACHED THE HORIZON, AMERica and I quietly left the apartment behind. We didn't speak on the way to Morgan. I was glad for the silence. I didn't want to talk, I didn't want to think, I just wanted to block out the last twelve hours. My body felt heavy and sore, as if I'd been in a car accident. When we walked into my room, I saw that Kara's bed was made.

"Can I stick around a while? I need to borrow your flatiron," America asked.

"Mare, I'm fine. Go to class."

"You're not fine. I don't want to leave you alone right now."

"That's all I want to be at the moment."

She opened her mouth to argue but sighed. There would be no changing my mind. "I'm coming back to check on you after class. Get some rest."

I nodded, locking the door behind her. The bed squeaked beneath me as I fell onto it with a huff. All along I believed that I was important to Travis, that he needed me. But in that moment, I felt like the shiny new toy Parker said I was. He wanted to prove to Parker that I was still his. His.

"I'm nobody's," I said to the empty room.

As the words sunk in, I was overwhelmed with the grief I'd felt from the night before. I belonged to no one.

I'd never felt so alone in my life.

FINCH SET A BROWN BOTTLE IN FRONT OF ME. NEITHER of us felt like celebrating, but I was at least comforted by the fact that, according to America, Travis would avoid the date party at all costs. Red-and-pink craft paper covered empty beer cans hanging from the ceiling, and red dresses in every style walked past. The tables were covered with tiny foil hearts, and Finch rolled his eyes at the ridiculous decorations.

"Valentine's Day at a frat house. Romantic," he said, watching the couples walk by.

Shepley and America had been downstairs dancing from the moment we arrived, and Finch and I protested our presence by pouting in the kitchen. I drank the contents of the bottle quickly, determined to blur the memories of the last date party I'd attended.

Finch popped open another cap and handed me another, aware of my desperation to forget. "I'll get more," he said, returning to the fridge.

"The keg is for guests, the bottles are for Sig Tau," a girl sneered beside me.

I looked down at the red cup in her hand. "Or maybe your boyfriend just told you that because he was counting on a cheap date."

She narrowed her eyes and pushed away from the counter, taking her cup elsewhere.

"Who was that?" Finch asked, setting down four more bottles.

"Random sorority bitch," I said, watching her walk away.

By the time Shepley and America rejoined us, six empty bottles sat on the table beside me. My teeth were numb, and it felt a bit easier to smile. I was more comfortable, leaning against my spot on the counter. Travis had proven to be a no-show, and I could survive the remainder of the party in peace.

"Are you guys going to dance or what?" America asked.

I looked to Finch. "Are you going to dance with me, Finch?"

"Are you going to be able to dance?" he asked, raising an eyebrow.

"There's only one way to find out," I said, pulling him downstairs.

We bounced and shook until a thin sheen of sweat began to form under my dress. Just when I thought my lungs would burst, a slow song came over the speakers. Finch peered uncomfortably around us, glancing at the people pairing off and getting close.

"You're going to make me dance to this, aren't you?" he asked.

"It's Valentine's Day, Finch. Pretend I'm a boy."

He laughed, pulling me into his arms. "It's hard to do that when you're wearing a short pink dress."

"Whatever. Like you've never seen a boy in a dress."

Finch shrugged. "True."

I giggled, resting my head against his shoulder. The alcohol made my body feel heavy and sluggish as I tried to move to the slow tempo.

"Mind if I cut in, Finch?"

Travis stood beside us, half amused, half prepared for my reaction. The blood under my cheeks immediately burst into flames.

Finch looked at me, and then at Travis. "Sure."

"Finch," I hissed as he walked away. Travis pulled me against him, and I tried to keep as much space between us as possible. "I thought you weren't coming."

"I wasn't, but I knew you were here. I had to come."

I looked around the room, avoiding his eyes. Every movement he made I was acutely aware of. The pressure changes of his fingers at the points where he touched me, his feet shuffling beside mine, his arms shifting, brushing against my dress. I felt ridiculous pretending not to notice. His eye was healing, the bruise had almost vanished, and the red blotches on his face were absent as if I had imagined them. All evidence of that horrible night had disappeared, leaving only the stinging memories.

He watched my every breath, and when the song was half over, he sighed. "You look beautiful, Pidge."

"Don't."

"Don't what? Tell you you're beautiful?"

"Just . . . don't."

"I didn't mean it."

I huffed in frustration. "Thanks."

"No . . . you look beautiful. I meant that. I was talking about what I said in my room. I'm not going to lie. I enjoyed pulling you from your date with Parker . . ."

"It wasn't a date, Travis. We were just eating. He won't speak to me now, thanks to you."

"I heard. I'm sorry."

"No you're not."

"Y-you're right," he said, stuttering when he saw my impatient expression. "But I . . . that wasn't the only reason I took you to the fight. I wanted you there with me, Pidge. You're my good-luck charm."

"I'm not your anything," I snapped, glaring up at him.

His eyebrows pulled in and he stopped dancing. "You're my everything."

I pressed my lips together, trying to keep the anger at the surface, but it was impossible to stay mad at him when he looked at me that way.

"You don't really hate me . . . do you?" he asked.

I turned away from him, putting more distance between us. "Sometimes I wish that I did. It would make everything a whole hell of a lot easier."

A cautious smile spread across his lips in a thin, subtle line. "So what pisses you off more? What I did to make you wanna hate me? Or knowing that you can't?"

The anger returned. I shoved past him, running up the stairs to the kitchen. My eyes were beginning to gloss over but I refused to be a sobbing mess at the date party. Finch stood beside the table and I sighed with relief when he handed me another beer.

For the next hour, I watched Travis fend off girls and suck down shots of whiskey in the living room. Each time he caught my eye, I looked away from him, determined to get through the night without a scene.

"You two look miserable," Shepley said.

"They couldn't look more bored if they were doing it on purpose," America grumbled.

"Don't forget . . . we didn't want to come," Finch reminded them.

America made her famous face that I was just as famous for giving in to. "You could pretend, Abby. For me."

Just when I opened my mouth for a sharp retort, Finch touched my arm. "I think we've done our duty. You ready to go, Abby?"

I drank the remainder of my beer in a quick swig and then took Finch's hand. As anxious as I was to leave, my legs froze when the same song that Travis and I danced to at my birthday party floated up the stairs. I grabbed Finch's bottle and took another swig, trying to block out the memories that came with the music.

Brad leaned against the counter beside me. "Wanna dance?"

I smiled at him, shaking my head. He began to say something else, but he was interrupted.

"Dance with me." Travis stood a few feet from me, his hand outstretched to mine.

America, Shepley, and Finch were all staring at me, waiting for my answer as anxiously as Travis.

"Leave me alone, Travis," I said, crossing my arms.

"This is our song, Pidge."

"We don't have a song."

"Pigeon . . ."

"No."

I looked to Brad and forced a smile. "I would love to dance, Brad."

Brad's freckles stretched across his cheeks as he smiled, gesturing for me to lead the way to the stairs.

Travis staggered backward, the hurt plainly displayed in his eyes. "A toast!" he yelled.

I flinched, turning just in time to see him climbing onto a chair, stealing a beer from the shocked Sig Tau brother closest to him. I glanced to America, who watched Travis with a pained expression.

"To douchebags!" he said, gesturing to Brad. "And to girls that break your heart," he bowed his head to me. His eyes lost focus. "And to the absolute fucking horror of losing your best friend because you were stupid enough to fall in love with her."

He tilted back the beer, finishing what was left, and then tossed it to the floor. The room was silent except for the music playing in the lower level, and everyone stared at Travis in mass confusion.

Mortified, I grabbed Brad's hand and led him downstairs to the dance floor. A few couples followed behind us, watching me closely for tears or some other response to Travis's tirade. I smoothed my features, refusing to give them what they wanted.

We danced a few stiff steps and Brad sighed. "That was kind of . . . weird."

"Welcome to my life."

Travis pushed his way through the couples on the dance floor, stopping beside me. It took him a moment to steady his feet. "I'm cutting in."

"No, you're not. Jesus!" I said, refusing to look at him.

After a few tense moments I glanced up, seeing Travis's eyes boring into Brad's. "If you don't back away from my girl, I'll rip out your fucking throat. Right here on the dance floor."

Brad seemed conflicted, his eyes nervously darting from me to Travis. "Sorry, Abby," he said, slowly pulling his arms away. He retreated to the stairs and I stood alone, humiliated.

"How I feel about you right now, Travis . . . it very closely resembles hate."

"Dance with me," he pleaded, swaying to keep his balance.

The song ended and I sighed with relief. "Go drink another bottle of whiskey, Trav." I turned to dance with the only single guy on the dance floor.

The tempo was faster, and I smiled at my new, surprised dance partner, trying to ignore the fact that Travis was just a few feet behind me. Another Sig Tau brother danced behind me, grabbing my hips. I reached back, pulling him closer. It reminded me of the way Travis and Megan danced that night at the Red, and I did my best to recreate the scene I had wished on many occasions that I could forget. Two pairs of hands were on nearly every part of my body, and it was easy to ignore my more reserved side with the amount of alcohol in my system.

Suddenly, I was airborne. Travis threw me over his shoulder, at the same time shoving one of his frat brothers hard, knocking him to the floor.

"Put me down!" I said, pounding my fists into his back.

"I'm not going to let you embarrass yourself over me," he growled, taking the stairs two at a time.

Every pair of eyes we passed watched me kick and scream as Travis carried me across the room. "You don't think," I said as I struggled, "this is embarrassing? Travis!"

"Shepley! Is Donnie outside?" Travis said, ducking from my flailing limbs.

"Uh . . . yeah?" he said.

"Put her down!" America said, taking a step toward us.

"America," I said, squirming, "don't just stand there! Help me!"

Her mouth turned up and she laughed once. "You two look ridiculous."

My eyebrows turned in at her words, both shocked and angry that she found any part of the situation funny.

Travis headed for the door and I glared at her. "Thanks a lot, friend!"

The cold air struck the bare parts of my skin, and I protested louder. "Put me down, dammit!"

Travis opened a car door and tossed me into the backseat, sliding in beside me. "Donnie, you're the DD tonight?"

"Yeah," he said, nervously watching me struggle to escape.

"I need you take us to my apartment."

"Travis . . . I don't think . . ."

Travis's voice was controlled, but frightening. "Do it, Donnie, or I'll shove my fist through the back of your head, I swear to God."

Donnie pulled away from the curb and I lunged for the door handle. "I'm not going to your apartment!"

Travis grabbed one of my wrists and then the other. I leaned down to bite his arm. He closed his eyes, and then a low grunt escaped through his clenched jaw as my teeth sunk into his flesh.

"Do your worst, Pidge. I'm tired of your shit."

I released his skin and jerked my arms, struggling against his grip. "My shit? Let me out of this fucking car!"

He pulled my wrists close to his face. "I love you, dammit! You're not going anywhere until you sober up and we figure this out!"

"You're the only one that hasn't figured it out, Travis!" I said. He released my wrists and I crossed my arms, pouting the rest of the way to the apartment.

When the car slowed to a stop, I leaned forward. "Can you take me home, Donnie?"

Travis pulled me out of the car by the arm and then he swung me over his shoulder again, carrying me up the stairs. "Night, Donnie."

"I'm calling your dad!" I cried.

Travis laughed out loud. "And he'd probably pat me on the shoulder and tell me that it's about damn time!"

He struggled to unlock the door as I kicked and waved my arms, trying to get away. "Knock it off, Pidge, or we're going to fall down the stairs!" Once he opened the door, he stomped into Shepley's room.

"Put. Me. Down!" I screamed.

"Fine," he said, dropping me onto Shepley's bed. "Sleep it off. We'll talk in the morning."

The room was dark; the only light a rectangular beam shooting into the doorway from the hall. I fought to focus through the darkness, beer, and anger, and when he turned into the light, it illuminated his smug smile.

I pounded the mattress with my fists. "You can't tell me what to do anymore, Travis! I don't belong to you!"

In the second it took him to turn and face me, his expression had contorted into anger. He stomped toward me, planting his hands on the bed and leaning into my face.

"WELL, I BELONG TO YOU!" The veins in his neck bulged as he shouted, and I met his glare, refusing to even flinch.

He looked at my lips, panting. "I belong to you," he whispered, his anger melting as he realized how close we were.

Before I could think of a reason not to, I grabbed his face, slamming my lips against his. Without hesitation, Travis lifted me into his arms. In a few long strides, he carried me into his bedroom, both of us crashing to the bed.

I yanked his shirt over his head, fumbling in the dark with his belt buckle. He jerked it open, ripped it off, and threw it to the floor. He lifted me from the mattress with one hand and unzipped my dress with the other. I pulled it over my head, tossing it somewhere in the dark, and then Travis kissed me, moaning against my mouth.

With just a few quick movements, his boxers were off and he pressed his chest against mine. I grabbed his backside, but he resisted when I tried to pull him into me.

"We're both drunk," he said, breathing hard.

"Please." I pressed my legs against his hips, desperate to relieve the burning between my thighs. Travis was set on us getting back together, and I had no intentions of fighting the inevitable, so I was more than ready to spend the night tangled up in his sheets.

"This isn't right," he said.

He was just above me, pressing his forehead against mine. I hoped that it was just halfhearted protesting, and that I could persuade him somehow that he was wrong. The way we couldn't seem to stay away from each other was unexplainable, but I didn't need an explanation anymore. I didn't even need an excuse. In that moment, I only needed him.

"I want you."

"I need you to say it," he said.

My insides were screaming for him, and I couldn't stand it a second longer. "I'll say whatever you want."

"Then say that you belong to me. Say that you'll take me back. I won't do this unless we're together."

"We've never really been apart, have we?" I asked, hoping it was enough.

He shook his head, his lips sweeping across mine. "I need to hear you say it. I need to know you're mine."

"I've been yours since the second we met."

My voice took the tone of begging. Any other time I would have been embarrassed, but I was beyond regret. I had fought my feelings, guarded them, and bottled them up. I had experienced the happiest moments of my life while at Eastern, all of them with Travis. Fighting, laughing, loving, or crying, if it was with him, I was where I wanted to be.

One side of his mouth turned up as he touched my face, and then his lips touched mine in a tender kiss. When I pulled him against me, he didn't resist. His muscles tensed, and he held his breath as he slid inside me.

"Say it again," he said.

"I'm yours," I breathed. Every nerve, inside and out, ached for more. "I don't ever want to be apart from you again."

"Promise me," he said, groaning with another thrust.

"I love you. I'll love you forever." The words were more of a sigh, but I met his eyes when I said them. I could see the uncertainty in his eyes vanish, and even in the dim light, his face brightened.

Finally satisfied, he sealed his mouth over mine.

◆ ◆ ◆

TRAVIS WOKE ME WITH KISSES. MY HEAD FELT HEAVY and fogged from the multiple drinks I'd had the night before, but the hour before I fell asleep replayed in my mind in vivid detail. Soft lips showered every inch of my hand, arm, and neck, and when he reached my lips, I smiled.

"Good morning," I said against his mouth.

He didn't speak; his lips continued working against mine. His solid arms enveloped me, and then he buried his face in my neck.

"You're quiet this morning," I said, running my hands over the bare skin of his back. I let them continue down his backside, and then I hooked my leg over his hip, kissing his cheek.

He shook his head. "I just want to be like this," he whispered.

I frowned. "Did I miss something?"

"I didn't mean to wake you up. Why don't you just go back to sleep?"

I leaned back against the pillow, pulling up his chin. His eyes were bloodshot, the skin around them blotchy and red.

"What in the hell is wrong with you?" I asked, alarmed.

He put one of my hands in his and kissed it, pressing his forehead against my neck. "Just go back to sleep, Pigeon. Please?"

"Did something happen? Is it America?" With the last question, I sat up. Even seeing the fear in my eyes, his expression didn't change. He simply sighed and sat up with me, looking at my hand in his.

"No . . . America's fine. They got home around four this morning. They're still in bed. It's early, let's just go back to sleep."

Feeling my heart pounding against my chest, I knew there

was no chance of falling back asleep. Travis put both hands on each side of my face and kissed me. His mouth moved differently, as if he were kissing me for the last time. He lowered me to the pillow, kissed me once more, and then rested his head on my chest, wrapping both arms tightly around me.

Every possible reason for Travis's behavior flipped through my mind like television channels. I hugged him to me, afraid to ask. "Have you slept?"

"I . . . couldn't. I didn't wanna . . ." his voice trailed off.

I kissed his forehead. "Whatever it is, we'll get through it, okay? Why don't you get some sleep? We'll figure it out when you wake up."

His head popped up and he scanned my face. I saw both mistrust and hope in his eyes. "What do you mean? That we'll get through it?"

My eyebrows pulled in, confused. I couldn't imagine what had happened while I was sleeping that would cause him so much anguish. "I don't know what's going on, but I'm here."

"You're here? As in you're staying? With me?"

I knew that my expression must have been ridiculous, but my head was spinning from both the alcohol and Travis's bizarre questions. "Yes. I thought we discussed this last night?"

"We did." He nodded, encouraged.

I searched the room with my eyes, thinking. His walls were no longer bare as they were when we had first met. They were now peppered with trinkets from places that we'd spent time together, and the white paint was interrupted by black frames holding pictures of me, us, Toto, and our group of friends. A larger frame of the two of us at my birthday party replaced the sombrero that once hung by a nail above his headboard.

I narrowed my eyes at him. "You thought I was going to wake up pissed at you, didn't you? You thought I was going to leave?"

He shrugged, making a poor attempt at the indifference that used to come so easily to him. "That is what you're famous for."

"Is that what you're so upset about? You stayed up all night worrying about what would happen when I woke up?"

He shifted as if his next words would be difficult. "I didn't mean for last night to happen like that. I was a little drunk, and I followed you around the party like some fucking stalker, and then I dragged you out of there, against your will . . . and then we . . ." He shook his head, clearly disgusted with the memories playing in his mind.

"Had the best sex of my life?" I smiled, squeezing his hand.

Travis laughed once, the tension around his eyes slowly melting away. "So we're okay?"

I kissed him, touching the sides of his face with tenderness. "Yes, dummy. I promised, didn't I? I told you everything you wanted to hear, we're back together, and you're still not happy?"

His face compressed around his smile.

"Travis, stop. I love you," I said, smoothing the worried lines around his eyes. "This absurd standoff could have been over at Thanksgiving, but . . ."

"Wait . . . what?" he interrupted, leaning back.

"I was fully prepared to give in on Thanksgiving, but you said you were done trying to make me happy, and I was too proud to tell you that I wanted you back."

"Are you fucking kidding me? I was just trying to make it easier on you! Do you know how miserable I've been?"

I frowned. "You looked just fine after break."

"That was for you! I was afraid I'd lose you if I didn't pretend to be okay with just being friends. I could have been with you this whole time? What the fuck, Pigeon?"

"I . . ." I couldn't argue; he was right. I had made us both suffer, and I had no excuse. "I'm sorry."

"You're sorry? I damn near drank myself to death, I could barely get out of bed, I shattered my phone into a million pieces on New Year's Eve to keep from calling you . . . and you're sorry?"

I bit my lip and nodded, ashamed. I had no idea what he'd been through, and hearing him say the words made a sharp pain twist inside my chest. "I'm so . . . so sorry."

"You're forgiven," he said with a grin. "Don't ever do it again."

"I won't. I promise."

He flashed his dimple and shook his head. "I fucking love you."

Chapter Twenty-One
Smoke

THE WEEKS PASSED, AND IT WAS A SURPRISE TO ME how quickly spring break was upon us. The expected stream of gossip and stares had vanished, and life had returned to normal. The basements of Eastern U hadn't held a fight in weeks. Adam made a point of keeping a low profile after the arrests had led to questions about what exactly had gone on that night, and Travis grew irritable waiting for a phone call to summon him to his last fight of the year, the fight that would pay most of his bills for the summer and well into the fall.

The snow was still thick on the ground, and on the Friday before break, one last snowball fight broke out on the crystalline lawn. Travis and I weaved through the flying ice to the cafeteria, and I held tight to his arm, trying to avoid both the snowballs and falling to the ground.

"They're not going to hit you, Pidge. They know better," Travis said, holding his red, cold nose to my cheek.

"Their aim isn't synonymous with their fear of your temper, Trav."

He held me against his side, rubbing my coat sleeve with his hand as he guided me through the chaos. We came to an abrupt halt when a handful of girls screamed past as they were pelted by the merciless aim of the baseball team. Once they cleared the path, Travis led me safely to the door.

"See? I told you we'd make it," he said with a smile.

His amusement faded when a tightly packed snowball exploded against the door, just between our faces. Travis's glare scanned the lawn, but the sheer numbers of students darting in every direction doused his urge to retaliate.

He pulled open the door, watching the melting snow slide down the painted metal to the ground. "Let's get inside."

"Good idea," I nodded.

He led me by the hand down the buffet line, piling different steaming dishes on one tray. The cashier, used to our routine, had given up her predictable baffled expression weeks before.

"Abby," Brazil nodded to me and then winked at Travis. "You guys have plans next week?"

"We're staying here. My brothers are coming in," Travis said, distracted as he organized our lunches, dividing the small Styrofoam plates in front of us on the table.

"I'm going to kill David Lapinski!" America announced, shaking snow out of her hair as she approached.

"Direct hit!" Shepley laughed. America shot him a warning glare and his laugh turned into a nervous chuckle. "I mean . . . what an asshole."

We laughed at his regretful expression as he watched her stomp to the buffet line, following quickly after.

"He's so whipped," Brazil said with a disgusted look on his face.

"America's a little uptight," Travis explained. "She's meeting his parents this week."

Brazil nodded, his eyebrows shooting up. "So they're . . ."

"There," I said, nodding with him. "It's permanent."

"Whoa," Brazil said. The shock didn't leave his face as he picked at his food, and I could see the confusion swirl around him. We were all young, and Brazil couldn't wrap his head around Shepley's commitment.

"When you have it, Brazil . . . you'll get it," Travis said, smiling at me.

The room was abuzz with excitement from both the spectacle outside and the quickly approaching last hours before break. As the seats filled, the steady stream of chatter grew to a loud echo, the volume rising as everyone began talking over the noise.

By the time Shepley and America returned with their trays, they had made up. She happily sat in the empty seat next to me, prattling on about her impending meet-the-parents moment. They would leave that evening for his parents' house. It was the perfect excuse for one of America's infamous meltdowns.

I watched her pick at her bread as she fretted about what to pack and how much luggage she could take without appearing pretentious, but she seemed to be holding it together.

"I told you, baby. They're gonna love you. Love you like I love you, love you," Shepley said, tucking her hair behind her ear. America took a breath and the corners of her mouth turned up in the way they always did when he made her feel more at ease.

Travis's phone shivered, causing it to glide a few inches across the table. He ignored it, regaling Brazil with the story of our first game of poker with his brothers. I glanced at the display, tapping Travis on the shoulder when I read the name.

"Trav?"

Without apology, he turned away from Brazil and gave me his undivided attention. "Yeah, Pigeon?"

"You might want to get that."

He looked down at his cell phone and sighed. "Or not."

"It could be important."

He pursed his lips before holding the receiver to his ear. "What's up, Adam?" His eyes searched the room as he listened, nodding occasionally. "This is my last fight, Adam. I'm not sure yet. I won't go without her and Shep's leaving town. I know ... I heard you. Hmmm ... that's not a bad idea, actually."

My eyebrows pulled in, seeing his eyes brighten with whatever idea Adam had enlightened him with. When Travis hung up the phone, I stared at him expectantly.

"It's enough to pay rent for the next eight months. Adam got John Savage. He's trying to go pro."

"I haven't seen him fight, have you?" Shepley asked, leaning forward.

Travis nodded. "Just once in Springfield. He's good."

"Not good enough," I said. Travis leaned in and kissed my forehead with soft appreciation. "I can stay home, Trav."

"No," he said, shaking his head.

"I don't want you to get hit like you did last time because you're worried about me."

"No, Pidge."

"I'll wait up for you," I said, trying to seem happier with the idea than I felt.

"I'm going to ask Trent to come. He's the only one I'd trust so I can concentrate on the fight."

"Thanks a lot, asshole," Shepley grumbled.

"Hey, you had your chance," Travis said, only half teasing.

Shepley's mouth pulled to the side with chagrin. He still felt at fault for the night at Hellerton. He apologized to me daily for weeks, but his guilt finally became manageable enough for him to suffer in silence. America and I tried to convince him that he wasn't to blame, but Travis would always hold him accountable.

"Shepley, it wasn't your fault. You pulled him off of me, remember?" I said, reaching around America to pat his arm. I turned to Travis, "When is the fight?"

"Next week sometime," he shrugged. "I want you there. I need you there."

I smiled, resting my chin on his shoulder. "Then I'll be there."

Travis walked me to class, his grip tensing a few times when my feet slipped on the ice. "You should be more careful," he teased.

"I'm doing it on purpose. You're such a sucker."

"If you want my arms around you, all you have to do is ask," he said, pulling me into his chest.

We were oblivious to the students passing and the snowballs flying overhead as he pressed his lips against mine. My feet left the ground and he continued to kiss me, carrying me with ease across campus. When he finally set me on my feet in front of the door of my classroom, he shook his head.

"When we make our schedules for next semester, it would be more convenient if we had more classes together."

"I'll work on that," I said, giving him one last kiss before making my way to my seat.

I looked up, and Travis gave me one last smile before making his way to his class in the next building. The students around me were as used to our shameless displays of affection as his class was used to him being a few minutes late.

I was surprised that the time ticked by so quickly. I turned in my last test of the day and made my way to Morgan Hall. Kara sat in her usual spot on her bed as I rifled through my drawers for a few needed items.

"You going out of town?" Kara asked.

"No, I just needed a few things. I'm headed over to the Science building to pick up Trav, and then I'll be at the apartment all week."

"I figured," she said, keeping her eyes on the pages of her book.

"Have a good break, Kara."

"Mmmhmm."

The campus was nearly empty, with only a few stragglers left. When I turned the corner, I saw Travis standing outside, finishing a cigarette. He wore a knit cap over his shaved head and one hand was shoved in the pocket of his worn dark-brown leather jacket. Smoke drifted from his nostrils as he looked down to the ground, deep in thought. It wasn't until I was just a few feet from him that I noticed how distracted he was.

"What's on your mind, baby?" I asked. He didn't look up. "Travis?"

His lashes fluttered when my voice registered and the troubled expression was replaced with a contrived smile. "Hey, Pigeon."

"Everything okay?"

"It is now," he said, pulling me against him.

"Okay. What's up?" I said. With a raised eyebrow and a frown, I made a show of my skepticism.

"Just have a lot on my mind," he sighed. When I waited expectantly, he continued. "This week, the fight, you being there . . ."

"I told you I would stay home."

"I need you there, Pidge," he said, flicking his cigarette to the ground. He watched it disappear into a deep footprint in the snow and then cupped his hand around mine, pulling me toward the parking lot.

"Have you talked to Trent?" I asked.

He shook his head. "I'm waiting for him to call me back."

America rolled down the window and poked her head out of Shepley's Charger. "Hurry up! It's freaking freezing!"

Travis smiled and picked up the pace, opening the door for me to slide in. Shepley and America repeated the same conversation they'd had since she learned she would be meeting his parents while I watched Travis stare out of the window. Just as we pulled into the parking lot of the apartment, Travis's phone rang.

"What the fuck, Trent?" he answered. "I called you four hours ago. It's not like you're productive at work or anything. Whatever. Listen, I need a favor. I've got a fight next week. I need you to go. I don't know when it is, but when I call you, I need you there within an hour. Can you do that for me? Can you do it or not, douchebag? Because I need you to keep an eye on Pigeon. Some asshole put his hands on her last time and . . . yeah." His voice lowered to a frightening tone. "I took care of it. So if I call . . . ? Thanks, Trent."

Travis clicked his phone shut and leaned his head against the back of the seat.

"Relieved?" Shepley asked, watching Travis in the rearview mirror.

"Yeah. I wasn't sure how I was going to do it without him there."

"I told you," I began.

"Pidge, how many times do I have to say it?" he frowned.

I shook my head at his impatient tone. "I don't understand it, though. You didn't need me there before."

His fingers lightly grazed my cheek. "I didn't know you before. When you're not there, I can't concentrate. I'm wondering where you are, what you're doing . . . if you're there and I can see you, I can focus. I know it's crazy, but that's how it is."

"And crazy is exactly the way I like it," I said, leaning up to kiss his lips.

"Obviously," America muttered under her breath.

IN THE SHADOWS OF KEATON HALL, TRAVIS HELD ME tight against his side. The steam from my breath entangled with his in the cold night air, and I could hear the low conversations of those filtering in a side door a few feet away, oblivious to our presence.

Keaton was the oldest building at Eastern, and although the Circle had been held there before, I was uneasy about the venue. Adam expected a full house, and Keaton wasn't the most spacious of basements on campus. Beams formed a grid along the aging brick walls, just one sign of the renovations taking place inside.

"This is one of the worst ideas Adam has had yet," Travis grumbled.

"It's too late to change it, now," I said, looking up at the scaffolds.

Travis's cell phone lit up and he popped it open. His face was tinged with blue against the display, and I could finally see the two worry lines between his eyebrows I already knew were there. He clicked buttons and then snapped the phone shut, gripping me tighter.

"You seem nervous tonight," I whispered.

"I'll feel better when Trent gets his punk ass here."

"I'm here, you whiny little girl," Trenton said in a hushed voice. I could barely see his outline in the darkness, but his smile gleamed in the moonlight.

"How ya been, sis?" he said. He hugged me with one arm, and then playfully shoved Travis with the other.

"I'm good, Trent."

Travis immediately relaxed, and then he led me by the hand to the back of the building.

"If the cops show and we get separated, meet me at Morgan Hall, okay?" Travis said to his brother. We stopped at an open window low to the ground, the signal that Adam was inside and waiting.

"You're fuckin' with me," Trenton said, staring down at the window. "Abby's barely gonna fit through there."

"You'll fit," Travis assured him, crawling down into the blackness inside. Like so many times before, I leaned down and pushed myself backward, knowing Travis would catch me.

We waited for a few moments, and then Trenton grunted as

he pushed off the ledge and landed on the floor, nearly losing his balance as his feet hit the concrete.

"You're lucky I love Abby. I wouldn't do this shit for just anyone," Trenton grumbled, brushing off his shirt.

Travis jumped up, pulling the window closed with one quick movement. "This way," he said, leading us through the dark.

Hallway after hallway, I gripped Travis's hand in mine, feeling Trenton pinching the fabric of my shirt. I could hear small pieces of gravel scrape the concrete as I shuffled along the floor. I felt my eyes widen, trying to adjust to the blackness of the basement, but there was no light to help them focus.

Trenton sighed after the third turn. "We're never gonna find our way out of here."

"Just follow me out. It'll be fine," Travis said, irritated with Trenton's complaining.

When the hallway grew lighter, I knew we were close. When the low roar of the crowd came to a feverish pitch of numbers and names, I knew we had arrived. The room where Travis waited to be called usually had only one lantern and one chair, but with the renovations, it was full of desks and chairs and random equipment covered in white sheets.

Travis and Trenton discussed strategy for the fight as I peeked outside. It was as packed and chaotic as the last fight, but with less room. Furniture covered in dusty sheets lined the edges of the walls, pushed aside to make room for the spectators.

The room was darker than usual, and I guessed that Adam wanted to be careful not to draw attention to our whereabouts. Lanterns hung from the ceilings, creating a dingy glow on the cash being held high as bets were still being called.

"Pigeon, did you hear me?" Travis said, touching my arm.

"What?" I said, blinking.

"I want you to stand by this doorway, okay? Keep hold of Trent's arm at all times."

"I won't move. I promise."

Travis smiled, his perfect dimple sinking into his cheek. "Now you look nervous."

I glanced to the doorway and then back to him. "I don't have a good feeling about this, Trav. Not about the fight, but . . . something. This place gives me the creeps."

"We won't be here long," Travis assured me. Adam's voice came over the horn, and then a pair of warm, familiar hands were on each side of my face. "I love you," he said. He wrapped his arms around me and lifted me off the floor, squeezing me to him as he kissed me. He lowered me to the ground and then hooked my arm around Trenton's. "Don't take your eyes off of her," he said to his brother. "Even for a second. This place'll get crazy once the fight starts."

". . . so let's welcome tonight's contender—JOHN SAVAGE!"

"I'll guard her with my life, little brother," Trenton said, tugging on my arm. "Now go kick this guy's ass and let's get out of here."

". . . TRAVIS 'MAD DOG' MADDOX!" Adam yelled through the horn.

The volume was deafening as Travis made his way through the crowd. I looked up to Trenton, who had the tiniest crook of a smile on his face. Anyone else might not have noticed, but I could see the pride in his eyes.

When Travis reached the center of the Circle, I swallowed. John wasn't much bigger, but he looked different from anyone Travis had fought before, including the man he fought in Vegas.

He wasn't trying to intimidate Travis with a severe stare like the others; he was studying him, preparing the fight in his mind. As analytical as his eyes were, they were also absent of reason. I knew before the fight began that Travis had more than a fight on his hands; he was standing in front of a demon.

Travis seemed to notice the difference as well. His usual smirk was gone, an intense stare in its place. When the horn sounded, John attacked.

"Jesus," I said, gripping Trenton's arm.

Trenton moved as Travis did, as if they were one. I tensed with each swing John threw, fighting the urge to shut my eyes. There were no wasted movements; John was cunning and precise. All of Travis's other fights seemed sloppy in comparison. The raw strength behind the punches alone was awe-inspiring, as if the whole thing had been choreographed and practiced to perfection.

The air in the room was heavy and stagnant; the dust from the sheets had been disturbed and caught in my throat each time I gasped. The longer the fight lasted, the worse the ominous feeling became. I couldn't shake it, and yet I forced myself to stay in place so Travis could concentrate.

In one moment, I was hypnotized by the spectacle in the middle of the basement; in the next, I was shoved from behind. My head jerked back with the blow, but I tightened my grip, refusing to budge from my promised spot. Trenton turned and grabbed the shirts of two men behind us and tossed them to the ground as though they were rag dolls.

"Back the fuck up, or I'll kill you!" he yelled to those staring at the fallen men. I gripped his arm tighter and he patted my hand. "I got ya, Abby. Just watch the fight."

Travis was doing well, and I sighed when he drew first blood. The crowd grew louder, but Trenton's warning kept those around us at a safe distance. Travis landed a solid punch and then glanced at me, quickly returning his attention to John. His movements were lithe, almost calculating, seeming to predict John's attacks before he made them.

Noticeably impatient, John wrapped his arms around Travis, pulling him to the ground. As one unit, the crowd surrounding the makeshift ring tightened around them, leaning in as the action fell to the floor.

"I can't see him, Trent!" I cried as I bounced on my tiptoes.

Trenton looked around, finding Adam's wooden chair. In a dancelike motion, he passed me from one arm to the other, helping me as I climbed above the mob. "Can you see him?"

"Yeah!" I said, holding Trenton's arm for balance. "He's on top, but John's legs are around his neck!"

Trenton leaned forward on his toes, cupping his free hand around his mouth, "SLAM HIS ASS, TRAVIS!"

I glanced down to Trenton and then leaned forward to get a better look at the men on the floor. Suddenly Travis was on his feet, John holding tight around Travis's neck with his legs. Travis fell on his knees, slamming John's back and head against the concrete in a devastating blow. John's legs went limp, releasing Travis's neck, and then Travis reared back his elbow, pummeling John over and over with his clenched fist until Adam pulled him away, throwing the red square on John's flaccid body.

The room erupted, cheering as Adam lifted Travis's hand into the air. Trenton hugged my legs, calling out victory to his brother. Travis looked up at me with a broad, bloody smile; his right eye had already begun to swell.

As the money passed hands and the crowd began to meander about, preparing to leave, my eyes drifted to a wildly flickering lantern swaying back and forth in the corner of the room behind Travis. Liquid was dripping from its base, soaking the sheet below it. My stomach sank.

"Trent?"

Catching his attention, I pointed to the corner. In that moment, the lantern fell from its clip, crashing into the sheet below, immediately bursting into flames.

"Holy shit!" Trenton said, gripping my legs.

A few men around the fire jumped back, watching in awe as the flames crawled to the adjacent sheet. Black smoke bellowed from the corner, and in unison, every person in the room flew into a panic, pushing their way to the exits.

My eyes met Travis's. A look of absolute terror distorted his face.

"Abby!" he screamed, pushing at the sea of people between us.

"C'mon!" Trenton yelled, pulling me from the chair to his side.

The room darkened, and a loud popping noise sounded from another side of the room. The other lanterns were igniting and adding to the fire in small explosions. Trenton grabbed my arm, pulling me behind him as he tried to force his way through the crowd.

"We can't get out that way! We'll have to go back the way we came!" I cried, resisting.

Trenton looked around, forming a plan of escape in the center of the confusion. I looked to Travis again, watching as he tried to make his way across the room. As the crowd surged, Travis was pushed farther away. The excited cheering from before was now horrified shrieks of fear and desperation as everyone fought to reach the exits.

Trenton pulled me to the doorway, and I looked back. "Travis!" I yelled, reaching out for him.

He was coughing, waving the smoke away.

"This way, Trav!" Trenton called to him.

"Just get her out of here, Trent! Get Pigeon out!" he said, coughing.

Conflicted, Trenton looked down to me. I could see the fear in his eyes. "I don't know the way out."

I looked to Travis once more, his form flickering behind the flames that had spread between us. "Travis!"

"Just go! I'll catch up to you outside!" His voice was drowned out by the chaos around us, and I gripped Trenton's sleeve.

"This way, Trent!" I said, feeling the tears and smoke burn my eyes. Dozens of panicked people were between Travis and his only escape.

I tugged on Trenton's hand, shoving anyone in my path. We reached the doorway, and then I looked back and forth. Two dark hallways were dimly lit by the fire behind us.

"This way!" I said, pulling on his hand again.

"You sure?" Trenton asked, his voice thick with doubt and fear.

"C'mon!" I said, tugging on him again.

The farther we ran, the darker the rooms became. After a few moments, my breaths were easier as we left the smoke behind, but the screams didn't subside. They were louder and more frantic than before. The horrific sounds behind us fueled my determination, keeping my steps quick and purposeful. By the second turn, we were walking blindly through the darkness.

388   **Jamie McGuire**

I held my hand in front of me, feeling along the wall with my free hand, gripping Trenton's hand with the other.

"Do you think he got out?" Trenton asked.

His question undermined my focus, and I tried to push the answer from my mind. "Keep moving," I choked out.

Trenton resisted for a moment, but when I tugged on him again, a light flickered. He held up a lighter, squinting into the small space for the way out. I followed the light as he waved it around the room, and gasped when a doorway came into view.

"This way!" I said, tugging on him again.

As I rushed through to the next room, a wall of people crashed into me, throwing me to the ground. Three women and two men, all with dirty faces and wide, frightened eyes looked down at me.

One of the boys reached down to help me up. "There's some windows down here we can get out of!" he said.

"We just came from that way. There's nothing down there," I said, shaking my head.

"You must have missed it. I know they're this way!"

Trenton tugged on my hand. "C'mon, Abby, they know the way out!"

I shook my head. "We came in this way with Travis. I know it."

He tightened his grip. "I told Travis I wouldn't let you out of my sight. We're going with them."

"Trent, we've been down that way . . . there were no windows!"

"Let's go, Jason!" a girl cried.

"We're going," Jason said, looking to Trenton.

Trenton tugged on my hand again and I pulled away. "Trent, please! It's this way, I promise!"

"I'm going with them," he said, "Please come with me."

I shook my head, tears flowing down my cheeks. "I've been here before. That's not the way out!"

"You're coming with me!" he yelled, pulling on my arm.

"Trent, stop! We're going the wrong way!" I cried.

My feet slid across the concrete as he pulled me along, and when the smell of smoke grew stronger, I yanked away, running in the opposite direction.

"ABBY! ABBY!" Trenton called.

I kept running, holding my hands out in front of me, anticipating a wall.

"Come on! She's gonna get you killed!" a girl said.

My shoulder crashed into a corner and I spun around, falling to the ground. I crawled along the floor, holding my trembling hand in front of me. When my fingers touched Sheetrock, I followed it up, rising to my feet. The corner of a doorway materialized under my touch and I followed it into the next room.

The darkness was endless, but I willed away the panic, carefully keeping my footsteps straight, reaching out for the next wall. Several minutes passed by, and I felt the fear well up inside me as the wails from behind rung in my ears.

"Please," I whispered in the blackness, "let this be the way out."

I felt another corner of a doorway, and when I made my way through, a silver stream of light glowed before me. Moonlight filtered through the glass of the window, and a sob forced its way from my throat.

"T-trent! It's here!" I called behind me. "Trent!"

I squinted, seeing a tiny bit of movement in the distance. "Trent?" I called out, my heart beat fluttering wildly in my chest. Within moments, shadows danced against the walls, and my eyes widened with horror when I realized what I thought were people, was actually the flickering light of approaching flames.

"Oh my God," I said, looking up at the window. Travis had closed it behind us, and it was too high for me to reach.

I looked around for something to stand on. The room was lined with wooden furniture covered in white sheets. The same sheets that would feed the fire until the room turned into an inferno.

I grabbed a piece of white cloth, yanking it from a desk. Dust clouded around me as threw the sheet to the ground and lugged the bulky wood across the room to the space beneath the window. I shoved it next to the wall and climbed up, coughing from the smoke that slowly seeped into the room. The window was still a few feet above me.

I grunted as I tried to shove it open, clumsily twisting the lock back and forth between each push. It wouldn't budge.

"Come on, dammit!" I yelled, leaning into my arms.

I leaned back, using my body weight with the little momentum I could manage to force it open. When that didn't work, I slid my nails under the edges, pulling until I thought my nails had pulled away from the skin. Light flashed from the corner of my eye, and I cried out when I saw the fire barreling down the white sheets lining the hallway I had traveled just moments before.

I looked up at the window, once again digging my nails into

the edges. Blood dripped from my fingertips, the metal edges sinking into my flesh. Instinct overcame all other senses, and my hands balled into fists, ramming into the glass. A small crack splintered across the pane, along with my blood smearing and spattering with each blow.

I hammered the glass once more with my fist, and then pulled off my shoe, slamming it with full force. Sirens wailed in the distance and I sobbed, beating my palms against the window. The rest of my life was just a few inches away, on the other side of the glass. I clawed at the edges once more and then began slapping the glass with both palms.

"HELP ME!" I screamed, seeing the flames draw nearer. "SOMEBODY HELP ME!"

A faint cough sputtered behind me. "Pigeon?"

I flipped around to the familiar voice. Travis appeared in a doorway behind me, his face and clothes covered in soot.

"TRAVIS!" I cried. I scrambled off the desk and ran across the floor to where he stood, exhausted and filthy.

I slammed into him, and he wrapped his arms around me, coughing as he gasped for air. His hands grabbed my cheeks.

"Where's Trent?" he said, his voice raspy and weak.

"He followed them!" I bawled, tears streaming down my face. "I tried to get him to come with me, but he wouldn't come!"

Travis looked down at the approaching fire and his eyebrows pulled in. I sucked in a breath, coughing when smoke filled my lungs. He looked down at me, his eyes filling with tears. "I'm gonna get us outta here, Pidge." His lips pressed against mine in one quick, firm movement, and then he climbed on top of my makeshift ladder.

He pushed at the window and then twisted the lock, the

muscles of his arms quivering as he used all of his strength against the glass.

"Get back, Abby! I'm gonna break the glass!"

Afraid to move, I could only take one step away from our only way out. Travis's elbow bent as he reared back his fist, yelling as he rammed it into the window. I turned away, shielding my face with my bloody hands as the glass shattered above me.

"Come on!" he yelled, holding his hand out to me. The heat from the fire took over the room, and I soared into the air as he lifted me from the ground and pushed me outside.

I waited on my knees as Travis climbed out, and then helped him to his feet. The sirens were blaring from the other side of the building, and red and blue lights from fire engines and police cruisers danced across the brick on the adjacent buildings.

We ran to the crowd of people standing in front of the building, scanning the dirty faces for Trenton. Travis yelled his brother's name, his voice becoming more and more hopeless with each call. He pulled out his cell phone to check for a missed call and then slammed it shut, covering his mouth with his blackened hand.

"TRENT!" Travis screamed, stretching his neck as he searched the crowd.

Those that had escaped were hugging and whimpering behind the emergency vehicles, watching in horror as the pumper truck shot water through the windows and firefighters ran inside, pulling hoses behind them.

Travis ran his hand over the stubble on his scalp, shaking his head. "He didn't get out," he whispered. "He didn't get out, Pidge."

My breath caught as I watched the soot on his cheeks streak with tears. He fell to his knees, and I fell with him.

"Trent's smart, Trav. He got out. He had to have found a different way," I said, trying to convince myself as well.

Travis collapsed into my lap, gripping my shirt with both fists. I held him. I didn't know what else to do.

An hour passed. The cries and wailing from the survivors and spectators outside the building had grown to an eerie quiet. We watched with waning hope as the firefighters brought out two people, and then continuously came out empty-handed. As the paramedics tended to the injured and ambulances tore into night with burn victims, we waited. Half an hour later, the bodies they returned with were those who were beyond saving. The ground was lined with casualties, far outnumbering those of us that had escaped. Travis's eyes didn't leave the door, waiting for them to pull his brother from the ashes.

"Travis?"

We turned at the same time to see Adam standing beside us. Travis stood up, pulling me along with him.

"I'm glad to see you guys made it out," Adam said, looking stunned and bewildered. "Where's Trent?"

Travis didn't answer.

Our eyes returned to the charred remains of Keaton Hall, the thick black smoke still billowing from the windows. I buried my face into Travis's chest, shutting my eyes tight, hoping at any moment I would wake up.

"I have to uh . . . I have to call my dad," Travis said, his eyebrows pulling together as he opened his cell phone.

I took a breath, hoping my voice would sound stronger than

I felt. "Maybe you should wait, Travis. We don't know anything, yet."

His eyes didn't leave the number pad, and his lip quivered. "This ain't fucking right. He shoulda never been there."

"It was an accident, Travis. You couldn't have known something like this was going to happen," I said, touching his cheek.

His face compressed, his eyes shutting tight. He took in a deep breath and began to dial his father's number.

Chapter Twenty-Two
Jet Plane

THE NUMBERS ON THE SCREEN WERE REPLACED WITH A name as the phone began to ring, and Travis's eyes widened when he read the display.

"Trent?" A surprised laugh escaped his lips, and a smile broke out on his face as he looked at me. "It's Trent!" I gasped and squeezed his arm as he spoke. "Where are you? What do you mean you're at Morgan? I'll be there in a second, don't you fucking move!"

I surged forward, my feet struggling to keep up with Travis as he sprinted across the campus, dragging me behind him. When we reached Morgan, my lungs were screaming for air. Trenton ran down the steps, crashing into both of us.

"Jesus H. Christ, brother! I thought you were toast!" Trenton said, squeezing us so tightly I couldn't breathe.

"You asshole!" Trayis screamed, shoving his brother away. "I thought you were fucking dead! I've been waiting for the fire-fighters to carry your charred body from Keaton!"

Travis frowned at Trenton for a moment, and then pulled him into a hug. His arm shot out, fumbling around until he felt my shirt, and then pulled me into a hug as well. After several moments, Travis released Trenton, keeping me close beside him.

Trenton looked at me with an apologetic frown. "I'm sorry, Abby. I panicked."

I shook my head. "I'm just glad you're okay."

"Me? I would have been better off dead if Travis had seen me come out of that building without you. I tried to find you after you ran off, but then I got lost and had to find another way. I walked along the building looking for that window, but I ran into some cops and they made me leave. I've been flippin' the fuck out over here!" he said, running his hand over his short hair.

Travis wiped my cheeks with his thumbs, and then pulled up his shirt, using it to wipe the soot from his face. "Let's get out of here. The cops are going to be crawling all over the place soon."

After hugging his brother once more, we walked to America's Honda. Travis watched me buckle my seat belt and then frowned when I coughed.

"Maybe I should take you to the hospital. Get you checked out."

"I'm fine," I said, interlacing my fingers in his. I looked down, seeing a deep cut across his knuckles. "Is that from the fight or the window?"

"The window," he answered, frowning at my bloodied nails.

"You saved my life, you know."

His eyebrows pulled together. "I wasn't leaving without you."

"I knew you'd come," I said, squeezing his fingers between mine.

We held hands until we arrived at the apartment. I couldn't

tell whose blood was whose as I washed the crimson and ash from my skin in the shower. Falling into Travis's bed, I could still smell the stench of smoke and smoldering skin.

"Here," he said, handing me a short glass filled with amber liquid. "It'll help you relax."

"I'm not tired."

He held out the glass again. His eyes were exhausted, bloodshot and heavy. "Just try to get some rest, Pidge."

"I'm almost afraid to close my eyes," I said, taking the glass and gulping the liquid down.

He took the glass and set it on the nightstand, sitting beside me. We sat in silence, letting the last hours sink in. I shut my eyes tight when the memories of the terrified cries of those trapped in the basement filled my mind. I wasn't sure how long it would take me to forget, or if I ever would.

Travis's warm hand on my knee pulled me from my conscious nightmare. "A lot of people died tonight."

"I know."

"We won't find out until tomorrow just how many."

"Trent and I passed a group of kids on the way out. I wonder if they made it. They looked so scared . . ."

I felt the tears fill my eyes, but before they touched my cheeks, Travis's solid arms were surrounding me. Immediately I felt protected, flush against his skin. Feeling so at home in his arms had once terrified me, but in that moment, I was grateful that I could feel so safe after experiencing something so horrific. There was only one reason I could ever feel that way with anyone.

I belonged to him.

It was then that I knew. Without a doubt in my mind, without worry of what others would think, and having no fear of mistakes or consequences, I smiled at the words I would say.

"Travis?" I said against his chest.

"What, baby?" he whispered into my hair.

Our phones rang in unison, and I handed his to him as I answered mine. "Hello?"

"Abby?" America shrieked.

"I'm okay, Mare. We're all okay."

"We just heard! It's all over the news!"

I could hear Travis explaining to Shepley next to me, and I tried my best to reassure America. Fielding dozens of her questions, trying to keep my voice steady while recounting the scariest moments of my life, I relaxed the second Travis covered my hand with his.

It seemed I was telling someone else's story, sitting in the comfort of Travis's apartment, a million miles away from the nightmare that could have killed us. America wept when I finished, realizing how close we came to losing our lives.

"I'm going to start packing now. We'll be home first thing in the morning," America sniffed.

"Mare, don't leave early. We're fine."

"I have to see you. I have to hug you so I'll know you're all right," she cried.

"We're fine. You can hug me on Friday."

She sniffed again. "I love you."

"I love you, too. Have a good time."

Travis looked at me and then pressed the phone tight against his ear. "Better hug your girl, Shep. She sounds upset. I know, man . . . me, too. See you soon."

I hung up seconds before Travis did, and we sat in silence for a moment, still processing what had happened. After several moments, Travis leaned back against his pillow, and then pulled me against his chest.

"America all right?" he asked, staring up at the ceiling.

"She's upset. She'll be okay."

"I'm glad they weren't there."

I clenched my teeth. I hadn't even thought about what might have happened had they not stayed with Shepley's parents. My mind flashed to the terrified expressions of the girls in the basement, fighting against the men to escape. America's frightened eyes replaced the nameless girls in that room. I felt nauseated thinking about her beautiful blond hair soiled and singed along with the rest of the bodies laid out on the lawn.

"Me, too," I said with a shiver.

"I'm sorry. You've been through a lot tonight. I don't need to add anything else to your plate."

"You were there, too, Trav."

He was quiet for several moments, and just when I opened my mouth to speak again, he took a deep breath.

"I don't get scared very often," he said finally. "I was scared the first morning I woke up and you weren't here. I was scared when you left me after Vegas. I was scared when I thought I was going to have to tell my dad that Trent had died in that building. But when I saw you across the flames in that basement . . . I was terrified. I made it to the door, was a few feet from the exit, and I couldn't leave."

"What do you mean? Are you crazy?" I said, my head jerking up to look into his eyes.

"I've never been so clear about anything in my life. I turned around, made my way to that room you were in, and there you were. Nothing else mattered. I didn't even know if we would make it out or not, I just wanted to be where you were, whatever that meant. The only thing I'm afraid of is a life without you, Pigeon."

I leaned up, kissing his lips tenderly. When our mouths parted, I smiled. "Then you have nothing to be afraid of. We're forever."

He sighed. "I'd do it all over again, you know. I wouldn't trade one second if it meant we were right here, in this moment."

My eyes felt heavy, and I took in a deep breath. My lungs protested, still burning from the smoke. I coughed a bit and then relaxed, feeling Travis's warm lips against my forehead. His hand glided over my damp hair, and I could hear his heart beating steady in his chest.

"This is it," he said with a sigh.

"What?"

"The moment. When I watch you sleeping . . . that peace on your face? This is it. I haven't had it since before my mom died, but I can feel it again." He took another deep breath and pulled me closer. "I knew the second I met you that there was something about you I needed. Turns out it wasn't something about you at all. It was just you."

The corner of my mouth turned up as I buried my face into his chest. "It's us, Trav. Nothing makes sense unless we're together. Have you noticed that?"

"Noticed? I've been telling you that all year!" he teased. "It's official. Bimbos, fights, leaving, Parker, Vegas . . . even fires . . . our relationship can withstand anything."

I lifted my head up once more, noticing the contentment

in his eyes as he looked at me. It was similar to the peace I had seen on his face after I lost the bet to stay with him in the apartment, after I told him I loved him for the first time, and the morning after the Valentine's dance. It was similar, but different. This was absolute—permanent. The cautious hope had vanished from his eyes, unqualified trust taking its place.

I recognized it only because his eyes mirrored what I was feeling.

"Vegas?" I asked.

His brow furrowed, unsure of where I was headed. "Yeah?"

"Have you thought about going back?"

His eyebrows shot up. "I don't think that's a good idea for me."

"What if we just went for a night?"

He looked around the dark room, confused. "A night?"

"Marry me," I said without hesitation. I was surprised at how quickly and easily the words came.

His mouth spread into a broad smile. "When?"

I shrugged. "We can book a flight tomorrow. It's spring break. I don't have anything going on tomorrow, do you?"

"I'm callin' your bluff," he said, reaching for his phone. "American Airlines," He said, watching my reaction closely as he was connected. "I need two tickets to Vegas, please. Tomorrow. Hmmmm . . ." He looked at me, waiting for me to change my mind. "Two days, round trip. Whatever you have."

I rested my chin on his chest, waiting for him to book the tickets. The longer I let him stay on the phone, the wider his smile became.

"Yeah . . . uh, hold on a minute," he said, pointing to his wallet. "Grab my card, would ya, Pidge?" He waited again for my reaction. I happily leaned over, pulled his credit card from his wallet, and handed it to him.

Travis called out the numbers to the agent, glancing up at me after each set. When he gave the expiration date and saw my lack of protesting, he pressed his lips together. "Er, yes, ma'am. We'll just pick them up at the desk. Thank you."

He handed me his phone and I set it on the night table, waiting for him to speak.

"You just asked me to marry you," he said, still waiting for me to admit some kind of trickery.

"I know."

"That was the real deal, you know. I just booked two tickets to Vegas for noon tomorrow. So that means we're getting married tomorrow night."

"Thank you."

His eyes narrowed. "You're going to be Mrs. Maddox when you start classes on Monday."

"Oh," I said, looking around.

Travis raised an eyebrow. "Second thoughts?"

"I'm going to have some serious paperwork to change next week."

He nodded slowly, cautiously hopeful. "You're going to marry me tomorrow?"

I smiled. "Uh-huh."

"You're serious?"

"Yep."

"I fucking love you!" He grabbed each side of my face, slamming his lips against mine. "I love you so much, Pigeon," he said, kissing me over and over.

"Just remember that in fifty years when I'm still kicking your ass in poker," I giggled.

He smiled, triumphant. "If it means sixty or seventy years with you, baby...you have my full permission to do your worst."

I raised one eyebrow. "You're gonna regret that."

"I bet I won't."

I smiled with as much deviance as I could muster. "Are you confident enough to bet that shiny bike outside?"

He shook his head, a serious expression replacing the teasing smile he had just seconds before. "I'll put in everything I have. I don't regret a single second with you, Pidge, and I never will."

I held out my hand and he took it without hesitation, shaking it once and then bringing it to his mouth, pressing his lips tenderly against my knuckles. The room was quiet, his lips leaving my skin and the air escaping his lungs the only sound.

"Abby Maddox..." he said, his smile beaming in the moonlight.

I pressed my cheek against his bare chest. "Travis and Abby Maddox. Has a nice ring to it."

"Ring?" he said, frowning.

"We'll worry about rings later. I sort of sprung this on you."

"Uh..." he trailed off, watching me for the reaction he expected.

"What?" I asked, feeling myself tense.

"Don't freak out," he said as he shifted nervously. His grip around me tightened. "I kind of...already took care of that part."

"What part?" I said, my head craning to see his face.

He stared up at the ceiling and sighed. "You're going to freak out."

"Travis . . ."

I frowned as he pulled one arm away from me, reaching for the drawer of his nightstand. He felt around for a moment.

I blew my damp bangs from my eyes. "What? You bought condoms?"

He laughed once. "No, Pidge." His eyebrows pulled together as he made more of an effort, reaching farther into the drawer. Once he found what he was looking for, his focus changed, and he watched me as he pulled a small box from its hiding place.

I looked down as he placed the small velvet square on his chest, reaching behind him to rest his head on his arm.

"What's that?" I asked.

"What does it look like?"

"Okay. Let me rephrase the question: When did you get that?"

Travis inhaled, and as he did, the box rose with his chest and fell when he pushed the air from his lungs. "A while ago."

"Trav . . ."

"I just happened to see it one day, and I knew there was only one place it could belong . . . on your perfect little finger."

"One day when?"

"Does it matter?" he rebutted. He squirmed a bit, and I couldn't help but laugh.

"Can I see it?" I smiled, suddenly feeling a bit giddy.

His smile matched mine, and he looked to the box. "Open it."

I touched it with one finger, feeling the lush velvet under my fingertip. I grasped the golden seal with both hands, slowly pulling the lid open. A glimmer caught my eye and I slammed the lid shut.

"Travis!" I wailed.

"I knew you'd freak out!" he said, sitting up and cupping his hands over mine.

I could feel the box pressing against both of my palms, feeling like a prickly grenade that could detonate at any moment. I closed my eyes and shook my head. "Are you insane?"

"I know. I know what you're thinking, but I had to. It was the One. And I was right! I haven't seen one since that was as perfect as this one!"

My eyes popped open and instead of the anxious pair of brown eyes I expected, he was beaming with pride. He gently peeled my hands from the case and pulled the lid open, pulling the ring from the tiny slit that held it in place. The large, round diamond glittered even in the dim light, catching the moonlight in every facet.

"It's . . . my God, it's amazing," I whispered as he took my left hand in his.

"Can I put it on your finger?" he asked, peering up at me. When I nodded, he pressed his lips together, sliding the silver band over my knuckle, holding it in place for a moment before letting go. "Now it's amazing."

We both stared at my hand for a moment, equally shocked at the contrast of the large diamond sitting atop my small, slender finger. The band spanned the bottom of my finger, splitting in two on each side as it reached the solitaire, smaller diamonds lining each sliver of white gold.

"You could have put a down payment on a car for this," I said under my breath, unable to put any strength behind my voice.

My eyes followed my hand as Travis brought it up to his lips. "I've imagined what this would look like on your hand a million times. Now that it's there . . ."

"What?" I smiled, watching him stare at my hand with an emotional grin.

He looked up at me. "I thought I was going to have to sweat five years before I'd feel like this."

"I wanted it as much as you did. I've just got a hell of a poker face," I said, pressing my lips against his.

Epilogue

Travis squeezed my hand as I held my breath. I tried to keep my face smooth, but when I cringed, his grip became tighter. The white ceiling was tarnished in some places by leak stains. Other than that, the room was immaculate. No clutter, no utensils strewn about. Everything had its place, which made me feel moderately at ease about the situation. I had made the decision. I would go through with it.

"Baby . . ." Travis said, frowning.

"I can do this," I said, staring at spots in the ceiling. I jumped when fingertips touched my skin, but I tried not to tense. I could see the worry in Travis's eyes when the buzzing began.

"Pigeon," Travis began again, but I shook my head dismissively.

"All right. I'm ready." I held the phone away from my ear, wincing from both the pain and the inevitable lecture.

"I'm going to kill you, Abby Abernathy!" America cried. "Kill you!"

"Technically, it's Abby Maddox, now," I said, smiling at my new husband.

"It's not fair!" she whined, the anger subsiding from her tone. "I was supposed to be your maid of honor! I was supposed to go dress shopping with you and throw a bachelorette party and hold your bouquet!"

"I know," I said, watching Travis's smile fade as I winced again.

"You don't have to do this, you know," he said, his eyebrows pulling together.

I squeezed his fingers together with my free hand. "I know."

"You said that already!" America snapped.

"I wasn't talking to you."

"Oh, you're talking to me," she fumed. "You are sooo talking to me. You are never going to hear the end of this, do you hear me? I will never, ever forgive you!"

"Yes you will."

"You! You're a . . . ! You're just plain mean, Abby! You're a horrible best friend!"

I laughed, causing the man seated beside me to jerk. "Hold still, Mrs. Maddox."

"I'm sorry," I said.

"Who was that?" America snapped.

"That was Griffin."

"Who the hell is Griffin? Let me guess, you invited a total stranger to your wedding and not your best friend?" Her voice became shriller with each question.

"No. He didn't go to the wedding," I said, sucking in a breath of air.

Travis sighed and shifted nervously in his chair, squeezing my hand.

"I'm supposed to do that to you, remember?" I said, smiling up at him through the pain.

"Sorry. I don't think I can take this," he said, his voice thick with distress. He relaxed his hand, looking to Griffin.

"Hurry up, would ya?"

Griffin shook his head. "Covered in tats and can't take your girlfriend getting a simple script. I'll be finished in a minute, mate."

Travis's frown deepened. "Wife. She's my wife."

America gasped once the conversation processed in her mind. "You're getting a tattoo? What is going on with you, Abby? Did you breathe toxic fumes in that fire?"

I looked down at my stomach, to the smeared black mess just to the inside of my hipbone, and smiled. "Trav has my name on his wrist." I sucked in another breath when the buzzing continued. Griffin wiped ink from my skin and began again. I spoke through my teeth, "We're married. I wanted something, too."

Travis shook his head. "You didn't have to."

I narrowed my eyes. "Don't start with me. We discussed this."

America laughed once. "You've gone crazy. I'm committing you to the asylum when you get home." Her voice was still piercing and exasperated.

"It's not that crazy. We love each other. We have been practically living together on and off all year. Why not?"

"Because you're nineteen, you idiot! Because you ran off and didn't tell anyone, and because I'm not there!" she cried.

"I'm sorry, Mare, I have to go. I'll see you tomorrow, okay?"

"I don't know if I want to see you tomorrow! I don't think I want to see Travis ever again!" she sneered.

"I'll see you tomorrow, Mare. You know you want to see my ring."

"And your tat," she said, a smile in her voice.

I clicked the phone shut, handing it to Travis. The buzzing resumed again, and my attention focused on the burning sensation followed by the sweet second of relief as he wiped the excess ink away. Travis shoved my phone in his pocket, gripping my hand with both of his, leaning down to touch his forehead to mine.

"Did you freak out this much when you got your tattoos?" I asked him, smiling at the apprehensive expression on his face.

He shifted, seeming to feel my pain a thousand times more than I. "Uh . . . no. This is different. This is much, much worse."

"Done!" Griffin said with as much relief in his voice as was on Travis's face.

I let my head fall back against the chair. "Thank God!"

"Thank God!" Travis sighed, patting my hand.

I looked down at the beautiful black lines on my red and angry skin:

MRS. MADDOX

"Wow," I said, rising up on my elbows to get a better look.

Travis's frown instantly turned into a triumphant smile. "It's beautiful."

Griffin shook his head. "If I had a dollar for every inked-up new husband that brought his wife in here and took it worse than she did . . . well. I wouldn't have to tat anyone ever again."

"Just tell me how much I owe, smart-ass," Travis mumbled.

"I'll have your bill at the counter," Griffin said, amused with Travis's retort.

I looked around the room at the shiny chrome and posters of sample tattoos on the wall and then back down to my stomach. My new last name shined in thick, elegant black letters. Travis watched me with pride, and then peered down at his titanium wedding band.

"We did it, baby," he said in a hushed voice. "I still can't believe you're my wife."

"Believe it," I said, smiling.

He helped me from the chair and I favored my right side, conscious of every movement I made that caused my jeans to rub against my raw skin. Travis pulled out his wallet, signing the receipt quickly before leading me by the hand to the cab waiting outside. My cell phone rang again, and when I saw that it was America, I let it ring.

"She's going to lay the guilt trip on thick, isn't she?" Travis said with a frown.

"She'll pout for twenty-four hours after she sees the pictures—then she'll get over it."

Travis shot me a mischievous grin. "Are you sure about that, Mrs. Maddox?"

"Are you ever going to stop calling me that? You've said it a hundred times since we left the chapel."

He shook his head as he held the cab door open for me. "I'll quit calling you that when it sinks in that this is real."

"Oh, it's real all right," I said, sliding to the middle of the seat to make room. "I have wedding night memories to prove it."

He leaned against me, running his nose up the sensitive skin of my neck until he reached my ear. "We sure do."

"Ow . . ." I said when he pressed against my bandage.

"Oh, dammit, I'm sorry, Pidge."

"You're forgiven," I said with a smile.

We rode to the airport hand in hand, and I giggled as I watched Travis stare at his wedding band without apology. His eyes held the peaceful expression I was becoming accustomed to.

"When we get back to the apartment, I think it will finally hit me, and I'll quit acting like such a jackass."

"Promise?" I smiled.

He kissed my hand and then cradled it in his lap between his palms. "No."

I laughed, resting my head on his shoulder until the cab slowed to a stop in front of the airport. My cell phone rang again, displaying America's name once again.

"She's relentless. Let me talk to her," Travis said, reaching for my phone.

"Hello?" he said, waiting out the shrill stream on the other end of the line. He smiled. "Because I'm her husband. I can answer her phone now." He glanced at me and then shoved open the cab door, offering his hand. "We're at the airport, America. Why don't you and Shep pick us up and you can yell at us both on the way home? Yes, the whole way home. We should arrive around three. All right, Mare. See you then." He winced with her sharp words and then handed me the phone. "You weren't kidding. She's pissed."

He tipped the cabby and then threw his bag over his shoulder, pulling up the handle to my rolling luggage. His tattooed arms tensed as he pulled my bag, his free hand reaching out to take mine.

"I can't believe you gave her the green light to let us have it for an entire hour," I said, following him through the revolving door.

"You don't really think I'm going to let her yell at my wife, do you?"

"You're getting pretty comfortable with that term."

"I guess it's time I admit it. I knew you were going to be my wife pretty much from the second I met you. I'm not going to lie and say I haven't been waiting for the day I could say it . . . so I'm going to abuse the title. You should get used to it, now." He said this all matter-of-factly, as if he were giving a practiced speech.

I laughed, squeezing his hand. "I don't mind."

He peered at me from the corner of his eye. "You don't?" I shook my head and he pulled me to his side, kissing my cheek. "Good. You're going to get sick of it over the next few months, but just cut me some slack, okay?"

I followed him through the hallways, up escalators, and past lines of security. When Travis walked through the metal detector, a loud buzzer went off. When the airport guard asked Travis to remove his ring, his face turned severe.

"I'll hold onto it, sir," the officer said. "It will only be for a moment."

"I promised her I'd never take it off," Travis said through his teeth.

The officer held out his palm; patience and amused understanding wrinkled the thin skin around his eyes.

Travis begrudgingly removed his ring, slammed it into the guard's hand, and then sighed when he walked through the doorway. He didn't set off the alarm, but he was still annoyed. I walked through without event, handing over my ring as well.

Travis's expression was still tense, but when we were allowed to pass, his shoulders relaxed.

"It's okay, baby. It's back on your finger," I said, giggling at his overreaction.

He kissed my forehead, pulling me to his side as we made our way to the terminal. When I caught the eyes of those we passed, I wondered if it was obvious that we were newlyweds, or if they simply noticed the ridiculous grin on Travis's face, a stark contrast to his shaved head, inked arms, and bulging muscles.

The airport was abuzz with excited tourists, the beeping and ringing of slot machines, and people meandering in every direction. I smiled at a young couple holding hands, looking as excited and nervous as Travis and I did when we arrived. I didn't doubt that they would leave feeling the same mixture of relief and bewilderment that we felt.

In the terminal, I thumbed through a magazine, and gently touched Travis's wildly bouncing knee. His leg froze and I smiled, keeping my eyes on the pictures of celebrities. He was nervous about something, but I waited for him to tell me, knowing he was working it out internally. After a few minutes, his knee bobbed again, but this time he stopped it on his own and then slowly slumped down into his chair.

"Pigeon?"

"Yeah?"

A few moments passed, and then he sighed. "Nothing."

The time passed too quickly, and it seemed we had just sat down when our flight number was called to board. A line quickly formed, and we stood up, waiting our turn to show our tickets and walk down the long hall to the airplane that would take us home.

Travis hesitated. "I can't shake this feeling," he said under his breath.

"What do you mean? Like a bad feeling?" I said, suddenly nervous.

He turned to me with concern in his eyes. "I have this crazy feeling that once we get home, I'm going to wake up. Like none of this was real."

I slid my arms around his waist, running my hands up the lean muscles of his back. "Is that what you're worried about?"

He looked down to his wrist and then glanced to the thick silver band on his left finger. "I just can't shake the feeling that the bubble's going to burst, and I'm going to be lying in my bed alone, wishing you were there with me."

"I don't know what I'm going to do with you, Trav! I've dumped someone for you—twice—I've picked up and gone to Vegas with you—twice—I've literally gone through hell and back, married you, and branded myself with your name. I'm running out of ideas to prove to you that I'm yours."

A small smile graced his lips. "I love it when you say that."

"That I'm yours?" I asked. I leaned up on the balls of my feet, pressing my lips against his. "I. Am. Yours. Mrs. Travis Maddox. Forever and always."

His small smile faded as he looked at the boarding gate and then down to me. "I'm gonna fuck it up, Pigeon. You're gonna get sick of my shit."

I laughed. "I'm sick of your shit now. I still married you."

"I thought once we got married, that I'd feel a little more reassured about not losing you. But I feel like if I get on that plane . . ."

"Travis? I love you. Let's go home."

His eyebrows pulled in. "You won't leave me, right? Even when I'm a pain in the ass?"

"I vowed in front of God—and Elvis—that I wouldn't, didn't I?"

His frown lightened a bit. "This is forever, right?"

One corner of my mouth turned up. "Would it make you feel better if we made a wager?"

Other passengers began to walk around us, however slowly, watching and listening to our ridiculous conversation. As before, I was glaringly aware of prying eyes, but this time was different. The only thing I could think about was the peace returning to Travis's eyes.

"What kind of husband would I be if I bet against my own marriage?"

I smiled. "The stupid kind. Didn't you listen to your dad when he told you not to bet against me?"

He raised an eyebrow. "So you're that sure, huh? You'd bet on it?"

I wrapped my arms around his neck and smiled against his lips. "I'd bet my firstborn. That's how sure I am."

And then the peace returned.

"You can't be that sure," he said, the anxiousness absent from his voice.

I raised an eyebrow, my mouth pulling up on the same side. "Wanna bet?"

Acknowledgments

I AM SO INCREDIBLY THANKFUL FOR MY BEST FRIEND and sister, Beth. Without her encouragement, I would never have embarked on this journey. It's because of her enthusiastic cheerleading that I am living my dream. I cannot say thank you enough. Thank you to my children for their endless patience, hugs, and understanding.

To my mother, Brenda, for her assistance in any way she could, whenever I asked. Many thanks to fellow authors and dear friends Jessica Park, Tammara Webber, Tina Reber, Stephanie Campbell, Abbi Glines, Liz Reinhardt, Elizabeth Reyes, Nichole Chase, Laura Bradley Rede, Elizabeth Hunter, Killian McRae, Colleen Hoover, Eyvonna Rains, Lani Wendt Young, Karly Blakemore-Mowle, Michele Scott, Tracey Garvis-Graves, Angie Stanton, and E L James for their overwhelming support, love, and advice. You are the best thing to come from my writing career. Truly.

Thank you to my agent Rebecca Watson, who is as brilliant as she is funny, and my agents at the Intercontinental Literary Agency for their diligence and hard work.

Enormous gratitude to Judith Curr at Atria Books for your unwavering support, and to my editor, Amy Tannenbaum, who has been passionate about this project from the very beginning. Thank you for believing in this story. And thanks to everyone else at Atria who made this happen so quickly, including Peter Borland, Chris Lloreda, Kimberly Goldstein, Samantha Cohen, Paul Olsewski, Isolde Sauer, Dana Sloan, Jessica Chin, Benjamin Holmes, Michael Kwan, James Pervin, Susan Rella, and James Walsh.

Thank you to Dr. Ross Vanhooser for your invaluable advice, and for believing in my talent before even I knew I had any.

Thank you so much to Maryse and Lily of Maryse.net and to reader Nikki Estep for loving Travis and Abby's story so much that they made it their mission to share it!

Last, but never least, endless love and appreciation to my darling husband who's infinitely supportive and patient, and loves me even when I'm ignoring him for fictional people. He is my everything, and I wouldn't think of doing any of this without him . . . I wouldn't want to. It's because of him that I know how to write about intense love. Jeff, thank you so much for being everything that you are.

About the Author

JAMIE MCGUIRE IS THE *NEW YORK TIMES* BESTSELLING author of three other novels: *Providence, Requiem,* and *Eden.* McGuire studied radiography at Northern Oklahoma College and Autry Technology Center in Enid, Oklahoma, during which time she wrote her first novel, *Providence.* She and her husband, Jeff, live with their children just outside Enid, Oklahoma, with four dogs, four horses, and a cat named Rooster.

To learn more about Jamie McGuire, visit her at:

Facebook
https://www.facebook.com/Jamie.McGuire.Author

Twitter
@JamieMcGuire_

Atria Books/Simon & Schuster Author Page
http://authors.simonandschuster.com/Jamie
-McGuire/408106960

Author website
www.jamiemcguire.com